BAKER'S DOZEN

13 SHORT ESPIONAGE NOVELS

ABOUT THE EDITORS

BILL PRONZINI is one of America's finest mystery/suspense/espionage writers, as well as one of its leading critics. He has published more than 30 novels and 280 stories. His fiction has been translated into 17 languages and he has edited or coedited some 40 anthologies, including, with Martin Greenberg, *Baker's Dozen: 13 Short Mystery Novels, A Treasury of World War II Stories,* and *A Treasury of Civil War Stories*. A longtime resident of San Francisco, he possesses one of the larger collections of pulp magazines in the world.

MARTIN H. GREENBERG, who has been called "the king of the anthologists," now has some 125 of them to his credit. Greenberg is Professor of Regional Analysis and Policital Science at the University of Wisconsin–Green Bay, where he teaches a course in American foreign and defense policy.

BAKER'S DOZEN

13 SHORT ESPIONAGE NOVELS

Edited by
Bill Pronzini
and
Martin H. Greenberg

BONANZA BOOKS
New York

Grateful acknowledgment is hereby given for permission to reprint the following:
The Traitor—Copyright 1927 by W. Somerset Maugham. Reprinted from *Ashenden* by W. Somerset Maugham by permission of Doubleday & Company, Inc. and the Executors of the Estate of W. Somerset Maugham and William Heinemann Ltd.
Tokyo, 1941—Copyright © 1960 by Cornell Woolrich. Reprinted by permission of the agents or the author's estate, Scott Meredith Literary Agency, Inc., 845 Third Avenue, New York, New York 10022.
Dealers in Doom—Copyright 1934 by Magazine Publishers, Inc. Reprinted by permission of Harold Ober Associates Incorporated.
The Sizzling Saboteur—Copyright 1944 by Leslie Charteris. Reprinted by permission of the author.
The Danger Zone—Copyright 1932 by Erle Stanley Gardner; copyright renewed © 1960 by Erle Stanley Gardner. Reprinted by permission of Curtis Brown, Ltd.
Betrayed—Copyright 1952; copyright renewed © 1980 by John D. MacDonald Publishing, Inc. Reprinted by permission of the author.
Deep-Sleep—Copyright © 1965 by Pamar Enterprises, Inc. Originally published in *Intrigue Mystery Magazine,* October 1965. Reprinted by permission of the author.
The People of the Peacock—Copyright © 1965 by Fiction Publishing Company. Reprinted by permission of the author.
Dr. Sweetkill—Copyright © 1965 by Pamar Enterprises, Inc. Originally published in *Intrigue Mystery Magazine*, January 1966. Reprinted by permission of the author.
The Giggle-Wrecker—Copyright © 1972 by Peter O'Donnell. Reprinted from *Pieces of Modesty* by Peter O'Donnell by permission of the Mysterious Press and Euro-Features Ltd.
The Spoilers—Copyright © 1965 by Michael Gilbert. Originally published in *Argosy* (U.K.), October 1965. Reprinted by permission of the author.
Octopussy—Copyright © 1963 by Ian Fleming. Reprinted from *Octopussy* by Ian Fleming by permission of New American Library, New York, New York, and Glidrose Productions Ltd., London.

Published 1985 by Bonanza Books, distributed by Crown Publishers, Inc.,
One Park Avenue, New York, New York 10016
Manufactured in the United States of America

Library of Congress Cataloging in Publication Data
Main entry under title:

Baker's dozen.

1. Spy stories, American. 2. Spy stories, English.
I. Pronzini, Bill. II. Greenberg, Martin Harry.
PS648.S85B35 1985 823'.0872'08 85-12820

ISBN:0-517-476479
h g f e d c b a

CONTENTS

INTRODUCTION

Baker's Dozen: 13 Short Espionage Novels brings together for the first time in book form thirteen outstanding spy and espionage novellas by some of the most accomplished writers in the field, both past and present.

These stories span more than seventy-five years of espionage writing in the United States and Great Britain, and they feature a wide variety of secret agents, counterspies, double agents, and espionage situations, as well as diverse settings (England; different locales in the United States; Japan; Germany; Italy; Switzerland; behind the Iron Curtain) and stylistic approaches to what has become one of the most popular forms of literature in the world. Taken together, they demonstrate how the spy story has evolved in form, structure, and content throughout this century; how the masters of this type of fiction have adapted to meet changing conditions and events. Indeed, the spy story is heavily dependent on actual history; thus the entries in this collection have various time frames: before and during World War I, the interwar period, World War II, and the continuing Cold War battle between agents of the West and those of the Soviet bloc and/or SMERSH-type organizations.

Several well-known fictional spies populate these pages. W. Somerset Maugham's justifiably famous operative, Ashenden, a character based on the author's firsthand experience in World War I espionage, who does his finest work in *The Traitor*; Ian Fleming's quintessential secret agent, 007 himself, James Bond, who stars in one of his most explosive and entertaining adventures, *Octopussy*; Peter O'Donnell's Modesty Blaise, the female James Bond, whose talents are nowhere better displayed than in the thunderous and often quite funny tale, *The Giggle-Wrecker*; and Michael Gilbert's genteel (but on occasion quite deadly) pair of British agents, Mr. Calder and Mr. Behrens, who work for the External Branch of the Joint Services Standing Intelligence Committee and who face one of their greatest challenges in *The Spoilers*. Also featured here is no less a personage than the world's greatest detective, Sherlock Holmes, in one of Sir Arthur Conan Doyle's few excursions into the realm of spy fiction, *The Bruce-Partington Plans*. Leslie Charteris's dashing rogue, the

Saint, makes an appearance as well in *The Sizzling Saboteur*, a tale of fifth-column activity in World War II. And Edward D. Hoch's popular police detective, Captain Leopold, finds himself enmeshed in a web of intrigue that has its roots in the volatile Middle Eastern political scene in *The People of the Peacock*.

Nonseries stories also form an important part of this anthology. The undisputed master of nail-biting suspense, Cornell Woolrich, serves up a powerful brew in his story of an American caught in *Tokyo, 1941*. Another fine suspense writer and creator of the best-selling Travis McGee series, John D. MacDonald, tells the bizarre top-secret story of a young widow who receives a letter from her dead husband in *Betrayed*. The father of Perry Mason, Erle Stanley Gardner, presents a retired army major playing a game of international intrigue with his life as the prize in *The Danger Zone*. William E. Barrett, the author of such critically acclaimed novels as *Lilies of the Field*, weaves a deadly net of plot and counterplot in pre–World War II Washington, D.C., in *Dealers in Doom*. Yet another best-selling writer, John Jakes, author of the enormously popular Kent Family Chronicles, offers an action-packed adventure in field espionage in *Dr. Sweetkill*. And Bruce Cassiday's Bondian secret agent Peter Baron meets his most clever and most dangerous adversary, Mr. Satin, "The Man from I.C.E.," in *Deep-Sleep*.

Baker's Dozen provides something for every lover of espionage fiction—memorable stories by expert writers, some of which are reprinted here for the first time since their original appearance in print. We hope you derive as much pleasure from reading these thirteen exciting and stimulating novellas as we did from selecting them.

BILL PRONZINI
MARTIN H. GREENBERG

1985

SIR ARTHUR CONAN DOYLE

The Adventure of The Bruce-Partington Plans

IN THE THIRD week of November, in the year 1895, a dense yellow fog settled down upon London. From the Monday to the Thursday I doubt whether it was ever possible from our windows in Baker Street to see the loom of the opposite houses. The first day Holmes had spent in cross-indexing his huge book of references. The second and third had been patiently occupied upon a subject which he had recently made his hobby—the music of the Middle Ages. But when, for the fourth time, after pushing back our chairs from breakfast we saw the greasy, heavy brown swirl still drifting past us and condensing in oily drops upon the window panes, my comrade's impatient and active nature could endure this drab existence no longer. He paced restlessly about our sitting room in a fever of suppressed energy, biting his nails, tapping the furniture, and chafing against inaction.

"Nothing of interest in the paper, Watson?"

I was aware that by anything of interest, Holmes meant anything of criminal interest. There was the news of a revolution, of a possible war, and of an impending change of government; but these did not come within the horizon of my companion. I could see nothing recorded in the shape of crime which was not commonplace and futile. Holmes groaned and resumed his restless meanderings.

"The London criminal is certainly a dull fellow," said he in the querulous voice of the sportsman whose game has failed him. "Look out of this window, Watson. See how the figures loom up, are dimly seen, and then blend once more into the cloud bank. The thief or the murderer could roam London on such a day as the tiger does the jungle, unseen until he pounces, and then evident only to his victim."

"There have," said I, "been numerous petty thefts."

Holmes snorted his contempt.

"This great and somber stage is set for something more worthy than that,'' said he. ''It is fortunate for this community that I am not a criminal.''

''It is, indeed!'' said I heartily.

''Suppose that I were Brooks or Woodhouse, or any of the fifty men who have good reason for taking my life, how long could I survive against my own pursuit? A summons, a bogus appointment, and all would be over. It is well they don't have days of fog in the Latin countries—the countries of assassination. By Jove! here comes something at last to break our dead monotony.''

It was the maid with a telegram. Holmes tore it open and burst out laughing.

''Well, well! What next?'' said he. ''Brother Mycroft is coming round.''

''Why not?'' I asked.

''Why not? It is as if you met a tram car coming down a country lane. Mycroft has his rails and he runs on them. His Pall Mall lodgings, the Diogenes Club, Whitehall—that is his cycle. Once, and only once, he has been here. What upheaval can possibly have derailed him?''

''Does he not explain?''

Holmes handed me his brother's telegram.

MUST SEE YOU OVER CADOGAN WEST. COMING AT ONCE.
Mycroft

''Cadogan West? I have heard the name.''

''It recalls nothing to my mind. But that Mycroft should break out in this erratic fashion! A planet might as well leave its orbit. By the way, do you what what Mycroft is?''

I had some vague recollection of an explanation at the time of the Adventure of the Greek Interpreter.

''You told me that he had some small office under the British government.''

Holmes chuckled.

''I did not know you quite so well in those days. One has to be discreet when one talks of high matters of state. You are right in thinking that he is under the British government. You would also be right in a sense if you said that occasionally he *is* the British government.''

''My dear Holmes!''

''I thought I might surprise you. Mycroft draws four hundred and fifty pounds a year, remains a subordinate, has no ambitions of any kind, will receive neither honor nor title, but remains the most indispensable man in the country.''

"But how?"

"Well, his position is unique. He has made it for himself. There has never been anything like it before, nor will be again. He has the tidiest and most orderly brain, with the greatest capacity for storing facts, of any man living. The same great powers which I have turned to the detection of crime he has used for this particular business. The conclusions of every department are passed to him, and he is the central exchange, the clearing house, which makes out the balance. All other men are specialists, but his specialism is omniscience. We will suppose that a minister needs information as to a point which involves the Navy, India, Canada, and the bimetallic question; he could get his separate advices from various departments upon each, but only Mycroft can focus them all, and say offhand how each factor would affect the other. They began by using him as a short-cut, a convenience; now he has made himself an essential. In that great brain of his everything is pigeon-holed and can be handed out in an instant. Again and again his word has decided the national policy. He lives in it. He thinks of nothing else save when, as an intellectual exercise, he unbends if I call upon him and ask him to advise me on one of my little problems. But Jupiter is descending today. What on earth can it mean? Who is Cadogan West, and what is he to Mycroft?"

"I have it," I cried, and plunged among the litter of papers upon the sofa. "Yes, yes, here he is, sure enough! Cadogan West was the young man who was found dead on the Underground on Tuesday morning."

Holmes sat up at attention, his pipe halfway to his lips.

"This must be serious, Watson. A death which has caused my brother to alter his habits can be no ordinary one. What in the world can he have to do with it? The case was featureless as I remember it. The young man had apparently fallen out of the train and killed himself. He had not been robbed, and there was no particular reason to suspect violence. Is that not so?"

"There has been an inquest," said I, "and a good many fresh facts have come out. Looked at more closely, I should certainly say that it was a curious case."

"Judging by its effect upon my brother, I should think it must be a most extraordinary one." He snuggled down in his armchair. "Now, Watson, let's have the facts."

"The man's name was Arthur Cadogan West. He was twenty-seven years of age, unmarried, and a clerk at Woolwich Arsenal."

"Government employ. Behold the link with brother Mycroft!"

"He left Woolwich suddenly on Monday night. Was last seen by his fiancée, Miss Violet Westbury, whom he left abruptly in the fog about

7:30 that evening. There was no quarrel between them and she can give no motive for his action. The next thing heard of him was when his dead body was discovered by a plate-layer named Mason, just outside Aldgate Station on the Underground system in London."

"When?"

"The body was found at six on the Tuesday morning. It was lying wide of the metals upon the left hand of the track as one goes eastward, at a point close to the station, where the line emerges from the tunnel in which it runs. The head was badly crushed—an injury which might well have been caused by a fall from the train. The body could only have come on the line in that way. Had it been carried down from any neighboring street, it must have passed the station barriers, where a collector is always standing. This point seems absolutely certain."

"Very good. The case is definite enough. The man, dead or alive, either fell or was precipitated from a train. So much is clear to me. Continue."

"The trains which traverse the lines of rail beside which the body was found are those which run from west to east, some being purely Metropolitan, and some from Willesden and outlying junctions. It can be stated for certain that this young man, when he met his death, was traveling in this direction at some late hour of the night, but at what point he entered the train it is impossible to state."

"His ticket, of course, would show that."

"There was no ticket in his pockets."

"No ticket! Dear me, Watson, this is really very singular. According to my experience it is not possible to reach the platform of a Metropolitan train without exhibiting one's ticket. Presumably, then, the young man had one. Was it taken from him in order to conceal the station from which he came? It is possible. Or did he drop it in the carriage? That also is possible. But the point is of curious interest. I understand that there was no sign of robbery?"

"Apparently not. There is a list here of his possessions. His purse contained two pounds fifteen. He had also a checkbook on the Woolwich branch of the Capital and Counties Bank. Through this his identity was established. There were also two dress circle tickets for the Woolwich Theatre, dated for that very evening. Also a small packet of technical papers."

Holmes gave an exclamation of satisfaction.

"There we have it at last, Watson! British government—Woolwich Arsenal—technical papers—Brother Mycroft, the chain is complete. But here he comes, if I am not mistaken, to speak for himself."

A moment later the tall and portly form of Mycroft Holmes was ushered into the room. Heavily built and massive, there was a suggestion of uncouth physical inertia in the figure, but above this unwieldy frame there was perched a head so masterful in its brow, so alert in its steel-gray, deep-set eyes, so firm in its lips, and so subtle in its play of expression, that after the first glance one forgot the gross body and remembered only the dominant mind.

At his heels came our old friend Lestrade, of Scotland Yard—thin and austere. The gravity of both their faces foretold some weighty quest. The detective shook hands without a word. Mycroft Holmes struggled out of his overcoat and subsided into an armchair.

"A most annoying business, Sherlock," said he. "I extremely dislike altering my habits, but the powers that be would take no denial. In the present state of Siam it is most awkward that I should be away from the office. But it is a real crisis. I have never seen the Prime Minister so upset. As to the Admiralty—it is buzzing like an overturned beehive. Have you read up the case?"

"We have just done so. What were the technical papers?"

"Ah, there's the point! Fortunately, it has not come out. The press would be furious if it did. The papers which this wretched youth had in his pocket were the plans of the Bruce-Partington submarine."

Mycroft Holmes spoke with a solemnity which showed his sense of the importance of the subject. His brother and I sat expectant.

"Surely you have heard of it? I thought everyone had heard of it."

"Only as a name."

"Its importance can hardly be exaggerated. It has been the most jealously guarded of all government secrets. You may take it from me that naval warfare becomes impossible within the radius of a Bruce-Partington's operation. Two years ago a very large sum was smuggled through Estimates and was expended in acquiring a monopoly of the invention. Every effort has been made to keep the secret. The plans, which are exceedingly intricate, comprising some thirty separate patents, each essential to the working of the whole, are kept in an elaborate safe in a confidential office adjoining the arsenal, with burglar-proof doors and windows. Under no conceivable circumstances were the plans to be taken from the office. If the chief constructor of the Navy desired to consult them, even he was forced to go to the Woolwich office for the purpose. And yet here we find them in the pockets of a dead junior clerk in the heart of London. From an official point of view it's simply awful."

"But you have recovered them?"

"No, Sherlock, no! That's the pinch. We have not. Ten papers were taken from Woolwich. There were seven in the pockets of Cadogan West. The three most essential are gone—stolen, vanished. You must drop everything, Sherlock. Never mind your usual petty puzzles of the police court. It's a vital international problem that you have to solve. Why did Cadogan West take the papers, where are the missing ones, how did he die, how came his body where it was found, how can the evil be set right? Find an answer to all these questions, and you will have done good service for your country."

"Why do you not solve it yourself, Mycroft? You can see as far as I."

"Possibly, Sherlock. But it is a question of getting details. Give me your details, and from an armchair I will return you an excellent expert opinion. But to run here and run there, to cross-question railway guards, and lie on my face with a lens to my eye—it is not my *métier*. No, you are the one man who can clear the matter up. If you have a fancy to see your name in the next honors list—"

My friend smiled and shook his head.

"I play the game for the game's own sake," said he. "But the problem certainly presents some points of interest, and I shall be very pleased to look into it. Some more facts, please."

"I have jotted down the more essential ones upon this sheet of paper, together with a few addresses which you will find of service. The actual official guardian of the papers is the famous government expert, Sir James Walter, whose decorations and subtitles fill two lines of a book of reference. He has grown gray in the service, is a gentleman, a favored guest in the most exalted houses, and, above all, a man whose patriotism is beyond suspicion. He is one of two who have a key of the safe. I may add that the papers were undoubtedly in the office during working hours on Monday, and that Sir James left for London about three o'clock taking his key with him. He was at the house of Admiral Sinclair at Barclay Square during the whole of the evening when this incident occurred."

"Has the fact been verified?"

"Yes; his brother, Colonel Valentine Walter, has testified to his departure from Woolwich, and Admiral Sinclair to his arrival in London; so Sir James is no longer a direct factor in the problem."

"Who was the other man with a key?"

"The senior clerk and draughtsman, Mr. Sidney Johnson. He is a man of forty, married, with five children. He is a silent, morose man, but he has, on the whole, an excellent record in the public service. He is unpopular with his colleagues, but a hard worker. According to his own account, corroborated only by the word of his wife, he was at home the whole of Monday evening after office hours, and his key has never left the watchchain upon which it hangs."

"Tell us about Cadogan West."

"He has been ten years in the service and has done good work. He has the reputation of being hot-headed and impetuous, but a straight, honest man. We have nothing against him. He was next Sidney Johnson in the office. His duties brought him into daily, personal contact with the plans. No one else had the handling of them."

"Who locked the plans up that night?"

"Mr. Sidney Johnson, the senior clerk."

"Well, it is surely perfectly clear who took them away. They are actually found upon the person of this junior clerk, Cadogan West. That seems final, does it not?"

"It does, Sherlock, and yet it leaves so much unexplained. In the first place, why did he take them?"

"I presume they were of value?"

"He could have got several thousands for them very easily."

"Can you suggest any possible motive for taking the papers to London except to sell them?"

"No, I cannot."

"Then we must take that as our working hypothesis. Young West took the papers. Now this could only be done by having a false key—"

"Several false keys. He had to open the building and the room."

"He had, then, several false keys. He took the papers to London to sell the secret, intending, no doubt, to have the plans themselves back in the same next morning before they were missed. While in London on this treasonable mission he met his end."

"We will suppose that he was traveling back to Woolwich when he was killed and thrown out of the compartment."

"Aldgate, where the body was found, is considerably past the station for London Bridge, which would be his route to Woolwich."

"Many circumstances could be imagined under which he would pass London Bridge. There was someone in the carriage, for example, with whom he was having an absorbing interview. This interview led to a violent scene in which he lost his life. Possibly he tried to leave the carriage, fell out on the line, and so met his end. The other closed the door. There was a thick fog, and nothing could be seen."

"No better explanation can be given with our present knowledge; and yet consider, Sherlock, how much you leave untouched. We will suppose, for argument's sake, that young Cadogan West *had* determined to convey these papers to London. He would naturally have made an appointment with the foreign agent and kept his evening clear. Instead of that he took two tickets to the theater, escorted his fiancée halfway there, and then suddenly disappeared.''

''A blind,'' said Lestrade, who had sat listening with some impatience to the conversation.

''A very singular one. That is objection No. 1. Objection No. 2: We will suppose that he reaches London and sees the foreign agent. He must bring back the papers before morning or the loss will be discovered. He took away ten. Only seven were in his pocket. What had become of the other three? He certainly would not leave them of his own free will. Then, again, where is the price of his treason? One would have expected to find a large sum of money in his pocket.''

''It seems to me perfectly clear,'' said Lestrade. ''I have no doubt at all as to what occurred. He took the papers to sell them. He saw the agent. They could not agree as to price. He started home again, but the agent went with him. In the train the agent murdered him, took the more essential papers, and threw his body from the carriage. That would account for everything, would it not?

''Why had he no ticket?''

''The ticket would have shown which station was nearest the agent's house. Therefore he took it from the murdered man's pocket.''

''Good, Lestrade, very good,'' said Holmes. ''Your theory holds together. But if this is true, then the case is at an end. On the one hand, the traitor is dead. On the other, the plans of the Bruce-Partington submarine are presumably already on the Continent. What is there for us to do?''

''To act, Sherlock—to act!'' cried Mycroft, springing to his feet. ''All my instincts are against this explanation. Use your powers! Go to the scene of the crime! See the people concerned! Leave no stone unturned! In all your career you have never had so great a chance of serving your country.''

''Well, well!'' said Holmes, shrugging his shoulders. ''Come, Watson! And you, Lestrade, could you favor us with your company for an hour or two? We will begin our investigation by a visit to Aldgate Station. Good-bye, Mycroft. I shall let you have a report before evening, but I warn you in advance that you have little to expect.''

An hour later Holmes, Lestrade, and I stood upon the Underground railroad at the point where it emerges from the tunnel immediately before Aldgate Station. A courteous red-faced old gentleman represented the railway company.

''This is where the young man's body lay,'' said he, indicating a spot about three feet from the metals. ''It could not have fallen from above, for these, as you see, are all blank walls. Therefore, it could only have come from a train, and that train, so far as we can trace it, must have passed about midnight on Monday."

"Have the carriages been examined for any sign of violence?"

"There are no such signs, and no ticket has been found."

"No record of a door being found open?"

"None."

"We have had some fresh evidence this morning," said Lestrade. "A passenger who passed Aldgate in an ordinary Metropolitan train about 11:40 on Monday night declares that he heard a heavy thud, as of a body striking the line, just before the train reached the station. There was dense fog, however, and nothing could be seen. He made no report of it at the time. Why, whatever is the matter with Mr. Holmes?"

My friend was standing with an expression of strained intensity upon his face, staring at the railway metals where they curved out of the tunnel. Aldgate is a junction, and there was a network of points. On these his eager, questioning eyes were fixed, and I saw on his keen, alert face that tightening of the lips, that quiver of the nostrils, and concentration of the heavy, tufted brows which I knew so well.

"Points," he muttered; "the points."

"What of it? What do you mean?"

"I suppose there are no great number of points on a system such as this?"

"No; there are very few."

"And a curve, too. Points and a curve. By Jove! if it were only so."

"What is it, Mr. Holmes? Have you a clue?"

"An idea—an indication, no more. But the case certainly grows in interest. Unique, perfectly unique, and yet why not? I do not see any indications of bleeding on the line."

"There were hardly any."

"But I understand that there was a considerable wound."

"The bone was crushed, but there was no great external injury."

"And yet one would have expected some bleeding. Would it be possible for me to inspect the train which contained the passenger who heard the thud of a fall in the fog?"

"I fear not, Mr. Holmes. The train has been broken up before now, and the carriages redistributed."

"I can assure you, Mr. Holmes," said Lestrade, "that every carriage has been carefully examined. I saw to it myself."

It was one of my friend's most obvious weaknesses that he was impatient with less alert intelligences than his own.

"Very likely," said he, turning away. "As it happens, it was not the carriages which I desired to examine. Watson, we have done all we can here. We need not trouble you any further, Mr. Lestrade. I think our investigations must now carry us to Woolwich."

At London Bridge, Holmes wrote a telegram to his brother, which he handed to me before dispatching it. It ran thus:

> SEE SOME LIGHT IN THE DARKNESS, BUT IT MAY POSSIBLY FLICKER OUT. MEANWHILE, PLEASE SEND BY MESSENGER, TO AWAIT RETURN AT BAKER STREET, A COMPLETE LIST OF ALL FOREIGN SPIES OR INTERNATIONAL AGENTS KNOWN TO BE IN ENGLAND, WITH FULL ADDRESS.
>
> *Sherlock*

"That should be helpful, Watson," he remarked as we took our seats in the Woolwich train. "We certainly owe brother Mycroft a debt for having introduced us to what promises to be a really very remarkable case."

His eager face still wore that expression of intense and high-strung energy, which showed me that some novel and suggestive circumstance had opened up a stimulating line of thought. See the foxhound with hanging ears and drooping tail as it lolls about the kennels, and compare it with the same hound as, with gleaming eyes and straining muscles, it runs upon a breast-high scent—such was the change in Holmes since the morning. He was a different man from the limp and lounging figure in the mouse-colored dressing gown who had prowled so restlessly only a few hours before round the fog-girt room.

"There is material here. There is scope," said he. "I am dull indeed not to have understood its possibilities."

"Even now they are dark to me."

"The end is dark to me also, but I have hold of one idea which may lead us far. The man met his death elsewhere, and his body was on the roof of a carriage."

"On the roof!"

"Remarkable, is it not? But consider the facts. Is it a coincidence that it is found at the very point where the train pitches and sways as it comes round on the points? Is not that the place where an object upon the roof might be expected to fall off? The points would affect no object inside the train. Either the body fell from the roof, or a very curious coincidence has occurred. But now consider the question of the blood. Of course, there was no bleeding on the line if the body had bled elsewhere. Each fact is suggestive in itself. Together they have a cumulative force."

"And the ticket, too!" I cried.

"Exactly. We could not explain the absence of a ticket. This would explain it. Everything fits together."

"But suppose it were so, we are still as far as ever from unraveling the mystery of his death. Indeed, it becomes not simpler but stranger."

"Perhaps," said Holmes thoughtfully, "perhaps." He relapsed into a silent reverie, which lasted until the slow train drew up at last in Woolwich Station. There he called a cab and drew Mycroft's paper from his pocket.

"We have quite a little round of afternoon calls to make," said he. "I think that Sir James Walter claims our first attention."

The house of the famous official was a fine villa with green lawns stretching down to the Thames. As we reached it the fog was lifting, and a thin, watery sunshine was breaking through. A butler answered our ring.

"Sir James, sir?" said he with a solemn face. "Sir James died this morning."

"Good heavens!" cried Holmes in amazement. "How did he die?"

"Perhaps you would care to step in, sir, and see his brother, Colonel Valentine?"

"Yes, we had best do so."

We were ushered into a dim-lit drawing room, where an instant later we were joined by a very tall, handsome, light-bearded man of fifty, the younger brother of the dead scientist. His wild eyes, stained cheeks, and unkempt hair all spoke of the sudden blow which had fallen upon the household. He was hardly articulate as he spoke of it.

"It was this horrible scandal," said he. "My brother, Sir James, was a man of very sensitive honor, and he could not survive such an affair. It broke his heart. He was always so proud of the efficiency of his department, and this was a crushing blow."

"We had hoped that he might have given us some indications which would have helped us to clear the matter up."

"I assure you that it was all a mystery to him as it is to you and to all of us. He had already put all his knowledge at the disposal of the police. Naturally he had no doubt that Cadogan West was guilty. But all the rest was inconceivable."

"You cannot throw any new light upon the affair?"

"I know nothing myself save what I have read or heard. I have no desire to be discourteous, but you can understand, Mr. Holmes that we are much disturbed at present, and I must ask you to hasten this interview to an end."

"This is indeed an unexpected development," said my friend when we had regained the cab. "I wonder if the death was natural, or whether the poor old fellow killed himself! If the latter, may it be taken as some sign of self-reproach for duty neglected? We must leave that question to the future. Now we shall turn to the Cadogan Wests."

A small but well-kept house in the outskirts of the town sheltered the bereaved mother. The old lady was too dazed with grief to be of any use to us, but at her side was a white-faced young lady, who introduced herself as Miss Violet Westbury, the fiancée of the dead man, and the last to see him upon that fatal night.

"I cannot explain it, Mr. Holmes," she said. "I have not shut an eye since the tragedy, thinking, thinking, thinking, night and day, what the true meaning of it can be. Arthur was the most single-minded, chivalrous, patriotic man upon earth. He would have cut his right hand off before he would sell a State secret confided to his keeping. It is absurd, impossible, preposterous to anyone who knew him."

"But the facts, Miss Westbury?"

"Yes, yes; I admit I cannot explain them."

"Was he in any want of money?"

"No; his needs were very simple and his salary ample. He had saved a few hundreds, and we were to marry at the New Year."

"No signs of any mental excitement? Come, Miss Westbury, be absolutely frank with us."

The quick eye of my companion had noted some change in her manner. She colored and hesitated.

"Yes," she said at last. "I had a feeling that there was something on his mind."

"For long?"

"Only for the last week or so. He was thoughtful and worried. Once I pressed him about it. He admitted that there was something, and that it was concerned with his official life. 'It is too serious for me to speak about, even to you,' said he. I could get nothing more."

Holmes looked grave.

"Go on, Miss Westbury. Even if it seems to tell against him, go on. We cannot say what it may lead to."

"Indeed, I have nothing more to tell. Once or twice it seemed to me that he was on the point of telling me something. He spoke one evening of the importance of the secret, and I have some recollection that he said that no doubt foreign spies would pay a great deal to have it."

My friend's face grew graver still.

"Anything else?"

"He said that we were slack about such matters—that it would be easy for a traitor to get the plans."

"Was it only recently that he made such remarks?"

"Yes, quite recently."

"Now tell us of that last evening."

"We were to go to the theater. The fog was so thick that a cab was useless. We walked, and our way took us close to the office. Suddenly he darted away into the fog."

"Without a word?"

"He gave an exclamation; that was all. I waited but he never returned. Then I walked home. Next morning, after the office opened, they came to inquire. About twelve o'clock we heard the terrible news. Oh, Mr. Holmes, if you could only, only save his honor! It was so much to him."

Holmes shook his head sadly.

"Come, Watson," said he, "our ways lie elsewhere. Our next station must be the office from which the papers were taken.

"It was black enough before against this young man, but our inquiries make it blacker," he remarked as the cab lumbered off. "His coming marriage gives a motive for the crime. He naturally wanted money. The idea was in his head, since he spoke about it. He nearly made the girl an accomplice in the treason by telling her his plans. It is all very bad."

"But surely, Holmes, character goes for something? Then, again, why should he leave the girl in the street and dart away to commit a felony?"

"Exactly! There are certainly objections. But it is a formidable case which they have to meet."

Mr. Sidney Johnson, the senior clerk, met us at the office and received us with that respect which my companion's card always commanded. He was a thin, gruff, bespectacled man of middle age, his cheeks haggard, and his hands twitching from the nervous strain to which he had been subjected.

"It is bad, Mr. Holmes, very bad! Have you heard of the death of the chief?"

"We have just come from his house."

"The place is disorganized. The chief dead, Cadogan West dead, our papers stolen. And yet, when we closed our door on Monday evening, we were as efficient an office as any in the government service. Good God, it's dreadful to think of! That West, of all men, should have done such a thing!"

"You are sure of his guilt, then?"

"I can see no other way out of it. And yet I would have trusted him as I trust myself."

"At what hour was the office closed on Monday?"

"At five."

"Did you close it?"

"I am always the last man out."

"Where were the plans?"

"In that safe. I put them there myself."

"Is there no watchman to the building?"

"There is, but he has other departments to look after as well. He is an old soldier and a most trustworthy man. He saw nothing that evening. Of course the fog was very thick."

"Suppose that Cadogan West wished to make his way into the building after hours; he would need three keys, would he not, before he could reach the papers?"

"Yes, he would. The key of the outer door, the key of the office, and the key of the safe."

"Only Sir James Walter and you had those keys?"

"I had no keys of the doors—only of the safe."

"Was Sir James a man who was orderly in his habits?"

"Yes, I think he was. I know that so far as those three keys are concerned he kept them on the same ring. I have often seen them there."

"And that ring went with him to London?"

"He said so."

"And your key never left your possession?"

"Never."

"Then West, if he is the culprit, must have had a duplicate. And yet none was found upon his body. One other point: if a clerk in this office desired to sell the plans, would it not be simpler to copy the plans for himself than to take the originals, as was actually done?"

"It would take considerable technical knowledge to copy the plans in an effective way."

"But I suppose either Sir James, or you, or West had that technical knowledge?"

"No doubt we had, but I beg you won't try to drag me into the matter, Mr. Holmes. What is the use of our speculating in this way when the original plans were actually found on West?"

"Well, it is certainly singular that he should run the risk of taking originals if he could safely have taken copies, which would have equally served his turn."

"Singular, no doubt—and yet he did so."

"Every inquiry in this case reveals something inexplicable. Now there are three papers still missing. They are, as I understand, the vital ones."

"Yes, that is so."

"Do you mean to say that anyone holding these three papers, and without the seven others, could construct a Bruce-Partington submarine?"

"I reported to that effect to the Admiralty. But today I have been over the drawings again, and I am not so sure of it. The double valves with the automatic self-adjusting slots are drawn in one of the papers which have been returned. Until the foreigners had invented that for themselves they could not make the boat. Of course they might soon get over the difficulty."

"But the three missing drawings are the most important?"

"Undoubtedly."

"I think, with your permission, I will now take a stroll round the premises. I do not recall any other question which I desired to ask."

He examined the lock of the safe, the door of the room, and finally the iron shutters of the window. It was only when we were on the lawn outside that his interest was strongly excited. There was a laurel bush outside the window, and several of the branches bore signs of having been twisted or snapped. He examined them carefully with his lens, and then some dim and vague marks upon the earth beneath. Finally he asked the chief clerk to close the iron shutters, and he pointed out to me that they hardly met in the center, and that it would be possible for anyone outside to see what was going on within the room.

"The indications are ruined by the three days' delay. They may mean something or nothing. Well, Watson, I do not think that Woolwich can help us further. It is a small crop which we have gathered. Let us see if we can do better in London."

Yet we added one more sheaf to our harvest before we left Woolwich Station. The clerk in the ticket office was able to say with confidence that he saw Cadogan West—whom he knew well by sight—upon the Monday night, and that he went to London by the 8:15 to London Bridge. He was alone and took a single third-class ticket. The clerk was struck at the time by his excited and nervous manner. So shaky was he that he could hardly pick up his change, and the clerk had helped him with it. A reference to the timetable showed that the 8:15 was the first train which it was possible for West to take after he had left the lady about 7:30.

"Let us reconstruct, Watson," said Holmes after half an hour of silence. "I am not aware that in all our joint researches we have ever had a case which was more difficult to get at. Every fresh advance which we make only reveals a fresh ridge beyond. And yet we have surely made some appreciable progress.

"The effect of our inquiries at Woolwich has in the main been against young Cadogan West; but the indications at the window would lend themselves to a more favorable hypothesis. Let us suppose, for example, that he had been approached by some foreign agent. It might have been done under such pledges as would have prevented him from speaking of it, and yet would have affected his thoughts in the direction indicated by his remarks to his fiancée. Very good. We will now suppose that as he went to the theater with the young lady he suddenly, in the fog, caught a glimpse of this same agent going in the direction of the office. He was an impetuous man, quick in his decisions. Everything gave way to his duty. He followed the man, reached the window, saw the abstraction of the documents, and pursued the thief. In this way we get over the objection that no one would take originals when he could make copies. This outsider had to take originals. So far it holds together."

"What is the next step?"

"Then we come into difficulties. One would imagine that under such circumstances the first act of young Cadogan West would be to seize the villain and raise the alarm. Why did he not do so? Could it have been an official superior who took the papers? That would explain West's conduct. Or could the chief have given West the slip in the fog, and West started at once to London to head him off from his own rooms, presuming that he knew where the rooms were? The call must have been very pressing, since he left his girl standing in the fog, and made no effort to communicate with her. Our scent runs cold here, and there is a vast gap between either hypothesis and the laying of West's body, with seven papers in his pocket, on the roof of a Metropolitan train. My instinct now is to work from the other end. If Mycroft has given us the list of addresses we may be able to pick our man and follow two tracks instead of one."

Surely enough, a note awaited us at Baker Street. A government messenger had brought it post-haste. Holmes glanced at it and threw it over to me.

> There are numerous small fry, but few who would handle so big an affair. The only men worth considering are Adolph Meyer, of 13 Great George Street, Westminster; Louis La Rothière, of Campden Mansions, Notting Hill; and Hugo Oberstein, 13 Caulfield Gardens, Kensington. The latter was known to be in town on Monday and is now reported as having left. Glad to hear you have seen some light.

> The Cabinet awaits your final report with the utmost anxiety. Urgent representations have arrived from the very highest quarter. The whole force of the State is at your back if you should need it.
>
> MYCROFT

"I'm afraid," said Holmes, smiling, "that all the queen's horses and all the queen's men cannot avail in this matter." He had spread out his big map of London and leaned eagerly over it. "Well, well," said he presently with an exclamation of satisfaction, "things are turning a little in our direction at last. Why, Watson, I do honestly believe that we are going to pull it off, after all." He slapped me on the shoulder with a sudden burst of hilarity. "I am going out now. It is only a reconnaissance. I will do nothing serious without my trusted comrade and biographer at my elbow. Do you stay here, and the odds are that you will see me again in an hour or two. If time hangs heavy get foolscap and a pen, and begin your narrative of how we saved the State."

I felt some reflection of his elation in my own mind, for I knew well that he would not depart so far from his usual austerity of demeanor unless there was good cause for exultation. All the long November evening I waited, filled with impatience for his return. At last, shortly after nine o'clock, there arrived a messenger with a note:

> Am dining at Goldini's Restaurant, Gloucester Road, Kensington. Please come at once and join me there. Bring with you a jemmy, a dark lantern, a chisel, and a revolver.
>
> S.H.

It was a nice equipment for a respectable citizen to carry through the dim, fog-draped streets. I stowed them all discreetly away in my overcoat and drove straight to the address given. There sat my friend at a little round table near the door of the garish Italian restaurant.

"Have you had something to eat? Then join me in a coffee and curaçao. Try one of the proprietor's cigars. They are less poisonous than one would expect. Have you the tools?"

"They are here, in my overcoat."

"Excellent. Let me give you a short sketch of what I have done, with some indication of what we are about to do. Now it must be evident to you, Watson, that this young man's body was *placed* on the roof of the train. That was clear from the instant that I determined the fact that it was from the roof, and not from a carriage, that he had fallen."

"Could it not have been dropped from a bridge?"

"I should say it was impossible. If you examine the roofs you will find that they are slightly rounded, and there is no railing round them.

Therefore, we can say for certain that young Cadogan West was placed on it.''

''How could he be placed there?''

''That was the question which we had to answer. There is only one possible way. You are aware that the Underground runs clear of tunnels at some points in the West End. I had a vague memory that as I have traveled by it I have occasionally seen windows just above my head. Now, suppose that a train halted under such a window, would there be any difficulty in laying a body upon the roof?''

''It seems most improbable.''

''We must fall back upon the old axiom that when all other contingencies fail, whatever remains, however improbable, must be the truth. Here all other contingencies *have* failed. When I found that the leading international agent, who had just left London, lived in a row of houses which abutted upon the Underground, I was so pleased that you were a little astonished at my sudden frivolity.''

''Oh, that was it, was it?''

''Yes, that was it. Mr. Hugo Oberstein, of 13 Caulfield Gardens, had become my objective. I began my operations at Gloucester Road Station, where a very helpful official walked with me along the track and allowed me to satisfy myself not only that the back-stair windows of Caulfield Gardens open on the line but the even more essential fact that, owing to the intersection of one of the larger railways, the Underground trains are frequently held motionless for some minutes at that very spot.''

''Splendid, Holmes! You have got it!''

''So far—so far, Watson. We advance, but the goal is afar. Well, having seen the back of Caulfield Gardens, I visited the front and satisfied myself that the bird was indeed flown. It is a considerable house, unfurnished, so far as I could judge, in the upper rooms. Oberstein lived there with a single valet, who was probably a confederate entirely in his confidence. We must bear in mind that Oberstein has gone to the Continent to dispose of his booty, but not with any idea of flight; for he had no reason to fear a warrant, and the idea of an amateur domiciliary visit would certainly never occur to him. Yet that is precisely what we are about to make.''

''Could we not get a warrant and legalize it?''

''Hardly on the evidence.''

''What can we hope to do?''

''We cannot tell what correspondence may be there.''

''I don't like it, Holmes.''

''My dear fellow, you shall keep watch in the street. I'll do the criminal part. It's not a time to stick at trifles. Think of Mycroft's note, of the Admiralty, the Cabinet, the exalted person who waits for news. We are bound to go.''

My answer was to rise from the table.

He sprang up and shook me by the hand.

''I knew you would not shrink at the last,'' said he, and for a moment I saw something in his eyes which was nearer to tenderness than I had ever seen. The next instant he was his masterful, practical self once more.

''It is nearly half a mile, but there is no hurry. Let us walk,'' said he. ''Don't drop the instruments, I beg. Your arrest as a suspicious character would be a most unfortunate complication.''

Caulfield Gardens was one of those lines of flat-faced, pillared, and porticoed houses which are so prominent a product of the middle Victorian epoch in the West End of London. Next door there appeared to be a children's party, for the merry buzz of young voices and the clatter of a piano resounded through the night. The fog still hung about and screened us with its friendly shade. Holmes had lit his lantern and flashed it upon the massive door.

''This is a serious proposition,'' said he. ''It is certainly bolted as well as locked. We would do better in the area. There is an excellent archway down yonder in case a too zealous policeman should intrude. Give me a hand, Watson, and I'll do the same for you.''

A minute later we were both in the area. Hardly had we reached the dark shadows before the step of the policeman was heard in the fog above. As its soft rhythm died away, Holmes set to work upon the lower door. I saw him stoop and strain until with a sharp crash it flew open. We sprang through into the dark passage, closing the area door behind us. Holmes led the way up the curving, uncarpeted stair. His little fan of yellow light shone upon a low window.

''Here we are, Watson—this must be the one.'' He threw it open, and as he did so there was a low, harsh murmur, growing steadily into a loud roar as a train dashed past us in the darkness. Holmes swept his light along the window sill. It was thickly coated with soot from the passing engines, but the black surface was blurred and rubbed in places.

''You can see where they rested the body. Halloa, Watson! what is this? There can be no doubt that it is a blood mark.'' He was pointing to faint discolorations along the woodwork of the window. ''Here it is on the stone of the stair also. The demonstration is complete. Let us stay here until a train stops.''

We had not long to wait. The very next train roared from the tunnel as before, but slowed in the open, and then, with a creaking of brakes, pulled up immediately beneath us. It was not four feet from the window ledge to the roof of the carriages. Holmes softly closed the window.

"So far we are justified," said he. "What do you think of it, Watson?"

"A masterpiece. You have never risen to a greater height."

"I cannot agree with you there. From the moment that I conceived the idea of the body being upon the roof, which surely was not a very abstruse one, all the rest was inevitable. If it were not for the grave interests involved, the affair up to this point would be insignificant. Our difficulties are still before us. But perhaps we may find something here which may help us."

We had ascended the kitchen stair and entered the suite of rooms upon the first floor. One was a dining room, severely furnished and containing nothing of interest. A second was a bedroom, which also drew blank. The remaining room appeared more promising, and my companion settled down to a systematic examination. It was littered with books and papers, and was evidently used as a study. Swiftly and methodically Holmes turned over the contents of drawer after drawer and cupboard after cupboard, but no gleam of success came to brighten his austere face. At the end of an hour he was no further than when he started.

"The cunning dog has covered his tracks," said he. "He has left nothing to incriminate him. His dangerous correspondence has been destroyed or removed. This is our last chance."

It was a small tin cash box which stood upon the writing desk. Holmes pried it open with his chisel. Several rolls of paper were within, covered with figures and calculations, without any note to show to what they referred. The recurring words, "water pressure" and "pressure to the square inch" suggested some possible relation to a submarine. Holmes tossed them all impatiently aside. There only remained an envelope with some small newspaper slips inside it. He shook them out on the table, and at once I saw by his eager face that his hopes had been raised.

"What's this, Watson? Eh? What's this? Record of a series of messages in the advertisements of a paper. *Daily Telegraph* agony column by the print and paper. Right-hand top corner of a page. No dates—but messages arrange themselves. This must be the first:

> "Hoped to hear sooner. Terms agreed to. Write fully to address given on card.
>
> "PIERROT

"Next comes:

> "Too complex for description. Must have full report. Stuff awaits you when goods delivered.
>
> "PIERROT

"Then comes:

> "Matter presses. Must withdraw offer unless contract completed. Make appointment by letter. Will confirm by advertisement.
>
> "PIERROT

"Finally:

> "Monday night after nine. Two taps. Only ourselves. Do not be so suspicious, payment in hard cash when goods delivered.
>
> "PIERROT

"A fairly complete record, Watson! If we could only get at the man at the other end!" He sat lost in thought, tapping his fingers on the table. Finally he sprang to his feet.

"Well, perhaps it won't be so difficult, after all. There is nothing more to be done here, Watson. I think we might drive round to the offices of the *Daily Telegraph*, and so bring a good day's work to a conclusion."

Mycroft Holmes and Lestrade had come round by appointment after breakfast next day and Sherlock Holmes had recounted to them our proceedings of the day before. The professional shook his head over our confessed burglary.

"We can't do these things in the force, Mr. Holmes," said he. "No wonder you get results that are beyond us. But some of these days you'll go too far, and you'll find yourself and your friend in trouble."

"For England, home and beauty—eh, Watson? Martyrs on the altar of our country. But what do you think of it, Mycroft?"

"Excellent, Sherlock! Admirable! But what use will you make of it?"

Holmes picked up the *Daily Telegraph* which lay upon the table.

"Have you seen Pierrot's advertisement today?"

"What? Another one?"

"Yes, here it is:

> "Tonight. Same hour. Same place. Two taps. Most vitally important. Your own safety at stake.
>
> "PIERROT."

"By George!" cried Lestrade. "If he answers that we've got him!"

"That was my idea when I put it in. I think if you could both make it convenient to come with us about eight o'clock to Caulfield Gardens we might possibly get a little nearer to a solution."

One of the most remarkable characteristics of Sherlock Holmes was his power of throwing his brain out of action and switching all his thoughts on to lighter things whenever he had convinced himself that he could no longer work to advantage. I remember that during the whole of that memorable day he lost himself in a monograph which he had undertaken upon the Polyphonic Motets of Lassus. For my own part I had none of this power of detachment, and the day, in consequence, appeared to be interminable. The great national importance of the issue, the suspense in high quarters, the direct nature of the experiment which we were trying—all combined to work upon my nerve. It was a relief to me when at last, after a light dinner, we set out upon our expedition. Lestrade and Mycroft met us by appointment at the outside of Gloucester Road Station. The area door of Oberstein's house had been left open the night before, and it was necessary for me, as Mycroft Holmes absolutely and indignantly declined to climb the railings, to pass in and open the hall door. By nine o'clock we were all seated in the study, waiting patiently for our man.

An hour passed and yet another. When eleven struck, the measured beat of the great church clock seemed to sound the dirge of our hopes. Lestrade and Mycroft were fidgeting in their seats and looking twice a minute at their watches. Holmes sat silent and composed, his eyelids half shut, but every sense on the alert. He raised his head with a sudden jerk.

"He is coming," said he.

There had been a furtive step past the door. Now it returned. We heard a shuffling sound outside, and then two sharp taps with the knocker. Holmes rose, motioning us to remain seated. The gas in the hall was a mere point of light. He opened the outer door, and then as a dark figure slipped past him he closed and fastened it. "This way!" we heard him say, and a moment later our man stood before us. Holmes had followed him closely, and as the man turned with a cry of surprise and alarm he caught him by the collar and threw him back into the room. Before our prisoner had recovered his balance the door was shut and Holmes standing with his back against it. The man glared round him, staggered, and fell senseless to the floor. With the shock, his broad-brimmed hat flew from his head, his cravat slipped down from his lips, and there were the long light beard and the soft, handsome delicate features of Colonel Valentine Walter.

Holmes gave a whistle of surprise.

"You can write me down an ass this time, Watson," said he. "This was not the bird that I was looking for."

"Who is he?" asked Mycroft eagerly.

"The younger brother of the late Sir James Walter, the head of the Submarine Department. Yes, yes; I see the fall of the cards. He is coming to. I think that you had best leave his examination to me."

We had carried the prostrate body to the sofa. Now our prisoner sat up, looked round him with a horror-stricken face, and passed his hand over his forehead, like one who cannot believe his own senses.

"What is this?" he asked. "I came here to visit Mr. Oberstein."

"Everything is known, Colonel Walter," said Holmes. "How an English gentleman could behave in such a manner is beyond my comprehension. But your whole correspondence and relations with Oberstein are within our knowledge. So also are the circumstances connected with the death of young Cadogan West. Let me advise you to gain at least the small credit for repentance and confession, since there are still some details which we can only learn from your lips."

The man groaned and sank his face in his hands. We waited, but he was silent.

"I can assure you," said Holmes, "that every essential is already known. We know that you were pressed for money; that you took an impress of the keys which your brother held; and that you entered into a correspondence with Oberstein, who answered your letters through the advertisement columns of the *Daily Telegraph*. We are aware that you went down to the office in the fog on Monday night, but that you were seen and followed by young Cadogan West, who had probably some previous reason to suspect you. He saw your theft, but could not give the alarm, as it was just possible that you were taking the papers to your brother in London. Leaving all his private concerns like the good citizen that he was, he followed you closely in the fog and kept at your heels until you reached this very house. There he intervened, and then it was, Colonel Walter, that to treason you added the more terrible crime of murder."

"I did not! I did not! Before God I swear that I did not!" cried our wretched prisoner.

"Tell us, then, how Cadogan West met his end before you laid him upon the roof of a railway carriage."

"I will. I swear to you that I will. I did the rest. I confess it. It was just as you say. A Stock Exchange debt had to be paid. I needed the money badly. Oberstein offered me five thousand. It was to save myself from ruin. But as to murder, I am as innocent as you."

"What happened, then?"

"He had his suspicions before, and he followed me as you describe. I never knew it until I was at the very door. It was thick fog, and one could not see three yards. I had given two taps and Oberstein had come to the door. The young man rushed up and demanded to know what we were about to do with the papers. Oberstein had a short life-preserver. He always carried it with him. As West forced his way after us into the house Oberstein struck him on the head. The blow was a fatal one. He was dead within five minutes. There he lay in the hall, and we were at our wit's end what to do. Then Oberstein had this idea about the trains which halted under his back window. But first he examined the papers which I had brought. He said that three of them were essential, and that he must keep them. 'You cannot keep them,' said I. 'There will be a dreadful row at Woolrich if they are not returned.' 'I must keep them,' said he, 'for they are so technical that it is impossible in the time to make copies.' 'Then they must all go back together tonight,' said I. He thought for a little, and then he cried out that he had it. 'Three I will keep,' said he. 'The others we will stuff into the pocket of this young man. When he is found the whole business will assuredly be put to his account. I could see no other way out of it, so we did as he suggested. We waited half an hour at the window before a train stopped. It was so thick that nothing could be seen, and we had no difficulty in lowering West's body on to the train. That was the end of the matter so far as I was concerned."

"And your brother?"

"He said nothing, but he had caught me once with his keys, and I think that he suspected. I read in his eyes that he suspected. As you know, he never held up his head again."

There was silence in the room. It was broken by Mycroft Holmes.

"Can you not make reparation? It would ease your conscience, and possibly your punishment."

"What reparation can I make?"

"Where is Oberstein with the papers?"

"I do not know."

"Did he give you no address?"

"He said that letters to the Hôtel du Louvre, Paris, would eventually reach him."

"Then reparation is still within your power," said Sherlock Holmes.

"I will do anything I can. I owe this fellow no particular goodwill. He has been my ruin and my downfall."

"Here are paper and pen. Sit at this desk and write to my dictation. Direct the envelope to the address given. That is right. Now the letter:

"DEAR SIR:

"With regard to our transaction, you will no doubt have observed by now that one essential detail is missing. I have a tracing which will make it complete. This has involved me in extra trouble, however, and I must ask you for a further advance of five hundred pounds. I will not trust it to the post, nor will I take anything but gold or notes. I would come to you abroad, but it would excite remark if I left the country at present. Therefore I shall expect to meet you in the smoking room of the Charing Cross Hotel at noon on Saturday. Remember that only English notes, or gold, will be taken.

"That will do very well. I shall be very much surprised if it does not fetch our man."

And it did! It is a matter of history—that secret history of a nation which is often so much more intimate and interesting than its public chronicles—that Oberstein, eager to complete the coup of his lifetime, came to the lure and was safely engulfed for fifteen years in a British prison. In his trunk were found the invaluable Bruce-Partington plans, which he had put up for auction in all the naval centers of Europe.

Colonel Walter died in prison toward the end of the second year of his sentence. As to Holmes, he returned refreshed to his monograph upon the Polyphonic Motets of Lassus, which has since been printed for private circulation, and is said by experts to be the last word upon the subject. Some weeks afterward I learned incidentally that my friend spent a day at Windsor, whence he returned with a remarkably fine emerald tie pin. When I asked him if he had bought it, he answered that it was a present from a certain gracious lady in whose interests he had once been fortunate enough to carry out a small commission. He said no more; but I fancy that I could guess at that lady's name, and I have little doubt that the emerald pin will forever recall to my friend's memory the adventure of the Bruce-Partington plans.

W. SOMERSET MAUGHAM
The Traitor

WHEN ASHENDEN, GIVEN charge of a number of spies working from Switzerland, was first sent there, R., wishing him to see the sort of reports that he would be required to obtain, handed him the communications, a sheaf of typewritten documents, of a man known in the secret service as Gustav.

"He's the best fellow we've got," said R. "His information is always very full and circumstantial. I want you to give his reports your very best attention. Of course Gustav is a clever little chap, but there's no reason why we shouldn't get just as good reports from the other agents. It's merely a question of explaining exactly what we want."

Gustav, who lived at Basle, represented a Swiss firm with branches at Frankfort, Mannheim and Cologne, and by virtue of his business was able to go in and out of Germany without risk. He traveled up and down the Rhine, and gathered material about the movement of troops, the manufacture of munitions, the state of mind of the country (a point on which R. laid stress) and other matters upon which the Allies desired information. His frequent letters to his wife hid an ingenious code and the moment she received them in Basle she sent them to Ashenden in Geneva, who extracted from them the important facts and communicated these in the proper quarter. Every two months Gustav came home and prepared one of the reports that served as models to the other spies in this particular section of the secret service.

His employers were pleased with Gustav and Gustav had reason to be pleased with his employers. His services were so useful that he was not only paid more highly than the others but for particular scoops had recieved from time to time a handsome bonus.

This went on for more than a year. Then something aroused R.'s quick suspicions: he was a man of an amazing alertness, not so much of mind, as of instinct, and he had suddenly a feeling that some hankey-pankey was going on. He said nothing definite to Ashenden (whatever R. surmised he was disposed to keep to himself) but told him to go to Basle, Gustav being then in Germany, and have a talk with Gustav's wife. He left it to Ashenden to decide the tenor of the conversation.

Having arrived at Basle, and leaving his bag at the station, for he did not yet know whether he would have to stay or not, he took a tram to the corner of the street in which Gustav lived, and with a quick look to see that he was not followed, walked along to the house he sought. It was a block of flats that gave you the impression of decent poverty and Ashenden conjectured that they were inhabited by clerks and small tradespeople. Just inside the door was a cobbler's shop and Ashenden stopped.

"Does Herr Grabow live here?" he asked in his none too fluent German.

"Yes, I saw him go up a few minutes ago. You'll find him in."

Ashenden was startled, for he had but the day before received through Gustav's wife a letter addressed from Mannheim in which Gustav by means of his code gave the numbers of certain regiments that had just crossed the Rhine. Ashenden thought it unwise to ask the cobbler the question that rose to his lips, so thanked him and went up to the third floor on which he knew already that Gustav lived. He rang the bell and heard it tinkle within. In a moment the door was opened by a dapper little man with a close-shaven round head and spectacles. He wore carpet slippers.

"Herr Grabow?" asked Ashenden.

"At your service," said Gustav.

"May I come in?"

Gustav was standing with his back to the light and Ashenden could not see the look on his face. He felt a momentary hesitation and gave the name under which he received Gustav's letters from Germany.

"Come in, come in. I am very glad to see you."

Gustav led the way into a stuffy little room, heavy with carved oak furniture, and on the large table covered with a tablecloth of green velveteen was a typewriter. Gustav was apparently engaged in composing one of his invaluable reports. A woman was sitting at the open window darning socks, but at a word from Gustav rose, gathered up her things and left. Ashenden had disturbed a pretty picture of connubial bliss.

"Sit down, please. How very fortunate that I was in Basle! I have long wanted to make your acquaintance. I have only just this minute returned from Germany." He pointed to the sheets of paper by the typewriter. "I think you will be pleased with the news I bring. I have some very valuable information." He chuckled. "One is never sorry to earn a bonus."

He was very cordial, but to Ashenden his cordiality rang false. Gustav kept his eyes, smiling behind the glasses, fixed watchfully on Ashenden and it was possible that they held a trace of nervousness.

"You must have traveled quickly to get here only a few hours after your letter, sent here and then sent on by your wife, reached me in Geneva."

"That is very probable. One of the things I had to tell you is that the Germans suspect that information is getting through by means of commercial letters and so they have decided to hold up all mail at the frontier for eight and forty hours."

"I see," said Ashenden amiably. "And was it on that account that you took the precaution of dating your letter forty-eight hours after you sent it?"

"Did I do that? That was very stupid of me. I must have mistaken the day of the month."

Ashenden looked at Gustav with a smile. That was very thin; Gustav a business man, knew too well how important in his particular job was the exactness of a date. The circuitous routes by which it was necessary to get information from Germany made it difficult to transmit news quickly and it was essential to know precisely on what days certain events had taken place.

"Let me look at your passport a minute," said Ashenden.

"What do you want with my passport?"

"I want to see when you went into Germany and when you came out."

"But you do not imagine that my comings and goings are marked on my passport? I have methods of crossing the frontier."

Ashenden knew a good deal of this matter. He knew that both the Germans and the Swiss guarded the frontier with severity.

"Oh? Why should you not cross in the ordinary way? You were engaged because your connection with a Swiss firm supplying necessary goods to Germany made it easy for you to travel backwards and forwards without suspicion. I can understand that you might get past the German sentries with the connivance of the Germans, but what about the Swiss?"

Gustav assumed a look of indignation.

"I do not understand you. Do you mean to suggest that I am in the service of the Germans? I give you my word of honor . . . I will not allow my straightforwardness to be impugned."

"You would not be the only one to take money from both sides and provide information of value to neither."

"Do you pretend that my information is of no value? Why then have you given me more bonuses than any other agent has received? The

Colonel has repeatedly expressed the highest satisfaction with my services.''

It was Ashenden's turn now to be cordial.

''Come, come, my dear fellow, do not try to ride the high horse. You are not under the impression that we leave the statements of our agents without corroboration or that we are so foolish as not to keep track of their movements? Even the best of jokes cannot bear an indefinite repetition. I am in peace time a humorist by profession and I tell you that from bitter experience.'' Now Ashenden thought the moment had arrived to attempt his bluff; he knew something of the excellent but difficult game of poker. ''We have information that you have not been to Germany now, nor since you were engaged by us, but have sat here quietly in Basle, and all your reports are merely due to your fertile imagination.''

Gustav looked at Ashenden and saw a face expressive of nothing but tolerance and good humor. A smile slowly broke on his lips and he gave his shoulders a little shrug.

''Did you think I was such a fool as to risk my life for fifty pounds a month? I love my wife.''

Ashenden laughed outright.

''I congratulate you. It is not everyone who can flatter himself that he has made a fool of our secret service for a year.''

''I had the chance of earning money without any difficulty. My firm stopped sending me into Germany at the beginning of the war, but I learned what I could from the other travelers, I kept my ears open in restaurants and beer cellars, and I read the German papers. I got a lot of amusement out of sending you reports and letters.''

''I don't wonder,'' said Ashenden.

''What are you going to do?''

''Nothing. What can we do? You are not under the impression that we shall continue to pay you a salary?''

''No, I cannot expect that.''

''By the way, if it is not indiscreet, may I ask if you have been playing the same game with the Germans?''

''Oh, no,'' Gustav cried vehemently. ''How can you think it? My sympathies are absolutely pro-Ally. My heart is entirely with you.''

''Well, why not?'' asked Ashenden. ''The Germans have all the money in the world and there is no reason why you should not get some of it. We could give you information from time to time that the Germans would be prepared to pay for.''

Gustav drummed his fingers on the table. He took up a sheet of the now useless report.

"The Germans are dangerous people to meddle with."

"You are a very intelligent man. And after all, even if your salary is stopped, you can always earn a bonus by bringing us news that can be useful to us. But it will have to be substantiated; in future we pay only by results."

"I will think of it."

For a moment or two Ashenden left Gustav to his reflections. He lit a cigarette and watched the smoke he had inhaled fade into the air. He thought too.

"Is there anything particular you want to know?" asked Gustav suddenly.

Ashenden smiled.

"It would be worth a couple of thousand Swiss francs to you if you could tell me what the Germans are doing with a spy of theirs in Lucerne. He is an Englishman and his name is Grantley Caypor."

"I have heard the name," said Gustav. He paused a moment. "How long are you staying here?"

"As long as necessary. I will take a room at the hotel and let you know the number. If you have anything to say to me you can be sure of finding me in my room at nine every morning and at seven every night."

"I should not risk coming to the hotel. But I can write."

"Very well."

Ashenden rose to go and Gustav accompanied him to the door.

"We part without ill-feeling then?" he asked.

"Of course. Your reports will remain in our archives as models of what a report should be."

Ashenden spent two or three days visiting Basle. It did not much amuse him. He passed a good deal of time in the bookshops turning over the pages of books that would have been worth reading if life were a thousand years long. Once he saw Gustav in the street. On the fourth morning, a letter was brought up with his coffee. The envelope was that of a commercial firm unknown to him and inside it was a typewritten sheet. There was no address and no signature. Ashenden wondered if Gustav was aware that a typewriter could betray its owner as certainly as a handwriting. Having twice carefully read the letter, he held the paper up to the light to see the watermark (he had no reason for doing this except that the sleuths of detective novels always did it), then struck a match and watched it burn. He scrunched up the charred fragments in his hand.

He got up, for he had taken advantage of his situation to breakfast in bed, packed his bag and took the next train to Berne. From there he was able to send a code telegram to R. His instructions were given to him verbally two days later, in the bedroom of his hotel at an hour when no one was likely to be seen walking along a corridor, and within twenty-four hours, though by a circuitous route, he arrived at Lucerne.

Having taken a room at the hotel at which he had been instructed to stay Ashenden went out; it was a lovely day, early in August, and the sun shone in an unclouded sky. He had not been to Lucerne since he was a boy and but vaguely remembered a covered bridge, a great stone lion and a church in which he had sat, bored yet impressed, while they played an organ; and now wandering along a shady quay (and the lake looked just as tawdry and unreal as it looked on the picture postcards) he tried not so much to find his way about a half-forgotten scene as to reform in his mind some recollection of the shy and eager lad, so impatient for life (which he saw not in the present of his adolescence but only in the future of his manhood), who so long ago had wandered there. But it seemed to him that the most vivid of his memories was not of himself, but of the crowd; he seemed to remember sun and heat and people; the train was crowded and so was the hotel, the lake steamers were packed and on the quays and in the streets you threaded your way among the throng of holiday makers. They were fat and old and ugly and odd, and they stank. Now, in wartime, Lucerne was as deserted as it must have been before the world at large discovered that Switzerland was the playground of Europe. Most of the hotels were closed, the streets were empty, the rowing boats for hire rocked idly at the water's edge and there was none to take them, and in the avenues by the lake the only persons to be seen were serious Swiss taking their neutrality, like a dachshund, for a walk with them. Ashenden felt exhilarated by the solitude, and sitting down on a bench that faced the water surrendered himself deliberately to the sensation. It was true that the lake was absurd, the water was too blue, the mountains too snowy, and its beauty, hitting you in the face, exasperated rather than thrilled; but all the same there was something pleasing in the prospect, an artless candor, like one of Mendelssohn's *Songs Without Words,* that made Ashenden smile with complacency. Lucerne reminded him of wax flowers under glass cases and cuckoo clocks and fancy work in Berlin wool. So long as all events as the fine weather lasted he was prepared to enjoy himself. He did not see why he should not at least try to combine pleasure to himself with profit to his country. He was traveling with a brand-new passport in his pocket, under a borrowed name, and this gave him an agreeable sense of owning a new personality. He was often slightly tired of himself, and it diverted him for a while to be merely a creature of R.'s facile invention. The experience he had just enjoyed appealed to his acute sense of the absurd. R., it is true, had not seen the fun of it: what humor R. possessed was of a sardonic turn and he had no facility for taking in good part a joke at his own expense. To do that you must be able to look at yourself from the outside and be at the same time spectator and actor in the pleasant comedy of life. R. was a soldier and regarded introspection as unhealthy, un-English and unpatriotic.

Ashenden got up and strolled slowly to his hotel. It was a small German hotel, of the second class, spotlessly clean, and his bedroom had a nice view; it was furnished with brightly varnished pitch-pine, and though on a cold wet day it would have been wretched, in that warm and sunny weather it was gay and pleasing. There were tables in the hall and he sat down at one of these and ordered a bottle of beer. The landlady was curious to know why in that dead season he had come to stay and he was glad to satisfy her curiosity. He told her that he had recently recovered from an attack of typhoid and had come to Lucerne to get back his strength. He was employed in the Censorship Department and was taking the opportunity to brush up his rusty German. He asked her if she could recommend to him a German teacher. The landlady was a blond and blowsy Swiss, good-humored and talkative, so that Ashenden felt pretty sure that she would repeat in the proper quarter the information he gave her. It was his turn now to ask a few questions. She was voluble on the subject of the war on account of which the hotel, in that month so full that rooms had to be found for visitors in neighboring houses, was nearly empty. A few people came in from outside to eat their meals *en pension*, but she had only two lots of resident guests. One was an old Irish couple who lived in Vevey and passed their summers in Lucerne and the other was an Englishman and his wife. She was a German and they were obliged on that account to live in neutral country. Ashenden took care to show little curiosity about them—he recognized in the description Grantley Caypor—but of her own accord she told him that they spent most of the day walking about the mountains. Herr Caypor was a botanist and much interested in the flora of the country. His lady was a very nice woman and she felt her position keenly. Ah, well, the war could not last forever. The landlady bustled away and Ashenden went upstairs.

Dinner was at seven, and, wishing to be in the dining room before anyone else so that he could take stock of his fellow guests as they entered, he went down as soon as he heard the bell. It was a very plain, stiff, whitewashed room, with chairs of the same shiny pitch-pine as in his bedroom, and on the walls were oleographs of Swiss lakes. On each little table was a bunch of flowers. It was all neat and clean and presaged a bad dinner. Ashenden would have liked to make up for it by ordering a bottle of the best Rhine wine to be found in the hotel, but did not venture to draw attention to himself by extravagance (he saw on two or three tables half-empty bottles of table hock, which made him surmise that his fellow guests drank thriftily), and so contented himself with ordering a pint of lager. Presently one or two persons came in, single men with some occupation in Lucerne and obviously Swiss, and sat down each at his own little table and untied the napkins that at the end of luncheon they had neatly tied up. They propped newspapers against their water jugs and read while they somewhat noisily ate their soup. Then entered a very old tall bent man, with white hair and a drooping mustache, accompanied by a little old white-haired lady in black. These were certainly the Irish colonel and his wife of whom the landlady had spoken. They took their seats and the colonel poured out a thimbleful of wine for his wife and a thimbleful for himself. They waited in silence for their dinner to be served to them by the buxom, hearty maid.

At last the persons arrived for whom Ashenden had been waiting. He was doing his best to read a German book and it was only by an exercise of self-control that he allowed himself only for one instant to raise his eyes as they came in. His glance showed him a man of about forty-five with short dark hair, somewhat grizzled, of middle height, but corpulent, with a broad red clean-shaven face. He wore a shirt open at the neck, with a wide collar, and a gray suit. He walked ahead of his wife, and of her, Ashenden only caught the impression of a German woman self-effaced and dusty. Grantley Caypor sat down and began in a loud voice explaining to the waitress that they had taken an immense walk. They had been up some mountain the name of which meant nothing to Ashenden but which excited in the maid expressions of astonishment and enthusiasm. Then Caypor, still in fluent German but with a marked English accent, said that they were so late they had not even gone up to wash, but had just rinsed their hands outside. He had a resonant voice and a jovial manner.

"Serve me quick, we're starving with hunger, and bring beer, bring three bottles. *Lieber Gott,* what a thirst I have!"

He seemed to be a man of exuberant vitality. He brought into that dull, overclean dining room the breath of life and everyone in it appeared on a sudden more alert. He began to talk to his wife, in English, and everything he said could be heard by all; but presently she interrupted him with a remark made in an undertone. Caypor stopped and Ashenden felt that his eyes were turned in his direction. Mrs. Caypor had noticed the arrival of a stranger and had drawn her husband's attention to it. Ashenden turned the page of the book he was pretending to read, but he felt that Caypor's gaze was fixed intently upon him. When he addressed his wife again it was in so low a tone that Ashenden could not even tell what language he used, but when the maid brought them their soup Caypor, his voice still low, asked her a question. It was plain that he was enquiring who Ashenden was. Ashenden could catch of the maid's reply but the one word *länder*.

One or two people finished their dinner and went out picking their teeth. The old Irish colonel and his old wife rose from their table and he stood aside to let her pass. They had eaten their meal without exchanging a word. She walked slowly to the door; but the colonel stopped to say a word to a Swiss who might have been a local attorney, and when she reached it she stood there, bored and with a sheeplike look, patiently waiting for her husband to come and open it for her. Ashenden realized that she had never opened a door for herself. She did not know how to. In a minute the colonel with his old, old gait came to the door and opened it; she passed out and he followed. The little incident offered a key to their whole lives, and from it Ashenden began to reconstruct their histories, circumstances and characters; but he pulled himself up: he could not allow himself the luxury of creation. He finished his dinner.

When he went into the hall he saw tied to the leg of a table a bull terrier and in passing mechanically put down his hand to fondle the dog's drooping, soft ears. The landlady was standing at the foot of the stairs.

"Whose is this lovely beast?" asked Ashenden.

"He belongs to Herr Caypor. Fritzi, he is called. Herr Caypor says he has a longer pedigree than the King of England."

Fritzi rubbed himself against Ashenden's leg and with his nose sought the palm of his hand. Ashenden went upstairs to fetch his hat, and when he came down saw Caypor standing at the entrance of the hotel talking with the landlady. From the sudden silence and their constrained manner he guessed that Caypor had been making inquiries about him. When he passed between them, into the street, out of the corner of his eye he saw Caypor give him a suspicious stare. That frank, jovial red face bore then a look of shifty cunning.

Ashenden strolled along till he found a tavern where he could have his coffee in the open and to compensate himself for the bottle of beer that his sense of duty had urged him to drink at dinner, ordered the best brandy the house provided. He was pleased at last to have come face to face with the man of whom he had heard so much and in a day or two hoped to become acquainted with him. It is never very difficult to get to know anyone who has a dog. But he was in no hurry; he would let things take their course: with the object he had in view he could not afford to be hasty.

Ashenden reviewed the circumstances. Grantley Caypor was an Englishman, born according to his passport in Birmingham, and he was forty-two years of age. His wife, to whom he had been married for eleven years, was of German birth and parentage. That was public knowledge. Information about his antecendents was contained in a private document. He had started life, according to this, in a lawyer's office in Birmingham and then had drifted into journalism. He had been connected with an English paper in Cairo and with another in Shanghai. There he got into trouble for attempting to get money on false pretenses and was sentenced to a short term of imprisonment. All trace of him was lost for two years after his release, when he reappeared in a shipping office in Marseilles. From there, still in the shipping business, he went to Hamburg, where he married, and to London. In London he set up for himself, in the export business, but after some time failed and was made a bankrupt. He returned to journalism. At the outbreak of war he was once more in the shipping business and in August 1914 was living quietly with his German wife at Southampton. In the beginning of the following year he told his employers that owing to the nationality of his wife his position was intolerable; they had no fault to find with him and, recognizing that he was in an awkward fix, granted his request that he should be transferred to Genoa. Here he remained till Italy entered the war, but then gave notice and with his papers in perfect order crossed the border and took up his residence in Switzerland.

All this indicated a man of doubtful honesty and unsettled disposition, with no background and of no financial standing; but the facts were of no importance to anyone till it was discovered that Caypor, certainly from the beginning of the war and perhaps sooner, was in the service of the German Intelligence Department. He had a salary of forty pounds a month. But though dangerous and wily no steps would have been taken to deal with him if he had contented himself with transmitting such news as he was able to get in Switzerland. He could do no great harm there and it might even be possible to make use of him to convey information that it was desirable to let the enemy have. He had no notion that anything was known of him. His letters, and he received a good many, were closely censored; there were a few codes that the people who dealt with such matters could not in the end decipher and it might be that sooner or later through time it would be possible to lay hands on the organization that still flourished in England. But then he did something that drew R.'s attention to him. Had he known it none could have blamed him for shaking in his shoes: R. was not a very nice man to get on the wrong side of. Caypor scraped acquaintance in Zürich with a young Spaniard, Gomez by name, who had lately entered the British secret service, by his nationality inspired him with confidence and managed to worm out of him the fact that he was engaged in espionage. Probably the Spaniard, with a very human desire to seem important, had done no more than talk mysteriously; but on Caypor's information he was watched when he went to Germany and one day caught just as he was posting a letter in a code that was eventually deciphered. He was tried, convicted and shot. It was bad enough to lose a useful and disinterested agent, but it entailed besides the changing of a safe and simple code. R. was not pleased. But R. was not the man to let any desire of revenge stand in the way of his main object and it occurred to him that if Caypor was merely betraying his country for money it might be possible to get him to take more money to betray his employers. The fact that he had succeeded in delivering into their hands an agent of the Allies must seem to them an earnest of his good faith. He might be very useful. But R. had no notion what kind of a man Caypor was, he had lived his shabby, furtive life obscurely, and the only photograph that existed of him was one taken for a passport. Ashenden's instructions were to get acquainted with Caypor and see whether there was any chance that he would work honestly for the British: if he thought there was, he was entitled to sound him and if his suggestions were met with favor to make certain propositions. It was a task that needed tact and a knowledge of men. If on the other hand Ashenden came to the conclusion that Caypor could not be bought, he was to watch and report his movements. The information he had obtained from Gustav was vague, but important; there was only one point in it that was interesting, and this was that the head of the German Intelligence Department in Berne was growing restive at Caypor's lack of activity. Caypor was asking for a higher salary and Major von P. had told him that he must earn it. It might be that he was urging him to go to England. If he could be induced to cross the frontier Ashenden's work was done.

"How the devil do you expect *me* to persuade him to put his head in a noose?" asked Ashenden.

"It won't be a noose; it'll be a firing squad," said R.

"Caypor's clever."

"Well, be cleverer, damn your eyes."

Ashenden made up his mind that he would take no steps to make Caypor's acquaintance, but allow the first advances to be made by him. If he was being pressed for results it must surely occur to him that it would be worth while to get into conversation with an Englishman who was employed in the Censorship Department. Ashenden was prepared with a supply of information that it could not in the least benefit the

Central Powers to possess. With a false name and a false passport he had little fear that Caypor would guess that he was a British agent.

Ashenden did not have to wait long. Next day he was sitting in the doorway of the hotel, drinking a cup of coffee and already half asleep after a substantial *mittagessen,* when the Caypors came out of the dining room. Mrs. Caypor went upstairs and Caypor released his dog. The dog bounded along and in a friendly fashion leaped up against Ashenden.

"Come here, Fritzi," cried Caypor, and then to Ashenden: "I'm so sorry. But he's quite gentle."

"Oh, that's all right. He won't hurt me."

Caypor stopped at the doorway.

"He's a bull terrier. You don't often see them on the Continent." He seemed while he spoke to be taking Ashenden's measure; he called to the maid, "A coffee, please, *fräulein.* You've just arrived, haven't you?"

"Yes, I came yesterday."

"Really? I didn't see you in the dining room last night. Are you making a stay?"

"I don't know. I've been ill and I've come here to recuperate."

The maid came with the coffee and seeing Caypor talking to Ashenden, put the tray on the table at which he was sitting. Caypor gave a laugh of faint embarrassment.

"I don't want to force myself upon you. I don't know why the maid put my coffee on your table."

"Please sit down," said Ashenden.

"It's very good of you. I've lived so long on the Continent that I'm always forgetting that my countrymen are apt to look upon it as confounded cheek if you talk to them. Are you English, by the way, or American?"

"English," said Ashenden.

Ashenden was by nature a very shy person, and he had in vain tried to cure himself of a failing that at his age was unseemly, but on occasion he knew how to make effective use of it. He explained now in a hesitating and awkward manner the facts that he had the day before told the landlady and that he was convinced she had already passed on to Caypor.

"You couldn't have come to a better place than Lucerne. It's an oasis of peace in this war-weary world. When you're here you might almost forget that there is such a thing as a war going on. That is why I've come here. I'm a journalist by profession."

"I couldn't help wondering if you wrote," said Ashenden, with an eager timid smile.

It was clear that he had not learnt that "oasis of peace in a war-weary world" at the shipping office.

"You see, I married a German lady," said Caypor gravely.

"Oh, really?"

"I don't think anyone could be more patriotic than I am, I'm English through and through and I don't mind telling you that in my opinion the British Empire is the greatest instrument for good that the world has ever seen, but having a German wife I naturally see a good deal of the reverse of the medal. You don't have to tell me that the Germans have faults, but frankly I'm not prepared to admit that they're devils incarnate. At the beginning of the war my poor wife had a very rough time in England and I for one couldn't have blamed her if she'd felt rather bitter about it. Everyone thought she was a spy. It'll make you laugh when you know her. She's the typical German *hausfrau* who cares for nothing but her house and her husband and our only child Fritzi." Caypor fondled his dog and gave a little laugh. "Yes, Fritzi, you are our child, aren't you? Naturally it made my position very awkward, I was connected with some very important papers, and my editors weren't comfortable about it. Well, to cut a long story short I thought the most dignified course was to resign and come to a neutral country till the storm blew over. My wife and I never discuss the war, though I'm bound to tell you that it's more on my account than hers, she's much more tolerant than I am and she's more willing to look upon this terrible business from my point of view than I am from hers."

"That is strange," said Ashenden. "As a rule women are so much more rabid than men."

"My wife is a very remarkable person. I should like to introduce you to her. By the way, I don't know if you know my name. Grantley Caypor."

"My name is Somerville," said Ashenden.

He told him then of the work he had been doing in the Censorship Department, and he fancied that into Caypor's eyes came a certain intentness. Presently he told him that he was looking for someone to give him conversation lessons in German so that he might rub up his rusty knowledge of the language; and as he spoke a notion flashed across his mind: he gave Caypor a look and saw that the same notion had come to him. It had occurred to them at the same instant that it would be a very good plan for Ashenden's teacher to be Mrs. Caypor.

"I asked our landlady if she could find me someone and she said she thought she could. I must ask her again. It ought not to be very hard to find a man who is prepared to come and talk German to me for an hour a day."

"I wouldn't take anyone on the landlady's recommendation," said Caypor. "After all you want someone with a good north-German accent and she only talks Swiss. I'll ask my wife if she knows anyone. My wife's a very highly educated woman and you could trust her recommendation."

"That's very kind of you."

Ashenden observed Grantley Caypor at his ease. He noticed how the small, gray-green eyes, which last night he had not been able to see, contradicted the red good-humored frankness of the face. They were quick and shifty, but when the mind behind them was seized by an unexpected notion they were suddenly still. It gave one a peculiar feeling of the working of the brain. They were not eyes that inspired confidence; Caypor did that with his jolly, good-natured smile, the openness of his broad, weather-beaten face, his comfortable obesity and the cheeriness of his loud, deep voice. He was doing his best now to be agreeable. While Ashenden talked to him, a littly shyly still but gaining confidence from that breezy, cordial manner, capable of putting anyone at his ease, it intrigued him to remember that the man was a common spy. It gave a tang to his conversation to reflect that he had been ready to sell his country for no more than forty pounds a month. Ashenden had known Gomez, the young Spaniard whom Caypor had betrayed. He was a high-spirited youth, with a love of adventure, and he had undertaken his dangerous mission not for the money he earned by it, but from a passion for romance. It amused him to outwit the clumsy German and it appealed to his sense of the absurd to play a part in a shilling shocker. It was not very nice to think of him now six feet underground in a prison yard. He was young and he had a certain grace of gesture. Ashenden wondered whether Caypor had felt a qualm when he delivered him up to destruction.

"I suppose you know a little German?" asked Caypor, interested in the stranger.

"Oh yes, I was a student in Germany, and I used to talk it fluently, but that is long ago and I have forgotten. I can still read it very comfortably."

"Oh, yes, I noticed you were reading a German book last night."

Fool! It was only a little while since he had told Ashenden that he had not seen him at dinner. He wondered whether Caypor had observed the slip. How difficult it was never to make one! Ashenden must be on his guard; the thing that made him most nervous was the thought that he might not answer readily enough to his assumed name of Somerville. Of course there was always the chance that Caypor had made the slip on purpose to see by Ashenden's face whether he noticed anything. Caypor got up.

"There is my wife. We go for a walk up one of the mountains every afternoon. I can tell you some charming walks. The flowers even now are lovely."

"I'm afraid I must wait till I'm a bit stronger," said Ashenden, with a little sigh.

He had naturally a pale face and never looked as robust as he was. Mrs. Caypor came downstairs and her husband joined her. They walked down the road, Fritzi bounding round them, and Ashenden saw the Caypor immediately began to speak with volubility. He was evidently telling his wife the results of his interview with Ashenden. Ashenden looked at the sun shining so gaily on the lake; the shadow of a breeze fluttered the green leaves of the trees; everything invited to a stroll: he got up, went to his room and throwing himself on his bed had a very pleasant sleep.

He went into dinner that evening as the Caypors were finishing, for he had wandered melancholy about Lucerne in the hope of finding a cocktail that would enable him to face the potato salad that he foresaw, and on their way out of the dining room Caypor stopped and asked him if he would drink coffee with them. When Ashenden joined them in the hall Caypor got up and introduced him to his wife. She bowed stiffly and no answering smile came to her face to respond to Ashenden's civil greeting. It was not hard to see that her attitude was definitely hostile. It put Ashenden at his ease. She was a plainish woman, nearing forty, with a muddy skin and vague features; her drab hair was arranged in a plait round her head like that of Napoleon's Queen of Prussia; and she was squarely built, plump rather than fat, and solid. But she did not look stupid; she looked on the contrary a woman of character and Ashenden, who had lived enough in Germany to recognize the type, was ready to believe that though capable of doing the housework, cooking the dinner and climbing a mountain, she might be also prodigiously well informed. She wore a white blouse that showed a sunburned neck, a black skirt and heavy walking boots. Caypor addressing her in English told her in his jovial way, as though she did not know it already, what Ashenden had told him about himself. She listened grimly.

"I think you told me you understood German," said Caypor, his big red face wreathed in polite smiles but his little eyes darting about restlessly.

"Yes, I was for some time a student in Heidelberg."

"Really?" said Mrs. Caypor in English, an expression of faint interest for a moment chasing away the sullenness from her face. "I know Heidelberg very well. I was at school there for one year."

Her English was correct, but throaty, and the mouthing emphasis she gave her words was disagreeable. Ashenden was diffuse in praise of the old university town and the beauty of the neighborhood. She heard him, from the standpoint of her Teutonic superiority, with toleration rather than with enthusiasm.

"It is well known that the valley of the Neckar is one of the beauty places of the whole world," she said.

"I have not told you, my dear," said Caypor then, "that Mr. Somerville is looking for someone to give him conversation lessons while he is here. I told him that perhaps you could suggest a teacher."

"No, I know no one whom I could conscientiously recommend," she answered. "The Swiss accent is hateful beyond words. It could do Mr. Somerville only harm to converse with a Swiss."

"If I were in your place, Mr. Somerville, I would try and persuade my wife to give you lessons. She is, if I may say so, a very cultivated and highly educated woman."

"*Ach,* Grantley, I have not the time. I have my own work to do."

Ashenden saw that he was being given his opportunity. The trap was prepared and all he had to do was fall in. He turned to Mrs. Caypor with a manner that he tried to make shy, deprecating and modest.

"Of course it would be too wonderful if you would give me lessons. I should look upon it as a real privilege. Naturally I wouldn't want to interfere with your work, I am just here to get well, with nothing in the world to do, and I would suit my time entirely to your convenience."

He felt a flash of satisfaction pass from one to the other and in Mrs. Caypor's blue eyes he fancied that he saw a dark glow.

"Of course it would be a purely business arrangement," said Caypor. "There's no reason that my good wife shouldn't earn a little pin money. Would you think ten francs an hour too much?"

"No," said Ashenden, "I should think myself lucky to get a first-rate teacher for that."

"What do you say, my dear? Surely you can spare an hour, and you would be doing this gentleman a kindness. He would learn that all Germans are not the devilish fiends that they think them in England."

On Mrs. Caypor's brow was an uneasy frown and Ashenden could not but think with apprehension of that hour's conversation a day that he was going to exchange with her. Heaven only knew how he would have to rack his brain for subjects of discourse with that heavy and morose woman. Now she made a visible effort.

"I shall be very pleased to give Mr. Somerville conversation lessons."

"I congratulate you, Mr. Somerville," said Caypor noisily. "You're in for a treat. When will you start, tomorrow at eleven?"

"That would suit me very well if it suits Mrs. Caypor.'

"Yes, that is as good an hour as another," she answered.

Ashenden left them to discuss the happy outcome of their diplomacy. But when, punctually at eleven next morning, he heard a knock at his door (for it had been arranged that Mrs. Caypor should give him his lesson in his room) it was not without trepidation that he opened it. It behooved him to be frank, a trifle indiscreet, but obviously wary of a German woman, sufficiently intelligent, and impulsive. Mrs. Caypor's face was dark and sulky. She plainly hated having anything to do with him. But they sat down and she began, somewhat peremptorily, to ask him questions about his knowledge of German literature. She corrected his mistakes with exactness and when he put before her some difficulty in German construction explained it with clearness and precision. It was obvious that though she hated giving him a lesson she meant to give it conscientiously. She seemed to have not only an aptitude for teaching but a love of it, and as the hour went on she began to speak with greater earnestness. It was already only by an effort that she remembered that he was a brutal Englishman. Ashenden, noticing the unconscious struggle within her, found himself not a little entertained; and it was with truth that, when later in the day Caypor asked him how the lesson had gone, he answered that is was highly satisfactory; Mrs. Caypor was an excellent teacher and a most interesting person.

"I told you so. She's the most remarkable woman I know."

And Ashenden had a feeling that when in his hearty, laughing way Caypor said this he was for the first time entirely sincere.

In a day or two Ashenden guessed that Mrs. Caypor was giving him lessons only in order to enable Caypor to arrive at a closer intimacy with him, for she confined herself strictly to matters of literature, music and painting; and when Ashenden, by way of experiment, brought the conversation round to the war, she cut him short.

"I think that is a topic that we had better avoid, Herr Somerville," she said.

She continued to give her lessons with the greatest thoroughness, and he had his money's worth, but every day she came with the same sullen face and it was only in the interest of teaching that she lost for a moment her instinctive dislike of him. Ashenden exercised in turn, but in vain, all his wiles. He was ingratiating, ingenious, humble, grateful, flattering, simple and timid. She remained coldly hostile. She was a fanatic. Her patriotism was aggressive, but disinterested, and obsessed with the notion of the superiority of all things German she loathed England with a virulent hatred because in that country she saw the chief obstacle to their diffusion. Her ideal was a German world in which the rest of the nations under a hegemony greater than that of Rome should enjoy the benefits of German science and German art and German culture. There was in the conception a magnificent impudence that appealed to Ashenden's sense of humor. She was no fool. She had read much, in several languages, and she could talk of books she had read with good sense. She had a knowledge of modern painting and modern music that not a little impressed Ashenden. It was amusing once to hear her before luncheon play one of those silvery little pieces of Debussy: she played it disdainfully because it was French and so light, but with an angry appreciation of its grace and gaiety. When Ashenden congratulated her she shrugged her shoulders.

"The decadent music of a decadent nation," she said. Then with powerful hands she struck the first resounding chords of a sonata by Beethoven; but she stopped. "I cannot play, I am out of practice, and you English, what do you know of music? You have not produced a composer since Purcell!"

"What do you think of that statement?" Ashenden, smiling, asked Caypor who was standing near.

"I confess its truth. The little I know of music my wife taught me. I wish you could hear her play when she is in practice." He put his fat hand, with its square, stumpy fingers, on her shoulder. "She can wring your heartstrings with pure beauty."

"Dummer Kerl," she said, in a soft voice. "Stupid fellow," and Ashenden saw her mouth for a moment quiver, but she quickly recovered. "You English, you cannot paint, you cannot model, you cannot write music."

"Some of us can at time write pleasing verses," said Ashenden, with good humor, for it was not his business to be put out, and, he did not know why, two lines occuring to him he said them:

> "Whither, O splendid ship, thy white sails crowding,
> Leaning across the bosom of the urgent West."

"Yes," Mrs. Caypor, with a strange gesture, "you can write poetry. I wonder why."

And to Ashenden's surprise she went on, in her guttural English, to recite the next two lines of the poem he had quoted.

"Come, Grantley, *mittagessen* is ready, let us go into the dining room."

They left Ashenden reflective.

Ashenden admired goodness, but was not outraged by wickedness. People sometimes thought him heartless because he was more often interested in others than attached to them, and even in the few to whom he was attached his eyes saw with equal clearness the merits and the defects. When he liked people it was not because he was blind to their faults, he did not mind their faults but accepted them with a tolerant shrug of the shoulders, or because he ascribed to them excellencies that they did not possess; and since he judged his friends with candor they never disappointed him and so he seldom lost one. He asked from none more than he could give. He was able to pursue his study of the Caypors without prejudice and without passion. Mrs. Caypor seemed to him more of a piece and therefore the easier of the two to understand; she obviously detested him; though it was so necessary for her to be civil to him her antipathy was strong enough to wring from her now and then an expression of rudeness; and had she been safely able to do so she would have killed him without a qualm. But in the pressure of Caypor's chubby hand on his wife's shoulder and in the fugitive trembling of her lips Ashenden had divined that this unprepossessing woman and that mean fat man were joined together by a deep and sincere love. It was touching. Ashenden assembled the observations that he had been making for the past few days and little things that he had noticed but to which he had attached no significance returned to him. It seemed to him that Mrs. Caypor loved her husband because she was of a stronger character than he and because she felt his dependence on her; she loved him for his admiration of her, and you might guess that till she met him this dumpy, plain woman with her dullness, good sense and want of humor could not have much enjoyed the admiration of men; she enjoyed his heartiness and his noisy jokes, and his high spirits stirred her sluggish blood; he was a great big bouncing boy and he would never be anything else and she felt like a mother toward him; she had made him what he was, and he was her man and she was his woman, and she loved him, notwithstanding his weakness (for with her clear head she must always have been conscious of that), she loved him *ach, was,* as Isolde loved Tristan. But then there was the espionage. Even Ashenden with all his tolerance for human frailty could not but feel that to betray your country for money is not a very pretty proceeding. Of course she knew of it, indeed it was probably through her that Caypor had first been approached; he would never have undertaken such work if she had not urged him to it. She loved him and she was an honest and an upright woman. By what devious means had she persuaded herself to force her husband to adopt so base and dishonorable a calling? Ashenden lost himself in a labyrinth of conjecture as he tried to piece together the actions of her mind.

Grantley Caypor was another story. There was little to admire in him, but at that moment Ashenden was not looking for an object of admiration; but there was much that was singular and much that was unexpected in that gross and vulgar fellow. Ashenden watched with entertainment the suave manner in which the spy tried to inveigle him in his toils. It was a couple of days after his first lesson that Caypor after dinner, his wife having gone upstairs, threw himself heavily into a chair by Ashenden's side. His faithful Fritzi came up to him and put his long muzzle with its black nose on his knee.

"He has no brain," said Caypor, "but a heart of gold. Look at those little pink eyes. Did you ever see anything so stupid? And what an ugly face, but what incredible charm!"

"Have you had him long?" asked Ashenden.

"I got him in 1914 just before the outbreak of war. By the way, what do you think of the news today? Of course my wife and I never discuss the war. You can't think what a relief to me it is to find a fellow countryman to whom I can open my heart."

He handed Ashenden a cheap Swiss cigar and Ashenden, making a rueful sacrifice to duty, accepted it.

"Of course they haven't got a chance, the Germans," said Caypor, "not a dog's change. I knew they were beaten the moment we came in."

His manner was earnest, sincere and confidential. Ashenden made a commonplace rejoinder.

"It's the greatest grief of my life that owing to my wife's nationality I was unable to do any war work. I tried to enlist the day the war broke out, but they wouldn't have me on account of my age, but I don't mind telling you, if the war goes on much longer, wife or no wife, I'm going to do something. With my knowledge of languages I ought to be of some service in the Censorship Department. That's where you were, wasn't it?"

That was the mark at which he had been aiming and in answer now to his well-directed questions Ashenden gave him the information that he had already prepared. Caypor drew his chair a little nearer and dropped his voice.

"I'm sure you wouldn't tell me anything that anyone shouldn't know, but after all these Swiss are absolutely pro-German and we don't want to give anyone the chance of overhearing."

Then he went on another tack. He told Ashenden a number of things that were of a certain secrecy.

"I wouldn't tell this to anybody else, you know, but I have one or two friends who are in pretty influential positions, and they know they can trust me."

Thus encouraged Ashenden was a little more deliberately indiscreet and when they parted both had reason to be satisfied. Ashenden guessed that Caypor's typewriter would be kept busy next morning and that that extremely energetic Major in Berne would shortly receive a most interesting report.

One evening, going upstairs after dinner, Ashenden passed an open bathroom. He caught sight of the Caypors.

"Come in," cried Caypor in his cordial way. "We're washing our Fritzi."

The bull terrier was constantly getting himself very dirty, and it was Caypor's pride to see him clean and white. Ashenden went in. Mrs. Caypor with her sleeves turned up and a large white apron was standing at one end of the bath, while Caypor, in a pair of trousers and a singlet, his fat, freckled arms bare, was soaping the wretched hound.

"We have to do it at night," he said, "because the Fitzgeralds use this bath and they'd have a fit if they knew we washed the dog in it. We wait till they go to bed. Come along Fritzi, show the gentleman how beautifully you behave when you have your face scrubbed."

The poor brute, woebegone but faintly wagging his tail to show that however foul was this operation performed on him he bore no malice to the god who did it, was standing in the middle of the bath in six inches of water. He was soaped all over and Caypor, talking the while, shampooed him with his great fat hands.

"Oh, what a beautiful dog he's going to be when he's as white as the driven snow. His master will be as proud as Punch to walk out with him and all the little lady dogs will say: good gracious, who's that beautiful aristocratic-looking bull terrier walking as though he owned the whole of Switzerland? Now stand still while you have your ears washed. You couldn't bear to go out into the street with dirty ears, could you? Like a nasty little Swiss schoolboy. *Noblesse oblige*. Now the black nose. Oh, and all the soap is going into his little pink eyes and they'll smart."

Mrs. Caypor listened to this nonsense with a good-humored sluggish smile on her broad, plain face, and presently gravely took a towel.

"Now he's going to have a ducking. Upsie-daisy."

Caypor seized the dog by the fore legs and ducked him once and ducked him twice. There was a struggle, a flurry and a splashing. Caypor lifted him out of the bath.

"Now go to mother and she'll dry you."

Mrs. Caypor sat down and taking the dog between her strong legs rubbed him till the sweat poured off her forehead. And Fritzi, a little shaken and breathless, but happy it was all over stood, with his sweet stupid face, white and shining.

"Blood will tell," cried Caypor exultantly. "He knows the names of no less than sixty-four of his ancestors, and they were all nobly born."

Ashenden was faintly troubled. He shivered a little as he walked upstairs.

Then, one Sunday, Caypor told him that he and his wife were going on an excursion and would eat their luncheon at some little mountain restaurant; and he suggested that Ashenden, each paying his share, should come with them. After three weeks at Lucerne Ashenden thought that his strength would permit him to venture the exertion. They started early, Mrs. Caypor businesslike in her walking boots and Tyrolese hat and alpenstock, and Caypor in stockings and plus-fours looking very British. The situation amused Ashenden and he was prepared to enjoy his day; but he meant to keep his eyes open; it was not inconceivable that the Caypors had discovered what he was and it would not do to go too near a precipice: Mrs. Caypor would not hesitate to give him a push and Caypor for all his jolliness was an ugly customer. But on the face of it there was nothing to mar Ashenden's pleasure in the golden morning. The air was fragrant. Caypor was full of conversation. He told funny stories. He was gay and jovial. The sweat rolled off his great red face and he laughed at himself because he was so fat. To Ashenden's astonishment he showed a peculiar knowledge of the mountain flowers. Once he went out of the way to pick one he saw a little distance from the path and brought it back to his wife. He looked at it tenderly.

"Isn't it lovely?" he cried, and his shifty gray-green eyes for a moment were as candid as a child's. "It's like a poem by Walter Savage Landor."

"Botany is my husband's favorite science," said Mrs. Caypor. "I laugh at him sometimes. He is devoted to flowers. Often when we have hardly had enough money to pay the butcher he has spent everything in his pocket to bring me a bunch of roses."

"*Qui fleurit sa maison fleurit son cœur,*" said Grantley Caypor.

Ashenden had once or twice seen Caypor, coming in from a walk, offer Mrs. Fitzgerald a nosegay of mountain flowers with an elephantine courtesy that was not entirely displeasing; and what he had just learned added a certain significance to the pretty little action. His passion for flowers was genuine and when he gave them to the old Irish lady he gave her something he valued. It showed a real kindness of heart. Ashenden had always thought botany a tedious science, but Caypor, talking exuberantly as they walked along, was able to impart to it life and interest. He must have given it a good deal of study.

"I've never written a book," he said. "There are too many books already and any desire to write I have is satisfied by the more immediately profitable and quite ephemeral composition of an article for a daily paper. But if I stay here much longer I have half a mind to write a book about the wild flowers of Switzerland. Oh, I wish you'd been here a little earlier. They were marvelous. But one wants to be a poet for that, and I'm only a poor newspaper man."

It was curious to observe how he was able to combine real emotion with false fact.

When they reached the inn, with its view of the mountains and the lake, it was good to see the sensual pleasure with which he poured down his throat a bottle of ice-cold beer. You could not but feel sympathy for a man who took so much delight in simple things. They lunched deliciously off scrambled eggs and mountain trout. Even Mrs. Caypor was moved to an unwonted gentleness by her surroundings; the inn was in an agreeably rural spot,it looked like a picture of a Swiss châlet in a book of early nineteenth-century travels; and she treated Ashenden with something less than her usual hostility. When they arrived she had burst into loud German exclamations on the beauty of the scene, and now, softened perhaps too by food and drink, her eyes, dwelling on the grandeur before her, filled with tears. She stretched out her hand.

"It is dreadful and I am ashamed, notwithstanding this horrible and unjust war I can feel in my heart at the moment nothing but happiness and gratitude."

Caypor took her hand and pressed it and, an unusual thing with him, addressing her in German, called her little pet names. It was absurd, but touching. Ashenden, leaving them to their emotions, strolled through the garden and sat down on a bench that had been prepared for the comfort of the tourist. The view was, of course, spectacular, but it captured you; it was like a piece of music that was obvious and meretricious, but for the moment shattered your self-control.

And as Ashenden lingered idly in that spot he pondered over the mystery of Grantley Caypor's treachery. If he liked strange people he had found in him one who was strange beyond belief. It would be foolish to deny that he had amiable traits. His joviality was not assumed, he was without pretense a hearty fellow, and he had real good nature. He was always ready to do a kindness. Ashenden had often watched him with the old Irish Colonel and his wife who were the only other residents of the hotel; he would listen good-humoredly to the old man's tedious stories of the Egyptian war, and he was charming with her. Now that Ashenden had arrived at terms of some familiarity with Caypor he found that he regarded him less with repulsion than with curiosity. He did not think that he had become a spy merely for the money; he was a man of modest tastes and what he had earned in a shipping office must have sufficed to so good a manager as Mrs. Caypor; and after war was declared there was no lack of remunerative work for men over the military age. It might be that he was one of those men who prefer devious ways to straight for some intricate pleasure they get in fooling their fellows; and that he had turned spy, not from hatred of the country that had imprisoned him, not even from love of his wife, but from a desire to score off the big-wigs who never even knew of his existence. It might be that it was vanity that impelled him, a feeling that his talents had not received the recognition they merited, or just a puckish, impish desire to do mischief. He was a crook. It is true that only two cases of dishonesty had been brought home to him, but if he had been caught twice it might be surmised that he had often been dishonest without being caught. What did Mrs. Caypor think of this? They were so united that she must be aware of it. Did it make her ashamed, for her own uprightness surely none could doubt, or did she accept it as an inevitable kink in the man she loved? Did she do all she could to prevent it or did she close her eyes to something she could not help?

How much easier life would be if people were all black or all white and how much simpler it would be to act in regard to them! Was Caypor a good man who loved evil or a bad man who loved good? And how could such unreconcilable elements exist side by side and in harmony within the same heart? For one thing was clear, Caypor was disturbed by no gnawing of conscience; he did his mean and despicable work with gusto. He was a traitor who enjoyed his treachery. Though Ashenden had been studying human nature more or less consciously all his life, it seemed to him that he knew as little about it now in middle age as he had done when he was a child. Of course R. would have said to him: why the devil do you waste your time with such nonsense? The man's a dangerous spy and our business is to lay him by the heels.

That was true enough. Ashenden had decided that it would be useless to attempt to make any arrangement with Caypor. Though doubtless he would have no feeling about betraying his employers he could certainly not be trusted. His wife's influence was too strong. Besides, notwithstanding what he had from time to time told Ashenden, he was in his heart convinced that the Central Powers must win the war, and he meant to be on the winning side. Well, then Caypor must be laid by the heels, but how he was to effect that Ashenden had no notion. Suddenly he heard a voice.

"There you are. We've been wondering where you had hidden yourself."

He looked round and saw the Caypors strolling toward him. They were walking hand in hand.

"So this is what has kept you so quiet," said Caypor as his eyes fell on the view. "What a spot!"

Mrs. Caypor clasped her hands.

"*Ach Gott, wie schön!*" she cried. "*Wie schön*. When I look at that blue lake and those snowy mountains I feel inclined like Goëthe's Faust, to cry to the passing moment: tarry."

"This is better than being in England with the excursions and alarms of war, isn't it?" said Caypor.

"Much," said Ashenden.

"By the way, did you have any difficulty in getting out?"

"No, not in the smallest."

"I'm told they make rather a nuisance of themselves at the frontier nowadays."

"I came through without the smallest difficulty. I don't fancy they bother much about the English. I thought the examination of passports was quite perfunctory."

A fleeting glance passed between Caypor and his wife. Ashenden wondered what it meant. It would be strange if Caypor's thoughts were occupied with the chances of a journey to England at the very moment when he was himself reflecting on its possibility. In a little while Mrs. Caypor suggested that they had better be starting back and they wandered together in the shade of trees down the mountain paths.

Ashenden was watchful. He could do nothing (and his inactivity irked him) but wait with his eyes open to seize the opportunity that might present itself. A couple of days later an incident occurred that made him certain something was in the wind. In the course of his morning lesson Mrs. Caypor remarked:

"My husband has gone to Geneva today. He had some business to do there."

"Oh," said Ashenden, "will he be gone long?"

"No, only two days."

It is not everyone who can tell a lie and Ashenden had the feeling, he hardly knew why, that Mrs. Caypor was telling one then. Her manner perhaps was not quite as indifferent as you would have expected when she was mentioning a fact that could be of no interest to Ashenden. It flashed across his mind that Caypor had been summoned to Berne to see the redoubtable head of the German secret service. When he had the chance he said casually to the waitress:

"A little less work for you to do, *fräulein*. I hear that Herr Caypor has gone to Berne."

"Yes. But he'll be back tomorrow."

That proved nothing, but it was something to go upon. Ashenden knew in Lucerne a Swiss who was willing on emergency to do odd jobs and, looking him up, asked him to take a letter to Berne. It might be possible to pick up Caypor and trace his movements. Next day Caypor appeared once more with his wife at the dinner table, but merely nodded to Ashenden and afterwards both went straight upstairs. They looked troubled. Caypor, as a rule so animated, walked with bowed shoulders and looked neither to the right nor to the left. Next morning Ashenden received a reply to his letter: Caypor had seen Major von P. It was possible to guess what the Major had said to him. Ashenden well knew how rough he could be: he was a hard man and brutal, clever and unscrupulous and he was not accustomed to mince his words. They were tired of paying Caypor a salary to sit still in Lucerne and do nothing; the time was come for him to go to England. Guess work? Of course it was guess work, but in that trade it mostly was: you had to deduce the animal from its jaw bone. Ashenden knew from Gustav that the Germans wanted to send someone to England. He drew a long breath; if Caypor went he would have to get busy.

When Mrs. Caypor came in to give him his lesson she was dull and listless. She looked tired and her mouth was set obstinately. It occurred to Ashenden that the Caypors had spent most of the night talking. He wished he knew what they had said. Did she urge him to go or did she try to dissuade him? Ashenden watched them again at luncheon. Something was the matter, for they hardly spoke to one another and as a rule they found plenty to talk about. They left the room early, but when Ashenden went out he saw Caypor sitting in the hall by himself.

"Hulloa," he cried jovially, but surely the effort was patent, "how are you getting on? I've been to Geneva."

"So I heard," said Ashenden.

"Come and have your coffee with me. My poor wife's got a headache. I told her she'd better go and lie down." In his shifty green eyes was an expression that Ashenden could not read. "The fact is, she's rather worried, poor dear; I'm thinking of going to England."

Ashenden's heart gave a sudden leap against his ribs, but his face remained impassive.

"Oh, are you going for long? We shall miss you."

"To tell you the truth, I'm fed up with doing nothing. The war looks as though it were going on for years and I can't sit here indefinitely. Besides, I can't afford it, I've got to earn my living. I may have a

German wife, but I am an Englishman, hang it all, and I want to do my bit. I could never face my friends again if I just stayed here in ease and comfort till the end of the war and never attempted to do a thing to help the country. My wife takes her German point of view and I don't mind telling you she's a bit upset. You know what women are.''

Now Ashenden knew what it was that he saw in Caypor's eyes. Fear. It gave him a nasty turn. Caypor didn't want to go to England, he wanted to stay safely in Switzerland; Ashenden knew now what the major had said to him when he went to seem him in Berne. He had got to go or lose his salary. What was it that his wife had said when he told her what had happened? He had wanted her to press him to stay, but, it was plain, she hadn't done that; perhaps he had not dared tell her how frightened he was; to her he had always been gay, bold, adventurous and devil-may-care; and now, the prisoner of his own lies, he had not found it in him to confess himself the mean and sneaking coward he was.

''Are you going to take your wife with you?'' asked Ashenden.

''No, she'll stay here.''

It had been arranged very neatly. Mrs. Caypor would receive his letters and forward the information they contained to Berne.

''I've been out of England so long that I don't quite know how to set about getting war work. What would you do in my place?''

''I don't know; what sort of work are you thinking of?''

''Well, you know, I imagine I could do the same thing as you did. I wonder if there's anyone in the Censorship Department that you could give me a letter of introduction to.''

It was only by a miracle that Ashenden saved himself from showing by a smothered cry or by a broken gesture how startled he was; but not by Caypor's request, by what had just dawned upon him. What an idiot he had been! He had been disturbed by the thought that he was wasting his time at Lucerne, he was doing nothing, and though in fact, as it turned out, Caypor was going to England it was due to no cleverness of his. He could take to himself no credit for the result. And now he saw that he had been put in Lucerne, told how to describe himself and given the proper information, so that what actually had occurred should occur. It would be a wonderful thing for the German secret service to get an agent into the Censorship Departmant; and by a happy accident there was Grantley Caypor, the very man for the job, on friendly terms with someone who had worked there. What a bit of luck! Major von P. was a man of culture and, rubbing his hands, he must surely have murmured: *stultum facit fortuna quem vult perdere*. It was a trap of that devilish R. and the grim major at Berne had fallen into it. Ashenden had done his work just by sitting still and doing nothing. He almost laughed as he thought what a fool R. had made of him.

"I was on very good terms with the chief of my department, I could give you a note to him if you liked."

"That would be just the thing."

"But of course I must give the facts. I must say I've met you here and only known you a fortnight."

"Of course. But you'll say what else you can for me, won't you?"

"Oh, certainly."

"I don't know yet if I can get a visa. I'm told they're rather fussy."

"I don't see why. I shall be very sick if they refuse me one when I want to go back."

"I'll go and see how my wife is getting on," said Caypor suddenly, getting up. "When will you let me have that letter?"

"Whenever you like. Are you going at once?"

"As soon as possible."

Caypor left him. Ashenden waited in the hall for a quarter of an hour so that there should appear in him no sign of hurry. Then he went upstairs and prepared various communicatons. In one he informed R. that Caypor was going to England; in another he made arrangements through Berne that wherever Caypor applied for a visa it should be granted to him without question; and these he despatched forthwith. When he went down to dinner he handed Caypor a cordial letter of introduction.

Next day but one Caypor left Lucerne.

Ashenden waited. He continued to have his hour's lesson with Mrs. Caypor and under her conscientious tuition began now to speak German with ease. They talked of Goëthe and Winckelmann, of art and life and travel. Fritzi sat quietly by her chair.

"He misses his master," she said, pulling his ears. "He only really cares for him, he suffers me only as belonging to him."

After his lesson Ashenden went every morning to Cook's to ask for his letters. It was here that all communications were addressed to him. He could not move till he received instructions, but R. could be trusted not to leave him idle long; and meanwhile there was nothing for him to do but have patience. Presently he received a letter from the consul in Geneva to say that Caypor had there applied for his visa and had set out for France. Having read this Ashenden went on for a little stroll by the lake and on his way back happened to see Mrs. Caypor coming out of Cook's office. He guessed that she was having her letters addressed there too. He went up to her.

"Have you had news of Herr Caypor?" he asked her.

"No," she said. "I suppose I could hardly expect to yet."

He walked along by her side. She was disappointed, but not yet anxious; she knew how irregular at that time was the post. But next day during the lesson he could not but see that she was impatient to have done with it. The post was delivered at noon and at five minutes to she looked at her watch and him. Though Ashenden knew very well that no letter would ever come for her he had not the heart to keep her on tenterhooks.

"Don't you think that's enough for the day? I'm sure you want to go down to Cook's," he said.

"Thank you. That is very amiable of you."

Later he went there himself and found her standing in the middle of the office. Her face was distraught. She addressed him wildly.

"My husband promised to write from Paris. I am sure there is a letter for me, but these stupid people say there's nothing. They're so careless, it's a scandal."

Ashenden did not know what to say. While the clerk was looking through the bundle to see if there was anything for him she came up to the desk again.

"When does the next post come in from France?" she asked.

"Sometimes there are letters about five."

"I'll come then."

She turned and walked rapidly away. Fritzi followed her with his tail between his legs. There was no doubt of it, already the fear had seized her that something was wrong. Next morning she looked dreadful; she could not have closed her eyes all night; and in the middle of the lesson she started up from her chair.

"You must excuse me, Herr Somerville, I cannot give you a lesson today. I am not feeling well."

Before Ashenden could say anything she had flung nervously from the room, and in the evening he got a note from her to say that she regretted that she must discontinue giving him conversation lessons. She gave no reason. Then Ashenden saw no more of her; she ceased coming in to meals; except to go morning and afternoon to Cook's she spent apparently the whole day in her room. Ashenden thought of her sitting there hour after hour with that hideous fear gnawing at her heart. Who could help feeling sorry for her? The time hung heavy on his hands too. He read a good deal and wrote a little, he hired a canoe and went for long leisurely paddles on the lake; and at last one morning the clerk at Cook's handed him a letter. It was from R. It had all the appearance of a business communication, but between the lines he read a good deal.

Dear Sir, it began, *The goods, with accompanying letter, despatched by you from Lucerne have been duly delivered. We are obliged to you for executing our instructions with such promptness.*

It went on in this strain. R. was exultant. Ashenden guessed that Caypor had been arrested and by now had paid the penalty of his crime. He shuddered. He remembered a dreadful scene. Dawn. A cold, gray dawn, with a drizzling rain falling. A man, blindfolded, standing against a wall, an officer very pale giving an order, a volley, and then a young soldier, one of the firing party, turning round and holding on to his gun for support, vomiting. The officer turned paler still, and he, Ashenden, feeling dreadfully faint. How terrified Caypor must have been! It was awful when the tears ran down their faces. Ashenden shook himself. He went to the ticket-office and obedient to his orders bought himself a ticket for Geneva.

As he was waiting for his change Mrs. Caypor came in. He was shocked by the sight of her. She was blowsy and disheveled and there were heavy rings around her eyes. She was deathly pale. She staggered up to the desk and asked for a letter. The clerk shook his head.

"I'm sorry, madam, there's nothing yet."

"But look, look. Are you sure? Please look again."

The misery in her voice was heart-rending. The clerk with a shrug of the shoulders took out the letters from a pigeon hole and sorted them once more.

"No, there's nothing, madam."

She gave a hoarse cry of despair and her face was distorted with anguish.

"Oh, God, oh, God," she moaned.

She turned away, the tears streaming from her weary eyes, and for a moment she stood there like a blind man groping and not knowing which way to go. Then a fearful thing happened. Fritzi, the bull terrier, sat down on his haunches and threw back his head and gave a long melancholy howl. Mrs. Caypor looked at him with terror; her eyes seemed really to start from her head. The doubt, the gnawing doubt that had tortured her during those dreadful days of suspense, was a doubt no longer. She knew. She staggered blindly into the street.

CORNELL WOOLRICH

Tokyo, 1941

THE TELEPHONE RANG in the Hong Kong hotel room. Lyons had been expecting it to for the better part of an hour, and the delay had started to get on his nerves. He stopped pacing nervously back and forth and went over to it. He was in a man's black silk Japanese kimono, with a single white idiograph embroidered on the back of it. It was too short for him, and his muscular bare legs, quite un-Japanese in their hairiness, stuck out ludicrously from it.

The desk clerk said, "There's a gentleman down here to see you, sir."

Lyons didn't ask the name. He just said, "Send him up," and put the phone back.

He went over to his valise, which was standing unlocked at the foot of the bed, and upended the lid. He took out a revolver, checked it for load and thrust it into the elastic waistband of his undershorts. Then he closed the kimono over it, but kept his hand near it on the outside.

Someone knocked.

"Come in," he said.

The door opened, and a man holding a briefcase came in. He closed it after him, and then stood there without coming any nearer. He was a Caucasian with tawny-colored hair and hazel eyes.

All Lyons knew was that he had never seen him before. By the same token, neither had the man ever seen Lyons before.

"Good evening," the man said in slightly accented English. "I'm selling cameras and photographic equipment. Could I interest you?"

"I already have a camera, thank you. It's a Nikko, a Japanese make."

Both of them spoke in a rather stilted, unlifelike way, as though they were repeating a lesson they had memorized. Or like actors running through their lines at a first reading of a play.

"Are you satisfied with it?" the man asked.

"I get very good results," said Lyons. "Would you like me to show you some of them?"

He went to the valise again and took out a pair of socks. They had been rolled into a ball, toe-to-heel, and the tops turned back over them. From within them he took out a small plastic vial, of the sort that usually contains pills or tablets.

The man was opening his briefcase. He took out a long Manila envelope, sealed but unaddressed, and put it on the table near him.

He took the vial and uncapped it. Lyons took the envelope and opened that.

The man unwound the first few frames of a tightly rolled strip of microfilm, held them against the light and scanned them. Lyons counted over American currency, in denominations of fifty and a hundred.

"You do get very good results with it," the man agreed.

As though this were some sort of mutually understood signal, the man put the vial away in his briefcase and Lyons put the Manila envelope away in his valise.

The man went to the door, opened it and looked out into the hall to see if anyone was in sight.

Then he said, "Good evening," once more, with a foreigner's typical unfamiliarity with English usage, evidently meaning it for good night.

"So long," Lyons answered.

The door closed, and the man was gone.

Lyons picked up the phone and asked the clerk: "What time does the ship for Nagasaki sail, did you say?"

"Not until nine in the morning, sir."

Lyons hung up. He had to kill the night here.

He put the gun back in the valise first of all. Then he counted several hundred dollars out of the Manila envelope and stacked the bills into his wallet. He started to get dressed, to go out and have a night on the town.

The Chinese girl in the ricksha said, in an astonishingly genuine Cockney accent that must have rubbed off on her from long association with merchant-mariners and limey tars, "Don't tyke too long, byeby. We imes to get there before the plyce closes down, doncher knaow."

"I'll be right with you, China-doll," Lyons tossed at her, hopping out and following the elderly Chinese gentleman into an unlighted shop entrance. "Wait outside here for me, till I see what this old gazabo has up his sleeve."

The old man was unlocking a padlock that secured the door. Then he went inside a short distance, lighted up a pumpkin-shaped, pumpkin-colored paper lantern and let it ride up toward the ceiling again. Then he went a little deeper in, repeating the process with a yellow-green one. He let down a bamboo roller shade that blanked out the shop window from the street outside.

"So what is this big deal?" Lyons asked him impatiently. "You've been pestering me for the past hour in the last bar we were in, until you got my sales resistance worn down to nothing. And my curiosity up to boiling point."

The old merchant giggled. "I show. I show." But first he transferred the padlock around to the inside of the door and refastened it.

"What's the idea of that?" Lyons asked, lidding his eyes at him with sleepy wariness but without showing any actual alarm. "Don't try to get funny with me, because I can handle myself, and the girl's right outside there, anyway."

"No, no, I am gentleman, not holdup bandit," protested the Chinese gravely. "Is just so no one can disturb while I am showing you this."

"That valuable, huh?" said Lyons ironically.

"Oh, very. Very." He went into the back and was gone a long time. Finally Lyons began to fidget. He called out, "Hey! you in there, how about it? Wha'd you do, go to sleep on me?"

The Chinese reappeared, holding something in his hand.

"I have to keep it in very exclusive safe place, you know."

It was a very small lacquered box. He opened it first, then removed a false bottom from it.

Lyons' face dropped for a minute. He thought it was just some sort of knickknack or curio.

"Come over here, by light." He placed a little mat of cotton batting on the counter. And on it throbbed a diamond, the biggest one that Lyons had ever seen.

Lyons' face was a study in impassivity. "Haven't you got any electricity in this place?" he grumbled. "I can't see a damn thing."

"No 'lectric." But he brought out a coal miner's lamp with a bright tin reflector. It cast a pool of bleach on the counter, as white as spilled borax. In it the diamond seemed to turn blue. Rays came from it like silver quills shooting from a porcupine.

Lyons took a long time before saying anything.

"What am I supposed to do, buy it?"

The Chinese merely dropped his eyes in complacent assent.

Lyons waited another long time. "Why me?"

"You have plenty money; I see you in bar. You American, you pay good. Also, you pay in American money, best money there is in world."

"How do I even know it's real?" parried Lyons.

"It has to be. Is too big not to be. If was going to be imitation, false, would be smaller, maybe only medium-size, to fool somebody easier, sell easier. Is so big, nobody want to believe it real. So what good is it? That show it must be real."

He had a point there, in a roundabout way.

Lyons had another question. "Suppose it is real. Still and all, what makes you think I want it?"

"I study you good, in bar. You the kind of man buy this, no other kind but you. It go with your character, you personality. You reckless, you take chance, you live dangerous. You not think you going live too long, and you not care. You live wild and fast while you can. I see how you act with money, with drink, with girl, even when music play for dancing. You the kind of a man to buy a diamond, sudden, from a stranger, in the middle of the night, even when you don't need. Live for the moment—because tomorrow maybe never come."

Lyons didn't answer, but his slow smile did. "How'd you happen to come across it?" he asked curiously.

The Chinese sighed. He sat down alongside of him and lit a cigarette reflectively. He left the cotton-bedded jewel exposed there on the counter, but took the precaution of moving it a good deal nearer to himself, and out of easy reach of Lyons. The Strand-accented night-flower outside was allowed to cool her heels and wait.

"Is a long chain of circonstances. Was in our own country for a while. They say two men fight a duel, and one kill the other with it. Maybe not so, maybe only story, I don't know. Then, they say, partner of man killed steal it from coffin his friend body lie in, run away, take it with him to where he go, big city, New York. Big high-up man there, boss whole city, buy it from him. How you say—like mandarin?"

"Boss?" repeated Lyons, trying to help him out. "Political boss, you mean?" Association of words brought back the only name he could readily recall in that bracket. "Someone like Boss Tweed?"

"Him," said the Chinese with instant certainty. "Same name."

"Quite a history," admitted Lyons, absorbed in spite of himself. "So then?"

"He gave it to actress, him sweetheart. He thrown out, lose job, because he too crooked."

"I've heard," said Lyons drily."

"She not have good luck anymore, either. All plays bad; one time police close for indecent, one time fire in theater, many people die. One night in play she fall downstairs on stage, break leg, have to wear thing like stone—"

"Cast."

"—for six month. When she walk, never can walk again without cane. No more good for acting. She retire, go to Europe, every night play gambling table at Monte Carlo—" He made a circle with his hand.

"Roulette?" suggested Lyons.

He nodded. "Wheel spin. Ball fall in hole. Every night she lose, every night more and more. Never win. Until everything gone. Everything she have from that man you say name of. She come out with diamond one night, only thing she got left. Casino won't accept, only can play with money. But Russian grand duke standing next to her at same table, he see it. He buy it from her."

"So after that she won, I suppose."

"She lose even what he give her. She go outside casino, take little lady gun—you know, pearl handle, only so big—"

"Killed herself."

"No. Only make herself blind in both eyes, from way bullet push in brain. She live very old, never see again."

"Very spooky," grimaced Lyons. "Only I don't believe a word of it."

"I only know what I hear from last man had it. He say all this. I no can tell is true or isn't."

"Go on," Lyons said. "How'd it get to you?"

"Grand duke go back to Russia with it. This before revolution. People not like czar or czar-government or czar official. Somebody put bomb underneath seat of his carriage. When he get in with family to go to church Sunday, all blown up. Him, wife, son and daughter. Even little pet dog on lap. Only one son escaped because sick in bed with mump, can't go to church."

"And what happened to him?"

"Came bad things afterward. He marry Russian princess, they have son. Little boy fall down, scratch knee, one day. All little boy do is fall down, scratch knee. But they find out he have sickness where once blood start, never can stop again."

"I've heard of that."

"Twenty-four hour after, he dead. From little bit of scratch on knee. When revolution come, revolution army burn down house while he not home. They take his wife, put her in a little room in military headquarter. All night long soldiers wait in line, go in there. Next morning they forget to watch her little bit. She take two silk stocking, hang herself from window bar."

"And him?"

''He hide in freight car, go across Siberia, many many days, finally get out of country. So cold he have to cut off own hand with hatchet.''

''Frostbite?''

''I see it, my own eyes. Arm end at wrist. I meet him in Harbin, up north, Manchuria. He have nothing left, only the diamond. He eat from garbage cans, sleep under newspapers on doorsteps of houses. He stop me and beg one day. I take him to restaurant, buy him meal. Then he take it out from between toes and show it to me. He have only rags on feet, no shoes. I give him money, buy it. He kneel down, kiss my feet, cry.''

''A grand duke's son,'' mused Lyons.

''I have to run away myself pretty soon after,'' the Chinese went on. ''I make enemy of warlords in Manchuria, they take my business, all my property. Send soldiers after me. If I stay, they shoot me. I come down here to Hong Kong, where man I used to know up there have this little store. He let me sleep in back, give me rice and tea.

''Once I rich businessman myself. Now—'' He looked at the diamond sadly.

Lyons looked at it, too.

He reached over, picked it up and held it in his open hand. It was like holding a ball of white fire, only without burning yourself.

The Chinese kept watching his expression closely, but Lyons wouldn't say the first word. He knew good psychology from bad.

His silence broke the Chinese down finally.

''You can have for five thousand American dollar.''

''You've been smoking opium,'' Lyons told him tersely.

''Two thousand.''

''You're not in a position to bargain. You're strapped. You talked so much you've boxed yourself in.''

''One.''

''Never mind the count-down. I'll name it, not you. Now look, I've had lot to drink so I'm an easy mark, a pushover, a sucker. Give you five hundred for it, and I'll hate myself in the morning.''

''Oh, no can do, no can do!'' cried the Chinese, agonized, pounding a fist against each side of his head.

''Sure can do,'' Lyons said, mimicking his way of speech. ''In fact, better can-do while the can-doing's good or can-do the hell without anything at all.''

The Chinese clasped his hands prayerfully before his face and rolled his eyes up to the ceiling.

''Make up your mind,'' Lyons said remorselessly. ''I've got to get back to my pussy cat outside.''

The Chinese submitted, spreading his hands out in mute helplessness and letting his head droop forward forlornly.

But, as though the transaction weren't already one-sided enough, a tricky afterthought had occurred to Lyons by this time. "I only have two-fifty on me," he said glibly. "The rest is in my room in the hotel."

"All right, I hold for you, you come back with rest tomorrow," suggested the Chinese, but only halfheartedly.

"Hold, nothing!" flared Lyons, raising his voice in pretended anger at the reflection on his integrity. "I either take it with me now or not at all. Don't crowd your luck. I change very quickly. I may not be in the mood to buy it anymore by tomorrow. I'm at the Victoria, the best hotel in town." He took out his room key and showed it to him, tag first. "There's my room number on it, see, right there." His hand pistoned in and out a number of times in quick succession. "Here's your two-fifty. You come round tomorrow and pick up the rest."

"What time?" said the Chinese, who was an outsmarted man and knew it.

"Not too early. I'm expecting to do quite some howling tonight," Lyons told him. His ship for Nagasaki sailed at nine, he knew. "Make it about eleven. Just come up and knock at the door."

"Oh, and by the way," he added, bringing out an additional five-dollar bill. "Got a bottle of perfume or some such around? My little lady friend outside doesn't need to know what I've just bought in here. First thing you know she'll expect me to give it to her. Or maybe even try to help herself while I'm dozing between tackles."

When he brought the neatly packaged perfume bottle out and handed it to her, she exclaimed: "Aow, I sye, is that for me? Haow nice. What's it caahled?"

"Spanish Fly," he said irreverently.

John Lyons' little house in Azabu-ku was a Western-type job. Which didn't mean it wasn't flimsy, only that it was less flimsy than its native counterparts. It was mainly of wood, white-painted, with a very small amount of stonework around the base and a slanting red-tile roof. It had its own garden at the back and sides, and he rented the whole thing for thirty-seven-fifty American a month. Which was good value for pre-occupation Tokyo. It was even furnished, although, in truth, somewhat scantily, with the Japanese idea of Western furniture. Chairs and tables all with legs too short for the average lanky Occidental build. And in addition, they had a girl come in who worked from seven to seven, for only seven a week more. Finally, he even had a beat-up '34 Chevy to go around in. He'd bought it second-hand and it was only held together with spittle and a hairpin, but he was a good mechanic, and it got him where he wanted to go.

The whole thing fitted nicely into the framework of the hundred and fifty a month he got from the Acme Travel Agency, Fifth Avenue and Forty-eighth, New York. Also Market Street, San Fran, but no Tokyo office. His check came in regularly on about the 15th of each month, and made a lot of yen when it was converted.

Where else, he used to tell Ruth when she got her periodic homesick-blues—about every second week, it seemed—could they live as well as this for the same amount of money?

"This is living?" she'd answered once.

She didn't like it here, he knew. They had no children. When they'd first married, it was the Depression that kept them from having any. They couldn't afford them. Now he found he didn't want them anymore, anyway. He liked it better this way. His tendencies had become completely wolflike, and it was too late to change. In fact, he didn't want to change, wasn't going to. He liked running around to bars and clubs every night, meeting his men friends. He never took her with him, so time hung heavy on her hands. She didn't know what to do with herself.

And it was worse when he made those quick flying trips in and out, to Manila, Hong Kong, places like that, which he did regularly every two or three months. No wonder she was lonely here, didn't like the place.

The taxi that had brought him home from the railroad station let him out in front of the house. Before that there'd been the train from Nagasaki, before that the ship, before that the Hong Kong hotel room. He'd been away a total of five days this time. Just there, turn around, and back.

He was tall and lean, lanky would almost be the word. He had a thatch of dingy-colored hair, actually a lifeless light-brown shade, with scarcely any recession along the hairline. His eyes had a piercing quality to them, and were spaciously shadowed underneath from too many drinks and too many girls. His cheeks were on the gaunt side, probably for the same reason. He was not at all a bad-looking man, but the first telltale traces of fast living were beginning to leave their marks on his face. He looked about forty; actually he was thirty-five.

He had a herringbone topcoat slung over one arm—it was warm in Tokyo for October—and was carrying a small overnight case with the other.

Ruth must have seen him drive up before the house. She had the door open and ready for him before he could get at it with his key.

She was just as tall as he was. Red of hair, blue of eye and with a nice, frank American-girl face. A few freckles on it instead of face powder.

"How's the girl?" he said offhandedly.

She put her arms to his shoulders and held up her face. He touched his mouth to hers.

"Hello, Johnnie," she said then.

He squeezed his eyes shut in distaste. "There goes that name again."

"Is that going to start again?" she said. "Something new."

"No, it isn't. I never could stand it, even as a kid. Little girls in pigtails—" He mimicked ferociously. "John-eee! John-eee!" After a moment he added, "It makes me feel like I've never grown up at all."

"Have you?" she countered.

"Thanks," he said.

"I've always called you that, all our married life."

"And I still don't like it."

"Is it the name itself you don't like to be called," she said with momentary insight, "or is it me you don't like to have say it?"

"Let's drop it, shall we?"

"All right, John," she agreed with a slight cutting edge to her voice. "How was the trip?"

"Same as usual," he answered carelessly.

She gave him an unfathomable look. Then they went inside together and closed the door.

Once he'd nearly sent her in his place. "Do you want to go instead of me?" he'd asked, giving her a keen appraising look. As though thinking it was about time she'd started to make herself useful, instead of moping around all day.

"Why can't we both go?"

"That's out," he told her flatly. "Somebody has to stay and watch the store."

"What's there to watch? You don't even have an office."

"We both can't go at once, and that's all there is to it. Do you want to go or don't you?"

All right," she said finally. "I'll go. What do I have to do?"

But he wasn't satisfied yet. "Do you promise to do exactly as I tell you?" he asked her. "And not ask any questions?"

"Yes, of course, if that's what you want."

The night before she was to have gone, as she was undressing for bed, he came into the room and handed her a tiny tight-packed roll of something wrapped in waterproof material, either oil-silk or plastic, she could not be sure which. It was about the diameter of a cigarette, but not nearly as long as one.

"Slip this inside your garter belt when you get dressed in the morning," he told her. "I'll have another one for the other side by then."

She must have lain and thought about it all night. In the morning she said quite abruptly, ''Johnnie, I don't think I want to go on this business trip for you after all. Something about it—scares me. Something about it—isn't on the up-and-up.''

He gave her a long hard look, then banged out of the house and went on the trip himself.

He was gone two weeks that time, and she knew he must have been with some woman at least part of that time. But she also knew it probably wasn't the first time.

Now, returning from this latest trip, he asked her, ''Anything new around here?''

''Harry Matsuko called.''

''I told him I'd be away—didn't he know that?''

''He said you'd told him. He was just checking to see if you were back yet.''

They seemed to have difficulty talking to one another. It was not that they were strained or ill at ease; it was more as though they'd run out of things to say. Not just now, but some time ago.

''Anything else?''

''Oh, and some roofing contractor came around. I had the hardest time making him understand—''

''I didn't send for anyone like that,'' he said, narrowing his eyes at her.

''I told him I was sure you hadn't, or you would have told me about it. I tried to explain there was nothing wrong with our roof whatever. But he spoke of some city ordinance about making sure loose tiles didn't slide off and hurt somebody below. And they went ahead and put a ladder against the house and climbed up on the outside.''

''How many were there?''

''Two. The contractor and his assistant. They poked around up there an hour. I even saw them lift up some of the tiles and look underneath.'' She stopped. ''Why'd you do that?'' she asked him curiously.

''Do what?''

''Stroke both sides of your face with one hand like that?''

''I was feeling to see if I needed a shave.''

''No,'' she said tonelessly. ''You did it when I spoke of that roofing contractor having been here.''

They were in the bedroom by this time. He shrugged off his coat and flung it across the back of a chair. ''Guess I'll shower up,'' he said, untying his necktie. ''That train coming up from 'saki was pretty sooty.''

She was standing there looking at him, but her thoughts seemed to be in another world.

He was down to his shorts and undershirt now. Suddenly he stopped and said, "Why do you have to stand there like that? Didn't you ever see me getting undressed before? I don't need help."

She came back to herself with a start. "I'll see how Micky's getting along with the dinner," she said and went out. Mikki was their maid of all work; her name was too long for them to handle, so they called her by just the first two syllables of it. Mikki, or, more often than not, Micky.

But she was back in the room again when he came out of the shower, toweling himself vigorously. He stopped for a moment, narrowly scanned the expression on her face, and then nodded. "So you wouldn't be happy until you nosed, would you?"

"No," she said wearily. "I only came back to see if you needed an extra towel." She pointed to the chair seat. There was a fresh one lying folded on it.

He turned his back and began putting on his clothes again.

"But when a husband tells his wife not to stand watching him undress," she went on, "it's not modesty, it can't be. It's because he has something to hide."

He didn't answer.

"I found the money belt, with five thousand dollars United States currency in it."

"You took the trouble to count it, too, I notice," he said over his shoulder.

"You don't trust me anyway," she pointed out. "So I may as well have the game as long as I've got the name."

"Go ahead, ask me," he defied her. "Ask me where I got it and what I got it for!"

"Would you tell me the truth?"

"No!" he said sharply.

She shrugged her shoulders to show she knew the futility of it. "And the unset diamond, where did that come from?"

"Oh, you saw that, too." He went over to her and held it out on the flat of his hand. "That's something I don't mind you asking about," he told her unhesitatingly. "Although you probably won't believe me about that, either. A Chinaman came up to me in Hong Kong and asked if I wanted to buy it. He was a refugee or something, needed money. I bought it off him for peanuts."

"You don't buy a diamond that size for peanuts," she said skeptically.

"It's probably hot."

She didn't seem too interested in the diamond bit. "I hope it brings you good luck," she said indifferently. And then, as though turning to something of more consequence, "I also found a woman's Chinese silk handkerchief stuffed in your breast pocket, reeking of some God-awful cheap perfume."

"That's something I picked up on the street."

"The handkerchief or the woman?" she asked sweetly.

"Gee, you've been a busy little bitch in the half-hour since I came home!" he yelled. And he gave the door a slam that shook the whole house.

The girl in the taxi was extremely frightened as it drew up before Secret Service Headquarters. It was written all over her face, and every move she made indicated it plainly. She lowered her head first and peered worriedly under and out at the ugly, blocklike concrete building. Her hands were too rapid and agitated as she opened her purse and fumbled for money to pay the driver. Then, when he returned change, she fumbled again and spilled some to the floor. Finally, when she opened the door and got out, she left her gloves lying on the seat. He had to call her attention to them.

She was extremely beautiful, tall and straight for a Japanese girl, and with particularly lovely, long, well-proportioned legs, again an exception. She wore a tailored suit of tan pongee silk, with a turned-down white collar and a flowing black satin bow tie, such as artists are sometimes pictured wearing.

But she was still very frightened as she went up the steps and inside. The apprehensive way she looked all about her seemed to say, Why have I been sent for like this? What have I done? Will I ever come out of here again?

She noticed a building attendant and approached him. "The office of Colonel Setsu, please. Which way?"

He pointed. "Right at the end there, facing you."

She went over to the door and stood there looking at it. Finally she went in.

The outer office was nothing to be frightened of. There were desks with typists seated at them, a receptionist, all the usual business office personnel. But they were all men; there wasn't a woman in sight.

She was directed into an inner office and told to wait there. She sat down on a straight-backed chair placed against the wall and began to slap her loose gloves nervously with one hand against the other. Suddenly a door opened, and a young man in army uniform stood there, rigid and impersonal as an automaton. "In here, please," he ordered her.

She got up and went in. The young man, closing the door behind her, remained outside.

The man at the desk in the center of the room was also in uniform. He was in his sixties, bald of crown and with a wizened but cracklingly intelligent face. A cigarette burned away in a little lacquered tray to one side of him, untouched.

He let her stand there for several minutes out in the center of the room before him, while he looked over papers. Then he said, as though reading from the papers, without looking up at her, "You are Tomiko."

She inclined her head. "Yes, Colonel."

"You are paid to dance each night at the Yeddo entertainment place."

She inclined her head again. "Yes, Colonel."

His voice became a droning mumble while he continued to read from the papers, as though he did not need any further confirmation from her. "Twenty-four years old. Born here in Tokyo. Grandfather gave his life in the glorious victory at Tsushima Straits. Older brother died in Service in the China incident."

He became less formal, discarded the papers and clasped his hands comfortably on the desk before him, although he still allowed her to stand there, almost at attention.

"An honorable family."

She bowed her gratitude.

"Would you too like to serve your divine Emperor?"

This time she bowed deeply, reverently, arms held stiffly close to her sides. "I would give my unworthy life itself."

The colonel gravely nodded his approval. "Spoken like a true daughter of Yamato."

"But who am I to dare offer this, a mere woman?"

The colonel was more and more pleased with her. His first instinctive antipathy to her Western apparel and her un-Japanese mode of earning a living began to wear off. Underneath that she was all Japanese, he could see. She had the white flame of patriotism in its holiest form.

"Men must give their lives on the field of battle, true. But there are other ways in which men cannot serve, and a woman may. These can be just as important for the good of our country. In the eyes of the gods, these smaller ways can be just as worthy."

Her eyes were smoldering now. "Command me."

He thawed completely, captivated by her—not personally, but patriotically. "Sit down, *san*." He took out a fresh cigarette for himself and offered her one.

"This is not our way," she said quietly. "This is the way of the Others. Smoking is for men."

"For over a year now," he began without further preamble, "there has been, somewhere in this city, a secret radio transmitter, sending out coded messages. Our detector units have picked up its call signals over and over. This can only mean one thing. An enemy agent or a group of enemy agents are operating right here in the capital. We have been unable to pinpoint the transmitter closely enough to locate it. Our radio detection equipment is not accurate enough. However, there are other ways of capturing and silencing it. By identifying and arresting the person or persons who are opening it. Starting with a list of almost two hundred possible suspects at the beginning, our investigations have now brought this down to not more than six all told. Five out of the six are being covered by my other operatives.

"In Azabu-ku lives an American—" he grimaced as he pronounced the word— "called Jo-hin Lai-hyon. This is your task. He is a possibility, if only because so many others have already been eliminated. Close watch from the outside has uncovered nothing. His house has been searched a number of times without result. It is only from the *inside,* where a man has not the same defenses, that success may come. You must get on the inside of him. Know him inside out. There is your assignment. You may have to lie in his arms, and be the body to his body. Is this too much to ask?"

"No."

"It will not be too difficult. He has a sort of fever for women on him. All men do, but with him it has already become sickness. There is no let and no stop to it, until finally the door of the mind closes without ever again reopening."

"Where shall I meet him? How shall I know him?"

"You will be given a photograph we have of him, to study before you leave here. We will arrange the meeting for you also. His house is being watched. When he is seen to leave it, and it is sure he will not answer the call himself, I will have someone ring up on the telephone, give the name of one of the other five I mentioned, a California Japanese, and ask to have him meet him at the place you work, the Yeddo. His wife, who is stupid in our ways of speech, will not know one voice from another. She will give him the message. His friend will not be there, of course, when he goes there. Instead, he will see you. The rest will follow. You will know what to do. This is nothing that comes out of books. It was born into you.

"I will arrange with the central telephone exchange to have a closed circuit set up, so that you can reach me direct at any hour of the night or day, either at my home or here at the office, without having to go through the usual switchboards and interception desks. Simply give my name and say your own. Precious moments may be saved that way."

She dropped down to her knees and inclined her forehead until it touched the floor.

"I serve my divine Emperor."

The Yeddo Club was just off the Ginza, Tokyo's Broadway-Piccadilly-Champs Élysées. A single ideograph, in coral tube-lighting, announced its name. There was no Western lettering in the accompaniment. And yet the evidences of Westernism on every hand could not be escaped, for a nightclub in itself was a Western product, unlike the native geisha-houses, which were something entirely different.

Everyone in the place, even the Japanese, wore Western clothing. The barmen were busy mixing martinis and daiquiris, not serving sake. And at the moment when Lyons entered, a small Japanese band was sawing away—and with no sense of the beat—at an antique American number called "Button Up Your Overcoat." A few couples were on the floor doing the old-fashioned walkaway fox trot.

He asked for and got a small table for one on the edge of the parquet, rather than one of the banquettes lining the walls. He ordered a Tom Collins and sat out a trio of jugglers and a magician with a kimonoed girl assistant, wondering what was holding Matsuko up, and whether he'd come to the right place.

Then the spotlight, which had been spread out to envelop the whole floor area, contracted to just an aspirin tablet of dazzling white intensity, and a girl came out and began to dance.

Instantaneously, at first glance, she did something to him. A sort of spitting, sizzling electrical charge seemed to come from her and form an arc to him. Simply because he was what he was, and who he was, and ready to be grounded.

At first she was in a rich purple silk kimono, embroidered with gold cranes and chrysanthemums, and obi of pale violet, a gold eye mask on her face. She postured gracefully this way and that for a moment, opened and discarded the kimono—which was whisked from sight by a girl attendant—and then really began to dance.

She was not unclothed in any sense of the word. But a tier of long silken fringe fell from her bosom to her waist, and a second tier from her waist to her lower thighs. It was the glimpses of her body, as the fringe continually parted and split with her movements, that did the damage. It stirred his senses so that he almost reeled, and had to grab the sides of his chair tight to stay on.

He was hers before she'd even taken her third step. Every nerve in his body wanted her. The rest of the dance passed in a blur; he was hardly able to see it through the spell that enveloped him. His breath kept coming faster than the music.

When it was over and she was gone, the room seemed to cool down considerably, his heartbeats slowed and he could breathe better again.

Taking a long drink and a long shaky pull on a cigarette, he stopped a waiter with a peremptory jerk at his jacket.

"What was her name? Her, just now. You've got to give it to me."

"Tomiko," said the waiter blandly, as though this weren't exactly a new experience.

"Wait," he said, holding onto him. "Tell her she's got to come out here. She's got to come to my table. If she doesn't, I'll go in there myself and bring her out."

"Maybe she no like that," said the waiter, bland as ever.

Lyons crushed a paper tip into his breast pocket and managed to regain control of himself. "Ask her if she'll please join me at my table. Say I'd like to meet her very much."

Now, as he sat waiting, he didn't want Matsuko to show up anymore. But that was all right, because Matsuko didn't, in any case.

She didn't keep him waiting too long, considering that she'd changed from head to foot into street clothes. Western, of course. A plain black wool dress with six strands of white milkbeads tight around her neck. Even her hair had been done over. The bulging Japanese pompadour studded with flowers and pins was gone—he saw now that it must have been a wig—and she wore it now in a sleek little doll-bob with doll-bangs across her forehead. She smelled faintly of jasmine.

She came to a posed halt just far enough away from the table so that she didn't seem overanxious to get to it, one hip a little out of line, one foot pointed toe-forward, both hands holding the patent-leather envelope bag against the indentation of her waist.

"Good evening," she said in very presentable English.

His chair clicked like a dice roll with the swiftness with which he stood up. "Will you give me the pleasure of your company?"

"If you wish," she said demurely.

He circled the table and held her chair for her, and she eased into it. He was gone. He didn't have a chance, and didn't want one.

The waiter was beside them, solicitously.

"An anisette," she said, but to Lyons, not directly to the waiter. She let him see that he was her host. She was tactful that way, she was knowing.

"An anisette," he repeated to the waiter, although the waiter was standing closer to her than he was to Lyons himself.

"Did you like my dance?" she asked him, to break the ice while they were waiting.

"I didn't see it," he said. She waited for him to finish, and he did. "I only saw you."

She smiled to show that she accepted it as a compliment and not a slur.

"Would you care for a cigarette?"

"I rarely smoke," she said. And then quite unexpectedly added, "I will, though, if you want me to."

There was a good cue there, and he took it. "I don't want you to do anything you don't care to." A moment's meaningful pause.

She didn't pretend not to understand. "We haven't come to that yet. That's far ahead of us."

The waiter put her glass down to one side of her in order not to block their view of one another.

She raised the glass. "To our friendship," she said politely.

"No good," he said.

"Why no good? Why can't we be friends?"

"Oh hell, you know damn well we can't," he groaned, half under his breath.

She made a very slight warding-off motion with one hand, and smiled a little, to take the sting out of it. "I don't like to disappoint anyone, you in particular, so let's have things well-regulated in advance. In a little while—not immediately—but in a little while I'm going to get up and go home. It's late, I've danced, I'm tired and I have to get up tomorrow."

"What makes you think I'm not going right with you? I have a car outside."

"Very well, then you may take me as far as where I live. It will save me the trouble of having to find a taxi at this hour of the night."

"What was that 'as far as'?" he asked suspiciously. "Don't I get to go inside with you? What is it, off-bounds or something?"

"I happen to live with my family."

"Oh, come on now," he groaned. "Don't pull that old thing."

"I honestly do," she insisted. "A complete assortment of them. Father, mother, two younger sisters, one baby brother. You can ask the manager here at the club, if you don't believe me. He had to interview them before they permitted me to sign the contract with him. They've accepted my Western ways, my way of earning a living, but still I can't bring someone into the house with me. That broad-minded they are not."

"I'm going to have some night!" he lamented, throwing his face up toward the ceiling.

"What makes you think there won't be others," she said chastely, "after this one is over?"

"Whatever became of that little radio you used to keep on in the end room upstairs?" Ruth asked him unexpectedly at breakfast the next morning.

"I sold it."

He took another sip of his coffee, then asked "Why do you ask about that now? That's been gone long ago."

"Kind of sudden, wasn't it? You used to spend hours tinkering with it, locked up in there."

"Locked up? How do you know I was locked up?"

"I tried the door accidentally once or twice."

"Accidentally, I bet," was all he said.

"Another thing I keep thinking about," she went on presently, "is all those people who keep coming to the house by mistake. A roofing contractor, when there was nothing the matter with the roof. An electrical repairman, when there was no power failure. I've watched from the window sometimes, when they leave. They never go to any of the other houses. It's always only to this house they come."

"So?"

She was silent for a short time. Then she said, "Look, I'm not a fool, John. I went to U.C.L.A., same as you did. In fact that's where we met, remember? Level with me. What's up?"

She waited for it to sink in.

"What do you mean, what's up?" he said finally.

"Just what I said. What's up? What are you up to? What are you doing? Do I have to draw you a picture?"

He stared at her silently.

"All right, then here it is—listen to it. You make a hundred and fifty a month with the Acme Travel Agency. You don't even have an office. So where and when do you sell your tickets? Yet you go away on these little side-trips, come back with five thousand dollars in your money belt. The time before that it was fifteen hundred."

"Maybe I'm a dope smuggler," he jeered. "Have a shot on me."

"That was what first occurred to me," she admitted gravely. "Only the drug traffic flows the other way. *Out* of China, not *into* it. So it wouldn't be that."

"You name it, then."

"It all adds up to only one thing. Why try to deny it? You're engaged in espionage work of some kind or another. You're nothing but a—a common, ordinary spy."

''How revolting!'' he said sarcastically.

''There's nothing in it to be proud of that I can see. Maybe I have the wrong slant. A soldier fights openly on the field of battle. That's honest, at least. But this is—is sneaky, behind-the-back, in-the-dark kind of fighting. I never could see where it was romantic or glamorous. Never could see that at all. It's dirty and it's below the belt. It's juvenile, it's adolescent, only an immature mind could think other—''

''Like mine,'' he supplied for her.

The door opened tentatively, and she said sharply, ''Stay in the kitchen, Mikki, until we call you.'' Mikki did not know enough English to make a very good eavesdropper, even if she'd wanted to.

They were silent for a long while.

Then she said, dully, shaking her head in continued disbelief, ''My own husband a spy. After nine years I find it out.''

''We're not married that long,'' he said almost facetiously, as though he enjoyed tormenting her.

''No, but we've known each other that long. I don't know, something about it sticks in my craw. Why didn't you tell me at the start?'' she cried out bitterly. ''Why didn't you give me a chance to decide at that time whether I wanted to go on with you or not? Not let me give up six or seven years of my life, and then stumble on it by accident.''

''You're sure taking it big.''

''Because there's something unclean about it. I can't stomach it.''

''Well, if you don't like it, you can damn well lump it!'' he burst out. ''Because I'm staying with it. It's my life, and it's too late to back out now. I couldn't even if I wanted to, and I don't want to.''

She rose from the table, but still stood there by it, half turned away. ''I'm glad we haven't any children.'' Then she went on to the door, turned and asked him, ''Is Matsuko in on it, too?''

''Look,'' he said roughly, ''no questions, hear? You've talked just about enough for one day. Now zip up your yap and leave me alone. I want a little peace.''

''You answered my question anyway, just then, whether you realized it or not. Sure he is, he must be. All those cryptic phone calls you get from him.''

He swung his arm around at her impatiently. ''Blow. Beat it. Take an aspirin.''

''They'll shoot you one of these days,'' she said hollowly from outside by the stairs.

''They don't shoot here in Japan, they hang,'' he called back flippantly.

''How many other places have you done it? Did you do it in Russia, too, that time you went there before we were married? It's a wonder they didn't shoot you there."

He was pouring himself a drink of Japanese whiskey, his own nerves frayed now by the prolonged dispute. "Why would they shoot me in Russia, you jerk?" he exclaimed, caught off guard. "That's where I—"

He stopped. She was coming back toward him now. He shrugged, as though to say, What the hell's the difference anyway? He downed his drink.

He'd never seen her face so white before. He'd never seen any face so white before.

"What did you say just then?"

"Nothing."

"Finish it. Finish what you started to say."

"You heard me the first time, so what do you want me to repeat for?"

"Tell me I didn't hear you right. Tell me. You've got to tell me that." She tried to shake him by the shoulders.

He backed his hand at her. "Knock it off or I'll belt you!"

"It *is* the United States? It *is* the United States?" She was almost incoherent by now, sobbing drily without tears. "That's bad enough, but at least it *is* the United States?"

"What is the United States?"

"—you're working for."

"Grow up, you fool, he said with lethal slowness, spacing each word. "How dumb can you be? It's Soviet Russia."

At the sound she made, Mikki stuck her head in at the door. "Somesing happen, Missy?"

"Yeah, he said, without lifting a finger to help her. "Missy's chicken-hearted. She just fainted dead away on the floor." And he poured himself another drink.

It didn't take her long to get ready. In less than an hour she was tottering clumsily down the stairs, swaying off-balance from the bulky valise she was lugging with both hands.

When he saw her go past toward the front door, he got up and went out into the hall after her.

"Here, you better take this with you," he said briefly.

This wasn't any ordinary husband-and-wife quarrel, and they both knew it. This was terminal.

She looked down at his hand first and then up into his face.

"Money from those people? That kind of money?" she said bitterly. "Thank you, no!"

"All right, Betsy Ross," he answered grimly. "It's still a whole lot better shake than I ever got from my own country. You never stopped to think of my side of it, did you? Selling apples and shoelaces on the street corner, unable to finish my schooling, pounding my feet off looking for a job and never finding one. Standing on soup lines like a beggar. Living in tin-can shanties. Fatso Hoover. 'Prosperity is just around the corner.' 'Happy days are here again.' Even when I finally did marry, I wasn't allowed the privilege of having children of my own, like a man should. Even that right was taken away from me. That's what's turned me into what I am today, lushing and wolfing. My own country couldn't offer me a living. Why shouldn't I turn to those people? They offered the only hope there was, for an underdog like me."

She'd put the valise down, but only momentarily.

"A hundred million other Americans went through that right along with you. How is it all the others didn't turn their backs on their country, too? Because they had guts, and you and a few like you didn't. Don't blame your own weakness on your country's shortcomings. Every country goes through a tough time at one time or another. To turn your back on it just because of that is like—is like turning down a friend when he needs your help." Her lip curled disdainfully. "I don't think the United States wants a man like you. I think she's better off without a man like you, if you want to know the truth of it."

"Three cheers for the red, white and blue," he said sourly.

She hoisted the valise and turned and went out into the street.

He watched her for a moment, his expression changing from anger to relief.

"You better let me call a taxi for you, at least," he called after her.

"I don't want a taxi. I'll walk downtown along the middle of the street, carrying my valise in my hand—until I get to the American consulate. They'll take care of me there, they'll see that I get back home."

"Are you going to inform on me?"

"No. I'm more loyal to the man I married, than you are to—the country you were born into. I'll simply say there was another woman, that's all."

She turned a corner and was lost to view.

Suddenly, without any warning, two members of the Kempetai, the terrible, the terrifying "thought-police," were standing one on each side of her. One riveted his hand upon her shoulder, the other riveted his hand around her arm.

"You come with us," one said in Japanese.

"What for?" she asked, her eyes widening with unalloyed fright. "Why are you arresting me?"

"Detain for questioning."

She came hurrying across the room to him at the Yeddo, the smile on her face far brighter than any lipstick could have been.

She was still in the same black dress with the same milk-beads around her throat, but she'd added two new touches tonight. She had on a tricky black satin cocktail-hat, pert as a kitten. And she'd changed her perfume. Tonight she was wearing muguet.

She held out both hands to him as he sprang to his feet, and he took them in both of his. Then they swung them in and out a few times, in affectionate greeting.

"Johnnie!" she piped gleefully, like a small child.

"I love it when you call me that," he purred.

"Johnnie. Johnnie," she said softly.

They became aware that they were still standing and that people were turning around to grin at them. They sat down with a little mutual laugh.

"Did I keep you waiting long? I never changed so fast in my life. And that girl in there, she's no help at all, poor thing. She's not used to Western zippers."

"I wouldn't care how long you took." He leaned across the table and put his hand on top of hers. "Tonight's an anniversary. You know of what, don't you?"

She nodded with a sort of conspiratorial animation. "One week ago tonight we first met."

He became serious. "Let's do something different tonight. Let's—A week's an awful long time for a fellow to wait. And I've been awfully good about it, haven't I? Admit it."

"Except for begging every other minute," she said mockingly.

Then she, too, became serious.

"I'm not like all the others, Johnnie. I want to know you inside out. What are you like, really? What do you do, really? What is your life, really?"

"I've told you everything, there isn't anything I've left out," he said earnestly. "I even told you about Ruth, the second night we met."

"Oh, Ruth," she said in contemptuous dismissal. "Every married man tells the girl he loves everything about his wife the very first thing. That's nothing. I want to know you *deeper* than that, *closer* than that."

"There isn't any deeper, there isn't any closer," he said stubbornly.

"Then there isn't any use for us to keep on meeting every night," she said, as stubbornly. ''What for, if you're going to keep part of yourself away from me?''

He was glumly silent, and she saw that this was going to require more than just ordinary persuasion.

''Suppose I were to say yes,'' she came out with suddenly. ''I'm not saying yes—this is just supposition, remember. But suppose I were to say yes. Then where would we go? My family's at my own home. I won't go to your house. And I'm not the sort of girl, Mr. Johnnie Lyons, would go with you to some disreputable hotel just for the night.''

His face lit up like a floodlight. A little pulse in his temple started to jazz. His carburetor was in business again.

''I have a little bungalow, a country place, outside the city, on the Peninsula, overlooking the bay. Would you come there with me? We could make it in a forty-minute drive.''

''What would we do there?''

He chuckled outright in her face.

''But I mean—'' she went on falteringly, ''has it got a radio, anything like that?''

He stopped short, and the air between them was filled with sudden tension.

''What made you ask that?'' he said in a cold, wary voice.

''Well,'' she said plausibly, ''we can't make love all the time. We can't drink all the time. We can't eat all the time. I simply wondered if there was something to help pass the time away, if I did decide to stay with you.''

He relaxed again. ''Oh, I didn't get you for a minute.''

She knew enough not to ask the question a second time, and finally he said, of his own accord but a trifle reticently, ''Yeah, it's got a radio.''

''What are you put out about, Johnnie?''

''Well, y'know, your asking that isn't exactly a compliment to me,'' he said sulkily. ''You worried I won't keep you busy enough? Don't worry, baby, you won't need any music out there with me. We'll make our own.''

''Johnnie!'' she reproached. ''Wait for me here a minute,'' she said then, smiling shyly. ''I'll be right back. I'll have to telephone home and make up some excuse to tell my family.''

In the dressing room she motioned the maid out, closed the door and picked up the phone, all in one swift motion.

''Tomiko. Colonel Setsu, official business.''

Setsu's voice came on with uncanny quickness, almost as though he'd had his hand ready on the instrument.

They didn't waste time exchanging names.

"He has a little bungalow on the Peninsula," she began in a low-voiced rush. "It has a radio. He's taking me there now. Do I refuse, do I delay, do I go at once—your order?"

"How did he react about the radio?"

"He stopped short. His pride as a man rebelled that I should ask about outside entertainment."

Colonel Setsu had the sixth sense typical of the good Secret Service man. "He is the right one," he said instantly. "That was not his pride as a man, that was his caution as a secret agent."

"Then I go?"

"Absolutely essential. It will have to be in your own hands entirely, at first. It may take all night until I can identify the exact location and have my men reach there. Report back as soon as you safely can. But be very careful. One thing I must warn you about—"

Lyons was standing in the dressing room doorway, looking at her. She had not heard the door open.

"Good-bye, honorable father," she said, and hung up.

She turned to him with a dazzling smile.

"What'd they say?" he grunted.

"What does any family in any part of the world say when the eldest daughter tells them she is spending the night with a girl friend? They *think* they know, they're *afraid* they're right, but they *hope* they are mistaken."

She shrugged as she turned toward the door. "Well, Johnnie. Here goes nothing."

"I wouldn't say that," he said, tightening his arm possessively around her waist. "I wouldn't say that at all!"

When she awoke in the morning he wasn't in the bed with her and wasn't in the room.

The overturned goblets, the empty champagne bottles in the bucket, floating now in water that had once been chopped ice, told the story of their night. Successful from his point of view, barren from hers. She hadn't learned a thing more than she'd already known in the city.

She put on a man's black silk kimono she saw lying there—his, for she hadn't brought anything of her own with her—and ran to the window.

The view from the little country house was as beautiful as a Japanese print. In the foreground were nothing but dwarf fir trees, glossy and dark green. Beyond and below them the pebbly beach, rosy-beige in color. And then past that the waters of the bay, an incomparable blue. Out from the shore a little fishing smack rode motionless, reflected upside down as on a sheet of glass. There was no sign of life aboard it. All under a porcelain-smooth sky.

No use to search the tiny little two-room place again this morning, even though he wasn't here. She had done that exhaustively during the night, in the intervals between their love-bouts, while pretending to roam aimlessly about.

She went to the telephone and dispiritedly gave Colonel Setsu's name.

"I have failed. I came out here for nothing."

"The radio?"

"It is nothing more than it seems. One our own inexpensive Japanese makes, table-top, that you can buy in any store."

"You're sure?"

"I have examined it all over. It has no transmitter, messages cannot be sent out over it. The back panel is even broken, which made it easier for me to see inside."

"Stay there until you find it," ordered the Colonel curtly. "It may be right before your eyes and you do not know it."

She hung up disconsolately.

A law of diminishing returns would soon set in, and she knew it. The second night she would already mean less to him than the first, the third night less than the second. Her cards were down, she had nothing left to play with. And his were still being nursed up close to his face.

She went back to the window. The fishing smack had moved in closer to shore since she had last seen it. And he was standing up on it; she could recognize his tall lanky figure even at that distance. He must have been below somewhere the first time.

It may be right before your eyes and you do not know it.

She made a sudden swift turn, as if to go back to the telephone she had just left and pick it up once more, then thought better of it. He would be back to the house in a matter of minutes.

But she knew where the radio was now. She knew unerringly where he kept it.

She ran out of the house and down the slope to the beach to meet him, naked as she was under the kimono and in bare feet, uttering gleeful little cries of "Johneee! Johneee!"

They were both sitting on the edge of the gunwale now, trailing their bare feet in the water. He'd taken off shoes and socks now, too.

"Why can't I go down inside the hatch?" she asked for the tenth time.

"You don't want to go down there. Nothing but a lot of greasy machinery. Get yourself all dirty."

"I bet you're hiding a woman down there. That's why you won't let me see."

"I'm a one-woman man. One at a time."

"Well then, what are we going to do, just sit here like this soaking our feet? This is no fun. Let's go in for a swim at least."

"I have no suit."

"This is the one country in the world where nude bathing isn't immoral. You ought to know that, foolish one." Then, to prod him on, she added, "I bet you can't swim, that's what it is."

"I swim better than you," he told her.

"Prove it then." That worked. He jumped to his feet, took off everything but his shorts and went arching in in a very graceful dive.

She promptly flung off the kimono and went in after him.

They horsed around for a while, laughing and splashing, the way people do in the water.

"You're good, you know it?" he spluttered admiringly.

"At what, this?" she laughed.

"And a couple of other things."

She pretended to tire first, climbed back onto the boat and sat watching him, huddled under the kimono like a towel. As she had half expected, now that he was in, he was enjoying it too much to come right out again. He was only starting to get warmed up now.

"Swim around the boat," she suggested, squeezing out her short black hair.

He went under, bobbed up again. "What's that," he scoffed. "That's no distance."

"Do it underwater then. See if you can stay under all the way around it."

He submerged obediently, and the seat of his white shorts went in last, after all the rest of him. Her hand snaked out on the split second almost, and burrowed into the pocket of his trousers, which were spread-eagled within easy reach on the deck. No key in the left one. She tried the right. No key in that one, either. But she came out with a crumpled scrap of paper, which he must have forgotten to throw away. On it, in lead pencil, were two rows of words printed in capital letters. A message that must have gone out over the transmitter.

It was scrambled, didn't make sense. That didn't matter, it was the evidence she'd been sent out to get, and Setsu would know how to have it decoded.

She had no place to hide it. The kimono had no pockets, and she was nude under it.

She snatched a cigarette from the pack he'd left lying on the deck, rolled the paper quickly around the outside of it, blank-side out, and stuck it between her lips. Then she deliberately threw the accompanying paper match folder into the water, just as his head broke surface and a thin sheet of water went streaming down in front of his face.

"Didn't think I could do it, did you?" he panted breathlessly.

"Johnnie, I'm going back now—I'm starting to shiver," she said. "It's October, after all. You bring the kimono back with you."

She knew he'd have to rest on the boat, if only a minute or two, after his underwater exertions.

And, without giving him a chance to object or stop her, she slipped back into the water just as he hauled himself up out of it right alongside of her. But not before she glimpsed the key to the hatch fastened by a safety pin to the waistband of his shorts, around at the side.

Timing is everything, particularly in moments of crisis. Timing is life and death.

She could have made it half a dozen times over if she'd only worked out her time better. He was still on the boat, hadn't left it, when she looked back from the doorway as she re-entered the house.

But she was dripping wet, freezing, and shaking uncontrollably all over. She had to rub herself off first and put on some things, and it was that that undid her. Had she gone straight to the telephone just as she was, she probably could not have made herself understood through her chattering teeth. Nor, on the other hand, could she have gone directly to the car and driven naked like that all the way in to Tokyo.

A precious minute to rub down. A precious minute to put on clothes. An added precious minute for the shoes and stockings—cigarette slipped inside the top of one of them. And a final precious minute to pour out a finger of Hennessy and down it.

She glanced from the window—and the boat had disappeared. He must have switched on the engine and been bringing it in under its own power. The landing stage was around on the other side and couldn't be seen from where she was.

She fled to the phone, still gambling on her timing—"Tomiko for Colonel Setsu, urgent, urgent!"—and her timing had run out. He was standing there in the outside doorway, looking in at her.

She turned, smiled innocently, and then hung up. He smiled back; he didn't appear to be suspicous or ill-tempered or anything.

"What'd you do, drop my matches in the water, you little devil?" he reproved her.

He lit a cigarette from a lighter first, and then helped himself in turn to the Three-Star Hennessy.

"If I'd know you were going to bring the boat in right after I left, I wouldn't have gotten all wet for nothing, the way I did," she said.

He slung one hip onto the edge of a table and nursed his glass. "I always bring it in. What do you think I do, leave it out there all night with nobody on it?" Then, without any change of voice, he asked her, "Who was that you were talking to?"

"My family, silly. Do you realize this is going to be my second night away from home?"

"How'd they take it?" he asked, grinning at her knowingly.

"Not too badly, all things considered."

He finished his drink and put down the glass.

"Why didn't you tell me you couldn't reach them—"

"But I did," she quickly interrupted. "I just this minute finished talking to them. You saw me put down the phone."

"—then I still wouldn't have been sure about you, one way or the other. At least not sure enough to do anything to you. But you lied to me about it—"

"Lied?" she breathed.

"Because I cut the wires outisde the house myself just now as I came in. So you couldn't have been talking to anybody—that's a dead phone. And, by lying to me, now you *have* made me sure of you. That makes all the rest of it hang together. The matches thrown in the water, so there'd be no risk of having to smoke away the evidence. Going down into the water with a cigarette held in your mouth. Doing the dog-paddle on the way back instead of your regular stroke, so you could keep it dry. One trouser leg was flipped over when I went to put them back on. I'd left them both pasted down flat on the deck. You'd been in my pockets. Little things. But it's the little things in my line of work that count."

She made one last gamble. One final one. She had the long, strong legs of a dancer, good for running. The car was only a few yards down the road, in the open; there was no such thing as a garage out here. He had a habit of leaving the keys sticking in it nine times out of ten—she'd been out in it with him enough to know that. About things that didn't directly concern his work he was apt to be careless, even slipshod. And finally, last night during her roving she had noticed that the key was standing in the lock on the other side of the door between the two rooms here.

So she threw the dice—winner take all. What else could she do?

"This conversation isn't helping me get any warmer," she said, shuddering. "I could use one more drink."

She went toward the hefty cognac bottle, empty glass in hand.

Still half sitting, he had turned to watch her, so she couldn't try to hit him over the head; he could catch it in time. Instead she let the glass go, grabbed the bottle by the neck with both hands and rammed it, bottom-first, square into his face with all her might. It was the equivalent of a good man-driven punch in the nose, if nothing else, and it stunned him for a minute and opened his lip.

Then she ran like one possessed, slammed the door, turned the key in it and fled from the house, down the road—and all the gods of old Japan and all the ghosts of ancient warriors must have been rooting for her.

She flung herself in the car, without bothering to shut the door. The keys were in it, and she turned on the ignition and floored the starter. . . .

He didn't bother with the room door. He leaped out the window and cut through the dwarf firs diagonally for the car. . . .

The motor turned over once, turned over twice, failed.

He had her.

"C'mon back, baby," he said, wrapping her in a double-armed bear hug and lifting her bodily out of the car. He dragged her back toward the cabin, breathing heavily. "I don't know whether to love you or kill you." He laughed harshly "Why not both?"

Her timing was what had destroyed her. It had worked out all wrong.

Her eyes remained closed for some time after. She almost seemed to be in a faint, from overemotion. When she stirred at last and opened her eyes, he was all the way across the room from her. He had a closet door open and was standing by it, his hand inside the pocket of an old gabardine topcoat that was hanging there.

She tried to sit up, failed, then succeeded.

"Wasn't it good?" she whispered exhaustedly, as though seeking to determine her own fate by the answer.

"Sure. Out of this world. That's why I'm sending you there with it."

She dropped her eyes demurely. "In Japan there are many old arts. Making love is one of them."

"Ready, baby?" was all he said.

The gun came out.

She looked at him without expression. "Dying is another of our arts," she said.

Outside the house there was a guttural shout of command. Then running feet started to converge on it from all sides, dozens of them it seemed, pattering over grass, scraping over gravel, slapping over flagstones.

The gun jerked spasmodically.

"I was almost going to let you go there for a minute," he confided rapidly. "But this does it."

They weren't in time. He was too close, and they were too far.

He sighted at her face first, but then changed his mind, as though thinking it was too beautiful to spoil. He lowered it to her heart instead, and the bullet slammed her backward. The blood came out with an effect almost like an iridescent, finespun garden spray revolving on the grass, until she clapped both hands over it to try to hold it in. Then it simply ran down flat against her skin.

She toppled over sideward on the bed, and dropped from there to the floor, limp as a drunk.

Then they were in. They poured in like water through a sieve. They even seemed to come through the walls.

He tried to point it at his own head, but his immunity had run out, and they caught it from him and bore him down.

Then Colonel Setsu strode in, dress-uniform sword at his side. "Help this woman," he ordered, pointing.

She made warding-off gesture with one hand, its palm out toward them, shiny orange-red with her own blood but the creases in it still white.

Then she lifted herself—agonizedly, by sheer will power, almost miraculously—grasping the bed until she stood fully erect for a moment, for a moment only.

Not to face them, for her face turned straight upward overhead, to where Ameratsu the sun goddess, ancestress of all Japan, blazed in all her glory.

"For the divine Emperor I die!"

Then she fell and died there.

"Tomiko!" cried Colonel Setsu in a ringing voice, holding his sword upright before his face in salute. "Let every man remember her name and tell it to his sons. Let every man look upon her face and behold true love of country."

They all bowed their heads mutely for a long moment.

Then Johnnie Lyons was hustled violently out, staggering from side to side with the fury of their hatred.

* * *

The cell door grated open at the usual time, but instead of the guard with the daily tin breakfast tray, the Commandant of Sugamo Prison himself entered, holding two official-looking documents in his hand.

Lyons' face whitened—he would have been more than human if it hadn't—but at least it stayed steady enough. "Is this it?" he asked.

The Commandant didn't answer. A turnkey brought in a folded campstool and set it up, and the official seated himself on it. The turnkey went out and relocked the cell door.

"You wish to eat breakfast first?"

Lyons sighed listlessly. "No. What is it?"

"Has been discussions going on for some time," began the Commandant by way of introduction.

"I wondered what was taking it so long," said Lyons, half to himself.

"Is politics involved. No harm if you know this. Politics can forgive anything, if necessary. Overlook everything, no matter what."

"Why the briefing? I know I'm going to die," said Lyons morosely. "This is no fun for me."

"Finally, agreement has been reached, after long delicate negotiations. Russia have in prison two, three very valuable Japanese secret agents we would like back. Also, Japan for political reasons, have no wish to be bad friends with Russia at this time. Want to conciliate. We already fighting one all-out war. So, in exchange for two, three Japanese agents Russia hand back to us, you be taken out of here some time this week, go under armed escort to Valadivostock, and be turned free on Russian territory."

It took several moments for it to sink in. Lyons blinked, and then blinked again. "In other words, I'm not going to hang at all. I'm being traded in for some Japanese agents Russia's holding."

"Exactly," said the Commandant. "This is not made known, of course, to public or newspapers. Is bad for morale in wartime. But people soon forget your name, think you already been executed. Is higher politics, that's all. Happen many times before in this world."

"I'd be a liar," Lyons admitted, "if I said I wasn't glad. Anybody'd rather live than die."

"Now all you have to do," said the Commandant, producing a fountain pen and uncapping it, "you sign one of these two paper, and everything taken care of."

"What is it? Can I read it?"

The Commandant handed it to him. It was short, just a bare couple of lines, and typed in English. He read it half aloud to himself.

"I, John Lyons, do hereby and for all future time to come renounce my citizenship in the United States of America."

He looked up at the Commandant blankly. "What's the other one, the one I don't have to sign?"

"That automatically grant you Soviet citizenship as soon as you sign this first one. But first one must be signed before it can do so."

"But why?" said Johnnie dazedly. "Why? I don't get it."

"Is very simple," said the Commandant impatiently. "You haven't heard about it here in prison maybe, but my country has been in state of total war with United States America since eight of December just past."

"What!" said Johnnie, stunned.

"With Russia we still continue at peace. Is impossible exchange you as American citizen. As American citizen you must pay death penalty, for spying. Only as Soviet citizen can you be exchanged. Is only technicality, anyhow. You been working for Russia all along, for past several years."

"Yeah," said Johnnie dimly. "But there was no war then. And I hadn't seen a girl named Tomiko die."

He huddled forward and ran his hands through his hair.

"How much time have I got to decide?"

"How much time you need, to know if you want to live or die?" said the Commandant ironically.

"Give me one night's time."

The Commandant rose to his feet. "I return at exactly this time tomorrow morning. You let me know then which you decide."

When the Commandant came in he was again holding the same two papers, but there was no campstool this time.

"Which?" he demanded tersely.

"Death," Johnnie said simply.

The Commandant looked at him hard, for a long time. Then he said, equally simply, "I think you are right."

"Can I have one last favor?" asked Johnnie.

"If possible."

"Can I have that paper? The one renouncing . . ."

The Commandant handed it to him. Johnnie put a match to it. Then he dropped it to the floor and scuffed his foot around on it until it wasn't there anymore.

The death procession walked slowly toward the execution place, the Commandant at its head, Lyons in the center, flanked by two rows of three guards each, in stiff military formation. They came out into an open yard, with a pastel-blue sky overhead and clouds like gobs of shaving lather. A door in the cement wall facing them, ominous as the lid of a coffin standing upright, opened by itself before they had reached it. They filed in without breaking step. Then it closed after them, shutting out the light of Lyon's last day.

It was dim inside. Incense sweetened the air, and tapers were burning like shimmering little fireflies along an altar, illumining from below the serene downcast face of Buddha, hope and belief of half the world. A priest stood off to one side.

This was not the death chamber itself, but a temple just outside it, the last way station just before eternity.

They halted briefly, and the Commandant turned to Lyons. "Would you like to pray?" he asked him respectfully.

"I'll take mine straight," said Lyons shortly.

"He will say one for you, then," said the Commandant, indicating the priest.

"Thanks," said Lyons. "That I won't object to." And as they moved on toward the rear, he suddenly added, "And to show my appreciation—" Impulsively he jerked loose the little chamois-skin pouch that he had worn around his neck ever since his arrest—they had examined it, of course—and placed the huge diamond it contained in a little lacquered dish that stood there on the altar to receive any last gifts the condemned might wish to make as they moved on by toward the death place.

Back to the god it belonged to, at long last.

Behind the temple was the execution place. They led him over where the rope was and turned him around, and he, of his own accord, neatly fitted his feet in between the chalkmarks traced on the floor that showed the place he was to stand.

And as he stood there, he was saying a prayer of a sort after all. His lips moved noticeably, and his eyes had a concentrated—and yet far-away—look. Not a prayer a church would know, not a prayer for himself or for his own soul. Not a prayer at all, maybe.

He was saying the names of the states. Not all in the right order—he'd never been that good in geography. And he couldn't get them all in; the time they gave him was too short. But he did what he could while he stood there.

"Arizona, Alabama, Arkansas . . ."

The ready-made noose was deftly fitted around his neck, and closed until it hugged him tight.

"North Carolina, South Carolina, Delaware . . ."

The executioner tugged at the upright lever with both arms, like a railroad switchman throwing open a section of track. The floor shot open under him, and he was gone, head all the way over to the side.

* * *

Ruth Lyons, still wearing the pallor of the four years of imprisonment that only the American Occupation had brought to an end, walked slowly along the gravelly cemetery path to where the grave was.

She crouched beside it when she had reached it, and arranged the flowers she had brought with her around the little upright stone marker, but in such a way as not to obliterate it. Then she stood in silence looking down at it.

It had just four words on it, above his initials. They had told her for what reason he had died. She knew now he would have wanted that to be on there. The words on the marker were:

Here Lies an American

J.L.

WILLIAM E. BARRETT
Dealers in Doom

1

ASSIGNED TO KILL

DON COOPER BREEZED into the shabby little office in a corner of the State Department Building at Washington with a gleam of anticipation in his eyes. He was still young enough to get a thrill out of the business that he was in, and he was wise enough to anticipate action in this call. He would have visited this little office some time during the week, in any case, and Ben Rockwell knew it. There was something extraordinary in the wind, therefore, or Rockwell would not have called Don Cooper down here during his first twenty-four hours back in Washington.

The tan of Asiatic suns still dyed Don Cooper's face. His last mission had taken him far. As he opened the door of the office, a square-rigged, baldheaded man rose from behind a scarred desk and held out his hand.

A man without a title, Ben Rockwell made no pretensions. His office was bleak, unpretentious, and a bit cluttered. No one spent an unnecessary minute in it. It was a workshop, and the baldheaded man used it as the hub of a vast net into which the spies of peace time flew, and were caught. Don Cooper was part of that net—a U.S. agent of counter-espionage.

''You're looking fit, Cooper.'' Rockwell's eyes swept the tall young agent in swift appraisal.

Don Cooper grinned. ''That's the way a man sizes up a horse that he's going to work to death,'' he drawled. ''I know you.''

''The tea brigade in Washington is recruited to full strength, Cooper.'' Rockwell's voice was dry, a little harsh. His eyes, however, were friendlier than his tone. He waved to a chair, and flipped a paper into the younger man's lap. ''Seen that yet?''

Don Cooper's eyes raced through the lurid headlines that set off the latest exposé featured in the Hirsch newspapers.

ACTIVITY OF FOREIGN POWER
IN SOUTH AMERICA VIOLATES
MONROE DOCTRINE, SAYS
BUSHMAN

Hairless corpses mark path of gas bomb as little nations fight useless wars to test foreign devices of death.

There was a lot of it—a sensational story, under the by-line of a former munitions salesman, in which veiled charges were hurled at an unnamed foreign power, with a hint that the name of the power would be revealed in future articles. According to the Benjamin Bushman quoted, the South American nations were being used by foreign war makers to test new war equipment. Revolutions were being financed, he said, by nations interested in seeing how newly discovered gas bombs would work in the field. Special emphasis was laid on the gas bomb which was so powerful that it left the slain hairless. Bushman claimed to have one of these bombs to substantiate his charges.

Don Cooper raised his eyes. "I read something about this in the Chicago papers as I came through. They didn't take it so seriously. They called this lad 'Babbling Benny' and—"

"I know. They wrote it up as the dandruff bomb—"

"Because it causes the hair to fall out," Cooper finished, grinning despite the gravity of the underlying story.

Rockwell did not smile. "No one outside of the Hirsch papers takes it very seriously," he said, "but it's a build-up, and it isn't funny. Somebody is planting an idea."

"And the bomb?"

"Is bunk. We've investigated, and we can't find any evidence to support the belief that Bushman has such a bomb, or that such a bomb ever existed."

Don Cooper frowned. "Isn't this lad putting himself out on a limb, then?"

"No. It's probably more accurate to say that somebody else is putting him out on a limb, and he's dumb enough to play along. He was a munitions salesman in South America, and he got fired for taking too many of his own bribes. Rather an unsavory character, all around."

"Where's the play heading?"

"That's what we want to know." Rockwell bit the end off a new cigar and worried it around on his lips without lighting it. He tapped the desk with one forefinger.

"You've been in Asia, Cooper, while the war clouds have moved over Europe. I'll give you the picture as I see it. Benny Bushman is going to be your job. and you'll have your hands full."

Cooper did not say anything. There was nothing indicated. Rockwell toyed with the cigar. "This Senate munitions probe has raised some hell," he said slowly, "and mostly because the public is getting the idea that the munitions people promote wars for profit. The public isn't going to stand much of that—and there are a lot of people who don't want the public to get too curious about how wars start—not all munitions people, either."

Don Cooper nodded. "The professional spies, for instance—such as Paul Zeron."

"Yes—such as Zeron." Rockwell's eyes were thoughtful. "The best two ways, Cooper, to stop this munitions investigation from spreading too far are to promote a hell of a big scandal and blame it on the probe—start a hell of a big war that will be so interesting that people won't care how it started until it's over."

"A small reason for starting a big war," Cooper suggested.

"Certainly. But you forget that over half the world wants war, wants a few million men killed to keep a lot more from starving to death. Selfish interests can just play along with the war-wishers. They always have and, Cooper, Europe is being held together by the most unnatural string of alliances in history. Every one of those nations is chafing against them, but the alliances can be broken only by war. The game is to make somebody else start the war."

"And Babbling Benny with his dandruff bomb is tied into big-time politics?"

"He is—somewhere."

"And what nation is he going to name as responsible for wars in South America?"

"Italy."

"Absurd!"

"Of course. But there's a deep play building up. What it is, I don't pretend to guess. Hatred of Italy is being built up in other nations. If Il Duce loses their friendship, the time will be ripe. The United States will be compromised by some overt act here, Italy's enemies will leap at Italy's throat and before we know it, we'll be in another foreign war ourselves, on the side of Italy's enemy. That's a hypothesis. I can be wrong."

"OK. Where do I start?"

"With Paul Zeron."

"Zeron?" Cooper's interest sharpened at the mention of his old enemy.

"Yes." Rockwell smiled grimly. "That's why I picked you for this job. He's an ancient foe of yours—and he's the man behind Benny Bushman."

Don Cooper rose to his feet. "Who is behind Zeron?"

Rockwell shrugged. "He's anybody's for hire. He's played this game close. It may be a foreign power. It may be munitions interest. It may be that pack of international vultures who pick well on war—the professional spies. Somebody wants war, and Zeron is their tool. There's your job."

"Thanks. I've got a hunch that I'll like it."

Rockwell's unblinking blue eyes were on his agent. He put one hand in the drawer. When he withdrew it, something thumped hard on the desk. Don Cooper looked down at a short-barreled .38 Colt Detective Special. Rockwell pushed it across the desk.

"Neat little job at close range," he said, "and you can carry it under a dinner jacket without a bulge."

Don Cooper picked it up. His eyes asked a question. Rockwell was worrying his cigar again. He talked around it.

"Human life is a cheap commodity in any game that Paul Zeron plays," he said slowly, "and I've got a hunch that the world would miss Zeron less than almost anybody who went against him."

Don Cooper picked up the weapon, hefted it, and slipped it into his pocket. His lips were tight. There was no mistaking the meaning of that weapon and the manner of its presentation. For the first time since he had entered the service, Don Cooper was being sent out on a job—to kill.

2

A DOUBLE THREAT

"Even if a job threatens to be nasty, one can start it pleasantly," Don Cooper decided as he surrendered his topcoat to the check girl at the Carlton.

He eyed the main door expectantly. He had a dinner engagement with Marion Brill, and he could charge the time to business and pleasure simultaneously. The best woman agent in counter-espionage work was also the most beautiful. He was meeting her here to avoid her father, the Honorable Stephen Brill. The esteemed senator made too many speeches.

The elevator doors on Cooper's left slid open with a barely audible click, and an exceedingly short, insignificant man emerged. He paused for a moment, his dark eyes roving. Then he saw Don Cooper, and he was no longer insignificant. Something came into his eyes, lighting them. He slid across the floor at a glide rather than a walk, with the effortless forward movement of a professional dancer, perhaps—or an expert fencer.

"Ah, my frien', you have done Asia in so short a time, no?" His eyebrows were raised, his hand outstretched. Don Cooper smiled and took the proffered hand. There was no clasp, no heartiness in the exchange; it was merely a polite gesture, like the glove touch of two opposing pugilists.

"Long time or short," Cooper replied, "one never does Asia, quite."

"True." The little man gestured to two chairs placed conveniently close together. "You await a party? We can sit down and talk—about Asia, perhaps."

Don Cooper sat down, lighted a cigarette, and shared an ash tray with the little man. His talk with Rockwell was still fresh in his mind and he was wary. Officially, this man who called himself *Monsieur* Zeron (and pronounced the name, ironically, as Zero) was the purchasing agent for half a dozen republics below the Panama Canal. Unofficially he was many things, and served many masters. He was a realist not a patriot; he undertook contracts only at a price.

"I am concerned about your health, my dear Cooper." Zeron's voice was dry, a little grating. "Washington at this season would be most bad for you. I have a little place in Maine. You could take it over for—let's say a month."

Don Cooper laughed. "I'm glad that we're not kidding each other. But why me? There are better men in my line in Washington."

Zeron seemed to consider that. His fingertips pressed together. "Let us talk only of your health," he said. "Let us say that the men in Washington become used to the climate. You have been away. You are rash. You take chances. You might at such a time as this acquire a fatal malady." He turned his eyes full on Cooper as he spoke, and there was a penetrating fire behind them. Don Cooper shrugged.

"I haven't been ill in Washington yet," he said lightly.

Paul Zeron rose. "We cannot talk as long as I would wish," he said. "Your party has arrived. You will think of your health, no?"

"No." Don Cooper also rose. Marion Brill had entered the Carlton. He wondered how Zeron knew—but why wonder in this business? The little man was looking at him out of piercing black eyes.

"No?" he asked thoughtfully. "Perhaps not. But the young lady—you would suffer if she should suffer, perhaps." His voice was soft. He'd watched Don Cooper's eyes when they saw the girl.

Cooper whirled on him. "Meaning what?" His voice was low, ominous.

The little man's teeth flashed briefly. "I was just thinking that perhaps if the father of the young lady should have grave trouble—disgrace, perhaps—because you were rash, my frien'—ah, that would not be so good."

The glances of the two met and locked. They hated each other in that moment, Don Cooper with a swift fury, and Zeron with a grim, long-nourished hatred.

The little man bowed. "I will not intrude further, but it is, my dear Cooper, mos' pleasant in Maine."

He did a military about-face, and was gone. Don Cooper stared after him for a split second. The gauge was down. The threat to Don Cooper's life—if he interfered again with Paul Zeron's schemes—was direct, despite the veiled language. Don Cooper had had threats before, but that thrust at Marion, through her father—that was something else, something more viciously subtle. . . .

He didn't have time to figure it out, for Marion Brill was already crossing the lobby. Marion did not make entrances—she just appeared. She seemed to float down upon him now, a slim vision in a black velvet dress. The skirt was slit audaciously, and a tiny jacket with a prim row of buttons fastened tightly under her chin.

"Don! It's been a long while."

"An age—nine generations. Time enough for you to be reincarnated more beautiful than ever."

"You're still nice, Don. Your work hasn't hardened you."

They moved toward the dining room, and many eyes followed them. Bronzed, and big, and keen-eyed, Don Cooper had an air of sea and sun about him. Marion Brill was the sort of girl that a good magazine cover artist would put in a picture with such a man. She did not look like the kind of a girl who would write airy letters of love and light gossip that veiled diplomatic dynamite in code—but she had.

A three-piece orchestra was playing soft music as the head waiter seated them. The girl opened a black velvet handbag, looked briefly at the mirror that it contained, and laid it down on the table. Before the bag was closed, Don Cooper had a glimpse of a tiny spool wound tightly with black paper, like a film roll for a miniature camera. His eyes gleamed. With his right hand, he spread his napkin flat on the table-top—full open. It was a large napkin.

"I saw a Jap agent do this one at a dinner in Dairen," he said softly. "Attend, *mademoiselle*."

Using only his right hand, he bunched the napkin with seeming carelessness. Then it seemed to flow through his fingers as though it would drop to the tablecloth, but it never quite dropped. Somewhere in the process of leaving his fingers, it vanished.

Don Cooper smiled with a naïve air. "I believe that Jap was a scalawag," he said. "He was probably getting rid of dangerous papers."

The girl's smile matched his own. "Or acquiring some," she said lightly. "You didn't need to go to Manchukuo to learn tricks like that. You could always do them."

"Oh, but I've improved." Don Cooper smiled again. "And you, young lady, have become careless. You watch tricks too carefully."

He turned his hand over, stretched his fingers lazily. A neatly folded napkin dropped from his fingers. He spread the folds with one gesture and, gleaming darkly against the white of the linen was a tiny spool, wound tightly with black paper, like a roll of film.

"Tut, tut," he said. "Didn't I see that a moment ago in your bag?"

Marion Brill laughed. "You win, and you lose," she said. "You did a good job, but suppose you examine your trophy."

Cooper raised his eyebrows. He picked up the black spool. It unreeled easily, and there was white paper beneath the black. Fine script challenged him. It read:

> DON COOPER—
> I'll give you one glimpse of this and bet you more than you'll collect that you have it within five minutes. Or have you slipped, darling?

Don shook his head ruefully. "I've slipped," he said. "I should have let it lie and won the bet. I'm curious about the stakes." He rewound the black paper as he spoke.

His eyes were challenging, but she turned their charge lightly. "If you'd won that bet," she said mockingly, "you would never have known that it had been made."

* * *

The three-piece orchestra in the corner broke softly into the "Blue Danube"—and a mood perished. Hauntingly beautiful the piece might be, but it was more. With the first strains, these two had to remember what they were. The aura of the Danube seemed to flow into the room with the melody—that fateful stream which flowed through the Balkan heart, where war forever had its red beginnings. The girl seemed to feel its spell most.

"That piece—it's like an omen, Don. I wish they hadn't played it now—here. You were talking to Zeron when I came in. He wouldn't beat about the bush. What did he want?"

Don Cooper hesitated a moment. He had a swift impulse to tell her of the hint against her father, then waved it down. He'd look into that first himself.

"He wanted me to go to Maine for my health," he said easily.

The girl nodded. "I thought as much. He's making another play, and he fears you, Don. You don't play according to the rules. He's got a big stake somewhere, Don. I've been sniffing action, big action."

"Babbling Benny's dandruff bomb, maybe?"

The girl's eyes remained grave. "You think that's funny?"

"No, I don't. I've inherited the job, Marion."

The girl pondered that. "I've been expecting it," she said. "You know that Benny Bushman has a suite here in this hotel, I suppose."

"Yes. What else do you know?"

"Zeron has an assistant. Female gender, very deadly." Marion Brill was toying with a fork. Her eyes lifted. "She's supposed to be the niece of Mrs. Barrington-Dorchester."

"And isn't?"

"Decidedly isn't. Zeron has enough on Barrington-Dorchester to make him crawl, I guess. She's a plant, and she's going to be working under 'nice' auspices."

Don Cooper thought that one over. The Barrington-Dorchesters had millions that years of munitions manufacture had given them. They were not aristocrats, even in the American sense of the term, but they had influence in national affairs, and used it ruthlessly. If Zeron, in turn, had the power to use them, he was going to be a hard antagonist to knock over.

The girl seemed to divine Cooper's thoughts. "You have to figure Walter Hirsch and his newspapers, too," she said. "Hirsch will play Zeron's game as long as it suits his purpose; and he'll play rough if it will serve to break up this munitions probe. It hits his own pocketbook, and he doesn't like it."

The play mood was gone. Their eyes met, and they were not man and woman so much, now, as they were fellow agents in the cause of their country. The orchestra was still playing the "Blue Danube."

Suddenly, from some place in the hotel, there came a deep, booming roar. The musicians faltered, and the waiters stiffened in their places. Don Cooper gripped the table edge. Marion's eyes flashed him a message.

"Benny Bushman! The bomb—it might be, must be. Don, it's your job. I'll play my own angles. Get me at home later. I'll wait up."

"Thanks, Marion." Don Cooper rose hurriedly, pressed a bill on the head waiter, and took the lobby in stride.

3

THE HAIRLESS CORPSE

The third floor of the hotel was the scene of wild excitement. The house detective was up there, with several employees of the hotel to assist him in keeping the guests at a safe distance from the door of Benjamin Bushman's suite. The doors of that suite were closed, but an ominous wisp of grayish vapor was curling under one of them. As far down the hall as the elevators, there was a biting odor, like that of ammonia.

The hotel employees, at considerable distance from the doors themselves, were pale and uneasy. They had read the sensational stories in the papers and, although the Carlton management had never suspected that Bushman would keep a deadly bomb in his suite, those stories were vivid to more than one man now.

Watching the vapor curls from under the door and remembering tales of hairless corpses was no nerve tonic. Blocks away, the wail of a fire siren sounded. No one was taking a laugh at newspaper wit and the dandruff bomb now.

Don Cooper met Bill Russell of the Department of Justice in the corridor. The man looked at him sharply. "Howdy, Cooper. Haven't seen you in a while. You on this?"

Cooper nodded. He hadn't seen Russell in three years, but Washington was like that. They hit the corridor together. The house detective turned a worried countenance to them.

"That's gas, probably," he said. "No telling what it will do. We can't crash in. We've got the guests off the floor. They're moving them out upstairs and down. The fire wagon is well on its way.''

Cooper waited for more details.

''There's a woman in the case.'' Russell was chewing licorice, his face expressing no emotion whatever. ''Claims she saw the murder. All hysterical.''

''Murder?''

''Yeah, So she says. Says he was stabbed before the bomb went off. Funny play, that.''

Don Cooper nodded. The woman's story would keep. The firemen of the chemical squad were already in the room—weird figures in masks. The battalion chief came out into the hall.

''You can get a look at him now,'' he said. He was shaking his head. ''For a gas bomb, that one was a queer trick. More smoke than anything else, no thick fumes, and no consistency. Wouldn't last two minutes in the open air. We've got samples of the vapor for a test, but—'' His shrug was eloquent.

Russell and Cooper moved forward. Russell grunted. ''That doesn't prove a thing,'' he said. ''It might be just a sample bomb—a capsule dose of the real thing.''

''For a capsule, it raised a pretty lively fuss.'' Don Cooper commented, frowning.

Lieutenant Dan Kling of the Metropolitan Police joined them before they reached the room; a short, red-faced man, he rolled when he walked. He wasn't talkative, and looked tough. A murder that was already developing a State Department smell was not going to be any rest cure for him, and he knew it.

The room was a wreck. A table in the center had been blown to pieces, and there was a gaping hole in an upholstered divan. All the pictures had been blown from the walls; there was a black hole in the rug, and a door mirror had been cracked twice across. The damage, however, seemed to be confined to one half of the room—to the area between the door and the stiff figure which sagged in an easy chair on the window-side of the room.

Benjamin Bushman hadn't been a very prepossessing human when he was alive, and he wasn't a nice sight dead. He had met the Reaper informally, in his dressing gown and pajamas. Some backdraught of the explosion had torn the dressing gown and whipped it back from his flabby body. The pajama coat hung by one button, but it needed no buttons at all. It was fastened close to the man's body with a skewer—a stiletto buried hilt-deep in his chest. . . .

It was not death, however—nor the manner of it—that stopped the three men as they stepped into the room. Three pairs of eyes focused on the one startling, unbelievable thing about that sagging corpse.

It was bald—not shaven, nor burned, but hairless.

Dan Kling growled deep in his throat and crossed the room. Don Cooper was beside him as he dropped to one knee and loosened the one button on Bushman's pajama coat. His own eyes narrowed thoughtfully.

There was not a bit of hair on Bushman's body. Pictured always with an unruly mop of hair on his head, and a thick mustache, he had been found by death with neither.

"It's no razor trick. You could tell. Looks like it just dropped out or—" Kling broke off, got up, scratching his head. His face showed that he would never laugh again at the so-called dandruff bomb which caused hair to fall out.

Don Cooper was frowning. Without moving the corpse, he made an examination of the man's pajamas, and the chair in which he was seated. There was nothing there which would explain the mystery. He straightened up. Russell was examining a battered piece of metal.

"Piece of the bomb," he said. "light stuff, built like a cheap kettle."

Dan Kling was moving toward the door. "I'm going to get that girl," he said. "I want to hear somebody talk about this."

Don Cooper scarcely heard either of them. He was staring at a find of his own—a crushed bit of cellophane. He picked it up carefully by one edge. It was the odd shape that had intrigued him. Cellophane was common enough, but this piece had been shaped to something round, and not too thick; an oversized fountain pen or . . .

He took a swift look at the corpse, then hurried after Kling. He caught him at the door and held the cellophane in his out-stretched palm. Kling looked at it impatiently.

"So what?"

Cooper shrugged. "I've got an idea that it would fit around the grip of that stiletto if it were smoothed out."

Kling stared. "But why in hell?" His manner was less truculent now.

Don Cooper shook his head. "Think of a good answer to that," he said, "and you've got a clue."

Dan Kling had received a jolt that slowed him down as he came in with his witness. As he entered the Bushman suite with the girl, he was walking wearily, resignedly, like a man playing out a hopeless string. By common consent, the interrogation was to take place in a room of

Bushman's suite adjoining that in which the murder had taken place. Kling waved the girl into the room.

"Miss Gaylord, this is Mr. Russell and Mr. Cooper. If you don't mind, we want a little information." Kling was perspiring, and mopping at his red face.

The girl took her entrance cue and paused with one jeweled hand lightly on the door jamb. Her eyes, warily appraising for the moment, retreated swiftly behind excessively long lashes after one sweeping glance around the room. Definitely, decidedly, she was a woman dramatizing herself in a crisis.

"You are kind," she said.

She was tall and she moved lithely, her figure pencil-slim in gleaming satin, with a long, metallic tunic. There was something serpentine in the long train, and in the way the light was reflected in the gleaming satin. She sank gracefully into an overstuffed chair, and closed her eyes briefly as she posed with one white arm behind her dark hair.

Dan Kling made another pass at his red face with a limp handkerchief. He cleared his throat noisily.

"You say you saw this murder?" he asked hoarsely.

The girl's body moved. It was not so much a shudder as it was a ripple.

"Yes, I did." Her voice was almost a whisper.

Don Cooper took the play from the fumbling police lieutenant. "Suppose you tell us about it," he said. "It's easier than answering questions."

She threw him a perfect screen-test look of gratitude. "You are very kind," she said. She bit her lip lightly; then her lids shielded her eyes again. "I have always been indiscreet,' she said.

She let that highly significant fact hit, and gave it time to stop bouncing before she extended her remarks. "Mr. Bushman was nothing to me," she said slowly. "But he was different. He was embarrassed by all the publicity recently given him. It was unkind. He invited me to dinner with him a week ago, but he asked me tonight if I would mind dining in his room. He was so upset about what people were saying." She sighed. "I am very indiscreet. I accepted his invitation."

The story threatened to end there, to fall of its own weight.

Bill Russell grunted. "You were in the room when he was attacked, then?" he asked gruffly.

The girl put one hand to her throat. Her eyes got very big. "But no. I was merely coming in. I heard noises inside, and I knocked at the door." She paused dramatically.

Bill Russell grunted. "You heard a struggle and you knocked. OK. Then what?"

"I opened the door. Mr. Bushman was fighting with another man. The other man had a long knife in his hand, or a dagger—I couldn't quite tell. Mr. Bushman was in a big chair, and he had something in his hand that looked like a Thermos bottle."

"Then what?"

The slim body undulated again, and the girl moved her hands helplessly. "Then Mr. Bushman called out to me. 'Run!' he warned me. 'This is a deadly bomb.' Then the other man looked around—and I saw him bring that dagger down at Mr. Bushman. I ran and—" She was panting as though she were still running. Then she spread her hands wide, sat back limply. "That's all," she murmured.

Dan Kling's face was seven shades redder than usual. He dabbed furiously at his forehead with the handkerchief and struggled to keep the angry roar out of his voice.

"When the bomb went off," he said, "where were you? What happened to the man?"

The girl looked blankly at him. "You confuse me," she said. "Where was I? Oh, yes—I ran. Then the bomb went off, and the man ran out of the room and slammed the door."

"You saw him?"

"Only vaguely—I was so frightened."

Kling swallowed hard. "He ran out of the room *after* the bomb went off?"

The girl seemed startled. "Perhaps it was before it went off."

"And you saw him—yet you had run away from the room? Where were you when he went out?"

"I was running."

Kling mopped harder with the handkerchief. "Still running. Where did he go?"

The girl spread her hands again. "I don't know. I fainted."

Russell came to the rescue of the man from H.Q. "When did you faint?"

Her eyes turned tragically to him. "Why, I told you—when the bomb went off."

Kling made a gurgling sound in his throat. "In view of your value as a witness, Miss Gaylord—" he was gagging a little on that— "we'll have to ask you to view the body, to identify the man who was murdered."

"Must I do that?" She paled genuinely. Her hands gripped the arms of the chair.

Kling nodded grimly. "I'm afraid so."

"Very well." She rose, drew herself to regal height.

Kling opened the connecting door to the other room, and Russell stepped close enough to take the girl's elbow. Don Cooper brought up the rear of the procession. He was smoking a cigarette, and he was very thoughtful. Irene Gaylord interested him. She was at once stupid and clever.

In the other room, the routine workers were at their jobs. The medical examiner had come and gone, and the body was booked for an autopsy. A plainclothes man was carefully making measurements of the room. Another was taking fingerprints. Outside, in the hall, there sounded the hungry growls of the press. The corpse alone was unmoved. It sat still in the big chair.

Kling stepped across the room and removed the sheet which had been thrown over the body. Irene Gaylord screamed from the back of her throat. The scream trailed off into a choked cry.

''Oh, how horrible,'' she moaned. ''I've seen enough. It is he. It is Mr. Bushman.''

''You're sure?'' Kling's eyes narrowed.

The girl covered her eyes. ''I'm sure—certain. I don't want to see any more.'' She turned abruptly, and all but fought her way past Russell into the other room. The D. J. man started after her.

Don Cooper looked at Kling, then at the corpse. ''Do we have to let her get away with that story?'' he asked.

Kling laughed harshly. ''I do. She's the niece of Mrs. Waldo Barrington-Dorchester.'' He laughed again, bitterly. ''Hell, Cooper, it's always like that in this town. Everybody is always the niece or the nephew or the maiden aunt of somebody important.''

He stamped toward the other room. Cooper followed a little more slowly, thinking of Irene Gaylord. So this was the new Zeron operative! There was food for thought in that. He didn't believe in coincidences. This woman did not just happen to be here—any more than had Zeron.

In the other room, Irene Gaylord seemed to have recovered her composure. Kling rocked on his heels in the middle of the room.

''Miss Gaylord,'' he said huskily, ''you saw the man who was in the room where the murder was committed. Did you recognize him?''

Don Cooper stopped in the connecting doorway. He watched the girl roll her eyes slowly toward the police lieutenant.

''Oh, I was afraid you'd ask that. I don't know. I'm not sure, that is. I'd have to talk to somebody.''

''Who did you want to talk to?'' Kling was still keeping his voice down, squeezing the boom out of it.

"I'll have to have time to think. It's all so sudden."

"But this is murder," Kling exploded. "You saw a man. What did he look like?"

"I can't tell you. My head aches. You are really cruel." The eyes were on full again, the hands pathetically moving.

Just then, a hard-eyed man in a gray suit came in without knocking, interrupting the scene.

"Lieutenant," he said, "we've got a man downstairs. He was sitting on the curb and is woozy as hell. He doesn't even know his own name." The man paused and moved his shoulders slightly. "He looks pushed around a bit—and he's bald as an egg."

Kling stopped rocking and almost lost his balance. "Bald? No hair?"

"No more than a baby."

Kling wheeled. "Wait for me, please, Miss Gaylord. Russell, Cooper." He was rolling for the door in the wake of the gray-suited man. Russell started after him, but Don Cooper dropped back.

"I'll see Miss Gaylord across the hall to more pleasant quarters," he said, "and join you downstairs."

The girl's face showed awakening interest. "You are very kind," she murmured.

4

THE TRAP IS BAITED

A babble of voices came through the door which Russell had closed when he and Kling rushed out. Don Cooper smiled grimly. That, of course, would be the press. He crossed the room and made sure that the door was locked. From the corner of his eye he could see Irene Gaylord as he did so. She looked interested. As he turned, her eyes dropped.

She seemed to be no longer overacting, now that she had only one man to play to—and because of that her acting was better. Don Cooper sat down where he could face her and offered her a cigarette. She took it and waited for him to light it.

Cooper squinted through the smoke. "Before I take you across the hall, Miss Gaylord," he said. "I want to warn you that the newspapermen will probably make every attempt to get a statement from you."

"Ah," she sighed. "The same newspapers who were so cruel to Mr. Bushman."

Don Cooper nodded. "Yes," he said gravely, "exactly the same newspapers."

She pondered that. Cooper inhaled slowly. "You, of course, will not tell them anything until Lieutenant Kling tells you that you may," he said quietly.

"Why?" Her eyes were wide.

"Because your story might be misunderstood, garbled." He reflected inwardly that it couldn't help being garbled, her story being what it was. "That," he said, "might work injustices on people and make this case very hard to solve."

Her eyes went so wide that the lashes seemed to touch her thin eyebrows. "But," she said, "if I tell them my story just as it happened, they will be kind to me."

Don Cooper knew when he was licked, and he didn't go in for waste notions. "Miss Gaylord," he said, "I've given you an opinion, and I've got nothing else to give you except one more opinion. I do not think that the newspapers will be kind to you if you talk before the police department authorizes it."

The girl scarcely moved, but she shed one personality and coiled into another before he was finished with his little speech. He had anticipated that, and he had a stall ready. His body suddenly stiffened, and he looked past her toward the door of the murder room. That stopped her. On the point of lashing out, she drew back, her eyes following his.

Don Cooper was already out of his chair. His body blocked her line of vision for a moment, then bent at the waist. His right hand, all too apparently empty, groped along the floor close to the wall on one side of the door. His fingers seemed to close upon something there. When he straightened up, a tiny spool wound with black paper lay in his hand.

The woman came out of her chair as though propelled by springs. "That is mine," she said.

Don Cooper's hand closed over the spool. "What is?" he asked blandly.

The girl faced him. "That roll of films. I lost it. It is mine."

He shook his head slowly. "When could you have lost it? You weren't in here until we all came in. You didn't have it with you then, did you?"

She made a fluttering motion with one hand, and the other gripped his arm as though she needed that arm for support.

"I told you that I am very indiscreet," she said. "That roll of films is—well, not pretty." Her eyes dropped. "It would compromise me terribly."

Don Cooper shook his head, removed her hand gently from his arm.

"I promise you," he said, "that if this is a roll of personal film, it will never compromise or embarrass you. I will take care of it myself.

"And now, shall we go across the hall?"

Irene Gaylord knew a stone wall, too, when she met one. She flung away from him like a tigress, her lithe body crouched. "You give me that film," she said. "You locked the door and kept me in here. I'll scream and keep screaming. . . ."

Her fingers locked into the metallic tunic in a significant gesture, and there was strength enough in those fingers to demolish it in one tug. Don Cooper knew that with a hall full of newspapermen outside, she could count on one hundred percent results from the trick. And her eyes left no doubt of her determination, and she was between him and the door. The act would start before he could reach it.

He smiled grimly. "You scream," he said, "and I'll tell them who threw that bomb in Benny Bushman's apartment."

The threat straightened her like a punch. Her hand rose involuntarily, the back of it to her lips. Her cigarette dropped to the floor, and Don Cooper stepped on it deliberately. He was calm again, confident, after a windy moment. It was only a great actress, he reflected, who could rise above any tampering with the script. This woman would never be a great actress. She wrenched her hand away from her mouth violently.

"You—you're accusing me of—" She broke off with a gasp. She had overstepped his inference, and the slip made Cooper grin a little. It was his point.

"I didn't accuse you of anything," he reminded her. "I said merely that I'd tell them who threw the bomb."

She swayed a little, and then fury blazed in her eyes. He could literally see her remembering that she was still a woman and that she was still locked in with him and that the press awaited.

"Don't do it!" His voice snapped like a whip. "I'm going to walk out of here now, and I'm not giving you the film."

"You're not!" She threw herself before him fiercely. Her eyes were still blazing, but there was a little wariness behind them. She wasn't ready to scream yet. She was keeping that card to play, but she waited for him to call the trump. He called it.

"Where is the bag that you carried tonight?" he challenged.

"I didn't—" She let the denial trail off. She was remembering that her bag was across the hall where she couldn't check up on it immediately. His look reminded her of that, and for a moment there was panic in her eyes. Then it snuffed out. She was remembering that evening bags are very small, and that this man was talking about bombs. She hoped that he was walking into something, and the hope showed in her face. Her dark eyes gleamed.

Don Cooper caught her triumphant expression in time. He had nearly walked into something. He'd been guessing desperately, of course. He, too, was remembering now that the bomb had been tea-kettle size. He pulled another idea out of the air, and spoke with a cold, confident smile.

"There was a thin layer of very fine grease," he said, "on the bomb fragments. You clutched your bag very tightly, and the grease from the bomb—" His voice trailed off.

He shrugged the implication. Fear leaped into her eyes. Don Cooper's lips tightened. He'd had nothing to go on, of course, except the hunch of an observant and intelligent man. Benny Bushman had been stabbed, and the girl's story of the stabbing did not hang together. Therefore the man had probably been stabbed before the bomb went off, unless a time device was used—and that was doubtful. Somebody had taken over the job of tossing the bomb in the room while the murderer went elsewhere to establish an alibi. Where could a more suitable bomb-thrower be found than a girl like this, who could avoid grilling?

And this girl had been too quick to recognize in a hairless corpse the Benny Bushman who had affected a bushy mane and flowing mustache in life.

She seemed suddenly to realize that she had made a mistake, and that he had been bluffing. She stiffened, and her hand came up fast. She slapped his face and her whole body vibrated with fury.

"Go!" she screamed. "You're a brute to torture me so, after all I've been through tonight—"

"To say nothing of all you're going to go through."

Don Cooper smiled again, stepped out into the corridor, and closed the door behind him.

The combined efforts of the police and the hotel officials had not sufficed to lift the corridor-siege of the press. He waved the eager interrogators aside.

"No soap," he said. "Later. Miss Gaylord is upset."

He grinned at the understatement as he made his escape. The grin faded as he ran down the stairs. He had taken more time than he intended, and he had an unholy curiosity about the man who had been found on the curb in a dazed condition, and without hair. The logical supposition would be that a man in such a condition had been in the room when the bomb went off, or was just leaving it. Still, logical explanations did not always suffice when there was an international flavor to a situation.

There was a tall, rather good-looking man turning away from the house phones as Cooper came down the stairs. He looked up, and with tight lips, and eyes steeled to a grim resolve, crossed to Cooper's side. There was an extraordinary number of people in the lobby, and since the young man and Don Cooper both wore conventional dinner jackets, they were not conspicuous. Cooper found himself crowded.

''Walk out of the hotel with me quietly or I'll shoot.'' The young man's lips scarcely parted as he spoke. Don Cooper looked at him, shrugged, and started for the door. The other pressed him closely.

Paul Zeron was seated near the main entrance. He was engaged in conversation with a heavy-set man, and he did not look up. Don Cooper found that rather strange, and amusing.

''All right. I'm out of the hotel,'' he said. They were under the marquee in front.

The young man pushed him a little. ''Not here. Walk down the block,'' he said.

They walked. Sixteenth Street was darker down near the Eye Street corner.

''All right. I'll take Miss Gaylord's films,'' the young man said briefly.

That was it, of course. There would be some lad like this planted at the house phone to take care of any little chores that the lovely Miss Gaylord might have to be done. Don Cooper looked at him with interest. The chap was built like a halfback.

''And suppose, my friend, that you don't get those films—if any?''

''Then I'll have to take them.''

The young fellow had a grim air of determination about him that was very young. Don Cooper sighed. He dropped his hand toward his trousers pocket, and it came up a fist—a fist that carried the weight of his body behind it.

The halfback never had a chance. He was wide open, and the right hand took him squarely on the button before he could pull in his head. Don Cooper stepped in behind the punch and caught his man as he fell.

''Too bad, kid,' he said, ''but if you'd really had a gun, it would have been in a shoulder holster. Dinner jacket pockets aren't built for them.''

There was a man running across the street toward what he fondly hoped was a fight—and the driver of a Ford parked at the curb was swinging down to investigate the little street scene. Don Cooper turned to the man from the Ford.

"Here!" he said. The man quickened his stride, his eyes inquisitive. Cooper shoved the sagging halfback at him. "Fine," he said. "You're just in time. You take him."

As the astonished Ford owner made a grab at the knockout victim, he wheeled and dashed toward the Carlton. He didn't look back. It would take Mr. Buttinsky a few seconds to get over being startled, and the youngster could make any explanation he wanted to.

Paul Zeron was still talking when Don Cooper reentered the hotel. This time he looked up sharply when Don passed him, but Don let him look. He was betting that Zeron was doing more serious thinking than he'd been doing when Cooper was headed the other way.

The supposed roll of films was working like a charm. It was making the enemy take the aggressive, and aggressors are prone to make mistakes. He fondled the spool in his pocket and thanked the fates that his hands were still quicker than most eyes. Marion Brill's little joke was paying dividends.

"At that," he said softly, "I wish it were a real roll of films, and that I had found it in Benny's apartment. It would be darned interesting."

Real or not, the bait had drawn the wolf pack—and they would stop at nothing to get it, and its owner. . . .

5

THE RUMBLE OF WAR

Kling and Russell were in the manager's office. So were the house physician and a reporter from the *Herald*. They were all studying a short, compact man lying on the couch. The *Herald* reporter was jubilant. He'd got in by right of conquest. He was the one who had found the hairless man sitting on the curb. The doctor was shaking his head.

"We'll have to get him to a hospital for a more thorough examination. He seems to be suffering the natural reaction to a violent blow in the head."

Don Cooper wasn't paying much attention. He had a full look at the face of the man on the couch, and recognition came to him with a chilling sense of shock. Rockwell had said that Italy was the soft spot in the European muddle at which the war makers were hammering. Italy was supposed to be the nation that Bushman would name in his South

American *exposé*—and the hairless man who had been sitting dazedly on the curb was Paolo Luca, of the Italian Embassy.

Cooper could almost hear bugles calling in the room. . . .

Bill Russell caught his eye, and the expression on the D. J. man's face told Cooper that he, too, was hearing the bugles. Russell nodded toward the phone.

"I've been talking to people," he said. "Italian Embassy and others."

He broke off. There was a soft knock at the door. The man who entered did not need to introduce himself. He was Count Adolfo di Carlo, of the Italian Embassy. Tall, grave, broad-shouldered, he wore evening clothes as though they were a uniform. His white Vandyke was trimmed to a precise peak, and his scalp gleamed pinkly through his sparse white hair. Contrary to the popular conception of his race, he was neither excited nor excitable. For several seconds he looked at the still figure on the cot.

"I wish to hear about it," he said simply.

By common consent, the others turned to Bill Russell. He was the nearest thing to a government representative present. Before starting his story, he looked at the reporter from the *Herald*.

"Son," he said, "you won't hear anything that you'll dare print, and you're going to be in a tough spot if you stay. How about it?"

The reporter hesitated, then gave in. "OK," he said, reluctantly turning to leave.

Don Cooper stepped out of the door after him. "Just a minute," he said. "I want to ask one question."

The reporter's eyes narrowed. "Shoot."

"Did you just stumble on that man, or were you tipped off that you'd find him?"

"I'm not supposed to tell—" The reporter was watching Cooper closely, appraising him. "We got a tip," he said finally. "Somebody phoned in."

"Thanks." Don Cooper turned back to the room, a look of grim satisfaction on his face. Somebody had phoned the paper, and that meant careful prearrangement. The Italian had not just happened to be outside the Carlton at a time when his hairless condition would bring suspicion on him. He'd been brought from somewhere and put there for a newspaper reporter to find. That was an angle to think about.

Back in the room, Bill Russell had just finished the story of events. The count stroked his beard, gestured toward the cot.

"He has been missing from the Embassy for three days," he said.

Kling stiffened. "The police of the District had no record of that, sir. If we had known—"

The count bowed. "I am sorry." He said it courteously, but it was just another way of saying that diplomats bury their own dead. Kling reddened slightly.

There was another knock, and this time it was the ambulance that the doctor had ordered. The doctor went out with his patient, and with a transparent apology, the manager withdrew. The count was alone with people to whom he could speak without embarrassment. He looked at them thoughtfully, and there were deep shadows in his eyes.

"Gentlemen," he said gravely, "I will speak with bluntness. This situation is most serious. A sensational story has been manufactured—built up—for your press. There is an evil background for the most unfortunate happenings of tonight, a background which your papers will not ignore."

He paced a little, with his hands behind his back, like a man thinking aloud, rather than a man making a speech. "There have been grave insinuations made against Italy without a shred of proof—absurd things. Italy has played no secret hand in South American affairs. That is fantastic. Yet people have been led to believe that Italy does play such a hand. This alleged bomb is one more trick. Italy has never had such a bomb. If Mr. Bushman had such an invention, he was most welcome to it. Italy had no interest in it."

He paused for breath, his thin hands opening and closing nervously. "Tonight a man dies who has insinuated that he holds secrets detrimental to my country, secrets that will cause a breach between your country and mine. He is murdered. Paolo Luca of the Italian Embassy is suspect in this murder, struck down, and unable to defend himself from the charge. Meanwhile, your great newspapers are publishing a story which has in it the inflammatory sparks of war."

"You believe then, *signor*, that some other agency has planned this with the intention of throwing the blame upon Italy? To what purpose, *signor?*" Russell was doing the questioning. Don Cooper was content to sit back with his arms folded. He was very thoughtful.

The Italian clenched one hand. "The purpose? To give courage to Italy's enemies. These happenings fit in a chain. Secretary Dolfuss is assassinated in Vienna and Italy loses her most powerful friend, Austria. His Majesty, King Alexander, is assassinated in Marseilles, and Italy is cursed in Yugoslavia. Today—next week—something happens in

America. The friends of Italy draw away—for who wishes the friendship of one with powerful enemies?'' His clenched fist opened into spread fingers that had a strange eloquence. ''Thus, my friends, does war come to the world.''

''You have some suggestion to make to us?'' Russell's voice was quiet, but there was a hardness to his jaw that betokened his understanding of the gigantic nature of the thing that was confronting that little group in the room.

Count di Carlo's lips tightened. ''Only this,'' he said. ''Your great people will learn from their papers tomorrow a tale that would be laughable in any group of informed officials. Your people will not laugh; on the contrary, they will read more than is printed.'' He leaned forward, a terrible, awe-inspiring sadness in his face.

''Gentlemen,'' he said, ''you must race with those monstrous machines that make war torches out of paper. Somewhere there is truth, and only one truth, about this murder—about this bomb. In the name of God, find that truth before base rumor fans a flame of hatred that not even truth will extinguish. Find the murderer tonight! I do not speak for Italy alone—but for all who want peace.''

When he finished, Kling sat very still and Russell was hunched forward in his chair. Don Cooper met the earnest eyes of the count.

''*Signor*,'' he said, ''I have one path of my own that I'd like to follow. Can you get me a list of the persons on whom your *attaché* might have called on the night that he disappeared?''

Count di Carlo nodded. ''It was a long list,'' he said, ''but we were careful. All denied seeing him. We proved conclusively that only three out of the—let us say—suspects could possibly be lying.''

He bent over the manager's desk to write the three names. There was a tap on the door, and the man in the gray suit beckoned to Kling. Kling mopped his forehead and rolled over to the door. He took the paper, and the gray-suited man withdrew. As he read, a change came over Kling. His jaw squared.

''*Signor*,'' he said, ''suppose Bushman did have a bomb that was a secret, and suppose it were proved that your man was killed in a fight over that bomb. What then?''

Count di Carlo finished writing, passed the slip of paper to Cooper, and straightened, ''Impossible,'' he said. ''His duties were nonmilitary. He had no interest in bombs.''

Kling's lips tightened. ''His fingerprints were on the hilt of that stiletto,'' he said brusquely.

As Don Cooper heard that grim, portentous statement, he was staring at the paper in his hand, and his eyes narrowed. The third name on the list was that of Irene Gaylord!

There was no formal leave-taking on the part of the three men as they left the manager's office at the Carlton. Each had his own lines to follow, and each worked best alone. When the time came for a pooling of forces, they knew how to cooperate. The Department of Justice and the Metropolitan Police were already active. Operators had been swarming over myriad trails ever since the smoke in the room cleared. Don Cooper had no department in back of him; he worked alone, with no allies save one. He wanted no allies—save that one, who was Marion Brill.

His lips were tightly pressed as he made a quick inventory of the lobby before crossing to the phone booths. He was in no mood to be tolerant with any halfbacks who got in his way now. The stakes loomed too large. Count di Carlo was no alarmist, and the grim picture that he had painted was all too real. This was one case that would have to be cracked quickly.

In his hand, Cooper crushed the paper that the count had given him. Two of those names might bear a little investigating, but there was no doubt at all about the third. The mere fact that the unfortunate Paolo Luca might have been in the company of Irene Gaylord on the night that he disappeared made it a good bet for Don Cooper. He had already accepted the hypothesis that the hairless man on the curb was as much a victim as was the hairless corpse in the Bushman suite. The police could run their fingerprint clue to whatever end it brought them.

If anyone in the lobby was interested in his movements, the fact was not apparent. Don Cooper slipped into a booth, called the number of the *Washington Post*, snapped a name at the languid voice that answered, and waited. When he heard a high-pitched squeak at the other end of the line, he relaxed. The years could not change that voice, any more than they could change the encyclopedic mind behind it.

''Jones?'' he said. ''This is Don Cooper. I need your help. Think fast, hard, and accurate as hell. What white elephants do the Barrington-Dorchesters own around here?''

''White elephants?'' snapped the squeaky voice. ''Everybody with money's got 'em. Guess you mean real estate. Old Ralph B-D's worst dull-care is the fortress out on the hill, the one they called International House. He'll always have it. Can't sell such a—''

''Swell. Never mind his other worries. I should have thought of that myself. Thanks, Jones, and keep this quiet, will you?''

He hung up, his eyes gleaming. He'd forgotten the fortress, hadn't linked it with the Barrington-Dorchesters, in fact. But now—well, Irene Gaylord was posing as the niece of the Dorchesters. She had, perhaps, been out with Paolo Luca on the night that he disappeared, and he'd been somewhere for three days. A picture of the gloomy old medieval-looking place on the hill came before Don Cooper's eyes. He nodded his head and turned again to the phone.

The connection was made. There was a sleep-laden voice on the other end—Doctor Hugh Martingale. Cooper snapped his words through.

"Doc? Don Cooper. Wake up, and put the lateness of the hour on the bill. I'm going to describe a corpse to you, and you tell me what made him like that . . . I've got a hunch. Listen, this corpse was hairless. Yep, bald all over. . . . He had a blue line along his gums, and he was a little too stiff for a new corpse. . . . No! I'm not asking you what he died of. I know. He was stabbed in the heart. But what was wrong before that?"

He held the earpiece away from his ear patiently for a few moments while Doctor Martingale unburdened himself of a few explosive comments. Then Cooper took over the conversation once more.

"The point is that the stiletto only punctured his heart. It didn't shave him and give him a haircut. It didn't blue his gums, either. Now . . ."

This time he listened intently, and this time the doctor was not explosive. He was fully awake and interested. Don Cooper heard him through ahd shook his head, lips tight.

"Four months? No good, Doc . . . Could it have taken place in three weeks?" He did a bit of calculating. "No, Doc. Come again." The doctor was explaining, a little more slowly now, a little more doubtfully. Don Cooper's face lighted up. "That's it, Doc. I'll thank you personally some day."

He swung away from the phone, with the bugles sounding in his blood. The only flaw in the case now was the fact that it didn't have a flaw. The men who had planned it were clever, careful, and unscrupulous, and they were playing for high stakes, yet their plot had a hole in it that a man could drive a truck through—a hole they had left open on purpose. They couldn't even stall past the autopsy on the case as it stood. There had to be another play. . . .

He couldn't anticipate that, and it worried him, even in the flush of triumph in having followed his slim clues as far as he had. He turned to cut across the lobby, stopped short, and went toward the desk. He knew the clerk slightly.

"Was Mr. Bushman in the habit of dining here, or did he usually go out?" he asked.

The clerk looked interested. "He had dined in the dining room every evening until the last four or five days,'' he said. ''He'd been ill since Friday, and he was taking his meals in his room.''

''Did the house physician attend him?'' Cooper asked.

''No, sir. He had his own physician. I might be able to find the doctor's name for you.''

''Never mind.'' Don Cooper would have bet him—and laid heavy odds—that he wouldn't be able to find out, but it didn't matter. He was turning away when the manager came hurriedly from his office.

''Ah, Mr. Cooper. Senator Brill is on the wire. He has been trying to locate you. He says that the matter is urgent.''

Cooper felt a thrill of alarm. He remembered suddenly that Zeron had known, in some manner, of his dinner engagement with Marion Brill. Suppose he and his ring knew, too, that Marion worked with him on counter-espionage. Suppose they made some move to eliminate him through her.

Cooper lost no time in getting to the phone. Senator Brill's voice boomed in his ear.

''Cooper? I've got to see you right away, as fast as you can get out here.''

Don Cooper took a deep breath. ''Marion—is she there?''

''Marion? No. . . . How do I know where Marion is? Probably at some silly social *soirée*. But this is no time for family salutations, man. A matter of the gravest import . . .'' The voice boomed on.

''All right. I'll be right out.''

Don Cooper hung up wearily. The senator was a pretty fair human, but he did tire a man. He could talk two hours in the Senate on foreign affairs, and his own daughter knew more about them in two minutes than he'd ever know. For all of which, he had his points.

6

THE MAN OF MANY FLAGS

Don Cooper's car was parked between Eye and K on Seventeenth Street. He'd left it while he was in Asia, and charged Marion with seeing that it got no dry rot or hoof and mouth disease. Despite the fact that she had a car of her own, she'd put five thousand miles on it.

It was a short walk over, and his footsteps echoed hollowly. The half-hour before midnight is quiet outdoors in Washington. No one was trailing him, and he was a little surprised at that. It would be more in character if Zeron had kept tabs on him.

There was little traffic on Seventeenth Street, and he was the sole pedestrian. He eyed the bushes close to the walk with interest, but they were a thin screen, and no on was lurking there. That had been a chance. Anyone who could know that he was having dinner at the Carlton with Marion Brill would also know his car and where he left it.

The keys jingled in his hand, and he unlocked the door. The car was a four-passenger Buick coupé and it was old enought not to be conspicuous. He rolled down the widow on the driver's side while his foot pressed the starter.

As the engine caught, a man loomed up from the ground, on the left-hand side of the car. A blue-barreled automatic came unpleasantly close to Don Cooper's eyes. The man who held it was masked, but he still wore evening clothes, and he was built like a halfback.

"I want that roll of film," he said, "and I don't want any argument."

Don Cooper cursed softly. He'd looked everywhere for lurkers except under his own car.

"You shoot and I'll shoot!" came another voice.

The challenge sounded clear, cool, and confident from immediately behind Don Cooper. His eyes snapped to the rear-vision mirror. He'd known the voice, of course, but it was still a miracle when he saw her.

Marion Brill was in the back of the car, with a wicked little Colt in her right hand—and the Colt was pointed unswervingly at the man on the running board.

The halfback did several things at once, and all of them wrong. He looked hard to make sure that it was really a woman who had challenged him; he was surprised about it, and he went through a mad mental debate as to whether it was ethical for him to do anything about a pretty woman with a gun. Don Cooper relieved him of the necessity for decision.

With one quick, sure movement, he reached out and took the gun from the man's hand. When he removed it, he did so with a twist—and he pushed. The Buick was already in gear, and he had nothing more to do than step on the gas. For a wild moment, the halfback fought hard for balance; then he went off the running board in reverse and sat down on Seventeenth Street. Don Cooper whipped the car around the Eye Street corner toward Connecticut Avenue.

"Young lady," he said, "you shouldn't go around pointing guns at people—but thanks."

Marion laughed softly and came over the back of the seat in a tantalizing whirl of soft colors that straightened themselves out magically as she slid down into her place beside the driver. She was slipping the gun back into her bag—a wicked little short-barreled .38. There was a mate to that gun under Cooper's left armpit. As the Buick hummed out Connecticut, Don watched the long avenue.

"All right," he said. "You done noble, child. Explain it to me in words of one syllable."

The girl settled herself. "Nothing much," she drawled. "I saw Apollo come back to the hotel after you'd spilled him around, and I was sorry that I missed it. I was just coming back again after being home—briefly." Her lips came together hard, and she seemed far away for a moment.

"Apollo had just gone into the hotel, and there was a long, lean old duffer with a Ford who was explaining how one man knocked his handsome youth around and then passed him over as if he were a gift. He described you quite well, by the way. But of course, I knew who did things like that, anyway, and I watched Apollo."

"So what?"

"So after a while he went out and I went out, and he walked over to where your car was parked. Then he went down half a block to the Claridge Hotel, and I figured that he'd wait for you, but he had to phone his headquarters first. I laid my own bet that you'd use the car, and I didn't need to make any phone calls. I crawled in, and just a little while before you came, the lad crawled under." She spread her hands. "That's all."

"Practically all." Don Cooper nodded soberly. "That's not explaining how you walked into a locked car."

Her smile was triumphant. "What kind of agent would I be if I had your car for a year and didn't make a set of keys for myself?"

Don Cooper let her have her minute. She'd earned it. There was a fairly stiff line of traffic rolling out Connecticut Avenue, and he had to play the wheel with precision, and do a choice bit of weaving to make any time at all. The girl lighted a cigarette from the lighter on his dash.

"Don," she said after a time, "You haven't told me a thing about tonight. And where are we going?"

"Your place. Your father called me and practically commanded it."

"We're not. Pull in to the curb, Don."

There was urgency in her tone, and Don Cooper knew her too well to ignore that tone. He pulled to the curb. Marion puffed hard on her cigarette.

"I—I—" She broke off with a shrug. "Tell me your version of the business, Don. I'll talk later."

He looked at her thoughtfully. Some new factor had moved into the piece. "All right," he said softly.

He was no orator, as Count Di Carlo was, and he had never had to tell stories that way. The narrative took him a minimum of time in the telling. Marion lighted another cigarette.

"I should have gone with you," she said. "You wouldn't have had to run away from Gaylord, and leave her with a nice little telephone to play with."

Don Cooper let that lie discreetly where it fell.

"Anyway, I'm glad I know about the little bedroom scene," the girl added. "It explains Apollo."

Don Cooper grinned. "I'm away ahead of you. He was too clumsy to belong to Zeron. His role was that of a noble youth who was glad to be a lady's trained seal."

"You reason well on some angles."

Don Cooper's eyes narrowed; then he grinned. "Let it go. We've got work to do, youngster—lots of it." His grin faded. "You're in trouble. Tell me."

"No, Don. I've got to think it over. I don't get it myself, yet. Run along to the house, and flag a cab for me. I'll wait for you at the Carlton."

Something in her face stopped Don Cooper's protest. She wasn't herself. Something had hit her hard, and it worried him.

"On one condition, Marion," he said. "Your word that you'll wait there for me."

"I'll try." She evaded the promise deftly.

Don Cooper hesitated, then he stepped out and flagged a passing Diamond. As the taxi's brakes squealed, the girl slid out almost into his arms. For a few seconds she was very close to him.

"Don," she said, "they're mixing Dad up in this some way. He's full up on this 'preparedness is patriotism' hooey and—Don, I'm afraid. He'd be a baby in the hands of—Zeron."

His brows drew down at that. He patted her shoulder. "I'll look around," he said. "Just park at the Carlton—right out in the middle of the lobby."

Lines deepened in his face as he slid under the wheel of the Buick. Zeron, then, had not been bluffing. He had a hold over Marion's father. Stephen Brill had slipped somewhere—and Zeron had an ace in the hole.

* * *

The Honorable Stephen Brill was mad. He was pacing the floor of his study when Don Cooper was ushered in, and he had a calm, patient audience of one—*Monsieur* Paul Zeron.

Don Cooper registered that picture, digested it, and laid it away behind a poker mask. The senator was drawn to his full height, a watch in his hand.

''You are inexcusably late,'' he said. ''You have wasted the time of *Monsieur* Zeron and myself at a time when moments were never so precious. You—''

''Unfortunately, I had a serious matter on my hands, too. I'm sorry.'' Don Cooper hadn't the time to be tactful, and he had no time to listen to a senator being a statesman.

Stephen Brill froze into an attitude, his face a stern mask. ''I'll overlook that,'' he said. ''I've just learned of the work that you've been doing—and you're too young for it. With the cocksureness of youth, you plunge into matters beyond the comprehension of one of your years. You . . .''

There was more of it, and this was from a man who ran errands for munitions manufacturers in the belief that he was doing his sacred duty to his country; a man who did not even know that his own daughter was an agent of counter-espionage. Don Cooper sighed wearily.

''Your time is valuable, senator. So is mine. Let's be specific. What does Zeron want that I have—or is he merely interested in shipping me to Maine?'' The question rang out like a shot.

He looked at the man of many flags. Paul Zeron was relaxed in a big chair. His expression did not change, nor did his eyes move. At the moment they were like the eyes of a very ancient and slightly torpid snake. Only Don Cooper knew that there was nothing torpid about the reactions of the man behind those eyes.

Stephen Brill hit the desk with his fist. ''Your imprudence, sir, does not help your cause. You have in your possession a roll of camera film, which, I am told, is a source of potential disaster to a vital program of the United States. Mr. Zeron—''

''Mr. Zeron claims this film?'' Don Cooper broke in.

''I do.'' There was no affability to Zeron now as he came into the argument.

Don Cooper raised his eyebrows. ''It is yours?''

Zeron met his eyes. ''By power of agent, yes.''

''Well, you can't have it.''

That was a bombshell. Zeron sat up straight. Stephen Brill looked incredulous. Cooper beat him to the punch. "Senator," he said, "if you found something, you'd make any claimant describe the object and give some reasonable proof of ownership."

He paused, leaned forward, his elbows resting on his knees. This was a laugh. The false bait was still working. Cooper's inward enjoyment did not show in his face. "There is only one way of describing film," he said. "If it is exposed, the claimant can prove his claim by describing the pictures taken." He looked significantly to Zeron, his face a mask of gravity.

Zeron rose. "That is impossible," he said. "Those pictures cover a confidential matter that may not be discussed with you." He was getting in deep over the pictures he imagined Bushman had taken. "The senator, in his official capacity, knows well what that matter is. His word should carry weight. Against his word, you have only your own stubbornness."

"Plus some slight acquaintance with the claimant, my dear Zeron."

Obviously, Don realized, he had told Brill they contained munitions secrets. The eyes of the two men locked. The exchange had taken place a little too swiftly for the senator. Now he unlimbered.

"Cooper," he said, "this is outrageous. I insist—"

"You have no authority to insist." Cooper was still looking at Zeron. The little man drew himself up stiffly.

"Senator," he said, "this man will interpret what I say now as a threat from myself. You know that I speak out of experience and knowledge. If he walks out of here with that little roll, he will not live an hour."

The senator was uncomfortable. He had found unexpected strength in Don Cooper, and his political training had taught him to walk wide of men with strong hands to play. Besides, he was in the middle, and he knew that, too. No good politician stays in the middle when two strong forces tangle—on the fence, perhaps, but never in the whipsaw area. Don Cooper saved him further embarrassment.

"Senator," he offered, "I'll compromise on this. I will permit you to keep the disputed object in your safe with the understanding that it is to be surrendered to no one until we have another meeting to discuss it."

The senator looked his relief. Paul Zeron studied Cooper curiously, then nodded his head. "I am satisfied with that arrangement," he said.

Don Cooper removed from his pocket a small spool that was wound in black. He could have that safe watched, if necessary. It might be interesting to see who would try to crack it. He smiled inwardly. It was not the first time that he had used bait, but he had seldom used such slight bait more effectively. He'd stirred the opposition up to a frenzy of anxiety about the supposed films. The man who is carrying the fight is always a mark for a punch, and that little roll on the table had shifted the burden of action to others than himself. He didn't blame Paul Zeron for his worry.

Pictures taken by a miniature camera are liable to be of the surreptitious variety—and pictures of that type, if taken by a man like Babbling Benny, would be dynamite.

A little unsteadily, the senator picked up the dark object. He looked at it regretfully, but he was a man of honor. He would abide by an agreement. He crossed the room, moved a picture on the wall, and started to twirl the combination. Don Cooper almost groaned aloud. The naiveté of a law-maker who would open his personal safe in the presence of two admitted international agents was beyond comprehension. Zeron's snakelike eyes were motionless, fixed upon the man at the safe.

Don Cooper rose, knocked over an ash tray, and succeeded in fumbling around long enough to block at least four turns of the dial from the man who was memorizing the combination. He straightened up with a smile on his lips. Zeron looked at him and through him. In Paul Zeron's world, one never admitted defeat.

Both men turned as the safe door gave a little click. The senator reached into it with the little roll in his hand, then stopped abruptly. He gave an exclamation of alarm, laid the roll down, and stepped back from the safe, staring. Zeron and Don Cooper started from their chairs. The senator turned halfway around.

"My God!" he said. "My papers—I've been robbed!"

Don Cooper looked squarely at Zeron, but the man wasn't looking at him. There was an odd look on his face. Half-crouched, he stared at the senator. His eyes were very much alive now, some inner flame kindling them.

"The papers that I intrusted to you?" There was an unconcealed fury in his voice that was very unusual with Zeron.

"Gone, with mine." Stephen Brill seemed dazed. He looked back at the safe, then turned away again, bewilderment deepening in his face. "Impossible," he said. "No one could—"

"Who has the combination? Secretaries?"

"No one but myself. Absolutely no one."

Paul Zeron turned his blazing eyes for a second on Don Cooper; then they flamed back at Brill. "Your daughter," he said.

Don Cooper took one step forward. ''Follow that line of reasoning into any action whatever, Zeron,'' he said, ''and you've less time to live than you gave me. That's not advice out of experience, either—it's a plain threat!''

Stephen Brill's eyes were puzzled. ''Gentlemen, I do not understand. My daughter knows nothing of matters in my safe.'' He looked at Don Cooper. ''Just what do you mean by 'a threat'?''

Zeron all but spat. ''He means that he is of the belief that your daughter knows more than you suspect.''

Don Cooper took two steps, slammed the safe door, and twirled the knob. ''Senator,'' he said, ''I'm leaving, and I'm holding you to your agreement on that object I entrusted to you. When another man speaks for me in your home, I leave him to continue.''

He turned on his heel and left without a backward look.

Taking the steps of the Brill home at a bound, Don Cooper made for his car. It had been good to see the consternation in Zeron's face when he learned that his papers had been taken from the safe, but this was no time for gloating. His smile was a bit thin.

The senator's childlike faith was touching. He had believed some story of Zeron's, and had taken papers from the man to keep in his safe. Anyone raised in Washington should have known better. Zeron would never trust papers of value in other hands—but he was capable of planting papers that would embarrass somebody else. This, then, was the ace in the hole.

At the height of whatever scandal was stirred up in the wake of the Bushman murder, a few words dropped in the right corner would cause the senator's safe to be investigated. Don Cooper didn't know—but he could guess—that those papers would make Stephen Brill appear as a ringleader in a plot against his own country—a bribed hireling, perhaps, of Italy. The sensation of that would fan the flames higher, too high to quench.

Don Cooper's Buick was streaking down Connecticut. It was passing the lights of the Shoreham, and he recalled suddenly that Paul Zeron could beat him to the Carlton by proxy if he used the telephone. It was a disturbing thought, but it was too late to hunt up a phone and try to beat him to it. Cooper could be at the Carlton in the time it woud take to put through a warning call to Marion. He leaned harder on the accelerator and made time. But when he swung into the Carlton lobby, he knew that he had lost.

Marion Brill was not there.

7

THE DEATH LIST

"Miss Brill left a message for you, Mr. Cooper."

The clerk was holding an envelope in his hand. Don Cooper took it gratefully, managed a casual air, and rammed it into his pocket. "How long ago?" he asked.

"About fifteen minutes."

He nodded, gave the lobby a quick glance, and found a quiet corner. There was a single page of script, and an enclosure. Marion had used the code which had carried most of her confidential messages to him in Manchukuo. Don could read it at sight.

> You probably know by now that I opened Dad's safe tonight. I had to. Zeron was there when I went home to change. He was talking to Dad about you. Dad thinks that Zeron is just a fellow-believer in preparedness. He trusts him. Zeron mentioned the fact that he had entrusted father with important papers. I got them. I had to.
>
> Father never read them, of course. Zeron knew he wouldn't. They link Dad up with every bit of bribery, corruption and conspiracy in the munitions deals of the last five years. No proof. Just inference. The plot against Italy is just hinted at, but he's supposed to be in that too. Those papers were meant to be found. It's the build-up of another newspaper sensation.
>
> Look at the enclosed list. I copied it verbatim. It's a war maker. Dad would be the goat, the possessor of murderous knowledge. I just called Rockwell. I'm going over. He's got to get behind this list before it's too late.

Marion had to be badly shaken to write like that. Don Cooper spread out the enclosed list and frowned. It was a list of the names of prominent people, people in altogether different walks of life. Still, something about the list was familiar to Cooper. Suddenly he stiffened.

"My God!" he said.

They were indeed prominent people—but all of those at the top of the list were dead. His face paled as he went over the list again. The dead were listed in the exact order in which they had died under the bullets of assassins.

Premier Duca, Rumania
Bronislaw Pieracki, Poland
Chancellor Dollfus, Austria
King Alexander, Yugoslavia.

His staring eyes were looking right through that paper to a monstrous conspiracy into which small groups were linked with the cold metal of greed. Here was a list of dead—among them, men who had served their respective countries so well that the war makers despaired of setting the stage for private gain while these men lived.

Across Europe spread the trail of the assassins, small, stupid men who were privates in the army of intrigue without knowing it—warped, inflamed men who wielded the weapons of murder in the cause of the very forces which had made them what they were. And behind these men . . .

Ah, there the trail would be hard to follow. The men who led soft lives while hard hands wielded weapons in peace time were the same men who would lead soft lives while armies marched to war. There were the Paul Zerons who had craft and intelligence for hire, but behind the Zerons there were men who hired that intelligence and that ruthlessness.

Don Cooper could not hope to strike at the shadowy beings in the background, but—his hand clenched. He could perhaps smash the tools which these men used in laying the assassination trail across the United States.

His eyes dropped to the list once more and his breath caught again. The first shock had worn off, and he saw now the thing that had made Marion hurry to Rockwell without waiting for him. The name that followed Alexander of Yugoslavia on the list was the name of a living man, an American.

It was the name of Walter R. Hirsch.

Hirsch would be in Washington tomorrow. He would arrive while the excitement of tonight's dramatic murder was still at fever heat; while people were still speculating on the damning evidence of Italian intrigue that the war makers had so adroitly planted. Walter Hirsch, head of the great newspaper chain that had published the Babbling Benny *exposé*, would be shot down in the street as the others had been shot before him.

And the war makers would have some hopped-up imbecile do the trigger work—some dull-witted Italian gunman, no doubt, who would never realize that he was a tool used to discredit the country of his birth and make money for the munitions barons.

Don Cooper's hand was crushing the paper. In his mind's eye, he could see headlines as yet unwritten, see the burning phrases that might send a nation to war. He was on his feet in an instant, and across the lobby to the telephone. His own voice sounded strange to him as he gave Rockwell's private number. A click sounded, and then Rockwell's dry voice.

"No, Cooper, she isn't here yet. . . . I've been wondering. She's had ample time. . . ."

Don Cooper took a deep breath. "I'll find her," he said, "but get this—Walter Hirsch is getting in tomorrow. Throw an army around him. He's on the murder book. Details later. I'm heading for the Barrington-Dorchester fortress."

He could have asked Rockwell for men, and descended in force upon the spot that he suspected as a nest, but Rockwell could act only with the aid of the Department of Justice in any mass movements. Don Cooper could wait for that; and men in his business always had to be certain before they brought others into anything.

"It's the fortress now," he muttered. "It's got to be."

He left the hotel and again slid under the wheel of his car, feeling for the little gun under his armpit. Reaching into the side pocket of the car, he took out his regulation .38 and stowed it away. His jaw was set grimly.

A few short hours ago, he hadn't like Rockwell's hint when the man had given him the gun. Now he thought the hint too mild.

If Marion Brill was going to be a pawn in Zeron's game, Cooper's guns were going to find a target tonight. . . .

The fortress stood bleakly outlined on a hill above Wisconsin Avenue, a touch of old Austria in the capital of a great democracy. About it spread acres of wooded estate. Don Cooper parked his car on the avenue, avoided the main gate, and went over a particularly dark section of wall.

There was no sound or sign of life, but he walked cautiously through the wooded approach. He cursed the dark topcoat which hampered him, but he kept it on. It was preferable to the gleaming target of a white shirt-front.

As he approached the fortress itself, he caught a gleam of light through one narrow window a flight above ground level. The impatience dropped from him, and he moved like a ghost in the shadow of the towering pile. He could still be wrong, but he didn't believe so. He worked slowly around until he commanded the massive arched entrance; then he knew that he was right.

There was a man on guard there, a hulking, stoop-shouldered man who kept his hands in his pockets, and his sullen eyes on the narrow, private road. There was gunman written in every line of him. The broad, brutal face, the flashy clothes, the slouching pose—all marked him as another private soldier in the army of intrigue, but a paid mercenary, this one.

Off the road, and all but hidden in the shadow of the tall trees, was a dark car. Don Cooper considered investigating that, but it would take time. He stood still, thinking fast. If there was another man in the car, the guard would probably be availing himself of the companionship instead of standing there and glowering.

Rear entrances to the fortress were out. The construction of it made any such notion impractical. The fortress had been built on the slope of a hill, and the walls got higher toward the rear. There would be barred gates back there, of course.

It would have to be the front, and there was no time for finesse. He'd have to crash it—and the open space between the trees and the guard made a bad gap to cross. His own mission made noise something to be avoided, so firearms were out.

He was deep in the shadows and clear of the trees. Light flowed out into the clearing about the guard. Don Cooper groped around for a heavy stone that would not be too big. He found one and hefted it. He had been a fair pitcher in his college days. He shed the overcoat, laying his heavy gun on top of it.

The guard was just standing there. Don Cooper's arm whipped back, and the stone went down on a line. He was charging in behind the stone, and he saw the agonized expression of surprise on the guard's face as the missile took him amidships.

The man never had a chance to draw his gun. He was off balance when Cooper hit him, and Cooper hit him swinging. A booming right stopped the cry on the man's lips; then Don Cooper's fist opened, and the edge of his hand snapped across the man's windpipe.

He'd brought that blow from Asia and he could have killed with it. It was enough to know that his man would be out for many minutes. He turned swiftly toward the door—and a gun boomed.

He felt the tug of the lead as it whistled past his body between his arm and his ribs. Then he was doubled over and diving for the door. Hell was loose with that shot, of course—but he'd never know how much hell if he stayed out there in the light to argue.

Another shot burned past him and smashed into the door. He cursed the decision not to investigate that dark car. The shots were coming from there.

He made the hall on his hands and knees, and scrambled up to charge the stairs, with his small gun in his fist. The big gun was another regret. He'd laid it down when he threw the stone. It had been too heavy in his pocket. He wanted it now. He started up behind the gun. There was nothing else to do. If he tried to shoot it out on the lower floor with the man who had been shooting at him, he'd be caught between two fires. If he could gain the upper floor somehow . . .

Oddly, there was no opposition, no noise, as he ascended. Pale light gleamed up there, but it was not shining directly on the broad stairs. It was somewhere down the corridor. The main hall downstairs was lighted brightly. He was moving out of light to twilight, out of noise to silence.

Then something dropped on him out of the dark, and he tried in vain to pull his head out of the way. Great, glaring balls of intense light danced before his eyes and receded gradually until they were mere pinpoints. After that there was complete darkness.

8

FIVE MINUTES TO LIVE

He came back to consciousness with Marion bending over him. He was in a library of tremendous proportions. Shelves ran around the room from floor to ceiling, broken only in three places—by the door and by two high, narrow windows. The windows were barred and cross-barred. There were very few books on the shelves.

''Don, Don, are you all right?''

Marion was on her knees, one arm around him. He struggled up groggily. It was bad enough to have played the fool, without being worried over by the girl he had come out to save. She had been crying.

''I thought they'd killed you. They just dumped you in.''

''Who?'' His voice was thick, husky.

''Apollo and some others.''

He groaned. ''I deserve even that. I walked into it.''

''So did I.'' The girl's voice was bitter. ''I was worrying about Dad, trying to hurry. They took me as easily as if I were a little Campfire Girl.''

Don Cooper was on his feet, swaying a little, but forcing the pain down by an effort of will that brought sweat to his forehead. One glance was enough to show that the room held no possibilities for escape. There were only three chairs and a table, and the only way out was the door.

''Damn! I only figured the guard. Didn't think anyone was in that car.'' He spoke half to himself. The girl nodded her head.

'The driver. He's a dummy. He hears all right, but he can't talk.''

A dummy—that, then, explained why he wasn't talking to the guard. Don Cooper shook his head grimly. He'd known long ago that one must expect the unexpected always; yet he could not have foreseen that.

"Don, we've got to get out, Hirsch—"

"I know. I told Rockwell. But we've got to get out, anyway. You're in danger. You know too much." His head was clearing now. "Those papers, Marion—did Zeron get them?"

Her voice dropped to a whisper. "No. They're in the Carlton safe; but they don't prove anything on anybody. As long as Dad hasn't got them, it's all right."

Don Cooper didn't agree with that, but he didn't raise any fears or doubts. Zeron played hard. He wouldn't want anything that he had planted to be examined closely by his foes.

The door opened. Irene Gaylord stood there for the moment, posing. Even under circumstances such as these, with an audience that could not be appreciative, she made a dramatic entrance. Behind her was the halfback, with something of a swagger in his manner. He was the man who came back, virtue triumphant, the conqueror of his lady's tormentor.

Irene Gaylord was looking at Don Cooper with a curl to her full lips. She was no misunderstood woman now, no actress playing a role—and she was not even trying to act like a niece of the Barrington-Dorchesters. Standing in this old-world room, with a sneer on her lips, she was as foreign as Paul Zeron—and of the same mercenary breed.

She moved into the room, and behind her came first the college wonder, clutching a big Luger, and then a broad, flabby man with dull eyes. Don Cooper's gun had been taken away from him, and his expression as he looked at the halfback's gun brought a flush to the man's face. As though he had just realized that the weapon was unnecessary, the halfback lowered it and tried to put it in his pocket. Cooper's gun was already in that pocket and the halfback had to transfer the smaller gun to his left sidepocket to make room for the Luger.

A glint came into the flabby man's eyes for a moment as he watched the performance with the guns—a gleam of something very like contempt. It was only a flash, but for that moment, the man was a human personality and not just something tagged onto the end of the woman's escort.

This, Don Cooper decided, would be the dummy—and the man was decidedly an Italian, just as he was decidedly drug-soaked. Tomorrow Walter Hirsch came to Washington. Here was a prime victim for the mob, the dull, dumb instrument destined for the label "assassin."

Irene Gaylord broke in on his line of thought.

"I had you brought here," she said cuttingly, "because I thought that you might like to share a room with a woman who would not threaten to scream."

Don Cooper seemed to lose his head completely. He crouched, clenched his fists, and charged at the woman, his mouth working. The halfback made a pass at the Luger, decided that there wasn't time for that, and threw his body in the way of Cooper's charge as the girl took a frightened step backward.

The bodies of the two men crashed, and for a few seconds they strained against each other. Then the dummy's gun was out and clubbed. Don Cooper wriggled free and stepped back out of range. One crowning was enough for an evening.

"I'm sorry," he said. "I lost my head." He ran his fingers through his hair, and looked at the floor. Irene Gaylord laughed at him.

"I was almost impressed with you," she said. "Come, Carl."

The halfback brightened and fell in behind her as she turned to the door. The dummy saw no more need for his services and went out into the hall. Irene Gaylord did not look back, but both Cooper and Marion stared steadily after her.

Then Don Cooper's eyes met Marion's. "They're waiting for Zeron, of course," he said.

She nodded. "We'll be here when he comes, too."

Don Cooper's eyes were thoughtful, distant. "I want to be. I've got one card to play."

Marion Brill smiled. "I know. I saw you get it."

"Get what?"

"The one card."

Don spread his hands and looked at them. "The hand is quicker than the eye, no?"

"No," she said. "It isn't."

Dawn was tinting the narrow windows of the old library when Zeron came. Irene Gaylord knew what his coming portended, and there was a greedy look of anticipation on her face as she entered the library behind the little internationalist. At her side walked a sleepy-looking college wonder. The dummy and the man who had guarded the door downstairs were ranged on either side of the exit.

Zeron ran the tip of his tongue over his lips. His eyes drilled the wearily defiant Marion Brill. There was no veneer of politeness covering his viciousness now.

"I cannot argue or temporize," he said harshly. "You have less than five minutes to live unless you tell me where you put the papers you stole from the safe of your father.''

''They are where you can't get them.''

''So!'' The little man stepped close. His hand moved, and came up with a flat automatic gripped tight. He snapped a command, and the dummy took Marion by the arm and escorted her the width of the room from Don Cooper. Then he went back to his post. The other gunman had been vigilant. Zeron pointed the muzzle of his gun and lifted it on a line with the girl's heart.

''I count three,'' he said. ''You will live that long. One!''

The girl was pale, defiant, looking out over his head.

''Two.'' She tensed, but did not flinch. Don Cooper stood like a statue, his unblinking eyes fixed on Zeron.

Suddenly the little man stepped back. ''It is too fast. You do not fear it that way.''

The girl swayed a little, caught herself, and straightened. Don Cooper wiped his forehead. He had been sure—and yet he'd died a hundred deaths. Zeron could not kill quickly. He had to make a play for those papers before he killed. Don knew that, but he had watched every muscle movement and every flicker of expression on the little man's face. He'd have seen the resolve to fire.

Zeron was holding the automatic up so that the girl could see it. ''You see the sight on this weapon? It slashes mos' cruel—and this gun, it is heavy. You are beautiful, *mademoiselle*, but the first blow breaks your nose. And then—'' Hs lips curled back from his teeth.

Marion Brill's eyes widened in terror. ''You wouldn't!''

''No?'' There was a flicker of movement in the man's tense body.

''Stop!'' Don Cooper took a step forward, ignoring the fact that three hands moved to ready guns. Paul Zeron had half-turned. His eyes met Cooper's.

''That doesn't buy you a thing, Zeron.'' Cooper's voice was grim. ''You're practically standing on the gallows now.''

''So?''

''Yes. You killed Benny Bushman yourself. You didn't trust that job to anybody else. That finishes you.''

Paul Zeron laughed. ''With another man's fingerprints on the stiletto, and with that man bearing the marks of the bomb—how can I be suspected?''

Don Cooper was ignoring everyone else in the room. He was throwing the whole weight of his will on Zeron. He had one card, but the spot had to be right for the laying of that card.

"That bomb never marked anything," he said. "It was built to make a noise and a stink and a lot of smoke. It made nothing else."

Zeron was caught momentarily on the hook that gets the egotist and the man who works with his brain. He wanted to hear his plans discussed by others. He wanted to defend his own wisdom. His eyebrows went up mockingly.

"This bomb did not remove hair?"

"It did not. No bomb ever built could take the hair from under a man's armpits and leave his clothes on him. Benny Bushman took the bomb inside of him. That's why he was sick for days and had to take his meals in his room. That's why Paolo Luca disappeared for three days. You've got a quack doctor on your staff somewhere who'll scurry to cover and stay hidden when you fall."

"And the bomb?" A deadliness had crept into Zeron's voice.

"Is thallium acetate, the drug that reputable doctors use over a three-month period to remove the hair in case of severe skin disease. You used a concentrate."

"And the fingerprints?"

"You wouldn't know about them if you hadn't put them on the stiletto when you had poor Luca helpless out here where your bomb-throwing girl friend lured him."

Irene Gaylord fairly leaped across the room. "That's the second time you've accused me of that!" Her hand cracked viciously across his face.

Don Cooper laughed. He had them coming at him again. "The police will say so, too," he said. "Your eye-witness account of a struggle will blow up when they get around to asking you why you had a dinner engagement with a sick man, and how you identified Benny Bushman so quickly without his hair, and failed to comment on it. You had nothing to do but flip a bomb into a room with a dead man and then tell a story. You boobed the story."

She slapped his face again, and he took a backward step. Zeron snapped his fingers. "Enough, Irene." The girl stepped back, and Zeron bent a cold look on Don Cooper.

"The police, too," he said, "will tell you that I would have destroyed the set of prints on that stiletto if I had clutched it to kill."

Don Cooper smiled at him. "That was good," he said, "but they have the sheath of cellophane that covered the haft of that weapon."

Zeron stiffened slowly. "You should have gone to Maine," he said frozenly. "You will never go now." His thin lips flattened over his teeth as he lifted the heavy gun. "First you will watch me break the nose of *mademoiselle* who does not speak. Then—"

He turned swiftly to Marion. Don Cooper's hand moved too fast for any eye to follow. The gunman who had guarded the door was vigilant, but his draw was too slow. Metal flashed in Don Cooper's hand, and a .38 slammed the gunman in the chest. The man grunted and went down like a knocked-out prize fighter in slow motion. Paul Zeron pulled his head down and crouched. He was out of position to fire, and he was a small target when he crouched. Don Cooper didn't risk his aim with the baby .38—Marion was too close. Instead, he swung his gun in an arc.

"Hold it, everybody!"

The mere fact of his having a gun had been a surprise in his favor. The dummy was glowering at him; Zeron's eyes had filmed over like a snake's; the halfback was wide-eyed, and . . .

"Look out, Don!"

The cry was wrung from Marion, and he knew what called it forth, knew suddenly, with a curse. He couldn't look out. Two of the men before him were tensing. . . . A cold voice sounded almost in his ear.

"Just move. I'd love it."

He didn't need to wonder if Irene Gaylord was bluffing. He knew that she wasn't. She wasn't actress enough to get that gloat into her voice.

"I began to suspect your little act as soon as it was put on. You aren't the type to hit a woman. You just wanted an excuse to crash into Carl and wrestle with him—and get his gun." She shrugged, and gave way to the temptation to play the scene. Head tilted, she gave a long, soft laugh of elation. . . .

Marion Brill had been leaning back against the book shelves as though exhausted, her eyes half-closed. But when she moved, her body was like a snapping spring. Her hand closed on a book and released it in one continuous, flowing movement—and it came on a line, straight for the laughing face.

Few women know how to get out of the way of anything that comes like that—and Irene Gaylord was not one of the few. She broke off in the middle of a trilled note, gasped, dropped her gun—and took the book head-on.

Guns roared in the room. Don Cooper had twisted the instant he saw that book leave the shelf, but he was not quite quick enough. He felt a blow that was like the impact of the hardest, ice-packed snowball that was ever rolled, and he went down with it, lights dancing in his brain.

Through the fog and the thunder, he saw Paul Zeron wheeling on Marion Brill, his gun coming up. Don Cooper fired from the floor, and the spy's gun stopped in mid-arc. The little man's body spun like a dancing doll, hit the bookcase, and bounced. Dimly, Don realized that there had been other shots, but he didn't see what Marion Brill saw with horror-filled eyes. . . .

The quick shot of the dummy that had felled Don was instantly followed by another that missed him by a hair after he had fallen, smashing Irene Gaylord back against the wall. Then came the quick, impetuous dive of the halfback toward the girl—which took him into the gunman's third shot. . . .

All that Cooper had missed, but his eyes found the gunman in the split-second pause that followed the fall of the devoted Carl. His gun came up desperately as the dummy's gun came down. His finger squeezed hard on the trigger, but the icy stab along his arm told him that he had been hit. His gun flew from his hand, and he felt the bony hand of death reaching for him. Then his head cleared, and again he saw his antagonist plainly.

The dummy had not started to fall yet. He was drawn upright, his mouth half-open. One of his hands was gripping hard on his chest. When he went down, the crash of his fall echoed in the huge room.

Feet pounded on the stairs, and the door burst open. Don Cooper fought an impulse to lie down and forget it all. He wobbled upright, and stood on braced legs as Bill Russell and Dan Kling crashed the room with a small army of cops behind them. He smiled wearily at them.

"Everybody but the coroner," he said, "and he's the only bird we need."

But Don Cooper was wrong about that. Irene Gaylord and Carl went to the hospital together with less to worry about, as far as wounds were concerned, than Don Cooper. He had two pellets of lead where the lead hurt, even if it didn't interfere with the necessary business of living.

Propped up on a hospital bed, with Marion Brill holding his hand, he heard the wind-up from the lips of Ben Rockwell. Ben had conferred with Russell when he heard nothing further from Marion or Don Cooper, and they had decided to follow up Cooper's visit to the fortress, in spite of his asking for the lone-hand play. Russell had taken Kling in on it, and they had just found Cooper's coat and gun on the grounds when the shooting started.

"And that's that." The bald-headed man stood up. "The Gaylord woman is scared to death. She's going to live, and it's liable to be tough living. The Barrington-Dorchesters have stepped out of it, with Zeron dead. They say he blackmailed them into sponsoring the girl. Maybe he did. Anyway, she's cracked wide open and so has the conspiracy. We're rounding up people now from a list of names that she's given us." He smiled grimly.

"It's enough to make Zeron turn in his grave, but that young Italian who was picked for the goat is liable to come out of this a hero. I've given a nice tale to some of the newspaper lads. And now—" he shrugged his shoulders— "I suppose I can't get any work out of you for a while. Where do you think you'll go?"

Don Cooper grinned. "Maine," he said. "I hear it's a healthy spot."

As the echo of Rockwell's dry chuckle died out in the corridor, Don Cooper looked up into eyes that gazed at him with unashamed tenderness. He lifted his one good arm slowly.

"Is the hand quicker than the eye?" he asked softly.

Marion Brill shook her head. "No," she said. "It isn't."

Deliberately, she closed her eyes.

LESLIE CHARTERIS

The Sizzling Saboteur

1

SIMON TEMPLAR HAD met a lot of unusual obstructions on the highway in the course of a long and varied career of eccentric traveling. They had ranged from migrant sheep to diamond necklaces, from circus parades to damsels in distress; and he had acquired a tolerant feeling toward most of them—particularly the damsels in distress. But a partly incinerated tree, he felt, was carrying originality a little far. He thought that the Texas Highway Department should at least have been able to eliminate such exotic hazards as that.

Especially since there were no local trees in sight to account for it, so that somebody must have taken considerable trouble to import it. The surrounding country was flat, marshy, and reedy; and the sourish salty smell of the sea was a slight stench in the nostrils. The road was a graveled affair with a high crown, possibly for drainage, and not any too wide although comparatively smooth. It wound and snaked along through alternating patches of sand and reeds like an attenuated sea serpent which had crawled out of Galveston Bay to sun itself on that desolate stretch of beach, so that Simon had seen the log a longish while before he was obliged to brake his car on account of it.

The car was a nice shiny black sedan of the 1942 or BF (Before Freezing) vintage; but it was no more incongruous on this ribbon of road than its driver. However, Simon Templar was noted for doing incongruous things. Enroute to Galveston via Texas City on Highway 146, he hadn't even reached Texas City. Somehow, back where the highway forked left from the Southern Pacific right-of-way, Simon had taken an even lefter turn which now had him heading southwards along a most erratic observation tour of the Gulf coastline. A long way from the metropolitan crowding of New York, where he had recently wound up a job—or even of St. Louis, where he had been even more recently. Now his only company was the purring motor and an occasional raucous gull that flapped or soared above the marshland on predatory business of its own. Which didn't necessarily mean that that that business was any less predatory than that of Simon Templar, who under his more publicized nickname of the Saint had once left sundry police departments and local underworlds equally flatfooted in the face of new and unchallenged records of predatoriality—if this chronicler may inflict such a word on the long-suffering Messieurs Funk, Wagnalls, and Webster. The most immediately noticeable difference between the Saint and the seagull was the seagull's protective parosmia, or perversion of the sense of smell. . . . Yet the sun was still three hours high, and it was still twenty miles to Galveston unless the cartographer who had concocted the Saint's road map was trying in his small way to cheer the discouraged pilgrim.

And there was the smoldering blackened log laid almost squarely across the middle of the road, as if some diehard vigilante had made it his business to see that no casehardened voyager rushed through the scenery without a pause in which its deeper fascinations might have a chance to make their due impression on the soul.

Simon considered his own problem with clear blue eyes as the sedan came to a stop.

The road was too narrow for him to drive around the log; and in view of the tire rationing situation it was out of the question to try and drive over it. Which meant that somebody had to get out and move it. Which meant that the Saint had to move it himself.

Simon Templar said a few casual things about greenhorns who mislaid such sizeable chunks of their camp fires; but at the same time his eyes were glancing left and right with the endless alertness hardening in their sapphire calm, and his tanned face setting into the bronze fighting mask to which little things like that could instantly reduce it.

He knew from all the pitiless years behind him how easily this could be an effective ambush. When he got out to move the smoldering log, it would be a simple job for a couple of hirelings of the ungodly to attack him. A certain Mr. Matson, for instance, might have been capable of setting such a trap—if Mr. Matson had known that Simon Templar was the Saint, and was on his way to interview Mr. Matson in Galveston, and if Mr. Matson had had the prophetic ability to foretell that Simon Templar was going to take this coastal road. But since Simon himself hadn't known it until about half an hour ago, it appeared that this hypothesis would have credited Mr. Matson with a slightly fantastic grade of clairvoyance.

The Saint stared at the log with all these things in his mind; and while he was doing it he discovered for the first time in his life the real validity of a much-handled popular phrase.

Because he sat there and literally felt his blood run cold.

Because the log moved.

Not in the way that any ordinary log would have moved, in a sort of solid rolling way. This log was flexible, and the branches stirred independently like limbs.

Simon Templar had an instant of incredulous horror and sheer disbelief. But even while he groped back into the past for any commonplace explanation of such a defection of his senses, he knew that he was wasting his time. Because he had positively seen what he had seen, and that was the end of it.

Or the beginning.

Very quietly, when there was no reason to be quiet, he snapped open the door of the car and slid his seventy-four inches of whipcord muscle out on to the road. Four of his quick light strides took him to the side of the huge ember in the highway. And then he had no more doubt.

He said, involuntarily: "My God . . ."

For the ember was not a tree. It was human.

It had been a man.

Instead of a six-foot log of driftwood, the smoldering obstacle had been a man.

And the crowning horror was yet to come. For at the sound of the Saint's voice, the blackened log moved again feebly and emitted a faint groan.

Simon turned back to his car, and was back again in another moment with his light topcoat and a whiskey flask. He wrapped the coat around the piece of human charcoal to smother any remaining fire, and gently raised the singed black head to hold his flask to the cracked lips.

A spasm of pain contorted the man, and his face worked through a horrible crispness.

"Blue . . . Goose . . ." The voice came in a parched whisper. "Maris . . . contact . . . Olga—Ivan—Ivanovitch . . ."

Simon glanced around the deserted landscape, and had never felt so helpless. It was obviously impossible for him to move that sickening relic of a human being, or to render any useful first aid. Even if any aid, first or last would have made any difference.

"Can you hold it until I get some help—an ambulance?" he said. "I'll hurry. Can you hear me?"

The burned man rallied slightly.

"No use," he breathed. "I'm goner . . . Poured—gasoline—on me . . . Set fire . . ."

"Who did?" Simon insisted. "What happened?"

"Three men . . . Met last night—in bar . . . Blatt . . . Weinbach . . . And Maris . . . Going to party—at Olga's . . ."

"Where?"

"Don't know . . . "

"What's your name? Who are you?"

"Henry—Stephens," croaked the dying man. "Ostrich-skin—leather case—in gladstone lining . . . Get case—and send . . . send . . ."

His voice trailed off into an almost inaudible rasp that was whisked away along with his spirit on the wings of the wind that swept across the flats. Henry Stephens was dead, mercifully for him, leaving Simon Templar a handful of unexplained names and words and a decided mess.

"And God damn it," said the Saint unreasonably, to no better audience than the circling gulls, "why do people like you have to read that kind of mystery story? Couldn't one of you wait to die, just once, until after you'd finished saying what you were trying to get out?"

He knew what was the matter with him, but he said it just the same. It helped him to get back into the shell which too many episodes like that had helped to build around him.

And then he lighted a cigarette and wondered sanely what he should do.

Any further identification of Henry Stephens was impossible. His hair was all burned off, his hands were barbecued from trying to beat out the flames of his own pyre, and the few remnants of his clothes were charred to him in a hideous smelting. Simon debated whether to take the body with him or leave it where it was. He glanced at his watch and surveyed the lonely country about him. There was still no living person in sight, although in the distance he could see a couple of summer shacks and the indications of a town beyond.

Simon moved the body gently to one side of the road, re-entered his car, and drove carefully around it. Then his foot grew heavy on the accelerator until the side road eventually merged with the main highway and took him on to Virginia Point.

It was inevitable that the Saint's irregular past should have given him some fundamental hesitations about going out of his way to make contact with the law, and on top of that he had projects for his equally unpredictable future which argued almost as strongly against inviting complications and delays; but he heaved a deep sigh of resignation and found his way to the local police station.

The sergeant in charge, who was sticking his tongue out over a crossword puzzle in a prehistoric and dog-eared magazine, listened bug-eyed to the report of his find, and promptly telephoned the police across the Causeway in Galveston proper.

"I'll have to ask you to stay until the Homicide Squad and the ambulance comes over to pick up the corpse," he said as he hung up.

"Why?" Simon asked wearily. "Don't you think they'll bring enough men to lift him? I've got business in Galveston."

The sergeant looked apologetic.

"It's—it's a matter of law, Mr.—er—"

"Templar," supplied the Saint. "Simon Templar."

This apparently meant no more to the local authority than John Smith or Leslie Charteris. He excavated a sheet of paper and began to construct a report along the lines which he had probably memorized in his youth, which had been a long time ago.

"You're from where, Mr. Temple?" he asked, lifting his head.

"Tem-*plar*," Simon corrected him with his hopes beginning to rise again. "I just came from St. Louis, Missouri."

The sergeant wrote this down, spelling everything carefully.

"You got any identification papers on you?"

"What for?" Simon inquired. "It's the corpse you're going to have to identify, not me. I know who I am."

"I reckon so; but we don't," the other rejoined stolidly. "Now if you'll just oblige me by answering my questions———"

Simon sighed again, and reached for his wallet.

"I'm afraid you're going to be difficult, so help yourself, Lieutenant."

"Sergeant," maintained the other, calmly squinting at the Saint's draft cards and driving licenses and noting that the general descriptions fitted the man in front of him.

He was about to hand the wallet back without more than glancing into the compartment comfortably filled with green frogskins of the realm quaintly known as folding money when his eye was caught by the design stamped on the outside of the leather where a monogram might ordinarily have been. It was nothing but a line drawing of a skeletal figure with a cipher for a head and an elliptical halo floating above it. The pose of the figure was jaunty, with a subtle impudence that amounted almost to arrogance.

The sergeant examined it puzzledly.

"What's this?"

"I'm a doodler," Simon explained gravely. "That is my pet design for telephone booths, linen tablecloths, and ladies' underwear."

"I see," said the sergeant quite blankly, returning the wallet. "Now if you'll just sit down over there, Mr. Templar, the Galveston police will be here directly. It's only a couple of miles across the Causeway, and you can lead the way to the spot."

"Aren't you going to call out the posse to chase the murderers?" Simon suggested. "If they brought a horse for me, I could save some of my gas ration."

"You got something there," said the sergeant woodenly. "I'll call the sheriff's office while we're waitin'."

Simon Templar groaned inwardly, and saw it closing around him again, the fantastic destiny which seemed to have ordained that nothing lawless should ever happen anywhere and let him pass by like any other peaceful citizen.

He fished out another cigarette while the second call was being made, and finally said; "I'm beginning to hope that by the time you get out there the seagulls will have beaten you to it and there won't be any body."

"There'll be one if you saw one," opined the sergeant confidently. "Nobody'll likely come along that beach road again today. Too early in the season for picnics, and a bad day for fishin'."

"I trust your deductive genius is on the beam, Captain, but at least two other parties have been on that road today already—the victim and the murderers."

"Sergeant," grunted the other. "And I don't know how you come to be on that road yet."

Simon shrugged, and spread his hands slightly to indicate that under the laws of mathematical probability the point was unanswerable. Silence fell as the conversation languished.

Presently there was a noise of cars arriving, and installments of the law filtered into the house. The sergeant put down his crossword puzzle and stood up to do the honors.

"Hi, Bill. . . . Howdy, Lieutenant Kinglake. . . . 'Lo, Yard. . . . Hiyah, Dr. Quantry. . . . This is the man who reported that burned corpse. His name is Templar and he's a doodler."

Simon kept his face perfectly solemn as he weighed the men who were taking charge of the case.

Lieutenant Kinglake was a husky teak-skinned individual with gimlet gray eyes and a mouth like a thin slash above a battleship prow of jaw. He looked as if he worked hard and fast and would want to hit things that tried to slow him up. Yard, his assistant, was a lumbering impression from a familiar mold, in plain clothes that could have done nicely with a little dusting and pressing. Dr. Quantry, the coroner, looked like Dr.

Quantry, the coroner. Bill, who wore a leather windbreaker with a deputy sheriff's badge pinned on it, was middle-aged and heavy, with a brick-red face and a mustache like an untrimmed hedge. He had faintly popped light-blue eyes with a vague lack of focus, as if he was unused to seeing anything nearer than the horizon: he moved slowly and spoke even slower when he spoke at all.

It didn't take Kinglake more than a minute to assimilate all the information that the sergeant had gathered, and to examine Simon's identification papers. He stopped over the line drawing which reminded him of the figures of boxers which he used to draw in the margins of successive pages of his Fiske's history and riffle to simulate a sparring match.

"Doodler?" he said in a sharp voice. "I———" He broke off as his eyes widened and then narrowed. "I've seen this picture before. Simon Templar, eh? Are you the Saint?"

"I bow to your fund of miscellaneous information," Simon responded courteously.

"Meaning?"

"That I am known in certain strata of society, and to a goodly number of the carriage trade, by that cognomen."

"Ah." Detective Yard spoke with an air of discovery. "A funny man."

"The Saint, eh?" rumbled the sheriff's deputy, with a certain deliberate awe. "Gee, he's the Saint."

"He said he was a doodler," persisted the sergeant.

Dr. Quantry consulted a gold watch in exactly the way Dr. Quantry would have consulted a gold watch, and said: "Gentlemen, how about getting on?"

Lieutenant Kinglake held the Saint's eyes for another moment with his hard stare, and gave back the wallet.

"Right," he snapped. "Cut out the eight-cylinder words, Mr. Templar, and lead us to the body. You can leave your car here and ride with me. Yard, tell the ambulance driver to follow us. Come on."

Simon turned back to the sergeant as the party trooped out.

"By the way," he said, "the word for 'a hole in the ground' is w-e-l-l, not what you have. Good-bye, Inspector."

He climbed resignedly into the seat beside Kinglake, reflecting that there was nothing much you could do when Fate was running a private feud against you, and that he must be a congenital idiot to have ever expected that his business in Galveston would be allowed to proceed as smoothly as it should have for anyone else. He got a very meager satisfaction out of rehearsing some of the things he would have to say to a certain Mr. Hamilton in Washington about that.

2

The mortal remains, as our school of journalism taught us not to call them, of Mr. Henry Stephens lay precisely where Simon had left them, proving that the sergeant at Virginia Point had been right in one contention and no one had come along that road in the meantime.

Lieutenant Kinglake and the coroner squatted beside the body and made a superficial examination. Detective Yard took his cue to demonstrate that he was something more than window-dressing. He began searching the area close to the body, and then thoroughly quartered the surrounding acre in ever-widening circles like a dutiful mastiff. Slow and apparently awkward, perhaps a little on the dull side, he was meticulous and painstaking. Bill the deputy sheriff found a convenient horizon and gazed at it in profound meditation.

Simon Templar stood patiently by while it went on. He didn't want to interfere any more than he had already; and for all his irrepressible devilment he made the mistake of underestimating the law, or of baiting its minions without provocation or good purpose.

Dr. Quantry eventually straightened up and wiped his hands on his handkerchief.

"Death by carbonization," he announced. "Gasoline, apparently. It's a miracle that he was able to speak at all, if this is how Mr. Templar found him. . . . Autopsy as a matter of course. Give you a full report later."

The hard-eyed lieutenant nodded and got to his feet, holding out the Saint's topcoat.

"This is yours, Templar?"

"Thanks."

Dr. Quantry beckoned to the ambulance crew.

"Remove," he ordered briskly. "Morgue."

Kinglake made his own inspection of the crown of the road where Simon showed him he had first seen the body.

"He didn't do all that burning here—the surface is hardly scorched," he concluded, and turned to wait for the approach of his assistant.

Detective Yard carried some souvenirs carefully in his handkerchief. They consisted of a partly burned crumple of newspaper, and an ordinary match folder bearing the name of the 606 Club in Chicago. Kinglake looked at the exhibits without touching them.

"Galveston paper," he said; and then: "When were you last in Chicago, Templar?"

"A few days ago."

"Ever been to the 606 Club?"

"As a matter of fact, I have," said the Saint coolly. "I'm making a survey of the United States on the subject of stage and floor-show nudity in the principal cities in relation to the per capita circulation of the *Atlantic Monthly*. It's a fascinating study."

Lieutenant Kinglake was unruffled.

"What's the story, Yard?

"There's a spot about twenty yards in off the Gulf side of the road where the reeds are all trampled down and burned. Can't tell how many men made the tracks, and they're all scuffed up by the deceased having crawled back over them. Looks as if a couple of men might have taken the deceased in there, and one of them could have poured gas or oil over him while the other lit the paper to set fire to him so as not to have to get so close like he wouldn't have to with a match. Then they scrammed; but there aren't any distinguishable tire marks. Victim must have staggered around, trying to beat out the flames with his hands, and found his way back to the road where he collapsed."

It was a pretty shrewd reconstruction, as Simon recognized with respect; and it only left out one small thing.

"What about the bottle or container which held the gasoline?" he inquired.

"Maybe we'll find that in your car," Yard retorted with heavy hostility. "You were at this club in Chicago where the matches came from———"

"The dear old match folder clue," said the Saint sadly. "Detective Manuel, chapter two, paragraph three."

The deputy sheriff removed his eyes wistfully from the horizon, cleared his throat, and said weightily: "It ain't so funny, pardner. You're tied up closer 'n anybody with this business."

"We'll check the newspaper and the match book for fingerprints," Kinglake said shortly. "But don't let's go off at half cock. Look."

He reached into his own pocket and brought out three match folders. One carried the advertisement of a Galveston pool hall, one spoke glowingly of the virtues of Tums, and the other carried the imprint of the Florentine Gardens in Hollywood.

"See?" he commented. "Where did I get this Florentine Gardens thing? I've never been to Hollywood. Advertising matches are shipped all around the country nowadays. This is as good a clue as saying that the other book proves I must have a bad stomach. Let's go back and get Templar's statement."

"Just so I get to Galveston before I'm too old to care," said the Saint agreeably.

But inwardly he took a new measure of the lieutenant. Kinglake might be a rough man in a hurry, but he didn't jump to conclusions. He would be tough to change once he had reached a conclusion, but he would have done plenty of work on that conclusion before he reached it.

So the Saint kept a tight rein on his more wicked impulses, and submitted patiently and politely to the tedious routine of making his statement while it was taken down in labored longhand by Detective Yard and Bill the deputy simultaneously. Then there were a few ordinary questions and answers on it to be added, and after a long dull time it was over.

"OK, Bill," Kinglake said at last, getting up as if he was no less glad than the Saint to be through with the ordeal. "We'll keep in touch. Templar, I'll ride back to Galveston in your car, if you don't mind."

"Fine," said the Saint equably. "You can show me the way."

But he knew very well that there would be more to it than that; and his premonition was vindicated a few seconds after they got under way.

"Now," Kinglake said, slouching down in the seat beside him and biting off the end of a villainous-looking stogie, "we can have a private little chat on the way in."

"Good," said the Saint. "Tell me about your museums and local monuments."

"And I don't mean that," Kinglake said.

Simon put a cigarette in his mouth and pressed the lighter on the dashboard and surrendered to the continuation of Fate.

"But I'm damned if I know," he said, "why the hell you should be so concerned. Brother Stephens wasn't cremated within the city limits."

"There's bound to be a hook-up with something inside the city, and we work with the sheriff and he works with us. I'm trying to save myself some time."

"On the job of checking up on me?"

"Maybe."

''Then why not let Yard worry about it? I'm sure he'd love to pin something on me.''

''Yeah,'' Kinglake assented between puffs of smoke. ''He could get on your nerves at times, but don't let him fool you. He's a first-rate detective. Good enough for the work we do here.''

''I haven't the slightet doubt of it,'' Simon assured him. ''But I've told you everything I know, and every word of it happens to be true. However, I don't expect that to stop you trying to prove I did it. So get started. This is your inspiration.''

Kinglake still didn't start fighting.

''I know that your story checks as far as it goes,'' he said. ''I smelt the liquor on that dead guy's mouth, and I saw your coat. I'm not believing that you'd waste good whiskey and ruin a good coat just to build up a story—yet. But I do want to know what your business is in Galveston.''

The Saint had expected this.

''I told you,'' he replied blandly. ''I'm making this survey of American night life. Would you like to give me the lowdown on the standards of undress in your parish?''

''Want to play hard to handle, eh?''

''Not particularly. I just want to keep a few remnants of my private life.''

Kinglake bit down on his cigar and stared impartially at the Saint's tranquil profile.

After a little while he said: ''From what I remember reading, your private life is always turning into a public problem. So that's why I'm talking to you. As far as I know, you aren't wanted anywhere right now, and there aren't any charges out against you. I've also heard of a lot of officers here and there leading with their chins by thinking too fast as soon as they saw you. I'm not figuring on making myself another of 'em. Your story sounds straight so far, or it would if anybody else told it. It's too bad your reputation would make anybody look twice when you tell it. But OK. Until there's evidence against you, you're in the clear. So I'm just telling you. While you're in Galveston, you stay in line. I don't want your kind of trouble in my town.''

''And I hope you won't have it,'' said the Saint soberly. ''And I can tell you for my part that there won't be any trouble that someone else doesn't ask for.''

There was a prolonged and unproductive reticence, during which Simon devoted himself wholeheartedly to digesting the scenic features of the approach over the channel of water known as West Bay which separates the island of Galveston from the mainland.

"The Oleander city," he murmured dreamily, to relieve the awkward silence. "The old stamping grounds of Jean Lafitte. A shrine that every conscientious freebooter ought to visit. . . . Would you like me to give you a brief and somewhat garbled résumé of the history of Galveston, Lieutenant?"

"No," Kinglake said candidly. "The current history of the town is enough to keep me busy. Turn at the next light."

Simon drove him to Headquarters, and lighted another cigarette while the Lieutenant gathered his rather ungainly legs together and disembarked.

"The inquest will probably be tomorrow," he said practically. "Where are you staying?"

"The Alamo House."

Kinglake gave him directions.

"Don't leave town till I'm through with you," he said. "And don't forget what I told you. That's all."

He turned dourly away; and Simon Templar drove on to register faithfully and with no deception at the Alamo House.

The colored bellhop who showed him to his room was no more than naturally amazed at being tipped with a five-dollar bill for the toil of carrying one light suitcase. But the Saint had not finished with him then.

"George," he said, "I presume you know the lay of the town?"

"Yes, sah," answered the startled Negro, grinning. "But my names is Jones, sah."

"Congratulations. But the point is, you should be more or less familiar with the Galveston police force—know most of them by sight, I mean."

"Well, sah, I—er—yes, sah."

"Then I must tell you a secret. Lieutenant Kinglake and some of his pals are investigating me for membership in a private club they have. I expect some of them to be nosing around to find out if I'm really respectable enough to associate with them. Don't misunderstand me. If they ask you any questions, you must always tell them the truth. Never lie to detectives, Jones, because it makes them so bad tempered. But just point them out to me quietly and tell me who they are, so I can say hullo to them when we meet. And every time you do that, I'll be good for another fin."

The negro scratched his head, and then grinned again.

"Don't reckon they's no harm in that Mistah Templah. That Mistah

Kinglake sho' is a hard man. They ain't a single killin' he don't solve here in Galveston. He . . . Say!'' The big brown eyes came alert. ''How come you know 'bout Mistah Kinglake?''

''We had a mutual interest in what is known as a *corpus delicti,*'' said the Saint solemnly, ''but I sold him my share. He's now checking the bill of sale. Do you follow me?''

''No, sah,'' said Jones.

''Then don't let it worry you. Read the morning paper for details. By the way, what is the leading newspaper here?''

''The *Times-Tribune*, sah. They put out a mawnin' an' evenin' paper both.''

''They must be as busy as bees,'' said the Saint. ''Now don't forget our agreement. Five bucks per copy, delivered on the hoof.''

''Yes, sah. An' thank yuh, sah.''

The Saint grinned in his turn, and went to the bathroom to wash and change his shirt.

It was much later than he had meant to begin his real errand in Galveston; but he had nothing else to do there, and he didn't know enough about the entertainment potentialities of the town to be tempted by other attractions. It was most inconsiderate of Lieutenant Kinglake, he thought, to have refused to take his question seriously and enlighten him. . . . But besides that, he knew that his unfortunate discovery of the expiring Mr. Henry Stephens meant that he couldn't look forward to following his own trail much further in the obscurity which he would have chosen. It looked like nothing but cogent common sense to do what he could with the brief anonymity he could look forward to.

Thus it happened that after a couple of grilled sandwiches in the hotel coffee shop he set out to stroll back down into the business district with the air of a tourist who had nowhere to go and all night to get there.

And thus his stroll brought him to the Ascot Hotel just a few blocks from the waterfront. The Ascot was strictly a business man's bunkhouse, the kind of place where only the much-maligned couriers of commerce roost briefly on their missions of peculiar promotion.

Simon entered the small lobby and approached the desk. The plaque above the desk said, without cracking a smile: CLERK ON DUTY: MR. WIMBLETHORPE. Simon Templar, not to be outdone in facial restraint, said without smiling either: ''Mr. Wimblethorpe, I'm looking for a Mr. Matson of St. Louis.''

''Yes, sir,'' said the clerk. ''Mr. Matson was staying here but—''

''My name,'' said the Saint, ''is Sebastian Tombs. I'm a mining engineer from West Texas, and I have just located the richest deposit of bubble gum in the state. I wanted to tell Mr. Matson about it."

"I was trying to tell you," said the clerk, "that Mr. Matson has checked out."

"Oh," said the Saint, a bit blankly. "Well, could you give me his forwarding address?"

The clerk shuffled through his card file.

"Mr. Matson didn't leave an address. A friend of his came in at five o'clock and paid his bill and took his luggage away for him."

Simon stared at him with an odd sort of frown that didn't even see the man in front of him. For the Saint happened to know that Mr. Matson was waiting for a passport from Washington, in order to take ship to foreign parts, and that the passport had not yet come through. Wherefore it seemed strange for Mr. Matson to have left no forwarding address—unless he had suddenly changed his mind about the attractions of foreign travel.

"Who was this friend?" Simon inquired.

"I don't know, Mr.Tombs. If you could stop by or call up in the morning you might be able to find out from Mr. Baker, the day clerk."

"Could you tell me where Mr. Baker lives? I might catch him at home tonight."

Mr. Wimblethorpe was a little hesitant, but he wrote his fellow employee's address on a slip of paper. While he was doing it, the Saint leaned on the desk and half turned to give the lobby a lazy but comprehensive reconnaissance. As he had more or less expected, he discovered a large man in baggy clothes taking inadequate cover behind a potted palm.

"Thank you, Mr. Wimblethorpe," he said as he took the slip. "And now there's just one other thing. In another minute, a Mr. Yard of the police department will be yelling at you to tell him what I was talking to you about. Don't hesitate to confide in him. And if he seems worried about losing me, tell him he'll find me at Mr. Baker's."

He turned and sauntered leisurely away, leaving the bewildered man gaping after him.

He picked up a taxi at the next corner and gave the day clerk's address, and settled back with a cigarette without even bothering to look back and see how the pursuit was doing. There were too many more important things annoying him. A curious presentiment was trying to take shape behind his mind, and he wasn't going to like any part of it.

Mr. Baker happened to be at home, and recalled the incident without difficulty.

"He said that Mr. Matson had decided to move in with him, but he'd had a few too many, so his friend came to fetch his things for him."

"Didn't you think that was a bit funny?"

"Well, yes; but people are always doing funny things. We had a snuff manufacturer once who insisted on filling his room with parrots because he said the old buccaneers always had parrots, and Lafitte used to headquarter here. Then there was the music teacher from Idaho who———"

"About Mr. Matson," Simon interrupted—"what was his friend's name?"

"I'm not sure. I think it was something like Black. But I didn't pay much attention. I knew it was all right, because I'd seen him with Mr. Matson before."

"Can you describe him?"

"Yes. Tall and thin, with sort of gray-blond hair cut very short—"

"And a military bearing and a saber scar on the left cheek?"

"I didn't notice that," Baker said seriously. "Mr. Matson made a lot of friends while he was at the hotel. He was always out for a good time, wanting to find girls and drinking a lot. . . . I hope there isn't any trouble, is there?"

"I hope not. But this guy Black didn't say where Matson was going to move in with him?"

"No. He said Mr. Matson would probably stop in and leave his next address when he sobered up." Baker looked at him anxiously. "Do you have some business connection with Mr. Matson, Mr.—ah———"

"Titwillow," said the Saint. "Sullivan Titwillow. Yes, Mr. Matson and I are partners in an illicit diamond buying syndicate in Rhodesia. I hope I haven't kept you up. . . . Oh, and by the way. Don't jump into bed as soon as I go, because you'll have at least one other caller tonight. His name is Yard, and he is the law in Galveston. Please be nice to him, because I think his feet hurt."

He left the baffled day clerk on the front stoop, and returned to the cab which he had kept waiting.

He was whistling a little tune to himself as he got in, but his gaiety was only in the performance. The presentiment in his mind was growing more solid in spite of trying to stave it off. He knew whatever happened, Fate had taken the play away from him.

"My name, if anybody should ask you, he said to his driver, "is Sugarman Treacle. I am a Canadian in the lumber business. I have sold myself on the job of investigating public vehicles with a view to equipping them with soft pine blocks and coil springs as a substitute for rubber during the present tire shortage. Please feel quite free to discuss my project with any rival researchers who want to talk it over with you.''

''OK, Colonel,'' said the Cabby affably. ''Where to now?''

And then the Saint's presentiment was much too firmly materialized to be brushed off. It was something too outrageously coincidental to have ever been intelligently calculated, and at the same time so absurdly obvious that its only concealment had been that it had been too close to see.

The Saint said: ''Do you know a joint called the Blue Goose?''

''Yeah,'' said the other briefly. ''You wanna go there?''

''I think so.''

''I can get you in. But after that your're on your own.''

Simon raised one eyebrow a millimeter, but he made no comment. He said: ''Do you think you could shake off anybody who might be following us before we get there? My wife has been kind of inquisitive lately, and I'm not asking for trouble.''

''I getcha, pal,'' said the driver sympathetically, and swung his wheel.

The Blue Goose had a sign outside and several cars parked in front; but the door was locked, and the chauffeur had to hammer on it to produce a scrap of face at a barred judas window. There was a line of muttered introduction, and then the door opened. It was all very reminiscent of prohibition, and in fact it was much the same thing, for the state of Texas was still working on the package store system and hadn't legalized any open bars.

''There y' are, doc,'' said the cabby. ''An' take it easy.''

Simon paid his fare and added a generous tip, and went in.

It was apparent as soon as he was inside that at least the adjective in the name was justified. The decorator who had dreamed up the trimmings must have been hipped on Gershwin. Everything was done in a bluish motif—walls and tablecloths and glass and chairs. There was the inevitable from hunger orchestra, with too much brass and a blue tempo, and the inevitable tray-sized dance floor where the inevitable mixture of sailors, soldiers, salesmen, and stews were putting their work in with the inevitable assortment of wild kids who had drunk too much and wise women who hadn't drunk enough. Even the lighting was dim and blue.

The only thing that wasn't clear from the entrance was whether the customer got goosed, or was merely a goose to be there.

Simon crossed to the bar and ordered a Scotch and water, saving himself the trouble of ordering Peter Dawson, which would have been no different anyway in spite of the label on the bottle. He got it with plenty of water in a shimmed glass, and saved his breath on that subject also.

He said to the bartender: "Throgmorton—"

"Call me Joe," said the bartender automatically.

He was a big blond man with big shoulders and a slight paunch, with a square face that smiled quickly and never looked as if the smile went very far inside.

"Joe," said the Saint, "do you know a gal here by the name of Olga Ivanovitch?"

The man paused only infinitesimally in his mopping.

At the Saint's side, a voice with strange intonations in it said: "My name is Olga Ivanovitch."

Simon turned and looked at her.

She sat alone, as certain other women did there, with a pale drink in front of her. He hadn't paid any attention to her when he chose his stool, but he did now. Because she had a real beauty that was the last thing he had expected there—in spite of the traditional requirements of a well-cast mystery.

Beauty of a stately kind that had no connection with the common charms of the other temptations there. A face as pale and aristocratic as that of a grand duchess, but with the more earthy touches of broad forehead and wide cheekbones that betrayed the Slav. Blond hair as lustrous as frozen honey, braided severely around her head in a coiffure that would have been murder to any less classic bone structure. Green eyes that matched her deep-cut green gown. By her birth certificate she might have been any age; but by the calendars of a different chronology she had been old long ago—or ageless.

"Why were you looking for me?" she asked in that voice of unfamiliar harmonies.

The bartender had moved down the counter and was busy with other ministrations.

"I wanted to know," said the Saint steadily, "what you can tell me about a character called Henry Stephen Matson—possibly known to you as Henry Stephens."

3

He had to admire the way she had handled the mask of her face, even with the underlying configuration to help her.

"But why should you ask me?" she protested, with seductive bewilderment.

The Saint put one elbow on the bar and pillowed his chin on the hand attached to it.

"Darling," he said, with every kind of friendliness and good humor and amiable sophistication, "you are an exceedingly beautiful creature. You've probably been told that at least once before, if not ten times an evening. You are now hearing it again—but this time from a connoisseur. Nevertheless, ready as I am to swoon before you, the few fragments of sense that I have left will not let me go along with the gag of treating you as an ingenue."

She laughed; and it was something that he registered in her favor, if only becuase she was probably the only woman in the place who could have unraveled his phraseology enough to know whether to laugh or not.

She said: "Then I won't do?"

"You'll do perfectly," he assured her, "if you'll just take my word for it that I'm strictly in favor of women who are old enough to have had a little experience—and young enough to be interested in a little more. But they also have to be old enough to look at an old tired monument like me and know when I don't want to sit up all night arguing about storks."

It was a delight to watch the play of her shoulders and neck line.

"You're priceless. . . . Would you buy me a drink?"

"I'd love to. I expect to buy the whole joint, a small hunk at a time. If I have a drink too, it should be worth two tables and a dozen chairs."

He signaled the square-faced bartender.

"And a cigarette?" she said.

He shook one out of his pack.

"You've got quite a sense of humor, Mr.—"

"Simon Templar," he said quietly, while the bartender was turning away to select a bottle.

Her perfectly penciled eyebrows rose in perfectly controlled surprise.

"Simon Templar?" she repeated accurately. "Then you must be—. Here, let me show you."

She reached away to remove a newspaper from under the nose of a recuperating Rotarian on the other side of her. After a moment's search, she refolded it at an inside page and spread it in front of the Saint.

Simon saw at a glance that it was the early morning edition of the *Times-Tribune,* and read the item with professional appraisal.

It was not by any means the kind of publicity that he was accustomed to, having been condensed into four paragraphs of a middle column that was overshadowed on one side by the latest pronunciamento of the latest union megaphone, and on the other by a woman in Des Moines who had given birth to triplets in a freight elevator. But it did state quite barrenly that an unidentified burned body had been found on the shore road east of Virginia Point by "Simon Temple, a traveling salesman from Chicago." The police, as usual, had several clues, and were expected to solve the mystery shortly.

That was all; and the Saint wondered why there was no mention of the name that the dying man had given him, or his gasped reference to the Blue Goose, and why Lieutenant Kinglake had been so loath to give out with any leads on the night life of Galveston. Perhaps Kinglake hadn't taken the Saint's question seriously at all. . . .

Simon turned his blue-steel eyes back to Olga Ivanovitch again, and gave her a light for her cigarette. Once more he was aware of her statuesque perfection—and perfect untrustworthiness.

He lifted his newly delivered dilution of anonymous alcohol.

"Yes," he acknowledged modestly, "I am the traveling salesman. But you aren't the farmer's daughter."

"No," she answered without smiling. "My name is Ivanovitch."

"Which means, in Russian, exactly what 'Johnson' would mean here."

"But it's my name."

"And so is 'Templar' mine. But it says 'Temple' in the paper, and yet you placed me at once."

"For that matter," she said, "why did you ask me about—Henry?"

"Because, my sweet, if you'd like the item for your memoirs, your name was on dear Henry's lips just before he passed away."

She shuddered, and closed her eyes for a moment.

"It must have been a gruesome experience for you."

"How did you guess?" he inquired ironically, but she either didn't feel the irony or chose to ignore it.

"If he was still alive when you found him. . . . did he say anything else?"

The Saint smiled with a soft edge of mockery.

"Yes, he said other things. But why should you be so interested?"

"But naturally, because I knew him. He was to have come to my house for cocktails this afternoon."

"Was he really?" said the Saint gently. "You know, I can think of one man in this town who'd be quite excited to hear that."

Her dark gaze was full of innocence.

"You mean Lieutenant Kinglake?" she said calmly. "But he has heard it. He's already talked to me tonight."

Simon took a gulp of his drink.

"And that's how you got my name right?"

"Of course. He asked me about you. But I couldn't tell him anything except what I've read in the papers."

Simon didn't take his eyes off her, although it called for a little effort to hold them there. His first reaction was to feel outstandingly foolish, and he hid it behind a coldly unflinching mask. He hadn't held anything back in his statement—he had no reason to—and so there was no reason why Kinglake shouldn't have been there before him. It was his own fault that he had made a slow start; but that was because he hadn't been receptive to a coincidence that was too pat to be plausible.

He couldn't tell whether her green eyes were laughing at him. He knew that he was laughing at himself, but in a way that had dark and unfunny undertones.

"Tovarich," he said frankly, "suppose we let our back hair down. Or are you too steeped in intrigue to play that way?"

"I could try, if I knew what you meant."

"I'm not one of Kinglake's stooges—in fact, the reverse. I just happened to find Henry. He mumbled a few things to me before he died, and naturally I repeated what I could remember. But on account of my evil reputation, which you know about, I end up by qualifying as a potential suspect. So I'd have to be interested, even if I wasn't just curious. Now it's your move."

Olga Ivanovitch eyed him for a long moment, studying his clean-cut devil-may-care face feature by feature.

She said at last: "Are you very tired of being told that you're a frighteningly handsome man?"

"Very," he said. "And so how well did you know Henry?"

She sipped her drink, and made patterns with the wet print of her glass on the bar.

"Not well at all. I work here as a hostess. I met him here like I meet many people. Like I met you tonight. It was only for a few days. We had a lot of drinks and danced sometimes."

"But he was coming to your house."

"Other people come to my house," she said, with a dispassionate directness that disclaimed innuendo and defied interrogation.

The Saint blew a careful smoke ring to bridge another uncomfortable gap; but this time he bowed to a rare dignity that he had seldom met, and would never have looked for in the Blue Goose.

"Did Henry tell you anything about himself?"

"Nothing much that I can remember. Perhaps I didn't pay enough attention. But men tell you so many things. I think he said he'd been working in a defense plant somehwere—I think it was near St. Louis."

"Did he say anything about where he was going next, or what his plans were?"

"He said he was going to work in another plant in Mexico. He said he was waiting for a ship to Tampico or Vera Cruz."

"What sort of people was he with?"

"All sorts of people. He drank a lot, and he was very generous. He was—what do you call it?—a Good Time Charlie."

"He had plenty of moula?"

"Please?"

"Dough. Cabbage. The blue chips."

"Yes, he seemed to have plenty of money. And he bought plenty of drinks, so of course he made many friends."

"Can you remember any particular guy with a name like Black?"

She wrinkled her brow.

"I don't think so."

"Tall and thin, with sort of gray-blond hair cut very short."

"How can I be sure?" she said helplessly. "I see so many people."

The Saint drew a long breath through his cigarette that was not audibly a sigh, but which did him as much good.

He was very humbly baffled. He knew that Olga Ivanovitch had told him almost as little as he had told her; he knew at the same time that she was holding back some of the things she knew, exactly as he was. He knew that she had probably told him precisely as much as she had told Kinglake. But there was nothing that he could do about it. And he guessed that there had been nothing that Kinglake had been able to do about it, either. She had a good straight story in its place, and you couldn't shake it. It was quite simple and plausible too, except for the omissions. The only thing a police officer could have done about it was to obscure the issue with some synthetic charges about morals and the illegality of the Blue Goose, which Kinglake probably wouldn't stoop to even if the political system would have let him.

And yet the Saint knew to his own satisfaction that Olga Ivanovitch was watching and measuring him just as he was watching and measuring her. And if he was tired of being told how fascinating he was, she was indubitably just as tired of hearing about her exotic harmonies of ivory skin and flaxen hair, and the undeniable allure that they connived at. He took stock of the plain pagan perfection of her lip modeling, and could have done without the illegitimate ideas it gave him.

"In that case," he said, "let's have some more colored water and go on seeing each other."

The small hours of the morning were starting to grow up when he finally admitted that he was licked. By that time he must have bought several gallons of the beige fluid which was sold by the Blue Goose as Scotch, and it made no more impression on Olga Ivanovitch than it had on himself. He decided that if the late Mr. Matson had cut a wide swath there, he must have worked diligently over lubricating his mower before he went in. But Olga Ivanovitch had given out nothing more. She had been gay and she had been glowing, and with her poise and intelligence she had really been a lot of fun; but every time the Saint had tried to cast a line into the conversation she had met him with the same willing straightforward gaze and been so genuinely troubled because she could add nothing to what she had already told.

"So," said the Saint, "I'm going to get some sleep."

They were back at the bar, after some time of sitting at a table through a floor show of special talent but questionable decorum. Simon called for his check, and decided that by that time he should own everything in the place except possibly the ceiling. But he paid it without argument, and added a liberal percentage.

"I'm going to check out too," Olga said. "Would you give me a lift?"

The square-faced bartender gave them his big quick skin-deep smile.

"Come again, folks," he said, and made it sound almost like a pressing invitation.

"Goodnight, Joe," said the Saint, and made it sound almost like a promise.

He took the girl out to a taxi that was providentially waiting outside. It was so providential that he was prepared to believe that some less altruistic agency had brought it there; but that detail didn't distress him. If the ungodly wanted to find out what they would have a chance to find out that night, it wouldn't be hard for them to find it out anyway. When he seriously wanted to exercise them, he would do a job on it.

After they had gone a short way, Olga Ivanovitch said very prosaically: "You owe me ten dollars for the evening."

In identically the same prosaic manner, he peeled a ten-dollar bill out of his pocket and handed it to her.

She put it away in her purse.

After a while she said: "I don't know what you're trying to find in Galveston, Saint, but don't find anything you don't want."

"Why should you care?" he inquired mildly.

He had his answer in something yielding and yearning that was suddenly all over him, holding his mouth with lips that fulfilled all the urgent indications that he had been doing his earnest best to ignore.

It was more or less like that until the cab stopped again on Seawall Boulevard.

"Won't you come in for a nightcap?" she said.

Her face was a white blur in the dark, framed in shadow and slashed with crimson.

"Thanks," he said, "but I have to think of my beauty. So do you."

"You won't have to spend any more."

"I'll see you again," he said.

"Are you sure?"

"Quite sure."

"You'll remember the address?"

"Yes."

He took the taxi back to the Alamo House, and found Detective Yard snoring in a leather armchair in the lobby. It grieved him sincerely to have to interrupt such a blissful orchestration; but these were circumstances in which he felt that noblesse obliged.

"Good evening, Brother Yard," he murmured. "Or, if you want to be literal, good morning. And don't tell me your first name is Scotland, because that would be more than I could bear at this moment. . . . I trust you have enjoyed your siesta."

The field representative of the Kinglake Escort Service had a chance to gather his wits together during the speech. He glared at the Saint with overcooked malignance which was only to have been expected of a man who had been rudely awakened with such a greeting.

"What's your name, anyhow?" he growled indignantly. "Giving your name as Sebastian Tombs at the Ascot! Telling that taxi driver you was Sugarman Treacle!"

"Oh, you tracked him down, did you?" said the Saint interestedly. "So by this time you know that I've been to the Blue Goose. Wait till you check back there and find that I've been masquerading all evening as Shirley Temple."

"What," demanded the detective cholerically, "is the idea of all these names?"

Simon shook a disappointed head at him.

"Tut, Mr. Yard. In fact, a trio of tuts. How can a man with a name like yours ask such kindergarten questions? Don't all suspicious characters use aliases? Isn't it an inviolable rule on page thirty-six of the Detective Manual that a fugitive may change his name but will always stick to his proper initials? I was merely following the regulations to make things easy for you. I could just as well have told any of these people that my name was Montgomery Balmworth Wobblehouse, and loused the hell out of things. The trouble is, you don't appreciate me."

Detective Yard explained in a few vivid phrases just how much he appreciated Simon Templar.

"Thank you," said the Saint gratefully. "And now if you'd like to rest for a while, you can go back to sleep. Or go home to your wife, if she's attractive enough. I promise you that I'm going to bed now and stay there for several hours. And if it'll help you at all, I'll phone you before I go out again."

He stepped into the elevator and departed toward his floor with the depressing conviction that he had added one more notch to his record of failing to Win Friends and Influence Policemen. More practically, he knew that his visit to the Blue Goose was now certain to be misinterpreted.

He consulted the mirror in the elevator about wiping lipstick off his mouth, and hoped that Detective Yard had had as much fun out of noting it as he himself had had out of acquiring it.

4

In spite of the lateness of his bedtime, the Saint was up reasonably early the next morning. He was expecting to be officially annoyed before noon, and he preferred to get some breakfast under his belt first.

Jones met him as he stepped out of the elevator.

"Mawnin', Mistah Templah, sah, Ah been waitin' for you. One of them gennelmen you was askin' about is sittin' in the co'nah of the lobby."

"I know, said the Saint. "His name is Yard. He's worried about me."

The bellboy's grin shrank so abruptly that Simon was sorry for him.

He said: "Never mind Jones. Here's five dollars anyway. Keep up the counter-espionage."

The Negro beamed again.

"Yes, sah, thank you, sah. And there was somethin' else———"

"What?"

"Another gennelman was nosin' around this mawnin', askin' questions about you. He didn't give no name, and Ah never saw him befo'."

"Was he tall and thin, with gray-blond hair cut very short?"

"No, sah. He was kinda short and fat, and he had a red face and red hair and pale gray eyes. Ah dunno nothin' 'bout him, but he wasn't no Galveston policeman."

"Jones," said the Saint, "you have exceeded my fondest hopes. Here is another V for Victory. Carry on."

He went into the coffee shop and ordered tomato juice and ham and eggs. His mind revolved ineffectually while he fortified himself with them.

The late Mr. Matson had considerately bequeathed him three names, besides Olga Ivanovitch. Blatt, Weinbach, Maris. Blatt, who sounded like Black, was probably the tall thin gray-blond one who had been seen at the Ascot. The guy with the red face and red hair was one of the other two. So there was still one without any kind of identification. But even that made very little difference. There was no other detail in their pictures—no links, no attachments, no place to begin looking for them. Unless it was the Blue Goose. But unless they were very stupid or very well covered, they wouldn't be going back there.

He certainly had something on his hands, and all he could do was to wait for something to lead at him.

It did, while he was smoking a cigarette and stretching out his coffee. It looked just like Detective Yard, in a different suit that needed pressing just as badly as the last one.

"If you've finished," Yard said heavily, standing over him, "Lieutenant Kinglake would like to see you at Headquarters."

"That's fine," said the Saint. "I was only waiting for you to issue the invitation, so I could get a ride in a police car or make you pay for the taxi."

They traveled together in an uncongenial aloofness which the Saint's efforts at light badinage did nothing to alleviate.

The atmosphere at Headquarters was very similar; but the Saint continued to hand it to Kinglake for a restraint which he hadn't anticipated from a man with that air of nervous impatience. The Lieutenant looked just as tough and irascible, but he didn't rant and roar.

He let the official authority behind him make the noise for him, and said with impeccable control: "I hear you were getting around quite a bit last night."

"I tried to," said the Saint amiably. "After all, you remember that survey I told you about. If the Blue Goose meant things to you, you should have tipped me off. You could have saved me a lot of dollars and a slight hangover."

"I didn't think it was any of your business," Kinglake said. "And I still want to know why it was."

"Just curiosity," said the Saint. "In spite of anything you may have read, it isn't every day that I pick up a lump of talking charcoal on the highway. So when it says things to me, I can't just forget them."

"And you didn't forget Ivanovitch, either."

"Of course not. She was mentioned too. I'm sure I told you."

"According to Yard, you came home last night with lipstick on you."

"Some people are born gossips. But I think he's just jealous."

Lieutenant Kinglake picked up a pencil from his desk and fondled it as if the idea of breaking it in half intrigued him. Perhaps as an act of symbolism. But he still didn't raise his voice.

"I'm told," he said, "that you asked a lot of questions about this Henry Stephens—only you knew that his name was Matson. And you were asking about him all over town under that name. Now you can explain that to me, or you can take your chance as a material witness."

Simon rounded a cigarette with his forefingers and thumbs.

"You want to ask me questions. Do you mind if I ask a couple? For my own satisfaction. Being as I'm so curious."

Kinglake's chilled gimlet eyes took another exploratory twist into him.

"What are they?"

"What did Quantry get out of his autopsy?"

"No traces of poison or violence—nothing that came through the fire, anyway. The guy burned to death."

"What about the newspaper and the matches?"

"Just a piece of local paper, which anybody could have bought or picked up. No fingerprints."

"And where did you get the idea that I was a salesman?"

"I didn't give out anything about you. if some reporter got that idea, he got it. I'm not paid to be your press agent." Kinglake was at the full extension of his precarious control. "Now you answer my question before we go any further."

The Saint lighted his cigarette and used it to mark off a paragraph.

"The deceased's name," he said, "was Henry Stephen Matson. Until recently, he was a foreman at the Quenco plant near St. Louis. You may remember that Hobart Quennel got into a lot of trouble a while ago, on account of some fancy finagling with synthetic rubber—and mostly because of me. But that hasn't anything to do with it. The Quenco plants are now being run by the government, and the one outside St. Louis is now making a lot of soups that go bang and annoy the enemy. Matson pulled out a while ago, and came here. He used his real name at the Ascot, because he'd applied for a passport to Mexico and he wanted to get it. But in his social life he called himself Henry Stephens, because he didn't want to die."

"How do you know all this?" Kinglake rapped at him. "And why didn't you—"

"I didn't tell you yesterday, because I didn't know," said the Saint tiredly. "The thing I found on the road said it was Henry Stephens, and it was all too obvious to bother me. So I was too smart to be sensible. It wasn't until I started hunting for Matson that it dawned on me that coincidences are still possible."

"Well, why were you hunting for Matson?"

The Saint pondered about that one.

"Because," he said, "a Kiwanis convention just picked him as Mr. Atlantic Monthly of 1944. So in the interests of this survey of mine I wanted to get his reaction to the Galveston standards of strip-teasing. Now, the grade of g-string at the Blue Goose . . . "

There had to be a breaking point to Detective Yard's self-control, and it was bound to be lower than Kinglake's. Besides, Mr. Yard's feet had endured more.

He leaned down weightily on the Saint's shoulder.

"Listen, funny man," he said unoriginally, "how would you like to get poked right in the kisser?"

"Pipe down," Kinglake snarled; and it was an order.

But he went on glaring at the Saint, and for the first time his nervous impatience seemed to be more nervous than impatient. Simon was irresistibly reminded of his own efforts to cover confusion with a poker pan, only the night before.

"Let me tell you something, Templar," Kinglake said dogmatically. "We've made our own investigations; and no matter what you think, our opinion is that Stephens, or Matson, committed suicide by pouring gasoline on himself and setting himself alight."

It took a great deal to shatter the Saint's composure, but that was great enough. Simon stared at the Lieutenant in a state of sheer incredulity that even took his mind off the crude conventional ponderance of Detective Yard.

"Let me get this straight," he said slowly. "Are you going to try and work off Henry as a suicide?"

Lieutenant Kinglake's hard face, if anything, grew harder.

"On all the evidence, that's what it looks like. And I'm not going to make a monkey out of myself to get you some headlines. I told you, I don't want any trouble in this town."

"So what're you gonna do about it?" demanded Detective Yard, with an aptness which he must have learned from the movies.

Simon didn't even notice him.

"Evidence my back door," he said derisively. "So this guy who was so reckless with his gas ration was careful enough to swallow the flask he carried it in so it could eventually be recovered for the scrap drive."

"We just didn't happen to find the container yesterday. But if we search again, we may find it."

"Probably the Coke bottle that Scotland Yard takes out with him to keep his brain watered."

"One more crack like that outa you," Yard said truculently, "an' I'll—"

"You might just tell me this, Kinglake," said the Saint bitingly. "Is this your idea of a brilliant trick to trap the killers, or are you just a hick cop after all? The only thing you've left out is the standard suicide note. Or have you got that up your sleeve too?"

The Lieutenant's thin lips tightened, and his battleship jaw stuck out another half inch. He had all the chip-on-the-shoulder characteristics of a man in the wrong who wouldn't admit it while there was a punch left in him; yet he met the Saint's half jeering and half furious gaze so steadily as to almost start Simon out of countenance.

"Get this, Templar," Kinglake said coldly. "We think Stephens committed suicide—"

"In the most painful way he could think of—"

"He must have been nuts. But I've met nuts before."

"And even while he was dying he tried to make up a story—"

"He was out of his mind. He must have been, after a burning like that. You haven't been burned yet, so you use your head. And if you want to keep your nose clean, you will forget the whole thing—or you may find yourself with your can in the can. Do I make myself clear?"

The Saint met his eyes lengthily.

"If you were rolled flat, you could rent yourself out as a window," he said. "Instead of which, you have the colossal crust to sit there and spew that pap at me even after I've told you that I know more about Matson than you did."

"Yes," was all Kinglake replied.

"You aren't even going to make an issue out of the Blue Goose and my going there."

"No," Kinglake said curtly.

For once in his life, Simon Templar was frankly flabbergasted. He searched the shreds of his brain for a better word, and couldn't find one. Theories whirled through his head; but they were too fast and fantastic to be coordinated while he had to think on his feet.

Which was where he was thinking, since Kinglake's impenetrable stonewall had brought him up there, shrugging off Detective Yard's clumsy physical obstruction as if it had been a feather which had accidentally drifted onto him out of a cloud.

"I've met an astonishing variety of cops in my time," he remarked absorbently; "but you, chum, are an entirely new species. You don't even attempt to give me the guileless runaround or the genteel brush-off. . . . Have you said your last word on the subject?"

"Yes," snapped the Lieutenant. "Now will you kindly get the hell out of here and go on with the survey you were talking about?"

"I will," retorted the Saint. "And don't blame me if you find G-men in your G-string."

He stalked out of there with another unique feeling which was the precise antithesis of the sensation he had had when a certain log moved on the shore road. His blood had run cold then. Now it was boiling.

He had had to cope with local politics and obstruction before, in different guises and for different reasons. But this game was something else. And in that swift invigorating anger, the Saint knew just what he was going to do about it.

Kinglake had taunted him about publicity. Well, the Saint didn't need to hire any press agents. . . . He had seen himself waiting and hoping for a lead; but he could always ask for one. He had used newspapers before, in sundry ways, when he wanted to lead with his chin and invite the ungodly to step up and introduce themselves while they looked at it.

Almost literally without looking to left or right, he followed Center Street toward the waterfront on the north or channel side of the city. He walked into the building that housed the *Times-Tribune,* and worked his way doggedly through the trained interference until he stood in front of the city editor's desk.

"My name is Simon Templar," he said for about the fourteenth time. "If you spelt me right, I'd be the traveling salesman who found that botched biscuit on the shore road yesterday. I want to cover that case for you; and all I want out of you is a by-line."

"The editor scrutinized him quite clinically.

"Our police reporter must have messed up his spelling," he said. "It's funny—the name started to ring a bell when I read it. . . . so you're the Saint. But what are you selling?"

"I'm selling you your lead story for the afternoon edition," said the Saint. "I may be nuts, but I'm still news. Now shall we play gin rummy, or will you lend me a typewriter and stop the press?"

5

If only to be different in one more way from most typical men of action, Simon Templar was perfectly happy with words and paper. He could play just as fluently on the legitimate or L.C. Smith form of typewriter as he could on the well-known Thompson variety, and he handled both of them in much the same way. The keys rattled under his fingers like gunfire, and his choice of words had the impact of bullets. He worked at white heat, while his wrath still had all its initial impetus.

He told his own full story of the finding of "Henry Stephens," and every word that the dying man had said, together with a general summary of the other facts as he knew them, in a fusillade of hardboiled sinewy prose that would have qualified him for a job on the toughest tabloid in the country. Then he squared off to a fresh sheet of paper and went into his second movement. He wrote:

> It now grieves me to have to break it to all you nice people that these sensitive nostrils, which long ago became extraordinarily appreciative of certain characteristic smells, have caught wind of the grand inspiration that this guy committed suicide, which Lieutenant Kinglake was feeling out this morning.
>
> Now I am in here with quite a different story, and it has got to be known that Bulldog Templar does not brush off that easy.
>
> I am remembering a legend, true or not, that once when S.S. Van Dine happened to be close to the scene of another murder, it was suggested by some newspaper that he might cooperate with the gendarmerie and help run the villain to earth in the best Philo Vance manner; whereupon Mr. Van Dine placed himself in the center of four wheels and trod on the loud pedal so rapidly that his shadow had to be sent after him by express.
>
> We Templars are made of sterner stuff. Just give us a chance to stick our neck out, and a giraffe is not even in our league.

So we are going to sign our name to this invitation to all of you voting citizens to take a good long look at the suicidal Mr. Stephens.

He was, we observe, the stern and melancholy type which can get along without life anyway. He proved that by the way he spent his last days here, drinking all night in speakeasies and dancing with the girls. He didn't go much for fun of any kind, which is said to soften people up. He was strictly an ascetic; and when he knocked himself off he was still going to be tough. He wouldn't jump out of a window, or take an overdose of sleeping tablets, or put a gun in his ear and listen to see if it was loaded. He deliberately picked the most painful way that a man can die.

He figured he had some suffering coming to him. After all, he wasn't broke, for instance, which has been known to make some people so unhappy that they have let air into their tonsils with a sharp knife. He seemed to have had plenty of spending money. So he was going to have his hard times on his deathbed instead of before.

He even went 20 miles out of town to do it, walking all the way, since the street cars don't go there, so that he'd have lots of time to look forward to it and enjoy the prospect.

He was a consistent guy, too. He didn't mean to be selfish about his suffering. He wanted somebody else to have some of it too. So after he'd taken his gasoline shower, and before he struck the match, he carefully chewed up and ate the bottle he'd brought it in, so that Lieutenant Kinglake could have something to worry about. Not knowing, of course, that Lieutenant Kinglake wouldn't worry about a little thing like that at all.

It always gives us Templars a great respect for the benignness of Providence to observe how frequently a hard-pressed police department, facing a nervous breakdown before the task of breaking a really difficult case, has been saved in the nick of time by discovering that there never was a murder after all. It makes us feel pretty good to think that cops are practically people, and God takes care of them as well as Pearl White.

The Saint was beginning to enjoy himself by then. He lighted a cigarette and gazed at the ceiling for a while, balancing his ideas for the finale. Then he went on when he was ready.

But let's pretend that we don't have the clear and penetrating vision of Lieutenant Kinglake. Let's just pretend that we are too dumb to believe that a man in the dying agonies of third-degree burns cooked up that wonderful story about three men who did it to him, just because he was too modest to want to take the credit. Let's pretend there might really have been three other men.

Men with names. Blatt, Weinbach, Maris. A nice trio of Herrenvolk.

Then we might go along with the gag and say, suppose Henry

Stephen Matson was a traitor. Suppose he'd gotten into some sabotage organization, and he'd been given a job to do in this explosives plant in Missouri. Suppose he'd even drawn payment in advance—just to account for what he was using for dough in Galveston.

Then suppose he welshed on the job—either from an attack of cold feet or a relapse of patriotism. He knew that the heat was on. He couldn't stay in this country, because they might have turned him in to the FBI. If they didn't do anything worse. He took it on the lam for here, hoping to get a passport, and hoping he'd shaken off his pals. But they were too good for him. They tracked him down, struck up an acquaintance with him, and gave him what he had coming. In a very nasty way, just to discourage imitators.

That's my fairy tale. And I like it.

Blatt, Weinbach, Maris. I have a description of two of those men, and I've got my own good ideas about the third. And I am hereby announcing that I shall now have to get them for you myself, since we must not disturb Lieutenant Kinglake in his august meditations.

The city editor read it all through without a change of expression. Then he tapped the page with his forefinger and said: "It's an ingenious theory, but what's your basis for it?"

"Nothing but logic, which is all you can say for any theory. The facts are there. If you can do better with them, you can join Kinglake's club."

"This last statement of yours, about the three men—is that a fact?"

"Some of it. But the main point of it is that that's what you pay me with. If I can make them believe that I know more than I do, I may scare them into making some serious mistakes. That's why I'm making you a present of all the rest of that luscious literature."

The editor pulled at his underlip. He was a pear-shaped man with a long forbidding face that never smiled even when his eyes twinkled.

"It's good copy, anyway, so I'll print it," he said. "But don't blame me if you're the next human torch. Or if Kinglake has you brought in again and beats hell out of you."

"On the contrary, you're my insurance against that," said the Saint. "Going my own way, I might have had a lot more trouble with Kinglake at any moment. Now, he won't dare to do anything funny, because it would look as if he was scared of me."

"Kinglake's a good officer. He wouldn't do a thing like this unless there was a lot of pressure on him."

Simon recalled the Lieutenant's tight-lipped curtness, his harried and almost defensive belligerence.

"Maybe there was," he said. "But whose was it?"

The editor put his fingertips together.

"Galveston," he said, "has what is now called the commission form of government. Commissioner Number One—what other cities would call the mayor—is coming up for reelection soon. He appoints the Chief of Police. The Chief controls such men as Lieutenant Kinglake. Nobody wants any blemish on the record of the Police Department at this time. I'm quite confident that neither the Commissioner nor the Chief of Police is mixed up in anything crooked. It's just best for everybody concerned to let sleeping dogs—in this case, dead dogs—lie."

"And that is perfectly jake with you."

"The *Times-Tribune,* Mr. Templar, unlike yourself, is not addicted to sticking its neck out. We are not a political organ; and if we did start a crusade, it would not be on the basis of this one sensational but insignificant killing. But we do try to print the whole truth, as you'll see by the fact that I'm ready to use your article."

"Then you still haven't told me where the pressure would come from."

The city editor's long equine face grew even more absorbed in the contemplation of his matched fingers.

"As a stranger in town, Mr. Templar, it may surprise you to know that some of our most influential citizens sometimes go to the Blue Goose for their—er—relaxation. The Blue Goose is one of the leads in this story as you have it. So while none of these people, from the Commissioner down, might want to be a party to hushing up a crime, you can see that they might not be keen on too comprehensive an investigation of the Blue Goose. So that the management of the Blue Goose, which naturally doesn't want the spot involved in a murder mystery, might find a lot of sympathetic ears if they were pointing out the advantages of forgetting the whole thing. I shall not allow you to print that in your next article, but it might help you personally."

"It might," said the Saint. "And thank you."

He spent several hours after that on a conscientious job of verifying his background material that would have amazed some people who thought of him as a sort of intuitive comet, blazing with pyrotechnic violence and brilliance to ends and solutions that were only indicated to him by a guardian angel with a lot of spare time and an incurable weakness for piloting irresponsible characters. His research involved visits to various public places, and ingenuous conversations with a large number of total strangers, each of them a cameo of personality projection that would have left Dale Carnegie egg-bound with awe. But the net yield was negatively and concisely nothing.

The Commissioner appeared to be a bona fide native of Galveston who had made his money in sulfur and still controlled an important business. There seemed to be no particularly musty bones in his family skeleton. He came of Texas stock from away back, and he was set solid with business and family ties.

The sheriff of the county came out with the same sort of background and clean bill of health. Nobody seemed to know much about the type of deputies in his office, but there had never been any scandal about his administration. He was frankly a member of the same political machine as the Commissioner.

Nor were there any crevices in the armor of the Chief of Police. Kinglake was not too popular, very likely because of his personalty; but his record was good. Quantry was negligible.

Which meant that the *Times-Tribune* editor's analysis stood unshaken, and there was no evidence to brand the official eagerness to turn a blind eye on a murder as anything but a local issue of political expediency.

Except for the one thin thread that curled into a question mark and asked who it was at the Blue Goose who had turned the heat on even a complaisant political machine.

Olga Ivanovitch?

The Saint knew she was beautiful, he thought she was clever, and he suspected that she was dangerous. But how clever and how dangerous? He could learn nothing about her that sounded at all important. If she had any political connections, they weren't common gossip. But he knew that she had a definite place in the picture.

He made another call at the Ascot Hotel; but Mr. Baker hadn't remembered anymore overnight, and could add nothing to his information about Blatt or Black.

"But I'm sure, Mr. Titwillow, he wasn't a local man. I've been here so long that I think I know all the important people in Galveston by sight."

Blatt, Weinbach, Maris.

The names made no impression on anyone to whom he mentioned them. But he did find some representatives of their clans in the telephone directory, and studiously checked on each of them. Each of them had the kind of unimpeachable clearance that it would have been simply a waste of time to investigate any further.

It was a long and strenuous day, and dusk was creeping over the city as Simon headed back toward the Alamo House. He bought an evening paper and a bottle of Peter Dawson on the way.

The *Times-Tribune* carried his article on the front page, unabridged and unexpurgated, but with a box that gave a brief explanation of the Saint's background for the benefit of the ignorant, and stated that Mr. Templar's theories were his own and did not necessarily represent the editorial opinion of the *Times-Tribune*.

There was special justification for that in a short column which ran alongside his, which reported succinctly that at an inquest held that afternoon the coroner's jury had brought in a verdict of suicide.

Simon Templar crushed the newspaper in his hand with a grip that almost reverted it to its original pulp, and said several things which even our freedom of the press will not allow us to print.

So Kinglake hadn't backed down. He had gone right out from their interview and helped to railroad that fantastic verdict through. Maybe he had a wife and children and just wanted to go on feeding them; but he had done it.

In his room at the Alamo House, Simon sent for ice and opened his bottle, and tried to simmer down again over a highball.

He only had one other clue to think about, and that was in another snatch of words that the dying man had managed to get out. He could hear them just as clearly now as when they had been dragged hoarsely through the charred tortured lips.

"Ostrich-skin—leather case—in gladstone lining . . . Get case—and send . . . send . . ."

Send where?

And why?

And anyhow, Black or Blatt had the gladstone now.

One of three practical killers, probably strangers to Galveston themselves, possibly from Chicago (he remembered the 606 Club match booklet) who had trailed Matson on their mission of vengeance, carried out the assignment, and vanished.

He had another drink, and didn't get any further on that one.

It was later still when the telephone rang.

He had an electric moment as he went to answer it. He knew that the call had to have some bearing on the case, since he had no personal friends in Galveston; but the exquisite suspense was in wondering—who? A soft-pedaling politician? A raging Kinglake? Or the first nibble at his bait?

It was a voice that he knew, even if he had not known it long—a deep musical voice with appealing foreign inflections.

"You aren't only handsome, but you have talent," she said. "Why didn't you tell me you were a writer too?"

"My union doesn't allow it."

"Am I going to see you again? I'd like to very much."

He reached for a cigarette.

"I'm flattered. But I've only just paid one installment on the Blue Goose."

"I don't have to be there till ten. What are you doing for dinner?"

"Eating with you," he said with abrupt decision. "I'll meet you in the lobby here at eight o'clock."

He hung up, and still wondered which category that belonged in. But anything would be better than waiting in idleness.

He washed and freshened himself and changed his shirt, and went downstairs a little before eight. There was a note in his box when he turned in his key.

"It was delivered by hand just a few minutes ago," said the clerk.

Simon slit open the envelope. The letter inside was written in pencil on a cheap lined paper of an uncommon but typical pattern. There was no address; but Simon knew what that would be even without the clues in the context.

> Dear Mr. Templar,
>
> I just read your piece in the paper, and I can tell you sure have got it over these dumb bastards. I am getting a chap to take this out for me. I can tell you a lot more about this case and I will tell you if you can fix it to talk to me alone. You are right all the way and I can prove it, but I will not talk to anyone except you. After that you can do what you like with what I tell you but I will not give these dumb cops anything.
>
> Yours truly,
> NICK VASHCETTI

Simon looked up from the note because someone was practically leaning on him and breathing in his face.

"Got a love letter?" asked Detective Yard. "Or is it fan mail?"

Simon put the letter in his pocket.

"Yes," he said. "But not for you. In fact I hate to tell you, but my admirer calls you a dumb bastard."

The detective's face swelled as if he were being strangled.

"Listen, you," he got out. "One of these days———"

"You're going to forget your orders and be unkind to me," said the Saint. "So I'll be kind to you while I can. In a few minutes I'll be going out to dinner. I'll try to pick a restaurant where they'll let you in. And if I start to leave before you've finished, just yell at me and I'll wait for you."

Simon thought afterwards that it was criminal negligence on his part that he was so seduced by the frustration of Detective Yard that he didn't even notice the thin gray-blond man and the fat red-haired man who occupied chairs in the farther reaches of the lobby. But there was an excuse for him; because while he had heard their names and heard their sketchy descriptions, he had never before laid eyes on Johan Blatt and Fritzie Weinbach.

6

He went back up to his room and phoned the city desk of the *Times-Tribune*.

''Could you work it for me to have a private chat with a prisoner in the City Jail?''

''It might be done,'' said the editor cautiously, ''if nobody knew it was you. Why—have you had a bite?''

''I hope so,'' said the Saint. ''The guy's name is Nick Vaschetti.'' He spelt it out. ''He says he won't talk to anybody but me; but maybe the jail doesn't have to know me. See what you can do, and I'll call you back in about an hour.''

He sat on the bed in thought for a minute or two, and then he picked up the telephone again and asked for Washington. He hardly had to wait at all, for although the hotel operator didn't know it the number he asked for was its own automatic priority through all long distance exchanges.

''Hamilton,'' said the phone. ''I hear you're a newspaper man now.''

''In self-defense,'' said the Saint. ''If you don't like it, I can pack up. I never asked for this job, anyway.''

''I only hope you're getting a good salary to credit against your expense account.''

The Saint grinned.

''On the contrary, you'll probably be stuck for my union dues. . . . Listen, Ham: I'd rather lay it in your lap, but I think I'd better bother you. These three men—''

''Blatt, Weinbach,and Maris?''

''Your carrier pigeons travel fast.''

''They have to. Is there anything else on them?''

Simon gave him the two rough descriptions.

''There's a good chance,''he said, ''that they may have come on from Chicago. But that's almost a guess. Anyway, try it.''

"You never want much, do you?"

"I don't like you to feel left out."

"You're not leaving out the beautiful swooning siren, of course."

"In this case, she's a blond."

"You must like variety," Hamilton sighed. "How much longer are you expecting to take?"

"Depending on what you can dig up about the Three Neros, and what breaks tonight," said the Saint, "maybe not long. Don't go to bed too early, anyhow."

Which left him laughing inwardly at the breathtaking dimensions of his own bravado. And yet it has already been recorded in many of these chronicles that some of the Saint's tensest climaxes had often been brewing when those almost prophetic undercurrents of swashbuckling extravagance danced in his arteries. . . .

Olga Ivanovitch was waiting in the lobby when he came downstairs again.

"I'm sorry," he said. "There was a letter I had to answer."

"*Nitchevo,*" she said in her low warm memorable voice. "I was late myself, and we have plenty of time."

He admitted to himself after he saw her that he had had some belated misgivings about the rendezvous. The lighting in the lobby of the Alamo House was a different proposition from the blue dimness of the Blue Goose: she might have looked tired and coarsened, or she might have been overdressed and overpainted into a cheap travesty of charm. But she was none of those things. Her skin was so clear and fresh that she actually looked younger than he remembered her. She wore a long dress; but the décolletage was chastely pinned together, and she wore an inappropriate light camelhair polo coat over it that gave her a kind of careless apologetic swagger. She looked like a woman that any grown man would be a little excited to take anywhere.

"I've got a car," he said. "We can take it if you can direct me."

"Let me drive you, and I'll promise you a good dinner."

He let her drive, and sat beside her in alert relaxation. This could have been the simplest kind of trap; but if it was, it was what he had asked for, and he was ready for it. He had checked the gun in his shoulder holster once more before he last left his room, and the slim two-edged knife in the sheath strapped to his right calf was almost as deadly a weapon in his hands—and even less easy to detect. It nested down under his sock with hardly a bulge, but it was accessible from any sitting or reclining position by the most innocent motion of hitching up his trouser cuff to scratch the side of his knee.

Simon Templar was even inclined to feel cheated when the drive ended without incident.

She steered him into a darkened bistro near the Gulf shore with bare wooden booths and marble-topped tables and sawdust on the floor.

"You have eaten *bouillabaisse* in Marseilles," she said, "and perhaps in New Orleans. Now you will try this, and you will not be too disappointed."

The place was bleakly bright inside, and it was busy with people who looked ordinary but sober and harmless. Simon decided that it would be as safe as anything in his life ever could be to loosen up for the length of dinner.

"What made you call me?" he asked bluntly.

He had always felt her simple candor at the most cryptic of complexities.

"Why shouldn't I?" she returned. "I wanted to see you. And you turn out to be such an unusual kind of traveling salesman."

"There are so few things you can sell these days, a guy has to have a side line."

"You write very cleverly. I enjoyed your story. But when you were asking me questions, you weren't being honest with me."

"I told you everything I could."

"And I still told you everything I knew. Why do you think I was—what do you call it—holding out on you?"

"I told you everything I know, tovarich. Even if you did place me for a salesman."

"You didn't ask me about Blatt, Weinbach, and Maris."

"Only about Blatt."

He had to say that, but she could still make him feel wrong. Her air of straightforwardness was so unwavering that it turned the interrogator into the suspect. He had tried every device and approach in a rather fabulous repertoire the night before, and hadn't even scratched the surface of her. He knew exactly why even Lieutenant Kinglake might have left her alone, without any political pressure. Take her into court, and she could have made any public prosecutor feel that he was the prisoner who was being tried. It was the most flawlessly consistent stonewall act that Simon Templar had ever seen.

"You could have asked me about the others," she said. "If I could have told you anything, I would have. I'd like to help you."

"What could you have told me?"

"Nothing."

At least she had told him the truth about the *bouillabaisse*. He gave himself up to that consolation with fearful restraint.

It was half an hour later when he made one more attempt to drag the conversation back from the delightful flights of nothingness into which she was able to lead it so adroitly.

"Aside from my beautiful profile and my great literary gifts," he said, "I'd still like to know what made you want to see me again."

"I wanted you to pay for my dinner," she said seriously. "And I do like you—very much."

He remembered the way she had kissed him at her door, and forced himself to consider that if he had gone for that he would probably have been going for something as calculated as her simplicity.

"It couldn't have been, by any chance, because you wanted to find out if I knew anymore?"

"But why should I? I am not a detective. Do I keep asking you questions?" She was wide open and disarming. "No, I am just guilty of liking you. If you wanted to tell me things, I would listen. You see, my dear, I have that Russian feeling which you would think stupid or—corny: that a woman should be the slave of a man she admires. I am fascinated by you. So I must be interested in what you are doing. That is all."

The Saint's teeth gripped together while he smiled.

"Then, sweetheart, you'll be interested to know that I'm going to make an important phone call, if you'll excuse me a minute."

He went to a coin phone at the rear of the restaurant and called the *Times-Tribune* again.

"It's all set," said the flat voice of the city editor. "Any time you want to pick me up."

"I'm just finishing dinner," said the Saint grimly. "If nothing happens on the way, I'll pick you up within thirty minutes."

He went back to the table, and found Olga placidly powdering her perfect nose.

"I hate to break this up," he said, "but I have a short call to make; and I have to deliver you back to the Blue Goose in time to catch the next influx of salesmen."

"Whatever you like," she replied calmly. "I don't have to be exactly on time though, so you do whatever you want to do."

It was impossible to stir her even with virtual insult.

But he drove the Ford himself this time, knowing that it could have seemed a much better moment for ambush than before dinner. Yet even then nothing happened, in such a way that the mere failure of anything to happen was a subtle rebuke in exactly the same key as all her refusals to rise to his varied provocations.

His sleepless sense of direction enabled him to drive without a mistake to the offices of the *Times-Tribune;* and he arrived there with no more alarm than a slight stiffness in muscles which had been poised too long on an uncertain fuse. But then, the egregious efficiency of Detective Yard had still conspired to blind him to the shift of concealing newspapers which had punctuated his exit from the Alamo House.

''I have to complain to my editor about the size of my headlines,'' he said. ''It's a union rule. Do you mind waiting a little while?''

''Of course not,'' she said with that sublime and demoralizing pliability. ''Waiting is an old Russian pastime.''

Simon went up to the editorial floor, and this time he swept through the interceptor command without interference, powered by the certainty of his route and destination.

The city editor saw him, and took his feet off the desk and crammed a discolored and shapeless panama on to the small end of his pear-shaped head.

''I'll have to go with you myself,'' he explained. ''Not that I think you'd sell out to the UP, but it's the only way I could fix it. Let me do the talking, and you can take over when we get your man.''

''What's he in for?''

''Passing a rubber check at his hotel. I hope you have some idea what strings I had to pull to arrange this for you.''

Simon handed him the note that had been delivered to the Alamo House. The editor read it while they waited for the elevator.

''Smuggled out, eh? . . . Well, it might come to something.''

''Is there a back alley way out of the building?''

''When I was a copy boy here, we used to know one. I haven't noticed the building being altered since.'' The city editor turned his shrewd sphinxlike face toward Simon with only the glitter of his eyes for a clue to his expression. ''Are we still expecting something to happen?''

''I hope, yes and no,'' said the Saint tersely. ''I left Olga in my car outside, for a front and a cover. I'm hoping she's either fooled herself or she'll fool somebody else.''

He knew that he had seldom been so vulnerable, but he never guessed how that flaw in his guard was to mature. He just felt sure that a prisoner in the City Jail couldn't be the trigger of any of the potential traps that he was waiting to recognize. Provided he took the obvious precautions, like leaving Olga Ivanovitch in his car outside the newspaper building while he slipped out through a back alley . . .

The *Times-Tribune* man's dry bulbous presence was a key that bypassed tired clerks and opened clanging iron doors, and exacted obedience from soured disinterested jailers, and led them eventually into a small barren and discouraging office room with barred windows where they waited through a short echoing silence until the door opened again to admit Mr. Vaschetti with a turnkey behind him.

The door closed again, leaving the turnkey outside; and Mr. Vaschetti's darting black eyes switched over the city editor's somnolent self-effacement and made one of their touch landings on the Saint.

"You're Templar," he stated. "But I said this had to be private."

"This is Mr. Beetlespats of the *Times-Tribune,*" said the Saint inventively. "He published the article you read, and he organized this meeting. But we can pretend he isn't here. Just tell me what you've got on your mind."

Vaschetti's eyes whirled around the room like small dark bugs exploring the intricacies of a candelabra.

"I can tell you," he said, "you were dead right about Matson. I've been a courier for the Bund for a long time. I took a letter to Matson in St. Louis, and I brought a letter to your Mr. Blatt and other people in Galveston too."

7

He was a rather small man, spare and wiry, with the heavy eyebrows and hollow cheeks which so often seem to go together. His hair needed combing and his chin needed scraping. His clothes were neither good nor bad, but they were rumpled and soiled as if they had been slept in, which they doubtless had.

The Saint gave him a cigarette and said: "I don't think there are any dictographs planted here, so just keep talking. What made you write to me?"

"Because I don't like cops. I see where you've made suckers out of the cops plenty of times, and I'd like to see you do it again. Especially to those sons of bitches who threw me in here."

"You did pass a bum check, didn't you?" Simon mentioned.

"Yeah, but only because I had to, because Blatt didn't come through with my dough and I was broke. I wouldn't have squawked just for that, though. I've taken raps before. I've stood for a lot of things in my time, but I don't want any part of this." Vaschetti puffed at his cigarette shakily, and moved about the room with short jerky strides. "Not murder. No, sir. I don't want to sit in the hot seat, or dance on the end of a rope, or whatever they do to you in this state."

Simon kindled a cigarette for himself, and propped himself on the window sill.

"Why should anyone do things like that to you? Or were you one of the three fire-bugs?"

"No, sir. But that Kinglake might find out any time that I'd seen Blatt and been asking for him at the Blue Goose, and what chance would I have then? I don't want Blatt gunning for me either, and I guess he might be if he thought I might put the finger on him. I'd rather squeal first, and then if they know it's too late to shut my mouth maybe they won't bother with me."

"I see your point," said the Saint thoughtfully. "Suppose you sit down and tell me about your life as a courier."

Vaschetti attempted a laugh that didn't come off, licked his lips nervously, and sat down on a creaky chair.

"I met Fritz Kuhn when I was doing time in Dannemora. We got on pretty well, and he said if I wanted to make some money when I got out I should see him. Well, I did. I got this job carrying packages from place to place."

"How did that work?"

"Well, for instance, I'd have a package to deliver to Mr. Smith at the Station Hotel in Baltimore. I'd go there and ask for him. Maybe he'd be out of town. I'd hang around until he showed up—sometimes I'd have to wait for a week and more. Then I'd give Smith the package; and he'd pay me my dough and my expenses, and maybe give me another package to take to Mr. Robinson at MacFarland's Grill in Miami. Anytime there wasn't anything more for me, I'd go back to Jersey and start again."

"These Smiths and Robinsons weren't anything to do with the joints you met them in?"

"Mostly not. I'd just ask a bartender if he knew Mr. Smith, and he'd point out Mr. Smith. Or sometimes I'd be hanging around and Mr. Robinson would come in and say he was Robinson and had anyone been asking for him."

"How much did you get for this?"

"Seventy-five a week and all my expenses."

"You got paid by the Smiths and Robinsons as you went along."

"Yeah."

"You knew that this was obviously connected with something illegal."

Vaschetti licked his lips again and nodded.

''Sure, sure. It had to be things they didn't want to send through the mail, or they didn't want to chance having opened by the wrong person.''

''You knew it was more than that. You knew it was for the Bund, and so it was probably no good for this country.''

''What the hell? I'm an Italian, and I got brothers in Italy. And I never did like the goddam British. This was before the war got here. So what?''

''So you still went on after Pearl Harbor.''

Vaschetti swallowed, and his eyes took another of those fluttering whirls around the room.

''Yeah, I went on. I was in it then, and it didn't seem to make much difference. Not at first. Besides, I still thought Roosevelt and the Jews were getting us in. I was scared, too. I was scared what the Axis people her might do to me if I tried to quit. But I got a lot more curious.''

''So—?''

''So I started opening these packages. I was taking one to Schenectady at the time. I steamed it open, and inside there was four smaller envelopes addressed to people in Schenectady. But they had wax seals on them with swastikas and things, and I was afraid it might show if I tried to open them. So I put them back in the big envelope and delivered it like I was told to. Sometimes I had big parcels to carry, but I didn't dare monkey with them. I still had to eat, and I didn't want no trouble either. . . . But then I got more scared of the FBI and what'd happen to me if I got caught. Now there's this murder, and I'm through. I been a crook all my life, but I don't want no federal raps and I don't want to go to the chair.''

Simon's sapphire blue eyes studied him dispassionately through a slowly rising veil of smoke. There was nothing much to question or decipher about the psychology of Signor Vaschetti—or not about those facets which held any interest for the Saint. It was really nothing but a microcosmic outline of Signor Mussolini. He was just a small-time goon who had climbed on to a promising bandwagon, and now that the road ahead looked bumpy he was anxious to climb off.

There could hardly be any doubt that he was telling the truth—he was too plainly preoccupied with the integrity of his own skin to have had much energy to spare on embroidery or invention.

''It's a fine story,'' said the Saint lackadaisically. ''But where does it get us with Matson?''

''Like you wrote in the paper, he must have been paid to do some sagotage. He didn't do it, but he kept the money and took a powder. But you can't run out on that outfit. That's why I'm talking to you. They traced him here and gave him the business.''

''That *is* about how I doped it out,'' Simon said with thistledown satire. ''But what are you adding besides the applause?''

''I'm telling you, I took one of those letters to Matson in St. Louis. That proves he was being paid by the Germans, and that proves you're right and Kinglake is a horse's—''

''But you made this delivery in St. Louis. Why are you here in Galveston now?''

Vaschetti sucked on the stub of his cigarette, and dropped it on the floor and trod on it.

''That's on account of Blatt. I came here from El Paso two weeks ago with a package to give to Blatt at the Blue Goose. I didn't know Matson was coming here. I didn't know anything about Matson, except he told me he was working for Quenco. Blatt only paid me up to date and kept me hanging around waiting for some letters he said he'd be sending out. I ran up a pretty big bill at the hotel, and Blatt never came around and I couldn't reach him. That's why I flew the kite.''

''Did you meet any of my other friends?''

''I met Weinbach. He's a fat kraut with a red face and red hair and the palest eyes you ever saw.''

Smon placed the word-picture alongside the description that Jones had given him of the stranger who had been inquiring about him at the Alamo House, and it matched very well. So that was Weinbach.

And that left Maris, whom nobody seemed to have seen at all.

The Saint went on staring at the twitching representative of the Roman Empire.

''You could have told Kinglake this,'' he said.

''Yeah. And I'd be here as an accessory to murder, if that sourpussed bastard didn't try to make out I was all three murderers in one. No, sir. It's yours now. Gimme a break, and I'll write it down and sign it. I'm not going to give any of these dumb cops a free promotion. I'd rather you showed 'em up instead. Then I'll feel better about the spot I'm in.''

Simon spun out his smoke in a few moments' motionless contemplation.

''If it was some time ago that you met Matson in St. Louis,'' he said, ''how come you connected all this up?''

''I remembered.'' The other's eyes shifted craftily. ''And I got notes. I didn't dare play with those inside envelopes, but I been writing down the names of people. And the places I went to in different cities. A fellow never knows when some things will come in handy. You can have that list too, if you take care of me, and I don't care what you do with it. None of those bastards tried to do anything for me when I got in this jam, so the hell with them.''

The Saint barely showed polite interest; yet he felt so close to one of the real things that he had come to Galveston for that he was conscious of rationing his own breathing.

"It's only fair to tell you, Comrade," he said very carefully, "that if you give me any information that seems worth it, I shall have to turn it straight over to the FBI."

Vaschetti's face was pale in the clearings between his eyebrows and the stubble on his chin, yet in a foolish way he looked almost relieved.

"What you do after you've got it is your affair," he said. "Just gimme a couple hundred dollars and a chance to blow this town, and it's all yours."

Simon glanced at the city editor of the *Times-Tribune*, who was reclining in a junk-pile armchair in the corner with his shabby hat tilted over his eyes, who might have been passed over as asleep except that the eyes were visible and open under the stained straw brim. The eyes touched the Saint briefly and brightly, but nothing else in the composition looked alive. The Saint knew that he was still on his own, according to the agreement.

He said; "What hotel were you working on?"

"The Campeche."

"How much for?"

"Fifty bucks. And my bill."

"I'll take care of all that. You can probably be sprung in a couple of hours. Then I'll meet you at the Campeche and give you two hundred bucks for that statement and your list of names. Then I'll give you two hours to start traveling before I break the story. After that, you're on your own."

"You made a deal, mister. And as soon as I get that dough, I'll take my chance on getting out of here or I'll take what's coming to me. I don't want anything except to be all washed up with this."

His cathartic relief or else his blind faith in his ability to elude the seines of the FBI was either way so pathetic that Simon didn't have the heart to freeze him down anymore. He hitched himself out of the window frame and opened the office door to call back the jailer.

The city editor rocked his antique panama back on his head and tried to keep step beside him as they left.

"I suppose," he said, "you want me to take care of everything and get the Campeche to withdraw the complaint."

"I suppose you can do it. You didn't say anything, so there it is."

"I can put a man on it. I'll have him out in a couple of hours, as you said. But don't ask what happens to me for conspiring to suppress evidence, because I don't know."

"We write up the story," said the Saint, "and we hand Kinglake a proof while the presses are rolling. He gets the complete dope, and we get the beat. What could be fairer?"

The city editor continued to look dyspeptic and unhappy with all of his face except his bright eyes.

He said; "Where are you going now?"

"Call me at the Alamo House as soon as your stooge has Vaschetti under control," Simon told him. "I've got to take Olga to her treadmill, if she hasn't run out by this time."

But Olga Ivanovitch was still sitting in the Saint's car, to all appearances exactly as he had left her, with her hands folded in her lap and the radio turned on, listening happily to some aspiring and perspiring local comedy program.

She was able to make him feel wrong again, even like that, because she was so naively and incontestably untroubled by any of the things that might have been expected to rasp the edges of deliberate self-control.

"I'm sorry I was so long," he said, with a brusqueness that burred into his voice out of his own bewilderment. "But they've started teaching editors two-syllable words lately, and that means it takes them twice as long to talk back to you."

"I've been enjoying myself," she said; and in her own Slavic and slavish way she was still laughing at him, enjoying the tranquility of her own uncomplaining acceptance of everything. "Tell me how you talk to editors."

He told her something absurd; and she sat close against him and laughed gaily aloud as he drove toward the Blue Goose. He was very disconcertingly conscious of the supple firmness of her body as she leaned innocently toward him, and the loveliness of her face against its plaque of yellow braided hair; and he had to make himself remember that she was not so young, and she had been around.

He stopped at the Blue Goose, and opened her door for her without leaving the wheel.

"Aren't you coming in?" she asked.

He was lighting a cigarette with the dashboard gadget, not looking at her.

"I'll try to get back before closing time," he said, "and have a nightcap with you. But I've got a small job to do first. I'm a working man—or did you forget?"

She moved, after an instant's silence and stillness; and then he felt his hand brushed away from his mouth with the cigarette still freshly lighted in it, and her mouth was there instead, and this was like the night before only more so. Her arms were locked around his neck, and her face was the ivory blur in front of him, and he remembered that she had been a surprising warm fragrance to him when she did that before, and this was like that again. He had a split second of thinking that this was it, and he had slipped after all, and he couldn't reach his gun or his knife with her kissing him; and his ears were awake for the deafening thunderbolts that always rang down the curtain on careers like his. But there was nothing except her kiss, and her low voice saying, docilely like she said everything: "Be careful, tovarich. Be careful."

"I will be," he said, and put the gears scrupulously together, and had driven quite a fair way before it coordinated itself to him that she was still the only named name of the ungodly whom he had met and spoken to, and that there was no reason for her to warn him to be careful unless she knew from the other side that he could be in danger.

He drove cautiously back to the Alamo House, collected his key from the desk, glanced around to make sure that Detective Yard had found a comfortable chair, and went up to his room in search of a refreshing pause beside a cool alcoholic drink.

Specifically, the one person he had most in mind was the venerable Mr. Peter Dawson, a tireless distiller of bagpipe broth who, as we recollect, should have been represented among the Saint's furniture by the best part of a bottle of one of his classic consommés. Simon Templar was definitely not expecting, as an added attraction, the body of Mr. Jones, trussed up and gagged with strips of adhesive tape, and anchored to his bed with hawsers of sash cord, and looking exactly like a new kind of mummy; which is precisely what he was

8

Simon untied him and stripped off the tape. The bellhop at least was alive, and apparently not even slightly injured, to judge by the ready flow of words that came out of him when his mouth was unwrapped.

"Two men it was, Mistah Templah. One of 'em was that fat man with red hair that Ah done tole you about. Ah'd been off havin' mah supper, and when I come back, there he is in the lobby. He's with another tall thin man, like it might be the other gennelman you was askin' me about. So Ah was goin' to call your room so you could come down and have a look at them, but the clerk tole me you just went out. Then these men started to get in the elevator, and Ah knew there was somethin' wrong, Ah knew they wasn't stayin' here, and with you bein' out Ah just figured they was up to no good. So Ah ran up the stairs, and sho' nuff there they were just openin' your doah. So Ah ask them what they was doin', and they tried to tell me they was friends of yours. 'You ain't no friends of Mistah Templah's,' Ah says, 'because Mistah Templah done tole me to keep mah eyes open for you.' Then the fat man pulled out a gun and they hustled me in here and tied me up, and then they started searchin' the room. Ah don't think they found what they was huntin' for, because they was awful mad when they went off. But they sho' made a mess of your things."

That statement was somewhat superfluous. Aside from the disorder of the furnishings, which looked as if a cyclone had paused among them, the Saint's suitcase had been emptied on to the floor and everything in it had been tossed around and even taken apart when there was any conceivable point to it.

"Don't let it get you down, Jones," Simon said cheerfully. "I know they didn't get what they wanted, because I didn't leave anything here that they could possibly want. Unless one of them coveted an electric razor, which it seems he didn't. Just give me a hand with straightening out the wreckage."

He began to repack his suitcase while Jones became efficient about replacing the carpet and rearranging the furniture.

He was puzzled about the entire performance, for he certainly had no precious goods or papers with him; and if he had had any he certainly wouldn't have left them in his room when he went out. The ransacking must have stemmed from his connection with the Matson murder, but it seemed a long way for the ungodly to have gone with the mere hope of picking up some incidental information about him. The only reasonable explanation would be that they suspected that Matson might have given him something, or told him where to find something, before he died. But Matson had only muttered about an ostrich-skin case in a gladstone lining; and they had the gladstone. If they had taken the trouble to collect the gladstone, hadn't they looked in the lining? Or had they just picked it up along with other things, in the broad hope of coming across what they were searching for?

He said: "This happened just after I went out?"

"Yes, sah. The desk clerk said you hadn't been gone more 'n few minutes. He said you went out with a lady."

"What about that Detective Yard?"

"Ah didn't see him, sah. Ah guess most likely he went out when you did."

It had been a nice job of contrivance anyhow. If the ungodly knew or assumed that the police were watching Simon Templar, they could also assume that the police would go out when Simon Templar went out. So the coast would be relatively clear when they knew he was going out.

He had been on his guard against uninvited shadows, when it seemed like a good idea to watch out for uninvited shadows. He hadn't bothered much about those who stayed behind, because he hadn't been thinking about anything worth staying behind for. But they had been.

The three faceless men. Blatt Weinbach, and Maris. Two of whom he had only heard described. And Maris, whom nobody had heard of and nobody had ever seen.

But Olga Ivanovitch must have known at least one of them. Or even more positively, at least one of them must have known her. They must have sat and looked at each other in the lobby while she was waiting for him. One way or another, the Saint was being taken out of the way for a safe period; and some of them had known it and watched it when he went out. Quite probably, Olga.

Simon's lips hardened momentarily as he finished refolding the last shirt and laid it on top of the stack in his bag. He turned back from the job to watch Bellhop Jones fastidiously fitting a chair back into the scars which its standard position had printed on the nap of the carpet. The room looked as tidy again as if nothing had ever happened there.

"Thanks, chum," said the Saint. "Have we forgotten anything?"

The colored man scratched his close-cropped head.

"Well, sah, Ah dunno. The Alamo House is a mighty respectable hotel—"

"Will you be in trouble on account of the time you've been shut up in here?"

"Nawsah, Ah can't say that. Ah goes off for mah supper, and then Ah comes back and just stays around as long as there's a chance of earnin' an honest tip. Ah don't clock out at no definite time. But with people breakin' into rooms and pullin' a gun on you and tyin' you up, it seems like the management or the police or somebody oughta know what's goin' on."

He was honestly confused and worried about the whole thing.

Simon took a ten-dollar bill out of his pocket and flattened it between his hands so that the numbers were plainly visible.

"Look," he said, as one man to another, "I don't want any trouble with the hotel. And I don't want any help from the cops. I'd rather take care of these guys myself if I ever catch up with them. Why can't we just pretend that you went home early, and none of this ever happened, except that you did spot two more of those people I asked you about and pointed them out to me; and I'll pay you off on that basis."

The scruples of Mr. Jones were probably no less sincere and confirmed than those of Mr. Henry Morgenthau; but he eyed the dangling sawbuck and was irresistibly swayed by its potentialities in his budget. You could see box cars rolling majestically over the murky tracks of his mind.

"Yassah," he said, beaming. "Ah don't wanna start no trouble. Ah'll just forget it if that's what you say, sah."

Simon watched him stow away the green consolation and close the door contentedly after him.

Then he poured himself the highball which he had come home for in the first place. He was glad that at least his guests hadn't been searching for something that might have been soluble in alcohol.

He was just getting acquainted with the drink when his telephone rang.

"I've just taken care of your friend," said the *Times-Tribune*. "He should be back at the Campeche in just a little while. One of the boys is taking care of him."

"Good," said the Saint. "I'll be over there in just a little while too."

"I was able to fix it with the hotel and get to the judge," persisted the voice, rather mournfully. "At this time of night, that's not so easy."

"Congratulations," said the Saint. "You must be *persona* very *grata*."

There was a brief hiatus where the city editor silenced as if he was digging out a new lead.

"I liked the way you talked to that man Vaschetti," he excavated at length, "and I think I ought to talk to you the same way. I'll hold everything while you bring in your story; but I have to live here too. So whatever you bring in, I'll have to turn over to the police and the FBI."

"I'll give you a personal commendation for your fine public spirit," said the Saint.

He could see the pear-shaped figure with its feet on the desk and the battered hat tilted over the eyes that were the only sparkle in the dried poker face, as if it were sitting directly in front of him.

"You've said things that sounded as if you had a hell of a lot of inside dope on this case," said the city editor finally. "What are you doing in Galveston anyway, and why don't you give me the whole story and earn yourself some real dough?"

"I'll think about it," said the Saint, "after I've talked to Vaschetti again."

He dropped the phone, and tried to resume relations with his highball.

He had absorbed one good solid sip when the bell rang again.

This time it was Washington.

"Hamilton," said the line. "I hope this is an awkward moment."

Simon grinned for his own benefit, and said: "No."

"This is all I've got so far on those names. During Prohibition, there were two trigger men in Milwaukee named Johan Blatt and Fritzie Weinbach. They usually worked together. Racketeers. One or two charges—assault, carrying concealed weapons, and so on. Associated with un-American activities in Chicago just before the War. I can read you their full records, but they just sound like a couple of mercenary hoodlums."

"Don't bother," said the Saint. "What about Maris?"

"Nothing yet. A name doesn't mean anything. Hasn't anyone even seen the color of his eyes?"

"Nobody ever sees Maris," said the Saint. "They don't notice anything about him at all. But I'll find him before you do. I'm still working. Have some more black coffee and wait up for me."

He pronged the transceiver again, and reached for his glass once more with indomitable determination.

Maris—the man nobody saw. The man who might be much more than the mere trick answer to a riddle that had been posed by the premature cremation of Henry Stephen Matson. The man who might materialize into one of those almost legendary spear-carriers who were primarily responsible for Simon Templar's excursions as a talent scout even to such outposts as Galveston. The man who might be more concerned than anyone about the contents of the ostrich-skin leather case which had consumed Matson's dying breath.

Or about the list or memory of Nick Vaschetti, a glorified errand-boy with a bad case of fright of fluctuating conscience.

He crumpled out the stub of his cigarette and went downstairs.

Jones, shining like refurbished ebony, intercepted him as he left the elevator.

"Mistah Templah, sah, that Detective Yard just gone home. Another detective took over for him. His name's Mistah Callahan. He's sittin' half behind the second palm across the lobby. A stout gennelman with a bald head in a gray suit———''

Simon slipped another Lincoln label into the bellboy's pink palm.

''If you keep on like this,'' he said, ''you're going to end up a capitalist whether you want to or not.''

It was a well-indicated move which should have been taken before, to replace the too familiar Mr. Yard with somebody else whom the Saint might not recognize. Simon's only surprise was that it hadn't happened sooner. But presumably the whimsical antics of the Selective Service System had not excluded the Galveston Police Department from the scope of their ruthless raids upon personnel.

That wasn't the Saint's business. But for the most immediate future, at least until he had consummated the Vaschetti diversion, Simon Templar preferred to get along without the politically complicated protection of the Galveston gendarmerie.

Wherefore he shelved Mr. Callahan by the rather kindergarten expedient of climbing very deliberately into his parked car, switching on the lights, fiddling with the starter, and then just as leisurely stepping out of the other door, boarding a passing cab, and going away in it while Mr. Callahan was still glued to the bridge of his municipal sampan and waiting for the Saint's wagon to weigh anchor so that he could pursue it.

Which was an entirely elementary technique, but didn't even begin to tackle the major problem of the law in Galveston.

What Simon wanted more than anything at that moment was Mr. Vaschetti's autographed statement, and the list of names and addresses which he had promised. Those things, as weapons, would be worth even more to him than the gun that still bulked under his left arm, or the knife which he could feel with every swing of his right leg.

The Campeche Hotel was down on Water Street, and it appeared to be a very popular bivouac, for there was such a large crowd of citizens clustered around the entrance that they obstructed the traffic, and the Saint left his taxi a few doors away and walked into the throng. As he edged his way through them he was conscious of the crunching of broken glass under his feet; but he didn't think much about it until he noticed some of the crowd glancing upwards, and he glanced upwards with them and saw the jagged gaping hole in the shattered marquee overhead. Then with the advantage of his height he looked over a few heads and shoulders and saw the thing that was the nucleus of the assembly. A rather shapeless lump of something in the center of a clear circle of blood-spattered sidewalk, with one foot sticking out from under a blanket that covered its grosser deformations.

Even then, he knew; but he had to ask.

"What gives?" he said to the nearest bystander.

"Guy just got discouraged," was the laconic answer. "Walked outa his window on the eighth floor. I didn't see him jump, but I saw him light. He came through that marquee like a bomb."

Simon didn't even feel curious about getting the blanket moved for a glimpse of anything identifiable that might have been left as a face. He observed the uniformed patrolman standing rather smug guard over the remains, and said quite coldly: "How long ago did this happen?"

"Only about five minutes ago. They're still waitin' for the ambulance. I was just goin' by on the other side of the street, and I happened to look around———"

The Saint didn't weary his ears with the rest of the anecdote. He was too busy consuming the fact that one more character in that particular episode had elected to go voyaging into the Great Beyond in the middle of another of those unfinished revelations which only the most corny of scenario cookers would have tolerated for a moment. Either he had to take a very dim view of the writing talent in the books of Destiny, or else it would begin to seem that the abrupt transmigration of Nick Vaschetti was just another cog in a divine conspiracy to make life tantalizing for Simon Templar.

9

The links went clicking through Simon's brain as if they were meshing over the teeth of a perfectly fitted sprocket.

The ungodly had ransacked his room at the Alamo House while they knew he would be out of the way, and had drawn a blank. But they would have had plenty of time to pick him up again, and it would have been childishly simple for them to do it, because they knew he was with Olga Ivanovitch, and the place where she was going to steer him for dinner had been decided in advance. The Saint had been alert for the kind of ambuscade that would have been orchestrated with explosions and flying lead, but not for ordinary trailing, because why should the ungodly trail him when one of them was already with him to note all his movements? He had left Olga Ivanovitch in his car outside the *Times-Tribune* building, as he said, for a front and a cover: it hadn't occurred to him that she might be a front and a cover for others of the ungodly. She sat there covering the front while they took the precaution of covering the other exits. When he came out by the back alley, they followed. When he went to the City Jail, they remembered Vaschetti and knew that that must have been the man he had gone to see. Therefore one of them had waited for a chance to silence Vaschetti; and when Vaschetti was released and led back to the Campeche, the opportunity had been thrown into their laps. It had been as mechanically simple as that.

And Olga Ivanovitch had done a swell job all the way through. All those items went interlocking through his mind as he stood at the desk inside and faced an assistant manager who was trying somewhat flabbily to look as though he had everything under perfect control.

Simon flipped his lapel in a conventional gesture, but without showing anything, and said aggressively: "Police Department. What room was Vaschetti in?"

"Eight-twelve," said the assistant manager, in the accents of a harassed mortician. "The house detective is up there now. I assure you, we—"

"Who was with him when he jumped?"

"No one that I know of. He was brought in by one of the men from the *Times-Tribune*, who redeemed his check. Then the reporter left, and—"

"He didn't have any visitors after that?"

"No, nobody asked for him. I'm sure of that, because I was standing by the desk all the time. I'd just taken the money for his check, and told Mr. Vaschetti that we'd like to have his room in the morning; and I was chatting with a friend of mine—"

"Where are the elevators?"

"Over in that corner. I'll be glad to take you up, Mr.—"

"Thanks. I can still push my own buttons," said the Saint brusquely, and headed away in the direction indicated, leaving the assistant manager with only one more truncated sentence in his script.

He had very little time to spare, if any. It could be only a matter of seconds before the accredited constabulary would arrive on the scene, and he wanted to verify what he could before they were in his hair.

He went up and found 812, where the house detective could be seen through the open door, surveying the scene with his hands in his pockets and a dead piece of chewing cigar in the corner of his mouth.

Simon shouldered in with exactly the same authoritative technique and motion of a hand toward the flap of his buttonhole.

"What's the bad news?" he demanded breezily.

The house detective kept his hands in his pockets and made a speech with his shoulders and the protruding cud of his cigar that said as eloquently as anything: "You got eyes, ain'tcha?"

Simon fished out a pack of cigarettes and let his own eyes do the work.

It didn't take more than one wandering glance to rub in the certainty that he was still running behind schedule. Although not exactly a shambles, the room showed all the signs of a sound working over. The bed was torn apart, and the mattress had been slit open in several places, as had the upholstery of the single armchair. The closet door stood wide, and the few garments inside had been ripped to pieces and tossed on the floor. Every drawer of the dresser had been pulled out, and its contents dumped and pawed over on the carpet. The spectacle was reminiscent of the Saint's own room at the Alamo House—with trimmings. He wouldn't have wasted a second on any searching of his own. The search had already been made, by experts.

So someone already had Vaschetti's diary; or else no one was likely to come across it there.

The Saint scraped a match with his thumbnail and let the picture shroud itself in a blue haze.

"What about the men who were up here with Vaschetti?" he asked.

"I never saw anyone with him" responded the house dick promptly.

He had a broad beam and an advancing stomach, so that he had some of the air of a frog standing upright.

"I didn't get your name," he said. "Mine's Rowden."

"You didn't hear any commotion up here, Rowden?"

"I didn't hear a thing. Not until the crash Vaschetti made going through the marquee. I didn't even know he was back out of jail until just now. Where's Kinglake? He usually comes out on death cases."

"He'll be along," Simon promised, with conviction.

There was one fascinating detail to consider, Simon observed as he narrowed down the broad outlines of the scene. In the middle of the strewn junk on the floor there was an almost new gladstone bag, empty and open, lying on its side. He moved to examine it more closely.

"Anybody else been up here?"

"Nope. You're the first. Funny I don't know you. I though I'd met all the plainclothes men in Galveston."

"Maybe you have," said the Saint encouragingly.

Indubitably that was the gladstone which he had heard about. It even had the initials "HSM" goldstamped beside the handle. But if there had ever been an ostrich-skin leather case in the lining, it wasn't there any more. The lining had been slashed to ribbons, and you could have found a long-lost pin in it.

It was a picturesque mystery-museum piece, but that was all. The current questions were, how had it come to rest there, and why? Johan Blatt had removed it from the Ascot; and by no stretch of imagination could his description have been confused with that of the latest failure in the field of empirical levitation. Vaschetti and Blatt were even more different than chalk and cheese: they didn't even begin with the same letter.

Simon Templar pondered that intensely for a time, while the house detective teetered batrachianly on his heels and gnawed on his bowsprit of cigar. The house detective, Simon thought, would surely have been a big help in detecting a house. Aside from that, he was evidently content to let nature and the Police Department take their course. He would have made Dick Tracy break out in a rectangular rash.

They remained in that sterile atmosphere until the sound of voices and footsteps in the corridor, swelling rapidly louder, presaged the advent of Lieutenant Kinglake and his cohorts.

"Ah," said Detective Yard wisely, as he sighted the Saint.

Kinglake didn't even take time out to show surprise. He turned savagely on the frog-shaped house detective.

"How in hell did this bird get in here?"

"I came in under my own power," Simon intervened. "I was thinking of moving, and I wanted to see what the rooms were like. Don't blame Rowden. He was trying to tell me about the wooden mattresses. If you look again, you'll see where he was even ripping them open to show me the teak linings."

The Lieutenant was not amused. He had never looked like a man who was amused very often, and this was manifestly not one of his nights to relax in a bubble bath of wit and badinage.

He glared at the Saint balefully and said; "All right, Templar. You asked for it. I told you what was going to happen to you if you didn't keep your nose clean in this town. Well, this is it. I'm holding you as a material witness in the death of Nick Vaschetti."

The arch of the Saint's brows was angelic.

"As a witness of what, Comrade? The guy bumped himself off, didn't he? He stepped out of a window and left off his parachute. He'd heard about the Galveston Police, and he knew that the most precious legacy he could bequest them was an absolutely water-tight suicide. What makes you leave your ever-loving wife warming her own nightie so you can come here and improve your blood pressure?"

Kinglake's mouth became a thin slit in his face, and his neck reddened up to his ears; but he kept his temper miraculously. The blood stayed out of his slate gray stare.

"Why don't you save the wisecracks for your column?" he said nastily. "You've been mixed up in too many fishy things since you've been here———"

"What makes you assume that I was mixed up in this?"

"You talked to Vaschetti in the City Jail this evening. You arranged for him to be sprung, and you arranged to meet him here. I call that being mixed up in it."

"You must be psychic," Simon remarked. "I know I got rid of your Mr. Callahan. Or who told you?"

"I did," said the voice of the *Times-Tribune*.

He stood in the doorway with a vestige of apology on his mild stolid face. Simon turned and saw him, and went on looking at him with acid bitterness.

"Thanks, pal. Did you bring out a special edition and tell the rest of the world too?"

"I did not," said the city editor primly. "I acted according to the agreement I made with you, as soon as I heard what had happened to Vaschetti."

"How did you hear?"

"The reporter who was supposed to be taking care of him and waiting for you arrived back at the office. I asked him what he thought he was doing, and he said he'd been given a message that I wanted him back at once. Since I hadn't sent any such message, I guessed something was going on. I wasn't any too happy about my own position, so I thought I'd better come over and look into it myself. I met Lieutenant Kinglake downstairs, and I told him what I knew."

"And so we come up here," Kinglake said comfortably, "and catch the Saint just like this."

The repetition of names ultimately made its impression on the comatose house detective.

"Gosh," he exhaled, with a burst of awed excitement, "He's the Saint!" He looked disappointed when nobody seemed impressed by his great discovery, and retired again behind his cigar. He said sullenly: "He told me he was the police."

"He told the assistant manager the same thing," Kinglake said with some satisfaction. "A charge of impersonating an officer will hold him till we get something better."

Simon studied the Lieutenant's leathery face seriously for a moment.

"You know," he said, "something tells me you really mean to be difficult about this."

"You're damn right I do," Kinglake said without spite.

At that point there was a sudden sharp exclamation from Detective Yard, who had been quartering the room with the same plodding method that he had used out on the flats where the late Henry Stephen Matson had become his own funeral pyre.

"Hey, Lieutenant, look what we got here."

He brought over the shredded gladstone, pointing to the initials stamped on it.

"H-S-M-," he spelt out proudly. "Henry Stephen Matson. This could of belonged to that guy we found yesterday!"

Lieutenant Kinglake examined the bag minutely; but the Saint wasn't watching him.

Simon Templar had become profoundly intereted in something else. He had still been fidgeting over that bag in the back of his mind even while he had to make more immediate conversation, and it seemed to be sorting itself out. He was scanning the hodge-podge of stuff on the floor rather vacantly while Yard burgeoned into the bowers of Theory.

"Lieutenant, maybe this Vaschetti was the guy who called himself Blatt an' got away with Matson's luggage. So after they throw him out the window, they tear that bag apart while they're rippin' up everything else."

"Brother," said the Saint in hushed veneration, "I visualize you as the next Chief of Police. You can see that whole slabs of that lining have been torn right out; but in all this mess I bet you can't find one square inch of lining. I've been looking to see if the ungodly had been smart enough to think of that, but I don't think they were. Therefore that bag wasn't chopped up in here. Therefore it was planted just for the benefit of some genius like you."

"What else for?" Kinglake demanded curtly.

"To throw in a nice note of confusion. And most likely, in the hope that the confusion might take some of the heat off Blatt."

"If there ever was a Blatt before you thought of him."

"There was a Blatt," the city editor intervened scrupulously. "I think I told you, Vaschetti spoke about him and described him."

The Lieutenant handed the gladstone back to his assistant, and kept his stony eyes on the Saint.

"That doesn't make any difference," he stated coldly. "All I care about is that whatever went on here was done inside the city limits of Galveston. There's no question about my jurisdiction this time. And I'm tired of having you in my hair, Templar. You wanted Vaschetti out of the calaboose. You arranged to meet him here. And I find you in his room in the middle of a mess that makes it look as if he could have been pushed out of that window instead of jumped. You've been much too prominent in every bit of this—from finding Matson's body to going around with Olga Ivanovitch. So I'm just going to put you where I'll know what you're doing all the time."

"Has there been a political upheaval in the last half-hour," Simon inquired with sword-edged mockery, "or do you happen to be kidding yourself that if you bring me into court on any charge I won't manage to tie this job in with the Matson barbecue and raise holy hell with all the plans for a nice peaceful election?"

Kinglake's jaw hardened out like a cliff, but the harried expression that Simon had noticed before crept in around his eyes.

"We'll worry about that when the time comes. Right now, you're going to do all your hell-raising in a nice quiet cell."

Simon sighed faintly, with real regret. It would have been so much more fun playing it the old way, but he couldn't take any more chances with that now. This game mattered so much more than the old games that he had played for fun.

"I hate to disappoint you," he said, "but I can't let you interfere with me tonight."

He said it with such translucent simplicity that it produced the kind of stunned silence that might exist at the very core of an exploding bomb.

Detective Yard, the least sensitive character, was the first to recover.

"Now, ain't that just too bad!" he jeered, advancing on the Saint, and hauling out a pair of handcuffs as he came, but moving warily because of his own affronted confidence.

Simon didn't even spare him a glance. He was facing Kinglake and nobody else, and all the banter and levity had dropped away from his bearing. It was like a prizefighter in the ring shrugging off his gay and soft silk robe.

"I want five minutes with you alone," he said. "and I mean alone. It'll save you a lot of touble and grief."

Lieutenant Kinglake was no fool. The hard note of command that had slid into the Saint's voice was pitched in a subtle key that blended with his own harmonics.

He eyed Simon for a long moment, and then he said: "OK. The rest of you wait outside. Please."

In spite of which, he pulled out his Police Positive and sat down and held it loosely on his knee as the other members of the congregation filed out with their individual expressions of astonishment, disappointment, and disgust.

There was perplexity even in Kinglake's rugged bony face after the door had closed, but he overcame it with his bludgeon bluff of harsh peremptory speech.

"Well," he said unrelentingly. "Now we're alone, let's have it. But if you were thinking you could pull a fast one if you had me to yourself—just forget it, and save the City a hospital bill."

"I want you to pick up that pnone and make a call to Washington," said the Saint, without rancor. "The number is Imperative five, five hundred. Extension five. If you don't know what that means, your local FBI agent will tell you. You'll talk to a voice called Hamilton. After that you're on your own."

Even Kinglake looked as briefly startled as his seamed face could.

"And if I let you talk me into making this call, what good will it do you?"

"I think," said the Saint, "that Hamilton will laugh his head off; but I'm afraid he'll tell you to save that nice quiet cell for somebody else."

The Lieutenant gazed at him fixedly for four or five seconds.

Then he reached for the telephone.

Simon Templar germinated another cigarette, and folded into the remnants of an armchair. He hardly paid any attention to the conversation that went on, much less to the revolver that rested for a few more minutes on the detective's lap. That phase of the affair was finished, so far as he was concerned; and he had something else to think about.

He had to make a definite movement to bring himself back to that shabby and dissected room when the receiver clonked back on its bracket, and Kinglake said, with the nearest approach to humanity that Simon had yet heard in his gravel voice: "That's fine. And now what in hell am I going to tell those muggs outside?"

10

The Saint could string words into barbed wire, but he also knew when and how to be merciful. He smiled at the Lieutenant without the slightest trace of malice or gloating. He was purely practical.

"Tell 'em I spilled my guts. Tell 'em I gave you the whole story, which you can't repeat because it's temporarily a war secret and the FBI is taking over anyhow; but of course you knew all about it all the time. Tell 'em I'm just an ambitious amateur trying to butt into something that's too big for him: you scared the daylights out of me, which is all you really wanted to do. Tell 'em I folded up like a flower when I tried to sell you my line and you really got tough. So I quit; and you were big-hearted and let me hightail out of here. Make me into any kind of jerk that suits you, because I don't want the other kind of publicity and you can get credit for the pinch anyway."

"Why didn't you tell me this in the first place?" Kinglake wanted to know, rather petulantly.

"Because I didn't know anything about you, or your political problems. Which were somewhat involved, as it turns out." The Saint was very calmly candid. "After that, I knew even less abou your team. I mean guys like Yard and Callahan. This is a small town, as big towns go, and it wouldn't take long for one man's secret to become everybody's rumor. You know how it is. I might not have gotten very far that way."

Kinglake dragged another of his foul stogies out of his vest pocket, glared at it pessimistically, and finally bit off the end as if he had nerved himself to take a bite of a rotten apple. His concluding expression conveyed the notion that he had.

"And I always knew you for a crook," he said disconsolately.

The Saint's smile was almost nostalgically dreamy.

"I always was, in a technical sort of way," he said softly. "And I may be again. But there's a war on; and some odd people can find a use for some even odder people. . . . For that matter, there was a time when I thought you might be a crooked cop, which can be worse."

"I guess you know how that is, too," Kinglake said, sourly but sufficiently. "You sounded as if you did."

"I think that's all been said," Simon replied temperately. "We're just playing a new set of rules. For that matter, if I'd been playing some of my old rules, I think I could have found a way to pull a fast one on you, with or without the audience, and taken that heater away from you, and made time out of here no matter what you were threatening. I've done it before. I just thought this was the best way tonight."

The Lieutenant glanced guiltily at his half forgotten gun, and stuffed it back into his hip holster.

"Well?" He repeated the word without any of the aggressive implications that he had thrown into it the last time. "Can you feed me any of this story that I'm supposed to have known all along, or should I just go on clamming up because I don't know?"

Simon deliberately reduced his cigarette by the length of two measured inhalations. In between them, he measured the crestfallen Lieutenant once more for luck. After that he had no more hesitation.

If he hadn't been able to judge men down to the last things that made them tick, he wouldn't have been what he was or where he was at that instant. He could be wrong often and anywhere, incidentally, but not in the fundamentals of situation and character.

He said quite casually then, as it seemed to him after his decision was made: "It's just one of those stories . . ."

He swung a leg over the arm of his chair, pillowed his chin on his knee, and went on through a drift of smoke when he was ready.

"I've got to admit that the theory I set up in the *Times-Tribune* didn't just spill out of my deductive genius. It was almost ancient history to me. That's what brought me to Galveston and into your hair. The only coincidence I wasn't expecting, and which I didn't even get on to for some time afterwards, was that the body I nearly ran over out there in the marshes would turn out to be Henry Stephen Maston—the guy I came here to find."

"What did you want him for?"

"Because he was a saboteur. He worked in two or three war plants where acts of sabatage occurred, although he was never suspected. No gigantic jobs, but good serious sabotage just the same. The FBI found that out when they checked back on him. But the way they got on to him was frankly one of those weird accidents that are always waiting to trip up the most careful villains. He had a bad habit of going out and leaving the lights on in his room. About the umpteenth time his landlady had gone up and turned them out, she thought of leaving a note for him about it. But she didn't have a pencil with her, and she didn't see one lying around. So she rummaged about a bit, and found an Eversharp in one of his drawers. She started to write, and then the lead broke. She tried to produce another one, and nothing happened. So she started fiddling with it and unscrewing things, and suddenly the pencil came apart and a lot of stuff fell out of it that certainly couldn't have been the inner workings of an Eversharp. She was a bright woman. She managed to put it together again, without blowing herself up, and put it back where she found it and went out and told the FBI—of course, she knew that Matson was working for a defense plant. But it's a strictly incredible story, and exactly the sort of thing that's always happening."

"One of these days it'll probably happen to you," Kinglake said; but his stern features relaxed in the nearest approximation to a smile that they were capable of.

The Saint grinned.

"It has," he said. . . . "Anyway, Matson had an FBI man working next to him from then on, so he never had a chance to pull anything."

"Why wasn't he arrested?"

"Because if he'd done other jobs in other places, there was a good chance that he had contacts with a general sabotage organization, and that's what we've been trying to get on to for a long time. That's why I went to St. Louis. But before I arrived there, he'd scrammed. I don't think he knew he was being watched. But Quenco was much tougher than anything he'd tackled before. You don't have any minor sabotage in an explosives factory. You just have a loud noise and a large hole in the ground. I think Matson got cold feet and called it a day. But he wasn't a very clever fugitive. I'm not surprised that the mob caught up with him so quickly. He left a trail that a wooden Indian could have followed. I traced him to Baton Rouge in double time, and when I was there I heard from Washington that he'd applied for a passport and given his address as the Ascot Hotel in Galveston. He was afraid that his goose was cooked. It was, too—to a crisp."

"You were figuring on getting into his confidence and finding out what he knew."

"Maybe something like that. If I could have done it. If not, I'd have tried whatever I had to—even to the extent of roasting him myself. Only I'd have done it more slowly. I thought he might have some informative notes written down. A guy like that would be liable to do that sort of thing, just for insurance. Like Vaschetti. . . . I want that ostrich-skin case that was in his gladstone lining; and I want Vaschetti's diary of his trips and meetings. With those two items, we may be able to clean up practically the whole sabotage system from coast to coast."

"What do you mean by 'we'?" Kinglake asked curiously. "I've heard of this Imperative number; but is it a branch of the FBI?"

Simon shook his head.

"It's something much bigger. But don't ask me, and don't ask anyone else. And don't remember that I ever mentioned it."

Kinglake looked at the chewed end of his stogie.

"I just want you to know," he said, "that I had Matson figured as an ordinary gang killing, and that's why I would have let it ride. If I'd known it was anything like this, nobody could have made me lay off."

The Saint nodded.

"I guessed that. That's why I've talked to you. Now we've spent enough time for you to be able to put over your story; and I've got to be moving."

"You know where you're going?"

"Yes." Simon stood up and crushed out his cigarette. "You may hear from me again tonight."

The Lieutenant held out his hand and said: "Good luck."

"Thanks," said the Saint, and went out.

Rowden and Yard and the *Times-Tribune*, standing in a little huddle down the corridor, turned and fanned out to stare at him as he strolled toward them. Then the Lieutenant's voice came from the doorway behind him.

"Mr. Templar is leaving. Now you can all come back here."

"You know," Simon said earnestly, to Detective Yard, "I do wish your first name was Scotland."

He sauntered on, leaving his favorite plainclothes man gawping after him like a punch-drunk St. Bernard whose succored victim has refused to take a drink out of its keg.

Kinglake's trephining eyes reamed the blank questioning faces of his returned entr'acteurs. He clamped his teeth defiantly into his stogie, and drew a deep breath. In that breath, every wisp of the convenient alibi that Simon Templar had suggested was swept away, and he was standing solidly on a decision of his own.

"If you want to know what we were talking about," he clipped out, "Templar was giving me a stall, and I pretended to fall for it. Now I'm going to see where he takes me. Yard, you can take charge here. I'm going to follow the Saint myself, and I'm going to bust this whole case if it takes me till Christmas."

"But Lieutenant," protested the dumbfounded Yard, "what about the Chief? What about . . . "

"The Chief," Kinglake said shortly, "and the Commissioner, and the sheriff, and everybody behind them, can—"

He did not say that they could jump in the lake, or go climb a tree, or perform any of the more conventional immolations. It is indeed highly doubtful whether they could have done what the Lieutenant said they could do. But Kinglake was not very concerned just then with literal accuracy. He had an objective of his own which mattered a lot more to him, and he left his extraordinary statement fluttering forgotten in the air behind him as he stalked out.

Simon Templar was also dominated by one single idea. The murder of Matson had been unfortunate, but he could exonerate himself from it. The murder of Vaschetti had been still more unfortunate, but the excuses he could make for himself for that were flimsy gauze before his own ruthless self-criticism. But his reaction to that had already reversed itself into a positive driving force that would go on until the skies fell apart—or he did. For the ungodly to have murdered two men almost under his nose and within split seconds of giving him the precious information that he had to get was an insolence and an effrontery that he was going to make them wish they had never achieved. The Saint was angry now in a reckless cold savage way, not as he had been when he first went from Police Headquarters to the offices of the *Times-Tribune*, but in a way that could only be soothed out in blood.

And now he thought he knew where he was going to find the blood that night.

A taxi took him to the Blue Goose; but this time he didn't need the driver to vouch for him. The doorkeeper remembered him, and let him in at once. He walked through the blue melodious dimness toward the bar, loose-limbed and altogether at his ease; yet there were filaments stirring through all the length of him that kept no touch at all with the lazily debonair demeanor. He caught sight of Olga Ivanovitch sitting at a table with another girl and two obvious wholesale bottle-cap salesmen, but he only gave her a casual wave and went on to find a stool at the bar. He knew she would join him, and he waited good-humoredly while the brawny blond bartender worked over complicated mixtures for a complicated quartet at the other end of the counter.

Then she was beside him; and he knew it by the perfume she used and the cool satin of her hand before he looked at her.

"I'm glad you got here," she said. "Did you get your job done?"

She was exactly the same, lovely and docile, as if she was only glad of him and wanting to be glad for him; as if death had never struck near her or walked with the men she knew.

Simon made a movement of his head that seemed to answer the question unless one stopped to wonder whether it meant yes or no. He went on before that could happen: "I nearly didn't come here. What I'd really hoped to do was curl up at home with a good book from the circulating library."

"What was the book?"

"Just a piece of some guy's autobiography. However, when I went to pick it up, it was gone. A man named Nick Vaschetti had it earlier in the evening. He hadn't finished wih it—but he has now. I suppose you wouldn't know where it is?"

Her eyes were still pools of emerald in the mask of her face.

"Why do you say that?" She seemed to have difficulty in articulating.

"Lots of people read. It occurred to me—"

"I mean that this—this Vaschetti—hadn't finished with the book—but he has now?"

"He's given up reading," explained the Saint carelessly. "He was so upset about having the book taken away from him that he stepped out of an eighth-floor window—with the help of a couple of your pals."

He watched the warm ivory of her face fade and freeze into alabaster.

"He's—dead?"

"Well," said the Saint, "it was a long drop to the sidewalk, and on account of the rubber shortage he didn't bounce so well."

The bartender was standing over them expectantly. Simon said: "Dawson for me; and I guess you know what the lady's drinking." He became absorbed in the way the man worked with his big deft hands.

And then suddenly he knew all about everything, and it was like waking up under an ice-cold shower.

He took his breath back gradually, and said without a change in his voice except that the smile was no longer there: "You don't know Brother Blatt and his playmates very well, do you, Olga? Especially Maris. But if I'd only been a little brighter I'd have just stayed here and found Maris."

She was staring at him rigidly, with wide tragical eyes. It was a good act, he thought cynically.

The bartender stirred their drinks and set them up, fastidiously wiping spots of moisture from the bar around them. Simon appealed to him.

"I should have asked you in the first place, shouldn't I, Joe? You could have shown me Maris."

The man's big square face began to crinkle in its ready accommodating smile.

And the Saint knew he was right—even though the conclusion had come to him in one lightning-flash of revelation, and the steps toward it still had to be retraced.

Maris, the man nobody knew. Maris, the man nobody had ever heard of. The truly invisible man. The man whom the assistant manager of the Ascot might have been referring to, and have forgotten, even, when Nick Vaschetti came home to die. The man nobody ever saw, or ever would see; because they never looked.

Simon lifted his glass and took a sip from it.

"You could have told me, couldn't you?" he said, with his eyes like splinters of blue steel magnetized to the man's face. "Because everybody calls you Joe, but they don't give a damn about your last name. And I don't suppose you'd tell them it's Maris, anyway."

It was strange that everything could be so clear up to that instant, and then be blotted out in an explosion of blackness that sprang from somewhere behind his right ear and dissolved the universe into a timeless midnight.

11

There were bells tolling in the distance.

Enormous sluggish bells that paused in interminable suspense between each titanic *bong!* of their clappers.

Simon Templar was floating through stygian space toward them, so that the clanging became louder and sharper and the tempo became more rapid as he sped toward it.

He was hauling on the bell cords himself. It seemed vaguely ridiculous to be ringing peals for your own funeral, but that was what he was doing.

His arms ached from the toil. They felt as though they were being pulled out of their sockets. And the knell was blending into pain and sinking under it. A pain that swelled and receded like a leaden tide . . . like a pulse beat . . .

His mind came back gradually out of the dark, awakening to the realization that the carillon was being played inside his own cranium, and the pain was synchronized with the beating of his own heart.

He became aware that he was in a windowless chamber with some sort of plastered rock walls. A naked light bulb shone in the middle of the low ceiling. It was a cellar. There were collections and scatterings of the kind of junk that accumulates in cellars. There was an ugly iron furnace; and lines and cross-crosses of pipe hung high under the ceiling, wandering from point to point on undivinable errands, like metal worms in exposed transit from one hole to another.

He was close to one of the walls, sagging downward and outward, his whole weight hanging from his outstretched arms. He had been tied by the wrists to two of the overhead pipes, about six feet from the floor and the same distance apart. That accounted for the ache in his arms. Otherwise, he was unconfined.

He found the floor with his feet and straightened his knees. That eased the racking strain on his joints and ligaments, and reduced the pain of the ropes biting into his wrists, and might eventually give the throbbing of his strangled circulation a chance to die down. But it was the only constructive movement he could make.

Then he saw Olga Ivanovitch.

She was against the wall at right angles to his, tied to the pipes in exactly the same manner; but she was quite conscious and standing upright. She didn't look trim and sleek as he had last seen her. One of the braids of her coiled hair had broken loose and fallen over her shoulder like a drooping wing, and the demure dark dress she had been wearing was disheveled and torn away from one creamy shoulder and the lift of a breast. She was watching the Saint's recovery with eyes like scorched holes in the desperate pallor of her beauty.

It was the shock of recognition as much as anything which helped to clear the rest of the fuzzy cobwebs from his brain. His headache was more bearable now, but he had an idea that he wouldn't want anyone to lay a heavy hand on the place behind his right ear where it seemed to come from.

"To digress a moment from what we were saying," he managed to remark aloud in a thick voice that grew clearer and stronger with each passing breath, "what the hell did Joe hit me with—a boomerang? I only took a sip of that drink, and it wasn't any worse than the stuff they served me before."

"Blatt hit you from behind," she said. "He came up behind you while you were talking. I tried to warn you with my eyes. He was very quick, and nobody would have seen it. Then he caught you, and they said you were drunk and passed out. They took you into a back room, and that was the end of it."

Simon glanced at his surroundings again. They were depressingly reminiscent of many similar surroundings that he had been in before. He seemed to have spent a great deal of his life being knocked on the head and tied up in cellars.

"And so, by one easy transfer," he observed, "we arrive in the bomb-proof doghouse."

"This is the cellar of my house. There is a back way out of the Blue Goose. They took you out and brought you here."

"Well, well, well. We certainly do lead a hectic life. Never a dull moment."

Her gaze was wondering.

"You jest in the face of certain death. Are you a fatalist, or are you only a fool?"

"I've certainly acted like a fool," Simon admitted ruefully. "But as for this death business—that shouldn't lose you any sleep. You didn't have any nightmares over Matson, did you?"

"I have seen too much to have nightmares," she said wearily. "But I give you my word that I have never had a hand in any murder. I didn't know they were going to kill Matson. I knew nothing about him, except that he was one of their men, and I was told to amuse him. But after he had been killed—what could I do? I couldn't bring him back to life, or even prove that they did it. And Vaschetti. I thought Vaschetti was safe in jail when I . . ."

"When you what?"

"When I went to his room this afternoon to see if I could find—anything"

The Saint wondered if the blow on his head had done something to him. He looked at her through a film of unreality.

He said: "such as a diary of names and places?"

"Anything. Anything I could find. I thought he might have kept something, and I wanted it."

"What for—blackmail?"

"To turn over to the FBI, when I had enough."

He had learned before that he couldn't needle her, but it was a discovery that she could astound him.

"You mean you were planning to sell your own gang down the river?"

"Of course."

Maybe it was better to occupy his twinging head with material things. On due consideration, he admired the basic ingenuity of the way he was tied up. It was so simple and practical and economical of rope, and yet it completely eliminated all the standard tricks of escape. There was no chance of reaching a knot with the fingertips or the teeth, or cleverly breaking a watchglass and sawing the cords on a sharp fragment, or employing any of the other devices which have become so popular in these situations. It was one of the most effective systems the Saint had encountered in an exceptionally privileged experience, and he made a mental note to use it on his next prisoner.

Meanwhile he said, without much subtlety: "But would that have been cricket, tovarich? Do you want me to believe that anyone so beautiful could sink so low?"

For an instant he thought that he actually struck a flash from her green eyes.

"Why do you think I'm here now—tovarich?"

"I had wondered about that," he said. "But I decided you might have a fetish about being crucified."

"I'm here because they don't trust me anymore. I helped to bring you here. I wanted them to believe I was still helping them. I couldn't do anything else. . . . And I was only waiting for a chance to help you. . . . They tied you up. I helped them. And then, suddenly, they took hold of me and tied me up too. I fought them, but it was no use."

"You have such a sweet honest face—why wouldn't they trust you?"

"That was because of what you said in the Blue Goose," she told him without resentment. "You asked me if I had Vaschetti's book. Before that, they thought it was you who had been there first. But when Maris heard you accuse me he was suspicious. They knew that I liked you, and I had seen you. And for Maris, a little suspicion is enough.''

Simon decided that there was not so much profit in standing upright as he had hoped. If he rested his arms, the cords gnawed at his wrists again; if he favored his wrists, the strain of fatigue on his shoulders tautened slowly into exquisite torture. He had had no sensation in his hands and no control of his fingers for some time.

''And you really expect me to swallow that without water?'' he asked scornfully.

''It doesn't matter much what you believe now,'' she replied tiredly. ''It's too late. We shall both be dead in a little while. We cannot escape; and Siegfried is pitiless.''

''Pardon me if I get a bit confused among all these people, but who is Siegfried?''

''Siegfried Maris. You call him Joe. I think he is the head of the Nazi sabotage organization in the United States.''

The Saint thought so too. He had that all worked out before Blatt hit him on the head. It explained why Matson had ever gone to the Blue Goose at all. It explained why Vaschetti had touched there in his travels. It explained why the Blue Goose played such a part in the whole incident—why it was the local focus of infection, and why it could send its tendrils of corruption into honest local political dishonesty, squeezing and pressing cunningly here and there, using the human failings of the American scene to undermine America. A parasitic vine that used the unassuming and unconscious flaws in its host to destroy the tree. . . . It was not incredible that the prime root of the growth should turn out to be Siegfried Maris, whom everyone knew as Joe. Simon had always had it in his mind that the man he was hunting for would turn out to be someone that everybody called Joe. And this was the man. The man who could have anything around and not be part of it; who could always be legitimately there. The man nobody saw, in the place nobody thought of . . .

''Comrade Maris,'' said the Saint, ''has been offstage far too much. It's not fair to the readers. What is he doing now?''

''I expect he's upstairs, with the others. Searching my house.''

''He must like the place. How long have we been here?''

''Not very long. Not long at all.''

''What's he searching for?''

''The book,'' she said. ''Vaschetti's little book.''

''Why here?''

''Because I did find it. Because it has half the code names and meeting places in this country listed in it. But Maris will find it. I couldn't hide it very well.''

Simon was able to shrug his left shoulder tentatively. No weight dragged on it. They would have found and taken the gun in his spring holster, of course. It wouldn't have been much use to him if they hadn't. However . . .

''So it was you who tore Vaschetti's room at the Campeche apart,'' he said. ''But your mob thought it was me. That's why my room was gone over this evening while we were out together, and a colored friend of mine nearly had colored kittens. You aren't overlooking any bets, are you? And since Vaschetti's indiscreet memoirs are still missing—not to mention Brother Matson's notes and papers———''

''They have those,'' she said listlessly. ''They were in the gladstone bag.''

He was shaken as if he had been jolted in the ribs; but he went on.

''So anyway, we now have a well-staged scene in the old torture chamber, where you trick me into revealing where I have hidden all these priceless documents. You're doing a great show, Olga. If I could get my hands together I would applaud. You must be a full-fledged member of this lodge of Aryan cutthroats.''

''Think what you please,'' she said indifferently. ''It makes no difference.''

She could always make him feel wrong. Like now, when she was not angry, but wounded in everything but dignity. Because that devastating ingenuousness of hers was real; because the bridges she walked on were firm and tried, and she had built them herself, and she was as sure of them and her way as he was sure of his own. There could be no facile puncturing of a foundation like that, with a skilled flick of the wrist.

She said, without any emotion: ''You think of me as a mercenary adventuress. I don't deny it. I have worked for Maris—and other men—only for money. But that was before the Nazis invaded Russia. You will not believe that a greedy adventuress could have a heart, or a conscience. But it made all the difference to me. . . . I pretended that it didn't. I went on working for them—taking their money, doing what they told me, trying to keep their trust. But I was only waiting and working for the time when I could send all of them to the hell where they belong. . . . Yet, I had my own sins to redeem. I had done wrong things, too. That's why I thought that if I could bring something with me, something big enough to prove that all my heart had changed—then perhaps your FBI would understand and forgive me, and let me begin again here. . . . I could swear all this to you; but what is swearing without faith?''

The Saint's head was much clearer now. He saw her again through the ruthless screen of his disbelief. And still she wasn't trying to sell him from behind the counter of any phony job of tying-up. Her wrists were lashed as cruelly tight as his own. He could see the livid ridges in her skin where the ropes cut. Her face was damp like his was from strain and pain.

''Damn it, tovarich,'' he said musingly, ''you could act anyone in Hollywood off the screen. You've almost convinced me that you're on the level. You couldn't possibly be, but you sound just like it.''

Her eyes were unwavering against his, and they looked very old. But that was from the patience of a great sadness.

''I only wish you could have believed me before the end. It would have been nicer. But it will not be long now. Sigfried Maris is one of the most important men that Hitler has in this country. He won't take any chances with us.''

''At least,'' said the Saint, ''we should feel flattered about getting the personal attention of the big shot himself.''

He had crossed his left leg over his right now, but it was not with the idea of striking an elegant and insouciant pose. He was pressing the outside of his legs together, feeling for something. He had been searched and disarmed, he knew; but there was his own special armory which the ungodly didn't always . . .

''If we could have caught Maris,'' Olga was saying, out of that passionless and regretful resignation, ''it would have meant as much as winning a battle at the front. I would have liked to do that very much. Then we could have been quite happy about this.''

It was too good to be true; but it was true. He could feel the solid flat hardness of the haft and blade between the movements of his legs. And with that, he had a fantastic inspiration that might grow into a fantastic escape. But he had seen fantasy come real too often to discard it for nothing but its name.

The glint in his eyes was like sunlight on cut sapphires.

''Maybe we can still be happy, Olga,'' he said; and there was a lilt of exultant vitality in his voice. ''We'll try to repeat a significant scrap of United Nations history. You, like some other Russians, were petting the wrong dog. Until you saw the error of your ways. And it bit you. Now I shall try to come through with the lend-lease matériel.''

12

Olga Ivanovitch stared at him as though she was certain now that he was out of his mind.

"No, darling, I'm not," he said before she could put her own words to it. "I was just remembering a movie serial that I saw as a boy, which starred the greatest of all escape artists—Harry Houdini."

"How interesting," she said blankly.

It was lucky, he thought, that he liked his shoes loose and comfortable. Otherwise, getting them off might have been quite a problem. As it was, he was able to tread on one heel with the opposite instep and force one shoe off with only a moderate amount of violence. The other shoe presented a little more difficulty, without a hard welt to scrape against, but he went on working at it.

"Now don't go all Russian on me and relapse into brooding despair," he pleaded. "You ought to be interested in the late Mr. Houdini. He was a real maestro at getting out of situations like this. I was thinking of one installment in which he was tied to some sort of Oriental torture wheel, in very much the same way as we're tied up now. He managed to worry his shoes and socks off, and neatly unfastened the knots on his wrists with his toes.

He had the other shoe off at last. The socks were easier. He only had to tread on a bit of slack at each toe in turn and pull his feet out.

"So what?" Olga said skeptically. "Can you even reach your wrists with your toes?"

"Now you're coming to life," Simon approved. "I used to be a fairly agile guy before I started drinking myself to death, and I think I can manage that." He twisted his body and balanced himself on one foot, and swung his other leg lithely up to kick his hand. "There. I always knew all those years I spent in the Follies chorus would come in handy some day," he said contentedly.

"But the knots," she said in the same tone as before; yet it was already being contradicted by the curiosity kindling in her eyes.

"I'm afraid I'm not quite that good," he confessed. "However, I have an alternative solution for them which Harry might not have considered entirely ethical."

He was already working up his right trouser leg with his naked left foot. Under the amazed eyes of the girl, the upper end of the sheath and the haft of his knife came into view. He grasped the haft with his toe and drew the blade gently out of the scabbard and laid it on the floor.

"When I was swinging through the trees in my last incarnation," he said, "this would have been duck soup for me. But I'm a bit out of practice these days."

He was concentrating singly on the knife, maneuvering it between his two feet, getting the firmest possible grip on the handle between his big toe and the one next to it, adjusting and testing it before he made a decisive move. There was no sound in the room but the faint scuff of his efforts. His wrists hurt like hell; but he had forgotten about them. The sweat was standing out on his forehead by the time he was satisfied.

"Now we get to the really fancy part of the trick," he said. "Like the man on the flying trapeze without a net, I won't be able to go back and start over if I muff it."

He poised himself in the same way as he had done for his preliminary experiment, but much more carefully gauged his distances, and drew a deep breath and held it.

Then he swung his leg, aiming the razor edge of the blade at the link of rope between his left wrist and the pipe. Once, twice, three times he repeated the same pendulum movement, trying to strike the same spot on the rope each time, feeling the keen blade bite the fibers at every stroke.

Then the knife twisted between his toes; but he managed to keep a precarious hold on it. He brought it gingerly down to the floor and adjusted it again, with the aid of his left foot, in an intolerable hush of intense patience and concentration.

He swung his leg again.

Once more.

Twice more.

The knife spun out of his hold and clattered to the floor.

It was beyond his reach, and beyond hers.

He heard the girl's pent-up breath break out of her lungs in a long throaty sob, and saw tears swimming in her eyes.

He knew then, at last, without thinking about it anymore, that she had told him the truth. He had been unsure. He had taken a chance on it, because he was forced to, but wondering all the time if this would end up as the supreme sadism of tantalization—if after he had revealed his secret weapon, and freed himself, if he could free himself, she would only call out, and Maris would walk in with a gun, and all the hope and struggle would have been for nothing. Now he knew. She couldn't have gasped and wept like that, otherwise; wouldn't have needed to, no matter how well she was playing a part.

It was worth something to be sure of that.

The Saint smiled grimly as he inspected the section of rope that he had been working on. He had done a good job, in spite of everything. It wasn't anything like the rope it had been before.

''I forgot to mention,'' he murmured, ''that when I was in the circus I also used to break chains and tow tanks around with one hand.''

Then with an abrupt and feral outburst of titanic effort he threw all his weight and strength together against the partly severed cords, dropping his weight on them with a plunging jerk, and simultaneously thrusting himself away from the wall with his feet and contracting his arms together with all the power of his torso. The veins swelled in his neck, and the muscles rippled over his body in quivering waves. For an instant it felt as if his wrists were being bitten off. . . .

And then, with a suddenness that was physically sickening, the frayed and slashed portion of rope parted with a snap that flung him whirling outward and around.

He heard the girl sob again; but this time it was with a note of almost hysterical laughter.

He retained his balance without a waste motion, and fell to attacking the knots that bound his right hand.

''I must be slipping,'' he said. ''I used to do things like that just to warm up.''

The knots weren't so easy. His hands were numb, and he had to drive deliberate commands through for every movement of his fingers. He worked as fast as he could through that nightmarish impediment.

At last he was free. His wrists were chafed and bleeding a little. But that was nothing. The sense of freedom, of triumph, was like an intoxicating wind blowing through the reviving spaces of his soul.

He scooped up his knife, a little awkwardly because of the cramp in his hands, and cut Olga loose. She almost fell against him, and he had to hold her up for a moment. Until her clinging grew up from the weakness of reaction into something else.

Then he steadied her on her feet and left her standing while he went back to put on his shoes and socks. The return of circulation was filling his hands with pins and needles; but gradually, with the relentless exertion, his fingers began to feel less like swollen frozen sausages.

''There is a way out of here without going through the house,'' she was saying breathlessly. ''We can slip out without them ever knowing that we've gone.''

''Slip out?''

He glanced up at her. ''Darling, that would be a hell of an anticlimax. I'm going upstairs now and get Matson's notes and Vaschetti's diary away from dear old Joe!''

"But how can you?" she cried. "He'll shoot you like a dog. They took your gun. I saw them. We can call the police—"

Simon straightened up, and looked down in silent reckless laughter at her desperate imploring face.

"I've got my knife," he said; "but I haven't got any guarantee that the police would get here in time. And meanwhile Maris and Co. might find out that we'd got away, and decide to take the brakes off themselves. We don't want to risk that now. And besides, we've got to deliver you as a certified heroine. Remember?" Her soft scarlet lips were only a few inches away, turned up to him below the liquid pools of her eyes; and once again he was aware of their distracting provocation. He said: "Thanks just the same for being so concerned about me. It ought to be worth at least . . ."

Then she was in his arms, her breath warm against his cheek, and all of her asking for him; and it would never be like that again, but there was no time for that now and perhaps there never had been. It was like so many things in his life: they were always too late, and there was never any time.

He disengaged himself very gently.

"Now," he said, "we will have the last word with Joe."

The door on the other side of the cellar was not locked. Simon went up the crude wooden stairs, very quietly, and was conscious of Olga Ivanovitch following him. But he didn't look back. He came out through another unlatched door into the hall of the house. There was no guard there either. Obviously, Maris and his crew had great faith in the durability of manila hemp and the efficacy of their trussing system.

Which was reasonable enough; just as the Saint's faith in his knife was reasonable. He knew what it could do, and what he could do with it. He knew how it could transform itself into a streak of living quicksilver, swift as the flash of light from its polished blade, true as a rifle, deadly as any bullet that was ever launched by erupting chemicals.

He held it delicately in his resensitized fingers, frail and strong as a bird, only waiting for him to release it into life.

He was outside another door then, listening, when the voice came firmly through it to his ears. Just a voice: the voice of Siegfried Maris, generally known as Joe. But coming with a clear suddenness that was like traveling back in time and never having heard a talking picture, and suddenly hearing a screen speak.

It said: "Keep your hands well up, Lieutenant. Please don't try anything stupid. It wouldn't do you any good."

And then Kinglake's savage growl: "You son of a bitch—how did you get out of the Blue Goose?"

The Saint's mouth opened and closed again in a noiseless gasp, and a ripple of irresistible laughter rose up through him like a stream of bubbles to break soundlessly at his lips. Even at a moment like that he had to enjoy the perfection of that finishing touch.

"We have our own way out," Maris replied calmly. "It's very useful, as you see. But if you didn't know about it, how did you follow us here?"

"I didn't. When I didn't find Templar at the Blue Goose, I thought he might have come here with Ivanovitch."

"An excellent deduction, Lieutenant. And quite correct. He did come here with Ivanovitch. But that wasn't his choice. . . . It's very fortunate that you're a detective and not a burglar, isn't it? If you'd been a burglar you wouldn't have made such a clumsy entrance, and it mightn't have been half so easy to catch you."

Simon settled fingers on the door knob as if it had been a wafer-shelled egg. He began to turn it with micrometric gentleness.

"You bastards," Kinglake said. "What have you done with them?"

"You'll see for yourself, when you join them in just a few minutes."

"So you're Maris, are you? I should have known it."

"A pardonable oversight, Lieutenant. But you may still call me Joe, if it will make you feel more comfortable."

Simon waited through an infinitesimal pause, with the door handle fully turned.

Kinglake said: "I guess you can have oversights too. You aren't getting away with anything, Joe. I've got men outside———"

The low hard chuckle of Maris came through the door.

"An old bluff, Lieutenant, but always worth trying. I know that you came alone. Fritzie was watching you outside, and we made sure of that before we let you break in. Now if you'll be very careful about holding your arms up while Blatt takes your gun———"

That was the pleasantly dramatic moment when it seemed right to the Saint to throw the door wide open.

It was a nice composition that framed itself through the opening, a perfect instant of arrested motion, artistic and satisfactory. There was Lieutenant Kinglake standing with his hands up and his jaw tensed and a stubborn snarl around his eyes, with Johan Blatt advancing toward him. Fritzie Weinbach stood a little off to the right, with a big snub-nosed automatic leveled at the detective's sternum. Simon could identify them both without ever having seen them before—the tall blond man and the fat red man with the cold bleached eyes.

He saw Siegfried Maris too, for the first time as the man he was instead of the forgotten bartender called Joe. It was amazing what a difference there was. He sat behind a desk, without the disguise of the white coat and the quick obsequious serving movements, wearing an ordinary dark business suit, and obviously the dominant personality of the group. For ultimate proof, he even had a flat light tan case and a shabby pocket memorandum book among some papers on the blotter in front of him. Simon knew even from where he stood that they must be the notes of Henry Stephen Matson and the diary of Nick Vaschetti. It was all there.

And Maris was there, with his square powerful face that hadn't a natural smile in any line of it; and he was turning toward the interruption with his eyes widening and one of his strong swift hands already starting to move; and the Saint knew without any further study, without a second's hesitation, that this was the one man he had to get and be sure of, no matter what else happened afterwards.

The knife sped from his hand like a glitter of leaping silver, flying like a splinter of living light straight for the newly retired bartender's throat.

Then Lieutenant Kinglake had taken advantage of the diversion to make a grab for his gun, and the room was full of thunder and the dry stinging tang of cordite.

13

Simon Templar didn't carve notches in the handle of his knife, because they would eventually have affected the balance, and he was used to it and he hoped it would last for a long time. He did worry about rust and the way it could dull a blade. He wiped the blade very carefully on Maris's shirt before he put the knife back in its sheath.

"Let's face it," he said; "he did pour some of the lousiest drinks I ever paid for."

Kinglake was reloading his Police Positive with the unconscious detachment of prehistorically rooted habit.

He said, almost awkwardly for him: "I just wanted to be in at the death."

"You were," Simon assured him somewhat unnecessarily.

"Are there any more of 'em?"

"Quite a lot—I hope. But not around here. And we don't have to bother about them. Just turn that stuff on the desk over to the FBI. The rest will be their routine.''

''I'd sure like to know what happened to you.''

The Saint told him.

Kinglake scratched his head.

''I've seen plenty in my time, believe it or not,'' he said. ''But you've topped all of it.'' He ended up with an admission. ''I'll have to think of a new story now, though; because I messed up the one you gave me.''

''It doesn't matter,'' said the Saint. ''Whatever you said, you can tell 'em you only said it for a stall, because you couldn't give out with what you really knew. The true story is your story now. Only leaving me out. There's plenty of evidence on that desk. Go on and grab yourself some glory.''

''But these are the three guys you named in the *Times-Tribune*.''

''So what? So I happened to know too much, and I was too smart for anybody's good. You knew just as much if not more, but you were playing a cagey game. You say that by shooting my mouth off like that I told Maris and Co. that they were hot, and nearly ruined all your well-laid plans. That's why you were so hopping mad about me. In fact, you had to perform superhuman feats to salvage the situation after I balled it up. Say anthing you like. I won't contradict you. It suits me better that way. And there's nobody else left who can call you a liar.''

The Lieutenant's steely eyes flickered over the room. The truth of that theorem was rather gruesomely irrefutable.

Then his glance went to Olga Ivanovitch.

She stood very quietly beside the Saint, her pale face composed and expressionless, her green eyes passing unemotionally over the raw stains and ungainly attitudes of violent death. You could tell nothing about what she thought or expected, if she expected anything. She waited, in an incurious calm that suddenly struck Simon as almost regal; she hadn't asked anything or said anything.

''What about her?'' Kinglake asked.

Simon's pockets had been emptied completely. He bent over one of the bodies and relieved it of a packet of cigarettes that it wouldn't be needing anymore.

''I'm afraid I was holding out on you about her,'' he answered deliberately. ''She's one of our people. Why the hell do you think she was tied up in the cellar with me? But I couldn't tell you before.''

He was so easy and matter-of-fact with it that the Lieutenant only tried to look unstartled.

''But what story am I supposed to give out?''

"Like me—the less you say about her the better," Simon told him. "She was just one of the hostesses at the Blue Goose, and Maris was making use of her through his role of bartender. He set her up in this house, so he had a key. But she wasn't here tonight. When the setup began to look too sticky, she scrammed. You don't think she's worth fussing about."

Simon hadn't looked at the girl until then. He did now.

"By the way," he said casually, "you'd better get a move on with this scramming act. Kinglake is going to have to call Headquarters in a few minutes. You can scram in my car—it won't take me more than ten minutes to check out of the Alamo House. Go and put some things in a bag."

"Yes," she said, impassively and obediently; and went out of the room.

Simon smoked his inherited cigarette with unalloyed enjoyment.

Kinglake gathered the papers on the desk together and frowned over them wisely.

The Saint made another search of the unlamented ungodly, and found his own automatic in Weinbach's pocket. He nested it affectionately back in his clip holster.

The Lieutenant gazed yearningly at the telephone, tightened a spartan stopper on a reawakening ebullience of questions, and got out another of his miasmic cigars.

Olga Ivanovitch came in again.

She had changed into a simple gray suit with plain white trimmings. Her honey-colored hair was all in place again, and her face was cool and freshly sweetened. She looked younger than Simon had ever remembered her. She carried a pair of suitcases. Kinglake really looked at her.

Simon hitched himself off the corner of the desk where he had perched.

"Well," he said, "let's be on our way."

He shook hands with Kinglake for the last time, and picked up Olga's bags and went out with her. They went down the crushed coral walk through a rambling profusion of poinsettias and bougainvillea that were only dark clusters under the moon. The Gulf waters rolled against the beach beyond the seawall with a hushed friendly roar. Simon Templar thought about Jean Lafitte again, and decided that in the line of piracy he could still look the old boy in the eye on his home ground.

They left the gate; and the girl's step faltered beside him. He slowed with her, turning; and she stopped and faced him.

"*Spassibo,*" she said, with an odd husky break in her voice. "Thank you, thank you, tovarich. . . . I don't think it's any use, but thank you."

"What do you mean, you don't think it's any use?"

Light seeping from a window of the house behind them like a timid thief in a dimout touched her pale halo of hair and glistened on her wide steady eyes.

"Where can I go now?"

The Saint laughed.

"My God, you Russians! Look, darling. You played along with Maris for quite a while. Several of the ungodly must know it. But they'll never know that Maris ever changed his mind about you. They'll only know that you got out of Galveston one jump ahead of the barrage. So you're all set to move in again somewhere else. That's what you wanted, isn't it? Well, I wasn't kidding either. That's what you're going to do. Only next time you'll do it legitimately—for the FBI or something like that. I'm taking you to Washington with me so you can meet a guy named Hamilton. I have to see him anyway. . . . Besides," he added constructively, "it's a dull trip, and we might make fun on the way."

ERLE STANLEY GARDNER

The Danger Zone

A FEW BLOCKS to the north of Market Street in San Francisco, Grant Avenue ceases to be a street of high class stores and becomes a part of China.

Major Copely Brane, freelance diplomat soldier of fortune, knew every inch of this strange section. For Major Brane knew his Chinese as most baseball fans know the strength and weakness of opposing teams.

Not that Major Brane had consciously confined his freelance diplomatic activities to matters pertaining to the Orient. His services were available to various and sundry. He had accepted employment from a patriotic German who wished to ascertain certain information about the French attitude toward reparations; and it was perhaps significant of the Major's absolute fairness, that the fee he had received from the German upon the successful completion of his task was exactly the amount which he had previously charged a French banker for obtaining confidential information from the file of a visiting ambassador as to the exact proposals which the German government was prepared to make as a final offer.

In short, Major Brane worked for various governments and various individuals. Those who had the price could engage his services. There was only one requirement: the task must be within the legitimate field of diplomatic activity. Major Brane was a clearing house of international and political information, and he took pride in doing his work well. Those who employed him could count upon his absolute loyalty upon all matters connected with the employment, could bank upon his subsequent silence; and best of all, they could rest assured that if Major Brane encountered any serious trouble in the discharge of his duties, he would never mention the name of his employer.

Of late, however, the Major's activities had been centered upon the situation in the Orient. This was due in part to the extreme rapidity with which that situation was changing from day to day; and in part to the fact that Major Brane prided himself upon his ability to deliver results. There is no one who appreciates results more, and explanations less, than the native of the Orient.

It was early evening, and the streets of San Francisco's Chinatown were giving forth their strange sounds—the shuffling feet of herded tourists, gazing open-mouthed at the strange life which seethed around them; the slippety-slop of Chinese shoes—skidded along the cement by feet that were lifted only a fraction of an inch; the pounding heels of plainclothesmen who always worked in pairs when on Chinatown duty.

Major Brane's ears heard these sounds and interpreted them mechanically. Major Brane was particularly interested to notice the changing window displays of the Chinese stores. The embargo on Japanese products was slowly working a complete change in the merchandise handled by the curio stores, and Major Brane's eyes narrowed as he noticed the fact. Disputes over the murder of a subject can be settled by arbitration, but there can be but one answer to a blow that hits hard at a nation's business.

Major Brane let his mind dwell upon certain angles of the political situation which were unknown to the average man. Would the world powers close their eyes to developments in Manchuria, providing these developments smashed the five-year plan and . . . ?

His ears, trained to constant watchfulness in the matter of unusual sounds, noticed the change in the tempo of the hurrying feet behind him. He knew that some man was going to accost him, even before he turned appraising eyes upon the other.

The man was Chinese, probably Western born, since he wore his Occidental clothes with the air of one who finds in them nothing awkward; and he thudded his feet emphatically upon the sidewalk, slamming his heels hard home with every step.

He had been hurrying, and the narrow chest was laboring. The eyes were glittering with some inner emotion of which there was no other external sign, save, perhaps, a very slight muscular tenseness about the expressionless mask of the face.

"Major Brane," he said in excellent English, and then stopped to suck in a lungful of air. "I have been to your hotel. You were out. I came here. I saw you, and ran."

Major Brane bowed, and his bow was polite, yet uncordial. Major Brane did not like to have men run after him on the street. Much of his employment entailed very grave dangers, and it was always advisable to keep his connections as secret as possible. Grant Avenue, in the heart of San Francisco's Chinatown, at the hour of eight forty-seven in the evening, was hardly a proper place to discuss matters of business—not when the business of the person accosted was that of interfering with the political situation in the Far East.

"Well?" said Major Brane.

"You must come, sir!"

"Where?"

"To my grandfather."

"And who is your grandfather?"

"Wong Sing Lee."

The lad spoke in the Chinese manner, giving the surname first. Major Brane knew that the family of Wong was very powerful, and that Chinese venerate age, age being synonymous with wisdom. Therefore, the grandfather of the panting youth must be a man of great importance in the social fabric of Chinatown. Yet Major Brane could recall no prominent member of the Wong family whose given name was Sing Lee. Somehow, the entire name sounded manufactured for the occasion.

Major Brane turned these matters over in his mind rapidly.

"I am afraid that I am not at liberty to accept," he said. "Will you convey my very great regrets to your estimable grandparent?"

The lad's hand moved swiftly. His face remained utterly expressionless, but the black lacquer of the eyes assumed a reddish glint which would have spoken volumes to those who have studied the psychology of the Oriental.

"You come!" he said fiercely, his voice almost breaking, "or I kill!"

Major Brane squared his shoulders, studied the face intently. "You might get away with it," he said, in a dispassionate voice that was almost impersonal, "but you'd be caught before you'd gone twenty feet—and you'd be hung for it."

The boy's eyes still held their reddish glint. "Without the help which you alone can give," he said, "death is preferable to life!"

And it was only because Major Brane knew his Chinese so well that he determined to accompany the boy, when he heard that burst of impassioned speech. When your Chinese resolves upon murder, he is very, very cool; and very, very wily. Only when a matter of honor is concerned, only when there is a danger of "losing face," does he resolve upon a heedless sacrifice. But when such occasions arise, he considers his own life of but minor moment.

Major Brane nodded. "Remove your hand from the gun," he said. "There is a plainclothesman coming this way. I will go with you."

He reached out, clamped a friendly hand about the arm of the youth, taking hold of the muscles just above the elbow. If the plainclothes officer should accost them, Major Brane wanted to prevent the youth from doing anything rash. And as his fingers clamped about the arm, Major Brane felt the quivering of the flesh, that tremor which comes from taut nerves.

"Steady!" he warned.

There is a popular belief that the Chinese is unemotional. The fallacy of that belief is on a par with the hundreds of fallacies which bar an understanding of the Orient by the Occident. Major Brane realized just how deadly dangerous the present situation was. If the officer should insist upon searching the youth for a weapon . . . But the officer was reassured by Major Brane's words.

"If it's real jade," said Major Brane in a loud tone of voice, regarding the bulge in the pocket of the youth's coat, "I'll look at it, but I want a bargain."

The officer veered off. The Chinese glittered his beady eyes at Major Brane and said nothing. A casual observer would have gathered that he was totally oblivious of the danger he had just escaped as well as the ruse by which he had been saved. But the reddish tinge left the surface of the eyes, and the boy took a deep breath.

"M'goy!" he muttered mechanically, which is a Cantonese expression of thanks, and means, "I am not worthy."

Major Brane made the prompt reply which etiquette demanded.

"Hoh wah!" he said, which in turn means, "good talk!"

And the fact that most Westerners would have found the words amusing as well as entirely unrelated to expressions of thanks and welcome is but illustrative of the gulf between the races.

The young Chinese led the way down a side street. Major Brane fell in slightly behind, walked unhesitatingly, his hand swinging free making no covert effort to reach toward the shoulder holster which was slung beneath his left arm. He had given his word, and his word had been accepted.

They paused before a dark door, which was the center one of a row of dark doors. Apparently these entrances were to separate buildings, huddled closely together in the congestion of poverty; but when the door swung open, Major Brane found himself in a courtyard enclosed by a brick wall. The enclosure was spacious and airy. The other doors had been but dummies set in the brick wall, and were kept locked. Had one opened any one of those other doors, he would have encountered nothing but brick.

Major Brane gave no evidences of surprise. He had been in such places before. The Chinese of wealth always builds his house with a cunning simulation of external poverty. In the Orient one may look in vain for mansions, unless one has the entree to private homes. The street entrances always give the impression of congestion and poverty, and the lines of architecture are carefully carried out so that no glimpse of the mansion itself is visible over the forbidding false front of what appears to be a squalid hovel.

"Quickly!" breathed the Chinese.

His feet pattered over flags, paused at an entrance, to the side of which was an altar and the Chinese characters which signify the presence of Toe Day, the god whose duty it is to frighten away the "homeless ghosts" who would attach themselves to the family, yet will permit free access to the spirits of departed ancestors.

A bell jangled. The door swung open. A huge Chinese servant stood in the doorway.

"The master awaits," he said.

The boy pushed his way into the house, through a reception room furnished in conventional dark wood furnishings, into an inner room, the doorway to which was a circle with a high ledge at the entrance, to keep away evil spirits.

Major Brane knew at once that he was dealing with an old family who had retained all the conventions of ten thousand years; knew, also that he would be kept with his back to the door if he were received as a prisoner, and given a seat across the room, facing the doorway, if he were an honored guest.

His eyes, suddenly grown as hard as polished steel, surveyed the interior of the room. An old man sat on a low stool. A wisp of white beard straggled down from either side of his chin. His face was withered and wrinkled. Most of the hair was gone from the head. The nails of the little fingers were almost three inches long. The left hand waved toward a stool which was at the end of the room facing the door.

"Cheng nay choh," he said to Major Brane, and the boy interpreted. "Please sit down," he said.

Major Brane heaved a sigh of relief as he sat down upon the rigidly uncomfortable chair which faced the doorway—the seat of honor.

The servant brought him a cup of tea and a plate of dried melon seeds, which he set down upon a stand of teakwood inlaid with ivory and jade. Major Brane knew that regardless of the urgency of the matter in hand, it would not be broached until he had partaken of the food and drink, so he sipped the scalding tea, took a melon seed between his teeth, cracked it and extracted the meat with a celerity which branded him at once as one who knew his way about. Chopsticks can be mastered with a few lessons, but not so with the technique of melon seeds.

The old man sucked up a bamboo pipe, the bowl of which was of soft metal. It was packed with *sook yen*, the Chinese tobacco which will eat the membranes from an uneducated throat. He gurgled into speech.

There was no doubt in Major Brane's mind but that the young boy would act as interpreter; and he guessed that the lad was quite familiar with the situation, and eager to express himself upon it. Yet such is the veneration for age that the boy kept his eyes upon the old man's face, listening intently, ready to interpret, not what he himself wanted to say, but what the head of the family should utter.

For some three minutes the old man spoke. Major Brane caught a word here and there, and, as his ears conveyed those words to his consciousness, Major Brane sat very rigidly attentive.

The boy interpreted, when the grandfather had finished speaking; and his voice held that absence of tone which comes to one who is repeating but the words of another.

"Jee Kit King has been taken by our enemies. She will be tortured. Even now, they are preparing to start the torture. She will be tortured until she speaks or until she dies, and she will not speak. You are to save her. You must work with speed. And your own life will be in danger."

Major Brane snapped questions. "Who are your enemies?"

"Enemies of China."

"Who are they?"

"We do not know."

"How long has the girl been missing?"

"Less than one hour."

"Why do they torture her?"

"To find out what she did with the evidence."

"What evidence?"

That question brought a period of silence. Then the boy turned to the old man and rattled forth a swift sentence of Cantonese. Major Brane understood enough of that question to know that the youth was asking the old man for permission to give Major Brane the real facts; but even as the old man pursed his puckered lips about the stained mouthpiece of the pipe, Major Brane sensed that the reply would be adverse.

In fact there was no reply at all. The old man smoked placidly, puffing out the oil tobacco smoke, his eyes glittering, fixed upon the distance.

The young man whirled back to Major Brane, lowered his voice.

"There is, in this city, Mah Bak Heng, who comes from Canton."

Major Brane let his eyes show merely polite interest. He already knew much of Mah Bak Heng, and of his mission, but he kept that knowledge from showing in his eyes.

The boy began to outline certain salient facts.

"Mah Bak Heng has power in Canton. Canton is in revolt against the Nanking government. The Nanking government wishes to unite China to the end that war may be declared upon Japan, over Manchuria. Until the Canton matter is fixed, there can be no war. Canton has money and influence. . . .

"Mah Bak Heng keeps peace from being made. He cables his men to yield to the Nanking government only upon terms that are impossible. Mah Bak Heng is a traitor. He is accepting pay from enemies of China, to keep the revolution alive. If we could prove that, the people of Canton would no longer listen to the voice of the traitor.

"Jee Kit King is my sister. This man is the grandfather. We talked it over. Jee Kit King has studied in the business schools. She can write down the words of a man as fast as a man can speak, and then she can copy those words upon a typewriter. She is very bright. She agreed that she would trap Mah Bak Heng into employing her as his secretary. Then, when the payment for his treason was delivered, she would get sufficient evidence to prove that payment, and would come to us.

"We know she secured that evidence. She left the place of Mah Bak Heng. But on the way here, two men spoke to her. She accompanied them to a cab. She has not been seen since."

The boy ceased speaking, drew a quivering breath.

The old man puffed placidly upon the last dying embers of the oily tobacco, reached a stained thumb and forefinger into a time-glazed pouch of leather for a fresh portion.

Major Brane squinted his eyes slightly in thought. "Perhaps she went with friends."

"No. They were enemies."

"She had the evidence with her?"

"Apparently not."

"Why do you say that?"

"Because, just before I went to you, three men came hurriedly to her room and made a search."

Major Brane puckered his forehead in thought.

"That means?" he asked.

"That they captured her, searched her but could not find that which they sought, and then went to the room, thinking it was hidden there."

"And not finding it?" asked Major Brane.

"Not finding it, they will torture Jee Kit King." The boy wet his lips with the tip of his tongue, gave a motion that was like a shudder. "They are very cruel," he said. "They can torture well. They remove the clothes, string the body by hands and feet, and build small fires in the middle of the back."

"The girl will not speak?" inquired Major Brane. "Not even under torture?"

"She will not speak."

"How can I save her? There is no time. Even now they will have started the torture," said Major Brane, and he strove to make his tone as kindly as possible.

The boy gave vent to a little scream. His hand flashed out from his pocket. The last vestige of self control left him. He thrust a trembling revolver barrel into the middle of Major Brane's stomach.

"When she dies," he screamed, "you die! You can save her! You alone. You have knowledge in such matters. If she dies, you die. I swear it, by the memory of my ancestors!"

Major Brane glanced sideways at the menace of the cocked revolver, the quivering hand. He knew too well the danger in which he was placed. He looked at the old man, saw that he was lighting a fresh bowl of tobacco and that the clawlike hand which held the flaming match was as steady as a rock. The ebony eyes were still fixed upon distance. He had not so much as turned his head.

Major Brane realized several things. "I will do my best," he soothed, and gently moved backward, as though to get to his feet. The motion pushed the gun a little to one side. "If this girl is your sister," he said, "why is she a Jee, when your grandfather is a Wong?"

"She is not my sister. I love her. I am to marry her!—You must save her. Fast! Quick! Go and do something, and prepare to die if you do not. Here, you can have money, money in plenty!"

The old man, his eyes still fixed upon space, his head never turning, reached his left hand beneath the folds of his robe and tossed a leather bag toward Major Brane. The mouth of the bag was open, and the light glinted upon a great roll of currency.

"Where does the girl have her room?" asked Major Brane, making no move to reach for the money.

The boy was too nervous to speak. He seemed about to faint or to become hysterical. The shaking hand which held the revolver jiggled the weapon about in a half circle.

"Quick!" snapped Major Brane. "If I am to be of help I must know where she lives."

But the boy only writhed his lips.

It was the old man who answered. He removed the stained stem of the pipe from his mouth, and Brane was surprised to hear him speak in excellent English.

"She has a room at Number Thirteen Twenty-Two Stockton Street," he said. "The room is maintained in her name."

Major Brane swung his eyes.

"I've seen you somewhere before . . ." he said, and would have said more. But as though some giant hand had snuffed out the lights, the room became suddenly dark, a pitch black darkness that was as oppressive as a blanket. And the darkness gave forth the rustling sound of bodies, moving with surreptitious swiftness.

Major Brane flung himself to one side. His hand darted beneath the lapel of his coat, clutched the reassuring bulk of the automatic which reposed in the shoulder holster.

Then the lights came on, as abruptly as they had been extinguished. The room was exactly as it had been three or four seconds before, save that Major Brane was the only occupant. The chairs were there. The old man's pipe, the bowl still smoking and the oily tobacco sizzling against the sides of the metal, was even propped against a small table.

But the old Chinese grandfather and the boy himself had disappeared.

A man came shuffling along the flags of the outer room. It was the same servant who had escorted Major Brane into the room.

"What you want here?" he asked.

"I want to see the master."

"Master not home. You go out now."

Major Brane holstered his weapon, smiled affably. "Very well."

The servant slip-slopped to the courtyard, unlocked the door.

"Good-bye," he said.

"Good-bye," observed Major Brane, and stepped out into the street.

A fog was coming in, and its first damp, writhing tendrils were clutching at the dim corners of the mysterious buildings. The sounds of traffic from the main avenues came to him, muffled as though they were the sounds of another world.

Major Brane moved, and as he moved a patch of shadow across the street slipped into furtive motion. A stooped figure hugged the patch of darkness which extended along the front of the dark and silent buildings. Another figure walked casually out of the doorway of a building at the corner, stood in the light, looking up and down the lighted thoroughfare. It might have been waiting for a friend. A bulky figure, padded out with a quilted coat, hands thrust up the sleeves, came from a doorway to the rear and started walking directly toward Major Brane.

Major Brane sighed, turned, and walked rapidly toward the lighted thoroughfare. The fact that the boy had been forced to accost him on the street made it doubly inconvenient. Things which happen upon the streets of Chinatown seldom go unobserved.

Major Brane had no way of knowing who those shadowing figures might be; they might be friends of the people who had employed him, keeping a watch upon him lest he seek to escape the trust which had been thrust upon him, or they might be emissaries of the enemy, seeking to balk him in accomplishing anything of value.

But one thing was positive. Somewhere in the city a Chinese girl was held in restraint by enemies who were, in all probability, proceeding even now to a slow torture that would either end in speech or death. And another thing was equally positive: unless Major Brane could effect the rescue of that girl, he could count his own life as forfeit. The young man had sworn upon the memory of his ancestors, and such oaths are not to be disregarded. Moreover, there had been the silent acquiescence of the old man.

''Grandfather! sputtered Major Brane under his breath. ''He's no more her grandfather than I am! I've seen him before somewhere, and I'll place him yet!''

But he knew better than to waste any mental energy in jogging a tardy recollection. Major Brane was having his hands full at the moment. He had a task before him which required rare skill, and the price of failure would be death.

He reached back for his tobacco pouch, and his hand touched something which swung in a dangling circle from the skirt of his coat. He pulled the garment around. The thing was the leather pouch which the old man had tossed to him. It was filled with greenbacks of large denomination, rolled tightly together.

That bag must have been pinned to his coat by the old servant as he was leaving the courtyard. The knowledge gave Major Brane a feeling of mingled security and uneasiness. That meant that at least one of his shadows must be in the employ of the old man who had posed as the girl's grandfather. That shadow would make certain that Major Brane found the sack of currency, that it did not come loose and roll unheeded into the gutter.

But there were three shadows. What of the other two? And there was the disquieting knowledge that even the friendly shadow would become hostile should Major Brane fail in his undertaking.

The young man had promised that Brane should not outlive the girl;

and the promise had been sworn by the sacred memory of the young man's ancestors.

Major Copely Brane walked directly to his room in the hotel, which was almost on the outskirts of Chinatown. That step was, at least, noncommittal, and Major Brane needed time to think. Also, he had a secret method of exit from that room in the hotel.

He opened the door with his key, switched on the lights, bolted the door behind him, and dropped into a chair. He held his arm at an angle so that his wristwatch ticked off the seconds before his eyes.

He knew that it was hopeless to plunge blindly into the case without a plan of campaign. And he knew that it would be fatal to consume too much time in thought. Therefore he allowed himself precisely three minutes of concentration—one hundred and eighty seconds within which to work out some plan which might save the life of the girl, and, incidentally, preserve his own safety.

He thought of Mah Bak Heng. Major Brane had some shrewd suspicion about Mah Bak Heng, but he had no proof. There was a chance that those suspicions could be converted into proof by the burglary of a certain safe. But that burglary would take time. Even with the necessary proof, Major Brane would be no nearer locating those who held the girl captive; and she would be dead long before he could bring sufficient pressure to bear upon the Chinese politician to force a trade or treaty.

Major Brane squirmed uneasily in his chair. Thirty seconds had ticked by. He might trust to blind chance, figure out who would probably be chosen to kidnap a girl who had acquired dangerous information, make a guess as to the location that would be picked upon for torture. But there was only one chance in a hundred that, with all of his shrewd knowledge of things Oriental, he would be able to make a correct guess. Then there would remain the task of effecting a rescue.

No. The girl would have died a slow death long before such a plan could be carried into execution.

Forty-five seconds gone.

Major Brane shifted the position of his legs. His eyes were cold and hard as polished steel. His jaw was thrust forward. His lips were a thin line of determination. The light illuminated the delicately chiseled lines of his aristocratic face.

He went back to the first principles of deductive reasoning. The girl was a spy. She had evidently secured the thing that would link Mah Bak Heng with interests that were inimical to China. That thing would, if Major Brane read his man right, be in the nature of cash. But cash leaves no trail. Therefore, the thing which the girl had secured was something equivalent to cash, which also indicated the person who had paid the cash. It was a safe bet that this something had been a check.

She had left the place, seeking her friends; and the enemy had known she was a spy—at least that soon, perhaps before. Had the girl been aware that her disguise had been penetrated? That was a question which could only be answered in the light of subsequent events. Those subsequent events proved that the girl had been "taken for a ride" by her enemies. Undoubtedly, she had been searched almost immediately; and the subsequent searching of her rooms would indicate that this search had been fruitless.

So far, then, the enemies were deprived of the evidence which they had sought to take from the girl. The girl had hidden it in some place that was not on her person. Where?

Obviously, those enemies had thought the most likely place was the girl's bedroom. Rightly or wrongly, they had reasoned that the check was hidden there. It was impossible now to find the girl within the time necessary to save her life; but the people who held her captive would torture her, not for the pleasure of torture, but for the purpose of securing that which they coveted—the check. Therefore, if they secured the check without torture, they would refrain from torture.

That thought lodged in Major Brane's mind, and he immediately seized upon it as being the key to the situation. His eyes stared unwinkingly, his brows deepened into straight lines of thought.

Then, after a few moments, he nodded his head. His eyes snapped to a focus upon the dial of the wristwatch. The time lacked thirteen seconds of the three-minute limit which he had imposed upon himself.

Major Brane crossed to a desk in one corner of his room. That desk contained many curious odds and ends. They were articles which Major Brane had collected against future contingencies, and they dealt with many phases of the Orient. He selected a tinted oblong of paper. It was a check upon a bank that was known for its connections in the far east. The check was, of course, blank. Major Brane filled it in.

The name of the payee was Mah Bak Heng. The amount caused Major Brane some deliberation. He finally resolved upon the figure of fifty thousand dollars. He felt that in all probability that amount would be the top price for the final payment, and he knew Mah Bak Heng well enough to believe that he would command the top price for the final payment, assuming that there had been several previous payments.

It was when it came to filling in the name of the payer at the bottom of the check that Major Brane pulled his master stroke. There was a slight smile twisting the corners of his lips as he made a very credible forgery of a signature. The signature was that of a man who was utterly unknown in the Oriental situation, save by a very select few. But Major Brane had always made it his business to secure knowledge which was not available to the average diplomat.

He blotted the check, folded it once, straightened the fold and folded it again. Then he began to fold it into the smallest possible compass, taking care to iron down each fold with the handle of an ivory paper knife. When he had finished, the check was but a tight wad of paper, folded into an oblong.

Major Brane took the cellophane wrapping from a package of cigarettes, carefully wrapping the spurious check in it, and thrusting the tiny package into his pocket.

He left his room by the secret exit: through the connecting door into another room; through another connecting door into a room that had a window that opened on a fire escape platform; out the window to the platform; along the platform to a door; through the door to a back staircase; down the stairs to an alley exit; out the alley to the side street.

He hailed a passing cab and gave the address of the building where Jee Kit King had her residence. As the cab swung into speed, Major Brane looked behind him.

There were two cars, following closely.

Major Brane sighed wearily. It was no surprise; merely what he had expected. He was dealing with men who were very, very capable. He didn't know whether he had shaken off one of the shadows, or whether one of the following cars held two men, the other holding one; but he was inclined to believe all three were following, two in one car, one in the other.

He made an abortive effort to shake off the pursuit. It was an effort that was purposely clumsy. The following cars dropped well to the rear, however, and switched off their lights.

A less experienced man than Major Brane would have believed that the ruse had been a success, and that the shadows were lost. Major Brane merely smiled and sent the cab rushing to the address where the girl had lived.

He found her apartment without difficulty.

It was on a third floor. The lodgings were, for the most part, given over to people of limited means who were neat and clean but economical.

The door of the girl's apartment was locked. Major Brane hesitated over that lock only long enough to get a key that would turn the bolt; and his collection of skeleton keys was sufficiently complete to cut that delay to a period of less than four seconds. He entered the apartment, leaving the door open behind him; not much, just a sufficient crack to insure against a surreptitious bolting from the outer side without his knowledge.

When he had jerked out a few drawers and rumpled a few clothes, Major Brane picked up a jar of cold cream. A frown of annoyance crossed his features as he saw that there was only a small amount of cream in the jar.

But in the bathroom he found a fresh jar, unopened. He unscrewed the top, thrust the cellophane-wrapped check deep down into the greasy mixture. He let it remain there for a few seconds, then fished it out again. In taking it out, he smeared a copious supply of cold cream over the edge of the jar, and wiped his fingers on a convenient towel, leaving the excess cold cream smeared about the edge of the jar, a deep hole in the center of the cream.

Unwrapping the cellophane, he left it on the shelf over the washstand, a transparent oblong of paper smeared with cold cream; left it in such a shape that it was readily apparent it had served as a container for some small object.

Then Major Brane, pocketing the spurious check, wiped his hands carefully to remove all traces of the cream from his fingertips, but was careful to leave a sufficient deposit under the nails of his fingers to be readily detected.

He walked to the door of the apartment, peered out. The hallway seemed deserted. As furtively as a thief in the night, Major Brane tiptoed down this hallway, came to the stairs, took them upon cautious feet, emerged upon the sidewalk.

He motioned to his cab driver.

"Married?" he asked.

The man nodded.

"Children?"

Another nod.

"Remember them, then, if anything happens," said Major Brane. "Your first duty is to them."

"I'll say it is!" agreed the cab driver. "What's the racket?"

"Nothing," commented Major Brane crisply. "I simply wanted to impress that particular thought on your mind. Swing toward Chinatown and drive as fast as you can. Keep to the dark side streets."

"Whereabouts in Chinatown?"

"It doesn't matter. Just in that general direction."

"And drive fast?"

''Take 'em on two wheels!''

''Get in!'' snapped the driver.

He slammed the door. The cab started with a jerk. The tires screamed on the first corner, but all four wheels remained on the pavement. The cabbie did better at the second corner. Then he nearly tipped over as he cut into a dark side street.

Major Brane gave no sign of nervousness. He was watching the road behind him, and his eyes were cold and hard, frosty in their unwinking stare.

They were midway in the block when a car swung into the cross street. It was a low roadster, powerful, capable of great speed, and it swept down on the taxicab as a hawk swoops upon a sparrow. The head lights were dark, and the car flashed through the night like some sinister beast of prey.

The cab had just turned into the second intersection when the roadster drew alongside. There sounded a swift explosion that might have been a backfire. The taxicab swerved as a rear tire went out. Then it settled to the rim and the *thunkety-thunk-thunk-thunk*, marked the revolutions as the cab skidded to the pavement and stopped.

The cab driver turned a white face to Major Brane, started to say something, then thrust his hands up as high as he could get them, the fingertips jammed into the top of the roof. For he was gazing directly into the business end of a large caliber automatic, held in the hands of one of the figures that had leapt from the roadster. The other figure was holding a submachine gun pointed directly at Major Brane's stomach.

Both of the men were masked.

''Seem to have tire trouble,'' said one of the men. He spoke in the peculiar accents of a foreigner whose language is more staccato than musical.

Major Brane kept his hands in sight, but he did not elevate them. ''Yes,'' he said.

The man with the submachine gun grinned. His flashing teeth were plainly visible below the protection of the mask.

He spoke English with the easy familiarity of one who has spoken no other language since birth. ''Better come ride with us,'' he said. ''You seemed to be in a hurry, and it'll take time to repair that tire.''

''I'd prefer to wait,'' said Major Brane, and smiled.

''I'd prefer to have you ride,'' said the man with the submachine gun, politely, and the muzzle wavered suggestively in a little arc that took in Major Brane's torso. ''You might find it healthier to ride.''

''Thanks'' said Major Brane. ''I'll ride, then.''

The man in the roadster snapped a command. "Open the car door for him," he said.

The one who held the automatic stretched back his left hand, worked the catch of the door.

"OK," said the man in the roadster.

Major Brane stumbled. As he stumbled, he threw forth his hand to catch his balance, and the other hand slipped the folded check from his pocket. He lowered his head, thrust check in his mouth.

The man with the automatic jumped toward him. The man with the submachine gun laughed sarcastically.

"No you don't," he said. "Get it!"

The last two words were cracked at the man who had held the automatic. That man leapt forward. Stubby fingers, that were evidently well acquainted with the human anatomy, pressed against nerve centers in Major Brane's neck. Brane writhed with pain, and opened his jaw. The folded bit of tinted paper dropped to the pavement. The man swooped down upon it, picked it up with eager hands.

A police whistle trilled through the night.

"In!" crisped the man with the submachine gun.

Major Brane felt arms about him, felt his automatic whisked from its holster. Then he was boosted into the roadster. The gears clashed. The car lurched into speed.

Behind him, Major Brane could hear the taxicab driver yelling for the police, so loudly as to send echoes from the sides of the somber buildings that lined the dark street.

The roadster's lights clicked on. The man who had held the submachine gun was driving. The other man was crowded close beside Major Brane's neck, the other jabbing the end of the automatic into Major Brane's ribs.

The man at the wheel knew the city, and he knew his car. The machine kept almost entirely to dark side streets and went swiftly. Within five minutes, it had turned to an alley on a steep hill, slid slowly downward, wheels rubbing against brake bands.

A garage door silently opened. The roadster went into the garage. The door closed. The roadster lights were switched off. A door opened from the side of the garage.

"Well?" said a voice.

"We got it. He found it. We grabbed him. He tried to swallow it, but we got it."

"Where was it?" asked the voice from the darkness.

"In a jar of cold cream in her apartment."

The voice made no answer. For several seconds the weight of the dark silence oppressed them. Then the voice gave a crisp command.

"Bring him in."

The man who had driven the car took Major Brane's arm above the elbow. The other man, an arm still around Major Brane's neck, jabbed the gun firmly against his ribs.

"OK, guy. No funny stuff," said the one who had held the machine gun.

Major Brane groped with his feet, found the floor. The guards were on either side of him, pushing him forward. A door opened, disclosing a glow of diffused light. A flight of stairs led upward.

"Up and at 'em!" said the man on Major Brane's left.

They climbed up the stairs, maintaining their awkward formation of three abreast. There was a landing at the top, then a hallway. Major Brane was taken down the hallway, into a room that was furnished with exquisite care, a room in which massive furniture dwarfed the high ceilings, the wide windows. Those windows were covered with heavy drapes that had been tightly drawn.

Major Brane was pushed into a chair.

"Park yourself, guy."

Major Brane sank into the cushions. His hands were on the arms of the chair. The room was deserted, save for his two guards. The man whose voice had given the orders to the pair was nowhere in evidence.

"May I smoke?" asked Major Brane.

The masked guard grinned. "Brother," he said, "if there's any smoking to be done, I'll do it. You just sit pretty like you were having your picture taken, and don't make no sudden moves. I've got your gat; but they say you're full of tricks, and if I was to see any sudden moves, I'd have to cut you open to see whether you was stuffed with sawdust or tricks. You've got my curiosity aroused."

Major Brane said nothing.

The man who had taken the check walked purposefully toward one of the draped exits, pushed aside the rich hangings and disappeared.

Major Brane eyed the masked figure who remained to guard him. The man grinned.

"Don't bother," he said. "You wouldn't know me, even if it wasn't for the mask."

Major Brane lowered his voice, cautiously. "Are you in this thing for money?" he asked.

The man grinned. "No, no, brother. You got me wrong. I'm in it for my health!" And he laughed gleefully.

Major Brane was earnest. ''They've got the check. That's all they're concerned with. There'd be some money in it for you if you let me go.''

The eyes glittered through the mask in scornful appraisal.

''Think I'm a fool?''

Major Brane leaned forward, very slightly. ''They won't hurt me,'' he said, ''and the check's gone already. But there are some other important papers that I don't want them to find. They simply can't find them—mustn't. Those papers are worth a great deal to certain parties, and it would be most unfortunate if they should fall into the hands of these men who were interested in the check. If you would only accept those papers and deliver them to the proper parties, you could get enough money to make you independent for years to come.''

The eyes back of the mask were no longer scornful. ''Where are those papers?'' asked the man.

''You promise you'll deliver them?''

''Yeah. Sure.''

''In my cigarette case,'' said Major Brane. ''Get them—quick!''

And he half raised his hands.

The masked figure came to him in two swift strides.

''No you don't! Keep your hands down. I'll get the cigarette case—In your inside pocket, eh? All right, guy; try anything and you'll get bumped!'' He held a heavy gun in his left hand, thrust an exploring right hand into Major Brane's inside coat pocket. He extracted the cigarette case, grinned at Major Brane, stepped back.

''I said I'd deliver 'em. That was a promise. The only thing I didn't promise was who I'd deliver 'em to. I'll have to look at 'em first. I might be interested myself.'' And he gloatingly held the cigarette case up, pressed the catch.

That cigarette case had been designed by Major Brane against just such an emergency. The man pressed the catch. The halves flew open, and a spring mechanism shot a stream of ammonia full into the man's eyes.

Major Brane was out of the chair with a flashing spurt of motion which was deadly and swift. His right hand crossed over in the sort of blow which is only given by the trained boxer. It was a perfectly timed blow, the powerful muscles of the body swinging into play as the fist pivoted over and around.

The man with the mask caught the blow on the button of the jaw. Major Brane listened for an instant, but no one seemed to have heard the man's fall. He walked swiftly to the doorway which led into the hall, then down the hall and down the steps to the garage. He opened the garage door, got in the roadster, turned on the ignition, stepped on the starter. The motor throbbed into life.

A light flashed on in the garage. A grotesque figure stumbled out through the door, silhouetted as a black blotch against the light of the garage. The man was waving his arms, shouting.

Major Brane spun the wheel, sent the car skidding around the corner. Behind him, there sounded a single shot; and the bullet whined from the pavement. There were no more shots.

Major Brane stepped on the gas.

He drove three blocks toward the south, headed toward Market Street. He saw a garage that was open, slowed the car, swung the wheel, rolled into the garage.

''Storage,'' he said.

''Day, week, or month?'' asked the man in overalls and faded coat who slouched forward.

''Just for an hour or two; maybe all night.''

The attendant grinned. ''Four bits,'' he said.

Major Brane nodded, handed him half a dollar, received an oblong of pasteboard with a number. He turned, walked out of the garage, paused at the curb and tore the oblong of numbered pasteboard into small bits. Then he started walking, directing his steps over the same route he had traveled in the roadster.

He heard the snarl of a racing motor, the peculiar screaming noise made by protesting tires when a corner is rounded too fast, and he stepped back into a doorway. A touring car shot past. There were three men in it; three grim figures who sat very erect and whose hands were concealed.

When the car had passed, Major Brane stepped out and resumed his rapid walk, back toward the house from which he had escaped.

He walked up the hill. The garage was dark now, but the door was still open.

Major Brane walked cautiously, but kept up his speed. He slipped into the dark garage, waited, advanced, tried the door which opened to the flight of stairs. The door was locked now, from the inside. Major Brane stopped, applied an eye to the keyhole. The key, he saw, was in the lock.

He took out his skeleton keys, also a long, slender-bladed penknife. With the point of the knife blade he worked the end of the key around, up and down, up and down. Gradually, as he freed the key, the heavier end, containing the flange, had a tendency to drop down. Major Brane manipulated the key until this tendency had ample opportunity to assert itself. Then he pushed with the point of the knife. The key slid out of the lock, thudded to the floor on the other side of the door.

Major Brane inserted a skeleton key, pressed up and around on the key, felt the bolt snap back, and opened the door. The little entranceway with the flight of stairs was before him. Major Brane walked cautiously up those stairs. His eyes were slitted, his body poised for swift action.

He gained the hallway at the top of the stairs, started down it cautiously. He could hear voices from a room at one end of the corridor, voices that were raised in excited conversation. Major Brane avoided that room but slipped into the room which adjoined it. That room was dark; and Major Brane, closing the door behind him, listened for a moment while he stood perfectly still, his every faculty concentrated.

He was standing so, when there sounded the click of a light switch and the room was flooded with light.

A rather tall man with a black beard, and eyes that seemed the shade of dulled silver, was standing by a light switch, holding a huge automatic in a hand that was a mass of bony knuckles, of long fingers and black hair.

"Sit down, Major Brane," said the man.

Major Brane sighed, for the man was he whose name Major Brane had forged to the spurious check.

The man chuckled. "Do you know, Major, I rather expected you back. Clever, aren't you? But after one has dealt with you a few times he learns to anticipate your little schemes."

Major Brane said nothing. He stood rigidly motionless, taking great care not to move his hands. He knew this man, knew the ruthless cruelty of him, the shrewd resourcefulness of his mind, the deadly determination which actuated him.

"Do sit down, Major."

Major Brane crossed to a chair and sat down.

The man with the beard let the tips of his white teeth glitter below the gloss of dark hairs which swept his upper lip in smooth regularity. The tip of the pointed beard quivered as the chin muscles twitched. "Yes," he said, "I expected you back."

Major Brane nodded. "I didn't know *you* were here," he observed. "Otherwise I would have been more cautious."

"Thanks for the compliment, Major. Incidentally, my associates here know me by the name of Brinkhoff. It would be most unfortunate if they should learn of my real identity, or of my connections."

"Unfortunate for you?" asked Major Brane meaningly.

The teeth glittered again as the lips swept back in a mirthless and all but noiseless laugh.

"Unfortunate for both of us, Major. Slightly unfortunate for me, but doubly—trebly—unfortunate for you."

Major Brane nodded. "Very well, Mr. Brinkhoff," he said.

The dulled silver eyes regarded him speculatively, morosely. "Rather clever of you to prepare a forgery which you could use as a red herring to drag across the trail," he said. "That's what comes of trusting subordinates. As soon as they told me how clumsy you were in your attempt to thrust the check into your mouth and swallow it, I knew they had been duped.—Fools! They were laughing over your clumsy attempt! Bah!"

Major Brane inclined his head. "Thank you, Brinkhoff."

Ominous lights glinted back of the dulled silver of the eyes. "Well," rasped the man, after a moment, "what did you do with it?"

"The original?"

"Naturally."

Major Brane took a deep breath. "I placed it where you could never find it, of course."

The teeth shone again as the man grinned. "No you didn't, Major. You took advantage of your arrival here to conceal it some place in the room—perhaps in the cushion of the chair. When you escaped, you went in a hurry to draw pursuit. You returned to get the check."

Major Brane shook his head. "No. The check isn't in the house. I placed it where it would be safe. I returned for the girl."

A frown divided the man's forehead. "You hid it?"

Major Brane chose his words carefully. "I feel certain that it is safe from discovery," he said.

The man with the beard rasped out an oath, started toward Major Brane.

"Damn you," he gritted, "I believe you're telling the truth! I told them you'd come back after the girl. That's why I had them carrying on a loud conversation in the next room. I thought you'd try to slip in here and listen, particularly if the room was dark."

Major Brane inclined his head. "Well reasoned," he said. His voice was as impersonally courteous as that of a tennis player who mutters a "well played" to his opponent.

For a long three seconds the two men locked eyes.

"There are ways," said the bearded man, ending that long period of menacing silence, "of making even the stoutest heart weaken, of making even the most stubborn tongue talk."

Major Brane shrugged his shoulders. "Naturally," he said, "I hope you are not so stupid as to think that I would overlook that fact, and not take steps to guard against it."

"Such as?"

"Such as seeing that the check was placed entirely out of my control before I returned."

"Thinking that would make you immune from—persuasion?" asked the bearded man mockingly.

Major Brane nodded his head. "Thinking you would not waste time on torture when it could do you no good, and when your time is so short."

"Time so short, Major?"

"Yes. I rather think there will be many things for you to do, now that that check is to be made public. There will be complete new arrangements to make, and your time is short. The Nanking government and the Canton government will be forced to settle their differences as soon as the knowledge of that check becomes public property."

The bearded man cursed, bitterly, harshly.

Major Brane sat perfectly immobile.

The bearded one raised his voice. "All right. Here he is. Come in."

The door of the room in which the loud conversation had taken place burst open. Four men came tumbling eagerly into the room. They were not masked. Major Brane knew none of them. They stared at him curiously.

The bearded man glowered at them. "He claims he ditched the original check in a safe place," he said. "He's clever enough to have done something that'll be hard to check up on. The check may be in the house. He may have left it in the room where he sat; or he may have picked it up when he came in the second time, and put it some place where we'd never think to look. He's that clever.

"Search him first, and then search the house. Then take up the trail of the car. He wouldn't have taken it far. He was back too soon. . . Still, he wouldn't have left it parked on the street. He'd know we'd spot it. He must have left it in the garage that's down . . ."

Major Brane interrupted, courteously. "Pardon me, it is in the garage. I left it there and tore up the ticket. I didn't know you were here, at the time, Brinkhoff, or I would have saved myself the trouble."

The bearded man gave a formal inclination of the head. "Thanks. Now, since we understand each other so thoroughly, and since you have shown such a disposition to cooperate, there's a possibility we can simplify matters still further. We can make a trade, we two. I'll trade you the girl for the check."

Major Brane smiled, the patronizing, chiding smile which a parent gives to a precocious child who is trying to obtain some unfair advantage. "No. The check will have to be eliminated from the discussion now."

"We'll get it eventually."

"I hardly think so."

"That which is going to happen to the girl is hardly a pleasant subject to discuss. You see there are very major political issues involved. You, my dear Major, and I, have long since learned not to grow emotional over political matters. Unfortunately, some of my subordinates—or perhaps I should refer to them as associates—are still in the emotional stage. If they feel that major political issues have been shaped by the theft of a check, and that this girl is the guilty party . . ." He broke off with a suggesive shrug.

Major Brane sighed. The sigh seemed to be almost an incipient yawn. "As you, yourself, have so aptly remarked," he said indifferently, "*we* have learned not to grow emotional over political matters."

The bearded man sneered. "I thought you came here for the girl."

"I did."

"You don't seem anxious to save her from an unpleasant experience."

Major Brane made a slight gesture with his shoulders. "I was employed to recover the check. I thought it might be a good plan to throw in a rescue of the girl for good measure."

The bearded man suddenly lost his semblance of poise, his veneer of culture. He took a swift step forward, his beard bristling, the strong white fangs behind it contrasting with the jet black of the beard.

"Damn you! We'll get that check out of you. We'll fry you in hot grease, a bit at a time. We'll pull off the skin and stick burning cigars in the flesh. We'll . . ." He choked with the very vehemence of his rage.

This time Major Brane yawned outright. "Come, come!" he said. "I thought we had outgrown these childish displays of emotion! We are playing major politics, we two. If you have lost the check, you have lost the fight. Torturing through vengeance won't help you any."

"It'll make you suffer! It'll eliminate you from any future interference. You've blocked too many of my plans before this!"

Major Brane nodded. It was as though he considered an impersonal problem. "Of course," he muttered politely, "if you look at it that way!"

The man turned his dulled silver eyes morosely upon the others, who had been standing at sullen attention. "Search him. Then the house. Then the streets."

The men came forward. They were thorough about the search and not at all gentle. Major Brane assisted them wherever he could. They pulled his pockets inside out, took away all of his personal belongings, searched his shoes, his coat lining, the lapels of his coat, under the collar.

Then they divided into two groups. One searched the house, the other group the street. The man with the beard remained with Major Brane, glowering at him, the nature of his thoughts indicated by the dark of his skin, the closed fists, the level brows.

Major Brane regarded him speculatively. "The girl is here?" he asked.

His answer was a scornful, mocking laugh.

"I merely asked," said Major Brane, "because it is so greatly to your advantage to see that she doesn't come to harm. I telephoned, of course, to friends of hers before I returned to the house."

The bearded man gave a sudden start. Despite himself, he changed color. "Yes?" he asked. "And just what do you expect her friends to do?"

Major Brane pursed his lips. "Probably," he remarked, "they would not be so unwise as to storm the house; but they are well versed in certain matters of indirection. You might have some trouble in leaving the house."

The dulled silver eyes regarded him scornfully. "You lie!" said the man who went under the name of Brinkhoff.

Major Brane made a gesture with the palms of his hands, a deprecating gesture, partially of apology.

"Sometimes," he said, "I despair of you, Brinkhoff: You have a certain shrewdness, yes. But you lack perspective, breadth of vision; and you are unspeakably common!"

That last remark was like the lash of a whip.

"Common!" yelled the infuriated man. "I, who have the blood of three thousand years of royalty in my veins! Common, you scum of the gutter! I'll draw the sight of this gun across your cursed face! Just a taste of what you can expect . . ."

He leaped forward, swinging his arm so that the sight of the gun made a sudden, sharp arc. But Major Brane's forehead wasn't there when the gunsight swished through the air. Major Brane had flung himself backwards in the chair; and as he went over, he watched the sweep of the arm, elevated his foot with every bit of strength he could muster. The foot caught the wrist of the enraged man, sent the gun swirling through the air in a lopsided flight. The chair crashed to the floor, Major Brane rolled clear.

Brinkhoff saw his danger and jumped back. His bony, capable hand went to the back of his coat collar, reaching for the hilt of a concealed knife.

He caught the knife, jerked it out and down. The lights glinted from the whirling steel. Major Brane flung his arms out in a football tackle. For a moment it seemed that the downward stroke of the knife would strike squarely between Major Brane's shoulders. But the Major was first to reach his goal, first by that split fraction of a watch tick which seems to be so long when men are fighting for life and death, yet is the smallest unit of measured time.

The Major's weight crashed against the shins of the man with the dulled silver eyes. The impact threw him back. The stroke of the knife swung wild. The two men teetered, crashed. The man with the beard shouted, squirmed.

Outside, the hallway pounded with running feet. There were other voices calling down from an upper floor.

Major Brane swung his fist. Brinkhoff's cries ceased. Instantly, Major Brane was on his feet, as lithely active as a cat. He swooped toward the chair which lay on the floor, lifted it bodily, held it poised for a moment, and then flung it straight through the glass of the window.

The chair smashed a great jagged hole in the glass. There sounded the crash, the tinkle, of falling glass fragments. Then the chair topped outward and vanished into the night. There came a thud from the ground below.

Major Brane jumped for a closed door on one side of the room. He flung it open and found that it led, not to an adjoining room as he had hoped, but into a closet. The closet was well filled with stacks of papers, papers that were arranged in bundles, tied with tape.

Major Brane leaped inside, scrambled atop the bundles, pawed at the door, trying to get it closed. He had but partially succeeded when he heard the door of the room burst open, and the sound of bodies catapulting into the room.

Of a sudden, the sounds ceased. That, reasoned Major Brane, perched precariously atop the slippery pile of documents, would be when the others entered the room and took in the situation, the unconscious form of Brinkhoff sprawled on the floor, the window with its great jagged hole.

"Gone!" a voice cracked, and added a curse.

"Jumped out of the window . . ."

"Quick! After him.—No, no, not that way! Close the block! Signal the others! He's got fifty yards the start of us. Turn on the red lights. Hurry!"

Once more, feet pounded in haste. Major Brane could hear excited shouts, comments that were called back and forth.

A small section of the lighted floor of the room showed through the half-open door of the closet. Major Brane watched that section of floor for a full two seconds, to see if there were any moving shadows crossing it. There were no shadows. The room seemed utterly silent.

Major Brane strove to step quietly from his perch, but a packet of documents tilted, slid. Major Brane flung himself back, lost his balance, put out his arms, and crashed through the closet door into the room.

Brinkhoff lay sprawled on the floor. A man was bending over him, and that man had evidently been in the act of going through Brinkhoff's pockets when Major Brane, catapulting from the closet, had frozen him into startled immobility.

He looked at Major Brane, and Major Brane took advantage of his first moment of surprise. He rushed. The man teetered back to his heels, jumped backward in time to escape the momentum of that first rush. Major Brane landed a glancing blow with his left. Then he caught himself, turned, and lashed out with his right.

He realized then that the man with whom he had to deal was one who was trained in jujutsu. Too late he strove to beat down the other's left. It caught his right wrist; a foot shot out; a hand darted down with bone-crunching violence.

Major Brane knew the method of attack well enough to know that there was but one possible defense. To resist would be to have his arm snapped. The hands of the other were in a position to exert a tremendous leverage against the victim's own weight. Major Brane therefore did the only thing that would save him. Even before the last ounce of pressure had been brought to play upon his arms, he flung himself in a whirling somersault, using the momentum of his rush to send him over and around.

He whirled through the air like a pinwheel, crashed to the floor. But even while he was in midair, his brain, trained to instant appreciation of all of the angles of any given situation, remembered the gun which had been kicked from Brinkhoff's hand.

Major Brane whirled, even as the flashing shape of his opponent hurtled at him. His clawing hand groped for and found the automatic. The other pounced, and the automatic jabbed into his ribs.

"I shall pull the trigger," said Major Brane, his words muffled by the weight of the other, "in exactly one and one-half seconds!"

The words had the desired effect. Major Brane had a reputation for doing exactly whatever he said he would do, and the figure that had been on top of him flung backwards, hands elevated.

Major Brane, still lying on the floor, thrust the gun forward, so that it was plainly visible.

From the yard, outside the window, could be heard the low voices of men who were closing in on the spot where the chair had thudded to the ground.

"Don't move!" said Major Brane.

The man who faced him, twisted back his lips in a silent snarl, then let his face become utterly expressionless.

Major Brane smiled at him. "I wonder," he said, "what you were searching for, my friend?"

The man made no sound.

"Back against the wall," said Major Brane.

The man hesitated, then caught the steely glitter of Major Brane's eye. He backed, slowly. Major Brane raised himself to his knees, then to his feet. His eyes were almost dreamy with concentration.

"You want something," mused Major Brane, "that Brinkhoff is supposed to have on him; but you don't want the rest of the gang to know that you want it. You'd yell, if you were really one of them, and take a chance on my shooting.—The answer is that you're hostile. Probably the others don't even know you're here."

The man who stood against the wall had been breathing heavily. Now, as Major Brane summed up the situation, he held himself rigidly motionless, even the rising and falling of his shoulders ceasing. It was as though he held his breath, the better to check any possible betrayal of his thoughts through some involuntary start of surprise.

Major Brane moved toward the unconscious form of the man who went under the name of Brinkhoff. From outside came a series of cries; rage, surprise, disappointment, shouted instructions.—The attackers had found that they had been stalking only a chair that had been thrown from a window.

Major Brane remained as calmly cool as though he had ample time at his disposal.

"Therefore," he said, "the thing to do is to search until I find what you were looking for, and . . ."

His prisoner could stand the strain no longer. Already the thud of running feet showed that the others were coming toward the house. The man blurted out in excellent English:

"It's in the wallet, in the inside pocket. It's nothing that concerns you. It relates to another matter. My government wants it. They'll kill me if they find me, and they'll kill you. Let me have the paper, and I'll show you the girl."

Major Brane smiled. "Fair enough," he said. "No, don't move. Not yet!" His hands went to Brinkhoff's inside pocket, scooped out the leather folder, abstracted a document. The man against the wall was breathing heavily, as though he had been running. His hands were clenching and unclenching. A door banged somewhere in the house, feet sounded in the corridor. Brinkhoff stirred and groaned.

Major Brane paused to cast a swift eye over the documents which he had abstracted from the leather folder. He smiled, nodded.

"OK," he said. "It's a go. Show me the girl."

"This way," said the man, and ran toward a corner of the room. He opened a door, disclosed another closet, pressed a section of the wall. It opened upon a flight of stairs.

Major Brane followed, taking care to close the closet door after him. He could hear the sound of steps dashing down the corridor, the sound of confused voices shouting instructions.

The man led him down a winding staircase, to a cellar stored with various and sundry munitions and supplies. The house was a veritable arsenal, on a small scale. He crossed the storeroom, opened another door; and Major Brane, half expecting that which he was to find, came to an abrupt pause and took a deep breath.

The Chinese girl sat in a chair. Her arms and legs were bound. The clothing had been ripped from her torso, and there were evidences that her captors had been trying to make her talk. But she was staring ahead of her with a face absolutely void of expression, with eyes that glittered like lacquer. She was not gagged, for the room was virtually soundproof.

The girl surveyed them with eyes that remained glitteringly inexpressive, with a face that was like old ivory; but she said nothing.

The man who had guided Major Brane to the room pulled a knife and slit the bonds.

"Devils!" said Major Brane. The man with the knife turned to him. "I have done my share. From now on each man for himself. They have the entire block well guarded. I can't be bothered with the woman. Give me the paper."

Major Brane tossed him the wallet.

The man dashed from the room. "Each man for himself.—Remember!" he said as he left.

Major Brane nodded. He picked up a ragged remnant of the girl's clothing, flung it over her shoulders, looked around for a coat.

From the cellar he heard a voice calling.

"He is down here, with the girl!"

It was the voice of the man who had just guided Major Brane to the torture chamber. The Major nodded approvingly. The man had warned him; it was to be each man for himself; and the devil take the hindmost.

The one who had guided him to the girl felt that he stood a better chance to escape if he guided the enemy to Major Brane. That would lead to conflict, confusion, and a chance for escape. It was the strategy of warfare.

Major Brane heard the men running, coming pell mell down the stairs which led to the room. And the block was surrounded, guarded. They were many, and they were ruthless. Here in the heart of San Francisco, he had stumbled into a spy's nest, perhaps the headquarters for the lone wolves of diplomacy, the outlaws who ran ahead of the pack, ruthlessly doing things for which no government dared assume even a partial responsibility.

Major Brane stepped out into the cellar. He could see a pair of legs coming down the cellar stairs.

Major Brane observed a can of gasoline. The automatic he had captured barked twice. One shot splintered the stairs, just below the legs of the man who was descending, caused him to come to an abrupt halt. The other shot ripped through the can of gasoline.

The liquid poured out, ran along the cement floor of the cellar, Major Brane tossed a match, stepped back into the room which had been used as a torture chamber, and closed the door.

From the cellar came a loud *poof!* then a roaring, crackling sound.

Immediately, Major Brane dismissed the cellar from his thoughts and turned his attention to the room in which he found himself. The girl had arranged the clothing about her, had found a coat. She regarded him with glittering eyes and silent lips.

Major Brane pursed his lips. There seemed to be no opening from the room; yet he knew the type of mind with which he had to deal, and he sensed that there would be an opening.

The crackling sound was growing louder now. Major Brane could hear the frantic beat of panic stricken feet on the floor above. Then there was an explosion, followed by a series of explosions, coming from the cellar. Those would be cartridges exploding.

Major Brane upset a chest of drawers to examine the wall behind it. He picked up a hammer and pounded the cement of the floor. He cocked a wary eye at the ceiling, studied it.

The girl watched him in silence.

The fire was seething flame now, crackling, roaring. The door of the room in which they found themselves began to warp under the heat.

Major Brane was as calm as though he had been solving a chess problem, over a cigarette and cordial. He moved a box. The box didn't tip as it should. It pivoted instead. An oblong opening showed in the wall as the swinging box moved back a slab of what appeared to be solid concrete.

A fire siren was wailing in the distance. There were no more sounds of running feet above the torture chamber.

An automobile exhaust ripped the night. There were heavier explosions from the seat of the fire; then a terrific explosion that burst in the warped door. An inferno of red, roaring flame showed its hideous maw. Heat transformed the room into an oven. The red flames were bordered with a twisting vortex of black smoke.

Major Brane gave the inferno a casual glance, stood to one side to let the girl join him. She walked steadily to his side, and together, they walked along the passage, climbed a flight of stairs.

They came to what appeared to be a solid wall. Major Brane pushed against it. It was plaster and lath, and doubtless swung on a pivot. Major Brane had no time to locate the catch which controlled the opening; he lashed out with his foot, kicked a hole in the plaster. When he looked through the opening, he was peering into a room, furnished as a bedroom. It was deserted.

His second kick dislodged the spring mechanism which controlled the door. The section of plastered wall swung around. Major Brane led the girl into the room, Brinkhoff's automatic ready at his side. They walked through the room to a passage.

The open door led to the night, revealed a glimpse of the street outside, which was already crowded with curious spectators, showed firemen running with a hose. But Major Brane turned in the other direction.

"This way," he said. "It will avoid explanations."

They ran down the corridor, toward a rear exit. Major Brane recognized the stairs which led to the garage. He piloted the girl toward them.

In the garage she paused, looked about her. There was a wooden jack handle lying on a bench. The girl stopped to pick it up.

Major Brane grinned at her, "You won't need it. They've all ducked for cover," he said.

The girl said nothing, which was as he had expected.

A fireman came running down the alley, motioning calling instructions to other men, who were dragging a hose. He glanced sharply at Major Brane and the girl.

"Get outa here!" he yelled. "You're inside the fire lines. You'll get killed, sticking your noses into danger zones."

Major Brane bowed apologetically. "Is this the danger zone?" he asked, wide-eyed in his innocence.

The fireman snorted.

"It sure is. Get out!"

Major Brane followed instructions. They came to the fire lines at the corner, turned into a dark building entrance. Major Brane peered out, whispered to the girl.

"We don't want to be seen coming out of this district. The thing to do is wait until they run in that second hose, then slip along the shadows, and . . ."

He sensed a surreptitious rustle behind him. He turned, startled, just in time to see the jack handle coming down. He tried to throw up his hand, and was too late. The jack handle crashed on his head. He fought to keep his senses. There were blinding lights before his eyes, a black nausea gripping him. Something seemed to burst in his brain. He realized it was the jack handle making a second blow, and then he knew nothing further, save a vast engulfing wall of blackness smothered him with a rushing embrace.

When next he knew anything, it was a series of joltings and swayings, interspersed with demoniacal screams. The screams grew and receded at regular intervals, split the tortured head of Major Brane as though they had been edged with the teeth of a saw.

Then he identified them. They were the wails of a siren, and he was riding in an ambulance.

A bell clanged. The screams died away. The ambulance stopped, backed. The door opened. Hands slid out the stretcher. Major Brane groaned, tried to sit up, was gripped with faintness and nausea. He became unconscious again.

The next thing he knew, there was a bright light in his eyes and something soothing on his head. He felt soft hands patting about in the finishing touches of a dressing.

He opened his eyes. A nurse regarded him without pity, without scorn, merely as a receiving hospital nurse regards any minor case.

"You got past the fire line and into the danger zone," she said. "Something fell on your head."

Major Brane had presence of mind enough to heave a sigh of relief that the Chinese girl had taken his automatic with her. To have had that in his possession when he was found would have necessitated explanation.

"A Chinese girl told them about seeing you try to run past the line, when something fell from a building," said the nurse. "Her name's on record, if you want a witness for anything."

Major Brane grinned. "Not at all necessary," he said. "I was simply careless, that's all."

"I'll say you were," said the nurse, helping him to sit upright. "Feel better?"

Major Brane slid his feet over the edge of the surgical table.

"I think I can make it all right," he said.

She helped him to a chair, gave him a stimulant. Fifteen minutes later he was able to call a cab and leave the hospital. He went at once to his hotel.

He brushed past the clerk, who stared at his bandaged head curiously; he took the elevator, went to his own room. He fitted a key, opened the door. The smell of Chinese tobacco assailed his nostrils.

"Do not turn on the light," said a voice, and Major Brane recognized it as that of the old Chinese sage who had started him upon his mission.

Major Brane hesitated, sighed, walked into the room, and closed the door.

"I came to give my apologies," said the old man, a huddled figure of dark mystery in the darkened room, illuminated only by such light as came through the transom over the door.

"Don't mention it," said Major Brane. "I was careless."

"But," said the sage. "I want you to understand . . ."

Major Brane laughed. "I understood," he said, "as soon as I saw the jack handle coming down on my head. The girl had the check hidden, and she wanted to get it right away. She couldn't be certain that my rescue wasn't merely a ruse on the part of her enemies. I didn't have anything to identify me as having come from her friends. Therefore, it was possible that her enemies, seeing that torture would do no good, had staged a fake rescue, hoping to trap her into taking her supposed rescuer to the place where the check was hidden. I should have anticipated just such a thought on her part."

The old man got to his feet.

Major Brane could hear him sigh.

"It's satisfying to deal with one who has understanding," he said.

Major Brane saw him move to the door, open it, saw the hunched figure silhouetted against the oblong of light from the corridor.

"She had dropped the check in the waste basket by the side of her desk when she knew her theft was discovered," said the old man, and closed the door.

Major Brane sat in the darkness for some seconds before he turned on the light. When he did so he saw two articles on the table near which the old man had sat. One was a white jade figure of the Goddess of Mercy, a figure that was carved with infinite cunning and patience, a figure that thrilled the collector's heart of Major Brane. Instantly he knew that it was something that was almost priceless. The second object was a purse, crammed with bills of large denomination.

Major Brane inspected the jade figure with appreciative eyes, touched it with fingertips that were almost reverent for a full ten minutes before he even thought to count the currency in the purse. The amount was ample.

Then Major Brane undressed, crawled into bed. He got up an hour later, took ten grains of aspirin, and drifted off to sleep. He awoke in the morning, jumped from bed, and pulled the morning paper out from under the door.

Headlines announced the representatives of the Cantonese government had consented to consult with Chiang Kai-shek at the international port of Shanghai, the object being to patch up their internal difficulties so that China could present an unbroken front to her external enemies.

Major Brane sighed. It had been a hard night's work, but the results had been speedy.

On his way to breakfast, he encountered the night elevator operator.

"There was an old Chinaman who called on me last night," he said. "What time did he come in?"

The operator stared at him with wide eyes. "There wasn't any Chinaman came in while I was on duty," he said.

Major Brane nodded. "Perhaps," he said, "I was mistaken."

When he came to think of it, the Chinese sage would never have left a back track which could be traced to Major Brane. Doubtless the events of the preceding night had been such that no man and no government wished to be officially identified either with their success or failure.

Major Brane was a lone wolf, prowling through a diplomatic danger zone; but he would not have had it otherwise.

JOHN D. MACDONALD
Betrayed

IT WAS AN Indian summer afternoon in mid-October—Sunday afternoon. Francie had gone back to the lab, five miles from the lakeside cabin, but Dr. Blair Cudahy, the Administrator, had shooed her out, saying that he was committing enough perjury on the civil service hours-of-work reports without having her work Sundays, too.

And so Francie Aintrell had climbed back into her ten-year-old sedan and come rattling over the potholed highway back to the small cabin. She sat on the miniature porch, her back against a wooden upright, fingers laced around one blue-jeaned knee.

Work, she had learned, was one of the anesthetics. Work and time. They all talked about the healing wonder of time. As though each second could be another tiny layer of insulation between you and Bob. And one day, when enough seconds and minutes and years had gone by, you could look in your mirror and see a face old enough to be the mother of Bob, and his face would remain young and unchanged in memory.

But she could look in the wavery mirror in the little camp and touch her cheeks with her finger tips, touch the face that he had loved, see the blue eyes he had loved; the black hair.

And then she would forget the classic shape of the little tragedy. West Point, post–World War II class. Second Lieutenant Robert Aintrell. One of the expendable ones. And expended, of course, near a reservoir no one had ever heard of before.

KIA. A lot of them from that class became KIA on the record.

When he had been sent to Korea, she had gone from the West Coast back to the Pentagon and applied for reinstatement. Clerk-stenographer. CAF 6. Assigned to the District Control Section of the Industrial Service Branch of the Office of the Chief of Ordinance.

And then they send you a wire and you open it, and the whole world makes a convulsive twist and lands in a new pattern. It can't happen to you—and to Bob. But it has.

So after the first hurt, so sharp and wild that it was like a kind of insanity, Francie applied for work outside Washington, because they had been together in Washington, and that made it a place to escape from.

Everyone had been sweet. And then there had been the investigation. Very detailed, and very thorough. "Yes, Mrs. Aintrell is a loyal citizen. Class A security risk."

Promotion to CAF 7. "Report to Dr. Cudahy, please. Vanders, New York. Yes, that's in the Adirondacks—near Lake Arthur. Sorry the only name we have for that organization is Unit Thirty."

And three miles from Vanders, five miles from the lake, she had found a new gravel road, a shining wire fence at the end of it, a guard post, a cinder-block building, a power cable marching over the hills on towers, ending at the laboratory.

She had reported to Blair Cudahy, a fat little mild-eyed man. She could not tell, but she thought that he approved of her. "Mrs. Aintrell, you have been approved by Security. There is no need, I'm sure, to tell you not to discuss what we are doing here."

"No, sir," she had replied. "I quite understand."

"We are concerned with electronics, with radar. This is a research organization. The terminology will give you difficulty at first. If we accomplish our mission here, Mrs. Aintrell, we will be able to design a nose fuse for interceptor rockets which will make any air attack on this continent—too expensive to contemplate."

At that, Cudahy hitched in his chair and turned so that he could glance over his shoulder at an enlarged photograph of an illustration Francie remembered seeing in a magazine. It showed the fat red bloom of the atom god towering over the Manhattan skyline.

Cudahy turned back and smiled. "That is the threat that goads us on. Now come and meet the staff."

Most of them were young. The names and faces were a blur. Francie didn't mind. She knew that she would straighten them out soon enough. Ten scientists and engineers. About fifteen technicians. And then the guards and housekeeping personnel.

The bachelor staff lived behind the wire. The married staff rented cabins in the vicinity. Dr. Blair Cudahy's administrative assistant was a tall, youngish man with deep-set quiet eyes, a relaxed manner, a hint of stubbornness in the set of the jaw. His name was Clinton Reese.

After they were introduced, Cudahy said, "I believe Clint has found a place for you."

"Next best thing to a cave, Mrs. Aintrell," Clint Reese had said. "But you have lovely neighbors. Mostly bears. You have a car?"

"No, I haven't," she said. His casual banter seemed oddly out of place when she looked beyond his shoulder and saw that picture on Cudahy's office wall.

"I'll take you to the local car mart and we'll get you one."

Cudahy said, "Thanks, Clint. Show her where she'll work and give her a run through on the duties, then take her out to that place you rented. We'll expect you at nine tomorrow morning, Mrs. Aintrell."

Clint took her to her desk. He said, "Those crazy people you met are scientists and engineers. They work in teams, attempting different avenues of approach to the same problem. Left to their own devices, they'd keep notes on the backs of match folders. Because even scientists sometimes drop dead, we have to keep progress reports up to date in case somebody else has to take over. There are three teams. You'll take notes, transcribe them, and keep the program files. Tomorrow I'll explain the problems involved in the care of madmen. Ready to go?"

They stopped at Vanders and picked up her luggage from the combination general store and bus depot. Clint Reese loaded it into the back of his late model sedan. He chattered amiably all the way out to the road that bordered the north shore of Lake Arthur.

He pulled off into a small clearing just off the road and said, "We'll leave the stuff here, in case it turns out to be a little too primitive."

The trail leading down the wooded slope toward the lake shore was hard-packed. At the steepest point there was a rustic handrail. When Francie first saw the small cabin, and the deep blue of the lake beyond it, her heart seemed to turn over. Bob had talked of just such a place. A porch overlooking the lake. A small wooden dock. And the perfect stillness of the woods in mid-September.

The interior was small. One fair-sized room with a wide, built-in bunk. A gray stone fireplace. A tiny kitchen and bath.

Clint Reese said, in the manner of a guide, "You will note that this little nest has modern conveniences. Running water, latest model lanterns for lights. Refrigerator, stove heater, and hot-water heater all run on bottled gas. We never get more than eight feet of snow, so I'm told, and you'll have to have a car. The unscrupulous landlord wants sixty a month. Like?"

She turned to him smiling. "Like very much."

"Now I'll claw my way up your hill and bring down your bags. You check the utensils and supplies. I laid in some food, on the gamble that you'd like it here."

He came down with the bags, making a mock show of exhaustion. He explained the intricacies of the lanterns and the heaters, then said that he'd pick her up in the morning at eight-fifteen.

"You've been very kind," she said.

"Dogs and children go wild about me. See you tomorrow."

After he had disappeared around the bend of the trail, she stood frowning. He was her immediate superior, and he had acted totally unlike any previous superior in the Civil Service hierarchy. Usually they were most reserved, most cautious. He seemed entirely too blithe and carefree to be able to do an administrative job of the type this Unit 30 apparently demanded.

But she had to admit that he had been efficient about the cabin. And so, on a mid-September afternoon, she had unpacked. The first thing she took out of the large suitcase was Bob's picture. She could imagine him saying, "Baby, how do you *know* there aren't any bears in those woods? Fine life for a city gal."

"I'll get along, Bob," she told him. "I promise you, I'll get along."

And with his picture watching her, she unpacked and cooked, and ate, and went to bed in the deep bunk, surrounded by the pine smell, the leaf rustle, the lap of water against the small dock.

The work had been very hard at first, mostly because of the technical terms used in the reports, and also because of the backlog of data that had piled up since the illness of the previous girl. During the worst of it, Clint Reese found ways to make her smile. He helped her in her purchase of the ten-year-old car.

The names and faces straightened out quickly, with Clint's help. Gray chubby young Dr. Jonas McKay, with razor-sharp mind. Tom Blajoviak, with Slavic slanting merry eyes, heavy-handed joshing, big shoulders. Dr. Sherra, lost in a private fog of mental mathematics and conjecture.

Francie had pictured laboratories as being gleaming, spotless places full of stainless steel, sparkling glass, white smocks. Unit 30 was a kind of orderly, chaotic jumble of dust and bits of wire and tubing and old technical journals stacked on the floor in wild disarray.

She soon caught the hang of their verbal shorthand, learned to put in the reports the complete terms to which they referred. McKay was orderly about summoning her. Tom Blajoviak found so much pleasure in dictating that he kept calling for her when he found nothing at all to report. Dr. Sherra had to be trapped before he would dictate to her. He considered progress reports to be a lot of nonsense.

With increasing knowledge of the personalities of the three team leaders came a new awareness of the strain under which they worked. The strain made them sometimes irritable, sometimes childish. Dr. Cudahy supervised and coordinated the technical aspects of the lines of research, treading very gently so as not to offend. And it was Clint's task to take the burden of all other routine matters off Cudahy's shoulders, so that he could function at maximum efficiency at the technical supervision at which he excelled.

It had been a very full month, with little time for relaxation. Francie sat on the porch of the cabin on the October Sunday afternoon, realizing how closely she had identified herself with the work of Unit 30 during the past month.

With the Adirondack tour season over, most of the private camps were empty. There were only a few fishermen about. She heard the shrill keening of the reel long before the boat, following the shore line, came into view through the remaining lurid leaves of autumn.

A young girl, her hair pale and blond, rowed the boat very slowly. She wore a heavy cardigan and a wool skirt. A man stood in the boat, casting a black-and-white plug toward the shallows, and reeling it in with hopeful twitches of the rod tip. The sun was low, the lake still, the air sharp with the threat of coming winter. It made a very pretty picture. Francie wondered if they'd had any luck.

The boat moved slowly by, passing just ten feet or so from the end of the dock, not more than thirty feet from the small porch. The girl glanced up and smiled, and Francie instinctively waved. She remembered seeing them in Vanders in the store.

"Any luck?" Francie asked.

"One decent bass," the man said. He had a pleasant weather-burned face.

As he made the next cast Francie saw him slip. As the girl cried out he reached wildly at nothingness, and fell full length into the lake, inadvertently pushing the boat away from him. He came up quickly, looked toward the boat, then paddled toward the end of Francie's dock. Francie ran down just as he climbed up onto the dock.

"That must have been graceful to watch," the man said ruefully, his teeth chattering.

The girl bumped the end of the dock with the boat. "Are you all right, dear?" she asked nervously.

"Oh, I'm just dandy," the man said, flapping his arms. "Row me home quick."

The blond girl looked appealingly at Francie. "If it wouldn't be too much trouble. I could row home and bring dry clothes here and—"

"Of course!" Francie said. "I was going to suggest that."

"I don't want to put you out," the man said. "Darn fool stunt, falling in the lake."

"Come on in before you freeze solid," Francie said.

The girl rowed quickly down the lake shore. The man followed Francie in. The fire was all laid. She touched a match to the exposed corner of paper, handed him a folded blanket from the foot of the bunk.

"That fireplace works fast," she said. "Get those clothes off and wrap yourself up in the blanket. I'll be on the porch. You holler when you're ready."

She sat on the porch and waited. When the man called she went in. She put three fingers of whiskey in the bottom of a water tumbler and handed it to him. "Drink your medicine."

"I ought to fall in the lake oftener! Hey, don't bother with those clothes!"

"I'll hang them out."

She put his shoes on the porch, hung the clothes on the line she had rigged from the porch corner to a small birch. Just as she finished she saw the girl coming back, rowing strongly. Francie went down and tied the bow line, and took the pile of clothes from her, so that she could get out of the boat more easily.

"How is he?" the girl asked in a worried tone.

"Warm on the inside and the outside, too."

"He wouldn't want me to tell you this. He likes to pretend it isn't so. But he isn't well. That's why I was so worried. You're being more than kind."

"When I fall out of a boat near your place I'll expect the same service."

"You'll get it," the girl said.

Francie saw that she was older than she had looked from a distance. There were fine lines near her eyes, a bit of gray in the blond temples. Late twenties, possibly.

The girl took the clothes, put out her free hand, "I'm Betty Jackson," she said. "And my husband's name is Stewart."

"I'm Francie Aintrell. I'm glad you—dropped in."

Francie waited on the porch again until Betty came out. "He's dressed now," Betty said. "If we could stay just a little longer—"

"Of course you can! Actually, I was sort of lonesome this afternoon."

They went in. Francie put another heavy piece of slabwood on the fire. Stewart Jackson said, "I think I've stopped shivering. We certainly thank you, Miss Aintrell."

"It's Mrs. Aintrell. Francie Aintrell."

She saw Betty glance toward Bob's picture. "Is that your husband, Francie?"

"Yes, he—he was killed in Korea." Never before had she been able to say it so flatly, so factually.

Stewart Jackson looked down at his empty glass. "That's tough. Sorry I—"

"You couldn't have known. And I'm used to telling people." She went on quickly, in an effort to cover the awkwardness. "Are you on vacation? I think I've seen you over in town."

"No, we're not on vacation," Betty said. "Stewart sort of semiretired last year, and we bought a camp up here. It's—let me see—the seventh one down the shore from you. Stew has always been interested in fishing, and now we're making lures and trying to get a mail-order business started for them."

"I design 'em and test 'em and have a little firm down in Utica make up the wooden bodies of the plugs," Stewart said. "Then we put them together and put on the paint job. Are you working up here or vacationing?"

"I'm working for the Government," Francie said, "in the new weather station." That was the cover story which all employees were instructed to use—that Unit 30 was doing meteorological research.

"We've heard about that place, of course," Betty said. "Sounds rather dull to me. Do you like it?"

"It's a job," Francie said. "I was working in Washington and after I heard about my husband, I asked for a transfer to some other place."

Jackson yawned. "Now I'm so comfortable, I'm getting sleepy. We better go."

"No," Francie said meaning it. "Do stay. We're neighbors. How about hamburgers over the fire?"

She saw Betty and Stewart exchange glances. She liked them. There was something wholesome and comfortable about their relationship. And, because Stewart Jackson was obviously in his mid-forties, they did not give her the constant sense of loss that a younger couple might have caused.

"We'll stay if I can help," Betty said, "and if you'll return the visit. Soon."

"Signed and sealed," Francie said.

It was a pleasant evening. The Jacksons were relaxed, charming. Francie like the faint wryness of Stew's humor. And both of them were perceptive enough to keep the conversation far away from any subject that might be related to Bob.

Francie lent them a flashlight for the boat trip back to their camp. She heard the oars as Betty rowed away, heard the night voices calling, "Night, Francie! Good night!"

Monday she came back from work too late to make the promised call. She found the flashlight on the porch near the door, along with a note that said, "Anytime at all, Francie. And we mean it. *Betty and Stew.*"

Tuesday was another late night. On Wednesday, Clint Reese added up the hours she had worked and sent her home at three in the afternoon, saying, "Do you want us indicted by the Committee Investigating Abuses of Civil Service Secretaries?"

"I'm not abused."

"Out, now! Scat!"

At the cabin Francie Aintrell changed to jeans and a suede jacket and hiked down the trail by the empty camps to the one that the Jacksons had described. Stew was on the dock, casting with a spinning rod.

"Hi!" he said, grinning. "Thought the bears got you. Go on in. I'll be up soon as I find out why this little wooden monster won't wiggle like a fish."

Betty Jackson flushed with pleasure when she saw Francie. "It's nice of you to come. I'll show you the workshop before Stew does. He gets all wound up and takes hours."

The large glass-enclosed porch smelled of paint and glue. There were labels for the little glassine boxes, and rows of gay, shining lures.

"Here, it says in small print, is where we earn a living," Betty said. "But actually it's going pretty well." She held up a yellow lure with black spots. "This one," she said "is called—believe it or not—the Jackson Higgledy-Piggledy. A pickerel on every cast. It's our latest achievement. Manufacturing costs twelve cents apiece, if you don't count labor. Mail-order price, one dollar."

"It's pretty," Francie said dubiously.

"Don't admire it or Stew will put you to work addressing the new catalogues to our sucker list."

Stew came in and said, "I'll bet if the sun was out it would be over the yardarm."

"Is a martini all right with you, Francie?" Betty asked.

Francie nodded, smiling. The martinis were good. The dinner much later was even better. Stew made her an ex-officio director of the Jackson Lure Company, in charge of color schemes on bass plugs. Many times during dinner Francie felt a pang of guilt as she heard her own laughter ring out. Yet it was ridiculous to feel guilty. Bob would have wanted her to learn how to laugh all over again.

She left at eleven, and as she had brought no flashlight, Betty walked home with her, carrying a gasoline lantern. They sat on the edge of Francie's porch for a time, smoking and watching the moonlight on the lake.

"It's a pretty good life for us," Betty said. "Quiet. Stew's supposed to avoid strenuous exercise. And he's really taking this business seriously. Probably a good thing. our money won't last forever."

"I'm so glad you two people are going to be here all winter, Betty."

"And you don't know how glad I am to see you, Francie. I needed some girl-talk. Say, how about a picnic soon?"

"I adore picnics."

"There's a place on the east shore where the afternoon sun keeps the rocks warm. But we can't do it until Sunday. Stew wants to take a run down to New York to wind up some business things. I do the driving. Sunday, OK then?" Betty stood up.

It was agreed and Francie stood on the small porch and watched the harsh lantern light bob along the trail until it finally disappeared beyond the trees.

Sunday dawned brisk and clear. It would be pleasant enough in the sun. Francie went down the trail with her basket. When she got to the Jackson camp, Betty was loading the boat. She looked cute and young in khaki trousers, a fuzzy white sweater, a peaked ball-player's cap.

The girls took turns rowing against the wind as they went across the lake. Stewart trolled with a deep-running plug, without much success. He was grumbling about the lack of fish when they reached the far shore.

They unloaded the boat, carrying the food up to a small natural glade beyond the rocks. Stew settled down comfortably, finding a rock that fitted his back. Betty sat on another rock. Francie sprawled on her stomach on the grass, chin on the back of her hand.

Stew took a bit of soft pine out of his jacket pocket and a sharp-bladed knife. He began to carve carefully. He lifted the piece of pine up and squinted at it.

"Francie, if I'm clever enough, I can now carve myself something that a fish will snap at," he said. "A lure. A nice sparkly, dancy little thing that looks edible."

"With hooks in it," Francie said.

He looked down at her benignly. "Precisely. With hooks in it. You stop to think of it, an organization isn't very different from a fish. Now, I'm eventually going to catch a fish on this, because it will have precisely the appeal that fish are looking for. Now, you take an organization. You can always find one person in it, if you look hard enough, that can be attracted. But then, it's always better to use real bait instead of an artificial lure.''

''Sounds cold-blooded,'' Francie said sleepily.

''I suppose it is. Now, let's take for example, that supersecret organization you work for, Francie.''

She stared at him. ''What?''

''That so-called weather research outfit. Suppose we had to find bait to make somebody bite on a hook?''

Francie sat up and tried to smile. ''You know, I don't like the way you're talking, Stew.''

''You're among friends honey. Betty and I are very friendly people.''

Francie, confused, turned and looked at Betty. Her face had lost its usual animation. There was nothing there but a catlike watchfulness.

''What *is* this anyway?'' Francie said, laughing. But her laughter sounded false.

''We came over here,'' Stew said, ''because this is a nice, quiet place to settle down and make a deal. Now don't be alarmed, Francie. A lot of time and effort has gone into making exactly the right sort of contact with you. Of course, if it hadn't been you, it would have been somebody else in Unit Thirty. So this is the stroke of midnight at the fancy-dress ball. Everybody takes off their masks.''

Slowly the incredible meaning behind his words penetrated to Francie's mind. She looked at them. They had been friends—friends quickly made and yet dear to her. Now suddenly they had become strangers. Stew's bland, open face seemed to hold all the guilelessness of the face of an evil child. And Betty's features had sharpened, had become almost feral.

''Is this some sort of a stupid test?'' Francie demanded.

''I'll say it again. We are here to make a business deal. We give you something, you give us something. Everybody is satisfied.'' Stewart Jackson smiled at her.

Panic struck Francie Aintrell. She slipped as she scrambled to her feet. She ran as fast as she could toward the boat, heard the feet drumming behind her. As she bent to shove the boat off, Betty grabbed her, reached around her from behind, and with astonishing strength, twisted both of Francie's arms until her hands were pinned between her shoulder blades.

The pain doubled Francie over. ''You're hurting me,'' she cried. There was an odd indignity in being hurt by another woman.

''Come on back,'' Betty said, her voice flat-calm.

Stew hadn't moved. He cut a long, paper-thin strip from the piece of pine. Betty shoved Francie toward him and released her.

"Sit down, honey," Stew said calmly. "No need to get all upset. You read the papers and magazines. I know that you're a well-informed, intelligent young woman. *Please* sit down. You make me nervous."

Francie sat on the grass, hugged her knees. She felt cold all the way through.

"I don't know what you expect me to do. But you might as well know that I'll never do it. You had better kill me or something, because just as fast as I can get to a phone I'm going to—"

"Please stop sounding like a suspense movie, Francie," Stewart said patiently. "We don't go around killing people. Just let me talk for a minute. Maybe you, as an intelligent young woman, have wondered why so many apparently loyal and responsible people have committed acts of treason against their country. To understand that, you have to have an appreciation of the painstaking care with which all trusted people are surveyed.

"Sooner or later, Mrs. Aintrell, we usually find an avenue of approach to at least one person in each secret setup in which we interest ourselves. And, in the case of Unit Thirty, the Fates seem to have elected you to provide us with complete transcripts of all current progress reports dictated by Dr. Sherra, Dr. McKay, and Mr. Blajoviak."

Shock made Francie feel dull. She merely stared at him unbelievingly.

Stewart Jackson smiled blandly. "I assure you our cover is perfect. And I believe you have helped us along by casually mentioning your nice neighbors, the Jacksons."

"Yes, but—"

"We thought at first my boating accident might be too obvious, but then we remembered that there is nothing in your background to spoil your naiveté."

"You're very clever and I've been very stupid. But I assure you that nothing you can say to me will make any difference."

"Being hasty, isn't she?" Stewart said.

With the warm, friendly manner of a man bestowing gifts, he reached into the inside pocket of his heavy tweed jacket and took out an envelope. He took a sheet of paper from the envelope, unfolded it, and handed it to her. It was the coarse, pulpy kind of paper.

In the top right hand corner were Chinese ideographs, crudely printed. In the top left hand corner was a symbol of the hammer and sickle. But it was the scrawled pencil writing that tore her heart in two as she read.

> Baby, they say you will get this. Maybe it's like their other promises. Anyway I hope you do get it. This is a crumb-bum outfit. I keep telling them I'm sick, but nobody seems to be interested. The

> holes healed pretty good, but now they don't look so hot. Anything you can do to get me out of this, baby, do it. I can't last too long here, for sure. I love you, baby, and I keep thinking of us in front of a fireplace—it gets cold here—and old Satchmo on the turntable and you in the green housecoat, and Willy on the mantel.

Francie read it again and instinctively held it to her lips, her eyes so misted that Stewart and the rock he leaned against were merged in a gray-brown blur.

Bob was alive! There could be no doubt of it. No one else would know about the green housecoat, about Bob's delight in the zipper that went from throat to ankles. And they had all been wrong. All of them! Happiness made her feel dizzy, ill.

Stewart Jackson's voice came from remote distances: ". . . find it pretty interesting, at that. That piece of paper crossed Siberia and Russia and came to Washington by air in a diplomatic pouch—one that we don't have to identify. When we reported your assignment to Unit Thirty, our Central Intelligence ordered an immediate check of all captive officer personnel. In that first retreat after the Chinese came into it, they picked up quite a lot of wounded American personnel.

"It was quite a break to find your husband reported as killed in action instead of captured. If he'd been captured they'd never have transferred you to Unit Thirty, you know. So they told Lieutenant Aintrell the circumstances and he wrote that letter you're holding. It got to you just as fast as it could be managed."

"He says he's sick!" Francie exclaimed indignantly. "Why isn't he being taken care of?"

"Not many doctors and not much medicine on the Chinese mainland, Francie. They use what they have for their own troops."

"They've got to help him!"

Betty came over, put her arm around Francie's shoulders, "I guess, Francie, dear, that is going to be up to you."

Francie twisted away from her. "What do you mean?"

"It's out of our hands," Stew Jackson said. "You can think of us as just messengers from the boys who make the decisions. They say that when, as an evidence of your good faith, they start to receive copies of Unit Thirty progress reports, they will see to it that your husband is made more comfortable. I understand that his wounds are not serious. You will get more letters from him, and he'll tell you in those letters that things are better. When your services are no longer needed they will make arrangements to have him turned over to some impartial agency—maybe to a Swedish hospital ship.

"He'll come home to you, and that will be your reward for services rendered. Now if you don't want to play ball, I'm supposed to pass the word along, and they'll see that he gets transferred from the military prison to a labor camp, where he may last a month or a year. Now, you better take time to think it all over."

"How can you stand yourselves or each other?" Francie asked. "How can two people like you get mixed up in such a filthy business?"

Stewart Jackson flushed. "You can skip that holier than thou attitude, Mrs. Aintrell. You believe in one thing. We believe in something else. Betty and I just happen to believe there's going to be a good spot for us when this capitalistic dictatorship goes bankrupt and collapses of its own weight."

Jackson leaned forward with a charming smile. "Come on, Francie. Cheer up. And you should know that, as an individual, you certainly are not going to affect the course of world affairs by the decisions you make. As a woman, you want your husband and your happiness. The odds are that Unit Thirty research will get nowhere anyway. So what harm can you do? And the people I work with are never afraid to show gratitude. Certainly your Bob won't thank you for selling him out, selling him into a labor camp."

"There's more than one way to sell Bob out."

"Sentimentality masquerading as patriotism, I'm afraid. Think it over. How about the food, Betty? Join us, Francie?"

Francie didn't answer. She stood up and walked down the shore of the lake. She sat huddled on a natural step in the rocks. There seemed to be no warmth in the sun. She looked at the letter. In two places the pencil had torn the cheap, coarse paper. His hand had held the pencil. She remembered the marriage vows. To honor and cherish. A sacred promise, made in front of man and God.

She felt as though she were being torn in half, slowly, surely. And she could not forget that he was in danger and frighteningly alone.

She walked slowly back to Stewart and Betty. "Is that promise any good?" she asked, in a voice which was not her own. "Would he really be returned to me?"

"Once a promise is made, Francie, it is kept. I can guarantee that."

"Like they've kept treaties?" Francie asked bitterly.

"The myth of national honor is part of the folklore of decadent capitalism, Francie," Betty said. "Don't be politically immature. This is a promise to an individual and on a different basis entirely."

Francie looked down at them. "Tell me what you want me to do?" she asked.

"We have your pledge of cooperation?" Stewart Jackson asked.

"I—yes." Her mouth held a bitter dryness.

"Before we go into details, my dear Francie, I want you to understand that we appreciate the risk you are taking. If you ever get the urge to be a little tin heroine—at your husband's expense, of course—please understand that we shall take steps to protect ourselves. We would certainly make it quite impossible for you to testify against us."

Betty said quickly, "Francie wouldn't do that, Stew." She laughed shallowly.

"Now, Francie," Stewart said softly, "I will tell you what you will do."

When they rowed away from her dock they waved a cheerful goodbye to her. Francie went in and closed the door carefully behind her, knowing that doors and bolts and locks had become useless. Then she lay numbly on the bunk and pressed her forehead against the rough pine boards. Until at last the tears came. She cried herself out, and when she awakened from deep sleep the night was dark, the cabin cruelly cold.

She awakened to a changed world. The adjustment to Bob's death had been a precarious structure, moving in each emotional breeze. Now it collapsed utterly. She was again the bride, the Francie Aintrell of the day before the telegram arrived. And as she moved about, she began, in the back of her mind, to stage the scene and learn the lines for the moment of his return, for the moment when his arms would be around her again.

She pumped up the lantern and carried it over to the table. She set it down, and stood very still looking at the object. There, on the table, was one of the plugs manufactured by the Jacksons. It was a gay red lure, with two gang hooks, with yellow bead eyes.

The doors were still locked. She tried to tell herself it was purposeless melodrama, the sort of thing a small boy might do. She turned down slightly the harsh white light of the lantern and slowly walked into her bedroom.

Early next morning she parked her car behind the lab and walked in and sat at her desk. The smiling guards at the gate had a new look.

Clint Reese came out and gave her an impersonal good morning, and spun the dial on the locked file for her. She took the current Sherra folder from the drawer back to her desk, found her place, continued the transcription of notes that had been interrupted on Saturday.

They would want a full report, she told herself. Not just the final three or four pages. No one watched her closely. It would be easy to make one additional carbon. She planned how she would do it. Fold the additional carbons and stick them in the blue facial-tissue box. Then take the box with her to the lavatory. There she could fold them smaller and tuck them into her bra. But she would do it with the next report. Not this one, because it was only a portion of a report.

Sherra's report took twice as long as it should have. She made continual errors. Twice Clint Reese stopped by to pick up the completed report for checking by Cudahy and each time she told him it would be ready soon. When she took it to him at last she imagined that he gave her an odd look before he went on into Cudahy's office, the report in his hand.

Big Tom Blajoviak's note was on her spindle: *Come and get it, sweetheart*.

She took her book and went toward the cubicle in the corner where there was barely room for Blajoviak and a desk.

The door was ajar a few inches. He glanced up at her and said, "Enter the place of the common people, Francie. Just because I'm not a doctor, it's no reason to—"

"Have you really got something this time, Tom? Or is it more repetition?"

"Child, your skepticism is on the uncomplimentary side. Open thy book and aim your little pointed ears in this direction. Hark to the Blajoviak."

"Honestly?"

His square strong face altered. The bantering look was gone. "At five o'clock yesterday, Francie, we began to get a little warm. Here we go." He held his copy of the last report in front of him. "This would be new main subject, Francie. I make it *Roman numeral nine*. Isolation of margin error in Berkhoff Effect. Sub A. Following the series of tests described in *Roman eight* above, one additional memory tube was added to circuit C. The rerunning of the tests was begun on October twenty-third—"

He dictated rapidly. Francie's pencil darted along the notebook lines with the automatic ease of long practice. It took nearly an hour for the dictation.

"So that's it," he said, leaning back, smiling with a certain pride.

"Not that it means anything to me, you know," she said.

"It just might, Francie. It just might mean that instead of getting fried into the asphalt, you might look out to sea and say, 'Ah' at the big white lights out there. Fireworks for the kiddies instead of a disintegration."

She glanced down at her whitened knuckles. "Is it that important, Tom?"

"Are you kidding?"

She shook her head. "No, I just don't understand—all this."

"There was a longbow, and some citizen comes up with body armor. And then the crossbow, and so they made heavier armor. And then gunpowder, which eventually put guys into tanks. Every time, it sounded like an ultimate weapon, and each time a defense just happened to come along in time. Now our ultimate weapon is the thermonuclear missile. Everybody is naked when that baby comes whining down out of the stratosphere. So we have to stop it up there where it won't do any harm."

He paused an instant, then went on earnestly. "We can't depend on the slow reaction time of a man. We've got to have a gizmo. And now, for the first time, I think we're getting close to the ultimate interceptor. If you-know-who could find out how close we are, I'll bet they'd risk everything to try to knock us out before we could get into production on the defensive end. Cudahy wants this one fast as you can get it out, honey."

She stood up. "All right, Tom. As soon as I can get it out."

Francie went to work. She watched her hands add the extra onionskin sheet to the copies required by office routine. At five o'clock Cudahy came out of his office to check the progress. He seemed to be concealing jubilation with great difficulty. He patted her shoulder.

"Take a food break at six, Mrs. Aintrell," he said, "and then get back to it. I'll be here, so you won't have to lock anything up."

"Yes, sir." she said in a thin voice.

Cudahy had not noticed the extra copy. But she could not risk leaving the extra copy in sight while she went to the mess hall. At five of six she took the tissue box, containing the folded sheets into the lavatory. She tucked the sheets into her bra, molding the papers into an inconspicuous curve.

She looked at her face in the mirror, ran the finger tips of both hands down her cheeks. Bob had told her she would be lovely when she was seventy.

She looked into the barren depths of her own eyes and she could hear the voice of Tom Blajoviak: "Fireworks for the kiddies instead of disintegration. Knock us out before we could—"

Francie Aintrell squared her shoulders and walked out of the lavatory. She took her red shortcoat from the coat tree.

Clint Reese sat on the corner of a desk, one long leg swinging. He said, "Remind me to put all my black-haired women in red coats."

She found that she was glad to see him. His lighthearted manner made the lab work seem a little less important, made her own impending betrayal a more minor affair. And she sensed that during the past month

Clint had grown more aware of her. A subtle game of awareness and flirtation would make her forget what she was about to do—or almost forget.

She said, "If you want to see a woman eat like a wolf, come on and join me."

He put on his wool jacket. "I'll take care of all the wolflike characteristics around here, lady."

They walked to the small mess hall. Wind whined around the corner of the building and they leaned into it.

"And after the dogs are gone, we can always boil up the harness," he said.

She heard the false note in her own laughter. They shut the mess-hall door against the wind, hung up their jackets. They filled their trays, carried them back from the service counter to a table for two by the wall. Clint Reese sat down and shut his eyes for a moment. She saw a weariness in his face that she had not noticed before.

Reese smiled at her. "Now make like a wolf," he said.

She had thought she was hungry, but found that she couldn't eat.

"OK, Francie," he said. "Let's have it."

She gave him a startled look. For once there was no banter in his voice, no humor in his eyes.

"What do you mean?" she asked him.

"As official nursemaid to all personnel, I keep my eyes open. Something has been worrying you all day."

"Then make some jokes, and cheer me up, why don't you?"

He was grave. "Sometimes I get tired of jokes. Don't you?"

'Aren't you a little out of character, Mr. Reese? I thought you were the meringue on the local pie."

He looked through her and beyond her. "Perhaps I am. Tonight, my girl, I am lonesome and in a hair-taking down mood. Want to see my tresses fall?"

"Sure," she said.

He took a sip of his coffee, set his cup down. "Underneath this tattered shirt beats the heart of a missionary."

"No!"

"And perhaps a fool. I own a tidy little construction business. I was making myself useful, and discovering that I had a certain junior-executive type flair for the commercial world, when the Army put its sticky finger in the back of my collar and yanked me off to the wars. I was flexing my obstacle-course muscles on Okinawa when they dropped those big boomers on the Nipponese.

"Now get the picture. There I was as intrigued by those big boomers as a kid at the country club on the night of the fourth. *Siss boom, ah!* A big child at heart. Still thinking I was living in a nice, cozy little world. I was in one of the first units to go to Japan. I wangled a pass and went to Hiroshima. It was unpretty. Very."

In the depths of his eyes she saw the ghosts that he had seen.

"Francie, you can't tell another person how it is to grow up in one day. I wandered around in a big daze, and at the end of the day I had made up my mind that this was a desperate world to live in, a frightening world. And it took me another month to decide that the only way I could live with myself was to try to do something about it.

"When they gave me a discharge I turned the management of the company over to my brother and went to school to learn something about nuclear physics. I learned that if I studied hard I'd know something about it by the time I was seventy-three, so I quit. What resource did I have? Just that little flair for administration, the knack of getting along with people and keeping them happy and getting work done.

"So I decided to be a dog-robber for the professional boys who really know what the score is. By being here I make Cudahy more effective. Cudahy in turn makes the teams more effective.

"And now I understand, we're beginning to get someplace. Maybe because I'm here we get our solution a month sooner than otherwise. But if it were only twenty minutes sooner, I could say that I have made a contribution to something I believe in."

Francie felt a stinging in her eyes. She looked away from him, said huskily, "I'm just a little stupid I guess. You seemed so—casual, sort of."

He grinned. "With everybody going around grinding their teeth, you've got to have some relief. If I landed in a spot full of clowns I'd turn into the grimmest martinet you ever saw. Any administrative guy in a lab setup is a catalyst. So let's get back to the original question, now that you've made me prove my right to ask it. What's bothering you Francie?"

She stood up so abruptly that her chair tilted and nearly fell over. She went through the door with her coat in her hand, put it on outside, walked into the night with long strides.

There was a small clump of pines within the compound. She headed blindly toward them. He caught her arm just as she reached them. He turned her around gently.

"Look. I didn't want to say the wrong thing. If this is just one of those days when you—remember too much, please forgive me, Francie. I'd never do anything to hurt you."

She held onto his wrist with both hands. ''Clint, I'm so—terribly mixed up I don't know what to do.''

''Let me help you if I can.''

''Clint, what is the most important thing in the world to any individual? It's their own happiness isn't it? Tell me it is?''

''Of course it is, but you don't need a definition of terms. Isn't happiness sort of a compound?''

''How do you mean?''

''Don't too many people confuse happiness with self-gratification? You can be happy if you have self-respect and also what an old-fashioned uncle of mine used to call the love of God.''

She was crying soundlessly. ''Honor, maybe?''

''That's a word, too. Little dogeared through misuse, but still respectable.''

''Suppose, Clint, that somebody saved your life and the only way they could do it was by violating all the things you believe in. Would you be grateful?''

''If someone saved me that way I think I'd begin to hate them, and hate myself too, Francie. But don't think I'm a typical case. I'm a little top-heavy in the ethics department, they tell me.''

''I married that sort of man, Clint. I understand.''

''You still haven't told me how I can help you.''

She turned half away from him, knowing that unless she did it quickly, she would be unable to do it at all. She unbuttoned the red coat, the jacket under it, the blouse under that. She found the folded packet of onionskin sheets and held it out where he could see it.

''You can help me by taking that, Clint. Before I change my mind.''

He took it. ''What is it?'' he asked.

''A copy of what Tom dictated today,'' she said tonelessly.

''Why on earth are you carrying it around?'' he demanded sharply.

''To give it to someone on the outside.''

After a long silence he said, ''Holy jumping Nellie!'' His tone was husky.

''I was doing it to save Bob's life,'' she said.

''Your husband? But he's dead!''

''I found out yesterday that he's alive, Clint. Alive and in prison.'' She laughed, dangerously close to hysteria. ''Not that it makes any difference. Now he *will* die.''

He shook her hard but she could not stop laughing. He slapped her sharply, and she was able to stop. He walked her across the compound, unlocked a door, thrust her inside, turned on a light. The small room contained a chair, table, double bed, and bookshelf.

"Please wait here," he said gently. "I'll be back in a few minutes with Dr. Cudahy. Handkerchiefs in that top drawer."

Cudahy and Clint Reese were with her for over an hour. Clint sat beside her on the bed, holding her hand, urging her on with the story when she stumbled. Cudahy paced endlessly back and forth, white-lipped, grim. When he interrupted her now and then to ask a question his voice was harsh.

At last they knew all there was to know. Cudahy stopped in front of her. "And you, Mrs. Aintrell, were planning to give them the—"

"Please shut up, Doctor," Clint said tiredly.

Cudahy glared at him. "I'll require some explanation for that comment, Mr. Reese."

Clint lit two cigarettes and gave Francie one, while Cudahy waited for the explanation. Clint said, "I don't see how a tongue-lashing is going to help anything, Doctor. Forget your own motivations for a moment and think of hers. As far as this girl knows, she has just killed her husband—just as surely as if she had a gun to his head. I doubt, Dr. Cudahy, whether either you or I, under the same circumstances, would have that same quality of moral courage. I respect her for it. I respect her far too much to listen to you rant at her."

Cudahy let out a long breath. He turned a chair around and sat down. He gave Clint a sheepish glance and then said, "I'm sorry, Mrs. Aintrell. I got carried away with a sense of my own importance."

Francie said, tonelessly, "Bob told me once that they put him in a brown suit and made him expendable. I married him knowing that. And I guess my life can be as expendable as his. He said we had to be tough. I know they made him write that. He isn't the kind of man who begs. I almost—did what they wanted me to do. It isn't courage, I guess. I'm just—all mixed up."

"Francie," Clint said, "Dr. Cudahy and I are amateurs in the spy department. This is a job for the experts. But I'm in on this, and I'm going to stay in. I'm going to make it certain that the experts don't foul up your chances of getting your husband back. We're going to make the Jacksons believe that you are cooperating. The experts can't get here until tomorrow. Do you think you can handle it all right when they contact you tonight?"

He looked at her steadily.

"I—I think so. I can tell them that I didn't do any transcriptions today."

"Don't give them any reason to be suspicious."

"I'll try not to."

Clint Reese walked her to her car, stood with the door open after she had slid under the wheel. "Want me to come along?" he asked.

"I'm all right now."

"The best of luck, Francie."

He shut the door. The guard opened the gates. She drove down the gravel road toward Lake Arthur.

Betty Jackson, in ski pants and white cashmere sweater, was sitting on the bunk reading a magazine. The fire was burning. Her jacket was on a nearby chair.

Betty tossed the magazine aside and smiled up at her. "Hope you don't mind, hon. I nearly froze on the porch and I only had to make a tiny hole in the screen, just where the catch is."

Francie took off her coat, held her hands toward the flames "It's all right."

"Got a little present for us, dear?"

"I couldn't manage it today. I took a lot of dictation and then I was put to work filing routine correspondence."

Betty leaned back, her blond head against the pine wall, fingers laced across her stomach. "Stew was pretty anxious. This might alarm him a little, hon. He might worry about whether you're cooperating or double-crossing. You know, he told me last night that lots of war widows got so depressed they killed themselves. I'm not threatening you. That's just the way his mind works sometimes."

"I dropped J. Edgar Hoover a personal note," Francie said bitterly. "It's so much simpler than getting a divorce."

"You don't have to be nasty, you know. This isn't personal with us, dear. We take orders just as you do."

"Tell your husband, if he is your husband, that I'll have something tomorrow."

After the woman left, Francie stood and bit at the inside of her lip until she tasted blood. "Forgive me, Bob," she said silently. "Forgive me." It had been done. Now nothing could save him.

She found the lure on the shelf over the sink, at eye level. The body carved to resemble a frog. After she stopped trembling she forced herself to pick it up and throw it on the fire.

The men arrived in mid-afternoon the very next day. Three of them. A slow-moving, dry-skinned sandy one with a farmer's cross-hatched neck. He was called Luke Osborne and he was in charge. The names of the other two were not given. They were dark, well-scrubbed young men in gleaming white shirts, dark-toned suits. Cudahy and Clint Reese were present for the conference.

Osborne looked to be half asleep as Francie told her story. He spoke only to bring out a more detailed description of the Jacksons.

"New blood," he said, "or some of the reserves. Go on."

She finished, produced the letter. Luke Osborne fingered it, and held it up to the light before reading it. He handed it to the nearest young man, who read it slowly and passed it on to the other young man.

Osborne said, "You're convinced your husband wrote that?"

"Of course!" Francie said wonderingly. "I know his writing. I know the way he says things. And then there are those references—the housecoat, Willy."

"Who is Willy?"

"We bought him in Kansas. He's in storage now. A little porcelain figure of an elf. We had him on the mantel. Bob used to say he was our good—"

Suddenly she couldn't go on. Osborne waited patiently until she had regained control.

"—our good luck charm," she said, her voice calm.

"It stinks," Osborne said.

They all looked at him.

"What do you mean?" Reese demanded.

"Oh, this girl is all right. I don't mean that. I mean, the whole thing implies an extent of organization that I personally don't believe they have. I just don't believe that in a little over thirty days they could fix it so Mrs. Aintrell, here, is balanced on the razor's edge. Three months, maybe. Not one."

"But Bob wrote that letter!" Francie said.

"And believing that he wrote it, you opened up for Reese here?" Osborne asked.

"I almost didn't," Francie told him.

"But you did. That's the point. You won't get any medals. There are a lot of people not getting any medals these days." Osborne's smile was an inverted U.

"What are your plans?" Dr. Cudahy demanded.

The office was very still. At last Luke Osborne looked over at Francie. "I'm going to go on the assumption that your husband is alive, Mrs. Aintrell, and that he wrote this letter. At least, until we can prove differently."

"Dr. Cudahy, have you got a file on some line of research that proved to be valueless? A nice, fat file?"

Cudahy frowned. "Things are so interrelated here that even data on unsuccessful experimentation might give us a line on the other stuff."

"Pardon me, sir," Clint Reese said. "How about that work Sherra was doing? And you couldn't make him stop. Wasn't that—?"

Cudahy thumped his palm with a chubby fist. "That should do it! I had to have progress files made to keep him happy. That work bore no relation to our other avenues of approach, Mr. Osborne."

"And if Mrs. Aintrell gives them Sherra's work, a bit at a time, as though it were brand-new stuff, it won't help them, eh?" He thought an instant, then asked: "But will it make them suspicious?"

"Only,' said Cudahy, "if they know as much about what is going on here as I do."

"Reese, you turn that file over to Mrs. Aintrell. Mrs. Aintrell copy enough each day to turn over to Jackson, so he won't get suspicious. Better make six copies or so and give him the last one. Fold it up as though you smuggled it out of here. Can do?"

"Yes," Francie said quickly.

"That should keep your husband alive, if he is alive. We have channels of communication into the likely areas where he'd be. It will take nearly two months to get any kind of a check on him, even if we started yesterday. The better way is to check through the Jacksons." Luke Osborne was regarding her steadily.

"What do you mean by that?" Francie demanded. "You can't go to him and—"

Osborne held up his hand and gave a rare smile. "Settle down, Mrs. Aintrell. Even if your husband weren't involved, we'd hardly go plunging through the shrubbery waving our credentials. They use their expendables on this sort of contact work, just the same as we do. We want the jokers who are buried three or four layers of communication back. I want Jackson to be given the dope, because I am anxious to see what he does with it, and who gets it."

"But—"

"Just trust us, Mrs. Aintrell."

Francie forced a smile. There was something about Luke Osborne that inspired trust. Yet she had no real confidence that he could match his cleverness with the Jacksons. Both Stewart and Betty seemed so supremely confident.

"I'll need your letters from your husband, Mrs. Aintrell. Every one of them."

Francie flushed. The overseas letters, since they had been subject to censorship, were written in a doubletalk understandable only to the two of them. But the letters he had sent her that had been mailed inside the country had been full of bold passages that had been meant for her eyes alone.

''Do you have to have them?''

''Please, Mrs. Aintrell. We will have them for a very short time. Just long enough to make photostats for study. When this case is over our photostats will be burned.''

''But I can't imagine why—''

He smiled again. ''Just call it a hunch. You have them at your cabin, I judge.''

''Yes I do.''

Clint Reese followed her home in his car at five-thirty that evening. They walked down the trail together. A fine, misty rain was falling and the rustic guard rail felt sodden under he hand.

Francie unlocked the door and went in. She looked on the porch and turned to Clint. ''Nobody here,'' she said, relief in her voice.

She took the candy box full of letters out of the bureau drawer and handed it to him. ''You'll be back at nine?''

''Thereabout,'' he said. He slipped the box into his jacket pocket. Then he put both hands on her shoulders. ''Take care,'' he whispered.

''I will,'' she said. She knew he wanted to kiss her, and also knew that he would not, that his sense of rightness would not permit him. He touched his lips lightly to her forehead, turned, and left.

She turned on the gas under the hot water heater, and when the water was ready she took a shower. While she was under the water she heard someone call her.

''In a minute,'' she called back. She dressed in tailored wool slacks, a plaid shirt cut like a man's. She walked out unsmiling. Betty sat on the bunk, one heel up, hands laced around her knee.

Francie said, ''I brought something this time.''

Betty smiled. ''We knew you would. Stew is on his way over now.''

Francie sat down across the room from her. ''Did you get Stewart into this sort of thing, or did he get you in?''

''Clinical curiosity? We met while I was in college. We found out that we thought about things the same way. He had contacts and introduced me. After they started to trust me I kept needling Stew until he demanded a chance to do something active. They told us to stay under cover. No meetings. No cells. We did a little during the war, and a little bit last year in Canada. Satisfied?''

Stewart came in the door, shivering. ''Going to be a long winter,'' he said.

''Here's what you want,'' Francie said, taking the folded sheets from the pocket of her slacks.

''Thank you, my dear.'' Stew said blandly. He sat down on the bunk beside Betty and they both read through the sheets skimming them.

"Dr. Sherra's work, eh?" Stewart said. "Good man, Sherra. I think he was contacted once upon a time. Got stuffy about it though, and refused to play. He could have lived in Russia like a little tin king."

Jackson refolded the sheets, put them carefully in his wallet. "Did you have any trouble getting these out, Francie?"

"Not a bit."

"Good!" Stewart said. He still held the billfold in his hand. He dipped into it, took out some money, walked over, and dropped it into her lap.

Francie looked uncomprehendingly at the three twenty-dollar bills. "I'm not doing this for money."

He shrugged. "Keep it. It isn't important. Buy something pretty with it."

Francie fingered the bills. She folded them once, put them in the top left pocket of her plaid shirt.

"That's better," Stewart said. "Everybody gets paid for services rendered. Canada and London, Tennessee and Texas."

Francie remembered her instructions from Osborne. She leaned forward. "Please let them know right away that I'm cooperating. Bob's letter said he was sick. I want to know that he's being cared for."

Osborne had said to cry if she could. She found that it was no effort.

Stewart patted her shoulder. "Now don't fret, Francie. I was so certain of your cooperation that I already sent word that you're playing ball with us in every way that you can. I'd say that by the end of this week, no later, Bob ought to be getting all the attention he can use."

"Thank you," she said, meaning it completely. "Thank you so much."

Betty stood up, stretched like a plump kitten. "We'll see you tomorrow night, huh? Come on, Stew."

"I'll have more for you."

Francie stood up, too. She made herself stand quite still as Jackson patted her shoulder again. There was something about being touched by him that made her stomach turn over.

She stood at the side window and watched their flashlights bob down the trail through the trees. She made herself a light meal. Clint Reese arrived a little after nine. She took the box from him and put it back in the bureau drawer.

Clint gave an exaggerated sigh. "Osborne's orders. We got to go to the movies together. That gives me an excuse for coming down here, if they happen to be watching you. Ready to follow orders?"

She shivered. "I—I know they're watching me. I can feel it," she whispered. "I do want to be out of here for a little while."

As they went out the door she stumbled on the wet boards. He caught her arm, held it tightly. They stood quite still for a few moments. It was a strange moment of tension between them, and she knew that he was as conscious of it as she was. The strain of the past few days, strain they had shared, had heightened an awareness of each other.

''Francie!'' he said, his voice deeper than usual.

Shame was a rising red tide. Certainly her loyalty to Bob was sinking to a new low. To take the step that must lead to his death, and then take a silly pleasure in a strong male hand clasping her arm.

She pulled away, almost too violently, and said with false gaiety, ''But I buy my own ticket, Mister.''

''Sure,'' he said with no lift in his voice.

When they were in the car Clint said, ''I'm always grabbing hold of females. Sort of a reflex. Hope you don't mind.''

The car lights cut a bright tunnel through the wet night. ''I didn't mind that. It was the sultry tone of voice that got me.''

''Look. Slap me down when I get out line. After the movies, to change the subject, we meet Osborne.''

''It frightens me, having those people around. Suppose the Jacksons catch on.''

''To everybody except you and me and Cudahy, they're new personnel on the project. And they're careful.''

The movie was a dull musical. The crowd was very slim and no one sat within twenty feet of them.

''I can't help it, Francie,'' he said suddenly blurting it out like a small boy. ''I—''

''Clint, please listen to me. You told me once that you would never do anything to hurt me. This whole thing has torn me completely in half. I don't know who I am or where I am. I'm attracted to you, Clint, and I don't like that. I must ignore it, get over it. I have no other choice.''

For a long time he did not answer. When he spoke again, the familiar light note had come back into his voice: ''If you will permit me, madame, I shall finish my statement. Quote: I can't help it, Francie. I've got to have some popcorn. End quote.''

She touched his arm. ''Much better.''

''What's better than popcorn?''

The movie ended and they filed out with the others. As they walked toward the car a match flared startingly close, and the flame-light touched the high, hard cheekbones of the face of Stewart Jackson. Betty was a shadow beside him. Francie caught hard at Clint's arm, stumbling a little, her breathing suddenly shallow.

''Evening, Francie,'' Stewart said, a mild, sly triumph in his tone.

"Hello, Stewart. Hello Betty," she forced herself to say, proud that her voice did not shake, knowing that the presence of Clint Reese had given her strength.

Once they were in the car and had turned out of the small parking lot, she said, "Oh, Clint they were—"

"They just went to a movie. That's all. And found a chance to rattle you."

Clint turned off the main road onto a narrower one, and turned off lights and motor and waited for a time. No car followed them. He drove slowly up the hill and parked in a graveled space near some picnic tables. He gave Francie a cigarette, and she rolled her window down a few inches to let the smoke out.

When Osborne spoke, directly outside her window, he startled both of them: "Let me in before I freeze, kids."

She opened the door and slid over close to Clint. Osborne piled in and shut the door. "Let's have it, Mrs. Aintrell."

"They seemed pleased. Mr. Jackson told me that he'd already sent word to have Bob looked after, knowing in advance that I'd cooperate. And he gave me sixty dollars. He made me take it. Here it is."

"Keep it all together. He'll give you more. They love to pay off. They take some poor, idealistic fool who wants to help the Commies because he was nuts about *Das Kapital* when he was a college sophomore. When the fool finds out what kind of dictatorship he's dealing with and wants out, they sweetly remind him that he had accepted the money and he thereby established his own motive, and it is going to make him look very bad in court. So bad he'd better keep right on helping. By the way, thanks for the loan of the letters. The boys are tabulating them tonight."

"What do I—?"

"Just keep doing what you're doing. Feed them dope from the Sherra file."

"Oh, I forgot. Jackson mentioned that Sherra was contacted once. Is that important?"

"We know about it. Sherra reported it."

"Can I have that last letter back? The one from the prison camp?"

"You'll find it in the box with the others. I'll get a report from the handwriting experts soon."

"That's a waste of time. I know Bob wrote it. It sounds like him."

"Take her home Clint, before she convinces me," Osborne said, getting out of the car, "Night, people." The blackness of the night swallowed him at once.

On Wednesday and Thursday Francie turned more copies of the

Sherra file over to the Jacksons, receiving each time, an additional twenty-dollar bill, given her with utmost casualness and good cheer by Stewart Jackson. On Friday afternoon Francie was called into Dr. Cudahy's office by Clint. Cudahy was not there. Just Luke Osborne. He looked weary.

As Clint paused uncertainly in the doorway Osborne said, "Sit in on this, Reese."

Clint pulled the door shut and sat down. Osborne was in Cudahy's chair.

"What have you found out?" Francie demanded.

"How long can you keep playing this little game of ours, Mrs. Aintrell?"

"Forever, if it will help Bob."

Osborne picked up a report sheet and looked at it, his expression remote. "There's this report of the handwriting. They say it could be his handwriting, or it could be a clever forgery. There are certain changes, but they might be the result of fatigue or illness."

"I told you he wrote it."

Osborne studied her in silence. He looked more than ever like a prosperous Midwestern farmer worried about the Chicago grain market.

"Now can you take it on the chin?"

Francie looked down at her licked hands. "I—I guess so."

He picked up another sheet. "Tabulation report. It has a cross reference of the words in previous letters. We have numbered all his letters chronologically. Letter Four uses the term 'crumb-bum.' In Letter Sixteen there is a sentence as follows: 'Put old Satchmo on the turntable, baby, and when he sings "Blueberry Hill," make like I'm with you in front of a fireplace. Letter Eighteen has a reference to Willy in it. And Letter Three mentions—uh—the green housecoat."

Osborne colored a bit, and Francie flushed violently as she remembered the passage to which he referred.

"What are you trying to tell me?" she asked, in a low voice.

"There are no new words or phrases or references in that letter Stewart Jackson gave you. They can all be isolated in previous letters. We can assume that Jackson had access to those letters during the first few weeks you worked here."

"I don't see how that means anything," Francie said. "Of course, Bob would write as he always writes, and talk about the same things in letters that he always talked about. Wouldn't that be so?"

"Could be. But please let us consider it sufficient grounds—that and the handwriting report—to at least question the authenticity of the letter

Jackson gave you. Remember, the handwriting report said that it *could* be a forgery.''

Francie jumped up. ''Why are you saying all this to me? I go though every day thinking, every minute that if you slip up, just a little, Bob is going to die, and die in a horrible way. I'm doing the very best I can to keep him alive. If you keep trying to prove to me that he's been dead all the time, it takes away my reasons to go through all this—and I just can't see it like—''

She covered her eyes and sat down, not trying to fight against the harsh sobs.

Osborne said, ''I'm telling you this, Mrs. Aintrell, because I want you to do something that may end all this, before you crack up under the strain. I never like to have anybody follow orders without knowing the reason behind the orders.''

Francie uncovered her eyes, but she could not answer.

Osborne leaned forward and pointed a pencil at her. ''I want you to reestablish friendly relations with these Jacksons. Talk about your husband, talk about him all the time. Bore them to death with talk about your husband. Memorize the three items on this little slip of paper and give the slip back to me. I want those three items dropped into the conversation every chance you get.''

Francie reached out and took the slip. There were three short statements on the paper: ''Willy wears a green hat.'' . . . ''Bob broke the Goodman recording of the 'Russian Lullaby' accidentally.'' . . .''You met in Boston.''

It gave Francie a twisty, Alice-in-Wonderland feeling to read the nonsense phrases. She read them again and then stared wildly at Osborne, half-expecting that it would be some monstrous joke. ''Are you quite crazy?'' she asked.

''Not exactly. And not all those words appear in the letters. We know you are clever, Mrs. Aintrell. We want you to tell the complete truth to the Jacksons, except for those three statements on that slip of paper. We assume they have a photostat of those letters, too. Nothing in the letters contradicts those three statements. You are not to repeat them so often that the Jacksons will become suspicious. Just often enough to implant them firmly in memory. Then we shall wait for one of those false statements to reappear either directly or by inference, in the next letter you get from your husband.''

''And if they do, it will mean that—''

''That the army's report of your husband's death was correct. And that the Jacksons have been working one of the nastiest little deals I have ever heard of. Very clever, very brutal, and, except for your courage, Mrs. Aintrell, very effective.''

With forced calmness Francie said, ''You make it sound logical, and it might be easier for me if I could believe it. But I know Bob is alive.''

''I merely ask you to keep in mind the possibility that he may not be alive. Otherwise, should that second letter prove to be faked, you may break down in front of them.''

''She won't break down,'' Clint said.

Francie gave him a quick smile. ''Thank you.''

''Just be patient,'' Osborne said. ''Keep turning data over to them. Skip a day now and then to make it look better. We're trying to find their communication channel. When we find it we'll want you to demand the next letter from your husband. Maybe we can have you risk threatening to cut off the flow of data unless you get a letter. But get friendly with them now, and work in that information.''

That night Francie walked down the shore path to the Jackson camp. She saw Stewart through the window in the living room. He let her in. Betty sat at the other end of the room, knitting.

''A little eager to deliver, this time, aren't you?'' Stewart asked. He shut the door behind her and she gave him the folded packet. He glanced at it casually.

''Is something on your mind, Francie?''

''May I sit down?''

''Please do,'' Betty said.

Francie sat down, sensing their wariness at this deviation from routine. ''This is something I have to talk to you about,'' she said. ''I—I know I'd never have the nerve to consciously try to report you. But I am afraid of giving Dr. Cudahy or Mr. Reese a clue involuntarily.''

''What do you mean?'' Stewart demanded, leaning forward.

''It's just this: I think about Bob all the time. I think about how he is going to come home to me. It is the sort of thing a woman has to talk about, and there is no one to talk to. Sooner or later I may slip and mention Bob to either Dr. Cudahy or Mr. Reese. On my record it says that Bob is dead. They both know that. You see, I just don't like this chance I have to take every day, of my tongue slipping.''

''You haven't made a slip, have you?'' Stewart asked.

''No. But today I—I almost—''

Betty came to her quickly, sat on the arm of the chair. ''Stew, she's right. I know how it would be. Hon, could you talk to us, get it off your chest?''

''It might help, but—''

"But you don't particularly care for our company," Stewart said.

"It isn't that exactly. I don't like what you stand for. I hate it. But you are the only people I *can* talk to about Bob."

"And perhaps get into the habit of talking about him? So that you'd be more likely to make a slip?" Stewart asked.

"Oh no! Just to have *someone* listen."

Stewart stood up. "I want to impress on your mind just what a slip might mean, Francie. Not only would it mean you'd never see Bob again, but you wouldn't be around long enough to—"

"Leave her alone!" Betty said hotly. "A woman can understand this better than you, Stew. We'll be substitute friends for a while, Francie. You go ahead and talk your head off. Stew, it will be safer this way."

Stewart shrugged. Francie said, uncertainly, "I may bore you."

"You won't bore me," Betty said.

"I'm bursting with talk. Saving it up. I've been wondering what to do when he gets back. He'll be weak and sick, I suppose. I won't want to be here. I'll try to get a transfer back to Washington. I could rent a little apartment and get our things out of storage. I keep thinking of how I'm going to surprise him. Little ways, you know. He used to love our recording of 'Russian Lullaby.' The Benny Goodman one. And then he stepped on it. I could buy another one and have it all ready to play.

"And after I got the—the telegram, when I packed our things I was sort of shaky. I dropped Willy and chipped his green hat. I save the piece, though, and I can have it glued on. You know, I can't even remember if I ever told him about saving the flowers. I pressed them—the ones I just happened to be wearing the day we first met in Boston. White flowers on a dark-blue dress. I can get some flowers just like them. When he comes into the apartment, I'll have the record of 'Russian Lullaby' playing and Willy with his green hat fixed on the mantel and a blue dress and those flowers. Do you think he'd like that, Betty?"

"I'm sure he will, Francie."

"He isn't the sort of man who notices little things. I mean, I could get something new for the apartment and I'd always have to point it out to him. He used to—"

She seemed to be two people. One girl was talking on and on, talking in a soft, monotonous, lonely voice, and the other girl, the objective one, stood behind her, listening carefully. But the ice had been broken. Now she could talk about Bob and they would understand just why she had to. The words came in a soft torrent, unbroken.

After that, the days went by, and the constant strain was something she lived with, slept with, woke up with. The Sherra file was exhausted, and after careful consideration of the three team leaders, Cudahy brought Tom Blajoviak into the picture. Tom was enormously shocked at learning what was transpiring, and he was able to go into his personal files to find the basis for a new report on work that would in no way prejudice the current operations.

Stewart Jackson, although disappointed at the way the Sherra reports had reached negative conclusions, was pleased to begin to receive the Blajoviak reports.

Francie knew that she was becoming increasingly dependent on Clint Reese. No one else could make her smile, make her forget her precious moments. It was a quality of tenderness in him, of compassion, yet jaunty in its clownface.

And since that one night he never again put any part of his heart into his voice when he spoke to her. She thought that she could not bear it if he did.

During a frigid mid-November week Betty Jackson went away on an unexplained trip. Stewart collected the daily portions of the Blajoviak report. He smiled at Francie too much, and made clumsy, obvious passes which she pretended not to notice.

Betty left on a Tuesday night. She was back Friday night. Saturday morning Luke Osborne talked to Francie alone in Tom Blajoviak's tiny plywood office. Osborne was having difficulty concealing his jubilation behind a poker face.

"What have you found out?" Francie demanded, her voice rising.

"Nothing about Bob," he said quickly.

She sagged back into the chair and closed her eyes for a moment.

Osborne went on, "But we've gone places in another direction. Can't tell you too much, of course. But I thought you'd like to know. Evidently, they've been under orders to keep contacts at a minimum. I believe that Mrs. Jackson acted as a courier for everything accumulated up to date. She has good technical training for the job, but I don't think she has the feel for it. We put enough people on her so that even if she could push a button and make herself invisible, we'd still stay with her.

"Her contact is from one of the control groups we've been watching. She met him on a subway platform and went through a tired old transfer routine. He gave the stuff to a deluded young lady who works in Washington, taking a one-day vacation in New York. She took an inspirational walk when she got back to Washington. Visited national shrines by night and was picked up by the traditional black diplomatic sedan. By now those no good reports have cleared Gander, chained to the wrist of a courier from one of the cold war countries."

''Why are you telling me all this, Mr. Osborne?''

''It's time to get impatient. We know all we have to know. It has been a month since the first letter. How has it been going?''

''All right, I think. I don't think I've overworked those three things you told me to say. But it seems so pointless. I've been friendly. I help her with those lures they make, enameling them. And we talk a lot.''

''Start tonight. No letter, no more reports. My guess is that they'll tell you one is on the way.''

''One probably is.''

''Please, Mrs. Aintrell, keep planning on the worst. Then if I'm wrong, it will be a pleasant surprise.'' Osborne smiled. ''Young lady, you are doing fine, but, remember, give them a bad time tonight.''

That evening fat, wet flakes of the first November snow were coming down as she walked down the trail toward the Jackson camp. She walked slowly, rehearsing her lines.

She went up on their porch, knocked, and opened the door.

Betty put her knitting aside. ''Well, hi!'' she said. ''Off early today.''

Stewart was near the fire, reading. He put his book aside and said. ''An afternoon nip to cut the ice?''

Francie stripped off her mittens, shoved them in her pocket. She unbuttoned the red coat, looking at them somberly. She saw the quick look Betty and Stew exchanged.

''I came over to tell you that I didn't bring you anything today. And I'm not going to bring you anything from now on.''

Stewart Jackson took his time lighting a cigarette. ''That's a pretty flat statement, Francie. What's behind it?''

''We made a bargain. I kept my end of it. A month is more than up. As far as I know, Bob may have died in that military prison. When I get the letter you promised me, the letter saying that he's better, then you get more data.''

''Hon, we can understand your being impatient,'' Betty said, in an older sister tone. ''But don't go off half-cocked.''

''This isn't just an impulse,'' Francie said. ''I've thought it over. Now I'm doing the bargaining. You must be reporting to somebody. They're probably pleased with what you've done. Well, until I get my letter they can stop being pleased, because you're going to have to explain to them why there aren't any more reports.''

''Sit down, Francie,'' Stew said. ''Let's be civilized about this.''

Francie shook her head. ''I have been civilized long enough. No letter, no reports. I can't make it any clearer.''

Stewart smiled warmly. ''OK; there's no need of hiding this from you,

Francie. We just didn't want to get you too excited. A letter is already on the way. I'm surprised we haven't gotten it already. Now, do you see how foolish your attitude is?''

It startled Francie to learn how accurate Luke Osborne's guess had been. And the rightness of his guess strengthened her determination. She turned from them, took a few steps toward the fire.

''No letter, no reports.''

Stewart's smile grew a bit stiff. ''You are being paid for those reports.''

''I thought you'd bring that up. But it doesn't matter. I don't care what might happen to me. Here is step two in my ultimatum: Either I get my letter within a week or I consider it proof that Bob is dead. Then I'm going to go to Dr. Cudahy and tell him about you and what I've been doing.''

She took pleasure in Stewart's look of concern, in Betty's muffled gasp.

''You wouldn't dare,'' Betty said.

''You're bluffing,'' Stewart said. ''Sit down and we can talk it out.''

Francie pulled her mittens on and turned toward the door.

Stewart barked, ''I insist that you act more reasonably, Francie!''

''Look me up when you've got mail for me,'' Francie said crisply.

She slammed the door behind her and walked along the lakeside trail. She felt neither strength nor weakness—just a gray, calm emptiness. When she got home the fire she had lit was blazing nicely. She sat on the floor in front of it, looking for Bob's face in the flames.

On Monday after listening to her report, Osborne said, ''Now, understand this: You'll get a letter. If the letter proves by content to be a fake, it will be up to my superiors to make a policy decision. Either we take them into custody or we flush them and see which way they run. If the letter doesn't prove anything one way or another, then we go on as we are and wait for the report through Formosa. That may take until Christmas.

''If—and I am recognizing this possibility—the letter shows beyond any doubt that your husband is still alive, we'll continue to play along and use every resource to try to get him back for you. Just remember one thing: No matter what the letter shows you are to act as though you have no doubt. Can you do that?''

''I can try.''

''We've asked a great deal of you, Francie. Just this little bit more.''

The Jacksons came over to the cabin on Wednesday, minutes after Francie's arrival from the lab. They stamped the snow off their feet, and came in smiling.

"So you doubted me, eh?" Stew said cheerfully. "It came this morning."

As he fumbled for his pocket, Francie realized that Osborne's doubts had shaken her more than she knew. She was afraid of the letter—afraid to read it.

It seemed to take Stewart an impossibly long time to undo myriad buttons to get at the pocket which held the letter. Francie stood, looking beyond him, hand half outstretched, and through the windows she saw the shale of new ice that reached tentatively out from the shore line into the lake. She heard Betty prodding the fire.

"Here you go!" Stewart said, holding out another folded sheet of the familiar cheap fibered paper.

Francie took it, her finger tips alive to the texture of it. Betty knelt in front of the fire, bulky in her ski suit, head turned, smiling. Stew stood in his shaggy winter clothes, beaming at her.

"Well go on!" Betty said. "You going to stand and hold it?"

Francie licked her lips, "Could I—read it alone please? It means so much."

"Read it now, honey," Stewart said. "We want to share your pleasure with you. It means a lot to us, too, you know."

She unfolded the letter. At first the pencil scrawl was blurred. She closed her eyes hard, turned her back to them, opened her eyes again.

> Baby, now I know they weren't kidding when they said you'd get that other letter. I guess you're doing all you can for me. Anyway, I seem to be a guest of honor now. Sheets, even. Baby, don't feel bad about helping them. Maybe it's for the best. They've got something I've never understood before. For the first time I'm beginning to see the world as it really is. And now, darling, that fireplace seems closer than ever. And so do you. You still got those two freckles on the bridge of your nose? When I get my hands on you, baby, we'd better turn Willy's face to the wall.

Francie stopped reading for a moment and took a deep breath. A breath of joy and thanksgiving. He had to be alive. Nobody else could sound like that.

> Remember that I love you and keep thinking that we'll be together again. That's what really counts, isn't it? Figure on me being back in the spring when all the world is turning as green as Willy's hat.

She stared at the last words. How could Bob have made such a grotesque and incredible mistake? The figurine wore no hat! How could he possibly—? And she read it again and saw the whole letter begin to go subtly false. This new letter and the one before it. False, contrived, artificial. It was all so clear to her now.

Bob, under the circumstances he described, would never have written in such a pseudo-gay way. His other letter had been like that because he had been trying to keep her from worrying about combat wounds or combat death. Now these letters, these fake letters, sounded absurdly light-hearted.

Still looking at the letter, her back turned toward them, Francie saw how they had taken the most precious part of her life and twisted it to their own ends. Bob was dead. He had died during the retreat. Had any doubt existed they would have labeled it *Missing in Action*. She had been the gullible fool. The stupid sentimental fool who clung to any hope, closing her eyes to its improbability.

Involuntarily she closed her hands on the letter, crumpling it, as though it were something evil.

Stewart Jackson had walked over to where he could see her face. "Why are you doing that?" he asked, his voice oddly thin.

She fought for control, masking her anger. "I—I don't know. Excitement, I guess. To think that he'll be back in the spring and—we can—" But that was a spring that would never come.

In it's own way this letter was far more ruthless than the original telegram. She couldn't pretend any longer, not with the two of them watching her so carefully.

She looked at them, hating them. Such a charming civilized couple. Stewart's face, which had seemed so bland and jolly, was now merely porcine and vicious. Betty, with features sharpening in the moment of strain, looked menacingly cruel.

"Filth!" Francie whispered, careless now of her own safety. "Filth! Both of you."

Stewart gave a grunt of surprise. "Now, now, after all we've done for—"

"Grab her, you fool!" Betty shouted. "It went wrong somewhere. Just look at her face!" Betty jumped to her feet.

Stewart hesitated a moment before lunging toward Francie, his arms outspread. In that moment of hesitation Francie started to move toward the door. His fingers brushed her shoulder, slid down her arm, clamped tightly on her wrist. The meaty touch of his hand on her bare wrist brought back all her fear.

His lunge had put him a bit off balance, and Francie's body contracted in a spasm of fright that threw her back. Stewart was pulled against the raised hearth of the fireplace. As he tripped, his hand slipped from her wrist and before she turned she saw him stumble forward, heard the thud his head made striking the edge of the fieldstone fireplace, saw both his hands slide toward the log fire.

As Betty cried out and ran toward Stewart, Francie found the knob and pulled the door open and ran in panic toward the trail. She went up the first slope, reached the handrail, caught it, used it to pull herself along faster.

She glanced back, gasping for breath, and saw Betty, her face set, her strong legs driving her rapidly up the hill.

Fear gave Francie renewed strength and for a few moments the distance between them remained the same. But soon she was fighting for air, mouth wide, while a sharp pain began to knot her left side.

Betty's feet were so close that she dared not look back. Her shoulder brushed a tree and then Betty's arms locked her thighs and they went down together, rolling across the sticky trail into the base of a small spruce.

Betty slapped her hard, using each hand alternately slapping until Francie's ears were full of a hard ringing and she could taste blood inside her mouth. But she could hear the ugly words with which Betty emphasized each blow.

"Stop!" Francie cried. "Oh stop!"

The hard slaps ceased and Francie knew that she had learned a great deal about Betty's motivations during those brutal moments.

"On your feet," Betty said.

Francie rolled painfully to her hands and knees. She reached up and grasped a limb of the small spruce to help herself to her feet. The limb she grasped was only a stub, two feet long. It broke off close to the trunk as she pulled herself up. She did not realize that, in effect, she held a club, until she saw Betty's eyes narrow, saw the woman take a step backward.

"Drop it Francie," Betty said shrilly.

Francie felt her lips stretch in a meaningless smile. She stepped forward and swung the club with all her strength. It would have missed the blond woman entirely, but Betty, attempting to duck, moved directly into the path of the club. It shattered against the pale-gold head.

Betty stood for a moment bent forward from the waist, arms hanging, and then she went down with a boneless limpness. She hit on the slope, and momentum rolled her over onto her back.

Francie, laughing and crying, dropped to her knees beside the woman. She took what remained of the club in both hands and raised it high over her head, willing herself to smash it down against the unprotected face, her temples pounding.

For a long moment she held the club high, and then, just as she let it slip out of her hands to fall behind her, Clint Reese came down the wet path. He was half running, slipping on the wet snow, his overcoat fanning out behind him. When he saw Francie the tautness went out of his face. He took her arm and pulled her to her feet.

"Get off the path," he said roughly.

"They—"

He pulled her with him, forced her down, and crouched beside her. She heard the shots then. Two that were thin and bitter. Whipcracks across the snow. Then one heavy-throated shot, and after an interval, a second one.

She moved and Clint said, "Stay down! I came along to see if you were getting all the protection Osborne promised."

"Oh, Clint, they—"

"I know, darling. Hold it. Somebody's coming."

It was Luke Osborne, walking alone, coming up from the house. He walked slowly and the lines in his face were deeper. They came out to meet him. Osborne looked down at Betty Jackson. The woman moaned and stirred a little.

One of the young men, a stranger, came down the road.

Betty sat up. She looked vaguely at Osborne and the young man. Then she scrambled to her feet, her eyes wild. "Stewart," she screamed. "Stewart!"

Osborne blocked her as she started forward. "Your partner is dead, lady," he said. "Quite thoroughly dead."

Betty pressed the knuckles of both hands against her bared teeth. Instinctively Francie turned to Clint, and pressed her face against the rough top-coat texture. She heard Osborne saying, "Get her up to the car, Clint."

After giving Francie a shot the doctor sent her to bed in the Cudahy guestroom. As the drug took hold she let herself slip down and down, through endless layers of black velvet that folded over her, one after the other.

On the fourth day, Clint Reese took her from the Cudahy house back to her cabin. He helped her down the trail and pointed out where Osborne's men had been trying to protect her as much as possible without alarming the Jacksons.

He lit a fire, and tucked a blanket around her in the chair. And then he made coffee for them. He lounged on the bunk with coffee and cigarette. "Take tomorrow off," he said expansively.

"Yes, boss."

"Remember when I was going to say something in bad taste and you stopped me?"

"I remember."

"Oh, I'm not going to try to say it again, so don't look so worried. I'm going to say something else. Lines I memorized last night, in front of my mirror, trying to wear in appealing expression. The trouble is, they still happen to be sort of—well, previous. So I won't say them, either.

"But I'll keep practicing. You see, I've got to wait until you give me the go-ahead. then I'll say them some day. Old Reese, they always said, a very patient guy. Got a master's degree in waiting, that one has."

"It is too soon, Clint. Especially after all that's just happened."

"Well, I'll stick around and wait. The way we work it, you show up some morning one of these years with a lobster trap in your left hand and a hollyhock in your teeth, humming 'Hail to the Chief.' That will be our little signal—just yours and mine. I'll catch on. Then I'll spout deathless lines you can scribble in your diary."

He stood up for a moment. His eyes were very grave.

"Is it a date?"

"It's a date, Clint."

"Thanks, Francie."

He left with an exaggerated casualness that touched her heart. She pushed the blanket aside and went to the window to watch Clinton Reese go up the trail.

Now the Adirondack winter was coming, and during the long months she would watch the frozen lake and let the snow fall gently on her heart. A time of whiteness and peace, a time of healing. By spring Bob's death would be a year old, and spring is a time of growth and change and renewal.

Francie recalled the look of gravity and warmth and wanting in Clint's eyes, the look that denied the casual smile.

Possibly with strength and luck and sanity, it might come sooner than either of them realized. For this might be the winter in which she could learn to say good-bye.

BRUCE CASSIDAY

Deep-Sleep

1

PETER BARON BLINKED and turned away from the incessant glare of the flash bulbs popped by the news photographers eagerly lining the walls of the gaudy Naples nightclub. His eyes smarted. He tightened his arm around the waist of the Countess, who had slid off his lap and was now sharing his chair.

Countess Elena Rondi turned to him to smile, sagging against him, rumpling his impeccable dinner jacket and absently stroking his ear. Her full attention was centered on the dancer.

On the table top in the middle of the room, a heavily made-up girl with coal-black hair, blood-red lips, and clad only in a two-piece bikini and high-heeled Spanish dancing shoes, pirouetted and stamped to the beat of a perspiring combo. In her navel she wore an enormous opal. At each gyration, the girl's breasts seemed about to escape from the strip of silk which bound them.

She was an Italian starlet, and she had just returned from Hollywood, where she had filmed a daring feature-length trifle about incest. Because of it, she was the sensation of Rome, Paris, the Riviera—and Naples. The *paparazzi*, the tabloid photographers, were avid for her. She was the toast of the Neapolitan social set.

Peter Baron sipped at the third-rate, expensive champagne and gazed about the lavish furnishings of the plush Naples night spot. The room smelled of money, of aristocracy, of status. Men in exquisite formal attire, women in lavish gowns, inverts in eccentric fripperies, all sat about watching the antics of the actress with jaded awareness, some clapping sardonically to the tempo of the dance, some sipping the flat champagne morosely. Decadence and boredom looked out of well-fed, well-fleshed, well-painted faces.

Wishing suddenly that he had opted for the sunshine and abandon of the Riviera and his villa there, rather than Capri and Naples this month, Peter Baron whispered to the woman at his side:

"*Andiamo, Contessa*. Let's go."

She was a lush, golden-bodied creature, with long, syrupy hair and eyes the color of Chinese ginger. Her carmine lips covered cat's teeth. She was splendidly built, with the North Italian woman's fine figure, and the South Italian woman's passionate temperament.

She smiled lasciviously, her eyes darting about the room at the hollow-cheeked aristocracy, at the *paparazzi*, these denizens of the night whose job it is to capture in black-and-white permanence the tawdriness, the shame, the evil of modern Italy.

"*Momentino,*" she whispered. She snuggled against him, and he felt the warmth of her flesh through her sleek gown. It stirred him sensually. He fingered the champagne glass.

On the table top, the obscene dance reached a crescendo. The mascaraed girl twisted suddenly, tore the scant silken ribbon from her bosom, and threw the scrap into the air. She thrust herself about with greater abandon. The *paparazzi* went mad; the air quaked with chained lightning. Someone shrieked. A bottle smashed and a chair went over backwards.

With a resounding crash the music stopped. The lights went out. The girl on the table jumped to the floor and escaped to the rear of the club.

The dance was done.

Peter Baron pulled Countess Elena to her feet. "Now."

"*Si*," the Countess murmured.

She clung to him, pressing her soft body against him as he steered her through the close-packed tables, past the manicured hands of bright-eyed fairies and the fat, sweaty palms of bankers and merchants.

A *paparazzo* wearing enormous sunglasses which stretched in a wide band from one ear to the other stepped in front of Peter to take a picture.

"*Aspettate!*" Baron said curtly. "No pictures!"

The photographer shrugged, his lips a line of contempt under the black eyeless strip-mask. His flash bulb popped.

Baron lashed out at the camera, throwing it savagely to the floor. He bent down, opened it, unrolled the film quickly, and tore it off.

"What's going on here?" the *paparazzo* cried in a woman's way.

"No pictures," Baron told him calmly. "I asked you nicely."

The photographer swaggered forward, grabbing Baron's shirt front in his fist. Baron struck the finicky hand away and flung the other man down. The news photographer sank to his knees. His sunglasses hung lopsidedly from one ear. His eyes were naked, furtive and small.

The night club went dead quiet.

Baron threw a wad of bills on the floor contemptuously. ''For your trouble, *signore*!'' Then he gazed around at the pale, tense faces turned toward him. Without another word he gathered in the Countess, regal and silent, and hustled her into the street.

''Peter,'' she whispered, kissing him on the cheek. 'What did you do that to him for?''

''I don't like my picture taken,'' Peter Baron said softly.

More than anything else, Peter Baron loved to drive his off-white Lancia over the dusty roads of Italy. He liked to feel the wind blowing down on him, cooling him and washing away the stench of stuffy nightclubs, the rich and the sick. He slid his hand onto the Countess's bare knee. He could see her gleaming thigh where her $2,000 Paris gown had hiked up.

''Elena,'' he said softly.

She was leaning her head back, letting the wind catch her long, fine hair. ''Where are we going?'' she asked sleepily.

''To bed,'' Peter said. ''I'm tired.''

''Where, specifically?'' asked the Countess, a smile curving her lips.

''In a pink *palazzo* near Avellino. You know it?''

''My second cousin Julia was born there. Before the Social Democrats turned it into an inn.''

''It has a view of a lovely lake. Sailboats in the moonlight and all that.''

''I thought you lived on Capri, Peter.''

''Occasionally. Also in Geneva. On the Riviera. The Isle of Crete. I like a change of scenery.''

''And the *palazzo*?''

''I've rented it for the night, thrown out all the paying guests, and reserved it for us.''

''You're a dear boy, Peter.'' She leaned over and kissed him.

Above them the sky spread up into eternity, and the stars looked down.

''Peter?''

''Yes.''

''It must have cost a mint.''

''Yes.''

''You Americans!''

''Yes, but I never go to America, except to visit,'' Baron said, smiling.

''An internationalist?''

"Something like that."

"Peter."

"Yes?"

"All that money. Where does it come from?"

He smiled and looked at her. "What an embarassing question. Where do babies come from, *carissima?* The dollars come from the birds and the bees."

"You have style," she said.

"We'll try it out together later," Baron promised.

She laughed throatily, expectantly.

They were climbing a country hill outside Naples. Not a single light was visible in the emptiness of space around them. The smell of open fields drifted over them.

"Peter. Can you stop a minute?"

He turned to her questioningly.

"That cheap champagne. I think I may be sick."

"Sorry." Baron slowed the Lancia and pulled over to the side of the road. He snapped off the lights. They sat there a moment in silence. Somewhere near crickets chirped. A night animal scuttled through the brush.

"I feel better now," Elena said weakly. "Let's just sit."

Peter Baron heard the sputter of a motor scooter on the road behind them. In the rearview mirror, he could see one glowing head lamp hurtling through the darkness like a fiery eye of an errant cyclops. A Vespa passed them noisily and turned off the main road into a side lane twenty feet ahead. They were parked on the slope of a hill, looking down into a wide, silent valley.

The narrow beam of the Vespa's head lamp wavered slowly down the dirt road. A young man was driving. The road wound across a rickety wooden bridge over a stream, and then into a clump of trees before passing up the slope of the next hill.

As Peter and the Countess watched idly, they saw the head lamp of the Vespa pick out what seemed to be a barricade of empty barrels in the middle of the road. To one side, a tree was leaning down at an angle, as if the wind had bowled it over.

"That's strange," Baron mused.

"What, darling?"

"The barricade."

They both watched as the young man stopped the Vespa and alighted.

In the dim glow of the head lamp, he stepped across a tangle of rope which lay on the road's surface.

Peter Baron's jaw dropped. Then he straightened in his seat, instantly alert. He pounded frantically on the Lancia's horn. Its bleat echoed in the night.

"What are you doing?" the Countess asked.

"The fool! Doesn't he see?"

"See what?"

The tree by the side of the road straightened with lashing swiftness, as if a rope which had held it pulled down had been released. Simultaneously, the tangle of ropes under the man's feet gathered themselves together and whipped up around him, forming an enormous net. It drew together at the top, and hoisted him in the air, so that he was caught like a fish.

He hung there trapped, suspended from the tree top.

"My God!" gasped the Countess, as if she could not believe her eyes.

"A varmint trap!" Peter Baron murmured. "I wonder . . ."

Instantly he pressed the Lancia starter, and flicked on the headlights. He drove swiftly to the turn-off and onto the dirt road.

"What happened?" the Countess asked.

"I haven't the foggiest," Baron said. "But I intend to find out."

"That man—he's hanging in the air! In a net!" She stifled a hysterical laugh. "It's almost funny!"

The Lancia sped down the dusty dirt road toward the wooden bridge. As they passed over the planks, the bridge almost shook itself to pieces.

"Look!" The Countess was pointing upward into the sky. "Peter, I'm afraid!"

Baron lifted his eyes from the road and saw an enormous black shape hovering over the clump of trees, high in the air. There were no lights inside the mass, only a bluish glow. Then, as he squinted, Peter made out the shape of a helicopter, painted black, without markings, and running without navigation lights. It was hovering like a hummingbird over the man-trap in the tree.

A chain appeared at the open hatch of the helicopter, lowering a jagged grappling hook down toward the tree. Expertly, the grappling hook engaged the top of the fish net and began to draw it upward. A slip knot in the net unfastened, and the net came loose from the tree. The hook drew the man upward toward the helicopter cabin.

Baron slammed the Lancia to a stop behind the parked Vespa and jumped out. As he did so there was a harsh report in the air. A thin pinpoint of rifle flame stabbed out from the helicopter. Near Baron's feet a bullet cracked into the earch.

"They're shooting!" he cried to the Countess. "Get down on the floor of the car and don't move!"

"Yes, Peter. Where are you going?"

"When somebody shoots at me, I shoot back!"

He rushed to the boot and tore it open, removing his Winchester. He raised it to his shoulder and aimed at the nose of the helicopter, firing three times. One shot splintered a part of the Plexiglas bubble, but the other two missed.

Man and net disappeared into the interior of the helicopter. The snout of an ugly machine pistol protruded from the chopper's nose. Bullets popped up dirt all around Baron. One hit the Lancia. The Countess uttered a muffled shriek.

Baron cursed and ran toward the cover of the trees to draw fire from the Lancia. The helicopter hovered overhead, descending slightly. Peter dashed through the aura of light from the Vespa's head lamp. A bullet almost hit him in the shoulder, but passed instead into the trunk of a tree behind him. He plunged into the densest part of the wood, whirling to take a bead on the helicopter.

The machine pistol chattered, spraying leaves and bark around him. He fired back. The 'copter came down lower, its nose toward him, like a mechanical dinosaur in some futuristic nightmare. Baron backed down into the undergrowth as best he could.

He fired again. The Plexiglas starred. A voice cursed in a gutteral, Balkan tongue. Instantly the chopper rose into the air and vanished over the trees, heading eastward overland.

Peter Baron ran out into the open, firing at the aircraft several times. The 'copter lowered quickly over the brow of the far hill and vanished into the darkened sky.

Baron investigated the Vespa briefly for signs of identification, found none, and snapped off the head lamp. Then he returned to the Lancia.

"Are you all right?" he asked Elena, who was sitting in the seat now, sobbing.

"Yes. What was that all about?"

Baron packed the Winchester back into the boot. "I haven't the vaguest." He stared thoughtfully into the eastern sky. Could it be . . .?

He shook his head. He did not want to speculate. Tonight had been set aside especially for recreation.

He climbed in and slammed the door. "To the *palazzo*, Contessa?"

"Please, Peter," she said, trembling against him. He put his arm around her and squeezed her tightly. With his nose in the fragrance of her hair, his eyes slowly lifted to the sky again.

He wondered who the man in the net could be. And he wondered who could be flying illegally in an unmarked, unlightened helicopter over Southern Italy—and why.

His neck itched. That was a bad sign. It meant he would be at work soon.

2

DEEP-SLEEP

The shrill tone alternated between high C and high D. It resembled the beep-beep of sonar on a submarine. In a way, the tones were the beginning of a great and profound symphony—except that no notes past the first two were ever to be heard.

Peter Baron shook himself awake and opened his eyes. On the ceiling shimmered the bright reflection of water. The pink *palazzo* had a tiny lake outside, he remembered. Also he remembered the Countess. Turning, he saw her bare, golden shoulder peeping from the downy blue coverlet. Her hair fanned out from her head.

He sighed deeply and Contessa Elena Rondi turned toward him, opening her sleep-drenched eyes. Her hands crept out to him. Quickly he was in her arms again, enflooded in warmth and comfort and sensuality.

But still the high C and the high D obtruded on his consciousness.

Encircling her waist with one arm, he reached behind him for the miniature radio-telephone, shaped like a cigarette case, which he always carried. He pushed it down behind his pillow where its tone was somewhat more muffled.

Elena giggled and kissed him.

The beeping continued.

Baron lifted the radio-telephone and put it down on the floor. Then he covered it with the bolster from the bed.

The beeping diminished somewhat in intensity, but not in zealousness.

He kissed the countess deeply and she turned to him. She smiled and closed her eyes, wrapping her arms tightly about him.

Beep-beep-beep-beep.

Very reluctantly, Peter Baron emerged from the pleasures of the boudoir and retrieved the radio-telephone from beneath the bolster where it continued its repulsive ululations. On the edge of the bed he sat observing it sourly. He pressed the button and the ignominious beeping ceased.

"Baron."

"Peter, this is Duke Farinese," a clipped Oxford voice said.

"Obviously."

"Emergency. Repeat, emergency. Chadwick is here. He demands a meeting."

"Chadwick?"

"Oren Chadwick. The Yank."

"Where is 'here'?"

"Capri."

"I thought you were at the house in Geneva?"

"I returned to Italy yesterday. Where are you?"

"Near Avellino."

"When can you be here?"

"Soon."

"Come then, immediately."

"Of course."

"*Ciao.*"

"*Ciao.*"

Peter Baron replaced the miniature radio-telephone, yawned, stretched, and stood. He reached out and yanked on the old-fashioned silken bell cord at the head of the bed.

"Darling," a drowsy voice asked from the tumbled bed. "What are you doing?"

"Ringing for breakfast. I must be leaving you."

"Beast."

"Of the lowest order."

"Will you have breakfast with me, at least?"

He lifted her chin and kissed her lips. "Sorry. Business, you know."

She sat up and ran her fingers through her hair. The bedsheet had tumbled away from her bosom. She adjusted it slowly.

Peter Baron smiled. "Fresh strawberries flown in from Palmyra. Melon from Damascus. Eggs shirred in 1907 Cognac. Coffee roasted yesterday in Lebanon and ground this morning. Fresh cream from cow's milk."

"Luxury," sighed the Countess. "And you have to miss it."

"I'll make do without the breakfast," Baron said. "But I'll never be able to make do without you, *carissima*."

"Darling."

* * *

By Lancia Peter Baron sped to the dock at Naples and there climbed aboard his launch, *La Bonne Chance*. Soon he was tying up at the small jetty at his villa on the far side of Capri. Now called Villa di Pietro, it had originally belonged to a fascist millionaire who sold it off to pay debts after Mussolini departed the scene in 1945 with his heels up and his head down in that famed square in Milan.

Peter Baron leaped from the launch and started up the long sandstone steps. He could see Il Duca Francesco di Farinese standing at the top of them in the courtyard of the villa, waiting for him.

Farinese was a Sicilian by birth, but looked completely unlike an ordinary Sicilian. Instead of dark hair he had hair of a strange lemon-yellow color, which bleached albino white in the sunshine. Instead of a squat athletic body, he had a trim, lithe physique. Instead of a rasping accent he spoke English with the purest Oxford inflection. *Il Duca*, the Duke, was called just that: ''Duke.''

''Peter,'' he said. ''You're late.''

''No. You're just early, as usual.''

They shook hands, both standing in the elegant courtyard at the rear of the pale yellow villa. Grapevines hung overhead, trailing new buds down from the heavy crossbeams of the trellis.

''Where's Chadwick?'' Baron asked.

''I woke him when I heard you coming. He was worn out from the Paris flight.''

''What's the problem?''

''First let me fill you in on some of the personnel,'' Duke said.

''Right. Shall we go inside?''

They walked into the living room of the villa, a sumptuously furnished room in excellent and opulent taste. Fine carpeting, lush wall hangings, and decorous chandeliers and lamps: that was the keynote of the *Villa di Pietro*—''Peter's Villa.''

''I hope I didn't interrupt anything beautiful,'' Duke observed pointedly.

''You terminated nothing more than an elegant companionship,'' Baron said. ''But I must change the tone of that damned radio-telephone. It grates on my nerves. How about low E and F natural?''

''You have the musical sense of a deaf cow!'' Duke protested, scandalized. ''We'll keep it C and D. Let your tin ear adjust.''

Baron nodded. The quarrel was an ancient one, ever since they had begun to use the long-range radio-telephone with which they could be kept in direct personal contact anywhere on the Continent.

Baron sat on a couch along the far wall and looked out the window at the sparkling waters of the Tyrrhenian Sea.

"Let's have it."

Duke Farinese lit a cigarette and sat down. "World War II. Remember Prince Filipo Rimini?"

Peter Baron frowned. "You're taxing my memory. But I have read about him. He was one of Mussolini's favorites. He went over to the Underground to work for the Allies. He was fantastically successful in uniting the Partisans. Is that the one?"

Duke nodded grudgingly. "He was murdered at the end of World War II by the Communists. They thought he was trying to keep them from seizing control of the *Partigiani*. Which he was."

"The books say his assassination created an offensive political scandal."

"It did. Now, a little geneology. Prince Filipo had two children—twins. His wife died in childbirth. The twins were Filipo's greatest treasures. They were brought up after his murder with strong emotional ties for one another. A boy and a girl—Paula and Mario Rimini."

Peter Baron squinted. "Wait a minute. That name Paula Rimini rings a bell. Isn't she married now?"

The Sicilian's face relaxed in a bemused smile. "Yes. she is, Peter. But, unfortunately, not with benefit of clergy."

"Of course! She's the mistress of Dr. Blake Forester, the American chemical tycoon!"

"Very good. And Forester?"

"I *do* know that. Forester left the States because of a marital entanglement. His wife wouldn't give him a divorce. Also, he was in a legal tussle with one of the big chemical combines in the States over the rights to a drug patent he claims was stolen from him."

Duke smiled. "You Yanks always fight over the wrong things. Imagine—marriage and patents!"

"Forester came over to Italy at the request of a fellow chemist and started that big plant outside Naples—Chimici Consolidati. And it's been a financial prodigy ever since."

"Jolly good recital, Peter. One hundred percent correct."

"What about all this?"

"One more point. Mario Rimini secured a job at the chemical plant as a section head through his sister Paula's influence. Paula runs dutifully in the social strata to which she is accustomed. As they say, she is a Princess. She does have her moments of revolt, however. Mario, even though he is a genuine Prince, thinks Italian high society is decadent, idiotic, and sick."

"He is right, of course," Baron murmured.

"Yes, but one can't *say* that. Mario prefers to live in seclusion in a tiny farmhouse once owned by a distant relative outside Naples. It's on the road to Avellino. He's somewhat of a recluse, an odd-ball. A European beatnik—that sort of thing. He is a sports car enthusiast, has his own Vespa, skin dives, flies a plane, sails a boat, and so on."

"Avellino?" Baron asked, suddenly alert at the mention of both the Vespa and Avellino.

There were footsteps outside and a man entered the living room. Peter Baron rose. So did Duke.

Oren Chadwick smiled and approached Baron with outstretched hand.

Chadwick was a cool, self-possessed, bland man of forty-five who wore suits with no shoulder padding, shirts with high collars, and trousers with no hips.

He was of medium height, with generous, even features, blue eyes, freckles, and thinning reddish hair. When he sat down opposite Peter Baron, he pulled a pipe out of the pocket of his tweed jacket and filled it with maple-scented tobacco from a plastic pouch.

"We met during the Dietz business in Berlin," Chadwick reminded Baron, his blue eyes direct and probing.

"I remember it vividly."

"You did a superb undercover job for Uncle Sam. When this thing broke on us last night, I immediately wired home and suggested your help. I explained that the situation demanded a free-lance agent totally uninvolved with the U.S.—someone exactly like yourself. I received a go signal early this morning. Here I am."

"In what capacity are you here?" Baron asked.

Chadwick hesitated. "I do not represent anyone officially. I am a direct emissary of that nebulous fellow, Uncle Sam. The relationship between Rome and Washington is extremely touchy because of the rather famous personalities implicated. Do you see?"

"I see," Baron nodded.

"Right. You were at Quantico and at Fort Holabird, weren't you?"

"For a time."

"Then you know that what I'm going to tell you has to be kept in the strictest confidence."

"What else?" Peter Baron said.

Chadwick got his pipe going. "Will you help us?"

"First let me have some inkling of the problem."

"Of course." Chadwick composed his thoughts. "The flap concerns Deep-Sleep."

"Deep-Sleep?" Peter Baron laughed outright. "You're putting me on."

"Seriously. Deep-Sleep is the working title of a battle gas developed by Dr. Blake Forester, a chemist whom you may know."

Peter Baron winked at Duke Farinese.

"The properties of Deep-Sleep are fantastic. It is a knock-out gas, but the essentially unique thing about it is that it does not enter the human system through the nose and mouth, but through the pores of the skin."

Baron whistled softly.

"I underwent an experimental dose of Deep-Sleep," Chadwick went on. "It is unbelievable. At first I simply felt a mild tingling on my skin. Then, within seconds, a furious burning sensation, almost like the itch of poison ivy, enveloped me. Within moments, I was in a deep sleep, from which I emerged after two hours—with absolutely no after-effects!"

Peter Baron nodded.

"You can imagine the possibilities. Spray with the gas, take the objective without shedding a drop of blood, and disarm the enemy!"

"What's the drawback?" Peter asked.

"The use of gas in warfare is controlled by means of masks. You spray the gas, knock out the enemy, don gas masks, and march over the fallen. With Deep-Sleep, the problem can't be solved that way. Since the gas enters the pores of the skin, an antidote must be used. Airtight plastic work clothes with self-contained breathing devices do not work: no maneuverability. So Dr. Forester has been working to come up with an antidote—and he never got it!"

Peter Baron sensed Chadwick's agitation. "You use the past tense. Is Dr. Forester dead?"

"No. Two nights ago he was assaulted on the streets of Naples and now lies in deep coma in a hospital. Simultaneously, someone tried to enter the heavily guarded vault at his plant to secure the master copy of the formula for Deep-Sleep. No one but Dr. Forester knows the ingredients, you see. He worked it out all by himself."

"You mean there's only one copy of the formula, and it's in the vault?" Baron asked incredulously.

"Not exactly. There is a duplicate of the formula in the Pentagon—its exact location so top secret it would take a bank of computers to locate it. It's there in case something should happen to Chimici Consolidati—physical destruction, that sort of thing. The point is, with Deep-Sleep in our hands, we're safe. But if the enemy should get hold of it—bingo!"

"Did the thief obtain the formula?"

"No. he was killed by a guard."

"Ah. Was the thief identified? Do we know who is after the formula?"

"He was a nonentity. There was no way of ascertaining who hired him."

Baron frowned with disappointment.

"Our security checks on the Russians indicate that they know nothing about it. Nor do the Chinese Communists. It looks as if some independent agency is bent on securing the formula and blackmailing both East *and* West with it."

"I.C.E.?" Peter Baron glanced at Duke Farinese, who shrugged. Baron faced Chadwick. "The problem then is to enter the guarded vault and destroy the formula?"

"I wish it were that simple," Chadwick said morosely. "The problem is more complicated. Last night one more development occurred. Mario Rimini, who is a section head at Dr. Forester's plant, was kidnapped somewhere on the way home from Chimici Consolidati."

Peter Baron blinked. "How, exactly?"

"He simply did not appear at his home after leaving the plant. Since the attempt to burgle the vault, we had increased the guard at the plant and put a loose check on several people. Mario Rimini was one of them."

"Quite a loose check," Baron murmured. "The plant is located on the road to Avellino outside Naples, is it not?"

Chadwick's brows shot up. "Yes. Why?"

"I believe Mario Rimini has been taken out of Italy completely," Baron said. Briefly, he explained the strange adventure with the helicopter the night before.

Chadwick was disconsolate. "Just our luck! Your theory is undoubtedly correct. Otherwise, why the helicopter? Why the unmarked fuselage? Why the eastward flight?"

"Yugoslavia?" Duke Farinese murmured. "Rumania?"

"Either, undoubtedly," Baron said.

Chadwick shifted in his seat. "You can now see why he cannot march in and destroy the Deep-Sleep formula. Whoever has seized Mario Rimini will demand the formula in return for Mario's life. And the demand will most certainly be made on Paula Rimini, his twin sister, the mistress of Dr. Forester."

"What makes you so sure?"

"Dr. Forester feared some such attack on himself. He has given strict orders to Paula Rimini to open the vault and destroy the formula if ever he should be killed."

"If you knew this, why didn't you have a watch on Mario Rimini?"

"We didn't know about it until last night, when we told Paula Rimini of her brother's disappearance. She hadn't done anything about the formula because technically Dr. Forester was not murdered, but simply assaulted."

"I still don't understand why we can't obtain the formula and destroy it."

"The Riminis are national heroes, Peter," Chadwick said nervously. "People still remember their father, Prince Filipo. And they *are* royalty. If anything happened to Mario—or Paula—Dr. Forester, and America, would be blamed. Harboring a dangerous U.S. gas formula in Italy, and all that—why, it could blow NATO apart."

"Then you're saying we must got through with the ransom, and *then* try to retrieve the formula?"

"Exactly. Only after Mario Rimini is safe in our hands."

"Can't we hand over a fake formula?"

Chadwick's head shook vehemently. "Under no circumstances. A chemical expert would spot a phony in an instant. It must be the real thing."

"What if we're dealing with the Red Chinese and they *do* get the formula?" Duke Farinese wondered.

"They'd use the stuff on us in Vietnam and drive us out of Asia!" Chadwick exploded. "Under no circumstances must that happen!"

"Indeed not," Baron assented softly. "What do we do first? Do you have a plan of action?"

"Keep Paula Rimini under surveillance. When the kidnappers contact her for the ransom, watch her so that she is not betrayed before she can secure her brother's release. Then get the formula back."

"I'd suggest apprehending the kidnappers when they make the contact and demanding Mario Rimini's release," Duke said acidly.

"Absolutely not!" Chadwick snapped. "They would simply send more men. We would have revealed our intent and be unable to keep the Princess under surveillance."

Baron nodded. "What if the contact men moved in and seize the Princess?"

"It's our calculated risk that they won't. Top Echelon has decided we must play it this way, assuming the exchange will go through in the usual fashion. You will simply be chaperones, no more and no less."

Baron made a face. "Is the vault guarded adequately?"

"High tension lines on the cyclone fence. Alsatian police dogs on the prowl for all strangers. Gate guard and inside guard alerted and instructed to shoot first and talk afterwards. No one but Paula Rimini can get to that formula."

Peter Baron breathed wearily. "The difficult we do immediately. The impossible takes a little longer."

Chadwick smiled thinly. "Not too much longer, I trust. We don't have much time."

3

THE MAN FROM I.C.E.

In the opulent lobby of the Appartamenti D'Annunzio in suburban Naples, Peter Baron leafed desultorily through the morning newspaper. He was seated in a satin upholstered chair under an enormous, glittering cut-glass chandelier.

It was 10:30 in the morning. Outside, the sun shone brightly. Birds in the trees chirped excitedly. Automobiles and trucks whirred by on the street. In the distance, the blue Tyrrhenian Sea sparkled brightly.

A telephone rang and the clerk answered it. His face brightened. A hush descended over the lobby. The operator glanced at the arrow on the elevator bank.

"*La Principessa!*" the clerk whispered loudly.

A cleaning woman disappeared into the rear. The mail clerk straightened his tie and also watched the elevator indicator.

Peter Baron lowered his newspaper as the elevator doors slid open. A dark-haired woman with enormous, haunted black eyes walked out into the lobby, staring straight ahead, her head regal as a queen's. She wore an original Dior street coat and a splash of orange hat on her blue-black hair. Brilliant coral earrings set off the black of her eyes.

The clerk on duty bowed from the waist, averting his eyes. She barely glanced at him. At the front entrance, a doorman pulled back with a flourish. Almost immediately the Princess was whisked away in a cab.

Peter Baron continued to read his newspaper. He did not look up as a man in a white workman's pull-over appeared carrying a service grip. He approached the desk.

"*Il telefono*," the newcomer murmured.

"*Si*," said the clerk. "Go right on up."

The man nodded and passed by Peter Baron toward the elevator. It was Duke Farinese. Each pretended not to see the other.

Baron smiled to himself at the thoroughness of Duke's disguise. On the lapel of the work cloak the name ''Giacomo Salzino'' was stenciled in black letters.

That was the beauty of Duke Farinese's background. As a Sicilian, he had many cousins in the International Mafia. The Mafia had its members in organization in almost every walk of life. Giacomo Salzino was an employee of the Naples Telephone Company.

Twenty minutes later, Baron folded his newspaper and walked by the clerk toward the front of the apartment. He gave and received a warm, blank smile.

In the Lancia, Baron slumped down and leaned his head back on the seat, absorbing the sun like a vacationing bather without a care in the world. Seven minutes and 30 seconds later, the R/T in his pocket let out its familiar beep-beep.

''Duke this end. It's all done. Her phone is tapped.''

''Good. Where's the tape recorder?''

''I've got a man in the basement. One of my Mafioso.''

''Get out of there fast and meet me. We'll divide her into four-hour stretches. I want every move on paper.''

''Right, Peter.''

The call they expected came at ten o'clock that night. Peter Baron was in the villa, listening to a late newscast on FM from London, when Duke strode in through the courtyard.

He held up a cardboard box of tape triumphantly. ''Here it is.''

''Good. Let's put it on the tape deck.''

Baron shut off the FM radio and switched over to the tape deck. Duke slid the aluminum reel out of the box, threading the tape through the empty sprockets on the deck. Baron flipped the switch to PLAYBACK.

A woman's voice spoke first. ''*Pronto*.''

Baron leaned forward. The Princess's voice was clear and full of vibrancy. Her accent was elegantly Italian—the true Italian of Firenze, without a trace of dirty Neapolitan.

''Is this *Principessa* Paula Rimini?'' It was a man's voice, full and heavy, with a menacing overtone of suppressed violence. He spoke with a strange inflection—as if he had learned Italian as a foreigner. Baron could not place the accent. Balkan?

''Yes. Who is this, please?'' The Princess's voice trembled slightly. Peter could tell that she knew who this was, that she had been expecting the call.

"It is about your brother."

Paula swallowed hard. When she spoke she was almost breathless. "*Si*."

"I have news of him. I must see you alone tomorrow evening. At Da Giacominio's on Via San Carlo. You know it?"

"*Si*."

Peter Baron knew it, too. It was a small, pleasant restaurant, a favorite of the sporting set. There would be no way for them to protect the Princess in the crowd, no way to rough up and seize the contact if he proved intractable. The place was too respectable.

The male voice continued. "Exactly 6:30 at Da Giacominio's."

"*Si*," the Princess responded.

"If you tell anyone about this, you will never see your brother again—alive."

"I understand," she whispered, her voice trembling pathetically. The Princess, for all her courage and aplomb, was obviously on the brink of despair.

Peter Baron bit his lip in anger.

The caller hung up. The tape flipped off. Baron rewound it on the first spool. Then he lifted the reel and slid it into the box.

"I want to hear every word of that scheduled meeting at Da Giacomino's," Baron told Duke.

"I've a friend in the kitchen. A cousin."

"Good. He can help you set up the listening device. Isn't there an alcove where I can observe out of sight? I want to see the contact man."

"Yes."

"Fix it up for me then." Baron rose. "Bring that tape downstairs. I want to check it out. It's quite possible we have a voice profile of the man."

Duke shrugged. "Maybe."

Peter Baron remembered the Balkan accent of the man in the helicopter which had taken away Mario Rimini. This was not the same man.

"The accent sounds definitely Balkan," Baron said.

"I wouldn't know. But the computer might."

They descended a stairway that wound down into the solid rock of Capri. Moisture glistened on the surface of the walls. Lights glimmered in the ceiling. They entered the wine cellar. High in one wall a tiny window looked out through bars onto the ocean. Stars were visible in the clear sky.

The walls were lined with cribs of wine bottles. Enormous casks stood about. One sat astride a rack. Peter and Duke moved in front of it. Duke reached out and opened the lid as one might open a cupboard door. Actually, it was not a wine cask at all. It was a computer, its front panel lined with buttons, lights, and slots.

Duke ran the reel onto the tape deck at the top of the control panel and pressed the ON button. Lights glowed and blinked in a strange flashing pattern and then stopped.

The tape reel spun around. Finally it stopped and a card came out of the slot at the panel's bottom. Duke picked it up. He read it and then handed it over to Baron.

IDENTITY UNKNOWN.
MALE. FORTY-SEVEN.
FOREIGN TO ITALY. BASIC
LANGUAGE POSSIBLY
RUMANIAN, HUNGARIAN,
YUGOSLAVIAN. SPEAKER IS
HEAVILY BUILT,
MUSCULAR, STRONG. I.Q.
LOW. RESOLUTION HIGH.

Peter Baron whistled. "You see? I was right. Probably Balkan. Let's go, Duke. I want you to set up Da Giacomino's for me."

"Right."

"I'll bet we're tangling with I.C.E. again." The thought did not make him any happier.

At 6:30, Peter Baron was seated at a tiny table in an alcove off the main dining room of Da Giacomino's restaurant in Naples, sipping an Americano with an olive. In his ear he wore a device which resembled a hearing aid. He could observe the main dining room, but no one in there could see him unless he looked hard.

A waiter hovered over him. He glanced up in annoyance. He had given Duke specific orders that he was not to be disturbed. When he saw who the waiter was, he smiled.

"You make a perfect *garçon*, Duke. You should have taken it up as a profession."

"More fun in the suicide games we play," Duke observed. "She is on her way. I followed her myself earlier this afternoon. She went to two shops in the Via Ciaia. Then she bought shoes at Renfro's on Via Roma. After that she came directly here."

Baron nodded. "Have you planted the device?"

"Yes." Duke stiffened. "There she is!"

Peter Baron waved him off. Duke Farinese strolled into the dining room and watched the maitre-d' seat the Princess. In the well-lighted room, she appeared under a great strain, her face pale and her eyes circled. She was beautiful, Baron realized, with the indefinable grace of royalty.

She removed her gloves slowly and scanned the room impersonally. Several of the more knowledgeable patrons recognized her; these began discreetly whispering to their companions behind their hands.

As the maitre-d' hovered about her, she flicked her finger down the menu. Then she turned to Duke Farinese and gave a curt order. He bowed and moved quickly toward the bar. A moment later he was back, carrying a martini with an olive in it.

He set it down in front of her and crossed to Peter Baron. Peter flicked the switch in his pocket where the batteries were located. He heard a humming sound in his ear. The maitre-d' spoke to the Princess.

"We shall serve you as soon as your guest arrives, *Principessa*," he told her in Italian.

Peter Baron nodded to Duke. Duke caught his eye and passed on through to the kitchen at the back of the restaurant. The miniature microphone-transmitter was shaped like an olive and floated in the Princess's martini. It was working perfectly. Peter Baron was constantly amazed at the resourcefulness of the electronics people in supplying listening and seeing devices for use in the Cold War. He blessed his luck that Duke understood electronics from A to Z. Peter was himself such an all-thumbs technician that he could scarcely change a light bulb.

Exactly five minutes later, a yellow-haired man with a stocky build and a square face with a bulldog chin stepped up to the Princess's table.

"My dear *Principessa,*" his voice said in Baron's ear. "How pleasant to find you alone in these delightful surroundings." Baron had heard the voice before—on the tape recording of the Princess's telephone call.

"Thank you," the Princess said in a clear, defiant voice.

"May I join you?" the heavy voice asked in the indefinable Balkan accent.

"But of course," said the *Principessa* without expression.

Peter Baron peered through the curtains of the alcove. The man who had joined the Princess sat with his back to him. Paula Rimini toyed with her drink.

"I shall not stay long, Princess," he continued. "I am simply here to give you the details of an assignment you must perform for us."

"Assignment?" The Princess smiled bravely.

"You are in Dr. Forester's complete confidence. We know that in the event of a serious accident to Dr. Forester, you have been entrusted with the safety of a valuable document in his vault at Chimici Consoladati."

"I do not know what you mean," the Princess murmured.

"I'm sure you do. You have access to Dr. Forester's office, where his vault is located. The guards will let you in. They have been instructed to do so. You will procure for us a specific formula, called Deep-Sleep, in return for which your brother Mario will be surrendered to you."

The Princess straightened in her chair. Peter Baron saw a tear glint in her eye. She apparently understood enough about Deep-Sleep to know that there was great danger to her country if it fell into enemy hands.

"I cannot do it!" she whispered.

The heavy-set man leaned closer to her, smiling for those around the table who might be gazing curiously at this mismatched pair.

"You have no choice! If you do not do as I say, your brother—your twin—will be dead within the hour."

The two gazed at each other. The Princess broke. "Yes," she said finally, lowering her head in agony. "As you say."

The heavy-set man patted her hand. "Good."

She withdrew her hand angrily. Her face flamed. "Don't touch me!"

Beyond the two at the Princess's table, Peter Baron saw another man enter the dining room, a man similar in dress and appearance to the kidnapper with the Princess. He was dressed in a rumpled cheap suit, and he wore enormous shoes. He was taller than the first, all bone and muscle.

Baron started to rise. Chadwick's calculated risk had failed to pay off. The alleged contact had become a pick-up. He must abort it immediately.

"Our limousine is outside. We go now, *Principessa*. You understand?"

The Princess looked about her in sudden terror. She gripped the edge of the table until her knuckles were white. But she whispered, "Yes."

Peter Baron silently cursed Chadwick's excessive optimism and lack of foresight. As Baron debated his next move, the R/T in his jacket pocket beeped warningly. That meant that Duke had spotted the trouble himself. Quickly Baron removed the cigarette case from his pocket, feeling a sudden dizziness as he did so. He looked down at the martini, shaking his head. Duke must have mixed him a double. Of course, the martini was for effect, so that no one would question his presence in the alcove. But why a double?

Baron flicked the button of the radio-telephone and heard Duke's agonized voice.

"Peter! I.C.E. I recognized one of the men. He's just come into the kitchen. Grab the Princess and . . ."

There was a click and the R/T went dead. Baron was alone now. They had neutralized Duke. With difficulty he lifted his eyes to the Princess's table, wondering what was wrong with his reflexes. The second man had joined the first; now both were helping her to her feet.

The room began to spin under Peter Baron. His knees were weak. Willing himself not to fall, he clutched the table top, trying to think. He knew then that he had been taken in by the simplest trick of them all—a drugged cocktail. The watchers had in turn been watched.

A high-pitched laugh came from behind him. He turned to look into a grinning face. He recognized the man. He had seen him before, in Berlin, on the case Chadwick had remembered. The laughing man was a known agent of I.C.E.

"This isn't your day, Mr. Baron!" he said, his eyes derisive.

Peter Baron held his breath to keep from falling. He lashed out with a left feint, chopping down with the edge of his right hand on the man's neck. The agent from I.C.E. fell back a step.

He recovered and pounded a doubled-up fist into Baron's stomach. Peter Baron gripped both hands together and brought them down on the nape of the man's neck. The two of them tumbled to the floor.

Baron's vision kept getting fainter. He could barely see now. Black clouds of ink crept into his vision from all sides. He staggered to his feet, moving groggily.

The man kicked out at him. Baron turned away, pushing aside the curtains of the alcove. Behind him he heard a scuffling sound. He tried to turn to ward off the blow, but his knees went to jelly, and he could neither see nor hear.

"Princess!" he tried to cry out. "Stop! You're in danger!"

No words came out.

A chair crashed down on his shoulders, splintering dismally. Blackness swallowed him up even before he hit the floor.

4

THE FORMULA

La Principessa Paula Rimini sat silently in the back seat of the black Cadillac in front of Da Giacomino's, trying to maintain her composure.

She was more frightened than she had ever been in her life, but she determined not to show it.

''Now we see the sights of Naples,'' said the driver with a contented purr. He was the man who had conversed with her at the table inside. ''At ten o'clock, you go into the vault, Princess.''

''Exactly, Josip,'' said the man seated beside Paula.

Josip started the Cadillac, suddenly jubilant. ''It's going to be what the British call 'a piece of cake,' Miko!''

Miko eyed Paula. ''Don't be too sure, Josip. There is always the American.''

''Nonsense. That one was well taken care of,'' snorted Josip, pushing the Cadillac into the stream of traffic on the avenue. ''I saw him go down in the alcove where he was watching us.''

''And the fellow in the kitchen?'' Miko wondered.

Smiling, Josip drew his finger across his throat. ''The Yank will be on Mr. Satin's yacht in minutes. There he will remain until the exchange is made.''

Paula Rimini shuddered. She made no sense of the conversation. Every nerve in her body was screaming. She felt as if she might slip into unconsciousness through sheer tension. But she held herself rigidly erect.

''Relax, Princess,'' said Josip, smiling coarsely as he drove the Cadillac through the heavy traffic. Paula could see his badly cared-for teeth. ''It's some time before your turn comes.''

Mike subsided in the cushioned back seat of the Cadillac. Paula closed her eyes. She wanted to cry, but she promised that these two boors would never see her shed a tear.

It seemed ages before the hands of her wristwatch showed ten. She had not once spoken to either of the men as the limousine prowled through the tumbledown streets of night-time Naples. The men had conversed in a foreign tongue most of the time.

While they had chattered, Paula had made up her mind. To give in to the mailed-fist tactics of these professional assassins was the easy way out. She was only a woman, but she was a Princess. She owed something to Italy. She would fight—like her father, Principe Filipo. Then, and only then, would Mario, her brother, be proud of her.

''Here we are,'' Miko growled. ''Princess, when the guard stops us, you tell him you want to go in. He'll let you through. *Comprendete?*''

They drove up to the main gate of the chemical plant. She could see the big letters painted on the side of a long shedlike building near a double-height cyclone fence: CHIMICI CONSOLIDATI. Along the top of the fence ran two strands of electrified wire, strung high to prevent anyone from climbing over. Behind the cyclone fence an enormous Alsation hound patrolled the grounds. He was trained to seize any stranger and not let go until commanded by his master.

All this Paula knew because Oren Chadwick had told her.

Josip, the driver, turned his head. ''If the guard asks any suspicious questions, Princess, you tell him that Dr. Forester has regained consciousness and has requested you to come to the plant to pick up a set of papers. That will explain why we'll be going in to the office.''

''Yes.'' She had been in the plant many times. Each time she had been with Blake. The guards knew her. It would be quite easy for her to enter the grounds without special written orders. No one at Chimici Consolidati would knowingly refuse her entrance. The kidnappers had hit on a completely foolproof plan to obtain the formula for Deep-Sleep.

The limousine pulled up to the gate. A bright spotlight shone directly in through the windshield. Josip, the driver, held up a hand to ward off the glare. Outside, a guard peered at them from behind the meshed steel gate. He drew out a handgun from a holster at his belt and gestured the driver to climb out of the car.

Josip exchanged a glance with Miko. Miko nodded. Paula heard a rustling movement in the seat beside her. Out of the corner of her eye she saw that Miko had pulled a gun from his jacket and was screwing a short barrellike silencer to the end.

She shivered.

Josip approached the gate jauntily. ''Good evening, guard!'' he said with a bright smile. ''In the car I have Princess Paula Rimini who wishes to enter the plant grounds to pick up a package for Dr. Forester.''

The guard frowned. ''I do not see the Princess.'' He lifted the handgun and aimed it at Josip's stomach. Josip ignored the weapon purposefully and waved his hand at the limousine.

''Princess? Will you please show yourself?''

Paula did not move. She was frozen with indecision. If she refused to appear, the guard would turn away the two kidnappers. They would not get the very important formula for Deep-Sleep.

''Princess!'' hissed Miko at her side. ''Remember your twin!'' She felt the painful jab of metal in her side. The silenced gun was pointed at her midriff.

She swallowed. Heroic opposition to these men might mean Mario's immediate death. She opened the door, leaned out, smiled, and waved at the guard. In the glare of the spotlight she recognized him—a middle-aged man with a bald head and a family of three children. She had seen him many times, once playing with his little daughter, a polite, dignified, dedicated man.

If he let these men into the plant, what would happen to him? Would he be dismissed—disgraced?

"Is it all right, *Principessa*?" he asked her pleadingly.

Paula could not respond. *No!* she wanted to scream. It was *not* all right! Miko sidled closer, aiming the gun at her chest. "Talk! Or it's the end of Mario!"

"It's all right!" she burst out suddenly, almost sobbing.

Obediently, the guard crossed to the padlock which hung from the center of the closed gate. As he reached out with the key Paula jumped out of the car and ran toward him, waving her hands.

"No! No! Don't let them in!"

The guard turned, stunned, caught in tableau. With the quickness of light, there were three hissing explosions next to Paula's ear. The guard stiffened, gripping his chest with the hand which held the key. He lifted his handgun to fire. He never did. The handgun clattered loosely on the pavement as he slumped limply to the ground.

Paula started to scream. Miko clapped his hand over her mouth, seizing her around the waist, holding her immobile against him. Angrily he signaled Josip with a jerk of the head. Josip ran for the gate, leaning down and clawing at the dead guard's uniform. He had fallen so that his body was wedged between the gate and the pavement.

Quickly Josip worked with his fingers through the meshed steel and twisted the guard so that his hand fell across his chest toward Josip. The key to the padlock dropped into Miko's hand.

He straightened and, with a savage twist, opened the padlock. Glancing over his shoulder, he gestured to Miko to bring the girl inside. Miko pushed Paula through the gate and the three of them stood in the darkness just outside the cone of light.

"The Alsatian dog!" Miko breathed. "He'll be on his way."

Josip pulled a coil of bare wire from his jacket. On the end Paula could see a group of hooks extending loosely in all directions. Josip glanced upward at the top of the electrified fence.

In the shadows, the Alsatian growled. Paula closed her eyes in despair. Miko held her tightly, one hand still over her mouth, the other twisting up on her arm behind her. Pain flooded through her body. She thought she would faint.

Josip made a sound in his throat. The dog growled again in the darkness. Paula saw the thick rubber gloves which Josip had quickly slipped on his hands, and the flash of bare wire as the kidnapper threw the hooked end of the wire high into the air. It caught in the top wire of the cyclone fence and hung there, attached by the loose hooks.

Now the Alsatian leaped out of the shadows, teeth flashing, mouth open, black lips snarling. He closed instantly on Josip—or what looked like Josip's gloved hand. There was a terrifying discharge of electricity. The Alsatian glowed blue for one horrifying instant.

Paula sobbed.

The dog's teeth tightened on the "glove," and ten thousand volts of electricity poured into him from the hot wire at the top of the fence, through the false metal hand which Josip held in his insulating rubber glove. There was a sulfurous smell of burned flesh and singed fur and the dog fell over dead on his side. As he lay there, his hideously burned mouth fell slowly open.

"Come on!" Josip cried, pulling the coil down from the charged wire, wrapping it quickly.

They ran on into the silent plant.

In the large room which Dr. Forester used as his main office, Josip switched on the light. Miko held the silenced gun in his hand, pointing it at Paula Rimini. The two men faced the Princess across Dr. Forester's desk.

"Quick, now!"

"I must get the combination to the vault," Paula said. "I know where it is."

"Hurry!"

Paula lifted out the top righthand drawer of Dr. Forester's desk. Attached by tape to the underside of the desk top she found the slip of paper, just where he had said it would be. In the light she read it.

Miko crowded around behind her, looking over her shoulder. She could smell his breath, heavy with peppermint. She felt sick.

"F-F-D-O," the paper said.

"That's no combination!" Miko raged. "Are you trying to play games?"

She shook her head. "It's code."

Josip's eyes brightened. "Each letter means a number. F is 6, the sixth letter of the alphabet. Is that it?"

She wrote down "6-6-4-15." Then she ran the numbers together and divided by 5. The sum was now 13,283. She separated the numbers into 13-28-3. With the slip of paper in her hand, she walked over to the corner of the office where the entrance to the vault stood.

Miko followed, holding the silenced gun at her back.

Shivering, she slid aside the door which covered the dial of the vault. Then she turned it to the specified numbers.

Noiselessly the door swung open.

"Hurry up!" Josip breathed nervously. "There's still one more guard walking around somewhere."

Hope surged in her, but only briefly. She remembered the death of the guard at the gate. She did not want another man's life on her conscience.

One of the folders inside the vault was stamped. DEEP-SLEEP—TOP SECRET. She lifted it out and stood with it clutched to her bosom.

Josip stared at her. "Is that the formula?"

She hoped her voice did not tremble. "It says Deep-Sleep."

Josip leafed through its pages. He cursed under his breath. "Miko! Can you read this?"

Miko riffled through the folder. "No." His eyes came up to Paula's. He moved menacingly toward her, thrusting the gun muzzle into her side. Perspiration crawled out on her forehead. "If this isn't it, Princess, your brother is a dead man!"

She closed her eyes.

Josip had lifted a fountain pen flashlight from his jacket to examine the inside of the vault. 'What's that?"

Miko kept the gun pressed into Paula's side, and pushed her around in front of him so he could see into the vault. "I see it. It's a film canister."

"Mr. Satin told me the formula was on film," Josip grated.

"Take it!" snapped Miko. "The Princess is playing games with us!"

Paula almost cried. The last safeguard had failed. The real formula of Deep-Sleep was on film in the tiny, pencil-thick, inch-long canister which Josip now held. The folder of papers was a decoy.

"That's it, isn't it?" Josip shouted at her.

She bit her lip.

"Of course it is," Josip cried. "Let's go!"

Miko took the canister from Josip and held it in his left hand.

Paula reached out for the film. "It's mine! My brother—"

"The film is what we came for, Princess. You'll see your brother again sometime—if you're lucky!"

Josip laughed.

Miko pointed the gun at Paula. She stood there with sinking heart. The two men backed from her, carrying the precious film toward the doorway.

"That's far enough!" snapped a voice from outside the office.

Miko whirled with the gun. Josip dropped away, going to the floor, reaching for a weapon in his jacket. Paula saw one of the guards in the doorway, his weapon pointed at Miko.

Miko fired first, the silenced shot hissing out. The guard fired once at Miko, and then twisted to shoot Josip. He fired again and again at Josip, who had almost gotten out his own gun.

Miko fell dead.

Paula dropped to her knees and picked up the film canister from the floor where it had rolled out of the dead Miko's hand.

Her face was flooded with relief. "You've saved my life!" she told the guard.

Then she saw that he was slowly wilting to the floor. He went down with a crash, and did not move.

Paula screamed and ran out into the corridor, sobbing uncontrollably.

Her apartment was quiet and dark. She sat a long time, trying to think what she must do. The men who had kidnapped her brother had never intended to let him go. They had meant to steal the film from her as soon as she had taken it from the vault. She could never trust them again. She did have one thing in her favor. Because she had the film of the formula for Deep-Sleep, she had the power to buy back her brother.

She held the gun she had taken from Miko, weighing it in her hand. It was heavy and cumbersome, but she had seen it kill.

In panic she had driven the kidnapper's Cadillac back to her apartment. When she had entered, she had quickly found the new pair of shoes she had purchased that afternoon at Renfro's.

The heel of the right shoe slid to one side; inside was a hollowed slot where the film canister would fit: it was an artifice she had ordered prepared by a very special friend who worked at Renfro's on Via Roma. It was in that slot that she would carry the precious film so that no one could take it from her. Her brother's life depended on her now. She would not let anything happen to the film.

Paula thought about the shoe with the false heel where it now lay in her closet, along with the rest of the purchases of the day. Dress, coat, shoes—all very innocent items. No one would guess the truth.

The shattering jangle of the telephone bell sent her heart skipping.

"Yes?"

"Princess?"

She recognized the heavy accent, but not the voice, "Yes."

"Our apologies, Princess. Some of my associates have delusions of grandeur. As a result of their cupidity, you now have the object which we want. With it, you may redeem your twin brother Mario's life. It is your only chance."

Paula was angry. "I do not trust you! How am I to deal with someone I do not trust? Your friends killed two decent human beings!" Her voice was rising. She felt like screaming.

"No melodramatics," the voice intoned indulgently. "As soon as it is practicable, I shall arrange a rendezvous for the exchange of your brother and the formula. I guarantee there will be no more attempts to harry you."

"I can never trust you."

"And well you shouldn't," the voice said softly. "Nevertheless, I shall be in touch."

"I hardly intend to . . ."

Paula stared at the phone. There was no point in talking any longer. The man at the other end had hung up.

It was then that she heard the noise in her bedroom. *The closet!* she thought, panicky.

She ran through the darkened living room and pushed open the far door, holding Miko's heavy gun in her hand. Quickly she snapped on the lights. White brilliance flooded the room.

She saw her closet in disarray.

She understood: the telephone call had taken her away from the shoes and the film. Somehow these people had known everything. They had come to steal the shoes while she was talking on the telephone.

She stepped forward and a man thrust himself against her, clamping a heavy hand over her mouth.

5

MR. SATIN

When Peter Baron regained consciousness, there was only a dim glow of blue light all around him. Then when his eyes focused, he could see a small, cell-like room. In one wall there was a circular window with bars across it. Under him the floor swayed gently.

After a moment he realized that he was not in a cell, but in a cabin on board a ship. The blue light was simply a night light. He had a roaring headache from a bump on the neck, and his shoulders ached.

Cautiously he felt himself over for injuries. He had been savagely beaten, but he had no broken bones. Crawling to his knees, he tried to stand. The rocking of the deck was not pronounced. The craft did not seem to be moving; he guessed that it was anchored at rest in some quiet bay.

He peered through the porthole at open sea and a cloudless sky. They were unidentifiable.

He felt his way around the cabin. There was no furniture and only one entrance, a door that was locked. It was of heavy oak, not likely to lend itself to being easily broken down.

Peter Baron sat in the middle of the deck and tried to draw his scattered thoughts together.

He knew that he was a prisoner aboard a craft of some kind. He knew that Duke was either dead, in captivity with him, or neutralized by the attack on him in the kitchen of Da Giacomino's. Princess Paula Rimini was in the hands of the kidnappers of her brother, obviously on her way to remove the formula of Deep-Sleep from Dr. Forester's plant vault.

Baron sat up straighter. There was one more thing. Hadn't Duke recognized an I.C.E. agent at the last moment before being assaulted? I.C.E. *was* in it.

I.C.E. International Combine of Entrepreneurs, commonly called International Combine for Evil. I.C.E.

I.C.E. was a recent outgrowth of the Cold War. The International Combine for Evil profited monetarily from friction between East and West, recruiting its agents, many of whom were professional spies dismissed from one country or another for double-dealing, for selling secrets, or for arcane diplomatic reasons.

I.C.E. was in the nasty game of espionage for the money it brought in from any side—by blackmail, by extortion, by murder. And it was making a fantastically successful job of bartering secrets.

I.C.E. had kidnapped Mario Rimini in order to obtain Deep-Sleep. Once it had Deep-Sleep, it would sell to Russia, or to the West, or to some small emerging nation which needed to establish itself. World peace would not be secure from that moment on.

Peter Baron clenched his hands in hopeless frustration. So long as he remained in this cabin, he would be unable to act against the insidious organization.

He was dozing when the cabin door opened quickly. A shaft of yellow light from the corridor widened and blinded him.

"Get up," a voice told him in Italian.

Baron stood.

"Follow me."

He was led down a companionway into a sumptuously furnished cabin with large portholes which looked out over a placid bay. Baron recognized Naples in the background, with the hulking shadow of Vesuvius in the distance. Rapid calculation told him that the craft in which he was imprisoned was anchored not far from the Island of Ischia somewhat to the west of Naples.

An enormous desk stood in the center of the cabin. At it sat a man who matched it—enormous, with white, almost translucent skin, rosebud lips, and intelligent blue eyes. He was utterly bald. His skull gleamed palely.

Baron's escort vanished and the cabin door closed behind him.

"Sit down, Mr. Baron, please," said the big man, smiling broadly.

Baron sat in an upholstered chair. He tried to analyze the fat man's accent, but, since it was next to imperceptible, he could not pinpoint it. The voice was silken and liquescent; the English impeccable, but unnatural; the timbre was slightly feminine, yet with a crude inner strength. This was a man of conflicting characteristics, certainly; a dangerous man.

"I have heard so much about you," the stout man said, laying his hands down on the desk in front of him, palms down. "It has taken an inordinate amount of energy to arrange this meeting. And a modicum of trouble." The rosebud lips moved into a smile.

Peter Baron waved a hand. "I'm afraid you have the advantage of me, sir."

"A thing not easy in the achievement, certainly," the big man murmured, pursing his lower lip. In a way, he resembled an overgrown babe—a Churchillian Kewpie-doll. "I am Mr. Satin."

Peter Baron smiled.

"If you do not understand my affiliation, sir," continued Mr. Satin, "I am with I.C.E."

Baron looked around, appraising the cabin's furnishings meaningfully. "With I.C.E.? Or simply I.C.E.?"

Mr. Satin chuckled. "Touché, Mr. Baron. Indeed, you are in the picture. I *am* I.C.E. For a new organization, we have come remarkably far in the short time at our disposal, have we not?"

"It isn't always the distance which counts, ultimately, Mr. Satin, but the direction," Peter observed quietly.

Mr. Satin rubbed his hands together appreciatively. "At last I am lucky enough to face a man with a sense of humor. It is the pity of my life that not only my colleagues, but also my adversaries, usually turn out to be cretins, completely devoid of intelligence, perception, or imagination. You are a breath of spring, sir."

"I find it a surprise that a man of your obvious intellectual capacities and social standing should stoop so low as to operate an organization like I.C.E."

Mr. Satin's eyebrows shot up. "But sir, what possible censure could attach to such an organization as the International Combine of Entrepreneurs?"

"International Combine for Evil, is the way we say it," Peter Baron responded.

"Poof. Assuredly you are loading your interpretation of I.C.E. with your own subjective prejudices. To be clearly objective about it, sir, I.C.E. is simply a group of intelligent and enterprising men who seek to make their fortune in a way somewhat removed from the routine."

"Decidedly removed."

"Pray tell me what is wrong with honest, individual enterprise? Was not the United States of America, the most powerful country in the world today, dedicated to that proposition by its founding fathers?"

"Perhaps it is in the interpretation that we differ so irrevocably."

Mr. Satin's eyes narrowed as he surveyed Peter Baron carefully. "You have in no way indicated to me yet, Mr. Baron, why you are involving yourself needlessly in what we have come to know as Operation Deep-Sleep."

Baron suppressed a smile. "The motivation for my involvement has something to do with freedom of choice and the privilege of individual enterprise."

"Touché, again, Mr. Baron!" cried Mr. Satin delightedly.

"Perhaps it is beyond my purlieu, but I would like to ask what the immediate future holds for me," Peter said.

Mr. Satin pursed his lips and folded his hands on the top of his desk. He shifted himself in his chair. Baron could see that he wore a smoking jacket with a soft scarf around his throat.

"Oh dear," he said after a moment. "That rather puts the question out into the open, doesn't it?"

"That was my intention."

"I suppose you might say you will be a privileged guest on my private yacht, the *Basilisk*," Mr. Satin replied.

"Ah."

"At least, until the successful conclusion of Operation Deep-Sleep."

Brilliant, cold eyes pierced Peter's. There was no weakness in Mr.

Satin, for all the softness and delicacy of his surface movements. Inside, he was all power and brooding evil.

"Conclusion?"

"I mean, of course, when the formula is in our hands and Mario Rimini is back with his sister."

"You intend to go through with the exchange?"

"But naturally!" Mr. Satin said softly. "I am a man of my word."

Peter Baron snorted.

Mr. Satin leaned back, smiling. "Of course, I never *did* give my word yet, you know."

"I know."

"I shall now proceed to give my word, Mr. Baron." The enormous man rose quickly from his chair, graceful and lithe as a huge jungle cat. He turned, his back to Baron, and paced quickly across the cabin to the portholes which looked out over Naples Bay.

Now Baron could see that the fat man's jacket was made of brilliantly patterned satin. Ochre slacks broke neatly over satin-lined slippers of rich imperial purple. The man's hands, which he clasped behind him, had the same pale translucence as his fleshy face.

At the porthole Mr. Satin turned. Peter Baron joined the big man, gazing out onto the deck of the yacht. He could see the sinister silhouettes of objects mounted to the deck: machine guns under tarpaulins.

"I promise you that if you venture outside this ship, Mr. Baron, before you are invited to do so specifically by me, you will be riddled with bullets. You may take my word for it that those are machine guns, sir. .50 caliber. American Brownings."

Baron nodded grimly. "I do not doubt you."

"You exhibit remarkable perspicacity, I would also like you to see another phenomenon which does not pertain to every craft in these waters." Mr. Satin turned and touched a button at the edge of his desk. "Observe."

Instantly the waters around the yacht were flooded with brilliant light.

"Is it not lovely? We like to keep the area well-lighted." Mr. Satin's smile vanished. "It discourages our guests from night bathing."

"Bathing with a view to long-range traveling, I take it," Baron drawled.

Mr. Satin instantly changed back into his smiling, gracious self. "Indeed, you are a perceptive guest." He gestured to Peter Baron to take his seat again. As Baron settled back, the big man got to his desk and leaned forward.

"You must excuse my dressing habit. My skin cannot stand the touch of the coarser linens, cottons, and so on. I must have satin. Only satin. Nor do I leave this cabin during the daytime. I cannot stand the sun. Or, rather, my skin cannot. A rare allergy, which could kill me. I prefer to do my dealings at night. A creature of the dark, you might say." Mr. Satin shrugged. "To each his own special albatross. His own private eccentricity."

"Like murder," Baron said flatly.

Mr. Satin's brows rose in astonishment. "Murder? Decidedly not. I abhor violence." Mr. Satin shuddered. "To what are you referring, Mr. Baron?"

"To the fate of my friend Francesco di Farinese."

"Ah, ha," Mr. Satin said. "*Il Duca*." He smiled broadly. "It has often been said, royalty does not work to good advantage in a public kitchen."

"In war strange occupations are the rule rather than the exception."

"War? We are at peace. The world is bursting with peace," Mr. Satin said sardonically. "Have you not heard?"

"Why did you kill Farinese?" Baron asked with a throb of anger.

Mr. Satin lifted his hand. "My reports do not show that he is dead. He is simply neutralized."

"Then he is on board the *Basilisk?* Incidentally, I must commend you on the appropriate name you have chosen for your yacht."

"Thank you," Mr. Satin beamed. "No, *Il Duca* Francesco di Farinese is not aboard. He is, as far as I can conjecture, still in Naples."

Baron rose. "Then, if you are finished, Mr. Satin, I assume our discussion is completed?"

"Certainly. The lesson for the day has been assigned. No swimming at all. Perhaps you would do well to sit in your cabin and brood over the implications of the text, Mr. Baron."

The door opened and the guard who had brought Baron appeared. Mr. Satin gestured, and the guard took Peter by the arm and led him out.

The cabin was impregnable, Baron found. He sank onto the deck finally, trying to rest as much as he could. After a while there was no movement on the yacht. The entire contingent of I.C.E. seemed to be asleep.

Once he thought he heard a slight sound toward the stern of the craft, but he could not be sure. He sank back, trying to let sleep come. Then he heard a muffled stirring at the door to his cabin. He moved quickly over and tapped once. Instantly he was rewarded with the sound of three quick raps.

Duke Farinese.

"In a moment, Peter," Duke said. "Stand back."

Baron moved to the porthole, and hugged the bulkhead. After 20 seconds he heard a harsh whisper. "Now."

At the count of three there was a flash of light, and a hissing sound. Smoke puffed out of the door handle. An acrid stench permeated the air. The door moved quickly inward, the lock burned out by the intense heat of burning paste. Duke Farinese appeared, clad in a black wet suit. He carried another empty wet suit with him, and a scuba breathing apparatus.

"Here you are!" Duke said.

"Where are your tanks?" Baron demanded.

"Hanging at the water line of the yacht," Duke explained quickly. "I climbed in through the garbage shaft into the galley."

"I thought they had disposed of you at Da Giacomino's."

"Cousin Dom saved my life. I.C.E. thought he had disposed of me. When I came to in Dom's house, I sent him out to the Chimici Consolidati to see what he could observe there. Then I came immediately after you. I am happy to report that your homing device is working A-OK."

Peter Baron grinned. "I always thought we were idiots to wear those things," he said. "I take it back now."

Baron referred to his homing device, a miniature radio transmitter which continually sent out UHF waves on a specific wavelength; the signal could be picked up by a radio direction finder in Duke Farinese's wristwatch tuned to the same wavelength. The RDF, a needle in the wristwatch, would then lead Duke directly to Baron. The homing device was hidden in a false mole in Baron's back.

Duke Farinese had a similar homing device; Baron carried its RDF in his own wristwatch. Each man could locate the other, by electronics, in dangerous situations when they were separated.

"Let's go!" Duke urged nervously.

"First I'd like to look the ship over for Mario Rimini," Baron said calmly.

Duke looked at Baron. "I've searched the whole bloody vessel already, Peter. He's not here. I thought we had decided he was definitely in Yugoslavia or Rumania."

"Just checking up on you," Baron grinned. "I agree that it's time to get out of here. The yacht has a lighting system which illuminates everything on the sea surface for miles. We've got to keep far under.''

''Right.''

''We'll both hook onto the tanks and swim buddy system,'' Baron explained.

They crept along the corridor and into the galley. Silently they went down the chute, hooked themselves into the scuba tanks, and fell back into the dark water.

In 40 minutes they were sitting in Baron's villa, in dry clothes, trying to reach Duke Farinese's cousin Dom by R/T.

''Duke?'' a voice answered finally, almost breathless with excitement.

''Dom?''

''Yes. I'm at Chimici Consolidati. There are four dead men here. Two guards. Two gunmen.''

Duke glanced at Baron, who winced. ''The Princess has gone. I think she's got whatever they were after. There's a manila folder here, labeled Deep-Sleep. I'll bring it in. But it's been tossed aside.''

''Did you just get there?'' Peter Baron asked.

''Yes.''

''Does anyone know about the trouble, yet?''

''The authorities don't.''

''Go to a telephone booth and notify the *carabinieri*. Then make yourself scarce.''

''Yes,'' Dom said.

''Have you any idea where the Princess went?''

''No idea.''

Baron shrugged and looked out the window at the darkened seascape.

Duke put up the R/T silently.

''The Princess is still free, we assume,'' Baron mused. ''In which case, she has probably panicked and run back to her apartment.'' He bit his lip. ''That's exactly where she should *not* be. When Mr. Satin hears the news, he'll be on his way there to pick her up.''

Duke's eyes narrowed. ''You think she took the formula?''

''Yes. the fact that a manila folder has been thrown aside means the formula must be in a more compact state. Say, in a film pack. And that would mean . . .''

Duke snapped his fingers. ''I tailed her when she was shopping, Peter. She bought a dress, a coat, and then she went into Renfro's on Via Roma and stayed a long time while she was being fitted for shoes.''

"Of course," Peter Baron said. "She's used the oldest trick in the history of espionage. It isn't intelligent enough to fool a ten-year-old child. She's put that film into a hollowed-out heel of her shoe! Come on, we've got to get to her before I.C.E. does!"

The Princess's apartment was dark when Peter Baron forced his way in through the outer window of her bedroom. He quickly found her clothes closet, and in no time at all had the new pair of shoes. Slipping the heel to one side, he turned on his fountain pen flashlight and saw the hollowed-out hole and the canister of film inside.

He hurried to the window. "Duke!"

Duke lifted his head. He was balanced on a ledge which ran around the building.

"Take this quickly. You know what to do. I'll get the girl out of here."

Duke nodded and jumped down onto a balcony of the floor below. Peter Baron turned back into the room. He hurried toward the door. At that moment someone opened it. Instantly the room flooded with light. The Princess stepped inside and looked about her in dismay. She saw the closet and the clothes thrown about.

Baron moved out of concealment behind the door and clapped his hand over her mouth.

"Princess!" Baron whispered. "Don't make a sound. We've got to get out of here. Do you understand?"

Her eyes widened and she tried to scream. Baron held her tightly. She bit his hand. Her gun dropped. He shook her roughly.

"No noise. You hear?"

She sagged in his arms, and he knew she would not cry out. He uncovered her mouth.

"I'm a friend. I want to save your brother's life. Do you believe me?"

She watched him hopelessly. "I have to," she admitted after a moment.

"Let's go. You'll get your shoes back. You've got to believe me. Princess! Please, please!"

She tried to form words with her lips, but could not. Then she burst out: "He will call tomorrow, telling me where to meet him to save Mario!"

"He telephoned you tonight?" Baron asked.

"A few minutes ago."

"Then he's liable to be here any moment. It was just a trick to see if you were here or not."

Peter Baron seized her and dragged her quickly into the living room. He moved to the front door where he turned off all the lights. Then he opened the door a crack and looked out into the hallway. It was deserted.

"Come on!"

They moved quickly into the corridor toward the elevators. As they did so, the doors of one opened quietly. A man stepped out. He was a large, ponderous man, wearing a trench coat. Underneath the trench coat Baron spotted flamboyant ochre slacks. It was Mr. Satin.

Baron pushed the girl behind him and ran quickly toward the fat man. Mr. Satin turned, startled, and saw Baron. He reached into his pocket for whatever weapon he carried there. Behind him stood the man Baron had seen on the yacht.

Peter Baron leaped feet first at the fat man in the classical savate attack. Both feet took the big man in the stomach. Baron jumped back, still upright. Mr. Satin let out his breath in a gasp and folded in the middle. He slammed back into the second man and both went to the floor of the elevator. Mr. Satin's head banged on the rear wall. He lay there stunned. The second man tried to get to his feet and leave the elevator.

The doors closed quickly, locking them both in, and the cage began to rise.

Mr. Satin bellowed in anger. It was too late. Peter Baron grabbed the Princess and the two of them ran toward the large window at the end of the corridor. Outside, they could see a fire escape. Baron opened the window quickly and thrust the Princess ahead of him onto the iron platform.

The two of them rushed down the iron stairs for two levels. Then Baron forced the window and they climbed inside. From there they went down to the basement along the inside stairs, until they found themselves in the building maintenance man's storeroom. At the rear wall stood an old-fashioned coal chute, now out of use. Baron and the Princess climbed through that and emerged in a garden behind the apartment. Bordering the garden, Baron saw a stone wall.

"Over we go!" he snapped, and handed the Princess up. She jumped down on the other side. Baron followed.

Instantly, a fusillade of bullets rained down on them from one of the balcony platforms at the back of the Appartamenti D'Annunzio.

Mr. Satin's curse floated down loudly in the silent night.

"Get them, you idiots! Find them! A thousand *lire* for whoever finds them! Ten thousand!"

Baron turned to the Princess. "You'd think he would have the decency to put a respectable price on our heads!" He made a wry face. "Bourgeois!"

6

RENDEZVOUS IN YUGOSLAVIA

Shortly before dawn, a small, ugly fishing craft moved out from Naples Harbor carrying three men in Neapolitan garb. The skipper was Cesar Maggio. Cesar was a cousin of Duke Farinese, who was the second member of the crew. He wore a turtleneck sweater, dungarees, and a wool cap. The third crewman was Peter Baron, dressed similarly, a heavy pair of Zeiss 10×50 binoculars slung around his neck.

The fisher moved through the placid, silent harbor, past the off-loading freighters at the docks. Her direction was westward, toward the Island of Ischia. Peter Baron leaned against the gunwale, peering through the powerful glasses.

"There she is," he said finally.

Duke joined him. "The *Basilisk*? Mr. Satin?"

"Take a look." Peter handed the glasses to Duke.

Duke focused them, grunted, and gave them back. "Get the wireless warmed up," Baron told him.

The smells of the bay hung heavily over the sluggish waters. To their right, the city of Naples slumbered peacefully. A few flickering lights were the only indication of any kind of life in the sprawling metropolis. A stench of dissolution, decadence, and decay seemed to emanate from the ancient city's bowels.

Baron's race through the streets of Naples with the Princess had been a near thing. At the docks, he had handed her quickly aboard *La Bonne Chance*. They had sped out to Capri and moored at Peter's villa. There he had put here safely to bed.

Duke had arrived soon afterward, accompanied by three armed guards who were even now hidden in strategic spots around the Villa di Pietro to stand off any invaders from I.C.E.

Taking the portable wireless set, Baron had commandeered Cesar Maggio's fishing boat to close in on Mr. Satin's yacht *Basilisk*. At close range—but not too close—he would establish communications with the fat man and set up the ransom of Mario Rimini.

"The wireless is ready, Peter," Duke announced finally, looking up from the portable receiver-transmitter. "Shall I try to raise *Basilisk*?"

"Yes. Give them the message I wrote." Baron squinted ahead at Mr. Satin's yacht through the grayness which hung over the harbor. "Cesar, you can stop the boat now."

Cesar nodded. The fisher came to a wallowing halt and rose and sank rhythmically.

"Calling *Basilisk*, calling *Basilisk*," Duke said in monotonous Italian. "Harbor Patrol calling *Basilisk*." Duke lifted a hand and crossed his two fingers. "Come in, *Basilisk*."

It was a good two minutes before Duke managed to raise the radio operator aboard Mr. Satin's yacht.

"*Basilisk* here," a voice said finally on the portable set. "Go ahead, please."

"Message for Mr. Satin. Urgent message for Mr. Satin, owner of *Basilisk*."

"What is the message?"

"Message reads: 'We've got the film. You must guarantee delivery of your property. Set time and place immediately. Signed: Peter Baron.'"

Baron smiled. Duke punched him affectionately in the shoulder. "In one minute, I'll wager we'll hear from Mr. Satin."

The boat rocked up and down steadily. Baron watched the *Basilisk* through the Zeiss lenses. It was almost three minutes, really, but the answer was not a message. Mr. Satin in person came on the air.

"Mr. Baron, is that you?" he asked tendentiously.

Baron took the microphone from Duke. "This is Peter Baron."

"You'll pay for that kick in the ribs!" Mrs. Satin said evenly.

Baron laughed. "I've a proposition for you. I've got the film."

There was a short pause. "I'll deal," Mr. Satin said grudgingly. "The twin for the film."

"Where and when?"

"Midnight, tonight. The girl must deliver the film in person. My own man delivers the twin. We meet on neutral ground."

"I'll be watching the exchange with a loaded rifle," Peter Baron promised.

"So shall I," Mr. Satin responded.

"Where?"

"Italy depresses me."

"Russia depresses me no less," Baron retorted. "Somewhere else."

"A neutral country," Mr. Satin suggested.

"Name it."

"Hallwag map of Yugoslavia. Coordinates—30 centimeters on the X axis, 23.5 centimeters on the Y axis from lower right zero. The mountain can be reached by air. Do you read me?"

"Loud and clear," Peter Baron said, repeating the coordinates on the Hallwag map. "I'll be there."

"Midnight," said Mr. Satin. "A bonfire at the end of the landing strip will lead you in. That is the rendezvous site."

Princess Paula Rimini lay on her side, sleeping contentedly in a black silken nightgown Baron had rescued from the emergency wardrobe. Peter Baron decided not to awaken her to give her the good news. Then, as he stepped back to close the door, he saw her stir. Her eyes opened wide, filled with horror, and she began to tremble. Then she saw where she was, and she recognized him. She fell back on the pillow in relief.

Peter Baron sat down on the bedside. The morning sun had just risen outside. A shaft of golden light passed through the grilled window and fell on the terra cotta flooring. Grapevines entwined the wrought-iron bars. A breeze stirred the leaves—a breeze tangy with the scent of the open sea.

"I'm so tired," Paula said ruefully, sitting up and patting her dark lovely hair.

"You had a full evening," Baron said soberly. "But we have good news this morning."

"Oh?"

"Your brother will be returned to you at midnight tonight. In exchange for him we will give over the film."

Her eyes clouded. "But I do not have the film."

Baron reached into his pocket and held it out to her. "Take it. You won't feel right unless you have it on your person."

"Thank you." Her dark eyes suddenly filled with tears. "You have been so good to me."

Baron's hand covered her slim one. "You've been through too much. Go back to sleep."

She watched him, her face disturbed.

"What's the matter?" he asked.

"I'm mixed up," she whispered. "Always I thought that every man was the same—a husband, a father, a brother."

"Now?" He smiled gently.

"You do not fit into the categories I have mentioned. You are . . ." She shook her head in frustration.

Baron's brow arched mockingly. "A lover?"

"You should not say that," she scolded. "Dr. Forester is a fine man. Like a husband. But like a father. Not like you."

Baron leaned toward her, kissing her gently on the lips. "Go to sleep. You tempt me too much."

She drew back, her eyes warm and full. "Perhaps you are not the only one tempted."

"Rest, Princess," said Baron, resolutely pulling away from her presence.

"I do not need rest," she laughed. Her hands reached out, warm and soft, and touched his shoulders. She drew him down toward her, and fastened herself to him as her lips joined his.

He embraced her tightly and kissed her hungrily. She responded, and that was the end of the foolish talk.

Birds chirped overhead. Fleecy clouds dotted the blue sky. Red, blue, white, and green sails glimmered on the horizon below. Seagulls shrieked as they dove against the cliffs. In the solitude of the courtyard of Villa di Pietro, Peter and Duke studied the Hallwag map spread out on the cast-iron table between them.

"They're clever," Baron murmured. "Yugoslavia is only a hop, skip, and jump from here. The helicopter which picked up Mario the other night could make the trip in no time."

"That puts us on foreign soil for the exchange," Duke grumbled.

"Exactly. That's Mr. Satin's strategy."

"You said he's not tied up with the Reds. I don't understand."

"In a country like Tito's—Reddish, but not totally crimson—it's at least possible to pull off an international exchange like this without the authorities kicking up a tremendous furor."

"You're sure Rimini is there now?"

"You said you'd searched the yacht for him before you found me on *Basilisk*."

"He's not on *Basilisk*," Duke said positively.

"Then he's in Yugoslavia. Right near Mount Krstaca, where Montenegro and Serbia meet."

"It may be a trap."

"Of course. And I've prepared a series of defense maneuvers," Baron said.

"What do you need from me?"

"I need the black box, the modified DX paste, and a bundle of sticks."

"Right, Peter."

"Is the Cessna checked out satisfactorily?"

"Done."

Peter Baron was referring to his private, specially equipped Cessna passenger plane which was right now serviced and ready to fly out of the Naples Airport.

"Good. We know the black box works—at least, it did on the test run. So we should be all ready for the flight."

Duke hunched over the map, lines of concentration furrowing his forehead. "Let's go over the action again, step by step. I don't want to miss anything."

Peter Baron nodded and began a detailed breakdown of his scheme of attack and counterattack.

Shortly before dusk Peter Baron, Duke Farinese, and Princess Paula Rimini checked into the Alamino Hotel overlooking Naples Harbor. As soon as they were inside their suite, Baron pulled the Zeiss glasses out of a small black bag and walked over to the window overlooking Naples Harbor.

"Five minutes to go," murmured Baron.

"Am I supposed to know what you are talking about?" the Princess asked in exasperation.

"No."

She smiled and sat down in a chair.

Peter Baron adjusted the ten-magnification power glasses, which he focused on the road that ran by the hotel. It was known as Highway N 19. It traveled from Reggio, in Calabria, at the southern tip of Italy, all the way to Rome. Through traffic north and south on the west coast of Italy passed along N 19.

"There's the car," he said.

Duke looked down into the street below.

Peter Baron's off-white Lancia moved along at the head of a group of cars.

Baron chuckled. "Your brother-in-law doesn't look much like me, Duke, but I think he passes muster."

"Best I could dig up on such short notice."

"The girl's a little on the plump side for the Princess," Baron mused, looking across the room at Princess Paula Rimini. She blushed prettily.

"How about me?" Duke asked. "You haven't even noticed *me* down there."

"You're not important enough," Baron laughed.

"Still, it is a good resemblance. Those three do look like us—definitely."

"It's the Lancia that proves the deception. That's the only real thing there."

"Is the masquerade successful?" Duke wondered anxiously.

Baron continued gazing at the highway. He saw the blue Fiat about a block in back of the Lancia. Two men were in it.

"I see it," Baron told Duke. "A blue Fiat? Isn't that what Dom said?"

"With two men in it," Duke added.

"It's following the Lancia," Peter said with satisfaction, lowering the glasses and putting them back in the black bag. "Princess, it's time we were on our way again."

Princess Paula Rimini frowned prettily. "I do not understand what has happened."

"The Lancia is a decoy, Princess," Baron explained cheerfully. "One of the Duke's men said someone followed us from Capri. So, we give them a fake Peter Baron to follow up N 19 and a fake Princess to ambush on the road for the formula."

"And then?"

"We get into my Cessna and we fly to Yugoslavia to keep our rendezvous with I.C.E."

"But don't the kidnappers know about your Cessna?"

"They do," Baron said softly. "But, for a handful of silver, a report went to interested I.C.E. agents that Peter Baron's personal plane is out of commission. If he flies today, he flies from Rome. Hence the trip of the off-white Lancia northward."

"A simple decoy," Duke explained.

The Princess sighed unhappily. "It's all Greek to me."

Baron beamed. "We simply go to the Naples airport, file a fake flight plan to Bari, and fly to the rendezvous in Yugoslavia."

At the controls of the Cessna, Peter Baron gazed out through the Plexiglas windshield at the dark blue of the Adriatic beneath him. Ahead, the mass of the Yugoslavian coast loomed up darkly. He glanced at Duke, seated behind him with the Princess. No one had said a word for many minutes, each absorbed in his own thoughts.

"Montenegro," Baron said, gesturing downward with his hand.

The Princess craned her neck and gazed into the distance. "Mario," she whispered.

Duke said reassuringly: "You'll see him soon."

"Any alien craft about?" Baron asked Duke uneasily.

"Not a thing."

"No helicopter visible?"

"Nothing."

"I don't trust these people. I'd hate to be gunned down so close to our objective."

Duke leaned over and lifted a modified C.E.T.M.O. machine pistol from the deck of the ship. He patted it lovingly. "We're waiting."

Peter Baron flew on, checking his compass again, marking off his location on the chart spread out beside him.

"Twenty minutes to go."

Duke looked out into the darkened sky, scanning the heavens for foreign objects.

Below him Baron could see the flatlands sloping gradually upward into the steeper hills of central Montenegro. In the distance there were higher mountains, jagged against the starlit sky. Serbia.

"On the nose," he said calmly, eighteen minutes later, pointing through the windshield. Duke came up beside him.

"Mt. Krstaca."

A tiny pinpoint of orange light shone from one of the humps of mountain below them. It was a bonfire, exactly as Mr. Satin had said.

Lowering the flaps, he sent the Cessna curving downward. He kept looking for the flat area of the landing strip. When he had completed half a 180-degree turn, he suddenly spotted the strip in a clearing. To hit the field at the speed he was traveling was about as easy as diving off a hundred-foot board into a teacup.

"Here we go. I want you fully armed when we land," Baron instructed Duke. "But don't shoot unless you get a signal from me. Understand?"

"Right."

"Have you got the black box?"

"Yes. In the suitcase."

"Hang onto it."

Duke nodded grimly.

The mountains loomed up all around them. The Cessna kept losing altitude. Baron straightened up and aimed for the end of the tiny strip. The trees skimmed by below, and more trees rose ahead, blotting out the sky. On both sides, ahead, and underneath, there were pines. At the far end of the strip, the bonfire burned cheerfully, sending smoke gouting into the sky.

The Cessna balked, dropped, steadied, and then touched the ground with a squeal of tires. Baron ran the ship quickly across the bumpy ground and came to a stop. He opened the cabin door, drew his handgun from his holster, and stepped down. He looked all around. There was no one in sight.

Duke followed, carrying the black suitcase and the machine pistol. When the Princess appeared at the door of the cabin, Baron lifted her down gently.

Suddenly at the side of the airstrip a brilliant spotlight blazed on. A voice bellowed out.

"You are extremely punctual, Mr. Baron. Please to step out so we can see you."

"OK," Baron whispered to Duke. "That's Mr. Satin on the bull-horn." He turned to the Princess. "Scared?"

"Frightened to death," she breathed.

He took her hand. "Let's go. It's the only way."

She straightened and moved with him into the blinding glare of light.

After all the complications in getting there, the exchange was ridiculously simple. In the pines on one side of the strip stood Mr. Satin and his party behind the enormous portable spotlight. Peter Baron and his party waited, armed and alert beside the Cessna.

Two men appeared from behind the spotlight and stood at the edge of the pines.

"It's Mario!" cried the Princess, tearfully happy.

"You're sure?" Baron asked quickly.

Paula froze him with a look. "He's my twin brother!"

The two men walked forward. The man behind Mario did not have a gun. He wore horn-rimmed glasses, like a Balkan intellectual.

"Let the Princess cross to meet my man, please," Mr. Satin ordered.

"Princess." Baron urged her forward. "Do you have the film?"

She lifted her shoe and removed the film from the heel. "Here."

"Go on."

When Mario and the guard had reached a point halfway to the Cessna, the Princess was already walking toward them.

"The man with Mario Rimini is a chemist, Mr. Baron," intoned Mr. Satin. "He must examine the film. I do not trust you."

Baron laughed. "I'm hurt."

Paula Rimini handed the film to the man who stood by Mario. Mario took Paula swiftly in his arms; they embraced. Paula was sobbing; her quiet crying was the only sound in the remote wooded area of southern Yugoslavia.

The chemist turned and signaled toward the spotlight with a wave of the hand.

"All right!" Mr. Satin's voice was jovial. "You may have your man, Mr. Baron!"

The chemist walked rapidly toward the spotlight. Arm in arm, Paula and Mario ran across toward the Cessna. By the wing of the ship, Peter Baron crouched, his gun aimed, waiting for some surprise move by Mr. Satin.

The chemist vanished into the darkness behind the spotlight. Almost as if that were a long-awaited signal, a volley of gunshots roared out from the pines.

Baron pulled the trigger on his handgun and blasted the spotlight out. He had anticipated such a move. There was good reason to suspect Mr. Satin would try to destroy all participants in the ransom plot: if there were anyone alive to tell of the exchange, I.C.E. would be in danger of exposure. It was Mr. Satin's aim to wipe out both the Riminis, Baron, and Duke.

The Princess and the Prince stumbled into the shelter of the Cessna.

"Duke!" cried Baron. "Now!"

"Right!" Duke's voice came from somewhere behind the Cessna.

Baron watched the woods where the chemist had disappeared and from where Mr. Satin's voice had come. Streaks of gunfire kept erupting out of the darkness. Then, surprisingly, a brilliant flash of blue light punctuated the darkness and immediately went out.

"Good work!" shouted Baron, blinking against the dazzling afterimage.

"What was that?" Paula asked.

Duke ran toward the Cessna, carrying his black suitcase.

"A little gadget of Duke's," Baron explained proudly. "A remote control device for detonating explosive paste. The canister holding the film was smeared with modified DX paste. The explosion destroyed the formula."

"Are there copies?" Mario Rimini asked.

"Yes," Baron said. "I have the original. You see?" He opened his hand. "What Mr. Satin got was an exact copy, set up for sacrifice. Come on, we've got to get into the ship."

A scream of anguish came from the woods. Mr. Satin was cursing volubly over the destruction of the formula for Deep-Sleep. The bullhorn came to life. "Into the valley of Death rode the six hundred!" Mr. Satin's voice bellowed.

Peter Baron frowned. It sounded almost as if . . .

Mario Rimini turned, grabbed the film out of Peter Baron's hand, ran quickly toward the Cessna, and leaped up into the cabin.

"Duke! Quick! Stop him!" Peter Baron cried, understanding instantly what had happened.

Before Duke could react, however, the cabin door slammed shut, locked from inside by Mario Rimini.

"Mario!" screamed Paula. "What are you doing?"

The Cessna starter ground and the engine burst into life. Quickly the engine revved up.

"Into the trees!" Baron cried. "When he moves the ship out, we'll be in the open!"

The three of them hurried across the uneven ground to shelter. Rifle fire burst from the spot where Mr. Satin and his men stood. The Cessna started down the strip, wobbling from side to side. At the far end, by the still burning bonfire, it stopped and turned around. The Princess was sobbing disconsolately. Baron held her in his arms.

"What's happened?"

"Post-hypnotic suggestion. He's been brainwashed. That phrase from the 'Charge of the Light Brigade' was the trigger mechanism that put him under their control again. He knows how to fly. I should have anticipated their maneuver. He's on his way to some prearranged spot where Mr. Satin will pick up the film."

"Oh, my God!" sobbed Princess Paula Rimini. "My own brother!"

The ship slammed across the strip and took off. From the darkness across the strip Mr. Satin's voice drifted out gratingly. "Checkmate, Mr. Baron, is it not?"

Baron did not answer. He led the Princess and Duke quietly into the trees.

7

THE ROAD BACK

Within five minutes Peter Baron had taken the others down the pine-clad slope and into a small field below the landing strip. Above them, a continuing volley of rifle fire echoed through the woods. Apparently Mr. Satin was content simply to fire after the three of them without effecting pursuit.

They sank into the grass, exhausted.

The Princess was in tears. "Mario! He's not himself! Mr. Baron, what will happen to him?"

''Posthypnotic suggestion will soon wear off, Princess. He'll be perfectly all right.''

''But I'll never see him again,'' she sobbed. ''My own twin brother—a traitor!''

Peter Baron slipped his arm around her comfortingly. ''Not a traitor. A dupe. Besides, there is always hope.''

''Not anymore,'' she sighed. ''He's the only thing I have left in the world. If he goes . . .''

''He isn't gone for good,'' Peter Baron said calmly.

Her eyes suddenly blazed with anger. ''You can be calm about this. To you it's just a job that went wrong. That's all. You don't care a bit. But there's a human being involved. My brother. How can you be so ice-cold and aloof?''

''I tell you, it isn't all over, Princess.'' Peter Baron squeezed the girl by the shoulder.

Duke Farinese glanced up from the black box, where he was turning knobs and switching toggles.

''Why did you make a copy of the formula, Peter? Mario would have had no reason to steal the ship if the only film had been blown up.''

''It's best that I.C.E. think there's only one copy of Deep-Sleep, still.'' Peter smiled. ''Particularly when the one they think is real isn't.''

Duke's eyes lighted up. ''You mean Mario Rimini has flown off with a worthless film?''

''Hardly worthless, Duke,'' Baron said blandly. ''There are six lovely color pictures of a nude dancing girl in unforgettable poses.''

''You're simply amazing, Peter!''

''We do have to bring the Cessna back though—for our own survival.'' Peter Baron leaned over the black box. ''Duke, I want you to show the Princess what you're working on.''

''I haven't the time, Peter,'' Duke frowned. ''It's already five minutes plus forty seconds. In another four minutes, we will have lost contact completely.''

''As you prefer,'' Baron said quietly. ''I'll tell her. You see the black box, Princess?''

''Yes, of course,' she responded. ''I've watched him carry it with him in that suitcase since he left the plane. What is it?''

''It's quite a complex little gadget. But to make it perfectly understandable to you, let me say it's a remote-control automatic-pilot for the Cessna.''

''I do not understand.''

"All I have to do to bring my airplane back here and land it is to guide it myself—with the black box."

"But my brother is flying the ship!"

"When the remote pilot takes over, the manual controls are no longer operative. No matter what Mario tries to do, I can bring him down. We brought the remote kit along because we had suspected Mr. Satin would try to hijack the plane somehow. I never thought he would use your brother! Have you got the Cessna meshed in yet, Duke?"

"Yes." Duke handed the box to Baron.

Sitting in front of it, he reached out and began moving the knobs and watching the needles of the dials.

Duke raised his head. "I think I hear the sound of an airplane engine."

"So do I," Baron said. "I have to land her before Mr. Satin realizes that I control the plane."

"I think he's already taken up the trail," Duke muttered nervously, cupping one ear in his hand.

"You'd better go out and set up that fire wall at the edge of the woods," Baron ordered. "That will prevent I.C.E. from outflanking us."

"Right." Duke moved off.

Baron leaned over the black box, concentrating intently.

"Are you sure the plane is safe?" Paula asked shakily. "Nothing must happen to my brother."

"I've tested the Cessna before, Princess," Baron said. "Trust me."

The throb of the Cessna's engine grew louder. When Baron looked up, he could see the red and green navigating lights blinking in the distant sky. He had once brought the Cessna down safely, but only under test conditions. No one had been searching the woods for him. And the plane had not had a live passenger in it as it had now. His hands shook on the dials.

Gunfire crashed in the woods. Then Mr. Satin's voice rose above the sound of the airplane.

"Stop!" he cried to his men through the bullhorn. "Don't leave the woods! Shoot from cover!"

Bullets began whipping through the grass around Baron.

"Lie down flat!" he cried to the Princess. Paula hugged the ground. Duke Farinese crawled back toward them out of the darkness. He raised the C.E.T.M.O. machine pistol to his shoulder, aimed at the woods which he had just departed, and blazed away.

"Done?" Baron asked cryptically.

"Done," Duke reported.

"I'll bring her down."

"Any time."

"You wait until I tell you, Duke."

"But of course."

The Cessna lowered slowly. Baron watched the dials on the black box, glancing every so often into the sky to be sure the ship was lined up at its proper attitude.

The firing from the woods increased in intensity. The shadow of a man darted out into the open, high and thin above the jagged silhouette of the fir trees. Duke Farinese stitched bullets across the darkness. The man dropped in his tracks.

"Don't go into the open!" shouted Mr. Satin in a frenzy. 'We'll get them when they board the ship!"

Silently Baron congratulated Mr. Satin. It took an intelligent man to realize when he was outmaneuvered. The I.C.E. chief would simply wait until his three adversaries were in a position where they could not defend themselves, then he would strike.

The plane came in for a landing and rambled onto the field, swaying from side to side. Baron slowed it to a graceful stop. Idling, the plane hulked not 40 yards away.

"Now, Duke," Baron commanded quietly. "Detonate it."

Duke pushed the button plunger he held in his hand. Instantly there was a jarring explosion from the edge of the woods. Dirt and rocks flew into the air. Branches tumbled down. There was smoke everywhere.

"A simple dynamite charge," Baron told Paula Rimini, lifting her to her feet. Behind the screen of smoke from the dynamite the three of them raced across the grass to the Cessna.

Peter Baron pounded on the cabin door.

Magically, it opened.

They climbed in. A dazed Mario Rimini was standing there, completely astonished to find himself alone in the ship, not remembering a thing he had done since the trigger phrase had lapsed him into post-hypnotic suggestion.

Baron took the precious film canister from him and put it in his pocket. Duke Farinese slammed the door and Peter climbed under the controls of the Cessna. The Princess and her brother fell into each other's arms again, sitting side by side. Paula burst out crying, this time with happiness.

The Cessna rose and climbed into the sky.

It was early dawn when Peter Baron circled Naples Airport and requested permission to land. After a lengthy wait, he was cleared for landing and told to report immediately to the Tower as soon as he was on the ground.

"An investigation by the Italian Air Commission," Baron murmured prophetically.

He landed the Cessna in a fresh morning breeze, and the four of them alighted and walked across the macadam to the Control Tower.

Leaning on the wire mesh fence separating the observers from the passengers was Oren Chadwick. The American was smiling inscrutably behind his pipe.

"You've a good deal of red tape to unwind with the Air Commission," he told Baron cheerfully. "But I've managed to smooth the way a bit. Have you that little surprise you promised me?"

"Right here." Baron reached into his pocket and handed over the film canister.

Chadwick flipped it open and rolled out the film, which he held up to the sun. "I say!" he marveled. "Pity your opposite number didn't get this! Wouldn't it have rocked him back on his heels!" He tucked it into his tweed jacket quickly. "Not a word you understand, until the Pentagon and Dr. Forester confer over the original."

"I'll make a confidential report soonest," Baron said.

"Oh, quite. And then we'll be in touch immediately about adjustments."

Baron smiled at Chadwick's circumlocution regarding the all-important object called money.

"Oh, by the way, *Signorina*," Chadwick said, turning to Paula Rimini.

"*Principessa*, Chadwick," Baron corrected. "Princess, this is Mr. Oren Chadwick, a friend."

"I'm sure," said the Princess, nodding politely.

"I've a message for you from Dr. Forester."

Paula's face went pale. She put her hand to her chest. "Is he worse?"

"He's conscious now," Chadwick said. "He wants to be sure you come to see him right away."

Paula blinked, trying to hold back tears of relief. "I'm so glad!"

Peter Baron looked directly into Chadwick's eyes. Neither man spoke.

"Peter," the Princess said. "I can never thank you enough." She leaned over and pecked him briefly and impersonally on the cheek. She turned to her brother. "Mario, I must go to Blake right away. Come!"

Mario and she hurried off.

Chadwick sucked on his pipe. Peter Baron leaned on the other side of the wire mesh fence and looked after the Princess as she hurried into the wind across the macadam toward the main building.

''That good-bye wasn't much,'' Chadwick said succinctly. ''Apparently you didn't impress the Princess.''

Peter Baron shrugged philosophically. ''A little too rich for my blood, possibly.''

''My dear fellow, she's only a Princess—not a Queen!''

''Yes, of course. But I've been trying to taper off. At the present moment I am down to Countess level.'' Peter Baron vaulted the fence, heading for the main building.

''Where the devil are you going, Peter?'' Chadwick called after him.

''To a pink *palazzo* and a matinee engagement.'' Baron waved a hand airily at Chadwick. ''I'll be in touch. Duke, will you take care of the Air Commissioner?''

Chadwick frowned and stared at Duke Farinese, who had sauntered up carrying his precious black suitcase. ''The man's mad, isn't he?''

''Just the reverse, I'd say,'' Duke observed sagely. ''Just the reverse.''

EDWARD D. HOCH

The People of the Peacock

THE MAN WHO called himself Tony Wilder had traveled three days by camel to reach the valley oasis not far from where the Euphrates River crossed the arid border between Syria and Iraq. It had been an uninteresting journey for the most part, broken only by the nightly chore of putting up the little tent that sheltered him against the uncommon chill of the desert dark. The Syrian guide who accompanied him knew only a few words of basic English, just enough to make any attempt at conversation a frustrating and inconclusive experience. And the camel ride itself was anything but pleasant.

But at last, just after noon on the third day, the bronze-skinned guide called a halt and dismounted from his grunting beast. "There," he pointed, indicating a cluster of low white buildings nestled in the green of the oasis. "Peacock."

Wilder nodded, passing over a few gold coins in final payment. For just twice the price he could have hired a private plane to fly him out from Baghdad in a matter of hours, but his instructions had been exact. Venice did not want to attract attention to the place in the desert. He hated attention almost as much as disobedience.

Tony Wilder had met Venice only once before, in a dim Paris hotel room. But now he recognized the face at once, and even the handshake had a disturbingly familiar pressure to it. Venice was not the sort of person one ever forgot, even after three years.

"I trust you had a good journey," he remarked, releasing Tony Wilder's limp hand.

"Camels aren't my animal, I guess. How are things going here?"

Venice turned and walked over to the wide arabesque window overlooking the green of the oasis. "It is a peaceful place, and these days I ask little more. I think the war for me is over, Tony."

"What?" Wilder could not really believe the words.

"Oh, I've already told Moscow, never fear. I was never really one of them anyway, you know. No more than I was a Nazi twenty years ago. I worked for the side that paid me best, and the color of money is the only political philosophy you need in this game."

Tony Wilder nodded, because the words might have been his own. "What are you going to do? One doesn't just retire, not with agents from a dozen countries after your head."

Venice turned from the window, a thin smile on his lips. "This is the eternal problem, my friend. The British—and the American CIA—will hardly call a halt to the chase simply because I choose to spend the rest of my life lounging beside a swimming pool. It is the fate of the spy to end his life violently and alone." He paused a moment. "But I intend to change the pattern. I intend to live out my days in the peaceful security of the United States of America."

"Under their very noses? But how?"

"I have been working on it for some time," Venice said, hurrying on now with a gleam of excitement in his eyes. "I have a cover identity all planned, an identity so foolproof that no one will ever penetrate it."

Tony Wilder had caught the feeling of excitement. "Could you tell me?"

But Venice only smiled that same thin smile. "I have told you too much already. You can join me in a glass of champagne, though. A sort of toast, if you will, to the past and to the future."

They drank their champagne, and then they shook hands for one last time.

Exactly fourteen months after the meeting in the desert, a tall slim man with a boyishly handsome face sat across the desk from Captain Leopold in a dingy office at the rear of police headquarters. The city was a small one, an hour's drive north from New York, and the man had come all the way up from Washington on the morning plane. He didn't look like a spy to Leopold. He didn't look like much of anything, in fact.

"The name is Jim Saunter," he said, "Here are my credentials."

Leopold looked them over with interest. "Central Intelligence Agency. I never met one of you fellows before."

The slim man smiled without humor. "We're working closely with the FBI in this matter," he said. "But they've been a bit handicapped until now because there's no evidence of a violation of federal law."

Leopold started to reach for a cigarette and then remembered he was trying to cut down. "You have the advantage of me Mr. Saunter. I have no idea what matter you have in mind."

"I think I can speak frankly, Captain. The FBI people have a very high opinion of you. They tell me you're one of the best local cops in the northeast.''

''There was a kidnap case a year or so back,'' Leopold said. ''I guess I helped them a little on it. Most of the things are pretty routine up here, though.''

''I don't think you'll find this routine. One of our agents was murdered in your city yesterday morning.''

''Yesterday?'' Leopold's mind was suddenly alive. ''Walter Moon? The poisoning case? He gave his address as New York.''

''He operated out of Washington. He was in my office three days ago. And it wasn't suicide, in case you're wondering.''

Leopold scratched his jaw. ''What was he doing up here?''

''Looking for a man named Venice.''

''Venice? He's not known up here.''

''He wouldn't be. Let me tell you about Venice, Captain Leopold. I'll try not to be too melodramatic.''

''Go ahead.'' Leopold was beginning to like the man.

''Well, Venice is the only name he's ever had in our records. He turned up in Europe during the early days of World War II, working for the Nazi cause.''

''Any description, age?''

''Nothing, except that he was still a fairly young man during the war. Probably under thirty.''

''Which would make him around fifty today.''

Saunter nodded. ''Give or take five years.''

''Nationality?''

''Perhaps Yugoslavian, but we're not even sure of that. In any event, he passed for an English citizen during the war, so we must assume he's equally able to pass for an American.''

''And you think he's here?''

The government man unzipped his bulging briefcase. ''Let me give you the whole story, if a bit quickly. Venice was working for the Germans, who apparently found him in an Italian black market operation. The story goes that he showed a flair for espionage from the very beginning, and before long he turned up in London, sending out information as to the damage done by the German V–1 rocket, and later the V–2. The British didn't let many spies escape, and they almost had our man Venice. But he killed a Scotland Yard man and escaped to France disguised as a woman.''

''How did he kill the man?'' Leopold asked, because that was his end of the business.'

''With a dagger he was carrying up his sleeve. He was a bit melodramatic in those days. Anyway, next time we heard from him was in '47, and he was working for the Russians in the Middle East. At about that time he became somehow involved with a secret society called the Order of the Peacock Angel."

"The what?"

Jim Saunter smiled a bit. "The mysterious East, you know. The society had an uncertain origin in the area that is now Syria and Iraq, some hundreds of years ago. It was imported into England by a mysterious Syrian back in 1913, and has enjoyed some success there. The peacock, of course, has always been a symbol of power to some people. The rites of the Peacock Angel consist mainly of white-robed worshippers dancing madly before an eight-foot ebony statue of a peacock."

"Sure you haven't been reading Fu Manchu?"

"I wish it were as simple as that. Our man Venice apparently has been using certain members of the order for his own devious purposes, both in London and the Middle East. One of his favorite hide-outs between assignments was a sort of mission out in the middle of the desert."

"Maybe that's where he is now," Leopold ventured.

"No," Saunter answered abruptly.

"You seem quite certain."

"He left the place more than a year ago. He retired from the espionage game and said he was planning to start a new life in the United States. My man was on his trail when he was murdered here yesterday."

Captain Leopold frowned down at the occasional notes he'd been taking. "Why were you on his trail if he'd retired?"

"You never retire from the game. He killed at least three people personally in his lifetime, and perhaps indirectly caused the deaths of a million more with his activities."

"So you must kill him in return."

The younger man stared at Leopold. "I hardly said that. I thought I could be frank with you, Captain. They said I could. But perhaps I've been too frank."

"Venice committed no crimes in this country."

"Not until yesterday."

"You're so sure he killed your man?"

"I'm sure. Walter Moon came here to investigate the formation of the first Peacock Angel group in this country."

"In this city?" Leopold had been taken by surprise.

"In this city. I believe Venice is one of the members."

"It's a long way from Iraq and London."

"The world is getting smaller every day."

"True." Leopold got up and began to pace back and forth in the tiny office. "What do you want me to do?" he asked finally.

"Just conduct your murder investigation in the usual manner. Question the Peacock Angel people—I'll give you the address. But keep in mind whom you're looking for."

"And when I find him? How will we know for sure, when there's no description?"

For a long time Saunter didn't reply. Then, apparently deciding to show all his cards, he said, "There's a witness under guard in Washington, perhaps the only man in the world who can identify Venice. His name is Tony Wilder."

For a time after the CIA man left, Captain Leopold busied himself with the morning's routine paperwork. There were other crimes to be investigated, some more violent than the poison death of a man in a hotel room. He issued a few brisk commands over the intercom, read the morning report through carefully, and finally paused to study the spring-like weather beyond his dirty office window. Winter was ending early, and that was something to be pleased about.

"Fletcher!" he barked into the intercom. Presently the tall sergeant appeared as he always did, and Leopold asked, "What do you know about this poisoning case? Walter Moon, found yesterday morning in his hotel room."

Fletcher scratched his head. "Not much. Looks a bit like suicide. The poison was prussic acid—hydrocyanic acid—and it must have killed him instantly, within about thirty seconds. Despite the detective stories, it's never been much of a murder weapon. But it's a good way to commit suicide."

"This one wasn't suicide. He was a counter-intelligence agent on an assignment."

Fletcher whistled. "We got the federal boys in on this?"

"It seems so. But they want to keep the thing quiet for now. Why do you say that prussic acid is more of a suicide's weapon?"

Fletcher slid down in the worn wooden chair that Saunter had occupied such a short time before. "Well, the odor, for one thing—bitter almonds, you know. And then it kills so fast. Nobody gave it to Moon. He took it himself."

"You'd catch the odor in liquid form, but what if it was a salt, in a capsule?"

"He did have a bottle of capsules with him. Allergy pills of some sort. But there was no prussic acid or cyanide crystals in any of them."

"It would only have had to be in one," Leopold observed. "He probably took these allergy capsules every morning, didn't he?''

Fletcher nodded. ''Twice a day, according to the instructions on the bottle. I didn't know spies had allergies.''

''He'd probably have resented you calling him a spy, at least while he was working in this country. They have so-called black agents and white agents. The white agents, like Saunter and Moon, admit they work for the CIA.''

''What was this Moon's assignment?'' Fletcher asked.

''He was trying to locate a Russian spy named Venice who retired from the game and slipped into this country to live out his days in luxury.''

''Isn't that an FBI job?''

Leopold gave in to temptation and took a cigarette. ''They were working on it too, but apparently until yesterday this man Venice had committed no crime in the United States. And they had no reason to suspect that he would. I have the distinct, if unpleasant, impression that the CIA planned to take unofficial action against the man.''

''Is he that important?''

''He was, when he was active. I gather they credit him with engineering much of Russia's success in the Middle East, as well as carrying on espionage in London and Paris. I had quite a long talk with this fellow Saunter.''

''He was the one who was in here before? Looked sort of young.''

''Young, yes, but there's no age for this sort of thing. I suspect he'd rather handle the whole thing himself, but he couldn't avoid asking our help. If the federal people took over the investigation they'd tip their hand.''

''Did he give you any leads?''

''The address here of a secret society called the Order of the Peacock Angel. Ever hear of them?''

''I think one of the boys mentioned it a few months back, but I didn't pay any attention. Some nutty religion. Harmless, I guess.''

''Maybe,'' Leopold said. ''Anyway, I'm going out to see them.''

''You think this guy Venice is hiding out there?''

''Saunter says Walter Moon visited them the night before he died, so I guess it's a good enough place to start.''

But it was still a long way from Iraq, and nobody knew it better than Leopold. He really didn't expect to find the man named Venice in his city, though he was willing to look.

The Order of the Peacock Angel had taken over a decaying old mansion in the Third Ward, a section of the city once noted for its fabulous homes and dinner parties that went on long into the night. Most of the houses, abandoned by their original owners, had long ago fallen into disrepair and been cut up into hundred-dollar-a-month apartments, to be shared by working girls with nothing more in common than their quest for a man. This one, though, was different. The aging widow who'd lived there alone for so many years, watching the neighborhood she remembered so well crumble and change before her eyes, had only recently died. The mansion now, for all its need of a paint job and plumbing, was still in one piece.

Leopold was greeted at the door by one Jerome Farngood, an impressively white-haired man who might have been a lawyer but wasn't. As he showed Leopold into the plush living room, he readily admitted that he was the high priest of the Peacock cult in America. "We have nothing to hide," he said simply, spreading his hands before in a gesture of submission to authority.

"The Peacock Angel is a secret society, is it not?" Leopold asked.

"True, in a sense. But like the Rosicrucians and the Masons, you can learn all of our secrets from a number of readily available texts. They tell you more than many of our members know."

Leopold took out his cigarettes. "Mind if I smoke?"

"Not at all, Captain."

"I understand a man named Walter Moon visited you two evenings ago."

"Yes, he did. He represented himself as a reporter for a weekly news magazine, but I must admit I had my suspicions. His death was a tragedy, though."

"He was murdered, of course," Leopold said, making it a statement.

The white-haired man showed no emotion. "Better, certainly, than the taking of one's own life."

"You speak with a bit of an accent," Leopold observed. "Have you been in this country long?"

"I came over with my daughter nearly a year ago."

"From England?"

"From England. It is the only civilized nation left in this shrinking world."

"Then why did you leave?"

Jerome Farngood shrugged his broad shoulders. "Perhaps to spread the word."

"Do you know a man named Venice?"

"Not personally, no. Walter Moon asked the same question."

"Venice is a Russian spy who often used your society as a cover and a hiding place between missions. Did you know that?"

The man's forehead wrinkled suddenly as if in that instant he were pondering the fate of nations. Perhaps he was. Then he said, very carefully, "Let me tell you what I know of Venice. It may not agree with your version, but then who is to say what truth is, these days. Venice was a professional spy who worked for the highest bidder. Since the war he happened to be working for the Russians. He often came to our settlement on the Syrian-Iraq border, though I never met him there myself. More than a year ago he retired from espionage, and joined our order as a full member."

"Where is he today?"

"I honestly do not know."

"Is he still in Iraq?"

The impressive gray eyes closed for just an instant. "You are not well informed, Captain Leopold. Your government's agents sent an unmarked plane over the Iraq oasis some eleven months ago. It dropped three bombs on the buildings there, and killed fifty-four people. A crude attempt at Venice, but it failed, since he'd already left."

The words had been bitter, and there was something like naked hatred in those eyes now. "Can I believe that?" Leopold asked.

"It's a matter of public record. Some blamed the Jews at the time, but we always knew who had done it, and for what reason."

"If that's true, I'm very sorry.

"They won't stop until Venice is dead," Farngood told him. "And the man simply wants to be done with it all."

"Perhaps it's too late to be done with it." Leopold took out another cigarette, against his best resolutions. "Did you poison Walter Moon out of some misguided loyalty to Venice?"

"Hardly. I know nothing of his death except that he lived and now he no longer lives."

"Did he talk to anyone else here the other night?"

"Only my daughter, Helen."

"Could I speak to her?"

"Certainly, if you wish." He rose, moving quickly for a man of his apparent age, and disappeared up the stairs to the second floor. When he returned a moment later, he was followed by a slender woman with dark hair and a striking face.

Helen Farngood was of an indeterminate age that might have been as low as thirty. After a few moments with her, one didn't think too much of her age but rather the vibrant charm and almost masculine tenacity with which she entered into a conversation.

"He was such a nice man," she volunteered. "Such a nice man. I hate to hear about people dying."

"Somebody poisoned him, Miss Farngood. Did you—or your father—notice him taking any pills while he was here?"

"Pills, yes! From a little brown bottle! I remember asking him what they were for, and he said he had an allergy. Poor man."

"Do you assist your father in the ceremonies of the Peacock Angel?" Leopold asked.

"No."

"I was mainly interested in how many members you have," Leopold said.

Jerome Farngood cleared his throat. "I can answer that. We have just seven members at present, the minimum number for a lodge. My daughter is not one of them, though she aids me in other ways."

"None of them were here when Moon came?"

"No. We were not meeting that night. But he did ask for—and receive—a list of members." He threw his hands wide in a gesture of goodwill. "You see, we have no secrets."

"When is your next meeting?"

"Friday. Two nights from now."

"Could I come and observe it?" Leopold asked.

Farngood hesitated a moment, and his daughter answered for him. "Of course he can, Father!"

The white-haired man nodded finally in agreement. "Certainly, the meeting is an open one. I ask only that you merely observe and do not try to interrupt the ritual with needless questions."

"For a policeman investigating a murder, no questions are needless," Leopold said. "But I can ask them after your so-called ritual."

"We will see you on Friday, then."

Helen Farngood rose to show him to the door. "If not before," Leopold threw in. Then, at the door, he paused to ask her, "You wouldn't happen to know if Moon called on any of the members after he left here, would you?"

"I have no idea. I can tell you where he went directly from here, though."

"And where was that?"

She stood with hands on hips, reminding him of nothing so much as a statue of some pagan goddess. "To the little church down the street. I watched him from the upstairs window."

Leopold frowned slightly. Was Walter Moon the sort of man to go to church in the middle of a mission? "Thank you," he said.

"Not at all. We'll be looking for you on Friday."

Leopold walked a block to a corner drugstore and telephoned Fletcher at his home. When he had the man on the phone, he asked, "Was there a list of names on Walter Moon's body?"

"Names? Sure, Captain. We've been checking them."

"Well, get out and check some more. They're the members of the Peacock Angel. I think Moon may have visited them the night before he died."

"Right. I'll see how the boys are coming with them."

"Fletcher, I want *you* to check them, every last one of them. And tonight!"

"Sure," the detective said, and hung up softly.

Leopold lit a cigarette and wondered why his nerves were suddenly going to pieces. He hadn't yelled at Fletcher like that in years. Somehow the interview with Farngood and his daughter had upset him, and he wasn't sure just why.

He stood on the corner of the street for a moment, looking in both directions. Finally he turned and walked toward the soft glow from the little church halfway up the next block.

The place, a modernistic sanctuary of glazed brick and pebbled glass, was half-filled for a Lenten service. Leopold stood in the back, aware of a silence so great he could hear the whispered prayers of the old women in the rear pews. When finally it was over, he went forward up the side aisle to where a lean-faced priest was carrying on a quiet conversation with an anxious teenager.

When she had gone, Leopold introduced himself and followed the priest's lead to the modernistic rectory next door. There, settled in a leather-covered chair that seemed somehow a bit too comfortable, Leopold said, "It's about a man who might have stopped in your church two nights ago, Father . . ."

"Father Regan. Many people stop in my church."

"This would have been a man named Walter Moon." He took the morgue shot from his pocket and showed it to the priest.

"Yes," the priest answered slowly. "I think I remember him."

"Could you tell me what he wanted, Father?"

"He was interested in the house down the street, an odd sort of religious cult. But I told him I'd been here only a few months myself and couldn't help him."

"Was that all?"

"Oh, we talked for a while, casually, about the neighborhood. I've forgotten most of it now."

"He died yesterday," Leopold said simply.

"Of course! The man in the hotel room! I hadn't connected them until now. What a tragic way to die! Do you think he took his own life?"

Leopold pondered the question and gave an honest answer. "I really don't know. There are some who think he was murdered, but I don't know."

"He didn't seem like a man at the end of his rope."

"One other question, Father—did you see him take any pills while he was here?"

"Pills? No, I don't believe so."

Leopold thanked him and departed. Something about the case was still bothering him as he walked back to his car.

The morning was unexpectedly foggy, with a mist that came up off the river and gradually flowed like an uncoiling serpent through the dreary streets. Leopold wasn't happy when he met Jim Saunter shortly after nine. It wasn't a happy sort of morning.

"Such fog," he mumbled, brushing aside the mass of papers that had collected on his desk overnight. "I wanted to be down here an hour ago."

Saunter unzipped his briefcase, all business. "Did you question the Peacock people last evening, Captain?"

"I talked with Jerome Farngood and his daughter. My man Fletcher is interviewing the others."

"Any leads on Venice?"

"None. I'm beginning to doubt that he even exists, except in the minds of you people."

"He exists, all right," Saunter said shortly. "He killed Walter Moon."

"But *did* he? Did anyone?"

"What do you mean by that? Are you back to the suicide theory again?"

Leopold sighed and buzzed Fletcher. "Send somebody out for coffee, will you, Fletcher? I need it this morning." Then he turned his attention to the CIA man once more. "Mr. Saunter, is it true that your crowd bombed a settlement in Iraq and killed fifty-odd innocent people in an attempt to get Venice?"

Saunter was still young enough to reflect embarrassment. "The incident to which you apparently refer was not an official action of the CIA or any other government agency. And I think the number of dead was closer to thirty than fifty.''

``I see,'' Leopold said, feeling irrationally sorry for the man, for all of them. ``Just an overly zealous agent in the field, is that it?''

``I can't discuss it. We're here to talk about Walter Moon.''

Leopold, red-faced and fighting for his temper, was suddenly on his feet. ``Listen, man, Moon's life is no more important than those Arabs half a world away!''

``Venice is a murderer, several times over. Perhaps he killed half of London with his reports during the war.''

The coffee came and Leopold passed a cup to Saunter. When he'd calmed down a bit, he said, ``About Moon. There's a theory I have that would support the idea of suicide, if you care to hear it.''

Saunter nodded. ``I'll listen, but I don't have to believe it.''

``Well, your man Moon visited Farngood and quite possibly heard the same story I did about the bombing of the oasis. After he left there, he went down the street to a church where he spoke with a priest, perhaps seeking spiritual comfort. When he didn't find it, he went back to his room and killed himself out of a horror for what had been done. I believe you people always carry cyanide pills for emergencies.''

The young man's lips twisted in a sort of smile. ``I'm afraid you have let your imagination run away with you, Captain. If you'll allow me to kill off your points in order; Walter Moon knew about the Iraq thing some months ago, he was not a religious man, and—despite the spy novels—we never carry suicide pills. A few agents may request them when entering foreign territory, but they are never issued as standard equipment.''

``All right,'' Leopold admitted. ``It was just a possibility. These suicide pills, though—Venice would probably be carrying them in case he was captured.''

``Undoubtedly.''

``Then it would seem that their paths crossed, that Venice observed Moon taking his allergy pill and arranged to place a cyanide pill in the bottle.''

``Something like that has been my contention from the very beginning.''

Leopold was thinking out loud. ``But would the pills be the same size, the same color?''

``They were capsules. It would take only a minute for Venice to empty the powder from one and substitute cyanide from his own supply.''

"All right," Leopold sighed. "So we're back on the trail of your master spy. If that's the correct designation for him."

Saunter nodded. "Any spy who runs other agents is considered a master. It's another technical term generally misused in fiction. But it applies in this case. Venice had quite a string of them during his recent years in Paris. We have reason to believe there might even have been a Venice agent behind the attempted assassination of de Gaulle, among other things. Tony Wilder, the man we have under wraps in Washington, was one of his Paris agents."

"What about Wilder? Could you have him up here tomorrow night? The Peacock people are meeting."

"I could have him here in two hours."

Leopold pondered a bit. "Well, they'll all be together tomorrow night, and I've already got an invitation to attend. How about flying him up tonight and we'll keep him in a hotel here, just so he's on the scene."

Saunter nodded in agreement. "I'll get on the phone."

"You're sure he can identify Venice?"

"He's sure, and I believe him."

"What if there's been plastic surgery?"

"It leaves scars. Besides, why should Venice bother when there's no description of him in existence? To our knowledge, Tony Wilder is the only living person who's ever seen him."

Leopold nodded. "All right, then. That seems to be our best bet. Call me when you've got this Wilder bedded down and I'll come over to see him."

After the government man had departed, Leopold turned his attention once more to the papers and reports on his desk. There was one from Fletcher, a rundown on the six members of the Peacock Angel whom he'd interviewed long into the previous night. Three of the six had come to the city during the past year, and one admitted having lived in Europe. Otherwise they seemed fairly ordinary. One was a woman Leopold knew slightly, a downtown shopkeeper who sold ladies' hats.

He read over the paper again and then put it down, more in the dark than ever.

Saunter phoned him that night just after seven. "He's here," the CIA man said simply. "Hotel Hudson. I'll meet you in the lobby."

"Right." Leopold hung up and got his coat.

The lobby was crowded with a convention of some sort when he reached it, but he had little trouble picking out the youngish government man standing on the sidelines. As he headed for him, he suddenly found himself face to face with Father Regan, the priest he'd met the previous night.

"Hello again, Father. Are you part of the convention?"

"A small part," the priest explained. "It's a Knights of Columbus gathering. Good to see you again."

"And you, Father."

Leopold kept going and shook hands with Saunter in a good imitation of unexpected encounter. He followed the young man into the elevator and they rode in silence to the seventh floor. There, two more youngish and casual-looking men lounged in the corridor, quite obviously on guard.

"Before we go in," Leopold said, "fill me in a bit on this Tony Wilder."

"There's really not much to tell. He's a Russian citizen who's been passing for English since the war years. We had nothing on him till quite recently, when his name turned up as one of Venice's Paris agents. We knew that he journeyed to the Middle East a year ago, apparently for a meeting with Venice. A few months later he turned up in Berlin, asking political asylum. He admitted he wasn't English, and confessed to a good many other things as well. During the questioning it came out that he'd met Venice twice and could positively identify the man."

"And that's when you got interested."

"Right." Saunter paused before one of the doors and knocked. "But he can tell you the rest himself. He's quite a talker."

After a moment the door opened, revealing a middle-aged man with an ordinary face and tired eyes. He stepped aside to let them enter, then closed the door and carefully snapped the lock. "What's all the noise?" he asked, with just a trace of a British accent.

"Convention in the hotel," Saunter explained. "You needn't worry." He turned his head to indicate Leopold. "This gentleman is from the local police, looking into the killing of Walter Moon. Captain Leopold, Tony Wilder."

Leopold accepted the firm handshake and sat down. His first thought was that this man didn't look like a spy, either. Wilder was more the aging playboy type, the retired adventurer who still viewed the world as fair game for someone on the make. The eyes were tired, yes—but there was still the trace of a twinkle deep within them.

"I was sorry to hear about Moon," he said.

"Did you know him?" Leopold asked.

"He came to question me one night, before he left for here. I warned him that Venice was a ruthless man."

"Just what did you tell him?"

"Oh, about the last time I was Venice, in Iraq."

"At the place that was bombed?" Leopold asked, shooting a glance toward Saunter.

"Yes. It was about fourteen months ago, some time before the bombing. I'd worked for Venice in Paris, and he summoned me to meet him at the oasis of the Peacock Angel. It took me three days by camel to reach him."

"You're sure it was really Venice."

"I'm sure. I remembered him from Paris. He told me he was finished with the game, told me he was retiring. He said he had a foolproof cover identity worked out that would enable him to live in the United States undetected."

"Did he say it was connected with the Peacock Angel?"

"No, but I suspected it might be. He used the society as a cover in London, I know."

Leopold frowned. "Just what does Venice look like?"

"That is what Moon wanted to know, too. He's very difficult to describe, quite ordinary looking, really. About my age, I'd say."

"You're Russian, Mr. Wilder?"

The man smiled slightly. "My real name is quite lengthy and almost unpronounceable. I've thought of myself as English for a good many years."

"But you chose to ask for political asylum with the Americans when you could have returned to England and lived as you had before. Why?"

"I don't know exactly." He turned to stare out the window. "With Venice gone and the network collapsing, there wasn't anything left for me. Maybe you could say I have a compulsion to betray secrets. The Russians didn't want me anymore, so I turned to your side."

"And now you're ready to betray Venice."

Tony Wilder shrugged. "I met the man twice. He was no friend, only a business acquaintance. He'd do the same thing to me, I'm sure."

"What are you getting in return?" Leopold asked, keeping his eyes on Saunter.

"Nothing. A place to live out my days in peace, that's all."

Leopold stubbed out his cigarette. "I don't like it. The whole thing's a filthy business and I don't like it."

"What don't you like, specifically?" Jim Saunter asked.

"I don't like setting up the entire membership of the Peacock Angel for this bird to look at, and maybe for your people to take potshots at. You know very well that identifying Venice—simply identifying him—

won't give me a shred of evidence for a murder indictment. But it will give you what you want, a target for a bullet or maybe even another bomb."

Saunter was biting his lower lip. "I really don't think we should discuss this in front of Wilder. But I can say you're all wrong. We're not trying to kill the man, only find him."

"Now is it all set for tomorrow night?"

"I'll be at the meeting. Hopefully, they'll allow Wilder here to come in and look them over. If they won't, we'll have to set him up outside the house and check them as they leave."

Saunter was frowning a bit. "When you tip you hand, Venice might run for it."

"So! At least we'll know who he is, then, won't we?"

"What about your reports? Did Walter Moon visit any of them the night before he was killed?"

"Only Jerome Farngood admits to seeing him. But of course Venice would hardly volunteer the information. Moon might have called on one of them, realized the man was Venice, and not bothered with the rest."

"He'd have phoned me in Washington if he had that information," Saunter insisted.

"Probably. Still . . ." Leopold paused, deep in thought. "Anyway, have Wilder out there about nine o'clock tomorrow night. Across the street from Farngood's place. I'll get word to you somehow."

Saunter nodded. At the door he turned to Wilder. "If there's anything you need, the men are right outside."

Leopold followed them out, and one of the men in the hall came forward. "We'd better go in for a while, Jim," he said. "A couple of people gave us suspicious looks out here."

"All right," Saunter told him. "Look, see if you can get a convention badge somewhere. Then they'll never notice you."

They rode down in a crowded elevator, next to a middle-aged woman complaining about the noise. The lobby, when they reached it, was a confusing maze of mid-evening activity. As they threaded their way through it, a familiar feminine face loomed suddenly before Leopold. It took him an instant to realize it was Jerome Farngood's daughter, Helen.

"Hello again," he said. "What brings you here?"

"Captain Leopold, isn't it? I was checking arangements for a dinner party next week. It seems I picked a bad night for it, though."

"Knights of Columbus convention," Leopold explained. "They're harmless enough."

She smiled, closing her eyes to narrow slits. "Do I know this gentleman too?"

"I don't believe so. Miss Farngood, Jim Saunter."

Saunter nodded casually, apparently missing the significance of the name. "Pleased to meet you," she told him. "I must be getting along now."

When they reached the street, Leopold said, "That was Farngood's daughter. The Peacock man."

"Yeah?" Saunter turned, as if hoping to catch another glimpse of her. "Is she one of them?"

"No. Though they do have women members. At least one, anyway. I know her slightly."

Saunter lit a cigarette. "I'm going to turn in early. Tomorrow looks like a long day."

"Are you at this hotel, too?"

The CIA man nodded. "Different floor, though. I'll phone you in the morning, Leopold."

After they parted, Leopold strolled back to his car and drove to Headquarters. He was looking for Fletcher, but the sergeant had already gone home. Leopold sat for a time at his desk, staring at the telephone, then called Fletcher at his home.

"This is Leopold."

"What's up, Captain?"

"Nothing."

"Oh."

"Fletcher?"

"What?"

"How many pills were there?"

"What pills?"

"Are you asleep or something? Walter Moon. The cyanide. How many capsules were left in the bottle? You said the lab checked them."

"Yeah. But I forgot the number. It was about half full, I guess. Maybe forty or fifty capsules."

"Thanks, Fletcher."

"Does it mean anything, Captain?"

"Probably not."

He hung up and started pacing the office. He was still pacing ten minutes later when the telephone jingled. It was Jim Saunter and he was excited. "Get down to the hotel fast, Captain. Somebody just tried to kill Tony Wilder."

* * *

The hotel corridor was crowded with confusion when he arrived. Confusion and the scent of recent violence. A doctor was in Wilder's room, along with Saunter and the two men who'd been on guard. All of them were grim-faced and tense, as if unsure of how to cope with the situation.

Wasting no time, Leopold asked Saunter, "What happened? How bad is it?"

The man from Washington stared down at the faded hotel carpet. "I don't know, I just don't know. We were guarding the door so carefully we forgot about the window."

"It's only a flesh wound," the doctor said. "Painful, but not serious."

Leopold glanced into the bedroom and saw Tony Wilder stretched out on top of the spread. His left shoulder was bandaged and his face was the color of chalk. "How did it happen?" Leopold asked again.

"He heard something knocking at the window," Saunter explained. "It was something on the end of a long string, and as he watched it, the thing fell. He naturally opened the window and leaned out, and our killer dropped a knife on him. Luckily, it just caught him in the fleshy part of the shoulder. Six inches to the right and it would have gotten the neck."

Leopold saw something glinting on the coffee table. "Is that the knife?"

"Yeah. You probably should check it for fingerprints."

Leopold took out a handkerchief and gingerly picked up the weapon. It was of Middle Eastern design, with a heavy curving hilt. The blade, too, might have curved at one time, but it had been narrowed through numerous sharpenings to a narrow shaft of steel. Now dried blood coated some two inches of it, and there were stains, too, on the coffee table where it had rested.

"I don't think our man left any prints," Leopold said. "What about the thing Wilder saw at the window?"

One of the nameless men from the hallway produced something from his pocket. It was a length of string some thirty feet long, with a bar of hotel soap tied to one end. "This is it," the man said. "We found it down in the alley."

While Leopold studied it, Saunter explained, "Somehow Venice found out he was here. He got a passkey to one of the rooms above, went in, and dangled this gimmick from the window. When he figured he had Wilder's attention, he let it drop—and when Wilder looked out the window, Venice used the knife. It might have worked, you know. In fact, if Wilder had fallen back into the room and died, we'd have had a pretty baffling murder on our hands."

"I suppose you've checked the rooms above?" Leopold asked.

Saunter nodded. "As soon as Wilder yelled out for the guards, they notified me. I checked the rooms myself with the hotel detective. The four floors directly above are all occupied, but were empty tonight. Everybody's down at the convention banquet. Venice could have used any of them."

"You're sure it was Venice?"

"Who else could it be? Besides, it's an Arab dagger of some sort. I think I told you he was known to carry one up his sleeve."

"Let's talk to Wilder," Leopold said. They went into the bedroom where he was sitting up now, getting a bit of his color back. "How you feeling?"

"I'll live," he said.

"You think it was Venice?"

Wilder nodded. "It was him."

"Still want to go through with it tomorrow?"

"More than ever. Now I know he's here. If I don't get him, he might get me."

Leopold nodded and turned away. It was the same with all of them—kill or be killed. Track down the hunter and slay him in the streets. He wondered how it all would end.

Jerome Farngood met him at the door, smiling what was intended as a sincere greeting. "Come right in, Captain Leopold. It's a chilly night."

"It is indeed. And I thought spring was here."

"We're just about ready for the ceremony," he said. "Come this way."

Leopold followed him down a dim hallway to the back of the house. There were six others in the room they entered, and he recognized the lone woman as the hat-shop lady. The men looked like bankers or doctors or lawyers. All were middle-aged and none looked like a murderer and spy. But the thing that riveted his attention was the great ebony stature of a peacock that completely dominated the room. It was as if, for the first time, he realized that these people were serious.

"Amazing," Leopold breathed.

"Please keep silent during the ceremony," Farngood whispered. "It is essential if you are to remain."

Leopold found a folding chair near the back of the room and settled down to watch in silence. The people of the Peacock were dressed in regular street clothes, but as he watched, Farngood passed out flowing white robes, each embroidered on the breast with the figure of a peacock.

Leopold noticed for the first time that the feet of the black peacock rested in a shallow pool of water, and that the floor around the pool was covered by crisscross patterns in the tile. The seven robed figures seated themselves on low hassocks and one of them took up a stringed instrument not unlike a guitar. As the first strains of music filled the air, the others began to sway, ever so slightly. The water around the feet of the peacock statue began to bubble.

For twenty minutes Leopold watched in silence, seeing first one and then another of the worshippers leap to his feet and do a sort of dance around the figure of the black bird. At the conclusion, the dancer would throw a rolled piece of paper into the water at the feet of the peacock.

Finally, as quickly as it had begun, the strange ritual was at an end. Farngood came over to Leopold's chair, slipping out of the white robe as he did so. The music had stopped and the others were apparently preparing to leave. "Were you impressed?" Farngood asked.

"I guess so, but I won't claim to have understood it. What were those rolled-up papers in the water, for instance?"

"Not coded messages, as you probably assume," the man answered with a smile. "You see, we believe the peacock to be the source of all power, and we throw him our innermost thoughts and hopes and fears, in the same way that you might pray to your god."

Leopold grunted. Then, "Before I leave, I do have one favor to ask, if I might."

"What, Captain?"

"We have a witness outside, a man who knows and can identify this Venice. We'd like to bring him in here."

Farngood's face went grim. "I'm afraid I could not allow that."

"He'll see them outside anyway, as they pass under the street light."

"So be it, then. But these people are here as my guests."

"You'll promise not to warn them or let them slip out the back?"

"I won't warn them. I don't need to. None of these is the man you seek."

"What makes you so sure?"

"I know them. None hides a secret past. They are just people. Uncomplicated."

"We'll see what our witness says about them," Leopold decided. The first of them were leaving already, and he walked over to the window to signal Fletcher and Saunter in the car with Tony Wilder. He hoped vaguely there would be no shooting.

When they'd all departed, he walked quickly out to the car himself and leaned in the open side-window. "Well?" he asked Wilder. "Which one was Venice?"

The man looked blank. "None of them."

Saunter sighed and lit a cigarette. "Maybe he used plastic surgery after all."

"And maybe he was never here," Leopold countered. "Maybe he's peacefully raising sheep in Australia or something."

"You forget a couple of things. Walter Moon came here to find him and was murdered. Tony Wilder came here to identify him and was almost murdered."

"All right," Leopold said. "Come with me, Wilder."

"Where?"

"Up to the front door. There's only one of them you haven't seen, and that's Farngood himself."

Fletcher slipped out from behind the wheel. "I'll cover you, Captain."

"I don't want any shooting."

Leopold led the way, and when he reached the door, Jerome Farngood was already waiting there. "I thought you'd want to see me," he said.

"Well?" Leopold asked, turning to Tony Wilder. "Yes or no?"

"No. I never saw him before."

They went back to the car. Ahead, hurrying along the sidewalk on some nighttime mission, Leopold caught a glimpse of Father Regan from the church up the street. Perhaps he was only going downtown to the convention. At that moment, his life seemed simple compared with Leopold's.

They went back to headquarters and sat around smoking cigarettes. After a while Leopold sent Fletcher out for coffee and they smoked some more cigarettes.

"Bad for your health," Saunter said once. "So much smoking."

"Being a cop's bad for your health too. Sometimes it's fatal."

"I'm sorry we took up your time."

"That's all right. How about it, Wilder? Describe him once more, huh?"

The Russian who looked like an Englishman leaned forward in his chair. "I've told you. Medium. Medium everything. How do you describe somebody like that?"

Leopold frowned and thought about it. "Somebody killed Moon. That's the only fact we have. Somebody here, in this city, is a murderer."

"It has to be Venice," Saunter insisted.

And Leopold nodded. "It has to be. Otherwise there's no motive at all. But where is he?"

"He's one of the Peacock people. He has to be. Who else did Moon see while he was here?"

Who else? Leopold thought about it, remembering the priest from the church up the street. "I have an idea," he said. "I need to check something."

"You're going?"

"Stick close to the telephone. I may need Wilder again tonight."

But it took Leopold only an hour to track down the records on Father Regan and see that he'd been wrong in his wild assumption. The priest had just come to the city, true, but he'd been stationed in Manhattan and was well known to half the other priests in town.

All right.

All right, then.

Leopold sat alone in the drugstore near Farngood's home, drinking a Coke, and watching the clock move slowly toward twelve.

All right, Venice. Come out and be killed. There's no retirement for a spy. Not even in a place like this, with tree-lined streets and a sweet scent of spring beginning to form in the air.

He saw Helen Farngood at the counter, buying a carton of cigarettes. "Hello, there. You're out late."

"It's that sort of night," she said with a smile. "Did you get your man?"

"You know we didn't."

"You've given up? You'll stop bothering us?"

He closed his eyes as if against a great pain or a flashing brilliance. "I suppose we never really give up. It's like in books."

"You really think you'll find Venice?"

"I think so," he said. "You see, there's one possibility I didn't consider until this very moment—the possibility that Venice is a woman."

A police station is a lonely place at two in the morning, lonely even with the constant hum of activity as shifts change and arrests are made. The corridors at times are lined with the drunks and degenerates that are any night's fair sweepings, but it is the bolted darkness of most offices that gives the place its lonely look. There is none of the daytime bustle of young secretaries or wandering politicians. There is only the slight smell of sweat from the cellblock and the late-burning lights in offices like Leopold's.

"It fits," Leopold was telling a tired Jim Saunter. "Don't you see that it fits? You told me yourself that Venice escaped from England disguised as a woman."

The man from Washington nodded. "I know, I know. But you heard what Tony Wilder said when we asked him. There's not a chance of it. Venice is a man."

"But perhaps disguised as a woman once more."

"Perhaps. But it's not Helen Farngood. The matron checked her carefully enough."

Leopold nodded, fighting the twin tortures of depression and exhaustion. He'd had too many wrong guesses in the case. Helen Farngood had been the latest, and now they'd had to release her. "Leave me alone for a while, will you?" he asked Saunter.

"Sure. Can we take Wilder back to the hotel?"

"Keep him here for a while," Leopold said. "I want to question him once more about his meetings with Venice. You two can stay in my office. I'm going upstairs with Fletcher."

He found the sergeant sleepily drinking a cup of coffee with the downstairs desk man. "Can we go home now, Captain?" Fletcher asked.

"In a little while. I want to take a look at the evidence again."

"What evidence?"

"Moon's bottle of capsules and the knife that was used on Tony Wilder."

"What are they going to tell us?"

"Where I went wrong, I hope. They're the only links we have with Venice."

"Venice! Sometimes I wonder if the guy really exists at all, Captain. I think it's a game these guys in Washington invented to pass the time."

Upstairs, Leopold inspected the bottle once more, spilling the capsules on to a glass-topped desk while he puzzled over them carefully. "These have all been checked by the lab?"

Fletcher nodded. "The poison musta just been in one of them."

Leopold picked up the oddly shaped dagger and hefted it once more. "He never carried this thing up any sleeve. Not the way that hilt curves."

Fletcher yawned at the wall clock. "Can't we go over this in the morning, Captain? Why don't we just get all the Peacock people down here tomorrow, and flip a coin or something?"

"What?" Leopold looked up. "Flip a coin?"

"Why not?"

His eyes went blank for a moment, and then gradually began to clear. "But the motive . . ." he said, almost to himself.

"You got something, Captain?"

"Something I should have had a long time ago. It was the motive that threw me off. We had the wrong motive for Moon's killing. The wrong motive all along."

"You mean this Venice didn't really kill him?"

"Oh, Venice killed him all right, but not for the reason we thought. Come on—we have to talk to Tony Wilder once more."

Downstairs, they found Saunter and Wilder together in Leopold's office, talking about Berlin. Leopold slid easily behind the desk, suddenly wide awake. "Any new thoughts?" Saunter asked him.

"I have one. It concerns the motive for killing Moon."

"What about it?"

Leopold leaned back in his chair. "Well, I don't think Moon was killed because he'd found Venice. I think he was killed so you'd *think* he'd found Venice."

"Huh?" Saunter looked puzzled.

"Venice wanted it to seem that Moon had found him, when nothing could have been further from the truth."

Tony Wilder slid a hand inside his jacket to scratch himself. "Why would he do that?"

"To make it seem that Venice was up here someplace when he was really safely hidden in Washington. The game is over, Wilder. You'll never find Venice for us because you are Venice."

Tony Wilder's hand was coming up fast, bringing something from his jacket pocket. Saunter hesitated only an instant, then shot him through the forehead.

"You didn't have to kill him," Fletcher said, stooping over the shattered, bloody body of the man they'd known as Tony Wilder. "He was only reaching for this capsule. More cyanide, I suppose."

Saunter laid the gun carefully on Leopold's desk as the office began to fill with people. "I couldn't take a chance," he said. "The man was a killer." Then he asked Leopold, "How did you know?"

"Let's get out of here and I'll tell you."

They went into one of the other offices and Leopold settled grimly into a chair. He didn't like the memory of Wilder's face when the bullet hit.

"Well," Saunter said, "they told me you were good, and you are. He had us buffaloed."

Leopold started talking. He'd gone through the scene many times before, in front of murderers and judges, but somehow this time his heart wasn't in it. "Of course Venice killed the real Tony Wilder during the last meeting in Iraq. He probably chose Wilder because the man was almost as unknown to the West as he himself. If you analyzed it, there really couldn't have been any other motive in luring Wilder into the middle of the desert. Certainly a man as careful as Venice—who was rarely seen even by his associates—would hardly have explained his retirement plans to a man he barely knew. He probably told Wilder about coming to America all right, and then killed him and assumed his identity. The body would have been buried somewhere in the desert, and probably destroyed forever when you bombed the place."

"We didn't bomb . . ." Saunter started to protest.

"I know, I know. Anyway, the bogus Wilder arranged to fall into your hands and got a free ticket to America on the grounds that he could help you to find Venice. What better gambit for a master-spy? What better cover identity than that of a man searching for himself? You'd guard him and wine him and dine him for a while, and finally after he'd failed to locate Venice you'd let him settle down peacefully and forget about it. Only things were getting dull in Washington and I imagine he needed something to convince you that Venice was over here. So he killed Moon."

"Just like that."

"Just like that. I don't imagine it bothered him too much. Those capsules were a bit of evidence too. You assumed—we all assumed—that one of the people Moon saw the night before he died made the switch. But actually the mathematics were against it. There were more than thirty capsules left in the bottle. Even if Venice dropped the poisoned one on the top, the odds would be greatly against Moon getting it the very next morning. When I thought about that, it was only a step to the probability that the poisoned capsule had been in the bottle for some time, possibly since several days earlier when Moon was in Washington. You see, Venice didn't care *where* Moon died, as long as he died. But it was doubly lucky for Venice that it happened up here, where the Peacock group could be blamed."

"But how could Venice have poisoned Moon's pills?"

"He told me Moon came to question him one night in Washington. And we know Moon had to take his allergy capsules every morning and evening. He took one in front of Farngood, remember? I suppose he left the bottle while he went to the bathroom or something. Venice-Wilder already had his own supply of cyanide, and it would only have taken him a minute to empty a capsule and substitute the poison.

"All right," Saunter conceded. "I'll grant you that Wilder could have done all you say. But is that all the evidence you had?"

"Well, there was the negative evidence that Wilder failed to identify any of the Peacock people as Venice. But more on the positive side, there was the faked attempt on his life. Take a look at that knife again and you'll note that the hilt is quite heavy and curved. Most knives, when dropped from a height, will land point first. But not that one. I haven't tried it myself, but I'm willing to bet that the curved hilt would cause the knife to start turning in midair after it had fallen a ways. A few feet, maybe, but twenty or thirty feet and it never would have gone into Wilder's shoulder like it did. It would have cut him, maybe, but never gone in straight for a couple of inches. Also, of course, there was the bar of hotel soap used to weight the rope and attract Wilder—supposedly—to the window. A man who stole a passkey and came prepared with a dagger wouldn't have been so *unprepared* that he had to rely on a bar of hotel soap. No, Wilder was improvising, just as when he killed Moon. He thought a murder attempt was needed to further convince us that Venice was in this city. He dropped the soap and string from his own window, of course."

"How'd he stab himself in the back of the shoulder?"

"There are at least three ways that come to mind. Probably he simply held the knife in a door jamb and backed into it. Painful, but he was playing for big stakes, remember. He was playing for his life."

"He lost."

"He lost," Leopold agreed.

"One more question. How'd he manage to hide the knife and that string and those pills from us for all these months?"

"You would have had no reason to conduct a careful search of his belongings. And I imagine a man with a lifetime in espionage knew enough tricks to avoid any routine searches."

"He was a clever man," Saunter said. "Did it all just come to you like that?"

"It never just comes to you. The capsule bit stuck in my mind from the beginning. And then tonight Fletcher said something about flipping a coin and I got to thinking of the dagger flipping over as it fell."

Fletcher poked his head in the door. "Could I see you for a minute, Captain?"

Leopold nodded and excused himself. He was tired once more, very tired. "What is it, Fletcher?" he asked in the hallway.

"They've got the body out. What should I put in my report?"

Leopold glanced back into the office where Saunter sat calmly smoking a cigarette. Somehow it was that instant which decided him. That instant and the memory of a man who'd traveled halfway around the world to get his brains splattered against Leopold's office wall.

"There's been too much killing, Fletcher," he said a bit somberly. "The real Wilder, and Moon, and now Venice himself. And a lot of nameless people out in the middle of a desert. It has to end somewhere, to end with a law and a court and a verdict. Otherwise, what good are we, any of us?"

"What do you mean, Captain?"

Leopold put a hand to his forehead. "I mean that I'm holding Saunter for the Grand Jury. I know they won't indict him! I know I'll have Washington on my neck, but I'm going to do it anyway! Call it a gesture if you want."

Fletcher nodded. "I guess maybe I understand."

Leopold stretched and seemed to come awake with decision. The night had passed. It would be morning very soon. "Book him, then, for manslaughter. I'll phone the district attorney."

JOHN JAKES
Dr. Sweetkill

1

FOR THREE WEEKS Nick Lamont heard nothing from Wilburforce. For three weeks he drank too much, stayed out too late in the clubs round Soho, and stared with eyes that grew more gritty with each successive hung-over morning at the credit notices piling up in the day's post.

Then finally, one drizzly evening when Nick had touched his last friend for a few pounds, he was forced to hang around the flat because he was broke. That was when Wilburforce rang him up.

''Kemptons Luggage has a little task for you, Nicky,'' Wilburforce said. Kemptons Luggage was a shadow-firm in a shadow-office. It was the cover behind which Wilburforce and his counterparts in British intelligence farmed out their nasty work to free-lances like Nick. ''Of course, this is rather a take-it-or-leave-it proposition.''

Nick Lamont kicked one of his expensive calfskin lounging slippers halfway across the room at the grate. He wished he could smash his fist into Wilburforce's white, narrow, no-nonsense face.

Take it or leave it. Did the bastard think he could do anything except take it after the Tenderly mess? He was nearly washed up in the trade as it was.

''I'll meet you,'' Nick said after a moment. ''Five tomorrow at the usual place?''

''Sooner. Luncheon.'' Wilburforce mentioned a posh grille. ''Actually, Nicky, I didn't think you'd hesitate as long as you did. I'm glad to hear you're so enthusiastic about working again.''

Nick Lamont's dark-burned face turned white around the edges of the lips. ''I haven't said I'd take the thing. I'll listen.''

Wilburforce clucked. ''Try to control that red temper of yours, please. You're hardly in favor. If you want to keep on working for the firm, you'll pick up our little—ah—sales errand and relish it.''

Nick's epithet was short.

Nick had made dozens of pleasant acquaintances among the British in his years in London. Not friends, really. You never could afford friends in the trade. But Wilburforce was another case. Wilburforce disliked Americans. He disliked reasonably competent Americans like Nick even more. Nick had done some jobs well.

But now Wilburforce had no reason to conceal his antipathy. As a result of the blunder in Gibraltar, Nick's stock as a free-lance was sharply down.

Wilburforce said: "Am I to interpret that filthy language to mean you are interested?"

Across the flat on the writing desk loomed the bills. Nick wanted the new silver-gray Jag so badly he could taste it.

And there was Tenderly. Tenderly, and the gun in Nick's hand in the frowsy little room upstairs over the restaurant.

"I'll be there tomorrow," he said.

"When you arrive," Wilburforce said, "try to be civil. This is not the state of Ohio, Nicky. Nor are you the muscular hero athlete who can dictate his own contract. We shall be writing the contract this trip, and you shall accept our terms, or none at all. Good evening."

Cursing, Nick slammed the dead phone down.

He walked to the windows opening onto the terrace. Rain dribbled down the glass. When he turned round to fix a whiskey-soda from the liquor cabinet, he passed the mantel mirror. He avoided glancing into it. He knew what he would see if he did; a big, husky man now turned thirty-five, and a little heavier than he should be.

But flat in the gut. Hard. His hair was still wild, curling black, though it was turning a little gray around the ears. Occasionally his hands shook when he lit a match to a cigarette. But the eyes still had the old temper-spark on occasion.

While the London rain pelted away, he drank three whiskey-sodas and then fell into bed, hoping for no dreams. He wanted to sleep soundly, in preparation for meeting Icy-Guts, as Wilburforce was calling him behind his back.

But he dreamed.

He dreamed intensely, vividly, yet disjointedly. There was the stadium in Ohio under a crisp purple and gold late afternoon sky. The stands thundered. Women's faces shone here and there, red with screaming. Suddenly, just before he made the field goal he heard an amplifier roar, *"Nick the Kick does it again!"*

Yet at the dream-moment when his foot should have connected with the ball and sent it sailing between the uprights, he was in the room in Gibraltar.

Nick had been flown over to bring back one Wing Commander Saltenham, who had, according to the evidence, been jobbing electrostatic copies of an air defense network alarm system to a notorious middleman on Gib. Wilburforce's section wanted Saltenham quietly withdrawn from circulation, in order to subject him to extended interrogation at a country estate discreetly maintained by the section in Kent. Along with Nick had gone one of Wilburforce's own operatives, an aging, modestly attired clerk type named Arthur Tenderly.

On Gib, Nick ran Saltenham to earth in the room above the restaurant. The Wing Commander was bounding a bawdy little girl with Moorish eyes and nothing on except several cheap rings. Nick threw her out, aimed his pistol at Saltenham and told him they were departing via a special flight which would take off shortly.

Tenderly had knocked, entering with hardly a sound. The 'copter was standing by, he reported. Saltenham knew he was finished. Fear coated his cheeks with acrid sweat. Yet he had guts.

Either he would be carried out dead, he announced, or he would not go. In other words, Nick would have to use the gun. Saltenham was snide about it, too. In a physical go, even with two against one, the Wing Commander promised to knock their jawbones down their throats. He looked as though he meant it. And he had one advantage—his correct guess that Nick Lamont and Tenderly had no orders to kill.

That didn't prevent Nick from going at the man with the raw sight-end of his pistol. He charged in, trying to counter-buffalo the suspected spy with a slash of the muzzle. Arthur Tenderly disapproved of Nick's gambit. What he didn't know was that Nick had, regrettably, lost his temper under Saltenham's snide needling. Tenderly chose the moment to intervene.

He seized Nick's arm to prevent serious damage being done by the rather notorious American.

"I'm running this and I'll run it my way," Nick shouted, trying to shake Tenderly's pale, small grip off his forearm. In that moment, as Nick gave his right arm a wrench to free it, the pistol, off safety, exploded.

The Wing Commander tried to escape through the window. Nick pumped one bullet into his right calf because it was already too late to do the task without a racket. Arthur Tenderly died of a gunshot wound forty-five minutes later in the naval base hospital.

After Nick had returned to London with his prisoner, his stock had begun to decline. He was questioned, requestioned and finally cleared. But the phone failed to ring—until tonight.

And now, in the tortured dream that brought him wide awake to hear the midnight toll of bells, he somehow still saw Tenderly at his elbow. The gun had exploded. Tenderly was falling back, aghast. Somewhere an announcer thundered, *"The Kick does it again!"*

Two more drinks managed to send Nick back into a dull, thick slumber.

At 11:30 the next day he took a cab to The Castlereagh Grille.

Smoking in the cab, Nick tried to think back. Where had he gone wrong?

He had started out fine in college. All-American. Some said he was the most powerful, accurate kicker ever seen on a football gridiron. Then came the Army. A stint with Intelligence. He didn't lack brains, and he preferred to be of some damn use, instead of playing ball for one of the base squads.

His Army record hadn't been bad. Afterward, he had no trouble landing on a pro club. For three years The Kick made them stand up and yell themselves silly.

Meanwhile a taste for good living built and built. It included liquor. The liquor unlocked the temper—and that led to the awful night he wrecked four rooms in a motel. After the team failed to renew his contract, he drifted to Europe. He'd grown to like a fast, expensive life. And rather quickly he found a way to earn money.

For a time he sold his services to the Allies: NATO, the French secret service twice. Then he was invited to London, with a pretty good guarantee of income as a free-lance. The work was sometimes dirty. The trade was never clean. But he enjoyed the cars and the wine and the girls the money bought. So long as he checked that temper, he was all right.

In Gib, one wild swipe of his arm had exploded a gun and killed a man. And the phone hadn't rung for a long time.

Well-dressed in a Saville Row suit and an expensive rainproof, Nick climbed out of the taxi in front of the Castlereagh Grille. He hurried inside. He didn't look like a man who was up against the fact that his luck had run out. But in the trade, you kept a hard face.

Three flights up, down a corridor and through a succession of small private dining rooms, he came to the elegant, thick-walled chamber with steel behind every inch of patterned wallpaper. Here executives of Kemptons Luggage now and then met for "conferences." Here, by a dim little table lamp that threw a long shadow of the senior agent's bald head on the wall, Nick lunched with Icy-Guts.

Wilburforce picked at his chop. ''Because of the Tenderly business, Nicky, you damn well may never get another assignment.'' He smiled. He had a gold tooth, which glowed. ''Unless you take this one.''

''How much is the fee?'' Nick felt sarcastic. ''Half the usual?''

''Twice,'' Wilburforce said.

Nick's scalp crawled. The jokes were over.

Thrusting aside his willow-patterned plate, Wilburforce began to speak in his flat, dry manner.

''You will be assigned a target which is a perfectly legitimate and prosperous chemical corporation near Munich. Chemotex Worldwide G.m.b.h. Some of our lads working in the East, on the other side of the Curtain, have come up with the news that while the factory is indeed legitimate, its department of basic research—a separate ring of the home building—is in fact a thriving laboratory doing research on nerve gas and bacteriological agents.''

''Who runs the outfit?''

''The firm's director is Herr Doktor Franz Staub. We suspect he's sympathetic with the East and that, at very least, the secret laboratory has his tacit approval. But he's small fry. The laboratory's director is much more important. His name is Yonov.'' Wilburforce glanced across the spotless linen, pointedly. ''Dr. Genther Yonov.''

An ugly memory ticked in Nick's mind. ''I saw a dossier a year ago. The Athens thing. Something he'd sold. A compound. They had a code name for him.''

Wilburforce nodded. ''Yes, Dr. Sweetkill.''

A long silence. The shadow of Wilburforce's head loomed malignantly on the wall.

''Dr. Sweetkill, the seller-to-all,'' he said at length. ''Pacific yet ghastly death available on the open market. Almost uniformly, he seems to sell to the East. A filthy man. We understand Yonov has delivered to the East the formula for a new, quite deadly nerve gas code labeled Pax 11-A.''

Nick lighted one of his cigarettes that cost twice as much as the ordinary kind. ''And I'm supposed to do the old formula-stealing bit?''

''Already done,' Wilburforce replied. ''By our lads in the East. The mechanics needn't concern you. We have Pax 11-A, right enough. But now we have another signal from Top Planning. The Yonov gas and germ factory is to be destroyed. Blown up, obliterated. This will represent a considerable setback for the other side. Years, perhaps. And you, dear Nicky, win the choice assignment. You are to penetrate the basic research laboratory within the Chemotex headquarters, and finish it off.''

Slowly, Nick blew out smoke.

''How do I get in? Knock politely?''

Once again Nick found himself amazed by the thoroughness of Wilburforce's preparations. Despite being a bastard, the man was good. There would be a six-week training period in England. During that time Nick would be melded into the personality of Nicholas Lamont of Ridgefield, New Jersey, a young man with an impeccable record in international sales for a leading U.S. chemical firm. No relation to the American football player who enjoyed some vogue a few years ago, et cetera. N. Lamont had been hired by a man in the U.S. who was on the payrolls of both Wilburforce and Chemotex. N. Lamont would work for Chemotex in its legitimate international sales operation, and would, on a date not far away, travel to Munich to take over his new post. He would be trained by Chemotex, at factory sales training sessions.

''We have the papers, we have the photos, we have everything but the man,'' Wilburforce said. ''We even have your wife for you.''

One of Nick's black eyebrows hooked up. ''Wife?''

''Chemotex Worldwide treats its new employees rather royally. She will be traveling with you, all expenses paid. She's one of ours, of course. And she will not be with you,'' Wilburforce added rather nastily, ''to gratify your sexual appetites. She will be there to aid and assist you in handling the necessary details. A man could do it alone, but a wife provides a better cover for a man your age. How you get out of the factory after you set the explosives—indeed, how you even get in to set them at all—is your affair.'' Wilburforce leaned forward. ''Do you still want the little task, Nicky?''

Nick was cold in his mid-section. He tried to check his temper. ''You hope I do.''

''I hope you do. You're a smart, cheeky so-and-so. Lots of flash and brag. And there's Tenderly. He was one of my best. A lifelong friend. I hope you want it.''

In the private, protected, sealed and guarded dining room, all Nick Lamont could think about was a ridiculous stack of unpaid bills. For his guilt there was no specific symbol. It was only a feeling, heavy on his mind, never concrete except in dreams.

''I want it,'' Nick said. ''And I'll come back in one piece.''

Wilburforce dabbed his lips with a napkin. ''That's doubtful. But I'm delighted you accepted all the same.''

2

Six weeks later, on another of those dim, wet London afternoons, Nick Lamont met his bogus wife at the airfield. He had seen photos of her while he was in training. A round-hipped, slim-waisted, high-breasted girl with a pretty, though not beautiful, face. She had been trained separately. Once Nick inquired pointedly about this unusual procedure. Wilburforce fobbed him off with a reply that made no sense: the less dilly-dallying between the two of them while in training, the better they'd learn their lessons.

She wore a lavender suit, a small, wifely hat, and very little makeup. Her diamond rings sparkled. She had a crisp, athletic stride, a pink mouth that suggested passion.

"Hello, Nicky darling," she said, kissing his cheek.

"Hello, Anne." His smile was easy. "Couldn't we have a more wifely greeting?"

"I think not." She said it low, but with a perfect smile. Something in her eyes bothered him. It was something hard and direct, which made him stop paying attention to the rather choice way her firm, high breasts thrust out.

He'd looked forward to this part of the trip even if the rest of the excursion promised to be grim. She was a damn fine-looking girl. He'd hoped they might act husband and wife in more than name. Now he was doubtful.

"I've checked my luggage aboard," the girl told him. "Including the cameras."

In the noisy, aseptic terminal, Nick chilled again. The cameras were the explosives.

They strolled toward the boarding area. "You don't seem overjoyed to see me," Nick said.

"Didn't Wilburforce tell you my real name?"

"No, just Anne Lamont."

"It's Tenderly." She paused, faced him. She stared directly into his eyes. "Charity Tenderly. I know what happened in Gib. He was my uncle, you see. We were both in the trade. I know his death was technically an accident. So I'll do my utmost to see that this job is a smasher." Her smile was bright and hollow. "I do want to make sure you succeed, you know."

Through the terminal came the mechanized scream of a BOAC jet taking off. Charity Tenderly—he was going to have a hell of a time thinking of her as Anne Lamont—walked a few steps ahead of him. She smiled again over her shoulder, as if beckoning for him to hurry. There was a red fury in Nick for a moment, which he quickly quelled. Then came a vast, fatalistic depression.

In the assignment of this girl to be his partner he sensed the hand of Wilburforce at work.

Destroy the factory.

And himself.

3

Below, the picture-book prettiness of a Germany that looked unreal and untroubled gradually came up to meet them. They would land in Munich shortly. Nick tried to open the conversation again, meeting the difficult subject square on:

''Look, I know I've got a reputation for a temper but—''

The hostess was passing in the aisle. For her benefit, Charity interrupted, ''Why, darling, I've grown used to your temper in all the years we've been married.''

Nick's fingers closed on her wrist. ''Don't play smart games. What happened was—''

''Final.'' She said it looking him straight in the eye. ''A bullet. My uncle. But it's over. We don't want to be harping on it, not on airliners, not anywhere.''

Nick momentarily forgot caution. ''Why the hell did you come on this trip?''

Charity Tenderly grew quite serious. All malice was gone. ''Because this kind of career—your career—is important to me. I do what I do—well, darling, not for cash, that's for certain.''

''Then it's going to be all business?''

''Let's not argue, shall we? We'll be forced to stay in the same room. But there will be separate beds.''

Nick scowled. The seat belt sign came on. Charity Tenderly said nothing more, only stared thoughtfully out the aircraft window.

A small reception and dinner party was scheduled for them at the colorful but rather touristy inn located in the tiny village not far from Munich. They had reached the inn via a limousine waiting at the airport courtesy of the Chemotex management. The Chemotex works itself was several kilometers from the city, and one kilometer past the village inn.

At the inn that evening, Nick and Charity dined by candlelight in company with Herr Doktor Franz Staub and several other executives of the firm.

The dinner was excellent. Nick avoided wine, concentrated on dark beer and told a great many American jokes. Dr. Staub, an ascetic figure in a narrowly cut suit and small, gold-rimmed glasses, dry-washed his hands and nodded, pretending to understand the humor. Charity was seated between two of the sales executives who directed the European operation. She acted properly wifelike.

They were seated in a private dining room with a glass wall which overlooked the winding inn driveway. Shortly after the dinner began, a chauffeur-driven Mercedes arrived. Its occupant came in to join the group. She was tall, rather shapely, wearing a billowy out-of-season print dress and a large picture hat. Nick, a shade fuzzy with beer, was introduced.

''Permit me to present Fraulein Judith Yonov,'' said Dr. Staub.

Nick took the woman's hand briefly. Under the shadowy hat, her eyes were luminous, challenging. They were dark brown above a strong nose and full, brightly made-up lips. He judged her to be about 30. She had large breasts, a low voice, pale cheeks. She seemed to wear a great deal of makeup. She did not remove her hat, even though the private dining room was dim.

''This is the young salesman from America?'' Judith Yonov said in lightly accented English. ''How pleasant.''

''Your father—'' Nick began. ''I've heard the name. Research director, isn't he?''

''Yes. I am most regretful that he could not be here to share the occasion. But his projects—and Herr Doktor Staub's insistence on Chemotex competing vigorously in the world market—keep him laboring late many nights, I'm afraid.''

Up his backbone Nick felt another oppressive crawling sensation. The daughter of Dr. Sweetkill. She reeked of Chanel. There was something eerie about her.

''I've heard among the competition in the States,'' Nick said, still trying to sound off-hand, ''that your father has led Chemotex into some interesting basic research areas. I'd like to know more about that, Fraulein Yonov.''

Was he pushing too hard? Across the table Charity's glance was a brief flicker of warning. Dr. Staub clinked his spoon against his demitasse, laughed politely.

''Ah, my dear young Herr Lamont. How fascinated you Americans are with all things new! Actually, the nature of our basic research program is a rather closely guarded secret. If I may put it as tactfully as possible, I am afraid that new employees are not permitted access to that area of our operations. At least not immediately. Indeed, we must insist upon heavy security to protect our patents and processes, as well as work in progress. In any case I'm certain you will be kept quite busy learning our current commercial line, and selling that in the U.S. markets."

Judith Yonov pushed one of the candle holders slightly to the side, in order to get an unobstructed look at Nick.

"Perhaps, Herr Doktor," she said, "if Herr Lamont is truly interested in product development—and he is one of the family now, so to speak—" There was a pause. "Perhaps I might talk with father and we might arrange a tour."

"The rules forbid—" Staub began.

"We shall see," Judith Yonov interrupted. Staub flushed, silent.

The smoke from his cigarette burned Nick's throat. It was plain to see who in the group had the clout. But he hadn't liked the shrewd, luminous glare of those eyes from beneath the big hat. He wished her face were not so heavily shadowed. The party was spoiled. He was sitting across the table from the daughter of a mass murderer. A concertina played a bright air in another room.

Had Wilburforce triple-crossed him? Was he somehow part of a game, the rules of which were known to every damn one of them except himself?

Or had there been a leak during preparations?

Judith Yonov had been baiting him.

Or had she?

Did she *know*?

Presently, as dusk fell over the spectacular scenery outside, the party broke up. Nick would report to the Chemotex works tomorrow to begin training, Dr. Staub said. Pleasantries were exchanged all around. The sliding doors of the private chamber were rolled back. Judith Yonov excused herself and disappeared, presumably into a powder room.

Charity—he could not think of her as Anne, though he had no difficulty calling her that in public—was still chattering brightly with several of the executives. Nick discovered he was out of cigarettes. He left the room to buy some.

Going through the door into the inn lobby, he noticed a big, thick-shouldered man with a shaven head and a splayed nose. The man was emerging from the main tap room. He wore a dark uniform and highly polished boots. He had several inches on Nick, who was by no means small, at just over six feet.

The man walked unsteadily. He halted and blinked toward the party breaking up. He had a chauffeur's cap clutched in one hand. His eyes were small, and he reeked of beer.

Nick crossed the lobby, purchased his cigarettes and was just turning round when he heard a quick, brittle exclamation of alarm. He knew the voice. Charity!

He whipped around fast. Several of the executives had gone to fetch their homburgs from the check rack. Charity had apparently walked into the lobby to wait for Nick. The big chauffeur had stumbled against her, because he was standing so close to her now, an idiot's smile on his lips.

"I think you've had too much to drink," Charity said.

"*Nein.*" The heavy man stroked her forearm. "American lady, *ja*? Very pretty. Looks pretty, feels pretty—"

Charity glanced past him, and her eyes for once were something other than cold. The man had her cornered. Nick crossed to her quickly, touched the man's shoulder.

"Beg pardon, but she's not for handling."

"Don't put hands on Rathke." The big man slobbered it, scowling.

"I'll put hands on anybody I damn please. Get away."

"Very pretty, very nice," the man called Rathke said, squeezing Charity's wrist. The girl made a face. That was all it took for the Lamont temper to crack.

His mouth wrenched as he punched Rathke hard twice in the belly. Rathke stumbled back, more surprised than injured. Nick's arm ached. His knuckles hurt. Several of the executives began to jabber. Staub bore down on them.

Thoroughly drunk and raging because of it, Rathke planted his big boots wide and swung a huge, flailing punch. It caught Nick's chin, spun him just enough to unbalance him and set off the red fury in him in earnest.

He went in fast. For a second or so, Rathke punished Nick's belly with big, brutal hands. Then Nick got through the man's guard, counter-attacking the beefy German face with four fast, vicious punches. One of them slammed Rathke against the wall, brought a dribble of blood and a wild bellow of rage out of his mouth. Rathke lunged for Nick's throat—

In between the men there was a swirl of print fabric.

Judith Yonov spoke curtly in German, ordering Rathke to control himself. Rathke lowered his hands. He swiped his mouth with his uniform sleeve.

Nick was waiting. His tie was askew and he was breathing hard. But he was pleased, because he'd caught a glimpse of Charity's face.

She was irritated. He interpreted this to mean she was secretly pleased.

"Rathke, *nein!*" Judith Yonov exclaimed as the chauffer made up his mind, and shoved past her. Nick's head ached. Afterward he wasn't quite sure what had happened, but he believed Judith Yonov reached into her handbag, then touched her hand to the bare flesh of Rathke's left fist.

The man stopped. He blinked again. He took one more faltering step. With an audible swallow, he put on his cap.

The chauffeur stood docile. Blood made a thin red tracery down from the corner of his mouth.

"I do extend my deepest apologies for my chauffeur's behavior, Herr Lamont," Judith Yonov said. "He is under strict orders not to touch alcohol in any form. But I cannot watch him constantly."

Now the executives pressed close, apologizing in turn. In a moment Judith Yonov and Rathke had gone. But not before Rathke glanced back once, and gave a black scowl before sinking back into placid-featured obedience.

Nick guessed that Rathke had been subdued by some sort of needle-prick. A Dr. Sweetkill special? Very likely. What a nice poison-flower Fraulein Yonov turned out to be.

As the party at last ended for good, Nick Lamont quietly cursed himself for the burst of temper. He might have handled it another way, though he couldn't think of a good one off hand. As he shook hands with Herr Doktor Staub and the others one by one, he noticed Charity watching him again. Not quite with approval, but without animosity.

That was worth it, he decided—that single look. Worth it even if Rathke did remember, caused more trouble and—God forbid—endangered the mission.

Charity said nothing about the incident as they went upstairs, however, and they slept in separate beds.

4

Two evenings later, Nick got a measure of satisfaction when Charity did at last mention the fight. Earlier they'd driven into Munich in a sea-blue Volkswagen which the factory had provided for the length of Nick's training session. After a good deal of beer, a sumptuous meal and some reasonably friendly if inane talk, they returned to the inn around midnight.

Nick flopped down on his twin bed. Charity stepped into the bathroom and closed the door. He lay sprawled, his hard chest speckled with cigarette ash as he squinted through the smoke at the black beams of the high-ceilinged room. In his mind he went over what he'd learned about Chemotex in his two days of attending classes.

He was being taught the company's products, its pricing policies, its distribution, and he had a crammed notebook full of scribbled facts. But the lunch periods had been more illuminating, because during those times he'd gotten to see more of the facilities. He dined in the company cafeteria with the various sales executives who were his tutors. Today Herr Doktor Staub had lunched with them too.

Nick's mind was drifting over the lunch talk about research—Staub had been guarded, as usual—when the bathroom door opened.

Charity walked out. She was applying a pink comb to her hair. Nick tried a whistle. He got little response except a nod which indicated the bathroom was his. Still, this was curious. On their first two evenings Charity had appeared ready for bed clad in hideous baggy striped pajamas of mannish cut. Tonight she had put on instead a black sleeping gown, lined so as to be opaque, but short. Her calves were tanned and attractive. The gown's front fell precisely away from the two ripe, high sharpnesses of her breasts.

''Don't get notions,'' Charity said. ''I ripped the pajamas.'' With her back to him she began to hang up her daytime things.

Nick grinned. ''Oh, here I thought it was the softening up for the kill.''

The girl spun. ''That's not particularly funny. I don't care to see anyone killed.''

With a twist of his hand, Nick flicked ash into a tray. ''I meant the romantic kill.''

Charity's auburn hair shone by the dim lamps. ''That's rather presumptuous of you, Nicky darling.'' The *darling* was acid.

''I thought so, too.''

''Oh, you did?''

''Yes, but I'd like to know your reason,'' he said.

''I didn't ask to have my honor defended the other night.''

''Aha!'' Up he came off the bed, pointing a finger. ''You're still thinking about it.''

''I am not thinking about it! You're trying to imply I owe you something which—''

''Did I say that?'' Nick cut in. ''You said it. Been bothering you, has it?''

Charity flung back the coverlet on her bed. ''Since we're getting so damn psychoanalytical, why did you tackle that big, vicious creature?'' Charity raised her feet, bending her knees to slip her toes beneath the covers. The brief black gown's hem fell away for a second from the gently curving bottoms of her thighs. The view was exquisite, painful and over virtually at once.

''Was it,'' Charity continued, ''just another case of the Lamont temper breaking way out of bounds?''

Nick had an urge to hit her. ''Listen, maybe I felt he shouldn't paw you. Did that occur to you?''

''Yes. But I really think it was guilt. Thanks anyway.''

And, with a yank of the coverlet up over her bare shoulder, she turned her back toward him.

Nick closed his eyes. He saw it all again. The room in Gib. Tenderly's pale face wrenching as the accidental bullet drove into his breastbone and brought death and surprise to his failing eyes. Nick jumped up and stamped into the bathroom, where he slammed the door and ran the tap loudly so it would disturb her.

When he came out again, yanking the knot of his pajama bottoms tight to secure it, he made a quick round of the room as he did every evening, checking for hidden listening gear. Even though Charity was sitting up watching him, he avoided her eyes.

Finally he crawled into his own bed, reached for the light. Across his outstretched arm he looked at her. Strange, drawn lines pulled down the corners of her warm, pink, mouth.

''Nick, that was a bitchy thing for me to say. About the guilt, I mean.''

''Forget it.'' Yet he was oddly aware of a new, unfamiliar intensity about her.

''No, really. You've a tough enough job ahead without me complicating it. I do understand why you hit that filthy boor. Just to be decent. There's not much forgiveness in me. I apologize. We're none of us perfect. I had a bad marriage, I ruined—well, forget that. But do accept my thanks. Also the promise of truce. Nick?''

''Truce.'' He snapped out the light immediately.

He didn't want to look too long at the black-wrapped swell of her breasts above the coverlet, nor speculate on what tiny but definite change had come over her.

She settled down with small murmurs and rumpling bedding noises. Nick smoked one more cigarette, staring into the dark. He tried to concentrate on what he had to do.

His sales training wouldn't last forever. The Chemotex research wing had to be destroyed. The gear was in the wardrobe, as part of their luggage. He had to transfer it to his attache case. Use it. By God, he would, and go back and shove a fragment of Chemotex's blown-up steel up Wilburforce's damn behind.

Well, he would come back.

After another 12 days, at the beginning of the third week, Nick Lamont had learned enough—or all he could. He was ready to move.

A means of entrance to the basic research wing had to be found. This he'd learned early. He'd been studying the problem since.

The central building of Chemotex Worldwide G.m.b.h. presented a face to the one main access road. That face was all tinted blue glass and aluminum. Structurally, the building resembled the crossbar of a gigantic letter T. Running straight back from the crossbar was the basic research wing. It was three floors high, exactly like the main headquarters section. But all the doors leading into it from the main building were guarded during the daylight hours, alarm-rigged at night, and were, in any case, made of thick steel.

So far Nick had not even seen Dr. Genther Yonov. But he saw many of the scientist's white-coated research associates. They had their own private, treed and sodded exercise park at the rear of the downstroke of the T. They checked in and out through a rear gate in a high, electrified fence. Their cars were parked in a small, separate pool alongside the secondary road which ran off the main one and serviced the rear compound-like area.

At noontime the scientists lunched in the fenced park much like highly educated animals. Other employees from the main building, as well as from the nearby but separate manufacturing buildings, lunched in the regular cafeteria. And so far as Nick could tell, there was no fraternization between those who labored for Dr. Sweetkill and all the rest.

At another lunch, Nick commented on the unusual arrangement.

"Necessary, necessary," Herr Doktor Staub replied, munching a morsel of bun. "Here in Germany, as in your United States, industrial espionage is not unknown. Thus we must guard our most precious commodity, our brainpower."

And crawling bottles full of bacteria for Eastern stockpiles? Nick wondered sourly.

Staub's explanation made a glib kind of commercial sense, though. The security even included the extra precaution of having the entire factory hooked into a master fire and police signal system which connected to the headquarters of the two municipal services in the nearby village.

Penetration looked next to impossible until the night Nick became aware of Rathke's evening habits.

On a crisp Monday morning Nick was ready.

He packed his attache case carefully. A small but potent automatic pistol was concealed inside a dummy text on chemical engineering. One large rectangular side of the case now contained jellied explosive layered between thin metal. Nick sweated as he carried this to his sales training class and gingerly opened the lid to take out his notepad.

A pair of sales engineers lectured at him all day. By evening, Nick was used to handling the case, which was good. Shortly after the works closed, he checked out the gate and walked down toward the regular employee car park.

The sun slanted low. The sea-blue roof of the waiting VW gleamed. Nick bent down to tie his shoe. Charity had been picking him up at the factory all the past week. Now, directly opposite the VW, Judith Yonov's Mercedes was parked.

Charity was leaning from the window of the VW, directing a sunny and seductive smile at the driver of the Mercedes, Rathke. The man stood against the left front fender of the smaller car, a witlessly pleased expression on his thick face.

One of the sales engineers who'd lectured Nick that day emerged from the gate. Nick used the man's presence as a pretext for a question. When they had exchanged goodnights, Nick turned round.

Sweat trickled down the back of his neck into his collar. He clutched the attache case handle and walked between small, puttering sedans leaving the car park, to the VW. The Mercedes was pulling away along the secondary road, going around the rear of the gleaming headquarters toward the research wing.

"How did it go?" Nick asked once the VW was in gear.

Charity was headed back toward the inn and the village. Smoothly she downshifted in the heavy factory traffic. "I must look the perfect bored wife," she said. "I didn't think it would work at all. But the poor beast evidently has so few brains—anyway, I was parked there as he drove past. I hailed him and apologized for your nasty behavior at the party. At first I think he was very suspicious. Then he smelled the gin I drank before I left the inn. When I petted his hand and gave him the smile business, I knew I had him. But it was crawly, touching him. He's an absolute brute."

They were speeding down the twisting road between fragrant pines. The peaked roofs of the village, gilt with sunset, appeared ahead. Nick felt obliged to say:

"Sorry to force it, but I was beginning to get desperate. Rathke's the one key. The Yonovs live inside the research wing. He takes care of the Yonovs. So he can get in and out. It was a damn godsend when I got to noticing that he came back tanked from the village every afternoon about the time the factory lets out. Have you set it up?"

Charity's pink tongue touched her coral-painted lips, nervously. "Yes, for this evening."

Nick was conscious of the keen of the wind past the car. "How?"

"I'm just to be walking somewhere on the main street after dark. He thinks I'll be waiting breathlessly because I have this fixation about large, powerful men with black boots—" She shuddered. Before Nick could say anything else, she swung the wheel of the Volks sharply.

The small tires skidded on the shoulder, shooting gravel backwards. The sedan slowed to a stop. Other factory traffic streamed by, going downhill to the village and the sunset. They were cool sitting in the shadow of great, soughing pines.

Quite unexpectedly, Charity gripped Nick's hand.

"I haven't forgotten my uncle. But don't let Rathke hurt you."

Startled, Nick hooked up his eyebrow again. "Does it really worry you?"

"Damnit, don't be flip. You're a decent sort. You really are. Maybe a little flashy and—oh, I don't know what's got into me. Is it living in the same room with you every night for two weeks running? Or—damn you, stop staring." And her arms, rough with the chic tweed of her suit jacket, came round his neck and her mouth came up firmly against his, moistening as her lips parted.

Nick thought, *This is idiotic. You're liable to be dead.*

But as he kissed her two things hit home hard. One, he'd grown fond of her. Two, in some strangely chemical way, the same thing had happened to her regarding him. Somehow it made what he had to do this evening all the worse, all the more frightening.

Yet for a moment it was all swept away as he wrapped his arms around her in the shadowy car, hugged her hard while her mouth opened and she kept murmuring between deep kisses that she was a bloody fool who ought to know better. Nick touched her left breast. He felt it shudder, harden beneath the fabric of her suit. She pulled back suddenly.

Her eyes were bright with a quick, amazed passion she could hardly believe herself. With both her hands she clasped his big-knuckled right one to her breasts.

"I'm crazy for you, Nicky." She was almost crying. "Damn fool blunder, isn't it? I hope you come back. Please come back. Please."

Then she tore away, almost angrily. She drove fast back to the village.

On one hand, Nick felt pleased that it had happened. On the other, he wished it hadn't. Having it happen made him all the more conscious of the attache case jouncing lightly between his knees, layers of leather containing layers of steel and layers of steel sandwiching between them the jellied explosive he must use tonight.

The chimes in the village church stroked half-past nine.

Nick waited in a dark place as a shadow in the center of the dim street—Charity, walking—turned. The shadow was outlined by the sudden bursting brilliance of headlights.

The auto slowed. Charity walked over, white-faced in the leakage from the lights. She leaned smiling toward the driver's side of the Mercedes.

Attache case in one hand, Nick glided from the shadows. He raced the distance to the Mercedes, yanked open the door opposite the driver and slammed inside. He shoved the automatic pistol square against the side of Rathke's muscled neck.

"Drive to the factory or I kill you right now."

In the dash light glare, Rathke's lumpy face became by turns baffled, then dimly comprehending, then full of rage. Charity backed quickly away from the side of the gently humming car. Rathke cursed low, not too stupid to have failed to understand the betrayal. His immense right hand speared out through the open window.

Nick ground the muzzle deeper into the man's neck flesh.

"Pull your hand back."

Rathke did. Charity was by then out of range.

"Either start this thing going or you're all done right here."

Rathke turned his head slowly, hatefully, toward Nick. Then he faced front. He engaged the automatic drive lever. Charity floated out of sight. Were there tears shining on her face? Nick dared not look round.

He changed the position of the gun so that it prodded into Rathke's ribs, while the Mercedes shot past the limits of the tiny village and up the winding road into the pines, toward the death works.

5

Perhaps the prospect of death made him euphoric. At any rate Nick found himself speaking in a fairly relaxed, conversational manner to Rathke as the Mercedes ground smoothly up the twisting mountain road.

"Now let me make one or two things clear before we hit the grounds, because unless you understand me, you'll try something or other and there'll be trouble. If there's any trouble, this car is going to crash and you're going to get it right along with me. Understand?"

No answer.

"I said understand?"

Rathke's peaked cap threw shadows far down over his face. His lips twitched. *"Ja."*

"I know this much. You work for Yonov. His quarters are in the research wing. So I figure you know how to get in without triggering the alarms. If there's one single alarm, one goddam jangle of a bell, or light—anything—all you'll get for your pains is your brains smeared over the dash. If I don't do anything else I'll pull this trigger. It's all business between us as far as I'm concerned. Living or dying's up to you."

The brutish mouth worked at the corners, as if Rathke were bright enough to feel contempt for what Nick had said. It was not all business from Rathke's end. His smallish eyes held a vengeful brightness in the dash glare. He hadn't forgotten, or forgiven, the fight at the inn.

Nick had, though. He had because he had so much else to think about. For the first time in weeks, or months, or years, he didn't give much of a damn about a new Jag or anything, except getting back to Charity. And now that it mattered, he had to work doubly hard to keep the tension-edge out of his voice, the nervous spasm out of his gun hand. Those who theorized that there were no frightened men in the trade were fools.

Ahead, the bonnet lamps of the Mercedes brushed across the high steeled crosshatching of the electrified fence. Rathke made a tentative reach with his left hand for a small red button on the dash.

"What's that?" Nick said.

"Automatic signal. It will turn off and open the fence. We drive through when it opens."

"It had better do that and nothing else." Nick gestured with the gun. "Go on."

Rathke's splay finger pressed the red stud. Somewhere under the bonnet, an electronic device sang low. Abruptly the massive gates in the high fence began to swing inward like a scene done in slow-motion frames. The Mercedes slid ahead along the service road.

The gates passed on either side of Nick's field of vision. Then the black of the lawn where the research workers exercised during the day. The Mercedes rolled up to a rear door in the three-story building. Two blue fluorescent lights in an aluminum fixture over the door cast a ghastly glow. Nick had to risk passing through the lights.

"Out, *bitte*," he said, mockingly, though he wasn't feeling funny. The night had grown chill. The air bit at the bone. The pine smell all around was stingingly sweet. Rathke climbed from the car bent over, then straightened up.

"Do you know how to get inside with no noise?"

"*Ja*, I know."

"You'd better."

Carefully the chauffeur fished in his smartly tailored black uniform blouse. He produced a pair of aluminum keys which he jingled. Nick nodded for him to proceed. The attache case weighed heavy in Nick's left hand.

Rathke slipped the first key into a lock, twisted. He withdrew the key, inserted the second one into a lock immediately below. Nick's senses felt raw. He was trying to listen, watch, take in more than human senses could. At any second Rathke might be planning to trip some alarm.

Using his shoulder, Rathke nudged the glass-and-aluminum door inward. A long corridor stretched into a dwindling vista of metal walls with pastel-colored office doors shut on either side.

"The pilot plant area," Nick said. "We'll go directly there."

"Then this stairway—we go up." Rathke led the way.

Footfalls had a hollow, eerie ring. Service lights burned here and there in the stairwell. Inset in the walls Nick noticed one of the black pull-toggle devices he had seen in the main plant. These were the fire and police alarms which were connected to the village.

On the third floor Rathke went down a hall identical with that on the first. It seemed endless. More of the black pull-toggle alarms were spaced at intervals. Ahead, a steel door brightly lacquered in red loomed. It bore *Keep Out* warnings stenciled in German, English and French.

When Nick asked whether the pilot plant lay beyond, he received a grunt in reply. The big chauffeur pushed the panic-bar and the door swung open. Rathke moved ahead, onto a kind of steel-floored gallery with a rail. Below, for two stories, there was emptiness crisscrossed with a weird tangle of glass piping.

Nick was starting through the scarlet door when he realized the wrongness of it all.

The pilot plant tanks, distillation apparatus, centrifuges, were two floors down on the cement.

Rathke had chosen to bring him into the plant on the third level—the catwalk went all the way round the big chamber in a square at the second level, too.

He was halfway through the door now, and Rathke was midway between door and rail.

Nick broke stride as the notion registered that it was all wrong. This brief hesitation was what Rathke had counted upon. Too late, Nick realized that the chauffeur's mind was less spongy than it seemed. For even as Nick's mind noted the arrangement of the pilot plant—huge windows; the chemical piping swooping up and down like big clear glass arteries in which colored liquids flowed sluggishly—Rathke turned and rolled his shoulder down and came charging in to kill.

Nick tried to keep hold of the attache case and get off a shot at the same time. Rathke's shoulder hit Nick violently at the waist. The attache case dropped, slid away on the catwalk floor. Rathke lifted hard, up and over in one immensely powerful lunge. Nick tumbled down the man's back—straight at the rail and the drop over, and death.

Wildly, Nick shot out his free hand, fingers in a claw.

He caught the top of the railing, grappled for purchase, closed his fingers.

A red-purple pain hit his mind, and his arm was nearly wrenched out of place as it took the whole brunt of his body dropping. But he hung on. He hung by his left hand, cheek smashed against the rail's middle rung.

Rathke threw his cap away. He wiped his sleeve across his upper lip. He smoothed the front of his uniform tunic. He started walking toward the rail. His great black boots gleamed with a leather luster as he came on, nailed heels going *clang-scrape, clang-scrape* with each step.

Nick lifted his right hand with the automatic pistol in it. He hurt from hanging there by one hand, two floors above the concrete of the pilot plant floor. His face contorted as he tried to steady his trembling right hand, aim between the railing rungs.

The chauffeur leaped, closed thick fingers, twisted the gun loose. He threw it, clanging, down the catwalk floor where it slid to a stop several yards away.

Sweat formed on the palms of Nick's left hand, on the inside of his fingers by which he was hanging. That left hand began to slip.

"Is the American growing tired?" Rathke said. He drew out something long that suddenly doubled its length with a *snick*, and shone bright blue.

"Tired of holding on, *jah*?" Rathke continued, pointing the knife blade down at Nick's bloodless left hand clawed around the top rail. Nick struggled to get his right leg up. He managed to do it, giving himself a little extra support on the catwalk's edge.

Rathke kicked his foot away. Nick nearly dropped again. His shoulder took another bad jolt.

"Perhaps we release the fingers with a cut, one at a time," Rathke said. He brought the knife down toward Nick's middle finger knuckle.

The blade edge touched skin, broke through, went down to bone.

Nick bit his tongue to keep from yelling. Every bit of power he had left went into the frantic surge as he brought his right foot up again to the catwalk edge, tore his left hand back, out from under the knife, away from the rail.

His middle finger burned. For a moment he held onto nothing.

Then his grappling right hand caught the rail. With his left he reached up and dragged hard at Rathke's white collar, one quick, strong jerk at the point where the chauffeur's tie was knotted. And suddenly Rathke was pitching over, dumb eyes growing as he sailed past the rail, past Nick.

Rathke seemed to spiral slowly. His boots shone. Then his head struck the concrete and burst.

Something hurt Nick's ears. A deep, throaty sound. As he clambered up over the rail and stumbled across the catwalk, he realized that Rathke had yelled loudly when he went over. Yelled in wild, frantic fear.

How loudly?

Yes. There were footfalls somewhere off the second level of the pilot plant.

Nick could barely move. But he had to move. He shambled over and picked up his gun. Then he headed for the metal service stair down to the main floor.

Halfway to the bottom he passed another of the black pull-toggle devices set in the wall. He was recovering a little from the shock of the fight now. The footfalls had stopped. Had he imagined?

As soon as he set the timer on the explosives, he wanted out of the plant. He wouldn't be able to get much beyond the exercise yard before the explosives blew, however. There were night guards in the main building. They would surely catch him in the open. Some diversion, confusion, might help. But he had to plan for that now, and then move very fast.

Police or fire-fighters from the village would create the right kind of diversion, keep the guards from the main plant busy and give him a chance to escape. Nick reached up and pulled down the toggle. He hoped the alarms really rang in the village.

He went lurching on down the iron steps and out onto the pilot plant floor. Overhead the glass pipes full of liquids—and several contained smokish gasses, he saw—soared and crisscrossed so that he moved through a weird checkerboard of shadows. He ran panting past Rathke's corpse to a central place on the floor, knelt, unfastened the snaps of the attache case.

"That will be quite all, Herr Lamont. *Quite all.*"

Nick twisted his head around. He'd been watching the corridor entrances at the back end of the research wing. Now he saw that the voice came from the opposite side entirely: an almost wholly shadowed doorway on the second level, but on the side leading into the main building.

At the railing was a woman in a dressing gown. Blurrily he recognized her as Judith Yonov. Beside her, gaunt, in an old maroon lounging jacket with black lapels, holding a pistol, was Dr. Sweetkill.

It was Dr. Genther Yonov who had spoken.

He was a tall, slope-shouldered man, mild of face and affecting a tuft of beard.

"Our apartments are on the end of the wing through which you entered," Yonov said as he headed toward the stairway. Judith followed. "We decided it might be prudent to circle around and approach from a different direction. Poor Rathke's yell carried, I'm afraid. Be so kind as to throw the pistol on the floor. Then you will stand back from the briefcase."

Feeling weary and defeated, Nick obeyed. Judith Yonov's voice was stridently sharp, bouncing back and forth across the pilot plant as she followed her father down the stairs:

"From the beginning it had all the smell of a penetration."

"Pity we had to lose Rathke to verify it," Yonov said. Like specters the two came toward him.

Judith Yonov came only part way, however. She stopped, standing back in the shadow thrown by a tall chemical mixing tank. Dr. Yonov appraised the disheveled Nick.

"I am aware," Yonov said, stroking his long scholar's nose with his free hand, "that you triggered the village alarm connections. All doors from this area are now locked, so the police cannot enter except by force. Still, they will be here. Their vans move rapidly. They should arrive at the back gate shortly. Well, I have already decharged that gate. They will have no difficulty getting in to the yard."

Nick's head pounded. What was there to say, or argue about? Yonov had him.

The man called Dr. Sweetkill was in his late fifties. He looked bright enough, but there was an odd, private-world gleam in his deeply set brown eyes.

Nick sucked in long breaths. Why the hell was Dr. Yonov so casual about the police arriving? Had he fixed them? Not all of them, he couldn't have, that wasn't possible. Nick would try talking his way out. Stupid idea, but what else was there now? The gun was gone, dropped on instructions. The attache case lay open several yards away, near a centrifuge recessed into the concrete floor. The case was useless, too.

Dr. Yonov stepped around Nick, instructing him to turn so as to keep his face toward him.

"Who you are makes little difference, though we may learn that in a moment," Yonov said. His thin free hand reached up to a vertical pipe of steel which rose through the floor. A big but delicately balanced wheel with four metal spokes spun at his touch.

Through one of the glass pipes overhead, a whitish fume of smoke went crawling and flittering. Then it twisted and leaped as blowers took over.

"For the moment," Yonov went on, "it's quite enough to say that we have long anticipated a penetration attempt. Obviously they have sent us an amateur. Ah, you're looking at the wheel. Well, out there—" The gun waved toward the high windows which overlooked the night-blackened grass of the exercise yard. "Out there we have an underground valve system. We frequently employ it to test our experimental gasses in the open air on small animals. When there are no humans—no staff members relaxing there, of course," Yonov added with a stilted chuckle. "What you see going through that tube overhead is now being pumped down through conduits and up again through the valves scattered in the grass. If I no longer have the required cover for operating in this facility, then I might just as well leave it in grand style, wouldn't you say so, whoever you are?"

"Red light!" Judith Yonov said from the shadow. "Coming up the road fast."

"The gas mists quite easily," Yonov explained. "They'll not see, feel, taste or smell it until they're in the midst of it. The alarm was an idle gesture on your part. I have not tried this special compound on small animals—or any animals. It will be interesting to note what happens."

Red light whirling, the police van screamed up to the gate in another 90 seconds. Men opened the gate. Others, also armed, followed the first pair across the lawn. Before any of them had reached the halfway point between the fence and the building, they had all dropped, white faces distorted, ugly.

Over the seven incredibly still bodies the revolving van light washed waves of dark red color. Nothing else moved.

"Satisfactory," Dr. Yonov murmured. "Yes, satisfactory." He smiled. "And now, dear friend, we turn to you."

6

Dr. Genther Yonov stroked the ball of his index finger up and down the side of his nose for a meditative moment. Nick's mind was dull, thick, struggling for some way to live, some way to even the wretched odds. Judith Yonov had not stirred from under the shadow of the huge chemical tank. She acted as if she were afraid of the light.

Yonov gave his gun hand a slight twist. The gesture seemed to indicate that he had made up his mind.

"First," he said in a conversational tone, "we had best cut off the gas flow into the yard, else we shall have half the neighborhood dead." Nimbly the man moved to the upright pipe, spun the delicately balanced wheel again. In the act of turning back around he suddenly seemed to move much faster, dancing across the concrete to hit Nick viciously across the side of the head with the pistol muzzle.

Nick stumbled. He tried to fend off the next blow, to right himself, to grab Yonov's gun. Yonov kicked hard with a high, telling kick to the small of the back.

Off balance, Nick skidded across the concrete floor. Suddenly there was nothing beneath him but a great, round circular darkness. Primitive panic brought a yell choking up in his throat.

Everything dropped away. He fell.

He hit hard, with a whanging sound and a cold, nasty smack to the side of his head. He sprawled on the bottom of one of the great stainless steel centrifuges whose upper rims were flush with the concrete floor.

Nick shook his head, crawled to hands and knees. The shadow of Yonov fell across the mirrored interior of the sunken centrifuge. Nick gauged the height up to the concrete floor as hardly more than four feet. But his arms and legs felt heavy, useless. He had to jump. He had to get up, get out of this sunken silvery dish—

Everything twisted again, distorted with pain. He came up on his feet, reached for the lip of the centrifuge. Yonov gave another of his little waves with the gun.

"Judith, please?"

A rasping click somewhere. Suddenly, beneath him, the slippery steel floor seemed to revolve.

The centrifuge was spinning.

Nick was slammed, hurled, around and around. Each time he tried to stand he was thrown helplessly further around the circular inside. Yonov's shadow flicked past, and past again.

Nick felt like he was in a fun-house device, crazy, laughable, but he could not stand up, nor grasp the concrete lip now because force hurled him always outward toward the wall.

Somehow Yonov's voice penetrated, filtering down: "Now, Herr Lamont, before I increase to the next highest r.p.m., perhaps you will tell me for whom you are working?"

Around and around everything went, sickeningly, a blur. Yonov's shadow was the only constant, black across Nick's field of vision every other second or so. Why couldn't he stand *up*?

Each time he tried he was thrown back to hit against the outer wall, revolving more swiftly now. Or was that all in his head?

Above, the next time round, a blue-shiny object glimmered. Yonov's voice as he called down alternately dinned and faded, depending upon the point to which the centrifuge had revolved.

"You are traveling slowly enough to see these objects which I have brought to the rim. Ten-gallon glass chemical vessels. I propose to kick one, then the next, then the third, down into the machine. Then I propose to throw a control which will slide the steel cover outward from its recess, completely covering you and all the broken glass. Instead of mixing up an intermediary as we do in production, I think 30 seconds with the cover closed and the glass flying into you will make a nice blend of blood and pain. Then I propose to slow the machine down again and you will have an opportunity to tell me who assigned you here."

Around and around.

The bell-shaped glass vessel was recognizable to Nick because Yonov's words had made it so. Already Nick could imagine the bits of shattered glass being whirled outward like deadly darts, at his cheeks, his wrists, his eyeballs.

"Say welcome to the first of the glass, my spy friend," said Yonov, pulling back to kick.

Glass shattering. Tinklings, crashings. There was a loud, flat report mingled with the breaking. Nick was still pinned against the wall of the spinning centrifuge. Only a moment later did he realize two peculiar things:

The centrifuge was slowing down.

And Yonov's shadow had vanished from the rim.

In a daze Nick swallowed hard, as the centrifuge came to a full stop by revolving one last time past the body of Dr. Sweetkill.

The scientist lay on his back. His mouth was open in dismay. His eyes were huge and fixed on the piping overhead. Blood bubbled out of a hole in his throat.

That had been the report Nick had heard. A shot. The huge glass vessels stood unbroken. Nick's sweat-blinded eyes finally found the source of all the sounds of shattering—a large lower pane in one of the pilot plant windows had smashed inward.

And threading a path through the litter, wrapped in an old tan trench coat that bore rips from where she'd climbed through the window, and looking pale and frightened, but with a small wicked gun in her right hand—

"My God," Nick said. "My God, Charity. My God."

"I—I thought you were down in there. I couldn't see exactly. I shot twice at the window first, to break it."

Through the night, out where the red van light still revolved, bells jangled.

"The alarms," Nick said. "The breaking glass triggered the plant alarms."

"I had to come after you," she said, her words overlapping his. "You'd told me about the police and fire bells being connected in the village. I was walking—just walking in the street, worrying about you and—" She fell against him. Then after she had buried her face for a moment, she drew back. "The police alarm rang in the station. I heard it from a block away. A van left. I came too. After I ran all the way up here, I saw all those men lying out there. All dead. I thought they would have things in control. I saw Sweetkill through the window. They do teach us how to fire one of these accurately, you know. It's part of the training."

Nick Lamont swallowed a long, sweet breath of air. His temples had stopped hurting. Things had settled into reasonable focus.

"Then we can get out of here. We can—"

"Not as you think," came her voice from the shadows, forgotten till now. "No, not as you think. The young lady's back presents a splendid target. She will please put her gun down, and turn."

Nick stared past Charity, who was frozen, trying to see in the mirrors of his eyes the source of the ugly feminine voice. Nick's belly iced again. He'd drawn a hand that looked like a lucky one at last, and now there was a trump.

Yonov's fallen gun had been retrieved by the girl who came walking out of the shadows.

Charity's fingers whitened about the trigger of her own weapon. Nick gauged the risk, then shook his head. Carefully he reached down and pried her fingers apart.

"I'll throw the gun off to the right," he said.

"Yes," said Judith Yonov. "Then the young lady will please stand to one side."

This Charity did, as Judith Yonov came all the way out of the chemical tank's shadow.

The strong nose, the full figure, the lipstick mouth were as Nick had remembered them. His mind created a beery image of a young woman hiding under a picture hat. Only this woman was not young.

Turkey-skin, all wrinkled and reddish, showed at the throat of her robe. Her hair was dyed. Her eyes veed with folds at the outer corners. Her makeup laid a hideous pink-orange patina over pale skin. She was not pretty, and she was at least Yonov's age.

"You needn't stare," she said. Nick heard false teeth clicking grotesquely. "I am not his daughter. I am his wife. But there are certain reasons why it was more secure for me to remain well hidden under large hats, in dark places." Her voice was dead level. Only a quick glance at Yonov's red-throated corpse betrayed her contempt. "Perhaps you might say I was his guardian. I was his contact, his link with the East, you see. I am the one who gave him a cause, a purpose for his work. Except for the affection the poor idiot felt for me, perhaps you Englishers—I suspect that's what you must be since the young lady has the sound of it in her voice—as I say, but for me, he might have sold you his little bottles instead. Well, I am not so fond of the theatrical as he was. I shall do this quickly. But with pleasure."

Again the eyes flicked bright and fanatic at the dead Sweetkill. She added: "I did not care for Genther personally. It was my duty to care for him. He was valuable. You have destroyed that value. I am duty-bound to finish what he began."

Nick stared at her. He heard the alarm bells still ringing, jangling down the night. He heard voices now, male voices, guards, shouting off in the direction of the main building. They hammered on the steel doors, unable to get in.

On the floor, perhaps a yard away, lay the attache case.

I wonder if I can? Nick thought.

His mind went briefly black. He heard a thunder of a hundred thousand voices on a Sunday afternoon under an Ohio sky. There was no other way. It would never work but he had to try. Up came Judith Yonov's gun muzzle.

With a wide bash of his arm, Nick threw Charity out of the way and did the run.

His right foot came up with less speed but as much fluid power as in the past. *The kick! The kick!* they were screaming somewhere. His foot connected.

Judith Yonov's gun flamed, missed. He had kicked the attache case hard but it seemed to slide forward slowly. Actually there was power in the kick. The case flew. It struck Judith Yonov in the left calf, not hard, but enough to distract her. Her gun hand jerked. A second bullet went upward.

A glass pipe burst, began to leak down viscous greenish fluid that smoked when it hit the concrete. Then, before Nick could stop her, Charity was past him, screaming like no civilized woman should scream.

Judith Yonov tried to shove her back. Charity clawed, pushed. Judith Yonov went tumbling into the centrifuge. Her foot caught the attache case handle. Charity saw the case skitter and gave it a swift kick, almost as an afterthought.

She moved on fast, a blur of hate, of foul words. Her nails broke as she punched and punched at the centrifuge control box.

With a whine, as Judith Yonov howled down there with the case, the centrifuge began to spin.

Now guards were battering at the steel doors with what sounded like sledges. ''Damn fool,'' Nick shouted in a rage at Charity. ''The spin of that thing may detonate all the juice in the case and—''

His chest hurt. Time was pitifully short. He quit squandering time and words and bowled broadside into Charity. *''Run!''*

He drove her along with his shoulder. They tore their clothing and their flesh getting through the shattered window. The dash across the field of dead policeman was nightmarish. Nick had to pick Charity up once when she faltered. He hurled her bodily out through the open gate. Then the black tore open behind them in one blinding, thundering red cloud of detonation that hurled them forward half a dozen yards onto their faces.

On his neck, Nick felt the heat of the death works dying.

7

''What a mess,'' Nick said.

He was panting so hard, he was barely able to speak. ''What a damned indescribable mess.'' He dragged tired hands over his clothes. They were covered with sap, quilled with pine needles.

He and Charity had run parallel with the winding road, all the way down to the village, while the fire vehicles roared up.

The inn was empty. All the personnel and guests were out in the narrow street, watching the furnace-hued sky. They had got in via the back stairs. Now, in the sanctuary of their room, Nick had shot home the iron bolt.

He sat heavy and tired on the bed, saying again, ''A mess. We both look like things off the garbage heap.''

"But we made it."

Charity's words came out as a bare squeak. She tried to laugh about it. Nick scowled. He scowled because her tan trench coat was an untidy collection of blood spots and tears and sap stains. She looked sick, wretched, tired and happy.

Nick said the first thing that came into his head:

"That was a stupid thing—"

Disbelief, utter fury sparked in the girl's eyes as her head came up.

"What?"

"Killing the Yonov woman. Going crazy. It was a callous, dirty thing."

"Are you so blasted tired you don't know what you're saying?"

"You murdered her."

"Who told you this was dancing class anyway, you son of a bitch?" Tears were on her cheeks, tears coming fast as she balled her fists at her sides. "I seem to remember a man named Tenderly in Gib. A man you killed, and here I'd got it into my head that maybe I had to forgive you and now you pull this on me!"

She sank down.

"Don't you know why? Don't you know why I did it?"

Slowly she lifted her head to look at him. She was no longer crying out of anger:

"Because, Nick, I wanted you to live, not her."

He let out a breath which was more like a choke. The relief came. An end to the guilt. Wiped clean. Understanding seeped into his fatigue-dulled mind. He went toward her and sat beside her. New shiny-bright Jaguars no longer existed. Even Wilburforce hardly seemed worth bothering about.

Charity kissed him, hungrily, open-mouthed. He tried to show her he understood, and wanted her. He reached and fumbled at her clothing. Finally, when he had her living, round breast cupped in his fingers, feeling the warm rising life of it, there was no longer a need for fear.

"The local police, Nicky."

"Tomorrow."

"But—"

"Old Icy-Guts will fix it."

"I still worry that—"

"Please shut up."

They fell back together, tired, wanting. Soon the antidote was there for both of them, close together. The curtains of the inn room had been drawn tight when they crept in, so they never saw the red light of burning anymore in the German sky that night.

PETER O'DONNELL

The Giggle-Wrecker

THE MINISTER LIGHTLY underlined a few words on the report in front of him, then looked across his desk at Sir Gerald Tarrant and said, "I'm advised that Professor Okubo is the best bacteriologist in the world. It's a vital aspect of defense today, and if he's available we want to have him. We must have him."

Tarrant sighed inwardly. He held Waverly in good esteem and liked the man personally. But, perhaps like all politicians, Waverly sometimes allowed his judgment to be swayed by a particular enthusiasm; and as Minister of Defense, Waverly's great enthusiasm was scientific research in the military field.

"If you want Okubo badly, Minister," Tarrant said, "then I think you should talk to somebody else about it. My organization in East Berlin isn't geared for getting a defector out."

Waverly began to fill his pipe. He was a stocky man with small, intelligent eyes in a heavy face. "I've persuaded the PM that this calls for a special effort," he said.

Sixteen years ago Okubo had slipped away from American surveillance in Tokyo and reappeared in Moscow. It had long been known that he was a brilliant young scientist, but of suspect political views. Until his defection it was not known that he was a dedicated Communist. Now, at the age of forty, he had become disenchanted with Marx's brave new world, and had defected anew, but it was a messy and poorly planned defection. Tarrant did not like it at all.

He said, "Even if we got him out, I don't think you could hold him for long. The Americans would offer him a million-pound laboratory set-up. Why should he stay with us and make do with a Bunsen burner and a bit of litmus paper?"

Waverly smiled. "Come now. You know I've wrung enormous increases from the Treasury for scientific work. And we seem to be Okubo's personal choice. Just get him out and leave the rest to me.''

First news of Okubo's disappearance from Moscow had come direct to Waverly from the Embassy Intelligence there. Within forty-eight hours there had been rumors in foreign newspapers, followed by denials. It was then that Tarrant had been called in. He did not like being handed a job that was already begun and had been botched, though there was nobody to blame for this but Okubo himself.

The Minister said, ''You've done very well so far.''

''I haven't had the chance to do either well or badly yet,'' Tarrant said courteously. ''You asked me to get a line on Okubo, and then he just turned up.''

''Yes.'' Waverly looked down at the report again. ''This is very brief. How did he get from Moscow to Berlin?''

''By way of Prague. After the Russians walked in there our Prague Section managed to recruit one or two embittered Czech party members. One was a scientist who knew Okubo well. Apparently they hatched this clumsy escape plan between them. Okubo got to Prague under his own steam without any difficulty and went to ground there. Then his friend informed Prague Control, and they managed to get Okubo as far as East Berlin. I don't think it was the best thing to do, but from the report sent to me I fancy Okubo is an awkward customer who likes things done according to his own ideas. Anyway, Prague found themselves holding this very hot potato and I don't blame them for getting rid of Okubo as fast as they could. If he'd given us any warning of his intention to defect we could have handled things much more smoothly. Even now, given time and given his cooperation, I can get Okubo out, either by the Baltic coast or back through Czechoslovakia and over the border into Austria. But the man who's keeping Okubo under wraps at the moment reports that he won't cooperate.''

Waverly shrugged. ''It's understandable. When you're little more than a stone's throw from freedom, you don't want to start traveling the other way. Besides, we have to make allowances for scientific genius. You'll just have to accept the situation, and bring him out from East to West Berlin.''

Tarrant said bluntly, ''I'm sorry. I haven't the facilities.''

The Minister frowned. ''If he can be got from Moscow to Berlin, surely you can get him over the Wall? It's only another hundred yards or so.''

''A very particular hundred yards, Minister. Okubo is Japanese, and only four feet ten inches high. In an Aryan country he couldn't be more obvious if he carried a banner with his name on it. Getting him out would require a major operation. Worst of all, we're not the only ones who know he's in East Berlin. The KGB knows it, too."

Waverly had been about to draw on his pipe. Now he paused. "How do you know that?"

Tarrant hesitated. He hated giving needless information, even to a Minister of the Crown. Reluctantly he said, "We've had a man in East German Security HQ for seven years now."

"I see. I won't mention it at cocktail parties," Waverly said with mild irony. He got up from his desk and walked to the window. "If the Russians know Okubo is there, I imagine they're turning East Berlin upside down, and as you say, it can't be easy to hide a Japanese. The sooner he's out, the better."

"The Russians aren't making a tooth-comb search," Tarrant said. "They know we have Okubo in a safe-house, and they're simply waiting for him to move. Then they'll net him. Starov's no fool."

"Starov?"

"Major-General Starov. Head of Russian Security in East Berlin. He's very devious. A man I fear."

Waverly returned to the desk. "You said it would require a major operation to bring Okubo out. I see what you mean. But you'll just have to mount one."

Tarrant kept a tight hold on the fear and anger he felt. "We've spent fifteen years building up the network we have in East Berlin," he said quietly. "It takes time to recruit safely and to get people planted, but we have a very nice tight little network now. Agents have been spotted carefully. They don't do anything. They're sleepers, and they've been placed there for one purpose only—so that we can activate them if and when the Berlin situation ever really catches fire. That's the real crunch, and they shouldn't be activated for anything else, however tempting. I suggest Okubo isn't worth it, Minister. It's like using *kamikaze* pilots to sink a row-boat."

Waverly stared into space for a while, then said, "Can you hire agents for the job? Money's no object for this."

Tarrent sat up a little. "No object to whom, Minister? The budget for all Secret Service departments was cut last year and again this year. We now have just over ten million pounds annually. I doubt if that would pay the CIA's telephone bill."

Waverly shook his head. "You're too old a hand to be disenchanted by Government parsimony. The Americans can afford it, and we can't. But you needn't touch your budget for this. I can secure money from the

Special Fund. Surely you can hire the necessary personnel? I understand there are more free-lance agents in West Berlin than we have civil servants in Whitehall."

"There are almost as many Intelligence groups as that," Tarrant said dryly. "Some agents have become so entangled in the situation that they find it hard to remember who they're working for. And since there's precious little liaison, they spend most of their time industriously liquidating each other's agents by mistake. The fact that many of the groups have been penetrated by Russian Intelligence complicates matters. Add in the free-lances, the doubles and the triples, and you have a situation which must make the Russians laugh themselves to sleep at nights."

Waverly smiled. It was a small and not very humorous smile. "Then if you can trust nobody else, you'll have to use your own people."

"I thought I'd covered that point, Minister."

"No." Waverly looked into Tarrant's eyes. "No, not really. You said Okubo wasn't worth risking your network for. But what Okubo is worth is a Ministerial decision. My decision."

There was a very long silence in the room. "Of course," Tarrant said at last, and got to his feet. "I'll keep you fully informed, Minister."

When Modesty Blaise came into the reception hall of the penthouse block she appeared to be accompanied by a small but very handsome walnut tallboy of Queen Anne's day, moving on human feet that protruded from beneath it.

Willie Garvin set the tallboy down and wiped his brow. He had sat with it resting across him in the back of Modesty's open Rolls while she drove the eighty-odd miles from the country house where the auction sale had been held.

She was looking apologetic now, as well as stunningly attractive in the powder-blue matching dress and jacket she wore. "I'm sorry, Willie," she said as he stretched his cramped muscles. "I ought to have let them send it."

"That's right," Willie agreed amiably.

"But I kept remembering how that lovely little table was ruined last year."

Willie nodded judicially. "That's right, too."

"So it was better to bring it with us, really."

"That's right, Princess."

She grinned suddenly, patted his arm and said, "You ought to get mad at me sometimes for my own good."

"Next time." He looked past her and registered mild surprise. "Look who's 'ere."

A man had risen from an armchair in the reception hall and was moving toward them. He carried a bowler hat and a rolled umbrella. His name was Fraser, and he was Sir Gerald Tarrant's personal assistant.

Fraser was a small bespectacled man with a thin face and a timorous manner. The picture he chose to present most of the time was one of nervous humility. This was a role he had acted for so long that it was a part of him. Sometimes, within a tiny circle of close intimates, the role was dropped and the real Fraser appeared. This was another man, and a very hard personality indeed. Fraser had served as an agent in the field for fifteen years before returning to a desk job, and he had been one of the great agents.

Now he said with an anxious smile, "I hope my visit isn't . . . I mean, I tried to telephone you, Miss Blaise, but—er . . . so I thought I'd come along and wait for you."

"That's all right. I wanted to go over the policy with you before I signed," Modesty said, and turned to the porter behind the reception desk. "George, will you give Mr. Garvin a hand to get this thing in the lift?"

A private lift served Modesty's penthouse. There was just room for the three of them and the tallboy. Going up in the lift, Fraser retained his servile manner, commenting fulsomely but knowledgeably on the tallboy.

Willie lifted it out and set it down in the tiled foyer. Modesty led the way into the big sitting-room, taking off her jacket, and said, "Is something wrong, Jack?"

Fraser grimaced, threw the hat and umbrella on to a big couch and stared at them sourly. "Tarrant's resigning," he said, discarding his image. "Bloody hell. The longer I live, the more I sympathize with Guy Fawkes, except that blowing up politicians is too good for them. Do you think I could have a drink?"

Modesty nodded to Willie, who moved to the bar and poured a double brandy. He knew Fraser's tastes.

"Why is he resigning?" Modesty asked.

"If I tell you that," Fraser said, "I shall be breaking the Official Secrets Act." He sipped the brandy, sighed, and said, "God, this is good. If anyone ever wants to ruin it with dry ginger, I hope you break their teeth."

Modesty and Willie glanced at each other. Fraser was a badly worried man, and that was so unlikely as to be alarming.

"So let's drive a truck through the Official Secrets Act," Fraser said with gloomy relish. "There's some bloody Jap bacteriologist who's been working for the Russians for years. Professor Okubo. He's defected and he's in East Berlin now, being kept under wraps by our liaison man. Our masters want him. Waverly's told Tarrant to get him out—even though Starov *knows* he's in hiding there. We can't do it without activating the sleeper network. Tarrant's been told to go ahead and do just that." Fraser shook his head. "My sister's husband would have more sense, and I wouldn't match *him* against a smart dog, the thick bastard."

Willie Garvin whistled softly. This was bad. He saw that Modesty was angry. Like him, she was thinking of the agents, the men and women who for years had lived the bleak, comfortless and restricted life of East Berliners, and who with luck might go on doing so for years more, simply so that they could be activated if ever a crisis got out of hand and the chips went down.

At very best the job was a sentence to long barren years of deprivation. At worst, a bad break would mean torture and death. God alone knew why they did it. But they did. And the very least acknowledgment they could be given was not to sell them down the river by needless exposure.

"If Tarrant resigns," Fraser said brusquely, "we lose the best man ever to hold the job. That's one thing. It's bad, but we seem to specialize in self-inflicted wounds, so it's nothing new. The second thing is this. If he resigns, they'll put in somebody who will agree to do what Tarrant won't. The new boy will activate the network to get this bloody Japanese measles expert out, and it's an odds-on chance that Starov will have the lot." He looked into his glass and said broodingly, "I've been where they're sitting now. It's not funny."

Modesty said, "You're asking us to do something?"

Fraser gave her a lopsided, humorless smile. He looked suddenly tired. "Not asking," he said. "I don't see what the hell you or anybody can do. I'm just telling you and hoping. Hoping you might think of *some* way to save those poor trusting buggers in East Berlin."

Nobody spoke for a while. Fraser looked up and saw that Willie Garvin was leaning against the wall by the fireplace, looking at Modesty with an almost comically inquiring air, as if they were sharing some faintly amusing joke.

She got up and moved to the telephone, saying, "Do you know where Sir Gerald is now?"

"At the office," Fraser said, hardly daring to acknowledge the flare of hope that leapt within him. "Composing his resignation, I imagine."

She dialed the direct number, waited a few seconds, then said, "It's

Modesty. Do you think you could call here very soon, Sir Gerald? Something urgent has come up.'' A pause. ''Thank you. In about twenty minutes, then.''

She put down the phone. Willie had moved and stood looking down at Fraser with a wicked grin. He said, ''Tarrant swore he'd never get the Princess tangled up in another caper. He's going to 'ave you guts for this, Fraser, my old mate.''

When Tarrant arrived, Willie Garvin was absent. The sight of Fraser, and his simple statement, ''I've told her,'' left no need for further explanation. Even Tarrant's immense control was barely sufficient to contain his fury.

Fraser went into his humble and pathetic act, was blasted out of it, and sat in dour silence, his face a little pale, as Tarrant lashed him with a cold but blistering tongue.

Modesty allowed time for the first shock to be absorbed, then broke in briskly. ''He came to me because he's concerned about your sleeper network, Sir Gerald. Let's talk about that now.''

''No, my dear.'' He turned to her. ''I wouldn't send one of my salaried agents into East Berlin for this job, much less you. Don't think me ungrateful. I even recognize Fraser's good intentions. But I won't allow you to attempt an impossible mission.''

''A few people who trust you are going to die if we don't do something.''

''I know.'' There was a gray tinge to Tarrant's face. ''If I thought you stood a chance of geting Okubo out . . .'' He shrugged. ''Perhaps I'd forget the promise I've made to myself, and ask your help. But there isn't a chance. The Berlin Wall is virtually impenetrable now. Oh, I know there have been plenty of escapes, but not recently. People used to escape over it, under it and through it. But not anymore.''

Absently he took the glass she handed him and muttered his thanks. ''It's different now,'' he said. ''And it was never easy. You'd need three figures to count the tunnels dug during the years since the Wall was built, but only a dozen succeeded. Now there are detection devices to locate tunnels. People have crossed the Wall in every possible way. By breeches-buoy on a high cable. By battering through it with a steamroller. They've used locomotives on the railway and steamers on the canal. They've swum and they've run and they've climbed. Over two hundred have died. With each new idea, the East Germans have taken measures to prevent it being used again. And the West Berlin people have stopped being cooperative now. They don't like messy incidents at the Wall.''

He gave her a tired smile. ''I can't send you into that. There's not only the Wall itself. There are guards by the hundred, highly trained guard dogs, and antipersonnel mines. There's a wired-off thirty-yard death strip even before you can reach the Wall from the east. That's where most people die. There are infrared cameras and trip wires and waterway patrols. And nobody gets smuggled through a checkpoint anymore, certainly not Okubo."

He emptied his glass and put it down. "I know your ability and resources. Perhaps you could find a way out, given time. But you can't even get inside safely at short notice. You could never enter East Berlin as yourself, and a sound cover-identity would take months to establish."

Modesty smiled at him. "Don't be such an old misery. I have a friend with special facilities for entering East Berlin."

Before Tarrant could answer there came the faint hum of the ascending lift. The doors in the foyer opened and a man stepped out. He was tall and wore a well-cut dark suit. His hair had once been fair but was now almost entirely gray, prematurely gray to judge by his face, which was rather round and bore a healthy tan. He wore horn-rimmed spectacles, and was beginning to thicken around the waist.

"Ah, there you are," Modesty said as he moved forward and down the three steps which pierced the wrought-iron balustrade separating the foyer from the sitting-room. "It's good of you to drop everything and come so quickly. Sir Gerald, I'd like you to meet Sven Jorgensen."

The man shook hands and said in good English with a slight accent, "A pleasure to meet you, Sir Gerald."

Tarrant said, "How do you do." He was puzzled and a little distressed. Why the hell had Modesty brought in a foreign stranger, right in the middle of a top-secret discussion? He trusted her judgment completely, but—

Why on earth was Jorgensen prolonging the handshake, gazing at him in that odd way?

Jorgensen said in Willie Garvin's voice, "You're not concentrating, Sir G."

Tarrant heard Fraser rip off a delighted oath, and struggled hard not to show his own surprise. Yes, he could see it now, as if suddenly seeing the hidden face in a child's puzzle-picture. The disguise was not heavy. There was the superb and undetectable wig, and the pads which altered the shape of the face, but the rest of the transformation lay mainly in manner, posture and movement.

Tarrant said, "Hallo, Willie. You're right. I wasn't concentrating."

"We go in from Sweden by air," Modesty said. "Willie is Herr Jorgensen, who runs a small antique and rare-book business in Gothenberg. I'm his secretary. I can't show you what I'll look like just now because I have to dye my hair, but I'll be equally convincing."

"I'm sure you will." Tarrant shook his head slowly. "But it still won't do, Modesty. Foreign businessmen or visitors are automatically suspect in East Germany, you know that. You'll be watched. Your rooms may be bugged, your passports intensely checked. You simply won't get away with it."

"We have got away with it for the last five years," Willie said in his rather stilted Jorgensen voice, and took out a packet of Swedish cigarettes. Tarrant looked at Modesty. She said, "We've made a ten- or twelve-day trip to East Berlin from Sweden every year for the last five. The antique business in Gothenberg is quite genuine and belongs to us."

Fraser said, "But for Christ's sake, *why* do you do it?"

She gave a little shrug. "We began it a year or two before we retired from crime. It seemed a useful provision, to see what went on behind the Curtain and to establish credible identities there. We kept it up because it seemed a pity to let the thing lapse. The East Berlin police have Herr Jorgensen and Fröken Osslund on record. We're been tailed and bugged and checked and politely questioned. They've given up tailing us now. We know that, because we always know if we're being tailed. They may still bug our rooms. We never bother to check, because even if the rooms were clean there might be three bugs in each when we got back from a trip. So when we talk in our rooms, we talk in character."

"You make trips?" Tarrant said. "Outside East Berlin?"

"Yes. We advertise in a few newspapers, and people with likely stuff to sell telephone us at the hotel. We go and see what they've got, and buy any reasonable antiques or books. Not just in Berlin, but in Potsdam, Dresden, Frankfurt and any number of small towns. We've kept our noses clean, we've done straight business and we make immediate payment in kroner or dollars, then ship the stuff to Gothenberg. Nobody can suspect that we're anything other than what we seem."

Fraser said in an awed voice. "You actually go there once a year? You go and spend ten days or so in that God-awful country, just to maintain these identities?"

"It's a chore," Modesty said, "but it always seemed potentially useful. And now it's going to be. The only thing the security people there might suspect is that I'm Willie's bird and that he takes me on business trips so he can have a little fun at a safe distance from his own doorstep." She grinned. "They won't have heard any confirmation of that over the bugs."

Willie lit a cigarette and moved to pour a drink. His walk and his mannerisms were still Jorgensen's. "We can be there in thirty-six hours," he said.

Tarrant rubbed his eyes with fingers and thumb, trying to collect his thoughts. "You'd still have to find a way of getting Okubo *out,*" he said slowly.

A hand was laid on his arm and he heard Modesty's voice, warm and understanding. She would know that his part—the safe, waiting part—was always the most agonizing. "Come on now," she said. "Don't worry so much. You know we've always come back before."

"Just," said Tarrant. "Only just." He opened his eyes to look at her. He was a widower and lost his sons in the war. With sudden and painful perception he realized that this dark-haired girl, smiling at him now, had in some measure filled the long emptiness in him. For a moment he hated his job with weary passion, and hated himself for letting sentiment lay its soft fingers upon him. It was as if he were throwing his own flesh and blood to wolves when he said, "Try to make coming back a little less marginal this time."

She slipped her arm through his and moved toward the foyer. "We'll be very careful. Come and see the tallboy I picked up at the Rothley Manor auction."

It was a beautiful piece, with inlaid intarsia panels and in almost perfect condition. For a moment the sight and touch of it lifted Tarrant's depression by a degree. He saw that Modesty was completely absorbed and that her face was lit with pleasure.

She said, almost apologetically, "Fifteen pounds."

He could not believe it. "My dear, you could get close to a thousand for it at Christie's any day. The dealers must have been blind."

"There weren't any. If you go far enough out of London for a sale, you often find the dealers haven't bothered. But I didn't buy it to sell. I just want to enjoy it."

The moment passed, and Tarrant felt aching anxiety descend on him again.

"For God's sake make sure you're able to," he said.

The printing shop lay in a narrow street not far from Alexanderplatz. Toller was a fair, thickset man in his late forties. He said, "Ah, yes. I don't know if the books have any great value, Herr Jorgensen, but when I read your advertisement I thought it worthwhile to telephone you. Come this way, please."

Willie Garvin and Modesty Blaise followed him through the printing shop, where half a dozen men were working. Her hair was dark chestnut now, and body padding made her look thirty pounds heavier. Contact lenses gave her eyes a different color, and a molded hoop of plastic round the gumline of her lower jaw had altered the shape of her face.

A small flat-bed machine was churning out propaganda pamphlets for the West. Bundles of these would be stuffed into papier-mâché containers, loaded into modified mortars, and fired across at different points along the 850-mile frontier of minefields, watchtowers and barbed wire. The pamphlets bore pinup pictures and enthusiastic accounts of the happy life led by one and all in the Democratic Republic.

In return, and because the prevailing wind was favorable, pamphlets from West Germany would come drifting across the frontier suspended from balloons with clockwork scatter-mechanism. It was all a heavy-handed exercise in pinprick irritation.

Toller closed the door of the print shop and opened another across the passage. They entered a small room, sparsely furnished, and when Toller closed the door all sound of machinery was muffled to a whisper.

"This room is safe," Toller said softly. His manner was steady, but looking beneath the surface Modesty saw the underlying tension.

"You have him here?" she asked. They spoke in German.

Toller jerked his head back slightly, lifting his eyes toward the ceiling. "Upstairs. It is three days since the courier brought instructions to me for making contact with you. Two days since I telephoned."

"We had to maintain our routine." Modesty said. "Is communication with West Berlin difficult?"

"There is always some risk. Couriers must be foreign nationals and can operate only for a limited time. But as foreigners you can pass freely yourselves."

"We won't do that. We've never gone to and fro before, and it would look suspicious if we started now. Zarov must be very much on his toes."

Toller said, "Very much. We use no radio. We have them, but for emergency only. The big emergency. Apart from that, communication with London Control must go through Local Control in West Berlin, by courier."

London Control had moved to West Berlin. Tarrant himself was there now. But Modesty did not tell Toller that. A spy dislikes holding more information than is necessary for what he has to do. She said, "I've arranged a new system of communication for this mission. I'll tell you about it after we've seen Okubo. We'll be taking him off your hands tonight."

Toller said fervently, "Thank God for that. He is very difficult. I have been more afraid in the last ten days than in the last ten years."

Okubo was in a small upper room with a single shuttered window overlooking an enclosed yard. There was a bed, a chair set at a plain deal table and a battered chest of drawers. A big china jug of water stood in a bowl on top of the chest. Okubo lay on the bed, smoking. He wore a rumpled dark gray suit and was very short but well proportioned. His thick black hair was sleek, and he had a vestigial mustache of which the hairs could almost be counted. His eyes were unfriendly and arrogant.

He sat up and spoke in rather high-pitched, liquid English, with a marked American accent. "Are these the people, Toller? I was beginning to wonder if they existed."

"The situation is not easy for them," Toller said. He sounded like a man who had said the same thing many times.

Okubo looked through Modesty, then stared at Willie without warmth. "You will explain your plan."

Modesty said, "It's a simple one—"

"I did not address you," Okubo broke in without looking at her.

Willie Garvin put his hands in his pockets, and Modesty saw his eyes behind the plain-glass spectacles go blank for a moment as he killed the instinctive flare of anger within him. Toller had not exaggerated in saying that Okubo was difficult. He was the best virus-man in the world, much sought after, and he knew it. Allied to his professional arrogance was the traditional male Japanese attitude toward the female. Okubo was not going to accept the idea of a woman running this operation.

She caught Willie's eye. He took over and said, speaking without his usual Cockney accent, "We're using an opportunity that happens to be available. De Souta is in Berlin this week—"

"De Souta?"

"Special United Nations Representative for U Thant. He's having talks on both sides of the Wall at local level, trying to reduce tension."

Okubo's mouth twisted in contempt. His reaction was justified. De Souta's efforts were futile. He no doubt knew this himself, but he was a dedicated man and had patiently suffered rebuffs in various parts of the world in the course of his peace-making attempts.

Willie said, "He's staying at his own Embassy here, and there's a set pattern to the talks. West Berlin in the morning, East Berlin in the afternoon. Every day at nine A.M. he goes through the checkpoint in his car, with his own chauffeur. The guards know the car. They just make sure he's in it, then wave it through. It's the only car that isn't checked. Tomorrow, you'll be in the boot. It's a Daimler, so there'll be plenty of room."

Okubo threw his cigarette on the floor. It was Toller who trod it out. "You must be a fool," Okubo said. "A United Nations representative would never involve himself."

"He won't know," Willie said. "The car's kept in a lock-up garage near the Embassy, and we've hired a lock-up in the same block. We've made a dry run on this, and it works. We'll get you into the garage and into the boot by eight o'clock, so you'll only have an hour to wait. I drilled some air-holes last night in the floor. The car stops at the Hilton. That's where De Souta talks to Mayor Klaus Schütz, to keep things informal. Wait five minutes after the car stops, then get out. I've fixed the lock so you can open the boot from inside. One of our men will be on the spot, waiting for you."

Okubo lit another cigarette and stared at Willie coldly. "It is a stupid plan," he said. "If your people want me, they should arrange a practical operation, meticulously organized, and covered by an experienced group—"

"Nobody's going to start a war to get you out," Willie said. "We're using an opportunity that's simple and that works." He gave Okubo no time to reply but said to Toller, "Can you bring him to that car park north of Rosenthaler Platz at midnight?"

Toller nodded.

"All right. We'll be there in a gray Skoda. I'll have the bonnet up and I'll be fiddling with the engine. Park alongside if you can. Have Okubo in overalls. He slides out and into the Skoda. Then you can forget him."

Okubo's face was hard with anger. He said, "I have told you—"

"I know you have," Willie cut in. "But don't. Don't tell us how to get you out of East Berlin, and we won't tell you how to breed foot-and-mouth bugs. All we want to know is if you're going to be in that car park at midnight."

The hatred of pricked vanity flamed in Okubo's dark eyes. He looked away. After a long silence he said, "Very well. You force me to agree."

Toller's sigh of relief was audible. He opened the door, and followed Modesty and Willie out. In the room below, Willie exhaled and rubbed a hand across the back of his neck. He swore softly and said in English, "We got a little beauty there. You signaled me to lean on 'im, Princess. I didn't make it too strong?"

"Just right. It worked. But he scares me."

Toller nodded his head in grim agreement. "It is a good plan. Very good. But Okubo has a great sense of his importance. I think he wished for some big, dramatic affair."

"Yes." Modesty took a compact from her handbag and checked her appearance. Her face was too taut, and she worked the muscles to relax them. "Dramatics are all right. But not when the man awarding the Oscars is Major-General Starov."

* * *

In the afternoon they drove out to a village north of Halle, to see a farmer who had telephoned after reading one of their advertisements. He had, he said, over two dozen carved wooden fairground animals for sale, cockerels and horses and ostriches. The small antique business in Gothenberg was managed by a competent Swede who kept abreast of the whims of fashion and who had told Modesty that there was a ready market at up to eighty pounds apiece for these curiosities from the old fairground roundabouts.

At the farm they were shown round three big barns, almost filled with circus and fairground equipment. The owner of a tenting circus, a Hungarian, had disappeared with all the cash takings at the end of last summer, leaving the season's rent unpaid and the performers and handling staff short of a month's wages.

Some of the circus acts had taken their gear and departed. But others, perhaps recognizing that theirs was a dying profession, had simply abandoned their gear and dispersed. Since the Hungarian had chosen to decamp with the lady lion-tamer, the farmer had found himself with six mangy lions to feed until they were taken over by a zoo. He had a long and harrowing story to tell about this.

Willie, who in his early twenties had once worked for a spell in a circus, was fascinated by the evocative sights and smells of the tawdry equipment. There were moldering tents, broken seating, sections of a dismantled roundabout and helter-skelter; rusting donkey engines and a miniature railway track; cages and cables, a huge cannon, a clowns' car with eccentric wheels and a set of distorting mirrors with most of the silvering gone. But only the roundabout animals were of any real value. Beneath the dirt and peeling paint they were exceptionally good specimens, free from worm and dry-rot, beautifully carved, and with the wooden eyes which set them above the cheaper type with eyes of glass.

After some uncertain bargaining on the farmer's part, Willie agreed to buy the twenty best for eighteen hundred kroner or the dollar equivalent, and to pay all transport charges. Modesty made a note of the transaction in a little book. She was pleased with the afternoon's work. Doing genuine business was important in strengthening their cover.

They drove out past Leipzig to look at some clocks, and were back in Berlin by seven that evening. Willie drove the car into one of the hired lock-up garages, only three doors from the garage where the Daimler of the United Nations representative was kept.

As he switched off he said softly, "I'll be glad when this one's over, Princess. That bug-fancier gets under my skin."

Modesty felt the same. It was a neat and beautifully simple caper.

Willie's idea. But like Willie, she felt that Okubo himself was the weak link, the dangerous element. And there was nothing they could do about that.

The pick-up at midnight went smoothly. Okubo was left to spend the night on the back seat of the Skoda in the garage. His manner was unchanged. He did not seem to be afraid, only resentful and ungracious, complaining of the inadequacy of the arrangements for his escape.

At eight in the morning, as Herr Jorgensen and his secretary, they left the hotel and took the Skoda out of the garage, with Okubo lying on the back seat. Willie immediately stalled it directly outside the door of the Daimler garage, and pretended to have difficulty in restarting. While he raised the bonnet and checked the leads, Modesty opened the door of the Daimler garage with the key Willie had made two days ago. Okubo slid out of the Skoda and into the darkness of the garage.

Surprisingly, he did not renew his complaints of the night before, but seemed subdued as he curled up in the big boot of the Daimler. She whispered, "Don't worry. We'll be watching you all the way." He nodded, saying nothing, and she closed the boot. A minute later she was in the Skoda with Willie, heading for Toller's yard.

Now, an hour later, Okubo was less than half a mile from Checkpoint Charlie and freedom. The Daimler moved smoothly along the Friedrichstrasse and crossed the intersection of Unter den Linden. Willie Garvin, driving a dirty brown van, kept on its tail. He wore overalls which covered his Jorgensen suit, and a beret pulled down low. Immediately behind him, Modesty was driving the Skoda.

Ahead lay Leipziger Strade. Willie prepared to turn off. He could go no farther without coming to the checkpoint.

It was then that shock hit him like a full-blooded jab under the heart. The Daimler was slowing, pulling into the curb, moving a little bumpily. The nearside tire was flat. He whispered, "*Jesus!*" The chauffeur would have to open the boot to release the spare wheel.

Willie Garvin became suddenly immensely calm. He put out his hand in a quick signal to Modesty, a wave-on followed by a chopping halt sign. As the Daimler stopped he pulled in behind it, leaving a space of no more than five feet between his front bumper and the rear of the Daimler. In the Skoda, Modesty came up alongside and stopped, covering the gap between the two vehicles.

She saw the flat tire, saw the chauffeur alighting. Willie was already out of the van. He glanced at her without interest and she gave him a fractional nod. From long years of working dangerously together their minds were sensitively attuned. His glance had simply asked for her confirmation to go ahead with what they both knew was the only way to snatch Okubo from disaster.

Willie would meet the chauffeur at the rear of the Daimler and offer to help. When the chauffeur opened the boot, Willie would drop him with a body-jab at close quarters. And while Modesty, anxious and fluttering, tapped on the Daimler window to tell De Souta his chauffeur had apparently fainted, Willie would get Okubo out of the boot and into the van.

The whole move was electric with danger, but it would take only five seconds and there was no other option now. A car hooted and swung out past Modesty. She made an apologetic gesture, started the engine and stalled as soon as it fired. The chauffeur had spoken to his master and was moving round to the rear of the Daimler. With an air of hopeful cupidity Willie said in German, "You want a hand with it?" The chauffeur looked slightly surprised. Then, grasping that goodwill was not the motive, he nodded indifferently and bent to open the boot. As he lifted the lid Modesty saw Willie's rigid hand poised to stab forward, his body hiding it from any passing pedestrian. Then he froze.

She could see into the boot, and it was empty. No Okubo. The chauffeur began to winch down the spare wheel from its resting place. Willie rubbed his chin and turned his head so that his gaze passed idly across her. Now what? She gave a little backward jerk of her head, then started the Skoda and moved off, turning down Leipziger Strade. Anger, relief and speculation all battled for a place in her mind.

An hour later Willie drove the van into Toller's yard. She was waiting for him in the big garage, and said, "We're alone. It's safe to talk."

He began to take off his overalls and said grimly, "Where's the little bastard now?"

"Back where he started. Up in Toller's room."

"You found 'im still in the lock-up garage?"

"Yes. He changed his mind at the last minute, he tells me, so he hid under a tarpaulin there when the chauffeur came to get the Daimler out."

"Changed 'is mind? He wants to go back to Moscow?"

She shook her head. "Changed his mind about accepting our plan for getting him out. I managed to smuggle him into the Skoda without anyone seeing, and I brought him back here. Toller was ripe to kill him when we turned up."

Willie took off the beret and inserted the rubber pads in his cheeks. His movements were taut and precise. She knew that he was boiling with anger. Her own fury had had time to cool now. She said, "It could have been worse, Willie love. I know that flat tire was a million-to-one chance, but it happened. We might have scooped Ocubo out of the boot and into the van safely, but we could only have brought him back here.''

Willie let out a long breath and nodded reluctant agreement. ''Did you tell Okubo what 'appened?''

She grimaced. ''No. He's bad enough without being given a chance to say I-told-you-so. I just tore him apart for fouling up the plan. But I'm female so he hardly listened. He just wants to know what the next move will be.''

''I wouldn't mind knowing that meself,'' Willie said bleakly, and put on his plain-glass spectacles.

''I told him that we'd have to lay on a major operation, but that it would take a few days to organize.''

''Willie stared. ''Activating Tarrant's lot?''

''Yes. That's what Okubo wants. A big show. I thought we might let him believe he'll get it.''

Willie relaxed, gazing at her curiously, trying to mesh with her thoughts. Then his eyebrows lifted and he gave a little nod of comprehension. ''Yes. You could be right, Princess.''

His anger had vanished now. They stood in silence for a while, their minds mutually preoccupied. At last Willie said, ''Tarrant should've got the message last night. It'll make 'im sweat when Okubo doesn't 'op out of that Daimler.''

''Yes.'' She gave a wry shrug. ''He's used to sweating. We'll get another message to him tonight.''

''Same way?''

''The same way. I don't want to use couriers. I don't want to rely on anybody but us. And Toller. We'll use the pamphlet bomb again. Toller says they're firing nightly for the next two weeks at least.''

Willie grinned. The idea was Modesty's, and he thought it a knockout. Toller printed the propaganda pamphlets and packed them in papier-mâché ''bombs'' which were fired over the border from crude mortars. He made a delivery of bombs nightly to gun sites along a four-mile stretch of the border south of Berlin.

It was easy to make a stronger bomb, a container which would not burst and scatter its contents. It would contain no pamphlets but would carry a homing device transmitting on a set frequency and activated by the shock of the discharge. Toller would deliver that bomb, with the usual issue, to a prearranged site. On the other side of the border, Tarrant had men on permanent listening watch, to get a cross-reference on the homing device in the fallen bomb. It would be located within minutes of landing, and it would contain whatever message Modesty wished to send.

Toller had been entranced by the idea. He hated using couriers, and the thought that the East German propaganda gunners would be acting as messengers gave him a pleasure that was rare in the unremittingly gray and dangerous life he lived.

Willie said, his grin fading, "So all we've got to do is figure another way of getting Okubo out."

"Just that small item."

He sighed. "There's only one good thing 'appened this morning," he said gloomily. "I got a dollar tip from that chauffeur for 'elping change the wheel."

Throughout the rest of the day they made no conscious efforts to formulate a plan, but simply left their minds open to recognize any opportunity. This was their method, and this was how Willie had hit upon the first plan, several days ago, when he had seen the United Nations car pass by on its daily journey through Checkpoint Charlie.

When night came they were still without inspiration. Modesty lay in bed and reviewed the chances of using the same escape plan again, except that this time they would knock Okubo unconscious before putting him in the boot. But his cooperation would be needed until the last moment, and she knew they could not fool him for long enough to ensure that cooperation.

It was eleven o'clock. Within the next hour or two the East Germans would obligingly shoot her message to Tarrant over the border. It would be some relief to him to know that even though one attempt had failed, at least they had not been caught. . . .

An association of ideas made her thoughts dart off at a tangent. She drew in a quick breath and sat up, her mind racing. The idea seemed hare-brained, but it might work. Yes . . . it just might. Willie would know, and he could make it work if it was in any way possible.

She got out of bed, pulled on a dressing-gown and went through the communicating door into his room. He woke at the faint sound of the door opening, sat up in bed and put on the bedside light. She beckoned him through to the bathroom and turned on the shower. It was possible the rooms were bugged, but unlikely that this included the bathroom. If so, then the sound of the shower would make the bug ineffective.

Willie sat beside her on the edge of the bath, his eyes eager, knowing she had an idea. She put her lips close to his ear and began to whisper. After the first ten seconds he suddenly hunched forward, a frantic expression on his face, then rammed the fingers of one hand into his mouth and closed his teeth on them, rocking back and forth in agonized struggle as he fought to subdue the gust of laughter that convulsed him, laughter so stupendous that if he had given vent to it the sound would have been heard through the walls.

She stared at him almost indignantly for a moment, then punched his arm gently in remonstrance. He shook his head in speechless apology, and doubled up again. Somehow he straightened, the breath rasping around the gag of his fingers. He looked at her, his face empurpled with strain, then nodded again and again, lifting his free hand to make a confirmatory circle with finger and thumb.

A new spasm gripped him, and suddenly she caught the infection. The same convulsive laughter welled up within her. Eyes closed, tears squeezing from under the lids, lips tightly compressed, she leaned against him and hugged her forearms across her stomach in the desperate struggle to keep silent.

Tarrant handed the sheet of paper to Berlin Control and fingered his mustache. Berlin Control read the message twice, a variety of expressions chasing one another over his face. At last he said simply, "They must be joking."

"That's the first impression one gets," Tarrant agreed. "But it's not tenable. So let's assume that this is just a typically unorthodox idea. We're going to comply with what they ask."

It was two days since the earlier message had come through, giving no details but stating baldly that the first plan had failed and that another would be devised. Now this new message had come over the border. Berlin Control read it once again and said, "It won't be easy to get this organized."

Tarrant eyed him coldly. "It's a bloody sight easier than what she and Willie have to organize, don't you think?"

"We only have thirty-six hours."

"Then that will have to be long enough." Tarrant frowned, trying to trap a fleeting thought of something he had seen or read in the last few days. He identified it and said, "There's a man in the States called John Dall. A tycoon with all kinds of diverse interests. Get him on the phone for me."

"I'll try. Tycoons usually have a screen of secretaries to shield them."

"Give my name and say it concerns Modesty Blaise," Tarrant said. "You'll get through that screen as fast as if you were the President."

It was an hour later, and four A.M. in New York, when Tarrant picked up the phone and heard Dall's voice. "Tarrant?"

"Yes. I'm sorry to disturb you at this hour—"

"Never mind. Have you got her into another peck of trouble?"

"I could have stopped her by putting her in a straitjacket, perhaps."

He heard Dall give a sigh of resignation. Then, "OK. I know what you mean. What can I do?"

"I believe you have a major interest in a film company which has a unit here at the moment, shooting scenes which include the Wall. They have, or can obtain, certain facilities she wants me to provide."

There was a silence. Tarrant knew that Dall wanted to ask if Modesty was on the wrong side of the Wall, but would not do so on an open line. He said, "Yes, she is, John."

Dall said, "Oh, my God. All right, the unit director is a guy called Joe Abrahams. I'll call him now. He'll make contact with you within the next couple of hours and he'll be under your orders for—how long do you want?"

"Thirty-six hours, please,"

"OK. Where does he contact you?"

Tarrant gave the address and number of a small travel agency. Dall said, "I've got that. Will you have her ring me as soon as she's able to, please?"

"Of course, And thank you." Tarrant put down the phone and looked at Berlin Control. "I've seen them shooting scenes close to the Wall. They must have permission for it from the West Germans."

"Yes. Are you going to ask the Gehlen Bureau for help? They have a lot of pull."

"I don't think we need it now we have the film-location cover, and the fewer people involved the better." Tarrant pointed to the message Berlin Control had picked up from the desk. "Study that sketch map and the figures, then go and look at the site and see how best to set the scene."

Okubo sat in the brown van with Modesty, in a lay-by on the Dresden road fifteen miles south of Berlin. It was just after half past eight, and night had fallen.

"There is to be a full conference?" Okubo said.

"Yes. Nobody likes the idea, but I persuaded them that we'd have to set up a major operation to get you out."

"So I have said all along. What is the plan?"

"I don't know yet. It's to be settled tonight."

"It must have my approval."

"That's why you're here now and out of cover," Modesty said dryly. "It's dangerous for you and it's bad security for our people, but they've accepted the risk."

An enormous furniture truck came rumbling along the road. It pulled into the lay-by behind them. The headlights were switched off, and Willie Garvin, dressed in overalls and a beret, climbed down from the cab of the truck and moved to the van. He nodded to Modesty. She said to Okubo, "We move into the truck now."

The little Japanese got out of the van and followed her round to the rear of the tall truck. A tarpaulin hung down from the back of the rectangular roof to join the tailboard. Willie lowered the tailboard and Okubo mounted it. He said, "It is to be a mobile conference, then?"

"The Group Controller decided it was the safest way," Modesty said, and followed Okubo as he ducked under the hanging tarpaulin.

There was nobody in the truck, but the vast bulk of some strange object filled it almost completely fore and aft, leaving a passageway on each side. Okubo stared in the darkness. The thing seemed to be an enormous cylinder, tapering slightly and angled up toward the rear of the truck. The cylinder was set on some kind of mounting or low carriage which seemed to be bolted to the floor.

It was a gun. A cannon. A caricature of a cannon. It was of metal and had once been brightly painted, but most of the paint had peeled off. The barrel was absurdly large. Large enough to take a man . . .

Watching, Modesty saw Okubo freeze with incredulity for a moment. Then he turned and sprang at her in the narrow gap between the side of the truck and the circus cannon. He jumped high, and one foot lashed out for her heart in a skilled karate kick. It was a reaction far quicker than she had anticipated, but instinct gave her a split-second warning of it.

She twisted, and his heel scraped her upper arm. She blocked the follow-up chop of his hand with an elbow driven paralyzingly against his forearm; and then, as he landed, she was inside his guard and the kongo in her fist rapped home sharply under his ear. He fell like an empty sack.

Behind her, Willie Garvin said, "Karate man, eh? And a lively little Professor all round. Caught on fast, but didn't fancy the idea much."

"It's not a very dignified way of going over the Wall," Modesty said, and took the hypodermic Willie handed her. "It ought to be dramatic enough for him, but there's a certain loss of face about it. Did you test the cannon again today?"

"Three times on a set trajectory, with a sack of sand the same weight as Toller gave us for Okubo. There wasn't more than thirty inches variation on landing. If Tarrant fixes the net on the measurements we want, Okubo ought to land pretty well dead center. And the size of net we asked for allows a margin of sixteen feet on width, and twice as much on length."

Willie Garvin sounded very confident. The circus he had worked for long ago had boasted a Human Cannonball act, and one of Willie's jobs had been to check and test the cannon, and to load it with the compressed air which provided the firepower.

Two days ago, undisguised and purporting to represent a Russian circus, Willie had visited the farm again and bought the cannon. He had spent a full day there, stripping down and adjusting the firing mechanism, scouring the inside of the barrel to mirror smoothness, getting the necessary compressed air cylinders, testing the cannon and hiring the furniture truck.

The farmer had been mildly surprised, but this brusque circus man was a Russian, and one did not argue with one's allies and protectors.

There was a crash-helmet to protect Okubo's head, a stiff leather collar for his neck and a small tarpaulin in which to wrap him up and so protect his limbs, since he would be unconscious while making the flight. The tarpaulin was oiled on the outside to give a smooth exit from the great barrel of the cannon. With the lightweight Okubo as projectile, the cannon's range was greater than usual. It had tested out well at just under ninety yards.

Modesty completed the injection of pentothal and straightened up. She said, "All right, Willie. Let's get him loaded."

Willie Garvin reached for the crash helmet and tarpaulin, and as he bent to the task his body shook with silent laughter.

Fifteen miles away, and on the other side of the Wall, Tarrant stood with Joe Abrahams in a side-street near Brunenstrade. Abrahams was a lean, eager man of great energy. At first resentful of interference by Dall from above, he had become ecstatic about the project as soon as Tarrant explained what was wanted. His only regret was that there was no film in the three cameras set up to cover the scene they were pretending to shoot.

Abrahams had conjured up a net, flown in from Bonn, after an urgent call to his property man there. It was forty yards long and fifteen wide. At this moment it lay carefully folded on top of three big trucks which stood facing the open ground between the end of the side-street and the Wall.

There was the usual apparent confusion that inevitably surrounds a film unit. Lights were being set up, powered by long cables run out from a generator. People sat around in canvas-backed chairs, drinking coffee served from a canteen-van. Others called instructions or made chalk marks on the ground for the actors to take up position when shooting began.

Abrahams ran his fingers through an untidy mop of hair and said, "Your artillery friends had better be spot on ten-fifteen. When we run that net out, the guys in the watchtowers won't see it because we've fixed the lighting that way. But it'll only take maybe five minutes before the West German cops get around to making guesses and having us take it down."

"My artillery friends are very reliable," Tarrant said. "Run the net out at twelve minutes past ten. I'm sure you can stall for seven or eight minutes from then. Once the fish is netted we'll whisk him away before anyone realizes what's happened. And don't worry about your crew. The East Germans won't fire into the West. Into the death-strip on their side, yes. But not over the Wall."

One edge of the net was attached to the upper windows of the empty building against which the three trucks were tightly backed. On Abrahams' signal the drivers would move the trucks forward slowly, in line abreast, to a precisely measured line marked on the open ground just over thirty yards from the Wall, and the net would then be tautly spread.

Berlin Control looked at his watch for the twentieth time and said, "Another eight minutes. I still think they're out of their minds."

"I hope you double-checked the map and the measurements," Tarrant said. "Accuracy is going to be vital."

"It bloody well is for Okubo," Berlin Control said with feeling. "I've triple-checked everything. But please don't ever send those two to get *me* over the Wall."

Abrahams grinned wolfishly. "They're creative people," he said. "I love 'em. Whoever they are, I love 'em."

Modesty turned off Weinbergstrade into the network of sidestreets. She was driving a different van now, a laundry van she had stolen from a car park only twenty minutes ago. She wore a plain head-scarf, and a loose sweater covered the upper half of the clothes she wore as Jorgensen's secretary.

Soon, in the headlights, she saw some way ahead of her the barbed-wire fence, eight-feet high, which ran parallel to the Wall, leaving a thirty-yard gap in which guards and dogs patrolled—the death-strip. Behind her the lights of the lumbering furniture truck disappeared as it turned off.

She looked at her watch and drove on slowly. Okubo would be making a flight of eighty-eight yards, thirty-one on this side of the Wall and fifty-seven on the far side. According to Willie the risk to Okubo was very small, providing the net was in the right position at the right time. That part of the job was Tarrant's, and she wasted no anxiety on it.

Turning again, she drove down the road which paralleled the Wall, the most westerly road where traffic was allowed. At each intersection the street to her right was a cul-de-sac leading only to the wire fence and the Wall beyond. The buildings in these cul-de-sacs were empty and derelict.

The next intersection was the one she wanted. Ahead and beyond it she saw the furniture truck turn into the road and come toward her. She moved into the center and stopped her engine. There was no room for the truck to pass. It halted. One or two people looked out from the window of a dingy café as Willie Garvin shouted to her in German.

She called back fluently, making her voice shrill, telling him she had stalled and her battery was flat. If he backed out of the way she could get started on the slight down-slope.

Grumbling, Willie Garvin put the big truck into reverse and backed slowly round the corner of the cul-de-sac. There was no laughter in him now. His eyes moved from side to side in total concentration as he centered the truck precisely . . . and kept backing.

Modesty let the laundry van roll forward a little. Now she could see obliquely along the side of the truck. When the back of it was within a yard of the barbed-wire fence she gave a short whistle. The truck stopped. She pushed back her sleeve and looked at the big stop-watch strapped to the inside of her forearm. It was ten-fourteen. Sixty seconds to wait. Her mouth became a little dry with tension.

The nearest observation platform was well over seventy yards away. Though the guards there could not see the truck now, they would have marked its passing along the road, and they were trained to suspicion. Their machine guns would be ready, covering the gap between wire and Wall, and they might well be calling the patrol guards by radio.

Distantly, from the far side of the Wall, a loud-hailer sounded harshly. An American voice. "Right folks, settle down. We're all set to shoot. All set to shoot. Roll 'em. *Action!*"

She did not wonder what Tarrant had arranged, but thanked God for his wit in saving a dangerous minute of waiting. Her hand moved in a signal to Willie.

In the cab of the truk there were two ropes which ran through holes into the back. Willie picked up the rope with a wooden toggle on the end and pulled hard. There was some resistance for the first few feet, and then the rope went slack. The tarpaulin fell from the back of the truck, leaving the great barrel of the cannon clear for an unobstructed shot. It still could not be seen, except from directly behind the truck, and no patrolling guards had arrived in the death-strip yet. Only twenty seconds had passed since the truck started backing.

Willie picked up the second rope and jerked it. The truck vibrated slightly. In the sawdust ring of the circus there would have been a puff of smoke and a loud explosion, a fake effect. Now there was surprisingly little sound as compressed air exploded from the firing chamber, only a heavy and sonorous plop.

From the laundry van, Modesty picked up a momentary sight of the black, sausage-shaped object soaring up over the death-strip, over the Wall, still rising, then dipping down, rotating slowly, end over end. It was gone, and she doubted that any other eye on this side of the Wall had seen it.

She started the engine. Willie was out of the truck and moving toward her, not seeming to hurry but covering ground fast. She swung open the passenger door for him and let in the clutch as he settled beside her. The distant voice sounded on the loud-hailer. *''Cut! OK folks—we'll print that one!''*

She turned a corner, heading away from the Wall, driving without obvious haste but keeping up a steady speed. Behind them a miniature searchlight beam stabbed along the Wall from the nearest watchtower, ranging back and forth uncertainly. An amplified voice began to call orders in German.

Five minutes later, when that section of the Wall was buzzing with activity and far behind them, they abandoned the laundry van in a poorly lit side street off Prenzlauer Allee. Willie had stripped off his overalls and was in his Jorgensen guise. Modesty had taken off the head-scarf and sweater, and was his secretary again. They walked out into Prenzlauer Allee and turned toward the cinema car park where she had left the Skoda.

When they were in the car with the doors closed, Willie leaned back luxuriously in his seat, hands resting on the wheel, utterly content, smiling dreamily. ''Psalm Eighteen, Verse ten,'' he murmured. *''Yea, he did fly upon the wings of the wind.''* He picked up her hand and touched it to his cheek for a moment. It was his salute to her, his accolade.

She gave an aggrieved sigh. ''You don't love me for myself, Mr. Jorgensen. Just for my nutty ideas.''

He shook his head. ''It worked. It was a cracker . . . a genuine twenty-two-carat masterpiece.'' He chuckled exuberantly and his voice changed to a hoarse, strident whisper, a muted impression of ring-master. ''Ladie-ees and Gentle*men*! We now present to you! For the first time anywhere in the world! That Mighty Midget, that Brilliant, Breath-taking Bacteriologist . . . *Professor Okubo—the Human Cannonball!*''

He choked and hunched forward. She had rarely seen him so delighted. She said, "For God's sake forget it and think Jorgensen for the next twenty-four hours, Willie love. We'll be out by then."

He nodded, controlling the rich and joyous emotion that bubbled within him. "Out," he said. "That's what I want, Princess. I got to 'ave room to laugh."

Three days later Tarrant sat in the Minister's Office once again. Waverly was in excellent humor. He said, "Fraser reported that you'd got the man out safely, but he gave no details. Congratulations, Tarrant."

"There were no important details to give at the time," Tarrant said. "And now I'm afraid you're going to be disappointed. The man wasn't Okubo."

Waverly stared. "I beg your pardon?"

"It wasn't Okubo. The first thing I did was to check identification. That took forty-eight hours, since we had to get hold of someone who knew Okubo personally."

Waverly looked very shaken. "And . . . it wasn't him? I don't understand."

"Okubo is still in Russia, and always was. The man who purported to defect was a Japanese agent called Yoshida, working for Major-General Starov. A put-up job. Starov banked on the fact that most Japanese look more or less alike to us, as we do to them, no doubt. He set up the whole thing to tempt us, hoping that we'd activate our sleeper network and expose it to Yoshida."

"Oh, my God," Waverly said softly.

"Yes. We'd have been wiped out there. Fortunately I didn't activate the network. I was able to make unofficial arrangements with two friends of mine who have some expertise in these matters."

"Friends of yours?"

Tarrant allowed himself a small smile. "I do have friends, Minister."

"I didn't mean that. I meant—"

"I can't tell you who they are," Tarrant cut in crisply. "They aren't employed by us, and they weren't hired."

Waverly gazed at him. "I find this very baffling. People don't risk their necks for nothing."

"It's unusual," Tarrant agreed, and left the point. "They came to suspect Okubo when their first escape-plan failed. He refused to go through with it at the last minute and kept pressing for a large-scale plan. If they had known for certain that he was an imposter, they would simply have killed him, because our liaison man who runs a safe-house there was already exposed. But there was no way to have Okubo identified, so they got him out.'' Tarrant paused for Waverly to absorb the implications, then added, ''Fortunately he killed himself with a cyanide pill soon after we'd had him identified in West Berlin.''

Waverly realized that his last part might nor might not be true. The man could not be held indefinitely, and as long as he was alive the safe-house and its agent were at risk. If Yoshida had not in fact killed himself, then Tarrant had seen to it. Waverly felt an inward chill, and for the first time realized with sharp clarity the awful and inexorable burdens of Tarrant's job.

He said, ''I must apologize to you. I made a serious error of judgment in the instructions I gave you.'' Tarrant inclined his head in acknowledgment, and Waverly went on, ''How the devil did these two get the man out? He certainly wouldn't cooperate, and they could hardly do it *without* his cooperation.''

''They're very resourceful. They rendered him unconscious and shot him over the wall from a cannon.'' Tarrant's face held no expression.

Waverly looked blank, then incredulous, then angry. Tarrant had been more than generous, but a Minister of the Crown could not be subjected to insolence. ''I asked you a serious question, Tarrant,'' he said sharply.

''They shot him out of a cannon,'' Tarrant repeated. ''Over the Berlin Wall. One of those Human Cannonball things they sometimes have in circuses. We caught him with a net.''

After twenty seconds Waverly said, ''Good God,'' and began to laugh. Tarrant warmed to him, but prepared to exact the mild retribution he had planned. ''The performance wasn't entirely free, Minister,'' he said. ''There are expenses. I shall want something from the Special Fund, as promised.''

Half an hour later, at a parking meter off Whitehall, Tarrant got into a Jensen and sat down beside Modesty Blaise. Once again he was intrigued by the fact that on her return from a situation of high danger she always looked younger, quite ridiculously young. He thought that perhaps this was how she had looked on the day Willie first saw her, when she was barely out of her teens.

She said, ''Willie sent his thanks for the lunch invitation but asked to be excused. He's gone away to forget his sorrows.''

''His sorrows?''

She smiled, almost giggled. ''He's very upset. This was the richest, funniest, most gorgeous caper he's ever known. But Yoshida ruined it. He killed the gag. Wrecked the giggle.''

''I don't quite follow.''

''Neither do I, quite. But then I'm not English and not a Cockney, so I don't always grasp the subtleties of Willie's weird sense of humor. I can only quote him.'' Her voice sank to a deeper pitch and became gravelly, in imitation of Willie. ''Shooting a big-'eaded, bloody-minded little Jap bug-expert over the Wall, that's one thing, Princess. But Yoshida was just a Commie agent, and that takes all the bubbles out of it.'' Her voice became normal. ''He's annoyed on my account. He takes the view that Yoshida ruined my punch-line.''

Tarrant reflected. ''Yes, I do see his point. Vaguely, perhaps, but I see it. Poor Willie.''

She was looking at him with an inquiring smile, and he remembered the little bunch of violets he was carrying. ''With my love,'' he said, and presented them to her.

''Why, thank you. They're beautiful.''

''I could think of nothing else,'' Tarrant said. ''The point is, they have a rarity value. They're not really from me, they'll be paid for out of the Special Fund. It's difficult to get money out of the Special Fund at any time, because the PM has to approve, but getting twenty thousand pounds would easier then getting two shillings, which is what I've put in for. Waverly wanted to give me two shillings out of his pocket, but I wouldn't have it. I wish you could have seen his face.''

She laughed, and put her lips briefly to Tarrant's cheek. ''They're just what I've always wanted. I'll ask for a vase when we get to Claridge's. You hold them while I drive.'' She started the Jensen and backed from the meter.

Tarrant said, ''How is Willie fogetting his sorrows?''

''With Mavis. He's flown to Jersey for a long weekend with her.''

''Mavis?''

''I haven't met her, but according to Willie she's a very tall showgirl with more and bigger curves than you'd think possible on any human being. Mentally as thick as two planks, but unfailingly cheerful and bursting with enthusiasm. He says it's like going to bed with four girls and a cylinder of laughing-gas. I think she's just the sort to take him out of himself.''

Tarrant sighed, baffled. ''You're a woman, and Willie is a part of you,'' he said. ''Why on earth aren't you possessive about him?''

He saw humor touch her face. ''I suppose it's just the pattern,'' she said patiently. With her eyes still on the road ahead she grinned suddenly. ''But if Mavis ever starts shooting people over the Berlin Wall with him, I might feel like bouncing some of those curves off her.''

Tarrant laughed. He felt very happy. It had started to rain, but for him the sun was shining today. ''I don't suppose it will ever come to that,'' he said.

MICHAEL GILBERT

The Spoilers

ON FRIDAY NIGHT Colonel Geoffrey Bax went down alone for a last visit to his weekend cottage in Sussex. It was a last visit, because the cottage had been put up for sale. He was alone because his wife was escorting her mother on her summer pilgrimage to Torquay.

On Saturday morning the farmer drove up with milk and eggs and discovered the colonel. He was seated in the chair at the head of the kitchen table, under the still-burning electric light. It was a hot June morning, and the flies were already gathering round the pool of blackening blood on the table top. The gun which had killed the colonel was in his right hand.

Mr. Behrens had known Colonel Bax. He read the news in his Sunday paper, and walked up the hill to discuss it with his old friend, Mr. Calder.

"It's in my paper too," said Mr. Calder. "But I didn't really know Bax. Wasn't he working for DI5?"

"Yes. He got a job with them when he retired from the Army. It wasn't anything hush-hush, you know. He did a lot of their positive vetting."

"I'd rather pick oakum," said Mr. Calder.

(Positive vetting was a palliative devised by the government in 1952 after a series of Security scandals. It meant, in practice, that any government servant who attained a certain degree of seniority had to supply the name of a referee; and it then became the duty of the positive vetter to interview the referee and inquire of him whether the officer concerned was reliable. The answer was predictable.)

"Most of those jobs went to officers who had been axed," said Mr. Behrens. "They got quite well paid for it. Add the salary to their service pensions and they could get by."

Mr. Calder looked up sharply. He had known Mr. Behrens long enough to ignore the plain meaning of what he said and jump to the thought behind it.

"Do you think there was some sort of pressure on Bax?"

"It's not impossible. The material was there. In his case it was a girl. Her parents were Poles. Geoffrey did them a good turn just after the war, and was godfather to their little daughter."

"Daddy Longlegs," said Mr. Calder, scratching the head of his deerhound Rasselas, who was stretched out under the breakfast table.

"It's all very well for you to sneer," said Mr. Behrens. "I've met the girl. She's very beautiful."

"Did Bax's wife know about her?"

"If she had, she'd have started divorce proceedings at once. She was that sort of woman."

"If she was that sort of woman, Bax would have been well rid of her."

"He'd have lost his job."

Mr. Calder, considering the matter, was inclined to agree. He knew that in certain branches of the Security Services sexual irregularity was considered a good deal worse than crime and nearly as bad as ideological deviation.

"He could have lived on his pension."

"*And* paid alimony to his wife?"

"He wouldn't have starved," said Mr. Calder. "There was no need to blow his brains out. *That* didn't help."

"That cottage of his," said Mr. Behrens. "He was very fond of it. He often talked about it. He was going to retire there."

"So?"

"I wondered why he had to sell it."

"You're making my flesh creep," said Mr. Calder. And from under the table Rasselas gave a rumbling snarl, just as if he had been following the whole conversation.

Her Majesty's Secretary of State for Education, Dermot Nicholson, read the news in his elegant flat on Campden Hill.

He said to his sister Norah—who had retired from the vice-principalship of an Oxford college to keep house and write his speeches for him—"Colonel Geoffrey Bax. Do we know a Geoffrey Bax? The name seems familiar."

"Wasn't that the name of the man who was round here a few weeks ago, asking you a lot of questions?"

"Oh, was that the chap? I thought I'd seen the name somewhere."

"What *did* he want? Did you ever find out?"

"It was some sort of routine check."

"We're getting so Security-minded," said Miss Nicholson, "that we might as well be living in a totalitarian state, under the control of the Gestapo."

Miss Nicholson, who was an intellectual liberal, often said things like this in letters to the Press and at public meetings, possibly because she had never lived in a totalitarian state and had no experience of the Gestapo. . . .

Professor Julius Gottlieb, a citizen of Czechoslovakia by birth, and of Great Britain by naturalization, read the news in his service flat in Northumberland Court. He took eight different Sunday papers and he found the story, with minor differences and embellishments, in all of them. It was clearly based on an official handout.

As he finished reading, the telephone rang. He hesitated for a long moment before answering it, but when he did so it was only his daughter Paula. She had gone down to Henley for the weekend.

"It's lovely," she said. "You ought to have come."

"I wanted to," said the professor. "But I had too much work."

"You'd be better off bathing and lying in the sun, than worrying about that silly paper. Fritz is enjoying it like anything. He had a fight with another dog. And he fell into the river and was hissed at by a swan."

"Good," said the professor. "Good." He spoke absently. When his daughter had rung off he seemed to be in no hurry to get on with the urgent work which was keeping him in London that fine June weekend. He sat in the window seat, watching the traffic swirl up Northumberland Avenue and turn down Whitehall Place. The telephone rang again. . . .

On the Thursday afternoon a coroner's jury came, without difficulty, to the conclusion that Colonel Geoffrey Bax had taken his own life while the balance of his mind was disturbed. Sympathy was expressed for his widow.

On Sunday morning the Prime Minister took breakfast at Chequers with the prime ministers of five of the newly independent African States. He thought that they looked politely surprised at the modest bacon and eggs and toast and marmalade.

"What the devil did they expect me to eat," he said to his private secretary when the last of his guests had gone, "boar's head and ambrosia?"

"I imagine Nwambe's idea of a suitable breakfast would be the head of the leader of the opposition, seethed in milk," said the private secretary. "Your next appointment's in five minutes. They've all arrived. I've put them in the small library."

The Prime Minister switched his mind to a problem which was worrying him a lot more than the growing pains of the new African

States. He said, "I want those papers. Particularly that rather odd letter that Gottlieb wrote me."

He found four men waiting for him. Ian Maver, the head of DI5, Air Vice-Marshal Pulleyne, the acting head of DI6—his boss was in America, engaged on one of their interminable wrangles with the CIA—and Commander Elfe, of the Special Branch. All of these the Prime Minister knew personally. The face of the fourth man was unfamiliar, and even when Maver introduced Mr. Fortescue it took him a moment to place him. Then he remembered that this sedate and respectable-looking man was ostensibly a bank manager, and in fact the controller and paymaster of a bunch of middle-aged cutthroats known as the "E" (or External) Branch of the Joint Services Standing Intelligence Committee. When the Prime Minister, on taking office, had shouldered, among other unwanted burdens, the supreme responsibility for all Security matters, his predecessor had explained to him, "If there's a job which is so disreputable that none of the departments will handle it, we give it to the 'E' Branch."

The Prime Minister looked a second time at Mr. Fortescue, who looked back at him kindly but firmly, as if preparing to refuse him an overdraft. An interesting face, thought the Prime Minister. Not unlike Arthur Balfour, in middle age.

"You're busy men," he said, "and I apologize for disrupting Sunday for all four of you. If I'd had a more accurate idea of what this trouble was, I could probably have let three of you off." He smiled the boyish smile which had won the hearts of so many of his constituents in the old days and was now collecting high TAM ratings on television. "But the fact of the matter is that, although I'm worried, I'm not at all sure which of you gentlemen is going to have to shoulder my worries for me. I'll put the problem to you in a nutshell. Certain key men in my government are being got at. You've got to find out who's doing it. And you've got to stop it."

Mr. Fortescue, who was himself an adept in the handling of conferences, found himself admiring the Prime Minister's technique. First the gentle introduction. Then the sharp slap.

"*Got* at, Prime Minister?" said Maver.

"That was the word I used. I can't be more specific, until you gentlemen find out more about it. They are being got at. Not by the opposition, which would be natural, or by the Press, which would be understandable, but by some private agency or group of persons who seem to be determined to get this government out of office."

The Prime Minister saw the quick look which Maver shot Pulleyne but gave no sign of having done so. He chalked it up as one more item on the debit account of the head of DI5. He had like Maver's predecessor, a garrulous, drunken, inefficient Irishman, a great deal more than the cold, self-contained, unquestionably efficient Scot.

"I think," the Prime Minister continued, "that when you hear the facts you will agree that I have some grounds for disquiet. A few months ago, Sir William Hamson, one of the most senior Revenue officials, and the man who did most of the work on last year's budget, came to me and told me that he wished to retire. He had eight years to go before his normal retirement. It was extremely inconvenient thought not, as it turned out, disastrous because he had a deputy who was capable of doing his job. But it might have upset the whole of our financial plans. Sir William gave me no reason, apart from saying that he was tired. I pointed out that he would lose a good slice of his pension. Since he had private means, that didn't worry him. We had to let him go, of course. He's now in the south of France, and seems to have recovered his health and spirits. By itself, such an incident meant nothing. Two months ago Dermot Nicholson who, as you know, is Minister of Education, and is therefore in charge of the most important measure of this session—a measure whose success might make the difference between defeat and victory—came to see me. I was at once reminded of Hamson. There was the same request—to be relieved of office. The same lack of any plausible reason. The same . . . I find it difficult to hit on the right word . . . it was something a great deal stronger than depression. There was an edge of fear to it. And a background of hopelessness." The Prime Minister paused, and then added, "If his doctor had told him that morning that he was suffering from inoperable cancer, I should have expected much the same sort of reactions."

The four men stirred uncomfortably in their chairs.

"I suppose," said Elfe, "that he wasn't—"

"I happen to know that there is nothing wrong with Nicholson's health at all. Let me finish. A fortnight ago I had to send for Professor Julius Gottlieb. You all know roughly what his job is, I expect? He is the leading town-planning expert in the world. Even the Americans admit it. Some months ago, at my request, he completed the first rough draft of a White Paper on Planning. It wasn't perfect, but believe me, it was two decades in advance of anything this country has yet seen. The departments concerned—particularly the Treasury and the Ministry of Agriculture—picked a few holes in it but they couldn't shoot it down. When all the criticisms had been collected, Gottlieb was to draw up the final version. He now says—" the Prime Minister paused again, not for effect this time Mr. Fortescue thought, but because he was really worried and angry—"he now says that he doesn't feel up to the job. He is thinking of retiring. He has a holiday chalet in Switzerland, in the Upper Vaud. I believe it's famous for its wildflowers. He has decided to retire and make it his permanent home."

Commander Elfe said, "It's disturbing, Prime Minister. But is it necessarily political?"

"When Education and Planning are the two cornerstones of this Session? What are people going to say—more to the point, what is the press going to say—if we have to tell them that the chief architect of the new Education Bill has thrown in the sponge—and the government's principal adviser on planning has refused to finish his own White Paper, and is retiring to Switzerland to pick wildflowers?"

"It was six months ago," said Pulleyne, in his precise voice, "when Hamson walked out. Two months ago when you first got worried about Nicholson. A fortnight ago when Gottlieb threatened to throw in his hand. Have no steps been taken?"

"Yes," said Maver. "It looked like a Home Security matter, so it was handed to us. We put one of our most reliable men onto it. He talked to Nicholson and Gottlieb."

"Did he come to any conclusion as a result of these talks?"

"We don't know. He committed suicide a week ago."

"Then you're talking about Colonel Bax?"

"Yes."

"And has he himself been investigated?"

Maver flushed and said, "Of course. And there *was* a background story, which could have accounted for it. We haven't got very far with it yet. But it's quite possible that he was being blackmailed, and had been driven too far."

"Well, that's the position, gentlemen," said the Prime Minister. "It could be organized pressure from an unscrupulous group in this country. I don't mean the official opposition. But there are plenty of extremist groups who wouldn't stop short of it. It could be foreign-inspired. I can think of four countries at this moment which would give a great deal to have the present government discredited. Or it may be simple blackmail. I leave you, gentlemen, to sort out the departmental priorities amongst yourselves. *I just want it stopped.*"

To his secretary when they had all gone away, he said, "Do you realize that all prime ministers have to live out the enthusiasms of their predecessors? Because of Lloyd George's lower middle-class habits I have to entertain official guests to breakfast. Because of Winston's boyish enthusiasm for cops and robbers I have to pretend to be personally responsible for Security. Do you remember that thing he wrote—?''

The private secretary didn't remember, but being a good private secretary he was able to put his hand on the reference his employer required. He fetched down a battered olive-green volume from the library shelf, found the place and read out: '' ' . . . plot and counterplot, ruse and treachery, cross and double-cross, true agent, false agent, gold and steel, the bomb, the dagger and the firing-party, interwoven in a texture so intricate as to be incredible, yet true, the high officers of the Secret Service revelled in these subterranean labyrinths, and pursued their task with cold and silent passion.' ''

''I didn't notice them reveling,'' said the Prime Minister. ''Did you?''

Ian Maver and Mr. Fortescue traveled back in the official car together. Maver said nothing until they were approaching the outskirts of London. Then he closed the glass panel to shut off the driver and said, ''The PM mentioned three possible explanations. There are at least two more that he omitted.''

''Yes,'' said Mr. Fortescue.

''The whole thing could be a coincidence. People crack up pretty quickly in government service these days. And all three of the people he mentioned had private means. There was no reason for them to kill themselves by going on doing a job which had got beyond them.''

''No,'' said Mr. Fortescue. ''And your other explanation?''

''The other possible explanation is that the Prime Minister has greatly exaggerated the whole thing as an excuse for getting rid of me. I'm afraid he doesn't like me very much.''

Mr. Fortescue did not make any comment on this.

On the following Monday Dermont Nicholson got back to his flat at Campden Hill at just after midnight. A threatened all-night sitting of the House had failed to develop. He was looking forward to a nightcap and bed.

His key went into the lock but he was unable to turn it, and when he tried to get it out again he found it was stuck. He rang the bell. Nothing happened. His sister very rarely went to bed before midnight and was most unlikely to be asleep.

Someone, or something, moved in the flat.

There was an indeterminate shuffling noise and, as he bent his head to listen, he thought he heard a faint moan.

In a sudden panic he rattled the door, shouted, put his shoulder to it, then turned and raced downstairs. There was a night porter, who had a master key.

"If your key's stuck in the lock, sir," he said, "it's no good trying to use my master key. We shall have to break the door down, and the police'll do that quicker than we will."

"Hurry," said Nicholson. "Hurry. Something's happened to my sister. She may have had a stroke."

Detective Sergeant Hallows, who was night duty officer at Notting Hill Gate, arrived inside five minutes. He and the police driver went up, carrying between them an assortment of housebreaking implements. It took them a further three minutes to deal with the front door. Nicholson pushed past them, and went straight to his sister's bedroom. She had been tied to the end of the bed with sheets, and gagged with a towel. The knots had been so savagely tightened that Nicholson was unable to do anything with them. He picked a pair of scissors from the dressing table, but his hands were shaking and he dropped them. The sergeant cut through the sheets with a knife; as soon as the gag was out of her mouth Miss Nicholson started to scream. . . .

"I have to announce," said the Prime Minister to the House, on Wednesday, "the news—to me, personally, it is very sad news—that the Right Honourable Member for Burnham Heath has had to offer me his resignation as Minister for Education. He has done this on the advice of his doctors. I have not yet finally decided on a successor, but I can assure the House that there will be no change in the government's education policy."

An opposition back-bencher said. "While we sympathize with the Prime Minister for having lost yet another of his already depleted team, we should be interested to know exactly what the late Minister of Education was suffering from? Could it be that he was sick of the Education Bill—"

The rest was lost in a roar of government protest and opposition laughter.

On the same Wednesday, Mr. Calder and Mr. Behrens both received telephone calls at home. Mr. Behrens said to his aunt, "I've some business in town. I'll probably stay at the Club for a few nights."

His aunt said, "You known that I don't like being left here alone."

"Why don't you visit Millicent?"

"It's tiresome you couldn't have given me more notice."

Mr. Calder got his old car out of the woodshed. To Rasselas, who was sunning himself in his favorite spot behind the woodpile, he said, "Back tonight.'' The big dog sighed windily, in exactly the same way that Miss Behrens had done.

Mr. Fortescue normally operated from the Westminster branch of the London and Home Counties Bank. But he had other offices. The one which he used on official occasions was in Richmond Terrace Mews, and it was here that Mr. Calder and Mr. Behrens found him.

When he had finished talking, Mr. Calder said, ''Mightn't there be some danger of getting our wires crossed over this? Most of it sounds like ordinary police work.''

''I agree that there's a police angle to it,'' said Mr. Fortescue. ''Since it involves the security of Ministers, it's the Special Branch which is involved. Elfe will be in charge of that side of it. DI5 and the police. Generally speaking, however, it's agreed that you're to have a free hand.''

Mr. Behrens said, ''I knew Gottlieb slightly. I met him in the 'forties, when he first came to England. I could have a word with him.''

''Then I'll start with Nicholson,'' said Mr. Calder. . . .

''It was a pigsty,'' said the detective sergeant. ''They did everything filthy they could think of. Over the floor, in the beds, everywhere. We've cleared up as best we could, but there's some things—well, come and have a look.''

He led the way into the living room. Someone had broken the glass in each of the half-dozen pictures on the wall and smeared filth over them. They were flower pictures, originals from Montessor's great folio. Looking closer, Mr. Calder saw that not only had the glass been smashed. The name of each plant was inscribed in copperplate at the foot of each picture. Someone had scored these through with an indelible pencil, and printed the word, PANSY.

''It's not only the pictures,'' said Hallows. ''It's the books too. Someone took a lot of trouble over this little job.''

There were a couple of hundred books in the fitted bookshelves between the windows. The back had been ripped out of each book, with a knife.

''We don't know just what they did to his sister,'' said Hallows. ''She's in a private nursing home. Maybe she'll be able to tell us something when she gets her wits back.''

''Did they take anything?''

''Nicholson says they took some money out of the desk, but it wasn't money they were after. It was a grudge job.''

''I agree,'' said Mr. Calder. He phrased his next question delicately, aware that it might give offense. "Seeing that he was a senior cabinet minister, I wondered if any special arrangements might have been made. I know the police can't keep a twenty-four watch on all these people—"

"He was guarded," said Hallows. "A private outfit was doing the job."

"Private?"

"That's right. We're so short of policement that government departments have started using private outfits lately. As a matter of act, some of them are ex-policemen."

"They seem to have slipped up on this occasion."

The doorbell rang.

Hallows said, as he went to open it, "They didn't slip. They were ditched. I asked the head of the firm to come round. This is probably him now. He can tell you about it."

Mr. Cotter, the managing director and founder of Cotter's Detectives, was a thickset, red-faced man with a brigade mustache. He shook hands with Mr. Calder and said, "Bad business. I've had to give Romilly his cards. No alternative. I don't know that it was one hundred percent his fault. He's never let me down before, anyway."

"What happened?"

"Someone telephoned the night porter, said he was Nicholson's secretary. The Minister had been detained at a meeting out at Finchley. Could Romilly pick up his car from the forecourt of the House, drive it out to Finchley, pick the old man up and bring him back to Westminster. It was plausible. After all, his main job's to look after the Minister."

"When this man telephoned?" said Mr. Calder, "did he actually say *Romilly*?"

Mr. Cotter thought for a moment, and then said, "Yes. I think he did. Why?"

"It would argue a pretty close knowledge of your setup if he knew the name of the man on duty at any given time. How many men do you have on a job like this?"

"It's a team of three. They do ten-hour stretches. That gives them a sort of dogwatch."

"Who are the other two?"

Mr. Cotter shot a glance at Sergeant Hallows, who said, "That's all right. Mr. Calder is from the Security Executive. He's helping us."

"I see," said Mr. Cotter. "My other two men on this assignment were Angel and Lawrie." He added stiffly, "They're both reliable men."

"Frank Angel," said Mr. Calder. "Small, dark, thick and Welsh?"

"That's him. Do you know him?"

"I worked with him on one or two jobs at Blenheim," said Mr. Calder. The atmosphere seemed to have become easier.

Mr. Behrens knew the Head of Records personally, and was thus able to get in to see this most closely guarded of all Home Office and Ministry of Defence officials. He said, "I want your full record on Gottlieb. The X *and* the Y file, please."

"You know as well as I do," said the Head of Records, "that you can't see the Y file without Cabinet authority."

Mr. Behrens laid his authority on the desk. The Head of Records read it through carefully and made a telephone call.

To the lump, serious young man with the middle-aged face who arrived in answer to it, he said, "This is Mr. Behrens, Smythe. Will you show him the X *and* Y files on Professor Julius Gottlieb."

Smythe said, in the manner of Jeeves, "If you would kindly step this way, sir," and conducted Mr. Behrens to the room in the basement of the building which contained, in numbered filing cabinets, enough high explosive to blow up both sides of Whitehall. He unlocked one of the cabinets, drew out two folders, one thick and one thin, placed a table and chair and said, "I'll leave you to it, sir."

As Mr. Behrens leafed through the folders he was smiling to himself. He was aware of the principles upon which this particular room was constructed, and he knew that anyone having access to a Y file was not only watched but normally photographed as well.

When he had finished he touched the bell. As he did so he smiled again. He knew that all he had to do was to say, without raising his voice, "Oh, Smythe—" and the guardian of the papers would have reappeared. By doing this he would have demonstrated that he knew that not only was every one of his movements being watched, but the room was wired for sound as well.

Mr. Behrens did no such thing. He had long outgrown any desire to give pointless exhibitions of his own expertise.

After a decent interval, Mr. Smythe reappeared.

"A lot of this Y file," said Mr. Behrens, "is in summary and précis. I imagine that the original documents—verbatim records of interrogations, and so on—were too bulky to file. Where would they be kept?"

"If they *were* kept," said Smythe, "I imagine they'd be at Brooklands. Or perhaps at Staines."

Mr. Behrens thanked him. Since it was then a quarter to one, he thought he would have lunch before tackling Gottlieb.

* * *

The girl who opened the door of the flat in Northumberland Court was, as Mr. Behrens saw even in the poor light of the front hall, pretty. When she had shown him into the drawing room, he changed his mind. Pretty was all wrong. A stupid word in any human context. She was attractive, with the attractions of dark hair, bright eyes, a good figure and youth.

She chased a dachshund off the sofa. "We call all our dachshunds Fritz," she said. "After the dog in that strip they used to have in the *Daily Mirror*. Do you remember? This one is Fritz the Third. He's the nicest and naughtiest of the lot. Daddy's mad about him."

She departed to summon her father. Mr. Behrens was not himself a susceptible man, but he made a mental note of the charm of Miss Gottlieb, since an attractive girl could be a relevant factor in any equation.

Professor Gottlieb who came in at that moment turned out to be a small man, with a suggestion of a humpback, a brown face and a mop of snowy white hair. He, like his daughter, was friendly. But it was clear to Mr. Behrens that he was on the defensive. They talked a little about the war. The professor had left Czechoslovakia in the summer of 1940 and had reached England in the autumn of that year by a round-about route, through Greece and Turkey. After being screened, he had been allowed to work on deep penetration bombs where his theoretical knowledge of electronics had been valuable. He had also done some work on DZ fuses, and, at the end of the war, on guided missiles.

"It is curious when you come to think of it," said the professor. "For the first twelve or fifteen years of my professional life, I worked on planning projects—in my own country, in Sweden and Denmark and America. I was hoping to contrive new and better towns for people to live in. Then for six whole years I worked at destruction. I helped to knock down whole cities—I was sorry for the people in them, of course. But even while I was doing it—yes, even when the bombs were falling on me in London—I could not help saying to myself, We are clearing the way for a gigantic reconstruction, a reconstruction such as the world has never seen before." For a moment, the professor's eyes were alight with an old enthusiasm. The glow died down. "The chance has been missed," he said. "And it will never come again."

"If it is missed," said Mr. Behrens, "it won't be your fault. When your paper is published—"

"Ah, my paper," said the professor, "I am afraid that too much reliance has been placed on that. You cannot change human nature with a piece of paper."

"You can't if it isn't published."

The professor looked up sharply. "I trust," he said, "that you are not going to turn what has been a very pleasant conversation into the channels of politics.''

''I'm not a politician,'' said Mr. Behrens. ''I'm a policeman. Of a sort. I can show you my credentials if you like.''

''Don't bother,'' said the professor. ''I was warned that you might be coming. It was not made clear to me how you could help, though.''

''I can only help,'' he said, ''if you tell me what's been happening.''

''Silly things. Stupid things. Things one hardly wants to talk about.'' He hesitated. ''Letters. Telephone calls. We had a word for it in my country. *Nadelstich*. You would translate it as pin-prickery.''

''When did it start?''

''About six months ago.''

''Did you report it at once?''

''Not until it became—unpleasant. Not until it started to involve my family as well as me. Paula, my daughter, was sent these one morning. They made her sick.''

The professor, as he was speaking, had moved across and unlocked a drawer in his desk. Now he handed Mr. Behrens a postcard-sized folder. On the outside was printed: ''A present for a nice girl.'' It opened out into a string of connected photographs. They were so revolting that even Mr. Behrens' lips wrinkled.

He said, ''Have the police tried to trace the origin of these?''

''I have shown them to no one. Paula forbade it. The thought of having to give evidence—''

''It wouldn't be nice,'' agreed Mr. Behrens. ''Can I keep them for the moment?''

''Please,'' said the professor. ''I never wish to see them again.''

Mr. Behrens paused before framing his next question. He said, ''These letters and messages. Have they been just general stuff? Or has there been anything specific?''

''The police have the letters. I cannot remember what was said on the telephone.''

''Of course not. But what line did they take? Pure xenophobia? 'Go home Czechoslovak.' That sort of thing?'' He paused invitingly.

''It was that sort of thing,'' agreed the professor.

He's lying, thought Mr. Behrens. And he's going to go right on lying. Because he's been frightened. I shan't get anything more out of him at the moment.

He said, ''I'll leave you this telephone number. It's on the London Code. Someone there will be able to contact me at once if I should be wanted.'' He took his leave. . . .

* * *

Richard Redmayne finished his whiskey, accepted a second one and said to Mr. Calder, "It's a bloody shame. The old man's the best prospect as Minister of Education this country has had this century. You think I'm prejudiced because I'm his secretary. Perhaps I am. But I can tell you this. Without Nicholson we're never going to get this Bill through."

"The PM said he had an able deputy, who would carry on with the same policy."

"Able deputy my foot. Morris is an old woman."

They were in a public house near St. James's Park underground station, much patronized by the junior staffs from Whitehall.

Mr. Calder said, "I suppose there's no chance he'll change his mind."

"None at all. He's made all his plans. As soon as his sister's fit to move, they're both going out to Canada."

"Why Canada?"

"That's were his family came from. He says they've got a really efficient Security Service out there, too. If *they* say they're going to look after you, they do it."

"We bought that one," said Mr. Calder. "Look here—you knew Nicholson as well as anyone. Better than most. Have you got any idea why—or, more to the point, how—anyone could have been getting at him?"

"Apart from politics, you mean?"

"Apart from politics. This wasn't the first attack, was it?"

"He'd had letters. And telephone calls. The sort of thing every public man gets."

"General abuse? Or specific?"

"I don't follow you."

Mr. Calder said, patiently, "There are two ways of attacking a public man. You can pick on some large, popularly believed sort of lie. If the man's a Jew, he's financially crooked. If he went to the London School of Economics and wears a red tie, he's a Communist. If he's a bachelor, he's homosexual. If you go on repeating the lie long and loud enough, someone will believe it in the end. The other method is to pick up some incident in their past life. It may be something quite silly, which wouldn't matter twopence if it were you or me—but which can be magnified out of all proportion if you're a public figure. You know what I mean?"

"Yes," said Redmayne. "I know exactly what you mean." He sat staring into his glass, and then said, "Well, he was a bachelor—"

* * *

The disposal of paper is a recurrent headache in government departments. Some of it can be destroyed and some of it must clearly be kept handy, but the bulk of it falls into that middle class of documents which no one can see any immediate use for, but which may conceivably be wanted some day. Having filled an abandoned motorcar factory near Staines Bridge, the Records Department has now taken over an airplane hangar at Brooklands and is fast filling that up too.

"Five cubic yards of paper a week," said the custodian to Mr. Behrens. "And it's getting worse. I haven't the staff to cope with it."

Mr. Behrens sympathized. He had found that a little sympathy went a long way with minor officials. "I'll do the searching myself," he said, "if you could just put me on the right track. For instance, I imagine that you index this stuff by departments. The papers I want would have come from the old MI5."

"The worst of the lot," said the custodian.

"I can tell you the approximate year of origin too. This would have originated at Blenheim in late 1940."

"When would it have been filed?"

"Probably after the end of the war."

"We got a lot of stuff from Blenheim in 1946. That's all at Staines, though."

Mr. Behrens went to Staines.

Late that afternoon he unearthed a bundle of yellow dockets. They were labeled: "Routine interrogation reports: Nov.-Dec. 1940. A-L." They appeared to be curiously incomplete.

He read them through, and then pressed the bell. When the official shuffled up, Mr. Behrens said to him, "Has anyone else been having a look at these particular records lately?"

The official said that he really couldn't say. All sorts of people came down every day to see papers. All *he* had to do was to be satisfied about their credentials. *He* couldn't keep a record of what papers they looked at.

Mr. Behrens reflected that if you paid people as little as they probably paid this particular civil servant it was idle to expect any enthusiastic or efficient service. He went back to London.

He had booked himself a room at Dons-in-London (or the "Dilly" Club), which occupies two large houses north of Lord's Cricket Ground and has the worst food and the best wine in London. It also has a unique library of classical pornography and several complete sets of the works of Dickens, Trollope and Thackeray. Mr. Behrens always used the D-I-L when he could, since he could rely on meeting a number of his cronies there.

"I understand that Sand-Douglas is up in London," he said to Mr. Calder. "I wanted to have a word with him—he was at Blenheim in 1940. You probably remember him. Why don't you join us at dinner?"

"*After* dinner," said Mr. Calder firmly.

At seven o'clock Mr. Behrens alighted from the Bakerloo tube at Marlborough Road station and started up toward the street. The evening rush was over, and the long escalator was nearly empty. Mr. Behrens sailed sedately upward, rapt in meditation. At the top he gave up his ticket and dawdled out into the street.

There were very few people about in the Finchley Road. Mr. Behrens noticed a policeman, strolling along the opposite pavement in a purposeful way which suggested that he was coming off duty and heading for home. Mr. Behrens crossed the road. When he reached the pavement, he stopped so abruptly that the man who had been crossing behind him bumped into him.

Mr. Behrens whirled round, glared at him and said, "Why are you following me?"

"What chew talking about," said the man. He was stout, bald and unremarkable except for a twisted upper lip which seemed to give him some difficulty in enunciating.

"You've been following me for more than an hour," said Mr. Behrens. "And doing it very badly."

"You're making a nerror there," said the man. Mr. Behrens was blocking his way, and he dodged to one side to get past him.

Mr. Behrens whipped up his umbrella and thrust the metal tip, hard, into the man's crotch. The man let out a scream.

"Now then," said the policeman. "What's all this?"

The man was doubled up, speechless. Mr. Behrens said, "This gentleman has been making a nuisance of himself. He accosted me, and tried to sell me some most unpleasant pictures."

"Thass a lie," said the man. But his eyes were flickering from side to side. "I never did anything to him. He poked me with his umbrella."

"*Did* you offer to sell anything to this gentleman?"

"Course I didn't."

"He's got them in his coat pocket," said Mr. Behrens.

"Thass a lie too." The man clapped a hand into his pocket, and his expression changed. He drew out the postcard-sized folder. As he did so, it fell open disclosing the photographs inside it.

"Do you mind if I have a look at those?" said the constable.

"It's a plant," said the man. "I never—"

He handed off the constable, dodged past Mr. Behrens and started off up the pavement. Mr. Behrens, reversing his umbrella, caught him round one ankle with the handle. The man crossed his legs and fell heavily.

"You'll have to come along to the station," said the constable. "I take it you'll be preferring a charge, sir."

"I shall certainly do so," said Mr. Behrens. "Here is my card. I think it disgraceful if one cannot pay a visit to London without being subjected to the attention of men like that."

Harry Sand-Douglas was a very large man, with a pink face, a mop of iron-gray hair and eyes the color of forget-me-nots. He finished his helping of marmalade pudding, pushed back his plate and lit a pipe.

"I think you did quite right," he said. "I hope you can make the charge stick."

"It might be difficult actually to charge him," said Mr. Behrens. "All I really hoped to do was to get rid of him. He was annoying me."

"They'll hold him overnight," said Mr. Calder. He had joined them at the port stage. "If you go round to the police station and withdraw the charge, they'll probably let him go. Then we could put a tail on him and see who's employing him. That really would be useful."

"It's an idea," said Mr. Behrens. "I'll telephone Elfe tonight. The interrogation originals at Staines were incomplete. Someone's been through them. But Harry tells me that duplicates *were* kept."

"They were microfilmed," said Sand-Douglas. "They were too bulky to be kept in any other way. When I think of the amount of paper we filled up questioning perfectly harmless people!"

"Where are the microfilm stored?"

"I've an idea it's somewhere at Oxford. I can find out. I'll ask Happold. He was in charge of that side of it."

"Good heavens," said Behrens. "Is Happold still alive? He must be ninety."

"Ninety-one," said Sand-Douglas. "And bathes in the Cherwell every morning."

At half-past ten Mr. Behrens said to Mr. Calder. "Why don't you stay the night here? I'm sure they can find you a bed."

"It's kind of you," said Mr. Calder, "but I told Rasselas I'd be back. He'll be worried if I don't turn up."

He caught the last train from Victoria to Swanly, picked up his car which he had left there and drove back to Lamperdown under a half moon, through the quiet lanes which smelled of tar and honeysuckle. A question about Mr. Behrens' assailant was teasing him. It was a matter of timing. The morning would probably solve it. He put it out of his mind.

Half a mile from the cottage a gray shape loomed. Mr. Calder braked sharply, and pulled the car up before a field gate. The great dog ran up to him and stopped, head cocked.

"All right," said Mr. Calder. "Message received and understood." He opened the gate, and manhandled his car in. It was a slight slope, and it was not a light car, but there was a surprising strength in Mr. Calder's barrel chest and stocky legs. When the car had been hidden, he started to walk home.

The dog ran ahead, silent as a cloud.

Two hundred yards from the cottage a roughly metaled track forked to the left. It led to a field, which was rented to a farmer. Rasselas went forward slowly. At a bend in the track he stopped again.

A van was parked, facing toward him. The offside door was open and there was a man standing beside it. Mr. Calder turned softly and went back the way he had come. Fifty yards down the track there was a gap in the hedge. He wriggled through it on hands and knees, and crept up the inside of the hedge until he could see the top of the van. Then, very gently, an inch at a time, he edged forward until he could see the whole van.

The man was standing beside the open door of the cab, one foot on the step. He was watching the track, and had one hand in his pocket. He looked remarkably wide-awake. Mr. Calder didn't like it. A van suggested numbers.

Half an hour passed slowly. Then there came the clink of shod feet against stone, and three other forms loomed.

Rasselas, who was lying almost on top of Mr. Calder inside the hedge, stiffened, and his lips drew back from his long white teeth. Mr. Calder clamped a hand firmly down on his head.

Two of the newcomers were carrying something heavy between them. It looked like an ammunition box. They opened the back of the van, pushed it in and climbed in beside it. The third man got up beside the driver. Under its own momentum the van rolled quietly down the track. As it reached the road, Mr. Calder heard the engine start up.

Not being a man who believed in taking chances against professional opposition, Mr. Calder spent the remaining hours of darkness in the ditch.

At a quarter to four, as the sky was whitening and the birds were starting to talk, he walked up the track and approached his cottage with caution. Rasselas moved beside him. They avoided the doors and went in by one of the side windows, which Mr. Calder opened with a long flat knife. Then, together, they made a very careful search. They both worked by sight but Rasselas had the additional faculty of smell to help him. And it was he who unearthed both of the booby traps. One was under the gas cooker, operated by the gas switch. The other was in the cistern of the lavatory, operated by the plug. Neither was exactly original but both, as Mr. Calder noted, had been very neatly and professionally done.

He telephoned Mr. Fortescue at his home in Leatherhead and gave him the registration number of the van, and a brief account of what had happened.

Mr. Fortescue, who sounded very wide-awake although it was still short of six in the morning, said, "Someone's got on to you very quickly, haven't they?"

"I thought the same," said Mr. Calder. "And another thing—they were trained men, working under discipline."

There was a long silence. Then Mr. Fortescue said, "When you come up to town you'd better come to the bank."

After breakfast Mr. Calder recovered his car and drove it back to the cottage. He was nearly out of petrol, but there was a can in his garage. When he pulled at the door it stuck, as it very often did. He gave it a sharp jerk. As he did so, the garage disintegrated and door came out to meet him.

When Mr. Behrens arrived at Swiss Cottage police station, he sensed that something had happened. The station sergeant showed him straight up to the CID room where he found Detective Inspector Larrymore in conference with a red-faced detective sergeant and a youngish, black-haired superintendent from the Special Branch.

"What's gone wrong," said Mr. Behrens, pleasantly.

"You've heard?" said Larrymore.

"I've heard nothing," said Mr. Behrens, "but you've all got faces like a wet Monday morning, and I've never known a station sergeant be affable before, so I guessed—"

"I'm afraid," said the Special Branch man, "that they've pulled a fast one on us. I got instructions from Commander Elfe late last night that a man might be released from here in the course of the morning, and that he was to be followed. I've got a two-car team waiting outside."

"Then—?"

"He was released at ten o'clock last night."

"What!"

Larrymore said, "Two men turned up, with a car. They had full DI5 credentials. They took over the prisoner. The man in charge ought to have checked back—"

The red-faced detective sergeant went even redder, and Mr. Behrens guessed that he had been the man in charge and felt sorry for him.

"It's easy to be wise after the event," he said. "Exactly what credentials did they produce?"

"They had identity cards with photographs, sir. As far as I could see they were properly signed and had the official stamp on them. And a letter on official notepaper to the officer in charge here, authorizing the handover. But it wasn't only that sir—"

The Special Branch man looked up sharply and said, "What else then?"

"Well, sir, it's difficult to say—but they *looked* right. When I was a recruit we did a three weeks' course with the Security people. As a matter of fact, I thought I recognized one of them as an instructor on the course. It was some time ago, of course, and I must have been mistaken—"

An uncomfortable silence was broken by the ringing of the telephone. Larrymore took the call and said, "It's for you, Mr. Behrens."

It was Mr. Fortescue. He said, "Would you come round to the bank at once. Use a police car. It can drop you at the Abbey, and you can use the back way. Don't waste any time."

"Has something happened?"

"Yes," said Mr. Fortescue. "Calder's in Gravesend Hospital. He's not dead, but he's quite far down the danger list."

"I got a message at my Whitehall office, when I got there this morning," said Mr. Fortescue. "Calder must have been conscious, because he gave the number to the senior houseman at Gravesend and it was he who rang me. It must have happened between six and nine in the morning. Because Calder had already telephoned me. . . ."

He told Mr. Behrens about it.

"I see," said Mr. Behrens. "He must have missed a third trap. They're very thorough, these people, aren't they? Were you able to trace the van?"

"The police traced it. It was stolen in the Borough yesterday."

"At about what time? Do they know?"

"Before two o'clock. Between one and two." Before Mr. Behrens could say anything, Mr. Fortescue stopped him. "I hadn't missed the point," he said. "Take it with the business at Swiss Cottage police station last night, and it adds up to something I'm not at all keen on thinking about. I gather that I'm to see the Prime Minister this afternoon. And I've gathered something else, too. Maver is *not* being invited to the meeting."

From Mr. Fortescue's office you could hear Big Ben quite clearly. First, the four sets of warning notes, then the ten strokes of the hour. It wasn't until the last of them had died away that either of them spoke again. It was Mr. Behrens who broke the silence. He said, "Of course, it was always on the cards that something like that might happen. It's happened often enough in other countries. We've never had it here. I think I'd better go down to Gravesend. If Calder can still talk, he'll find it easier to talk to me than anyone else."

"Very well," said Mr. Fortescue. "I don't need to tell you to be careful."

"I shall be extremely careful," Mr. Behrens assured him.

He was so careful that it took him three hours to reach Gravesend, and he entered the hospital by the tradesmen's entrance. He found a policeman standing in the corridor that led to the private wards, identified himself and was allowed into an anteroom. Here he found a grim-faced Sister seated at a table, guarding the inner door. She said, "No one can go in without Dr. Henfry's permission."

"Then perhaps," said Mr. Behrens, "you would be kind enough to send for Dr. Henfry."

This was clearly a breach of protocol. Sisters in hospitals do not run errands for visitors. She rang a bell, summoning a porter. The porter disappeared and silence fell.

Dr. Henfry, when he arrived five minutes later, was large and red-headed, the sort of man who would be a welcome addition to the pack in any hospital rugger team. He said, "If your name's Behrens, you can come in for five minutes."

"Thank you," said Mr. Behrens.

"Will you want the blood transfusions, doctor?"

"I'll let you know," said Dr. Henfry. "Come along, Mr. Behrens. And very quiet, please."

The bed in the room was entirely hidden by screens. Dr. Henfry closed the door carefully and bolted it. Then he moved the nearest screen and Mr. Behrens saw Mr. Calder. He was sitting up in bed reading the *Times*. On the table by his bed were the remains of a pork pie and two bottles of beer.

"It's not what we like to give our invalids for breakfast," said Dr. Henfry with a grin. "Particularly when they're at death's door. But it's all I could manage. I had to buy it myself and smuggle it in in my instrument case."

"Do I gather," said Mr. Behrens, "that you are *not* dying?"

"That's right," said Mr. Calder. "But you and Dr. Henfry are the only people who know it, and it's going to stay that way for a bit. The deputation who called at my cottage last night left a third visiting card, in the form of a few pounds of gelignite controlled by a trembler fuse and a detonator. They left it in the inspection pit in my garage. If I'd driven the car over it, I'd have been blown to Jericho. Luckly I set it off from outside by banging the door. The door hit me and knocked me cold. But it also protected me. I was still unconscious when the milkman came along. He put me straight into his van, bless him, and brought me down here. I'd come round by that time, and I realized what a stroke of luck the whole thing was. I put Dr. Henfry wise, and he's done the rest."

"I've had a gaggle of reporters round here already," said Dr. Henfry. "I told them you might recover—with luck and devoted nursing. You'd had three blood transfusions already."

"Excellent," said Mr. Calder.

"I'd better take Mr. Behrens out now, or Sister will start worrying. I'll show him the back way in along the balcony."

When they were alone together, Mr. Calder said, "You can tell Fortescue, of course. But no one else. I'm going to clear out as soon as it's dark. Dr. Henfry is fetching me."

"I assume you're going under cover?"

"We both are. We'll use Mrs. Palfrey's."

"Is this just general caution . . . or something special?"

Mr. Calder was busy pouring out the second bottle of beer and did not answer for a moment. Then he said, "That fuse on the plastic explosive under the grill was micrometer set. I shouldn't have needed to turn the gas on. The lightest touch on the switch would have set it off. When I'd immobilized it, I took some photographs. The whole thing had been beautifully concealed. even if you stooped down you could hardly see a thing. All the wires were taped, and the tapes themselves had been fish-tailed and folded under at the end. Do you remember that sergeant at the demolition school? 'Five minutes' extra work, gentlemen. But it may well make the difference between success and failure.' *He* always fish-tailed the ends of *his* tapes. It was when I saw those tapes that I decided to go undercover."

"I have on my books at this moment," said Mr. Fortescue to the Prime Minister, "twenty men and four women, any two of whom—they usually work in pairs—I *might* have allotted to this particular assignment. I selected Calder and Behrens, and I telephoned both of them on Wednesday evening. The line which I used is, I can assure you, secure. They both saw me on Thursday morning. It is true that they came quite openly, and my office in Richmond Terrace might be watched—although, as Commander Elfe will tell you, the Security precautions are such that it would be very difficult for anyone to do so without themselves being observed.''

Commander Elfe, who was the only other person present, nodded and said, ''Not impossible, but so difficult that I think we might rule it out.''

''In any event,'' went on Mr. Fortescue, ''Calder and Behrens were not the only people who saw me that morning. I had routine matters to discuss with at least six other members of my department.''

''So,'' said the Prime Minister, ''up to that time, no one would have any reason to connect them with this particular job. What did they do next?''

''Behrens visited the Records Department in the new Defence building and went from there to call on Professor Gottlieb. Calder went to Campden Hill to talk to the inspector in charge of the Nicholson inquiry.''

''At either of which points they could have been picked up and followed.''

''Oh, certainly,'' said Mr. Fortescue. ''Only Mr. Behrens did not reach the Gottlieb flat until a quarter past two, and Mr. Calder went to Campden Hill even later—at three o'clock. The van which was used for the visit to Mr. Calder's cottage was stolen between one and two. It was clearly stolen for that job, and was abandoned when it had been done.''

The Prime Minister looked at Elfe, who looked at Mr. Fortescue, and said, ''What it amounts to is this: the only people who could have known by midday that Behrens was on this job were the staff of the Defence Ministry. If they knew Behrens was on it, they would have assumed Calder was involved as well.''

''I'm afraid that's right,'' said Mr. Fortescue.

''Gentlemen,'' said the Prime Minister, ''I am not an alarmist. And thirty years in politics has taught me not to jump to conclusions. But if you add that last fact to certain others—the way in which Behrens' assailant was liberated; the method and execution of the attack on Calder—I'm afraid that a very distasteful possibility emerges.''

''You mean,'' said Commander Elfe bluntly, ''that Security executive are playing politics.''

In a comfortable bed-sitting room, in that area of bed-sitting rooms which lies between the station and the Rugby football ground at Twickenham, Mr. Behrens poured out a cup of tea for Mr. Calder and said, ''How many so far?''

''Seventeen near certainties,'' said Mr. Calder. ''Seventeen cases of public servants driven out. Nine of them have gone to live abroad. Two are in institutions. Six, including Bax, have taken their own lives. And, if those are the ones we know about, you can be certain that the true total is twice or three times as great."

Mr. Behrens said, "It was the technique which convinced me, much more than all that working out of times and places. It was such an exact reproduction of the interrogation techniques which both sides brought to horrible perfection during the war. If you wanted to break a man down, what did you do? First you made him uncomfortable. It was far more demoralizing for a man to be cold, or filthy, or sleepless, or thirsty than actually to be hurt. Discomfort weakens. Torture builds up a resistance. The Russians discovered that long ago. The interrogator's second weapon was to find something—it didn't matter what—but something which his victim was ashamed of. Some weakness, some slip. If he harped on it skillfully he could take the man to pieces."

Mr. Calder stirred his tea, and looked round the comfortable, lower-middle-class sitting room. Mrs. Palfrey's grandfather and grandmother stared back at him from fading brown oleographs over the mantelpiece. He found reassurance in their Victorian rigidity. He said, "Public servants are sitting ducks. They loathe fuss. They eschew scandal. And they can't run away. That's the point. They're nailed to their jobs. Take a man like Nicholson. He had to be within reach of Westminster and Whitehall. The only way to go out was to go right out. I wonder what they had on him. And how many times he paid up."

The arrival of Mrs. Palfrey, with a kettle of hot water and the evening paper, saved Mr. Behrens from having to reply. He found an item at the foot of the front page which seemed to interest him. He read it out: "A party of birdwatchers on the Cooling Marshes yesterday discovered, in one of the saltwater dikes, the body of a man. He has not yet been identified. The following description has been issued. Age, about forty-five. Height, five foot six. Stoutly built. A marked malformation of the upper lip."

"Do we know him?" said Mr. Calder.

"My acquaintance with him," said Mr. Behrens, "was limited to poking him with my umbrella. I cannot regard him as a great loss."

"Quick work, all the same," said Mr. Calder. "They don't believe in leaving loose ends about, do they? I wonder what they'll do next. . . . "

Richard Redmayne and Paula Gottlieb sitting on the seat in Green Park made a handsome couple.His conventional dress could not conceal a certain long-limbed, coordinated strength, the product of a school which was unfashionable enough to think athletic prowess important; the girl, dark, lively and very young.

She said, "Have you heard from Mr. Nicholson?"

"He's arrived in Canada," said Richard. "I had a short letter. He and his sister have got a flat in Toronto. He says they're settling down very happily."

"'We that had loved him so, followed him, honoured him, lived in his mild and magnificent eye, learned his great language, caught his clear accents, made him our pattern to live and to die.'"

"That's poetry," said Richard suspiciously.

"Robert Browning, 'The Lost Leader.' You remember? 'Just for a handful of silver he left us.'"

"It wasn't money in his case," said Richard. "It was fear. How's your father?"

This change of subject did not appear to surprise Paula. She had reached a stage of intimacy with Richard when such sudden jumps were part of the fun. She said, "If only he'd make up his mind. It's the uncertainty which is so horrible. If he'd only tell me—tell someone—what it's all about. He just sits at home. He hardly goes out at all. I had a job to persuade him to go out this morning and get his hair cut."

"That's two o'clock striking now," said Richard. "I've got to get back. But I'll walk home with you first."

As soon as Paula opened the door of the flat, she knew something was wrong.

"What's up?" said Richard.

"Where's Fritz?" There was panic in the girl's voice. "We left him to guard the house . . . he always runs out to meet me."

Through the open door of the drawing room they could glimpse the chaos within. Overturned chairs, broken glass, something seeping under the floor and staining the hall carpet.

Richard said urgently, "Don't go in there—stop." But he found himself unable to hold her. She burst past him and threw herself into the room. As he grabbed the telephone, he heard her give a single choked scream.

When the police and her father arrived together five minutes later, she was still on her knees, sobbing uncontrollably, with a brown and black head cradled on her lap. . . .

In the hot blacked-out room, half laboratory, half office, two men pored over the microfilm reader. "It's here if it's anywhere," said Sand-Douglas. "November 2nd, 1940. That was the day he arrived. The main interrogation would have started the day after. We usually gave them a night's rest."

Old Mr. Happold, as thin and as indestructible as dried seaweed, fed a second roll of microfilm into the reader and adjusted the reading glass.

He was unaffected by the heat and closeness of the room. "This looks like the one," he said. "Do you know exactly what it is we're looking for?"

"We're looking for a name," said Sand-Douglas. "A name out of the past. And I do believe"—he wiped a hand across to clear the sweat out of his eyes—"yes, that's it. I'll have to use your telephone. I think we'll risk an open line this time."

Professor Gottlieb looked round the table. There were four men there. Commander Elfe of the Special Branch he knew; and he had met Mr. Fortescue once, and was aware that he was connected with Security. The other two were a thickset man whom they called Mr. Calder, and Mr. Behrens.

"I don't think" said the professor, "that they could do anything more horrible than they did this morning. It was a mistake. Since there is nothing worse they can do, I have no motive not to speak. When I came to this country in 1940, I brought with me a secret of which I was bitterly ashamed. I am not a man of action. I could never have arranged my own escape from Prague. I should not have known how to start. It was arranged for me. When I told my story to your interrogators, I said that it was arranged by the Czech underground. That was a lie. It was arranged by the Germans. They bartered my escape with me for some information I was able to give them. I didn't know why they wanted it—that's no excuse. It led to the execution of two of my colleagues in Prague University. I thought, for a long time, the secret had died with them. I still have no idea how anyone could have found out."

"The man who interrogated you," said Mr. Fortescue, "also dealt with other compatriots of yours. He heard a rumor from them, and was able to verify it after the war from German sources. But please go on."

"There is no more. Seven years ago, when I began to be well known here, and well paid—the blackmail started. For seven years I have paid away about a third of all my income. Lately the demands were increased. I dug in my toes. Different forms of pressure were applied. I could do nothing to stop them. I was afraid that if I complained the whole truth would come out. I see now that I have been stupid. I should have spoken at once. But it is difficult to see these things when you are on your own."

"Have you any idea at all who the blackmailers were?" asked Commander Elfe.

"None at all. I never saw them, or spoke to them except on the telephone. I drew the money every month in notes and sent it to what I imagine was an accommodation address." He paused, and looked round the table at the four men. Mr. Calder and Mr. Behrens were looking impassive. The burly Commander Elfe had a scowl on his face. Mr. Fortescue was looking out of the window. He had a cold and clinical glint in his eye. It reminded Professor Gottlieb of a surgeon he had once watched, weighing up the chances of a delicate and critical operation. "And that's really all I can tell you," he said. "Do you think there is any chance of catching these men?"

Mr. Fortescue swiveled his head round so that he was looking directly at the professor. He said, "Oh, yes. We have found out who these men are, and where they operate from. It would be comparatively simple to render them harmless. But if we are actually to catch and convict them, we shall need a lot of luck—and your help. . . . "

"I am glad that my worst suspicions were wrong," said the Prime Minister, "and I apologize for them." He had invited Ian Maver, the head of DI5, to dinner and they were sitting together over their brandy.

"Not so far wrong," said Maver. The apology and the brandy were working on him. "Most of them are either ex-MI5 or ex-policemen. The leader is a man called Cotter. I knew him quite well. A guardsman. A very able officer, an excellent linguist and a good organizer. A bit ruthless for peacetime operations. He left us in the mid-'fifties. I think he was disappointed over promotion. Then he set up this private inquiry organization, Cotter's Detectives. We've been using him quite a bit lately ourselves. Guarding VIPs and that sort of thing."

"And it was his men who were put in charge of Nicholson?"

"That wasn't very clever," said Maver, "but if they keep us short of policemen it's bound to happen. Businesses use private gunmen to look after their payrolls now. Private watchmen patrol building estates. Private guards for VIPs? It was a logical step."

"How did you find out about him?"

"We went right back to the record of Gottlieb's first interrogation. Cotter was the man who conducted it. We got a cross-reference when we found out that Cotter and one of his men, Lawrie, had been the two 'referees' given by Smythe when he got his job in our Records Department. That was a bad slip, and it was entirely my fault."

The Prime Minister was aware that the head of DI5 was offering him his resignation if he chose to take it. He rejected the offering. His opinion of Ian Maver had changed in the course of the evening.

He said, "Everyone's allowed one mistake. Even in politics. What are you doing about Smythe?"

"For the moment, we're leaving him where he is. He happens to form rather a useful channel of communication. One of his jobs is to monitor the Records room. If we want to get a piece of information across to Cotter, without appearing to do so, all that's necessary is a little calculated indiscretion between two of our men when searching the files.''

''Do I gather from that,'' said the Prime Minister, ''that some definite action is contemplated?''

''Mr. Fortescue has the matter in hand,'' said Maver.

''It's not going to be at all easy,'' said Mr. Fortescue, ''but we have three points in our favor.'' He ticked them off with one finger of his right hand.

''First, they have no reason at all to think that we suspect them. And of course they most continue in this happy state of ignorance. Secondly, we can, if we are careful, leak information to them through Smythe. Third, and most important, I think they are bound to react to Professor Gottlieb. Like all bullies, if one of their victims rebels and they do nothing about it, other victims will follow suit. I am arranging for Professor Gottlieb to show fight.''

''They might go for his daughter,'' said Elfe.

''I had thought of that myself,'' said Mr. Fortescue, and Elfe looked up sharply.

''Do I understand that you're going to use the girl as bait?''

''It seems to me the simplest of a number of possible methods,'' said Mr. Fortescue. ''We'll keep the professor in town, and put such a ring fence of guards round him that they can't touch him. As a preliminary precaution, the girl will be sent into the country. Not too far. I had in mind the Thetford area in Norfolk. The army used it as a battle school during the war, and parts of it are still quite deserted.''

''And you're going to let them know she's there?''

''It will come to their ears in about a week's time.''

''I don't like it,'' said Elfe. ''It's too risky.''

''Any plan will be risky,'' said Mr. Fortescue. ''This plan will, I think have less risk than most. I always prefer to play a match on ground of my own choosing.''

''Who are you going to send with her? Calder—or Behrens?''

''If I sent either of them, it would be stupid of Cotter to go near her and Cotter is not a stupid man. No. I had in mind that Nicholson's secretary, young Redmayne, would be the man for the job. They know each other and are, I believe, good friends. They'll be suitably chaperoned, of course.''

* * *

Harwood Farm lay at the e
rambling, yellow-brick buildir
for some months, since the la
were now farmed by a man w

One of the pleasantest
mayne, had been the effor
For a fortnight he and P
scrubbed and scoured
several unexpected s
engine and dynamo whic
aid of a carload of technical stor
output, so that bulbs which had previo
brightly as though they were on mains.

''My father taught me not to be afraid of electricit
just like water. You see water coming out of a tap. A nice s
Halve the outlet, and you double the power. Like this.'' She was hol
a length of hosepipe in her hand, swilling down the choked gutters in the yard. As she pinched the end of the hose, a thin jet of water hissed out.

''All right,'' said Richard, ducking. ''You needn't demonstrate it. I understand the principle. I didn't know it applied to electricity, that's all.''

''Tomorrow,'' said Paula, ''I'm going to get Mrs. Mason to stoke up the boiler, and I'm going to run a hose into the big barn. I'll use a proper stopcock, and we'll build up the pressure. Then you'll see what steam can do. Did you know that if you got a fine enough jet and sufficient pressure you could cut metal with steam?''

''For goodness' sake, don't try it,'' said Richard. ''We shall blow ourselves up.''

''You're a coward,'' said Paula. ''By the way, did you see the *Times* this morning? It's got something about Daddy in it.''

It was a paragraph on the Home News page. It said that Professor Gottlieb was confident of finishing his final revision of the White Paper on Planning before the end of the month. The professor had held a news conference, in which he had said that certain minor technical difficulties which had been holding him up had been satisfactorily disposed of.

''He's trailing his coat,'' said Paula.

''What do you mean?''

''You must think me an idiot if you imagine I don't know what's going on. He's provoking those people to attack him, isn't he? And that's why I've been stowed away here, to be out of harm's way.''

''Well—'' said Richard.

ard. There's no need to apologize. I'm enjoying
rying about Daddy."
ooked after," said Richard.
after, he couldn't help thinking, than Paula herself. He
ngle afternoon of instruction he had been given—on the
llington Barracks—with the automatic pistol which he now
ked under his left armpit by day and placed under his pillow
nt. It was comforting to have a gun, but he was still far from
that he could hit anything with it. Mrs. Mason, he knew, was
ected with Fortescue's organization, but if real trouble devel-
ed . . .

"What are *you* looking so serious about?" said Paula.

"Nothing," said Richard. "I was working out what we had to do to the barn now that we've got the house in order."

Visitors to the farm were few but regular, and already their visits had fallen into a pattern. The grocer from East Harling delivered on Tuesday and Friday. The fishmonger and butcher came out from Diss on Thursday. Twice every day the little red post van came bowling down the lane with letters and newspapers. And on Friday the dustcart arrived to carry away the week's rubbish.

Mrs. Mason, doubtless acting on orders, allowed none of them near the house but went out to the gate to collect their offerings herself. To Richard they were blurred faces seen behind a windshield, except for the rubbish collectors, whose names were Ernest and Leonard and with whom he had exchanged local gossip.

The postman was a plump cheerful man. He operated from Diss, and had taken over the round which included Harwood Farm on the day before Richard and Paula arrived. He lodged in a back street and, although apparently a temporary, carried out his work in an efficient manner.

Indeed, so conscientious was he that in the evenings, after his rounds were completed, he would often take the van and tour the district, memorizing roads and lanes, houses and farms, and the position of telephone kiosks and AA boxes.

That Thursday night, when he returned to his lodging, he found a postcard propped up on the mantelpiece. The front showed a stout lady in a bathing dress, whose toe was being eaten by a crab. On the back was written: "Uncle Tom and the three boys planning to start for country tomorrow." It was signed "Edna," and the name was underlined three times.

"Three-line whip," said the postman to himself. He went across to the cupboard and took out a violin case. But what he took out of it was certainly not a violin. . . .

Friday was a perfect day. The sun rose through a cloak of early morning mist, scattered it and sailed in majesty across the heavens. Life at Harwood Farm pursued its unexciting course. The grocer came with groceries, and the postman on his morning round stopped for a gossip with Mrs. Mason. He seemd to do most of the talking. Mrs. Mason contented herself with nodding. She was a woman of few words. Her only relaxation was the *Times* crossword puzzle which she regularly finished in the kitchen when they had given it up in the drawing room. In the afternoon Paula rigged her steam hose, a fearsome contraption of plastic pipe and chromium fitting, and cleaned out the cowstalls at the end of the barn. The thin scalding jet stripped the filth of ages from the floors and wooden walls with the speed of a rotary plane.

It was five o'clock in the afternoon when the dustcart drove up. The driver reversed the lumbering vehicle in the space in front of the gate. He did it clumsily, crashing his gears, as if he was unused to driving it. Three men got out of the back. They walked quickly through the yard, ignoring the two dustbins and pushed into the kitchen.

Mrs. Mason jumped up, saw the gun in the hand of the leading man and said, calmly, "What do you want?"

"Take it easy," said the man, "and you won't get hurt." As he said this the second man walked round behind her and smacked her across the back of the neck with a leather-covered cosh. The third man caught her as she fell forward.

"Put her in that cupboard," said the leader. "There's a bolt on the outside."

Mr. Calder, turning the post van in at the top of the lane, saw signs of the ambush. The surface of the road was broken where the heavy dustcart had lurched to a halt, and the hedge was broken too. Mr. Calder jumped out to investigate, and found Ernest and Leonard in the ditch, their elbows and ankles strapped and their heads in paper dust sacks. He undid them and they sat up, swearing. Mr. Calder cut them short.

"There's a public telephone three hundred yards down the main road," he said. "Get there as quick as you can—ask for this number—and just say the word *Action*."

Leonard, who was the younger and more spirited of the two, said, "Couldn't we get after those bastards first?"

"No," said Mr. Calder. "You'd be in the way. Just do what I told you. And quick."

As they lumbered off down the road, he got back into his van. He could be heard coming, but that couldn't be helped. Speed was now more important than surprise. Anyway, he had no intention of driving up to the house. He had long ago located a field track, usable in dry weather, which led off the lane to a point behind the barn. . . .

The farmhouse being old and its walls thick, Richard, who was writing in the drawing room, had heard nothing of the goings-on in the kitchen. He did, however, hear heavy footsteps coming along the stone-floored passage, footsteps which could not belong to Mrs. Mason or Paula. He had time to get his gun out. It wasn't a bad shot for a first attempt. He missed Cotter who led the rush through the door, but hit the man behind him in the knee.

Cotter, steadying himself, shot Richard through the right shoulder, knocking him off his chair onto the floor. Then he picked up his gun and took no further notice of him.

"We'll look after Lawrie in a moment," he said. "We've got to grab the girl before she runs for it."

It was unfortunate for them that, being in a hurry, they came out of the door and into the yard together. Cotter realized their mistake when he heard the girl's voice from behind them. She said, "This gun's loaded, both barrels. Even I couldn't miss you from here."

The two men turned. Cotter's gun was back in its shoulder holster. The other man had not drawn his. And the girl was holding a twelve-bore, double-barreled sporting rifle.

"Into the barn," she said.

They moved slowly ahead of her. Cotter looked at the door as he went through to see if he could slam it, but it was too heavy and had been firmly wedged open with a stake.

"Down that end," she said. "Now. Take your guns out slowly and drop them on the ground."

The two men had spread themselves out. It was a deliberate movement. They knew very well that the odds were still on their side. As Cotter pulled his gun and dropped it onto the floor in front of him, he let it fall even farther to one side, and shuffled after it. The other man did the same. The gun barrel wavered. They were now so far apart that one shot could not hit both of them.

"What are you planning to do?" said Cotter, edging over a little farther. He was now almost up against the side wall of the barn. "Keep us here till it's dark?" He had seen the side door of the barn move and guessed that it was the fourth man, the driver of the van, coming to lend a hand. Keep her attention, and the driver could jump her from behind. No point in shooting her.

Paula saw the danger out of the corner of her eye. She swung round and fired both barrels. The first missed altogether. The second hit the driver full in the chest. As she fired, she dropped the gun, put out a hand without hurry, laid hold of the steam hosepipe and flicked open the faucet.

A jet of scalding steam, thin and sharp as a needle, hissed from the nozzle and seemed to hang in the air for a moment, then hit Cotter full in the face as he stooped for his gun. He went forward onto his knees. The hose followed him down, searing and stripping.

The second man got hold of his gun. Mr. Calder, standing square in the doorway of the barn, shot his legs from under him with his tommy gun.

When the carload of Special Branch men arrived they found Mr. Calder in the barn. The officer in charge was the same dark-haired young man whom Mr. Behrens had encountered at the police station. He introduced himself to Mr. Calder as Superintendent Patrick Petrella.

"We got your message," he said, "and passed it on to London. Behrens will have rounded up Smythe and the others by now. I don't think they're going to give us much trouble. Cotter was the mainspring of the whole thing."

"He's a busted mainspring now," said Mr. Calder. "There's going to be a lot of clearing up to do. I've got three wounded men for you. And two dead."

"I've yet to learn," said Petrella, "that it's a crime to resist an armed attempt at kidnaping. She'll get a vote of thanks." He moved across to the other end of the barn where two shapes lay, covered by sacks. "Which is Cotter?"

"This one," said Mr. Calder. "He isn't a very nice sight."

"Good God," said Petrella, shaken out of his phlegm. "What did she do that with?"

"She used a high-pressure steam hose," said Mr. Calder. "Cotter made a mistake. He killed her dog and mutilated it. I know just how she felt. I've got a dog myself."

IAN FLEMING

Octopussy

"YOU KNOW WHAT?" said Major Dexter Smythe to the octopus. "You're going to have a real treat today if I can manage it."

He had spoken aloud, and his breath had steamed up the glass of his Pirelli mask. He put his feet down to the sand beside the coral boulder and stood up. The water reached to his armpits. He took off the mask and spat into it, rubbed the spit round the glass, rinsed it clean, and pulled the rubber band of the mask back over his head. He bent down again.

The eye in the mottled brown sack was still watching him carefully from the hole in the coral, but now the tip of a single small tentacle wavered hesitatingly an inch or two out of the shadows and quested vaguely with its pink suckers uppermost. Dexter Smythe smiled with satisfaction. Given time—perhaps one more month on top of the two during which he had been chumming the octopus—and he would have tamed the darling. But he wasn't going to have that month. Should he take a chance today and reach down and offer his hand, instead of the expected lump of raw meat on the end of his spear, to the tentacle. Shake it by the hand, so to speak? No, Pussy, he thought. I can't quite trust you yet. Almost certainly other tentacles would whip out of the hole and up his arm. He only needed to be dragged down less than two feet for the cork valve on his mask to automatically close, and he would be suffocated inside it or, if he tore it off, drowned. He might get in a quick lucky jab with his spear, but it would take more than that to kill Pussy. No. Perhaps later in the day. It would be rather like playing Russian roulette, and at about the same five-to-one odds. It might be a quick, a whimsical, way out of his troubles! But not now. It would leave the interesting question unsolved. And he had promised that nice Professor Bengry at the Institute. . . . Dexter Smythe swam leisurely off toward the reef, his eyes questing for one shape only, the squat, sinister wedge of a scorpionfish, or, as Bengry would put it, *Scorpaena plumieri*.

Major Dexter Smythe, O.B.E., Royal Marines (Retd.), was the remains of a once brave and resourceful officer and a handsome man who had had the sexual run of his teeth all his life, particularly among the Wrens and Wracs and ATS who manned the communications and secretariat of the very special task force to which he had been attached at the end of his service career. Now he was fifty-four and slightly bald, and his belly sagged in his Jantzen trunks. And he had had two coronary thromboses, the second (the "second warning" as his doctor, Jimmy Greaves, who had been at one of their high poker games at Prince's Club when Dexter Smythe had first come to Jamaica, had half jocularly put it) only a month before. But, in his well-chosen clothes, with his varicose veins out of sight, and with his stomach flattened by a discreet support belt behind an immaculate cummerbund, he was still a fine figure of a man at a cocktail party or dinner on the North Shore. And it was a mystery to his friends and neighbors why, in defiance of the two ounces of whiskey and the ten cigarettes a day to which his doctor had rationed him, he persisted in smoking like a chimney and going to bed drunk, if amiably drunk, every night.

The truth of the matter was that Dexter Smythe had arrived at the frontier of the death wish. The origins of this state of mind were many and not all that complex. He was irretrievably tied to Jamaica, and tropical sloth had gradually riddled him so that, while outwardly he appeared a piece of fairly solid hardwood, inside the varnished surface, the termites of sloth, self-indulgence, guilt over an ancient sin, and general disgust with himself had eroded his once hard core into dust. Since the death of Mary two years before, he had loved no one. (He wasn't even sure that he had really loved her, but he knew that, every hour of the day, he missed her love of him and her gay, untidy, chiding, and often irritating presence.) And though he ate their canapés and drank their martinis, he had nothing but contempt for the international riffraff with whom he consorted on the North Shore. He could perhaps have made friends with the more solid elements—the gentleman-farmers inland, the plantation owners on the coast, the professional men, the politicians—but that would mean regaining some serious purpose in life which his sloth, his spiritual accidie, prevented, and cutting down on the bottle, which he was definitely unwilling to do. So Major Smythe was bored, bored to death, and, but for one factor in his life, he would long ago have swallowed the bottle of barbiturates he had easily acquired from a local doctor. The lifeline that kept him clinging to the edge of the cliff was a tenuous one. Heavy drinkers veer toward an exaggeration of their basic temperaments, the classic four—sanguine, phlegmatic, choleric, and melancholic. The sanguine drunk goes gay to the point of hysteria and idiocy; the phlegmatic sinks into a morass of sullen gloom; the choleric is the fighting drunk of the cartoonists who spends much of his life in prison for smashing people and things; and the melancholic succumbs to self-pity, mawkishness, and tears. Major Smythe was a melancholic who had slid into a drooling fantasy woven around the birds and insects and fish that inhabited the five acres of Wavelets (the name he had given his small villa was symptomatic), its beach, and the coral reef beyond. The fish were his particular favorites. He referred to them as "people," and since reef fish stick to their territories as closely as do most small birds, he knew them all, after two years, intimately, "loved" them, and believed that they loved him in return.

They certainly knew him, as the denizens of zoos know their keepers, because he was a daily and a regular provider, scraping off algae and stirring up the sand and rocks for the bottom-feeders, breaking up sea eggs and sea urchins for the small carnivores, and bringing out scraps of offal for the larger ones. And now, as he swam slowly and heavily up and down the reef and through the channels that led out to deep water, his "people" swarmed around him fearlessly and expectantly, darting at the tip of the three-pronged spear they knew only as a prodigal spoon, flirting right up to the glass of the Pirelli, and even, in the case of the fearless, pugnacious demoiselles, nipping softly at his feet and legs.

Part of Major Smythe's mind took in all these brilliantly colored little "people" and he greeted them in unspoken words. ("Morning, Beau Gregory" to the dark blue demoiselle sprinkled with bright blue spots—the jewelfish that exactly resembles the starlit fashioning of a bottle of Guerlain's Dans La Nuit; "Sorry. Not today, sweetheart" to a fluttering butterflyfish with false black eyes on its tail; and "You're too fat anyway, Blue Boy," to an indigo parrotfish that must have weighed a good ten pounds.) But today he had a job to do and his eyes were searching for only one of his "people"—his only enemy on the reef, the only one he killed on sight, a scorpionfish.

The scorpionfish inhabits most of the southern waters of the world, and the rascasse that is the foundation of bouillabaisse belongs to the family. The West Indian variety runs up to only about twelve inches long and perhaps a pound in weight. It is by far the ugliest fish in the sea, as if nature were giving warning. It is a mottled brownish gray with a heavy wedge-shaped shaggy head. It has fleshy pendulous "eyebrows" that droop over angry red eyes and a coloration and broken silhouette that are perfect camouflage on the reef. Though a small fish, its heavily toothed mouth is so wide that it can swallow whole most of the smaller reef fishes, but its supreme weapon lies in its erectile dorsal fins, the first few of which, acting on contact like hypodermic needles, are fed by poison glands containing enough dotoxin to kill a man if they merely graze him in a vulnerable spot—in an artery, for instance, or over the heart or in the groin. It constitutes the only real danger to the reef swimmer, far more dangerous than the barracuda or the shark, because, supreme in its confidence in its camouflage and armory, it flees before nothing except the very close approach of a foot or actual contact. Then it flits only a few yards, on wide and bizarrely striped pectorals, and settles again watchfully either on the sand, where it looks like a lump of overgrown coral, or among the rocks and seaweed where it virtually disappears. And Major Smythe was determined to find one and spear it and give it to his octopus to see if it would take it or spurn it—to see if one of the ocean's great predators would recognize the deadliness of another, know of its poison. Would the octopus consume the belly and leave the spines? Would it eat the lot? And if so, would it suffer from the poison? These were the questions Bengry at the Institute wanted answered, and today, since it was going to be the beginning of the end of Major Smythe's life at Wavelets—and though it might mean the end of his darling Octopussy—Major Smythe had decided to find out the answers and leave one tiny memorial to his now futile life in some dusty corner of the Institute's marine biological files.

For, in only the last couple of hours, Major Dexter Smythe's already dismal life had changed very much for the worse. So much for the worse that he would be lucky if, in a few weeks' time—time for an exchange of cables via Government House and the Colonial Office to the Secret Service and thence to Scotland Yard and the Public Prosecutor, and for Major Smythe's transportation to London with a police escort—he got away with a sentence of imprisonment for life.

And all this because of a man called Bond, Commander James Bond, who had turned up at ten-thirty that morning in a taxi from Kingston.

The day had started normally. Major Smythe had awakened from his Seconal sleep, swallowed a couple of Panadols (his heart condition forbade him aspirin), showered, skimped his breakfast under the umbrella-shaped sea almonds, and spent an hour feeding the remains of his breakfast to the birds. He then took his prescribed doses of anticoagulant and blood-pressure pills and killed time with the *Daily Gleaner* until it was time for his elevenses, which, for some months now, he had advanced to ten-thirty. He had just poured himself the first of two stiff brandy and ginger ales (The Drunkard's Drink) when he heard the car coming up the drive.

Luna, his colored housekeeper, came out into the garden and announced ''Gemmun to see you, Major.''

''What's his name?''

''Him doan say, Major. Him say to tell you him come from Govment House.''

Major Smythe was wearing nothing but a pair of old khaki shorts and sandals. He said, ''All right, Luna. Put him in the living room and say I won't be a moment.'' And he went round the back way into his bedroom and put on a white bush shirt and trousers and brushed his hair. Government House! Now what the hell?

As soon as he had walked through into the living room and seen the tall man in the dark tropical suit standing at the picture window looking out to sea, Major Smythe had somehow sensed bad news. And, when the man had turned slowly toward him and looked at him with watchful, serious gray-blue eyes, he had known that this was officialdom, and when his cheery smile was not returned, inimical officialdom. And a chill had run down Major Smythe's spine. ''They'' had somehow found out.

''Well, well. I'm Smythe. I gather you're from Government House. How's Sir Kenneth?''

There was somehow no question of shaking hands. The man said, ''I haven't met him. I only arrived a couple of days ago. I've been out round the island most of the time. My name's Bond, James Bond. I'm from the Ministry of Defense.''

Major Smythe remembered the hoary euphemism for the Secret Service. He said bonhomously, ''Oh. The old firm?''

The question had been ignored. ''Is there somewhere we can talk?''

''Rather. Anywhere you like. Here or in the garden? What about a drink?'' Major Smythe clinked the ice in the glass he still held in his hand. ''Rum and ginger's the local poison. I prefer the ginger by itself.'' The lie came out with the automatic smoothness of the alcoholic.

''No thanks. And here would be fine.'' The man leaned negligently against the wide mahogany windowsill.

Major Smythe sat down and threw a jaunty leg over the low arm of one of the comfortable planters' chairs he had had copied from an original by the local cabinetmaker. He pulled out the drink coaster from the other arm, took a deep pull at his glass, and slid it, with a consciously steady hand, down into the hole in the wood. ''Well,'' he said cheerily, looking the other man straight in the eyes, ''what can I do for you? Somebody been up to some dirty work on the North Shore and you need a spare hand? Be glad to get into harness again. It's been a long time since those days, but I can still remember some of the old routines.''

"Do you mind if I smoke?" The man had already got his cigarette case in his hand. It was a flat gun-metal one that would hold around twenty-five. Somehow this small sign of a shared weakness comforted Major Smythe.

"Of course, my dear fellow." He made a move to get up, his lighter ready.

"It's all right, thanks." James Bond had already lit his cigarette. "No, it's nothing local. I want to . . . I've been sent out to . . . ask you to recall your work for the Service at the end of the war." James Bond paused and looked down at Major Smythe carefully. "Particularly the time when you were working with the Miscellaneous Objectives Bureau."

Major Smythe laughed sharply. He had known it. He had known it for absolutely sure. But when it came out of this man's mouth, the laugh had been forced out of Major Smythe like the scream of a hit man. "Oh Lord, yes. Good old MOB. That was a lark all right." He laughed again. He felt the anginal pain, brought on by the pressure of what he knew was coming, build up across his chest. He dipped his hand into his trouser pocket, tilted the little bottle into the palm of his hand, and slipped the white TNT pill under his tongue. He was amused to see the tension coil up in the other man, the way the eyes narrowed watchfully. *It's all right, my dear fellow. This isn't a death pill.* He said, "You troubled with acidosis? No? It slays me when I go on a bender. Last night. Party at Jamaica Inn. One really ought to stop thinking one's always twenty-five. Anyway, let's get back to MOB Force. Not many of us left, I suppose." He felt the pain across his chest withdraw into its lair. "Something to do with the Official History?"

James Bond looked down at the tip of his cigarette. "Not exactly."

"I expect you know I wrote most of the chapter on the Force for the War Book. It's fifteen years since then. Doubt if I'd have much to add today."

"Nothing more about that operation in the Tirol—place called Oberaurach, about a mile east of Kitzbühel?"

One of the names he had been living with for fifteen years forced another harsh laugh out of Major Smythe. "That was a piece of cake! You've never seen such a shambles. All those Gestapo toughs with their doxies. All of 'em hog-drunk. They'd kept their files all ticketty-boo. Handed them over without a murmur. Hoped that'd earn 'em easy treatment I suppose. We gave the stuff a first going-over and shipped all the bods off to the Munich camp. Last I heard of them. Most of them hanged for war crimes I expect. We handed the bumf over to HQ at

Salzburg. Then we went on up the Mittersill valley after another hideout.'' Major Smythe took a good pull at his drink and lit a cigarette. He looked up. ''That's the long and the short of it.''

''You were Number Two at the time, I think. The CO was an American, a Colonel King from Patton's army.''

''That's right. Nice fellow. Wore a mustache, which isn't like an American. Knew his way among the local wines. Quite a civilized chap.''

''In his report about the operation he wrote that he handed you all the documents for a preliminary run-through as you were the German expert with the unit. Then you gave them all back to him with your comments?'' James Bond paused. ''Every single one of them?''

Major Smythe ignored the innuendo. ''That's right. Mostly lists of names. Counterintelligence dope. The CI people in Salzburg were very pleased with the stuff. Gave them plenty of new leads. I expect the originals are lying about somewhere. They'll have been used for the Nuremberg Trials. Yes, by Jove!''—Major Smyth was reminiscent, pally—''those were some of the jolliest months of my life, haring around the country with MOB Force. Wine, women, and song! And you can say that again!''

Here, Major Smythe was saying the whole truth. He had had a dangerous and uncomfortable war until 1945. When the commandos were formed in 1941, he had volunteered and been seconded from the Royal Marines to Combined Operations Headquarters under Mountbatten. There his excellent German (his mother had come from Heidelberg) had earned him the unenviable job of being advanced interrogator on commando operations across the Channel. He had been lucky to get away from two years of this work unscathed and with the O.B.E. (Military), which was sparingly awarded in the last war. And then, in preparation for the defeat of Germany, the Miscellaneous Objectives Bureau had been formed jointly by the Secret Service and Combined Operations, and Major Smythe had been given the temporary rank of lieutenant colonel and told to form a unit whose job would be the cleaning up of Gestapo and Abwehr hideouts when the collapse of Germany came about. The OSS got to hear of the scheme and insisted on getting into the act to cope with the American wing on the front, and the result was the creation of not one but six units that went into operation in Germany and Austria on the day of surrender. They were units of twenty men, each with a light armored car, six jeeps, a wireless truck, and three lorries, and they were controlled by a joint Anglo-American headquarters in SHAEF, which also fed them with targets from the Army Intelligence units and from the SIS and OSS. Major Smythe had been Number Two of "A" Force, which had been allotted the Tirol—an area full of good hiding places with easy access to Italy and perhaps out of Europe—that was known to have been chosen as funkhole Number One by the people MOB Force was after. And, as Major Smythe had just told Bond, they had had themselves a ball. All without firing a shot—except, that is, two fired by Major Smythe.

James Bond said casually, "Does the name of Hannes Oberhauser ring a bell?"

Major Smythe frowned, trying to remember. "Can't say it does." It was eighty degrees in the shade, but he shivered.

"Let me refresh your memory. On the same day as those documents were given to you to look over, you made inquiries at the Tiefenbrünner Hotel, where you were billeted, for the best mountain guide in Kitzbühel. You were referred to Oberhauser. The next day you asked your CO for a day's leave, which was granted. Early next morning you went to Oberhauser's chalet, put him under close arrest, and drove him away in your jeep. Does that ring a bell?"

That phrase about "refreshing your memory." How often had Major Smythe himself used it when he was trying to trap a German liar? *Take your time! You've been ready for something like this for years.* Major Smythe shook his head doubtfully. "Can't say it does."

"A man with graying hair and a gammy leg. Spoke some English, he'd been a ski teacher before the war."

Major Smythe looked candidly into the cold, clear blue eyes. "Sorry. Can't help you."

James Bond took a small blue leather notebook out of his inside pocket and turned the leaves. He stopped turning them. He looked up. "At that time, as side arms, you were carrying a regulation Webley-Scott forty-five with the serial number eight-nine-six-seven-three-sixty-two."

"It was certainly a Webley. Damned clumsy weapon. Hope they've got something more like the Luger or the heavy Beretta these days. But I can't say I ever took a note of the number."

"The number's right enough," said James Bond. "I've got the date of its issue to you by HQ and the date when you turned it in. You signed the book both times."

Major Smythe shrugged. "Well then, it must have been my gun. But"—he put rather angry impatience into his voice—"what, if I may ask, is all this in aid of?"

James Bond looked at him almost with curiosity. He said, and now his voice was not unkind, "You know what it's all about, Smythe." He paused and seemed to reflect. "Tell you what. I'll go out into the garden for ten minutes or so. Give you time to think things over. Give me a hail." He added seriously, "It'll make things so much easier for you if you come out with the story in your own words."

Bond walked to the door into the garden. He turned around. "I'm afraid it's only a question of dotting the *i*'s and crossing the *t*'s. You see I had a talk with the Foo brothers in Kingston yesterday." He stepped out onto the lawn.

Something in Major Smythe was relieved. Now at least the battle of wits, the trying to invent alibis, the evasions, were over. If this man Bond had got to the Foos, to either of them, they would have spilled the beans. The last thing they wanted was to get in bad with the government, and anyway there was only about six inches of the stuff left.

Major Smythe got briskly to his feet and went to the loaded sideboard and poured himself out another brandy and ginger ale, almost fifty-fifty. He might as well live it up while there was still time! The future wouldn't hold many more of these for him. He went back to his chair and lit his twentieth cigarette of the day. He looked at his watch. It said eleven-thirty. If he could be rid of the chap in an hour, he'd have plenty of time with his "people." He sat and drank and marshaled his thoughts. He could make the story long or short, put in the weather and the way the flowers and pines had smelled on the mountain, or he could cut it short. He would cut it short.

Up in that big double bedroom in the Tiefenbrünner, with the wads of buff and gray paper spread out on the spare bed, he hadn't been looking for anything special, just taking samples here and there and concentrating on the ones marked in red, KOMMANDOSACHE—HÖCHST VERTRAULICH. There weren't many of these, and they were mostly confidential reports on German top brass, intercepts of broken allied ciphers, and information about the whereabouts of secret dumps. Since these were the main targets of "A" Force, Major Smythe had scanned them with particular excitement—food, explosives, guns, espionage records, files of Gestapo personnel. A tremendous haul! And then, at the bottom of the packet, there had been the single envelope sealed with red wax and the notation ONLY TO BE OPENED IN FINAL EMERGENCY. The envelope contained one single sheet of paper. It was unsigned, and the few words were written in red ink. The heading said VALUTA, and beneath it was written: WILDE KAISER. FRANZISKANER HALT. 100 M. ÖSTLICH STEINHÜGEL. WAFFENKISTE ZWEI BAR 24 KT. Under that was a list of measurements in centimeters. Major Smythe held his hands apart as if telling a story about a fish he had caught. The bars would be about as wide as his shoulders and about two by four inches. And one single English sovereign of only eighteen carats was selling nowadays for two to three pounds! This was a bloody fortune! Forty, fifty thousand pounds worth! Maybe even a hundred! He didn't stop to think, but, quite coolly and speedily, in case anyone should come in, he put a match to the paper and the envelope, ground the ashes to powder, and swilled them down the lavatory. Then he took out his large-scale Austrian ordnance map of the area and in a moment had his finger on the Franziskaner Halt. It was marked as an uninhabited mountaineers' refuge on a saddle just below the highest of the easterly peaks of the Kaiser mountains, that awe-inspiring range of giant stone teeth that gave Kitzbühel its threatening northern horizon. And the cairn of stones would be about there—his fingernail pointed—and the whole bloody lot was only ten miles and perhaps a five hours' climb away!

The beginning had been as this fellow Bond had described. He had gone to Oberhauser's chalet at four in the morning, had arrested him, and had told his weeping, protesting family that Smythe was taking him to an interrogation camp in Munich. If the guide's record was clean he would be back home within a week. If the family kicked up a fuss it would only make trouble for Oberhauser. Smythe had refused to give his name and had had the forethought to shroud the numbers on his jeep. In twenty-four hours, "A" Force would be on its way, and by the time military government got to Kitzbühel, the incident would already be buried under the morass of the Occupation tangle.

Oberhauser had been a nice enough chap once he had recovered from his fright, and when Smythe talked knowingly about skiing and climbing, both of which he had done before the war, the pair, as Smythe intended, became quite pally. Their route lay along the bottom of the Kaiser range to Kufstein, and Smythe drove slowly, making admiring comments on the peaks that were now flushed with the pink of dawn. Finally, below the peak of gold, as he called it to himself, he slowed to a halt and pulled off the road into a grassy glade. He turned in his seat and said with an assumption of candor, "Oberhauser, you are a man after my own heart. We share many interests together, and from your talk, and from the man I think you to be, I am sure you did not cooperate with the Nazis. Now I will tell you what I will do. We will spend the day climbing on the Kaiser, and I will then drive you back to Kitzbühel and report to my commanding officer that you have been cleared at Munich." He grinned cheerfully. "Now. How about that?"

The man had been near to tears of gratitude. But could he have some kind of paper to show that he was a good citizen? Certainly. Major Smythe's signature would be quite enough. The pact was made, the jeep was driven up a track and well hidden from the road, and they were off at a steady pace, climbing up through the pine-scented foothills.

Smythe was well dressed for the climb. He had nothing on except his bush shirt, shorts, and a pair of the excellent rubber-soled boots issued to American parachutists. His only burden was the Webley-Scott, and, tactfully, for Oberhauser was after all one of the enemy, Oberhauser didn't suggest that he leave it behind some conspicuous rock. Oberhauser was in his best suit and boots, but that didn't seem to bother him, and he assured Major Smythe that ropes and pitons would not be needed for their climb and that there was a hut directly up above them where they could rest. It was called the Franziskaner Halt.

"Is it indeed?" said Major Smythe.

"Yes, and below it there is a small glacier. Very pretty, but we will climb round it. There are many crevasses."

"Is that so?" said Major Smythe thoughtfully. He examined the back of Oberhauser's head, now beaded with sweat. After all, he was only a bloody kraut, or at any rate of that ilk. What would one more or less matter? It was all going to be as easy as falling off a log. The only thing that worried Major Smythe was getting the bloody stuff down the mountain. He decided that he would somehow sling the bars across his back. After all, he could slide it most of the way in its ammunition box or whatnot.

It was a long, dreary hack up the mountain, and when they were above the treeline, the sun came up and it was very hot. And now it was all rock and scree, and their long zigzags sent boulders and rubble rumbling and crashing down the slope that got steeper as they approached the final crag, gray and menacing, that lanced away into the blue above them. They were both naked to the waist and sweating, so that the sweat ran down their legs into their boots, but despite Oberhauser's limp, they kept up a good pace, and when they stopped for a drink and a swabdown at a hurtling mountain stream, Oberhauser congratulated Major Smythe on his fitness. Major Smythe, his mind full of dreams, said curtly and untruthfully that all English soldiers were fit, and they went on.

The rock face wasn't difficult. Major Smythe had known that it wouldn't be or the climbers' hut couldn't have been built on the shoulder. Toeholds had been cut in the face, and there were occasional iron pegs hammered into crevices. But he couldn't have found the more difficult traverses by himself, and he congratulated himself on deciding to bring a guide.

Once, Oberhauser's hand, testing for a grip, dislodged a great slab of rock, loosened by five years of snow and frost, and sent it crashing down the mountain. Major Smythe suddenly thought about noise. "Many people around here?" he asked as they watched the boulder hurtle down into the treeline.

"Not a soul until you get near Kufstein," said Oberhauser. He gestured along the arid range of high peaks. "No grazing. Little water. Only the climbers come here. And since the beginning of the war. . . ." He left the phrase unfinished.

They skirted the blue-fanged glacier below the final climb to the shoulder. Major Smythe's careful eyes took in the width and depth of the crevasses. Yes, they would fit! Directly above them, perhaps a hundred feet up under the lee of the shoulder, were the weatherbeaten boards of the hut. Major Smythe measured the angle of the slope. Yes, it was almost a straight dive down. Now or later? He guessed later. The line of the last traverse wasn't very clear.

They were up at the hut in five hours flat. Major Smythe said he wanted to relieve himself and wandered casually along the shoulder to the east, paying no heed to the beautiful panoramas of Austria and Bavaria that stretched away on either side of him perhaps fifty miles into the heat haze. He counted his paces carefully. At exactly one hundred and twenty there was the cairn of stones, a loving memorial perhaps to some long dead climber. Major Smythe, knowing differently, longed to tear it apart there and then. Instead he took out his Webley-Scott, squinted down the barrel, and twirled the cylinder. Then he walked back.

It was cold up there at ten thousand feet or more, and Oberhauser had got into the hut and was busy preparing a fire. Major Smythe controlled his horror at the sight. "Oberhauser," he said cheerfully, "come out and show me some of the sights. Wonderful view up here."

"Certainly, Major." Oberhauser followed Major Smythe out of the hut. Outside, he fished in his hip pocket and produced something wrapped in paper. He undid the paper to reveal a hard wrinkled sausage. He offered it to the major. "It is only what we call a *Soldat*," he said shyly. "Smoked meat. Very tough but good." He smiled. "It is like what they eat in Wild West films. What is the name?"

"Pemmican," said the major. Then—and later this had slightly disgusted him with himself—he said, "Leave it in the hut. We will share it later. Come over here. Can we see Innsbruck? Show me the view on this side."

Oberhauser bobbed into the hut and out again. The major fell in just behind him as he talked, pointing out this or that distant church spire or mountain peak.

They came to the point above the glacier. Major Smythe drew his revolver, and at a range of two feet, fired two bullets into the base of Hannes Oberhauser's skull. No muffing! Dead-on!

The impact of the bullets knocked the guide clean off his feet and over the edge. Major Smythe craned over. The body hit twice only, and then crashed onto the glacier. But not onto its fissured origin. Halfway down and on a patch of old snow! "Hell!" said Major Smythe.

The deep boom of the two shots, which had been batting to and fro among the mountains, died away. Major Smythe took one last look at the black splash on the white snow and hurried off along the shoulder. First things first!

He started on the top of the cairn, working as if the devil were after him, throwing the rough, heavy stones indiscriminately down the mountain to right or left. His hands began to bleed, but he hardly noticed. Now there were only two feet or so left, and nothing! Bloody nothing! He bent to the last pile, scrabbling feverishly. And then! Yes! The edge of a metal box. A few more rocks away, and there was the whole of it! A good old gray Wehrmacht ammunition box with the trace of some lettering still on it. Major Smythe gave a groan of joy. He sat down on a hard piece of rock, and his mind went orbiting through Bentleys, Monte Carlo, penthouse flats, Cartier's, champagne, caviar, and, incongruously (but because he loved golf), a new set of Henry Cotton irons.

Drunk with his dreams, Major Smythe sat there looking at the gray box for a full quarter of an hour. Then he looked at his watch and got briskly to his feet. Time to get rid of the evidence. The box had a handle at each end. Major Smythe had expected it to be heavy. He had mentally compared its probable weight with the heaviest thing he had ever carried—a forty-pound salmon he had caught in Scotland just before the war—but the box was certainly double that weight, and he was only just able to lift it out of its last bed of rocks onto the thin alpine grass. Then he slung his handkerchief through one of the handles and dragged it clumsily along the shoulder to the hut. Then he sat down on the stone doorstep, and, his eyes never leaving the box, he tore at Oberhauser's smoked sausage with his strong teeth and thought about getting his fifty thousand pounds—for that was the figure he put it at—down the mountain and into a new hiding place.

Oberhauser's sausage was a real mountaineer's meal—tough, well-fatted, and strongly garlicked. Bits of it stuck uncomfortably between Major Smythe's teeth. He dug them out with a sliver of matchstick and spat them on the ground. Then his Intelligence-wise mind came into operation, and he meticulously searched among the stones and grass, picked up the scraps, and swallowed them. From now on he was a criminal—as much a criminal as if he had robbed a bank and shot the guard. He was a cop turned robber. He *must* remember that! It would be death if he didn't—death instead of Cartier's. All he had to do was to take infinite pains. He would take those pains, and by God they would be rich and happy. After taking ridiculously minute trouble to eradicate any sign of entry into the hut, he dragged the ammunition box to the edge of the last rock face and, aiming it away from the glacier, tipped it, with a prayer, into space.

The gray box, turning slowly in the air, hit the first steep slope below the rock face, bounded another hundred feet, and landed with an iron clang in some loose scree and stopped. Major Smythe couldn't see if it had burst open. He didn't mind one way or the other. He had tried to open it without success. Let the mountain do it for him!

With a last look around, he went over the edge. He took great care at each piton, tested each handhold and foothold before he put his weight on it. Coming down, he was a much more valuable life than he had been climbing up. He made for the glacier and trudged across the melting snow to the black patch on the icefield. There was nothing to be done about footprints. It would take only a few days for them to be melted down by the sun. He got to the body. He had seen many corpses during the war, and the blood and broken limbs meant nothing to him. He dragged the remains of Oberhauser to the nearest deep crevasse and toppled it in. Then he went carefully around the lip of the crevasse and kicked the snow overhang down on top of the body. Then, satisfied with his work, he retraced his steps, placing his feet exactly in his old footprints, and made his way on down the slope to the ammunition box.

Yes, the mountain had burst open the lid for him. Almost casually he tore away the cartridge-paper wrappings. The two great hunks of metal glittered up at him under the sun. There were the same markings on each—the swastika in a circle below an eagle, and the date 1943—the mint marks of the Reichsbank. Major Smythe gave a nod of approval. He replaced the paper and hammered the crooked lid half-shut with a rock. Then he tied the lanyard of his Webley around one of the handles and moved on down the mountain, dragging his clumsy burden behind him.

It was now one o'clock, and the sun beat fiercely down on his naked chest, frying him in his own sweat. His reddened shoulders began to burn. So did his face. To hell with them! He stopped at the stream from the glacier, dipped his handkerchief in the water, and tied it across his forehead. Then he drank deeply and went on, occasionally cursing the ammunition box as it caught up with him and banged at his heels. But these discomforts, the sunburn and the bruises, were nothing compared with what he would have to face when he got down to the valley and the going leveled out. For the time being he had gravity on his side. There would come at least a mile when he would have to carry the blasted stuff. Major Smythe winced at the thought of the havoc the eighty pounds or so would wreak on his burned back. "Oh well," he said to himself almost lightheadedly, *"il faut souffrir pour être millionaire!"*

When he got to the bottom and the time had come, he sat and rested on a mossy bank under the firs. Then he spread out his bush shirt and heaved the two bars out of the box and onto its center and tied the tails of the shirt as firmly as he could to where the sleeves sprang from the shoulders. After digging a shallow hole in the bank and burying the empty box, he knotted the two cuffs of the sleeves firmly together, knelt down, and slipped his head through the rough sling, got his hands on either side of the knot to protect his neck, and staggered to his feet, crouching far forward so as not to be pulled over on his back. Then, crushed under half his own weight, his back on fire under the contact with his burden, and his breath rasping through his constricted lungs, coolie-like, he shuffled slowly off down the little path through the trees.

To this day he didn't know how he had made it to the jeep. Again and again the knots gave under the strain and the bars crashed down on the calves of his legs, and each time he had sat with his head in his hands and then started all over again. But finally, by concentrating on counting his steps and stopping for a rest at every hundredth, he got to the blessed little jeep and collapsed beside it. And then there had been the business of burying his hoard in the wood, amongst a jumble of big rocks that he would be sure to find again, of cleaning himself up as best he could, and of getting back to his billet by a circuitous route that avoided the Oberhauser chalet. And then it was all done, and he had got drunk by himself off a bottle of cheap schnapps and eaten and gone to bed and fallen into a stupefied sleep. The next day, MOB "A" Force had moved off up the Mittersill valley on a fresh trail, and six months later Major Smythe was back in London and his war was over.

But not his problems. Gold is difficult stuff to smuggle, certainly in the quantity available to Major Smythe, and it was now essential to get his two bars across the Channel and into a new hiding place. So he put off his demobilization and clung to the red tabs of his temporary rank, and particularly to his Military Intelligence passes, and soon got himself sent back to Germany as a British representative at the Combined Interrogation Center in Munich. There he did a scratch job for six months, during which, on a weekend's leave, he collected his gold and stowed it in a battered suitcase in his quarters. Then he resigned his post and flew back to England, carrying the two bars in a bulky briefcase. The hundred yards across the tarmac at each end of the flight, and the handling of his case as if it contained only papers, required two benzedrine tablets and a will of iron, but at last he had his fortune safe in the basement of an aunt's flat in Kensington and could get on with the next phase of his plans at leisure.

He resigned from the Royal Marines and got himself demobilized and married one of the many girls he had slept with at MOB Force Headquarters, a charming blond Wren from a solid middle-class family named Mary Parnell. He got passages for them both in one of the early banana boats sailing from Avonmouth to Kingston, Jamaica, which they both agreed would be a paradise of sunshine, good food, cheap drink, and a glorious haven from the gloom and restrictions and Labour Government of postwar England. Before they sailed, Major Smythe showed Mary the gold bars from which he had chiseled away the mint marks of the Reichsbank.

"I've been clever, darling," he said. "I just don't trust the pound these days, so I've sold out all my securities and swapped the lot for gold. Must be about fifty thousand pounds' worth there. That should give us twenty-five years of the good life, just cutting off a slice now and then and selling it."

Mary Parnell was not to know that such a transaction was impossible under the currency laws. She knelt down and ran her hands lovingly over the gleaming bars. Then she got up and threw her arms around Major Smythe's neck and kissed him. "You're a wonderful, wonderful man," she said, almost in tears. "Frightfully clever and handsome and brave, and now I find out that you're rich as well. I'm the luckiest girl in the world."

"Well, anyway we're rich," said Major Smythe. "But promise me you won't breathe a word, or we'll have all the burglars in Jamaica around our ears. Promise?"

"Cross my heart."

Prince's Club, in the foothills above Kingston, was indeed a paradise. Pleasant enough members, wonderful servants, unlimited food, cheap drink—and all in the wonderful setting of the tropics, which neither of them had known before. They were a popular couple, and Major Smythe's war record earned them the entrée to Government House society, after which their life was one endless round of parties, with tennis for Mary and golf (with the Henry Cotton irons!) for Major Smythe. In the evenings there was bridge for her and the high poker game for him. Yes, it was paradise all right, while in their homeland people munched their Spam, fiddled in the black market, cursed the government, and suffered the worst winter's weather for thirty years.

The Smythes met all their initial expenditures from their combined cash reserves, swollen by wartime gratuities, and it took Major Smythe a full year of careful sniffing around before he decided to do business with the Messrs. Foo, import and export merchants. The brothers Foo, highly respected and very rich, were the acknowledged governing junta of the flourishing Chinese community in Jamaica. Some of their trading was suspected to be devious—in the Chinese tradition—but all Major Smythe's casually meticulous inquiries confirmed that they were utterly trustworthy. The Bretton Woods Convention, fixing a controlled world price for gold, had been signed, and it had already become common knowledge that Tangier and Macao were two free ports that, for different reasons, had escaped the Bretton Woods net; there a price of at least one hundred dollars per ounce of gold, ninety-nine fine, could be obtained, compared with the fixed world price of thirty-five dollars per ounce. And, conveniently, the Foos had just begun to trade again with a resurgent Hong Kong, already the port of entry for gold smuggling into the neighboring Macao. The whole setup was, in Major Smythe's language, "ticketty-boo." He had a most pleasant meeting with the Foo brothers. No questions were asked until it came to examining the bars. At this point the absence of mint marks resulted in a polite inquiry as to the original provenance of the gold.

"You see, Major," said the older and blander of the brothers behind the big bare mahogany desk, "in the bullion market the mint marks of all respectable national banks and responsible dealers are accepted without question. Such marks guarantee the fineness of the gold. But of course there are other banks and dealers whose methods of refining"—his benign smile widened a fraction—"are perhaps not quite, shall we say, so accurate."

"You mean the old gold brick swindle?" asked Major Smythe with a twinge of anxiety. "Hunk of lead covered with gold plating?"

Both brothers tee-heed reassuringly. "No, no, Major. That of course is out of the question. But"—the smiles held constant—"if you cannot recall the provenance of these fine bars, perhaps you would have no objections if we were to undertake an assay. There are methods of determining the exact fineness of such bars. My brother and I are competent in these methods. If you would care to leave these with us and perhaps come back after lunch . . . ?"

There had been no alternative. Major Smythe had to trust the Foos utterly now. They could cook up any figure, and he would just have to accept it. He went over to the Myrtle Bank and had one or two stiff drinks and a sandwich that stuck in his throat. Then he went back to the cool office of the Foos.

The setting was the same—the two smiling brothers, the two bars of gold, the briefcase—but now there was a piece of paper and a gold Parker pen in front of the older brother.

"We have solved the problem of your fine bars, Major———"

Fine! Thank God, thought Major Smythe.

"———And I am sure you will be interested to know their probable history."

"Yes indeed," said Major Smythe, with a brave show of enthusiasm.

"They are German bars, Major. Probably from the wartime Reichsbank. This we have deduced from the fact that they contain ten percent of lead. Under the Hitler regime, it was the foolish habit of the Reichsbank to adulterate their gold in this manner. This fact rapidly became known to dealers, and the price of German bars, in Switzerland for instance, where many of them found their way, was adjusted downward accordingly. So the only result of the German foolishness was that the national bank of Germany lost a reputation for honest dealing it had earned over the centuries." The Oriental's smile didn't vary. "Very bad business, Major. Very stupid."

Major Smythe marveled at the omniscience of these two men so far from the great commercial channels of the world, but he also cursed it. *Now what?* He said, "That's very interesting, Mr. Foo. But it is not very good news for me. Are these bars not 'Good delivery,' or whatever you call it in the bullion world?"

The older Foo made a slight throwaway gesture with his right hand. "It is of no importance, Major. Or rather, it is of very small importance. We will sell your gold at its true mint value, let us say, eighty-nine fine. It may be re-fined by the ultimate purchaser, or it may not. That is not our business. We shall have sold a true bill of goods."

"But at a lower price."

"That is so, Major. But I think I have some good news for you. Have you any estimate as to the worth of these two bars?"

"I thought around fifty thousand pounds."

The older Foo gave a dry chuckle. "I think—if we sell wisely and slowly—you should receive one hundred thousand pounds, Major, subject that is, to our commission, which will include shipping and incidental charges."

"How much would that be?"

"We were thinking about a figure of ten percent, Major. If that is satisfactory to you."

Major Smythe had an idea that bullion brokers received a fraction of one percent. But what the hell? He had already as good as made forty thousand pounds since lunch. He said ''Done'' and got up and reached his hand across the desk.

From then on, every quarter, he would visit the office of the Foos carrying an empty suitcase. On the broad desk there would be one thousand new Jamaican pounds in neat bundles and the two gold bars, which diminished inch by inch, together with a typed slip showing the amount sold and the price obtained in Macao. It was all very simple and friendly and highly businesslike, and Major Smythe didn't think that he was being submitted to any form of squeeze other than the duly recorded ten percent. In any case, he didn't particularly care. Four thousand net a year was good enough for him, and his only worry was that the income tax people would get after him and ask him what he was living on. He mentioned this possibility to the Foos. But they said he was not to worry, and for the next four quarters, there was only nine hundred pounds instead of a thousand on the table and no comment was made by either side. Squeeze had been administered in the right quarter.

And so the lazy, sunshiny days passed by for fifteen happy years. The Smythes both put on weight, and Major Smythe had the first of his two coronaries and was told by his doctor to cut down on his alcohol and cigarettes, to take life more easily, to avoid fats and fried food. Mary Smythe tried to be firm with him, but when he took to secret drinking and to a life of petty lies and evasions, she tried to backpedal on her attempts to control his self-indulgence. But she was too late. She had already become the symbol of the caretaker to Major Smythe, and he took to avoiding her. She berated him with not loving her anymore. And when the continual bickering became too much for her simple nature, she became a sleeping pill addict. And one night, after one flaming drunken row, she took an overdose—''just to show him.'' It was too much of an overdose and it killed her. The suicide was hushed up, but the cloud did Major Smythe no good socially, and he retreated to the North Shore, which, although only some thirty miles across the island from the capital, is, even in the small society of Jamaica, a different world. And there he had settled in Wavelets and, after his second coronary, was in the process of drinking himself to death when this man named Bond arrived on the scene with an alternative death warrant in his pocket.

Major Smythe looked at his watch. It was a few minutes after twelve o'clock. He got up and poured himself another stiff brandy and ginger ale and went out onto the lawn. James Bond was sitting under the sea almonds gazing out to sea. He didn't look up when Major Smythe pulled up another aluminum garden chair and put his drink on the grass beside him.

When Major Smythe had finished telling his story, Bond said unemotionally, ''Yes, that's more or less the way I figure it.''

''Want me to write it all out and sign it?''

''You can if you like. But not for me. That'll be for the court-martial. Your old corps will be handling all that. I've got nothing to do with the legal aspects. I shall put in a report to my own Service of what you've told me, and they'll pass it on to the Royal Marines. Then I suppose it'll go to the Public Prosecutor via Scotland Yard.''

''Could I ask a question?''

''Of course.''

''How did they find out?''

''It was a small glacier. Oberhauser's body came out at the bottom of it earlier this year. When the spring snows melted. Some climbers found it. All his papers and everything were intact. His family identified him. Then it was just a question of working back. The bullets clinched it.''

''But how did you get mixed up in the whole thing?''

''MOB Force was a responsibility of my, er, Service. The papers found their way to us. I happened to see the file. I had some spare time on my hands. I asked to be given the job of chasing up the man who did it.''

''Why?''

James Bond looked Major Smythe squarely in the eyes. ''It just happened that Oberhauser was a friend of mine. He taught me to ski before the war, when I was in my teens. He was a wonderful man. He was something of a father to me at a time when I happened to need one.''

''Oh, I see.'' Major Smythe looked away. ''I'm sorry.''

James Bond got to his feet. ''Well, I'll be getting back to Kingston.'' He held up a hand. ''No, don't bother. I'll find my way to the car.'' He looked down at the older man. He said abruptly, almost harshly—perhaps, Major Smythe thought, to hide his embarrassment—''It'll be about a week before they send someone out to bring you home.'' Then he walked off across the lawn and through the house, and Major Smythe heard the iron whirr of the self-starter and the clatter of the gravel on the unkempt drive.

Major Smythe, questing for his prey along the reef, wondered what exactly those last words of the Bond man had meant. Inside the Pirelli his lips drew mirthlessly back from the stained teeth. It was obvious, really. It was just a version of the corny old act of leaving the guilty officer alone with his revolver. If the Bond man had wanted to, he could have telephoned Government House and had an officer of the Jamaica Regiment sent over to take Major Smythe into custody. Decent of him, in a way. Or was it? A suicide would be tidier, save a lot of paperwork and taxpayers' money.

Should he oblige the Bond man and be tidy? Join Mary in whatever place suicides go to? Or go through with it—the indignity, the dreary formalities, the headlines, the boredom and drabness of a life sentence that would inevitably end with his third coronary? Or should he defend himself—plead wartime, a struggle with Oberhauser, prisoner trying to escape, Oberhauser knowing of the gold cache, the natural temptation of Smythe to make away with the bullion, he, a poor officer of the commandos confronted with sudden wealth?

Should he dramatically throw himself on the mercy of the court? Suddenly Major Smythe saw himself in the dock—a splendid, upright figure, in the fine bemedaled blue and scarlet of the ceremonial uniform that was the traditional rig for court-martial. (Had the moths got into the japanned box in the spare room at Wavelets? Had the damp? Luna would have to look to it.) A day in the sunshine, if the weather held. A good brushing. With the help of his corset, he could surely still get his forty-inch waist into the thirty-four-inch trousers Gieves had made for him twenty, thirty, years ago. And, down on the floor of the court, at Chatham probably, the Prisoners' Friend, some staunch fellow, at least of colonel's rank in deference to his own seniority, would be pleading his cause. And there was always the possibility of appeal to a higher court. Why, the whole affair might become a cause célèbre . . . he would sell his story to the papers, write a book. . . .

Major Smythe felt the excitement mounting in him. Careful, old boy! Careful! Remember what the good old snip-cock had said! He put his feet to the ground and had a rest amidst the dancing waves of the northeast trades that kept the North Shore so delightfully cool until the torrid months—August, September, October—of the hurricane season. He would soon be having his two pink gins, skimpy lunch, and happily sodden siesta, after which he would have to give all this more careful thought. And then there were cocktails with the Arundels and dinner at the Shaw Park Beach Club with the Marchesis. Then some high bridge and home to his seconal sleep. Cheered by the prospect of the familiar routine, the black shadow of Bond retreated into the background. Now then, scorp, where are you? Octopussy's waiting for her lunch! Major Smythe put his head down, and his mind freshly focused and his eyes questing, continued his leisurely swim along the shallow valley between the coral clumps that led out toward the white-fringed reef.

Almost at once he saw the two spiny antennae of a lobster, or rather of its cousin, the West Indian langouste, weaving inquisitively toward him, toward the turbulence he was creating, from a deep fissure under a coral boulder. From the thickness of the antennae, it would be a big one, three or four pounds! Normally, Major Smythe would have put his feet down and delicately stirred up the sand in front of the lair to bring the lobster farther out, for they are an inquisitive family. Then he would have speared it through the head and taken it back for lunch. But today there was only one prey in his mind, one shape to concentrate on—the shaggy, irregular silhouette of a scorpionfish. And, ten minutes later, he saw a clump of seaweedy rock on the white sand that wasn't just a clump of seaweedy rock. He put his feet softly down and watched the poison spines erect themselves along the back of the thing. It was a good-sized one, perhaps three-quarters of a pound. He got his three-pronged spear ready and inched forward. Now the red angry eyes of the fish were wide open and watching him. He would have to make a single quick lunge from as nearly the vertical as possible; otherwise, he knew from experience, the barbed prongs, needle-sharp though they were, would almost certainly bounce off the horny head of the beast. He swung his feet up off the ground and paddled forward very slowly, using his free hand as a fin. Now! He lunged forward and downward. But the scorpionfish had felt the tiny approaching shockwave of the spear. There was flurry of sand, and it had shot up in a vertical takeoff and whirred, in almost birdlike flight, under Major Smythe's belly.

Major Smythe cursed and twisted around in the water. Yes, it had done what the scorpionfish so often does—gone for refuge to the nearest algae-covered rock, and there, confident in its superb camouflage, gone to ground on the seaweed. Major Smythe had only to swim a few feet, lunge down again, this time more accurately, and he had it, flapping and squirming on the end of his spear.

The excitement and the small exertion had caused Major Smythe to pant, and he felt the old pain across his chest lurking, ready to come at him. He put his feet down, and after driving his spear all the way through the fish, held it, still flapping desperately, out of the water. Then he slowly made his way back across the lagoon on foot and walked up the sand of his beach to the wooden bench under the sea-grape. Then he dropped the spear with its jerking quarry on the sand beside him and sat down to rest.

It was perhaps five minutes later that Major Smythe felt a curious numbness more or less in the region of his solar plexus. He looked casually down, and his whole body stiffened with horror and disbelief. A patch of his skin, about the size of a cricket ball, had turned white under his tan, and, in the center of the patch, there were three punctures, one below the other, topped by little beads of blood. Automatically, Major Smythe wiped away the blood. The holes were only the size of pinpricks. Major Smythe remembered the rising flight of the scorpionfish, and he said aloud, with awe in his voice, but without animosity, "You got me, you bastard! By God, you got me!"

He sat very still, looking down at his body and remembering what it said about scorpionfish stings in the book he had borrowed from the Institute and had never returned—*Dangerous Marine Animals*, an American publication. He delicately touched and then prodded the white area around the punctures. Yes, the skin had gone totally numb, and now a pulse of pain began to throb beneath it. Very soon this would become a shooting pain. Then the pain would begin to lance all over his body and become so intense that he would throw himself on the sand, screaming and thrashing about, to rid himself of it. He would vomit and foam at the mouth, and then delirium and convulsions would take over until he lost consciousness. Then, inevitably in his case, there would ensue cardiac failure and death. According to the book the whole cycle would be complete in about a quarter of an hour—that was all he had left—fifteen minutes of hideous agony! There were cures, of course—procaine, antibiotics, and antihistamines—if his weak heart would stand them. But they had to be near at hand. Even if he could climb the steps up to the house, and supposing Dr. Cahusac had these modern drugs, the doctor couldn't possibly get to Wavelets in under an hour.

The first jet of pain seared into Major Smythe's body and bent him over double. Then came another and another, radiating through his stomach and limbs. Now there was a dry, metallic taste in his mouth, and his lips were prickling. He gave a groan and toppled off the seat onto the beach. A flapping on the sand beside his head reminded him of the scorpionfish. There came a lull in the spasms of pain. Instead, his whole body felt as though it were on fire, but, beneath the agony, his brain cleared. But of course! The experiment! Somehow, somehow he must get out to Octopussy and give her her lunch!

"Oh Pussy, my Pussy, this is the last meal you'll get."

Major Smythe mouthed the refrain to himself as he crouched on all fours, found his mask, and struggled to force it over his face. Then he got hold of his spear, tipped with the still flapping fish, and clutching his stomach with his free hand, crawled and slithered down the sand and into the water.

It was fifty yards of shallow water to the lair of the octopus in the coral cranny, and Major Smythe, screaming all the while into his mask, crawling mostly on his knees, somehow made it. As he came to the last approach and the water became deeper, he had to get to his feet, and the pain made him jiggle to and fro, as if he were a puppet manipulated by strings. Then he was there, and with a supreme effort of will, he held himself steady as he dipped his head down to let some water into his mask and clear the mist of his screams from the glass. Then, blood pouring from his bitten lower lip, he bent carefully down to look into Octopussy's house. Yes! The brown mass was still there. It was stirring excitedly. Why? Major Smythe saw the dark strings of his blood curling lazily down through the water. Of course! The darling was tasting his blood. A shaft of pain hit Major Smythe and sent him reeling. He heard himself babbling deliriously into his mask. *Pull yourself together, Dexter, old boy! You've got to give Pussy her lunch!* He steadied himself, and holding the spear well down the shaft, lowered the fish down toward the writhing hole.

Would Pussy take the bait? The poisonous bait that was killing Major Smythe but to which an octopus might be immune? If only Bengry could be here to watch! Three tentacles, weaving excitedly, came out of the hole and wavered around the scorpionfish. Now there was a gray mist in front of Major Smythe's eyes. He recognized it as the edge of unconsciousness and feebly shook his head to clear it. And then the tentacles leaped! But not at the fish! At Major Smythe's hand and arm. Major Smythe's torn mouth stretched in a grimace of pleasure. Now he and Pussy had shaken hands! How exciting! How truly wonderful!

But then the octopus, quietly, relentlessly pulled downward, and terrible realization came to Major Smythe. He summoned his dregs of strength and plunged his spear down. The only effect was to push the scorpionfish into the mass of the octopus and offer more arm to the octopus. The tentacles snaked upward and pulled more relentlessly. Too late, Major Smythe scrabbled away his mask. One bottled scream burst out across the empty bay, then his head went under and down, and there was an explosion of bubbles to the surface. Then Major Smythe's legs came up and the small waves washed his body to and fro while the octopus explored his right hand with its buccal orifice and took a first tentative bite at a finger with its beaklike jaws.

The body was found by two young Jamaicans spinning for needlefish from a canoe. They speared the octopus with Major Smythe's spear, killed it in the traditional fashion by turning it inside out and biting its head off, and brought the three corpses home. They turned Major

Smythe's body over to the police, and had the scorpionfish and the seacat for supper.

The local correspondent for the *Daily Gleaner* reported that Major Smythe had been killed by an octopus, but the paper translated this into "found drowned" so as not to frighten away the tourists.

Later, in London, James Bond, privately assuming "suicide," wrote the same verdict of "found drowned," together with the date, on the last page and closed the bulky file.

It is only from the notes of Dr. Cahusac, who performed the autopsy, that it has been possible to construct some kind of a postscript to the bizarre and pathetic end of a once valuable officer of the Secret Service.